Amish Turns
OF TIME
TRILOGY

Three Romances Weather Cultural Shifts in Amish History

Amish Turns
OF TIME
TRILOGY

OLIVIA
NEWPORT

SHILOH RUN PRESS

ISBN 978-1-63409-945-5

eBook Editions:
Adobe Digital Edition (.epub) 978-1-68322-139-5
Kindle and MobiPocket Edition (.prc) 978-1-68322-140-1

Cover design: Faceout Studio, www.faceoutstudio.com

Published by Shiloh Run Press, an imprint of Barbour Publishing, Inc., P.O. Box 719, Uhrichsville, Ohio 44683, www.shilohrunpress.com

Our mission is to publish and distribute inspirational products offering exceptional value and biblical encouragement to the masses.

Member of the
Evangelical Christian
Publishers Association

Printed in the United States of America.

CONTENTS

Wonderful —

LONESOME

CHAPTER 1

Elbert County, Colorado
May 1914

The front right wagon wheel, below Abigail Weaver, dipped sharply then lurched out of the hole. At its creak, she winced and eyed Willem Peters on the bench beside her.

Willem pulled the reins in, and the dark stallion responded. "I'd better look."

Willem dropped off the bench, stepped mindfully over the hitch, and squatted to inspect the bent hickory wheel.

Abbie twisted to watch. "Did it break?"

Willem scratched his forehead with his middle finger. "Not that I can see. Maybe the back side of one of the spokes cracked."

Abbie expelled a breath. "When did that hole happen anyway?"

"Who can say? At least it doesn't seem too deep." Willem stood. "We will be all right."

We will be all right. Willem's favorite expression.

Willem hoisted himself up to the bench. "There's an *English* wheel maker in Limon. I can ask him to take a look while you wait for Ruthanna's train."

Abbie nodded, glad to have Willem beside her again. He clicked his tongue and the horse began to move. Limon was only another two miles.

"Do you have your mother's list for Gates Mercantile?" Willem asked.

"She hates having to buy flour." Abbie squinted her brown eyes. "It's like losing last year's wheat all over again."

"Your family is not alone in losing the crop. We all feel it."

"I know. I hope they'll take her eggs in payment."

"They always do. Everybody needs eggs." Willem glanced at Abbie. "Do you think your mother wants to go home?"

Abbie shook her light brown-haired head. "Colorado is home now. She wants to be here as much as I do. I think she's written to every relative we have, though." Abbie reached into the leather bag and ran her fingers along the ridges of the coarse envelopes.

"I promised Albert Miller I would check for his mail. Remind me, please."

Abbie turned her face away and allowed herself a small smile. She liked it when Willem said things like that, the way he depended on her in the mundane.

"Where first?" Willem raised his green eyes in the direction of Limon. "Mercantile? Feed store? Post office? Wheel maker?"

"Someday we'll be able to do more of those things for ourselves." Abbie set her jaw. "Once a few more families join our settlement, we'll have the tradesmen to provide what we need."

"Speaking of tradesmen, remind me to check with our very own cobbler about my new boots. We're blessed to have someone to make our shoes."

"God is *gut*." Abbie peered toward the outline of Limon. "How much time do we have before Ruthanna's train?"

"I'll tell you what. Give me your list and letters, and I'll drop you at the station and start on the errands. That way you can enjoy Ruthanna. She'll be ready to talk your ear off as usual."

"That's one of the things I love about her." Abbie smiled. "Does it count if I remind you now to pick up the Millers' mail?"

One of Willem's cheeks twitched in amusement. "No one can accuse you of not fulfilling your promises."

⊱✦⊰

Abbie stood on the platform and bent at the waist, back straight, to peer down the tracks. Her dark dress seemed somber among the spray of colors and hats of *English* women preparing to board trains, but the sensation was fleeting. Abbie had no wish to be *English*. Perhaps Ruthanna would bring news of other families who wanted to join the settlement. The price of land was certainly attractive. Abbie's father had put his savings into his Colorado farm and tripled the acreage he had owned in Ohio. Willem had rented his acres in Ohio, but here he was a landowner. Every family in the settlement had a similar story.

Twenty-four trains a day shuddered into this station. Limon, Colorado, was on the Union Pacific line as well as the Rock Island. As much as Abbie wanted her Amish church members to be able to take care of their own needs and provide for each other, she knew this town of five hundred was crucial to the settlement's survival. The trains made the distance from their families seem less daunting.

Distant rumbling turned thunderous as the train approached. Abbie sucked in her bottom lip, her stomach fluttering. Four weeks without her best friend was too much time apart. Ruthanna's only letter in that interim had revealed she would travel with cousins into western Kansas and then continue to Limon alone and arrive on this day. Brakes squealed now as the mass of steel slowed to a lumber and halted. Abbie scanned in both directions, not knowing which train car Ruthanna would emerge from. She did know that Ruthanna's favorite apron to wear over her black dress was the blue one. Abbie instinctively looked for fabric dyed in this distinctive Amish shade. Her intuition was rewarded when her friend stepped off the train just two cars forward of where Abbie stood.

In only seconds, they locked in an embrace that wobbled from side to side.

Ruthanna finally pulled back, her blue eyes gleaming under white blond hair. "I'm thrilled to see you, of course, but where is Eber?"

Of course Ruthanna would have been expecting her husband to meet the train. "He's under the weather," Abbie said.

"Eber is ill?"

"Just the last few days, but it keeps him up at night. I saw him this morning and sent him back to bed. He was pale as a corpse, and Willem was coming into town anyway."

Concern flushed through Ruthanna's face.

"He'll be fine, Ruthanna."

"You sound like Willem. I should not have left Eber."

"Of course you should have." Abbie picked up Ruthanna's small suitcase and they began walking. "You must insist that he hire some help, though. A bit more rest would work wonders. Now tell me all about Pennsylvania."

Ruthanna's face brightened. She put her hand on a gently rounding belly. "I am so glad I waited to tell my parents about the baby in person."

Abbie grinned. "Your *daed* loves the *kinner*."

"Now they will have to visit us. Perhaps next spring, after they can see how well we've done with this year's harvest. They cannot resist a grandchild."

Ruthanna adjusted her *kapp*. The train ride had worn her out more than she wanted to admit to Abbie. She had seen other women sick while they were with child, but she had not known how exhausting it could be to fight the nausea for hours on end. At night she slept in exhaustion, but still she dragged through the days.

"Have you heard of anyone who wants to come and join us?"

Abbie's question was just what Ruthanna expected. "Not precisely."

"Is anyone even considering it?"

Ruthanna sighed. "Everyone thought we would have a minister by now."

"So did we. We have twelve households—some of them are even three generations. That's enough for our own minister."

"I'm not sure anyone else will come until we have a minister. They have a hard time imagining how we can go an entire year without a church service and communion." Ruthanna inhaled the loose dirt that always hung in the air on the Colorado plain and coughed. This did nothing to settle her stomach.

"I suppose I cannot blame them," Abbie said, "but surely

God could put the call on a minister to visit us more often until someone from our congregation can be ordained. I shall pray more fervently."

Ruthanna moistened her lips with what little saliva she could muster. "Also, everyone knows what happened to last year's crops. I received many questions about that as well."

"But that is not fair. Even farmers in Pennsylvania or Ohio can lose a crop if the weather is not favorable."

"You have to admit that the advertisements that brought us out here failed to mention some important factors."

Abbie waved a hand. "I do not believe anyone intended to deceive. The first men did not yet know for themselves how little rain there was. Acres and acres of land were available with no need to clear thousands of trees before planting. A new family can get a crop in the first spring they are here. Certainly that's still an attractive truth."

Ruthanna smiled and put a tongue in the corner of her mouth. "You are nothing if not persistent, Abigail Weaver. I cannot think of anyone who wants our settlement to succeed more than you do."

"We are so close! A few more families, a minister, a good crop this year."

Abbie's pace had quickened with her enthusiasm, and Ruthanna could not keep up. "Abbie, I need some cold refreshment and a place to sit that is not in motion."

"Of course! We can find a bench inside the depot. Willem will look for us there anyway. And we can talk about something happier."

❧❦❧

Willem watched the two heads bent toward each other as he held the door for a couple leaving the depot with four children stringing behind them. With a tall tin cup in her hand, Ruthanna looked relaxed. Eber had done well to marry her. Ruthanna balanced Eber's subdued demeanor with an exuberance that allowed her to talk to anyone about anything. Between them they had all the traits an Amish household would need to survive on the Colorado plain. Twenty years from now, Willem predicted, they would be watching their firstborn son take a bride in a congregation with three ministers, and they would be hard put to squelch their pride. *Demut,* they would remind each other. *Humility.*

Willem certainly hoped it would be so. Perhaps he and Abbie would follow soon enough. Maybe their daughter would love Eber and Ruthanna's son. A new generation would rise up from the dust of their parents' acreage. *Gottes wille.* God's will. May it be so.

As he walked toward the two friends, Ruthanna's face cheered and incited Willem's curiosity about what the women were discussing. A few seconds later Abbie smiled as well. No doubt Abbie was hanging on every word Ruthanna said, listening to stories, news, information, even gossip from the congregations their two families had left behind when they decided to settle in new territory. Abbie was the intense one. Ruthanna brought her the same balance she brought Eber. Abbie's shoulders now dropped, as if for a few minutes she had released her load. Willem wished she would do that more often. Her head turned toward him in a serendipitous way, and he waved.

"The wanderer has come home." When he reached them, Willem grinned and picked up Ruthanna's suitcase. "I'm sure Eber is anxious to see you."

"Did you mail the letters?" Abbie asked.

"Yes."

"And pick up the Millers' mail?"

"Under the wagon bench."

"And my mother's flour and pickles?"

"Sugar, dry beans, and baking powder, too."

"And the wheel maker?"

"No cracks. A squeaky axle."

Ruthanna laughed. "You two are quite a pair."

Willem gave her a half smile. Most of the community—both Amish and *English*—paired him with Abbie. Many expected him to make a proposal in the fall, after the harvest. After all, he was twenty-six and she was twenty-three, well old enough to begin their own household.

"That's Rudy Stutzman in the ticket line," Abbie said.

Willem glanced toward the counter. Abbie scowled, stood, and marched toward the window. Whatever Rudy's reasons were for being there, his explanation was not likely to satisfy Abbie. Willem admitted his own curiosity and made no move to constrain Abbie.

CHAPTER 2

Rudy, I hadn't heard you planned to travel."

Rudy jumped at the sound of Abbie's voice. "I thought I might make some inquiries about the price of fares."

"Are your parents unwell?" Abbie asked. Rudy had few extended family members, she knew, but he had come west with the blessing of his parents. They would have his two younger brothers to care for them as they aged.

"My family is well. Thank you for asking."

"Visiting someone?" Abbie said. Rudy's pitch sounded distant.

"No, I don't think so."

"Next," the ticket agent called.

Rudy stepped forward. The angle of one shoulder raised a wall between them. When he leaned in to speak to the agent, Abbie could not hear his words.

"Are you sure you just want a one-way ticket?" the agent said at a volume anyone within twelve feet would have heard.

Abbie stepped forward and grabbed Rudy's wrist. "No. Don't do this." Rudy glanced at her grip, and Abbie released it.

"Sir?" the agent said. Two people in line behind Rudy raised their eyebrows.

Rudy sighed and said to the ticket agent, "Perhaps for today you could just tell me what the cost is."

"One way all the way to Indiana?"

Rudy nodded. Abbie's heart sank.

The agent consulted a chart and announced the price.

"Thank you." Rudy stepped aside and Abbie followed.

"One way, Rudy?"

"Abigail, not everyone is as stalwart as you are. After four or five years, some of us are admitting that this is a lot harder than we thought it would be."

"We're all in this together, Rudy. We all need each other. That includes you."

"I am alone," Rudy said. "Willem and I, and Widower Samuels. What good is it for us to have a farm or dairy if we cannot keep up with the work?"

"Then hire somebody to help."

"No Amish families can spare their young men. My cash is in my land. I have nothing to pay an *English* with until the fall harvest. I only have what I make selling them milk."

"All the more reason to stay and make a go of it. You cannot just get on a train and leave your land and milk cows." Abbie's heart pounded. As far as she could influence anyone, she would not let a single settler give up.

"I thought I would make a listing with a land agent. I may not get back everything I put in, but I would have something."

"You know it is not our way to abandon each other in times of need. Speak to some of the other men. They will help you."

"The need is greater than we are," Rudy muttered.

"That is not true. That is never true." Below the hem of her skirt, Abbie lifted a foot and let it drop against the depot's oak decking.

Rudy looked past Abbie's shoulder. "I see Willem. Is he waiting for you?"

"Yes. We came to pick up Ruthanna. Eber is feeling poorly, but you can be sure no one is going to let his farm fail either."

"You cannot fight God's will, Abbie."

"You think it is God's will for us to fail?" Abbie refused to believe the settlers had obediently followed God into a new opportunity only to be forsaken.

"It must be," Rudy said. "It would take a miracle for us to succeed."

"Then a miracle we will have. Believe!"

Rudy leaned back against the wall. He had known plenty of stubborn people in his twenty-eight years, but none was a match for Abigail Weaver. He appreciated how hard she worked helping to bake and clean for the single men of the Amish community, but when she crawled into bed at night, she still slept under her parents' roof. He and Willem had ventured west without parents or wives. Rudy wasn't sure Abbie understood the risk they had taken.

And Willem, apparently, did not understand his ability to make Abbie happy or they would have wed two years ago.

"Abbie," Rudy said, "you are an example of great faith, but there is something to be said for realism as well."

"Not today. This is not the day that you are giving up."

Her dark eyes bore into him, and his resolve went soft. "You're right. One day at a time."

Her face cracked in a smile. "That's right. One day at a time. We *will* get through this summer and have a bountiful harvest. You will see."

Rudy lifted his eyes at the approaching sound of boots. "Hello, Willem. Abbie tells me the two of you have fetched Ruthanna home from Pennsylvania."

"That's right."

As soon as Willem stood beside Abbie, Rudy saw the hopefulness in the turn of her head, the wish for what Willem had not yet given her.

Willem seemed in no hurry about anything except that his farm should succeed. He and Abbie were so different that Rudy often wondered if the predictions that they would one day wed would come true. Abbie's one-day-at-a-time conviction might exasperate her when it came to waiting for Willem, and she might yet turn her head in that way toward another man.

Perhaps even toward Rudy.

When Rudy first arrived in Colorado, he regretted not bringing a wife with him. Then he met Abbie. He hated to think how he might have wounded a wife who saw through him.

"It's good to see you both," Rudy said. "We should all be on our way back to the farms, don't you think?"

Willem squinted at Rudy's retreating back. "Is Rudy all right?"

Abbie pressed her lips together. "I hope so. I suppose no one can blame him for a moment of indecisiveness."

"Is that what it was?"

Abbie was not inclined to answer. Willem was not inclined to press.

"We should get Ruthanna home," he said. "She's worried about Eber."

"Of course. If you are sure we remembered everything."

"Even if we have forgotten something, Limon is not going away. We will be back." Willem followed Abbie's line of sight to where Rudy stepped off the depot platform and stroked the neck of his midnight black horse.

"We should make sure Ruthanna has plenty to drink," Abbie said in a thoughtful murmur. "I can see she is weary, and Eber is ill. They will need something for supper tonight. I'm sure my mother can spare part of tonight's stew."

Willem nodded. Abbie, as always, thought of everything.

When they returned to the bench where they had left Ruthanna, she was standing and engaged in conversation with a man in a black suit. Willem's mind tried to sort out which Amish man this might be.

"Is that Jake Heatwole?" Abbie asked.

Willem nodded slowly as memory came into focus. "I believe so."

"What is he doing talking to Ruthanna?"

"You have to admit, they are two of the friendliest people we could ever hope to meet. They've met each other several times before."

"But—"

Willem cut off Abbie's protest. "But he's a Mennonite minister. Yes, I know. Does it really make a difference when we can't find a minister of our own?"

Abbie drew up her height. Willem ignored the *whoosh* of air she sucked in.

"Jake," Willem said, "what you brings you all the way from La Junta again?"

"Thought I would come and see how folks are," Jake answered with a smile. "Ruthanna tells me Eber is ill. Perhaps I'll pay him a call while I'm here."

"Jake says he plans to stay for at least a week," Ruthanna said. "Of course, I hope Eber will be feeling better long before that."

"He probably just needs his wife back," Jake said.

"If you're planning to stay a few days," Willem said, "why don't you stay with me? My home is small, but there's room for another bedroll."

❦

Abbie barely managed to swallow words she would have regretted and hoped the flush she felt move through her face was not visible. What was Willem thinking? The four of them began moving toward Willem's wagon.

"Where did you leave your horse?" Willem asked.

"At the blacksmith's," Jake answered. "She seemed to be favoring one foot on the ride up, so I thought he should look at her shoes. He should be just about finished."

"We'll give you a ride over if you don't mind sitting in the wagon. I am afraid the bench is full with the three of us."

Abbie admired many things about Willem. He was kind and generous and determined and hardworking. But this was going too far.

"It's only a few blocks," Jake said. "I don't mind the fresh air."

"It is at least a mile," Willem pointed out. "The blacksmith refuses to have a shop closer to town."

Slightly more than a mile, Abbie thought, which raised the question of what Jake was doing at the train station in the first place if he had left his horse. He carried no burlap sacks or packages tied with string from the mercantile. If he had not come to Limon for supplies unavailable in La Junta, then he had only one purpose.

Abbie set her jaw against what she knew to be true.

"In fact," Willem said, "why don't we pick up your horse and then you can ride alongside us? We can chat about how your plans are coming for starting a Mennonite church in Limon."

There it was. Leave it to Willem to speak it aloud. Abbie heard the whistle of an approaching freight train on the Rock Island track.

Jake dipped his head, the black brim of his hat swooping low. "Now that, my friend, is a subject I never tire of talking about."

"Willem, Mr. Heatwole might have other business in town," Abbie said. "We ought not to rush him."

"It is no problem," Jake said. "In fact, I appreciate the hospitality."

The train stirred up the wind around them, and its shuddering volume silenced the moment.

At Willem's wagon, he put Ruthanna's suitcase in the bed and extended a hand toward her. "I promise you'll be home soon."

Ruthanna accepted Willem's assistance onto the bench. "I admit a certain amount of curiosity about the new church myself."

Abbie half rolled her eyes. She and Ruthanna had discussed this topic more than once, and Ruthanna had been steadfast that she would never leave the true church. What was there to be curious about?

Ruthanna swallowed hard. The ride home would be just over eight miles to the point where her farm touched the corners of Abbie's, Willem's, and Rudy's. She had made it dozens of times before with Eber, and the miles always passed pleasantly enough. The child had changed that. Now every jostle, every dip, every sway required utmost concentration to keep her meals where they belonged. It would be good to sleep in her own bed again, beside Eber.

Their small home was hardly more than a lean-to compared to the homes of her parents and their friends in Pennsylvania, but at least it belonged to Eber and her. Ruthanna had a cast-iron stove for cooking, a firm rack for dry goods, a real mattress on an iron frame, and a table and four matching chairs. The baby would not need much at the beginning. Eber would build on next year, after the harvest. The baby would have plenty of room by the time she was ready to walk.

She.

Ruthanna smiled at the thought as Abbie settled in beside her.

"How long did you say Eber has been ill?" Ruthanna asked. "He didn't mention it in any of his letters."

"Just a couple of days, as far as I know," Abbie answered. "I only saw him a few times while you were gone."

"I do not suppose you would have reason to see him often. It's not like him to be sick."

"I admit I've never seen him ill before this, but everyone gets tired, Ruthanna."

"Not Eber."

Willem took up the reins. Ruthanna glanced over her shoulder at Jake stretching his legs in the wagon bed. He was a warm, sincere man with an infectious devotion. It seemed unjust to dislike him simply because he was a Mennonite, so she didn't. Surely Abbie did not truly dislike him, either.

It was the threat that Jake Heatwole carried in his every step that disturbed Abigail Weaver.

Abbie watched Jake Heatwole, relaxed in the wagon, as he conversed with Willem about why he thought Limon needed another church. It mattered nothing to Abbie whether Jake Heatwole started another *English* church. He had left the true faith when he joined the Mennonites. All that remained was to pray that he would not lure any of the Elbert County Amish. Willem had many responsibilities that demanded his best effort. Why would he think it profitable to spend time with Jake Heatwole?

Unless. Abbie sat up straighter. Unless Willem thought Jake would repent and return to the Amish.

Abbie wrapped three still-warm loaves in a soft flour sack and laid the bundle beside two similar offerings on the small table beside the hearth. The day was half gone, its first hours spent making bread dough, waiting for it to rise, heating the small oven, and baking bread two loaves at a time.

Esther Weaver silently counted on her fingers. "Twenty loaves. Nine for the single men leaves eleven for us."

"They came out well this week, don't you think?" Abbie resisted the urge to slice into a loaf that very moment and slather a thick serving with the butter she had churned the day before.

"The way your brothers have been eating lately," Esther said, "they'll go through three loaves a day if I don't stop them."

"I'll make more tomorrow," Abbie suggested.

Esther shook her head. "There's too much to do. We can't get in the habit of giving more than one day a week to baking. It's time the boys learned some self-control."

Abbie had to agree Daniel, Reuben, and Levi seemed to have bottomless stomachs, but she also noticed that all their trousers were too short again.

"Are you taking the open cart?" Esther asked.

Abbie nodded. "I don't mind the sun, and sadly, it is not likely to rain."

"No, I suppose not, though I pray every day for that particular blessing." Esther hung an idle kettle above the hearth. "On baking days at this time of year, the temperature is no different inside or out."

25

"*Daed* keeps talking about building a summer kitchen. I saw his sketch. It would have shade but no walls."

"He has many plans, but just when we need a summer kitchen the most, he must spend all his time thinking about getting water to the fields."

"He has ideas for an ingenious irrigation system," Abbie said. "It will not always be this hard. Not every summer will be a drought."

Esther smiled and tilted her head. "Abigail, my child, we have been here five years. Have we seen a single summer that was not drought compared to Ohio—and this one worse than all the others?"

"Then we are just about due for a nice wet summer."

"You had better get going. Where are you cleaning today?"

"Rudy's." And she would scrub his home spotless. She did not want to give Rudy any more reason to feel defeated.

Three weeks had passed since Abbie caught Rudy in the ticket line. She saw little of him, but he did not leave her mind. She would give encouragement in any form she could manage, including a sparkling house. Rudy Stutzman had a gift for understanding animals and keeping them healthy. If he left, who would be able to put a hand on the side of a cow and know that the animal's temperature was too high?

The wide brim of Abbie's bonnet, tied over her prayer *kapp*, allowed her to watch the road ahead of her without squinting. When she saw the Millers' buggy swaying toward her in the narrow road, she smiled. In a few more seconds she could see that both Albert and Mary were on the bench. That would mean that little Abraham was with them, probably in the back of the small black buggy.

Abbie lifted a hand off the reins to wave, and the Millers responded almost immediately. She guided her horse as far to the side of the road as she dared to take the cart's wheels. By the time her cart and the Millers' buggy were side by side, eighteen-month-old Abraham was peeking out from his miniature straw hat and had a thumb under a suspender strap in imitation of his father.

"Hello, Little Abe," Abbie said.

The little boy waved, his fingers squeezing in and out of his fist.

Abbie thought Abraham was the most beautiful child she had ever seen, though to speak the sentiment would tempt his parents to pride, so she did not. His chubby, shiny face, with its constant half smile, never failed to charm her.

Abbie raised her eyes to the child's parents. "How are the Millers today?"

Albert gave a somber nod. "We look for God's blessing of rain."

"As do I."

"We have just come from Eber and Ruthanna's."

"I was there yesterday to see how Ruthanna was feeling. How is she today?"

"She was having a good morning. Eber's health is of some concern to her, it seems."

"Yes, I was sorry to hear that he has a difficult day from time to time." Abbie suspected Eber's difficult days were more frequent than he admitted, and that was the reason for Ruthanna's concern.

"They've been hearing coyotes," Albert said. "We should all be watchful."

"By God's grace they will not come close."

Abraham rubbed his eyes, and his mother said, "It's time for us to get this little one home for a nap."

Albert nudged the horse and the Millers moved on. Abbie pulled her cart back onto the road, sighed, and smiled at the thought of Little Abe, and now Ruthanna's baby. These precious children were the future of the settlement. Whatever their parents suffered now would be worthwhile when they had strong, thriving farms to pass on to their sons.

A few minutes later, Abbie could tell from the stillness outside Willem's house that he was not there. Even the chickens had found a settled calm. Willem rarely was in the house when she came. He was running a farm, after all. Yet each time she hoped this would be the visit that he would be there to greet her.

She let herself in, making a point to look for an extra bedroll. Seeing only one, Abbie exhaled in relief. At least Jake Heatwole was not in residence this week. She moved across the undivided space to the area that would be called a kitchen were the structure a proper house. Last week's flour sack was empty, neatly folded, and laid precisely in the middle of the table. Abbie picked it up and put the new sack, holding three loaves of bread, in its place.

Then she scanned the room. Next week would be Willem's turn for a thorough cleaning, but Abbie looked for any task that appeared urgent for this day. Willem had been more generous with space in building his house than many of the settlers, and this pleased Abbie. There was plenty of room for a wife, and even a child or two. Willem also had partitioned off a true bedroom. Abbie peeked in there now, something she had come to be able to do without blushing at the thought that this would one day be her bedroom as well.

She found little to do. Although Willem ate the bread she brought and appreciated her cleaning efforts, he was remarkably neat for someone who lived alone. His habits were thoughtful and purposeful, features she believed she would appreciate even more when she was his wife.

By the time Abbie tidied up at Widower Samuels's house and made the wide circuit back to Rudy Stutzman's farm, bordering in a narrow strip on the Weavers', midafternoon had pressed in on the plain with the fiercest heat of the day. A wisp of humidity made Abbie reconsider her position that there was no reason to think it might rain that day. The whole community would raise hearts of gratitude if it were God's will to answer their prayers for moisture.

Rudy stood in a pasture with two *English* men about half a mile from his house. Abbie slowed the horse and cart long enough to try to recognize the *English*, but she could not see their faces well and could not be sure whether she had ever seen them before. At their ankles nipped a black and white dog. The mixed breed had turned up one day as a pup not more than ten weeks old and attached himself to Rudy. Because of his shaggy coat, Rudy had dubbed him Rug. When Abbie caught Rudy glancing up at her now, she had half a mind to tie up the horse and traipse through the pasture, but she would have no good explanation for doing so. With reluctance, she nudged the horse onward.

Rudy's house was built for a bachelor, one modest room for

sleeping, cooking, and eating, and a functional covered back porch for storing an unsystematic array of household and hardware items. Abbie put the bread in the middle of a table and found the previous week's limp flour sack hooked over the unadorned straight back of one of Rudy's two mismatched chairs. Then she looked in the water barrel and mentally gauged how much she would want for a proper cleaning. She would not use that much, of course. Rudy had a well, and as far as Abbie knew it did not threaten to run dry for household use and watering the animals, but water was too dear to use a drop more than necessary.

Abbie reached for the broom propped in one corner and began carefully dragging it through the dusty footprints on the floor of patchwork linoleum strips. She hung Rudy's extra pair of trousers on a hook, decided that the weak seam in his quilt would have to wait till another day, slid aside the few plates he owned so she could wipe down the shelves, and cleaned the dirty bowls in the bin that served as a sink. Every few minutes Abbie's gaze drifted out the open front door. She wished Rudy would walk through it and she could find out once and for all what was happening in that pasture.

Rudy chided himself. He ought to have known better than to agree to a meeting with the *English* on an afternoon when Abbie was due to come. But the visitors had gone to the trouble to track him down in his farthest field, where he fought a battle against weeds that only grew more futile in the face of strangled crops, and rode with him to the pastures where his eight cows and three horses grazed.

"You have some fine animals," Mr. Maxwell said, "though the coats on several of the cows lack a healthy sheen. That will, of course, affect the price we can offer. We cannot offer top dollar for unhealthy specimens."

Rudy said nothing. The cows were healthy. He would not engage in a discourteous conversation to prove his point. Only two days has passed since he mentioned to the owner of the feed store that he might sell his cows to the right owner, along with one of his horses. With his crop choking, the dairy cows were his livelihood. He would have to be certain of the decision he made.

Nothing required him to accept the offer the Maxwells might make. He was inclined to, though, unless the number they offered was grossly insulting. He could always list the property with an agent on short notice. He would not have to be present for the agent to show the land or close a deal. The animals were another question. If he sold them now, they would be worth more than they would be a few weeks later when they had chewed the pasture's scrabble down to the dust and he had nothing more to feed them and could not keep up with a growing bill at the feed store.

Rudy shook hands with the Maxwells, agreed to wait to hear from them, and watched as they mounted their horses and turned toward the road leading off his land. He had intended to retreat to one of the fields until he was sure Abbie was gone, but he spun around now at the clack of her cart behind him.

❦

"Hello, Rudy," Abbie said. She scrutinized him and then peered down the lane at the dust the two *English* stirred up in their departure.

"Hello, Abbie. Any problems up at the house?"

She shook her head. "I hope you will be pleased with my work."

"You never disappoint."

Abbie searched his eyes. Rudy was not so foolish as to think she had not seen the *English* on his land. "I don't think I've ever seen *English* visitors on your farm before."

"It's the first time."

Indignation welled. Why would Rudy be talking to *English* on his own land if it were not about a sale? "What's going on, Rudy?"

"We had some business to discuss. That is all."

"Business? What are you getting ready to sell to them?"

"I have come to feel that I do not need eight cows."

"Are you giving up on the dairy?"

Rudy waited a second too long to answer.

"Rudy, you cannot live out here by yourself without a cow. Have yours all dried up?"

"No, that's not the problem."

Abbie slipped off the cart's bench and paced toward Rudy. "You are not still thinking of leaving, are you?"

When his response was again delayed, Abbie's stomach tightened.

"I bought a voucher for a train ticket," Rudy said finally. "It does not have a date on it yet, but I wanted to buy one while I could still scrape together the cash to pay for it."

"Oh, Rudy. No. Please, no."

"Why not, Abbie? My wheat looks more pitiful by the day, even though I planted half what I put in last year because I cannot afford to irrigate my acres no matter how much milk I sell. I'm sure your *daed* knows how expensive it is to truck in water."

"But you belong here." Abbie dug her heels into the dirt. "We all do. We are here together."

"And we are stretched thin. Even you cannot dispute that."

"It will not always be this way."

Rudy turned in a full circle, gesturing to the flat dustiness of his land with upturned palms. "It might be."

"You have so much to look forward to here, Rudy. You have a future here." Abbie slapped a hand in Rudy's still outstretched hand.

He looked her straight in the eye. "Do I?"

"Of course you do."

"I mean apart from the land, Abbie." He closed his fingers around hers.

She shrugged, not understanding his meaning.

"Has Willem declared himself to you, Abigail?"

Abbie withdrew her hand and stepped back. "Not in so many words, no."

"But you feel certain that he will?"

"Nothing is certain except God's will."

"What if Willem does not meet your hopes, Abbie?"

Abbie broke her gaze.

❦

As Abbie cut through the back road that tied Rudy's farm with her family's land, the rain started with little warning other than the darkening clouds that blew across the plain on most summer afternoons without dispersing their moisture.

In her cart, halfway back to the Weaver farm, Abbie laughed out loud. She did not care that she had no covering, nor how drenched she might become. Rain! All around the region, farm families would be pausing in their work and looking up in exultation. Abbie turned her face to the sky, closed her eyes, and stuck out her tongue. She had not done that she since was a little girl in Ohio, but it seemed the only appropriate response now. The rain gathered in a thunderous drumbeat, and Abbie hastened the horse. In relief, she realized her dress already was damp enough that it was sticking to her skin.

Rain!

Abruptly the sound changed to a clatter of stones pouring from the heavens. Pea-size at first, then larger. The icy rock that struck her nose made Abbie's breath catch. The horse's feet danced while Abbie's chest heaved in protest. *Not hail. Please, God. Not hail.*

The nearest farm was Ruthanna and Eber's. They kept a hay shed near the road, but it stood empty now. By the time Abbie reached the shed, unhooked the mare from the cart, and dragged the horse under the shed's narrow overhang, tears streamed down her face. Abbie tied the horse tightly so it could not stray, then took refuge in the empty shelter.

She looked out at Ruthanna and Eber's tender crop and knew it could not survive this vicious pelting. No one's crop could.

The force that had destroyed the hope of harvest last summer once again rent in two the yearning of Abbie's heart.

CHAPTER 4

Ruthanna yanked open the door and stood in its frame screaming regret.

"Eber!"

Ruthanna had bitten her tongue two hours ago when Eber said he wanted to walk the fence line. He did not want to take the chance that a neighbor's hungry cow would nudge a loose post out of its earthy pocket in search of a scrabbly patch of grass to nibble on. If he had any grass, Eber would gladly share it with a cow. What he feared was that the animal would start in on his tenuous field of barley just as it showed signs of taking root. Eber had not regained his full strength. That was plain as day. But she could not hold him back from doing the only thing he could think to do as an obstinate summer yawned before them.

"Eber!"

Ruthanna's mind told her it was pointless to shriek into the wind, but she could not help it. The clanging smash of hail dumping from the sky against the tin roof drowned the sound of her voice even from her own ears. Eber had declined to take a horse with him, and he had been gone long enough that he could be anywhere on their acreage. When Ruthanna stepped out far enough to scan the horizon around the house—just to be sure Eber was not near—hail stung her cheeks. White icy mounds swelled around her as ever-larger hail pelted the finer base layer.

With one hand on her rounded abdomen, Ruthanna shielded her eyes with the other and peered through the onslaught of white.

Eber's white shirt would be lost against the hail. His black trousers would be her only hope of glimpsing him. Methodically, she scanned the view from left to right for any movement. Chickens in the yard scurried into the henhouse, but Ruthanna expected at least one or two would not survive the storm. Horses whinnied on the wind in their pasture. Ruthanna offered a quick prayer of thanks that their two cows were safely in the barn at the moment.

But she did not see Eber.

Within minutes, the hail was five inches deep. Ruthanna stepped back into the shelter of the doorframe, watching this mystery of spring. Only a few weeks ago five inches of snow would have been cause for rejoicing. Precious moisture would have melted into the ground and prepared the soil to welcome seed meticulously buried at precise depth and intervals. Even if hail had come before the seeds sprouted, the crop might have survived. But this! This was only terror.

Her father would have reminded her *Gottes wille.* God's will. Could it really be God's will for twelve obedient Amish families to suffer this racking devastation?

And then it was over. The sky had emptied and stilled. Drenched, Eber limped from around the back side of the barn.

Willem shoved open the barn door and hurtled toward the horse stalls. The stallion bared his teeth and raised his front legs in protest against the commotion. Willem slushed hail in on his boots. Frozen white masses in various sizes melted into the straw that lined the barn floor. Willem's tongue clucked the sequence of sounds that he had long ago learned would calm the frightened horse. He would not enter the stallion's stall until he was sure the animal had settled, but Willem spoke soothing words and familiar sounds. In the stall next to the stallion, the more mild-tempered mare hung her head over the half door hopefully, making Willem wish he had a carrot to reward her demeanor.

On the other side of the barn were the empty cow stalls. Intent on farming, not husbandry, Willem only had one cow. The hail's beating had been brief but swift, and Willem could not predict how the cow would have responded. He hoped it had not tried to bolt through Eber's fences.

Bareheaded, Willem stood in the center aisle that cut through the barn and stroked the mare's long face. Only two drops plopped on the top of his head before he raised his eyes and saw daylight through the barn's roof. Dropping his gaze, he saw that his feet stood in a mass of freshly damp hay. Hail had beaten its way through two wooden slats only loosely thatched over. Willem had hoped for proper shingles this year, but that required cash.

He put a hand across his eyes and bowed his head. Any of his fellow Amish worshippers might have thought he was praying, but Willem knew the truth. The thoughts ripping through his mind at that moment were far from submissive devotion to God's will. He forced himself to take several deep breaths before moving his hand from his eyes and again surveying the damage to his barn and the distress of his stallion. He could only imagine what his fields must look like.

Months of praying for favorable weather. Weeks of coaxing seeds to sprout in undernourished soil. Evening upon evening spent bent over the papers on his rustic wooden table writing out calculations and scenarios essential to the survival of his farm.

A hail storm was not part of the equation.

Willem pushed breath out and said aloud, "We will be all right."

The stallion shuffled but no longer protested.

The mare gave up looking for a treat in Willem's hand and nuzzled the straw in her stall.

Willem turned on one heel and left the barn. Outside the sun once again shone brilliant, as if the last twenty minutes had been a bad dream. Willem marched out to the pasture in search of his cow.

Abbie's heart rate slowed—finally.

The clattering of hail stopped as suddenly as it had begun. Cautious, Abbie pushed open the shed door. The extra resistance of several inches of hail required her to put her shoulder into the effort. Outside, fields of white glinted and forced her to squint. Abbie grabbed fistfuls of skirt and raised her hem above the slosh as she moved to where she had tied the horse. The animal was reasonably dry and unperturbed, Abbie was glad to see. As she hooked the cart to the horse again, she inspected her immediate surroundings. The size of the hail and its sheer quantity in the last few minutes twisted a lump in her stomach. In the distance she could see Ruthanna and Eber's house and wanted to see for herself that they were safe before continuing her journey home. The path was difficult to discern at first, covered by hail, but Abbie found signs of the familiar entry and guided the horse. Under the animal's feet and the cart's wheels, each sound of crunching hail reverberated through Abbie's mind with the implications of the storm.

A few minutes later, Abbie pulled up in front of the house. She saw boot prints leading from the barn to her friends' home, where the front door stood open and she could see clear through the structure. On the cooking side of the cabin, Eber sat in a straight-backed wooden chair with his boots off and his shoulders slumped, suspenders down around his waist. Behind him, Ruthanna worked at toweling his head dry. Abbie paused long enough at the door to knock and announce her presence. With a gasp, Ruthanna abandoned the towel and crossed the sparse sitting area to embrace Abbie.

"You're all right?" Squeezing her friend, Abbie felt the growing babe between them.

Ruthanna sniffled. "What does all right mean? Physically we are unharmed, but Eber. . ."

Abbie glanced across the room. "Eber, did you get caught out in the storm?"

Eber responded by putting his elbow on the table and hanging his head in his open palm.

Abbie tried again. "I hope you don't mind. I took shelter in your empty hay shed. You'll be glad to know it seems quite watertight."

Eber stood, pulled his suspenders over his shoulders, and retreated into the bedroom.

Ruthanna turned to Abbie. "What will we do now?"

"You're not alone. We have the church. We are all together, whether rejoicing or suffering."

"I cannot imagine anyone rejoicing today."

"Then we will suffer together and rejoice another day when

God shows us His will for the next step."

"Eber is tired." Ruthanna wiped the back of her hand across her face. "In body and spirit. He is tired."

The bedroom door closed with a thud.

With a promise to return the next day, Abbie said her farewell to Ruthanna. They both knew that a wife should go to her husband in a moment like this.

By now most of the hail had melted and puddled. In some places, miniature rivulets carved a downward path. As thirsty as the ground was, it could not absorb the moisture as quickly as icy chunks transformed into liquid on a warm afternoon. At first, Abbie willed herself to keep her eyes on the road and not to turn her gaze toward the fields on either side.

Ruthanna and Eber's fields.

Willem's fields.

Her father's fields.

What good would come from pausing to look at the damage so soon after the storm? After all, it was possible some shoots would have bent under pressure but might revive during the night, was it not? And Colorado hail sometimes dumped mercilessly in one area, while only three miles away the sun shone uninterrupted. The Amish farms were spread over miles and miles. She would be jumping to conclusions to presume that everyone's farm suffered equal fate. Perhaps the damage was more like a heavy, welcome rain. Surely no one would speculate about the severity or widespread nature of the loss on the same afternoon.

Abbie urged the horse's trot into a canter and kept her eyes straight ahead. She made her ears focus on the rhythmic beat of hooves and the swaying creek of the cart and breathed deeply of the spring scent after a rain.

Only once she turned down the ragged lane that led to the Weaver farm did Abbie allow herself to slow and observe. Her father stood in a field with two of her younger brothers. Abbie pulled on the reins, jumped out of the cart, and stepped delicately into the field.

She could see immediately that she need not have bothered with such care.

"Oh, *Daed*." Her voice cracked as the lump bulged in her throat. Ananias Weaver was beyond hearing range, but Abbie fixed her eyes on him until he at last looked up and met her gaze. Slowly, he shook his head before kneeling. Whether he bent in prayer, inspection, or resignation, Abbie did not know.

Abbie drew a knife through a loaf of bread and laid the resulting slice on the small plate her youngest brother held. Somber faced, Levi carried the plate to the table and sat down.

"Would you like to have two slices?" Abbie poised the knife over the bread again.

Levi shook his head. "We should be sure there's enough for everybody."

"I made four loaves today. You can have more."

The boy declined again.

Abbie laid the knife down. "I suppose we don't want to ruin your appetite for supper."

Levi picked at his bread. At eight, he was a skinny child with a usually infinite appetite.

"What's wrong, Levi?"

"I'm not hungry."

"*Mamm* has a bit of ham for supper, and some vegetables we canned last fall."

"If I tell her I'm not hungry, she won't make me eat."

He was right about that. Esther Weaver did not force children to eat supper, but she did make clear that if they chose not to, they would not have another opportunity until breakfast.

"*Mamm* asked me to give you an afternoon snack." Abbie dropped into a chair next to Levi. "Don't you feel well?"

"I feel fine." Levi put his hands in his lap. "Why don't you wrap this up for someone to have later? I'll go do my barn chores."

Levi nearly knocked his mother over on his way out the rear door of the family's narrow two-story house.

"Did he eat?" Esther set a basket of washed and sun-dried shirts on the floor.

"No. He believes we are running out of food." Abbie caught her mother's hand, forcing the older woman to look at her. "We aren't, are we?"

"The chickens still lay nicely, and the cows give milk morning and night, don't they?" Esther snapped a shirt flat on the table and began to smooth the sleeves. "It's all this talk about losing the summer crop. I've told your *daed* he must be more careful about who is listening."

"It's never been his way to coddle children."

"Surely there is something in between coddling and frightening."

"Yes, I suppose so." Abbie stood and returned to the butcher block to slice more bread. The family of seven would easily consume at least one loaf for supper.

"It's getting hotter every day," Esther said. "We may have to start doing our baking in the middle of the night."

"I haven't seen *Daed* in the fields since the hail."

Esther folded the shirt she had smoothed, wordless.

"*Mamm?*"

"He does not tell me what he is thinking."

"Surely he is going to put in a fall crop."

"Have you put the water on to boil?" Esther abandoned the laundry basket and moved toward the stove.

❧❀❧

"I'm going to make a quilt," Abbie announced.

Willem looked up from the patch of ground he was assaulting with a shovel. Sweat oozed out from under his straw hat and down the sides of his face.

"It's a hundred degrees out here," he said. "Just thinking about a quilt is more than I can take."

"But it won't always be a hundred degrees, and we won't always be in a drought."

"Why then, I suppose a quilt is an act of faith." Willem stabbed at unyielding earth once more. It was not too far into summer to put in a few vegetables—something that did not require much water.

"That's exactly right." Abbie folded the empty flour sack she had exchanged for Willem's weekly ration of bread inside his cabin. "An act of faith. It's going to be a tree of life quilt."

Willem chuckled. "The attraction of this land was that we didn't have to clear trees before we could plant. Right now I could do with a bit of shade."

"It's a beautiful pattern. I can make one tree for each of the twelve families in our settlement."

Willem nodded. It seemed unlikely the Elbert County settlement would attract more families anytime soon. He tipped his hat back and looked at Abbie full on. "And what will become of this quilt once it is finished? Will it be big enough for two?"

That blush. That was the reason he said these things.

She unfurled the folded flour sack at him. "You would like to think you're deserving, wouldn't you?"

He grinned. "I'm just choosing my moment."

"And what excuse will you have when the fall harvest is over and it's marrying season?"

"Ministers are as scarce as trees out here." Willem raised the shovel above his shoulders and let its point drop directly into the cracked soil.

"Maybe you'd better start solving that problem now."

"There's always Jake Heatwole."

He heard her gasp but refused to meet her eyes, instead scraping at the thin layer of soil he had managed to loosen. "What if it comes down to a Mennonite minister or no wedding at all?"

"Aren't you getting the cart before the horse? I don't recall hearing a proper proposal of marriage." Abbie folded the sack once again.

"You know I'm irresistible."

"Willem Peters! That is the most prideful thing to say."

"Perhaps. But it is a legitimate question, considering we haven't had a minister even visit us in a year to preach, much less baptize or marry."

"That's not going to last forever. The drought will end. The settlement will grow. We will have a minister."

Willem wiped a sleeve across his forehead. He hoped she was right. He hoped the day would not come that he would have to tell her that the optimism had worn off his own faith.

❧

"Are you tempted to use some prints?" Ruthanna smoothed the folded blue apron one last time before handing it to Abbie.

"Oh my, no." Abbie clutched the apron to her chest. "I don't want to use any fabric that our people would not wear."

"Some do, you know. Nothing too outrageous, but remnants or old skirts from the *English*." Ruthanna sat in one of her four kitchen chairs and wished she had washed the morning dishes before Abbie arrived.

In another chair, Abbie shook her head. "Not me. My tree of life quilt will be a symbol of our growing settlement. I don't want the suggestion of anything *English*."

Ruthanna gave a small shrug. "You wouldn't have to go all the way to the *English*. The Mennonite women are beginning to wear small prints."

"I wish them well in their own settlement, but I do not want their worn dresses."

"I wish I had more to give you. I only have three dresses. I feel I can spare the apron because I spilled ink all over it and couldn't get it out. But there are plenty of unspoiled patches that will do fine in a piece quilt."

"Don't feel badly," Abbie said. "My *mamm* says it is time for her to give her quilt scraps to me anyway. If I have even one item from each of our households, the quilt will truly represent the settlement."

"How much do you have so far?"

Abbie tilted her head to think. "I still need to go by the Millers', but Mary promised me one of Albert's old shirts. And I haven't spoken to Rudy yet." She had contributions from the Yoders, Nissleys, Chupps, Yutzys, Mullets, Troyers, and now the

Gingeriches. Even Willem and Widower Samuels had found something to donate. Her mother's scraps would fill in many gaps.

"Do you really think Rudy will have something you can use?" Ruthanna stroked her stomach. "Most of his clothes look ready for the rag pile as it is."

"I know. I ought to make him a shirt."

"He's sweet on you. You know that, right?"

Abbie bristled. "I most certainly do not. Where do you get such nonsense?"

"I see the way his eyes follow you when everyone is together."

"Without church services, that hardly ever happens. You're imagining things."

"Would it be so bad if he were? Willem is not exactly..."

"Willem is Willem."

"Right." Ruthanna cleared her throat. "Are you sure you don't want a cup of *kaffi?*"

"Positive. I'm perspiring as it is, and I still need to take eggs and cheese to some of the other families of the settlement."

Ruthanna breathed in and out slowly. "Do you think we'll ever stop calling it that?"

"Calling it what?"

"The settlement. Nobody at home in Pennsylvania or Ohio uses that word."

"Because they are all in established districts, with ministers."

"That's what I mean," Ruthanna said. "If no minister ever comes, we'll never be more than a settlement."

Abbie stood. "I am far too busy to let such doubts into my mind, and I suggest you banish them as well. You have a baby to get ready for!"

Ruthanna received the kiss her friend offered her cheek and watched as Abbie skittered across the cabin and out the front door. Last year's failed crop. A horrific winter. Spring hail. Summer drought. Yet Abigail Weaver believed.

Rudy Stutzman leaned on a fence post and wiped his eyes against his shoulder to contain the dripping sweat. Even when he came out to work in his fields at first light, long before the sun slashed the sky with full-fledged rays, he was drenched in his own perspiration before breakfast. Indiana summers were hot, but mature oaks and elms dotted the countryside, and creeks and rivers ran with as much cool water as a man could ask for. Here Rudy reminded himself to swallow his spit because drinking water was scarce and he had the animals to think of—never mind sufficient water to irrigate.

After the hail, Rudy had dutifully begun turning his soil again, inch by backbreaking inch. Not all of it. He did not have seed for a second planting even for half of his acres—not even a third. He only turned as much earth as he needed for sparse rows he could afford. Without any delusions that he would have enough crop to generate cash in the market, he settled for hoping for enough wheat to grind and mill. If the Weaver women were going to continue to bake his bread, he ought at least to contribute grain to the process. He had not intended to be anyone's charity case when he came to this land he could only describe as desolate. Unyielding. Ever-thirsty. Stingy. Yes, desolate.

Rudy wanted to throw off his hat, stick his head in a bucket of cold water, and gulp freely. And when he pulled it out again, he wanted to see the rolling green hills of Indiana, the smile of his mother's face, fresh clean sheets on his bed. He still had the voucher for a train ticket that he bought the morning when Abbie Weaver pleaded with him not to leave. Alone in the evenings, he sometimes took it out of its envelope and fingered the edges.

She still stopped him from going. If he left now, he would never see her sweet face again. In all the weeks since that day, he had heard nothing new about what was between Abbie Weaver and Willem Peters. Perhaps it was not as much as many people presumed.

CHAPTER 6

Let me help you, Eber." Ruthanna reached for the metal pail. Eber grunted and turned away from her without releasing his grip on the handle. "Do you think I cannot manage a milk pail on my own?"

"That's just it." Ruthanna moved one hand to the achy spot at the side of her back more out of habit than pain. "It's only a milk pail. I can carry it to the house while you get started with the other cow."

"There's no need. I can bring them both when I come. You have the child to think of."

"The baby is not coming for months," Ruthanna said. "There is no need for me to give up simple tasks, at least not yet."

"You have a tendency to overwork yourself."

Ruthanna bit her bottom lip. How could Eber not see that he had taken his own tendency toward overwork to extremes? Every day that he spent outside in the heat worried her more. Even the brown tones the sun gave his skin did not hide his underlying pallor, and he was breathing too fast for her liking.

"Eber, please let me take the pail. It's not even half-full. I will be careful."

He relented. "We are going to need all the cheese you can make. We may not have much else to see us through the winter."

Ruthanna took the pail before he could change his mind. "Let me bring you some water."

Eber shook his head. "That isn't necessary. We must conserve."

"One glass of water is not going to save the crop, Eber. But it might save you."

He grunted again, running a dry tongue over chapped lips.

Ruthanna pivoted as smoothly as she could with her growing bulk and left the barn.

Inside the cabin, Ruthanna set the milk pail in the corner of the kitchen and took a glass from the cupboard. With the dipper in the water barrel, she filled the glass before looking around for some bit of nourishment to take to Eber as well. He had so little appetite these days. Ruthanna had already taken in his trousers twice. In the evenings, he sat in his chair and stared at her swelling belly. His early exuberance about the child had long ago faded. Ruthanna was sure he would love the baby when it arrived in November, but he wanted to provide a better start for their child's life than a failed crop and a hungry winter.

Ruthanna settled on a boiled egg. They still had hens, and the hens still laid. Ruthanna had boiled a batch that morning, carefully setting aside the leftover water to use again for another purpose. With a glass in one hand and an egg in the other, Ruthanna began the trek back to the barn.

The cow whose udder still hung heavy mooed in protest at Eber's inattention. He sat on a bale of hay with his head hanging between his hands. Just as Ruthanna entered the barn, he looked up for a fraction of a second, then slid off the hay.

Ruthanna hastened her swaying progress, gripping the water glass. She wanted to cast it away and run, but her intuition told her Eber needed the precious water more than ever. When she reached him, she cradled his head in her lap and slapped gently at his cheek.

"Eber! Open your eyes!"

He obliged, to her great relief. He was breathing far too heavily, and his skin was clammy under her touch.

"You must drink some water. Don't argue with me." She gripped the back of his head and raised it, while at the same time tipping the water glass against his lips. But he seemed to part his lips only to let his faltering breath escape. Water dribbled down his chin rather than down his throat.

"Eber! You must drink!"

He seemed to want to speak, but he did not have the strength.

Ruthanna's heart pounded. Her husband needed help. The closest neighbors, the Weavers, were miles away even by crisscrossing the back road. She picked up the hem of her dress and dipped it in the water glass, then moved the damp fabric around Eber's face and against his lips. When his mouth opened again, she squeezed the hem so loose drops would fall into his throat.

He closed his eyes again.

"Eber! No!"

He moaned but did not open his eyes. His head fell to one side.

Ruthanna laid his head back in the straw and opened the front of his shirt before drenching her hem again and dabbing his chest. He breathed evenly now and not so heavily, but Ruthanna was not fooled. He was not simply asleep.

She pushed herself upright and left the empty water glass beside the egg in the hay. The buggy was outside the barn, and the horse in the pasture. Ruthanna mustered a whistle, and the horse turned his head. She whistled again, and he began to trot toward her. She opened the gates. The hundreds of times she had fastened horse to cart guided her muscles now with efficiency beyond her thought. Ruthanna could not get herself astride a horse in her condition. The buggy was her only option.

She drove recklessly, abandoning all sensibility to the thought of losing Eber. Even when she turned into the rugged lane leading to the Weaver home, she did not slow down. Chickens in the yard scattered. The young Weaver sons looked up from their chores. Ruthanna screamed her friend's name.

The front door opened and Abbie appeared.

❧❦❧

Abbie drove the rig with firm determination and little sympathy for the performance she demanded from Ruthanna's horse. Beside her, Ruthanna gripped the bench with both hands, and behind them, Abbie's mother clutched a large jug of water and a sack of herbs and cloths. Esther had refused to stay behind, and Abbie was grateful. Her mother had far more experience coping with a crisis than she did. Ruthanna's face was a sopping mess of tears by the time they turned toward Eber and the barn. Abbie pulled the buggy up as close to the barn as she could. Even in her clumsy state, Ruthanna was out of the rig before it fully stopped, and Esther clamored out behind her. Abbie opted to leave the buggy harnessed to the horse in case they should need the animal's service again soon, but she allowed a rapid gesture to tie him to a post while Esther and Ruthanna ran into the barn.

When Abbie entered, she could not see Eber. Ruthanna and Esther were on their knees, bent over him.

"Is he—?" Abbie asked.

Ruthanna gave a cry. "He's still breathing. We're not too late."

"Hold his head, Ruthanna." Esther fished in her bag. "He's burning up. We have to get him cooled down before we do anything else."

As Ruthanna arranged her lap under her husband's head, Abbie fell to her knees on the other side of Eber. "*Mamm*, tell me what to do."

"Get this cloth good and wet." Esther flung the scrap of an old flour sack at Abbie and thrust the water jug toward her.

Perspiration drenched Abbie's dress as the afternoon's heat pressed in. She handed the sopping rag back to her mother, who exchanged it for a dry one. Abbie drenched the second rag as her mother opened Eber's shirt as far as it would go. With cool damp rags on Eber's chest and face, Esther proceeded to force water down his throat a spoonful at a time.

"Shall we try to take him into the house?" Ruthanna asked.

Esther nodded. "Soon. I hope it's cooler in there."

"It is," Ruthanna said. "Eber insisted on building a generous overhang for the extra shade."

"His own wisdom may help save his life."

"I should pray." Ruthanna looked stricken. "I can't think what to say. Why can't I pray when I have never needed to pray so hard in my life?"

"God hears your prayers." Esther handed a rag to Abbie to dampen again. "Words are not necessary. Now, Abbie, you help me get Eber upright. Ruthanna, you make sure a damp rag stays on his head at all times. Do you understand?"

While her mother tended Eber, Abbie finished milking the cow Eber had left in distress. With three younger brothers she did not often milk a cow anymore, but she managed. Then she took a slop bucket out to the chickens and made sure the horse had food and water.

Evening's waning light gave way to blackness, and still Eber's skin threw off heat. Each time he moaned, the three women jumped to their feet. Ruthanna pulled a chair up to the side of the bed and draped herself across her husband, finally finding words for her prayers. Abbie watched her friend's lips move silently but steadily.

Well after midnight, Abbie lit a lantern and rummaged around Ruthanna's pantry. She found the boiled eggs and a wedge of cheese and prepared a plate, which she set on the bed next to Ruthanna.

Ruthanna shook her head, struggling to swallow. "I cannot eat."

"You must. For the baby."

Ruthanna slowly drew herself up. "I am not sure I can."

"You must try. You must."

"Abigail is right." Esther Weaver's voice came from a dark corner at the foot of the bed.

Abbie peeled a boiled egg and handed it to Ruthanna. "I'll get you something to drink."

"Take care of my Ruthie." The sound from the bed startled them all.

"Eber!" Ruthanna put a hand against his face then turned toward Abbie. "He's cooling off!"

Esther laid a hand across his forehead. "She's right. The fever has broken."

"Will you drink something now, Eber?" Ruthanna asked.

He nodded. "If you will."

Abbie let out a joyful breath. "I will be right back with two glasses."

Esther followed Abbie out of the cramped bedroom and into the cooking area.

"Do you know where to find the doctor in Limon?" Esther whispered.

Abbie swallowed. "I think so. But Eber is better. Haven't we sat through the worst of it?"

Esther glanced toward the bedroom. "I am concerned that he is truly ill."

"He was too much in the heat," Abbie said. "He'll listen to Ruthanna now. He'll be more sensible."

Esther shook her head. "The Lord whispers to my spirit that it is more than that. You should go at first light."

CHAPTER 7

Three days later, Abbie hung up her apron and brushed the loose flour from her skirt. While the bread rose, she had time to go visit Ruthanna and Eber, particularly if she took a horse and buggy rather than walking the miles between the farms. Outside she stood for a moment surveying the Weaver land. The barn and chicken coop were close to the house. Beyond them her father had marked off the corners of a proper stables and training area for new horses. Abbie knew he had hoped to build the structure by now, rather than cramming horses into the barn at night and leaving the weather-beaten buggy outside.

Abbie blew out her breath, swallowed, and crossed the yard to the barn for a horse. Inside, the barn was dim, and it took a few seconds for Abbie to realize that her father knelt next to an open sack of seed. He scooped up a handful then spread his fingers and let it run back down to the sack. She watched him do this three or four times before she spoke.

"*Daed?*"

He looked up.

"Is it all right if I take the buggy? I want to check on Eber and see if Ruthanna needs anything."

"That is fine, daughter. I am sure God is pleased at how you are caring for your friend. You make sure they are following the doctor's instructions."

"I will." Slowly, she reached to remove a harness from the wall. "Are you getting ready to plant again?"

He resumed the rhythm of lifting and sifting seed.

"*Daed?*"

"This seed is the most valuable thing I have. Our family's future depends on the decision I make."

"It's not too late. Others are planting again now."

Ananias Weaver lifted his head and looked at his daughter full on. "It is difficult to discern whether that is foolishness or faith."

"If we don't plant, we won't have a crop."

"And if I cannot irrigate sufficiently, and we don't get rain, we will have wasted a valuable resource."

Abbie moistened her lips. For all of her childhood, her father had held closely any hint of difficulty in the family's finances from year to year or the reasons for his decisions. But she was no longer a child. She was of an age where she could have married and remained in Ohio. Abbie had chosen to move to the new settlement as an adult. At the time, she thought she knew the risks. They all did. No one could have foreseen the difficulty they would face in the quest to root an Amish congregation in the unyielding Colorado plain.

"Take the dark mare, please," Ananias said. "She hasn't been out of the pasture for several days. I don't need a horse that becomes accustomed to idleness."

Willem Peters stabbed a pitchfork into the soiled hay in the end stall of the Gingerich barn. The stench assaulted his breath. Willem was well accustomed to the smells that came with housing and caring for animals, but this seemed extreme. He could not help but wonder how long it had been since Eber felt well enough to adequately muck stalls. The doctor Abbie had fetched from Limon three days ago was clear that Eber needed complete rest for the next few weeks. Word of Eber's decline had spread quickly through the Amish families, and the men soon enough volunteered for the outdoor work to keep the farm operating. Eber would have no crop again this year and had no seed to plant again, but his animals would be milked and fed and cleaned up.

Rudy positioned a wheelbarrow as close to Willem as possible.

"We should have come sooner," Rudy said.

"*Ya.*" Willem emptied the fork into the wheelbarrow and attacked the stall with the implement again. "Eber doesn't like to ask for help."

"He should know that pride is a sin."

"He only wants to know he can take care of his family. You and I are not married men. We don't know what that responsibility must feel like."

"I guess not." Rudy picked up a shovel and began to work alongside Willem. "Why have you not married?"

Willem shrugged. "Perhaps I feel as Eber does—I want to feel sure I can provide."

"So you are waiting for the right time?"

"I suppose so."

"Not the right girl?"

"Of course I want the right girl."

"But haven't you found her?"

Willem eyed Rudy in his peripheral vision. "Do you mean Abigail Weaver?"

"No man could ask for a finer wife. Lovely in appearance, loyal in spirit, unafraid of hardship, devoted to the church."

Willem diverted his gaze now. "You seem to have given a lot of thought to Abigail."

"I am merely an observant man. I have not yet drawn a conclusion about the extent of her patience." Rudy dropped his shovel and gripped the handles of the wheelbarrow again. It was full enough to take out and dump in a place where the manure could do some good.

Willem watched as Rudy navigated down the short length of the barn and turned out of sight at the open door. He stood the pitchfork straight up and leaned on it, wishing Rudy would just say what was on his mind. What did he mean about Abbie's patience?

Willem heard a buggy clatter to a stop outside the barn and abandoned his task to see who had arrived. Abbie Weaver descended from the driving bench and leaned her head attentively toward Rudy.

A week later, Ruthanna worked as quietly as she could along the one wall of the cabin that she called her kitchen. It was a far cry from the sprawling kitchen of the home she grew up in and that she had always imagined her own kitchen would be like.

She *would* have a kitchen someday. Ruthanna refused to believe that she and Eber would have anything less than what they dreamed of when they left Pennsylvania. After all, they had a baby on the way finally—and owned more land than they could have hoped for in Pennsylvania. If they had to live in a small cabin for a year or two longer than they expected, that was not too great a sacrifice.

Ruthanna glanced toward the bedroom. If Eber were well, he would scowl at the thought of two men cleaning out his barn. He might even be displeased at the dishes of food that had been turning up in the hands of Amish visitors eager to be of some practical help during his illness. As it was, he did not question the origin of the food his wife offered to him at frequent intervals and ate very little before saying again that he wished to sleep.

The doctor had been vague. Ruthanna was not persuaded he knew what was wrong with Eber. Prescribing complete rest and generous food was safe advice. Anyone could see Eber was exhausted and thin. Rest and food could not possibly hurt him, but was it enough to help? Ruthanna murmured prayers every time fear welled within her. Eber *would* get well. She would not let her mind dawdle over any other possibility.

The knock at the door was soft, and Ruthanna knew it was Abbie before she turned to look. Abbie had heard the doctor's instructions with her own ears. Each time she visited she kept her voice low and movements soft. The door opened and Abbie entered.

"How are you?" Abbie touched Ruthanna's cheek. "Are you taking care of yourself?"

"I'm fine." Ruthanna gestured to a chair for Abbie to sit in. "The men have been coming to do all the chores. I barely have to leave the house."

"Good. If Eber needs you, you want to be here."

Ruthanna nodded.

From the bedroom came an insistent, deep-chested cough.

"When did that start?" Abbie looked alarmed.

"During the night."

"It sounds terrible."

"It is not constant. He has a fit every few hours. I think it is only the dust. I can't seem to keep it out of the house."

"I will ask my *mamm* if there is something else you should be doing."

"Thank you." Ruthanna swallowed. "I wish I could ask my own *mamm*."

"Have you written? I could mail a letter for you."

Ruthanna shook her head. "I don't want to alarm anyone at home. By the time a letter reached Pennsylvania and my *mamm* could write back, Eber will be well."

"Levi asked me to tell you he is praying in his heart all day long."

A strained smile stretched Ruthanna's lips, and she put her hand on her abdomen. "I hope my *kinner* is as sweet as Levi."

Abbie did not stay long at Ruthanna's. She knew her friend well enough to know she needed to use nervous energy by keeping her hands busy and feeling that she was accomplishing something. While Eber slept, Ruthanna would sweep and scrub and mend and cook, and Abbie would not suggest she should do otherwise. Abbie chatted with Rudy and Willem while she served them cold water and cornbread, provisions sent by her mother. Something was odd between the two of them. Whatever it was, they would have to work it out. Abbie had more on her mind.

Leaving Eber and Ruthanna's farm on the main road, Abbie saw Albert and Mary Miller approaching. She reined in the mare as she came alongside them and could see that Mary held in her lap a dish wrapped in towels. The generosity that poured out of all the Amish neighbors nearly made Abbie's chest burst. They might not have a minister of their own or the twice-monthly worship services they all yearned for, but they could still be a church and care for each other.

Little Abe peeked out from behind his mother and gave Abbie a grin. She grinned back. He lifted one bare foot for her inspection.

Mary laughed. "We were talking about having the cobbler make him some shoes. We have a piece of leather he can use, but we have not had time to take Abe to be measured."

"Why don't I take him?" Abbie said. "I could come by tomorrow and pick up Little Abe and the leather. I would be delighted to do it."

Mary glanced at her son. "He always loves spending time with you."

"Then please let me do this for you. I'll come in the morning so I can have him home in plenty of time for his nap."

CHAPTER 8

It all seemed so secretive, and Abbie did not understand why.

She put her father's breakfast plate in front of him and waited for his silent prayer before she asked, "What will the men be talking about this morning?"

"Church matters, of course." Ananias looked over his round-rimmed glasses at his daughter.

Abbie poured coffee and pushed the mug toward him. "Are we going to get a minister?"

"That is a question for God." He bit into his toast.

"We've been praying for a minister for years." Perhaps it was time for God to answer the pleas of the believers.

"In God's time."

Abbie thought back to more than a year ago. Her father and a few other men gathered on a morning not so different from this one. Hot. Dry. Cloudless.

But a bishop had been with them for that meeting. The men were behind closed doors for hours with Bishop Lehman. He had come from Kansas, which was not so far compared to Ohio or Pennsylvania. Even still, the bishop had not visited for months before that. Another minister, also from Kansas, had come to preach during a break in the February weather. By June of 1913, the twelve Amish families scattered around the outskirts of Limon ached for worship, for the discipline of hearing sermons, for the slow, careful harmonies of their hymns.

For communion, the body and blood of the Lord.

But the bishop cut his visit short without explanation. None but the handful of men on the church council knew the nature of the conversation that would cause him to leave abruptly without preaching and leading the communion service.

And none of them would speak of it, not even to their wives. Abbie had heard enough whispers among the women to know that her ignorance of the circumstances had nothing to do with her age or marital status. The men simply would not speak. Not a word for over a year.

"Maybe a minister would visit us again," Abbie said now, "if we asked."

Why had the ministers stopped visiting the new settlement? The question rang in Abbie's mind, though she dared not ask it aloud.

Ananias cleared his throat. "Abigail, I can see that you are disturbed by your own curiosity. I will not satisfy it, so you may as well release it and put your energy into something needful."

Abbie turned around and set the coffeepot on the stove. Did her father think the women did not miss having church services? Did he believe them incapable of understanding whatever had sent the bishop away?

This time all the men, even the unmarried ones, would attend the meeting. As her father finished his breakfast and put on his hat, Abbie cleaned the dishes with a minimum of water and pondered whether to ask Willem or Rudy later to tell her what happened.

Sitting on the wooden stoop outside his cabin, Willem raised his eyes to the sun. He judged he had a good thirty minutes before he must leave for the meeting and raised his coffee to his lips. It was strong and black and bitter, and he relished the sensation of its thickness oozing down his throat. Before too many more hours, the day would be blistering and he would not want coffee. In this moment he could enjoy it as he gazed across his land and watched as shadows dissipated and the day came into crisp focus.

Open on the step beside Willem was his mother's latest letter.

His brother was considering taking a job in an *English* factory to pay the bank what he owed on his farm. To finance new farm equipment, one of his cousins had sold a parcel of land that had been in the family for 150 years. Willem's gut clenched at the thought of those enchanting rolling acres lost to the Peters family forever. His cousin had been threatening to sell for years and even offered the acres to Willem. But they would have made for a small farm with no good place to situate a house, and Willem wanted a large farm. He wanted plenty of earth to receive as his own, a gift from God. He wanted more than to eke out a living. His parents had taught him generosity from before he ever held a coin in his hand. Over the years since he became a man, Willem had come to see that generosity was a measure of the spirit and not of land or money. Nevertheless his heart swelled with yearning to give. If God blessed him with abundance, Willem would gladly give to all in need.

Eber, for instance. Willem wished he could do something for Eber and Ruthanna. They deserved to know their child would have everything he needed.

Willem took another gulp of coffee. He was not a man for meetings. Last year, when the church council met, Willem had no curiosity about their discussions. He was as surprised as everyone else that the bishop left without serving communion, but Willem never thought to ask about the meeting. Like all Amish men, when he was baptized, he agreed to serve as minister if he should ever be called on, but the possibility could not be further from his mind. Especially now. A minister would have to be ordained, and if they could not even get ministers to visit and preach every few months, it was unlikely a bishop would suddenly agree to ordain one of the men. Besides, Willem was not married. No one would think to nominate him to be minister.

The coffee mug was empty now. The four men who made up the council had been firm that all men should attend this meeting, so Willem stood up, tucked in his shirt, raised his suspenders, and trudged to the barn for his horse.

❧❦❧

"I am sure the council will understand if you are not present for the meeting." Ruthanna followed Eber around the cabin, hesitant about every unstable step he took. "They shouldn't even have come out here to ask it of you."

"They asked all the men." Eber leaned over to pick up a boot and sat in a chair to put it on. He turned his head to cough.

"You are not well, Eber." Ruthanna presented herself in front of him with hands on hips.

"I have been in bed for weeks while other men do my work. I believe I can manage to sit upright for one meeting."

"Eber, you barely stay out of bed long enough to eat a meal at the table with me. You cannot even walk to the outhouse."

Ruthanna regretted pointing out this last reality.

Eber's eyes flashed at her. "Perhaps you can find it in yourself to leave me a small portion of my dignity."

"I'm sorry, Eber. You know I love you. I want you to be well. I want you to be strong. Then you can do all the things you want to do."

"Today I want to be strong enough to go to this meeting." Eber laced his boot and tied it snugly.

Ruthanna briefly considered blocking his view as he looked around for his second boot. He had not even had them on since the day she found him collapsed in the barn, yet he thought he was recovered enough to travel twenty miles and sit upright and awake. He did not know what the meeting was about. How could he be so sure he must be present? When Willem Peters delicately asked if Eber planned to go and Ruthanna immediately brushed away the impossible idea, Eber had announced his startling intention.

She stepped across the room and fetched Eber's other shoe. When she handed it to him, she said, "Why don't you let me drive you? I'm sewing for the baby. I can take my things and find a bit of shade to wait for you. That way, if you tire, I can bring you home."

He eyed her briefly before returning his attention to his feet. "I will drive. But you may come."

"Do you promise to let me drive home? You'll be exhausted by then."

Eber put his hand on his stomach and groaned. Ruthanna

winced at the sound.

"All right," he said. "Bring some food. For the sake of the baby."

When Ruthanna carried food and a jug of water out to the buggy, she also took a quilt and a pillow. Even if Eber did not want to admit it, she knew he was going to need them.

~❦~

Rudy did not see the point.

What could the men possibly have to talk about that would make a difference?

Crops? As far as he knew, no one seriously believed there would be a harvest.

A prayer meeting? Perhaps they intended to pray for the miracle of favorable weather. Rain to drench the fields and fill the water troughs. The stilling of the incessant wind. Clouds to protect their burnished faces from further assault. Such an effort would require more faith than Rudy could muster.

News of a visiting minister? That hardly required a meeting of all the men. The council would have arranged that.

A particular financial need? Rudy could not think what he had to share. Perhaps he would slaughter a cow to mercifully save it from starving to death and revive the long-forgotten taste of meat in everyone's mouths.

Whatever decision was to be made could be made without Rudy. He would go collect the morning's eggs—oh, how he was tired of subsisting on eggs—and go back to bed for another hour. There was no point in going into the fields.

The day's yield was seventeen eggs. Rudy placed them in a tin bowl and shuffled back toward the house, turning only when he heard the sound of a horse and buggy.

Willem Peters.

"You're a mess," Willem said. "Have you even washed your face this morning?"

"I'm not going." Rudy reached for the door.

"Of course you are." Willem dropped down from the buggy bench. "I'll wait for you."

"Willem—"

"Rudy, you're an able-bodied Amish man. The council has asked us to attend, and we will respect them. We knew when we joined the settlers that we might face some difficult decisions."

Rudy did not appreciate Willem's authoritative tone, but he took his point. "I think I have a clean shirt."

Or at least one that was less thick with dust.

CHAPTER 9

The Weaver house filled with women and small children. Abbie knew her mother had invited Mrs. Chupp, the cobbler's wife, and Mrs. Nissley to stop by while their husbands were meeting. The others must have come out of anticipation for what the men's conference might yield. Abbie put a fresh pot of coffee on the stove and fanned herself with an envelope from her cousin Leah in Indiana. Abbie would have to cut the coffee cake and canned apples into small portions to extend hospitality to a dozen extra women and children. The house was crowded and tepid, but Abbie did not mind. Having so many of the Amish women together in one place was almost as satisfying as a shared meal after a church service, an event beginning to fade in memory.

When Abbie heard one more buggy clatter into the yard, she threaded her way through the visiting women to look out the front window.

Mary Miller. And Little Abe.

Abbie grinned wide as she held the door open for them and scooped up Little Abe as soon as his bare feet and wiggly toes crossed the threshold. He showed her all his teeth and put a playful hand over her face.

"He is so adorable that I don't know how you can stand it," Abbie said. She slobbered a kiss on the boy's cheek.

Mary laughed. "He is not always so well tempered. When he has a tantrum I'm grateful we live miles from anyone else or we would have to supply the neighbors with something to plug their ears."

"We'll have to see if we have a treat for you." Abbie gently poked the child's tummy. She looked at Mary. "I'll bring you some *kaffi*. Mrs. Chupp is here. Perhaps she knows when her husband will have Little Abe's new shoes ready."

"He's excited to have shoes, but he is so used to bare feet that I don't know if he'll wear them."

"It will be good for him to have them. The ground here is not like the soft grass at home. Anything that grows is scratchy, and there are so many pebbles. Once he has shoes you can let him play more freely."

"He's not a baby anymore." Mary looked around. "Speaking of babies, is Ruthanna here?"

Abbie shook her head. "I'm sure she wouldn't want to leave Eber at home just to visit. She hasn't left their farm since the day he fell ill."

"I want to ask her what she needs for the baby. I would be happy to share the things Little Abe has outgrown."

"I'm sure she would be grateful."

Little Abe wriggled out of Abbie's arms and squatted to touch the nearest pair of shoes.

"How is your quilt coming along?" Mary asked.

"I have almost all the pieces cut out." Abbie tickled Little Abe under the chin. "I can't wait to start piecing."

"I'm eager to see your progress." Mary looked around. "I suppose everyone is here for the same reason. It's too nerve-racking to wait alone at home for news of what the men are discussing. I hope it is news of a minister. Without church for over a year, this is a wonderful lonesome place to be."

The men gathered on a motley arrangement of chairs, milking stools, barrels, and bales in the Mullet barn. It was the only space that would allow them to sit in a lopsided circle where most of them could see each other's faces. Willem sat beside Rudy at the curve in the circle nearest the open barn doors. He had also carried two jugs of water in from his wagon and now offered this token of refreshment as he studied the mostly bearded faces of the assembly.

Only two gave the slightest sign that they knew the purpose of the meeting. Everyone else appeared as uninformed as Willem and Rudy were.

Eli Yoder cleared his throat. As one of the first Amish men to arrive in Elbert County five years ago, Eli held a certain if unofficial role when the families gathered. Around the circle, conversation ceased as he commanded attention by the gutteral signal that he was ready to begin.

"I thank you all for coming." Eli nodded at Eber Gingerich. "We are blessed to have some among us who have been ill and brought back to us by the grace of God."

Murmurs confirmed the shared gratitude for Eber's presence.

Eli continued. "We will begin with a time of silent prayer so that we may know that we are acting in accordance with the Lord's will in our decisions today."

Willem glanced at Rudy, while around them others bowed their heads. Willem was accustomed to prayer, and he supposed Rudy was, too. Living and working alone on a wide expanse of plowed land allowed ample time to hum the hymns of the *Ausbund* and speak the words of Holy Scripture as prayer. Generally, though, when Willem was instructed to pray he preferred to know what he was praying for. What decisions did Eli Yoder expect they would be making? Willem inhaled softly and bowed his head. He could pray for the Holy Ghost to make His presence known. Such a prayer seemed relevant to any situation Willem had ever encountered.

Eli waited a good long time before speaking an audible "Amen." Willem heard the relief on the breath of other men that they would now find out why they had gathered.

"We need a minister," Eli said. "I have come to feel certain that if we were to nominate a faithful man from among our midst, we could invite a bishop to come and ordain him."

Rudy's hand went up.

Eli raised his eyebrows. "Do you have a nomination already, Rudy?"

"No sir. I have a question."

Eli shifted his considerable weight on the small wooden chair.

"A year ago a bishop was here and left without preaching or

giving us communion. I would be dishonest if I said I have not been wondering for many months why this was so."

Heads turned from Rudy to Eli.

"We are not here to discuss the past," Eli said. "Our need is for a future, and if we have no minister, we have no future. Now, I myself have come prepared to make a nomination."

The only shade Ruthanna saw was in the shadow of her own buggy. She kept her word to Eber and did not situate herself anywhere near the Mullet barn. This was the first time he was out of her sight since that day in their own barn, and every moment stretched interminable. At intervals that did not exceed fifteen seconds, she lifted her eyes to make sure Eber was not emerging from the barn overheated and freshly ill.

Ruthanna spread the blanket on the ground beside the buggy, lowered herself onto it, and unfolded the bundle of sewing she had brought. She was nearly finished with a small quilt and just had to put the hem into two long white infant dresses. Feeling the tension rising in her chest with each glance toward the barn, she began to recite Psalm 23. When she came to, "Yea, though I walk through the valley of the shadow of death," Ruthanna stopped. A lump rising in her throat threatened to cut off her air and she skipped ahead to, "Surely goodness and mercy shall follow me all the days of my life."

Then she made herself take a deep breath and begin stitching without looking up at the barn. She determined to finish a six-inch row of binding along the edge of the quilt before she raised her eyes again.

The wind was oddly still for the Colorado plain. Ruthanna was not sure whether to be grateful not to have hot, dusty air blasting into her face or to think that any movement at all would bring some relief to the perspiration trickling down her neck. She moistened her lips and focused on her row of stitching.

Ruthanna never knew what it was that made her sit up straight and look over her shoulder, through the undercarriage of the buggy, and into the eyes of a coyote. She froze, staring into the unmoving animal's eyes. Every farmer in the region knew what it was like to have a coyote get into the henhouse before dawn—and in one attack destroy the steady flow of eggs that fed the family. Ruthanna had not heard any tales of settlers coming face-to-face with one in the day's light, though.

If she moved, she might startle him into attack. But if he attacked first, her swelling belly and aching back would slow her down. And what was to keep him from leaping into the buggy if she tried to drive away? If he would come this close to begin with, what else might he do?

She started again at the beginning of Psalm 23, speaking the words in her mind over her pounding heart. This time she did not skip the unpleasant part as she held perfectly still and locked eyes with the coyote.

Finally the animal lost interest, turned around, and sauntered away. All Ruthanna wanted was to feel Eber's arms around her.

Rudy meant no disrespect, and he did not pursue his question. Eli did not intend to respond, and the only other two men present who knew the answer would never defy Eli. Unsatisfied about why the rest of the men should remain uninformed and confused, Rudy crossed his arms and tilted his stool back on two legs while Eli made his nomination.

Noah Chupp. The cobbler.

Eli methodically listed Noah's virtues. His mild temperament. His patience. His spiritual depth. His friendly relationships with everyone in the community. His family heritage of ministers, and the certainty that had he remained in Pennsylvania he would have been a minister before now. His grandfather had even been a bishop.

Noah Chupp humbly responded that he would need time to seek out the will of God in this matter. The assembly agreed that of course he should take as much time as he required to be sure. No one wanted to misinterpret the leading of the Lord.

As the meeting broke up, Rudy leaned toward Willem.

"Do you think we will ever know what happened last year?" Rudy asked.

Willem shrugged. "Do we need to?"

"If there is a reason why we have not been able to establish a true church before this, it affects us all. There may be division among us."

"Everyone seemed of one accord about Noah Chupp," Willem said softly. "Unless you are not."

Rudy scratched his chin. "Noah is a fine man."

"Then what is your hesitation?"

"I sense something must come into the light."

Willem stood. "Let's see what comes of praying over this matter. In the meantime, let's see if Eber needs help."

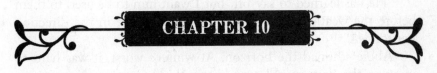

But I thought Noah Chupp was to be our minister." Abbie scrunched her face in confusion.

In Mary Miller's arms, Little Abe twisted to lean over and touch his new brown leather miniature boots.

"Mrs. Nissley says her husband believes it would be better if we began our church with a more experienced minister," Mary said. "He thinks one might come from Kansas."

"Does this minister know. . .the challenges of the settlement? He might need to find a way to make a living other than farming." Abbie tried to picture where a new family might live. Plenty of land was for sale closer to Limon, or perhaps in the other direction toward Colorado Springs. Considering the nearly nonexistent crop yield last year, the price per acre might even have fallen since her father purchased land.

"I don't think Mr. Nissley has anyone particular in mind just yet."

Mary relented and set Abe on his feet, which Abbie thought sensible. That was the point of having shoes made. They stood beside the treeless cow pasture on Weaver land, so the boy would not wander out of sight.

Abbie's confusion compounded. "If Mr. Nissley does not yet know of anyone willing to come, isn't it premature to talk about the possibility? Besides, we all heard what the men decided. Noah Chupp was to pray over the matter and give an answer in two weeks. What if he says yes? Wouldn't it be easier to find a bishop to ordain him than to persuade a minister who is already serving another district to move out here?"

"What if Noah says no?" Mary countered.

Then they would be back where they started. But if Adam Nissley thought enticing a minister from Kansas truly was an option, surely it would have happened by now.

"Let's walk a little bit," Abbie said, "and let Little Abe try out his shoes."

"He has learned to say 'off,' but I want him to be used to them before the weather turns." Mary began to amble in the direction her son led.

Abbie scanned the horizon. At winter's worst, it was hard to imagine the days would ever blister this hot again. Now it was difficult to think of the weather turning. Snow could fall as early as mid-September—too late for the crop and too soon to hope a minister might come before spring.

"I think Noah Chupp would do a fine job," Abbie said. "He makes wise decisions, and he was one of the first settlers to come. He loves the church, and he listens to the Holy Ghost."

"I wonder why they didn't think to ask him before this." Ahead of them, Mary's son lost his balance and fell on his bottom.

Abbie watched the tenacious child. While other toddlers might have wailed at falling in the dirt, Little Abe did the obvious thing. He put his hands on the ground and pushed himself upright again. Abbie's imagination drifted forward forty years when Little Abe would just be Abe, or Abraham, and he might be called upon to lead the congregation that nurtured him from infancy under the leadership of many ministers.

"We all must pray," Abbie said. "We followed God's leading to come and settle here. We must not think that He would abandon us. Finding the right minister is a matter of God's timing. Perhaps God has only begun to prepare the heart of our minister."

"I long for communion." Mary put a hand to the side of her head and pushed an errant braid into place. "I long for the unity that comes when we gather around the Lord's table."

"As do I," Abbie murmured. Without a spiritual leader for much longer, she hated to think what would happen to morale among the settlers.

The knock on the door startled Ruthanna. It was a man's knock, heavy fisted and insistent. She put down the baby's quilt and pulled herself out of the chair before Eber stirred. Though he would deny it, in Ruthanna's opinion Eber's outing to the men's meeting had sent him back to his bed in worse condition. He simply did not have the strength to spend half a day riding in a wagon and sitting upright. By God's grace Ruthanna had refrained from chastising her husband about his choice, instead caring for him with the same tenderness she offered before their disagreement. She did not tell him about the lurking coyote that day, though she had folded the blanket and moved back up into the buggy, and instead of watching for Eber every fifteen seconds she moved her eyes back and forth across the horizon, turning also to look behind her.

She opened the door now expecting Willem or Rudy or one of the other men inquiring whether she needed help with anything beyond the usual chores.

Instead she stared into brown eyes above ruddy cheeks on the face of Jake Heatwole.

Jake offered a warm, broad smile. "Good morning, Mrs. Gingerich. The Lord's blessing be on you."

"Thank you." Ruthanna moved aside, wondering what refreshment she might offer. Perhaps bread and strawberry preserves. "Please come in."

"I suppose you're surprised to see me."

Jake stepped into the room and removed his black hat nearly identical to Eber's. He wore the same collarless black suit and white shirt the Amish men wore. The townspeople of Limon never understood the difference between Amish and Mennonite, but Ruthanna did. The Amish had parted ways from the Mennonites more than two hundred years ago. Ruthanna did not claim certainty about the original dispute or the sometimes hostile chasm it opened between the two groups, but she did feel certainty that she belonged to the heritage her family had claimed for generations. She had no need to test the liberties the Mennonites might allow upon which the Amish would likely frown—especially if they had a minister. Ruthanna would much rather rest secure in belonging to the true church.

Still, it was hard not to like Jake Heatwole. She wondered why he had never married.

"I've just come from Willem Peters's," Jake said. "He tells me that your Eber is still ill and that he has not truly been well since that day we all encountered one another at the train station."

Ruthanna nodded and gestured to the only chair with a hint of padding on its seat. "Let me get you something. *Kaffi?* I have fresh cream."

Jake sat in the chair but waved away her offer. "I have not come to cause you inconvenience. Quite the opposite. I want to help."

"The men are doing the essential chores until Eber gets back on his feet."

"So Willem tells me. He also says that he looks around and sees work that they cannot keep up with because of their own farms. The henhouse, for instance, has a hole in the roof that is only going to get bigger. And he says you never leave the farm because you do not want to leave Eber alone."

Ruthanna nodded. This was all true. She depended heavily on Abbie and Esther to stop in and see if she needed anything from town before they went. Rain was unlikely, so she had not worried about the hole in the henhouse roof, though since her encounter with the coyote she wondered just how much of an opening the animal would require to wreak havoc.

"We're getting by." Ruthanna wiped her hands on her apron, turned a chair toward Jake, and sat down. "The others are doing everything they can to help."

"Of course they are," Jake said. "That is what the church does. I am here to help for the same reason."

Ruthanna furrowed her brow. "But you are Mennonite. We are Amish."

"We serve the same God."

"But your own farm—"

"It's in the capable hands of my two brothers. They know that I will move to Limon eventually to open a church there. They hardly let me lift a hand around the farm anymore."

"Surely you must have a thousand things to do."

"No doubt." Jake leaned forward, his elbows on his knees. "But this comes to the top of my list."

"Mr. Heatwole, your offer is most generous, but—"

"We can talk it over with Eber. I propose to camp out behind your barn for two weeks. I won't ask anything of you in the house except a bit of water if you can spare it. I'll give the other men a break by looking after all the chores, and if you need to go into town or want to visit with your friend Abbie, you can do so knowing that someone is here with Eber."

Ruthanna swallowed as she considered. What he suggested had merit. "Only for two weeks. Not a day more."

Jake turned a palm up. "We all hope Eber will be better soon."

"And only if Eber agrees."

"Of course."

❧

The committee assembled at the crossroads that joined three farms. Two miles away was Noah Chupp's land, with a promising vegetable garden despite the drought and a separate structure he used for a small tannery and cobbler's shop. He made shoes for the *English* as well, along with other leather goods, and it seemed to Willem that Noah's livelihood was thriving better than most. Willem was glad for the whole Chupp family, which included seven children under the age of twelve.

Willem never intended to be on this committee. Certainly he did not volunteer for it. Unlike Rudy, Willem hesitated to decline anything Eli Yoder asked him to do, so here he was with Eli. They stood beside their horses as they waited for the widower Samuels to join them. The trio would proceed together to hear Noah's discernment of the Lord's leading about becoming the first minister of the fledgling congregation, provided a bishop would agree to ordain him.

Martin Samuels trotted toward them, slowing his gelding but not dismounting.

Eli crossed his wrists in front of him. "Shall we have a word of prayer before we proceed?"

Willem hoped God had already made His will plain to Noah Chupp. Most congregations chose their ministers by lot, and the man chosen rarely had grounds to refuse. Noah already enjoyed the privilege of private discernment. But once again Willem found it impossible to refuse Eli.

"I agree," Martin said. "If Noah feels the calling of God to take up this mantle, he will bear the burden of healing the divide among us. It will not be an easy task. Will we wait until he agrees before we explain why the bishop left last year?"

Eli's eyes flashed at Willem before lowering in a posture of prayer. "We will not speak of that. We will pray only for our future."

Willem would have been hard-pressed to say he was praying in the moments of silence that followed. Too many questions flashed through his mind. He did not even close his eyes, instead gazing first at Eli and then at Martin. Eli stood motionless, head bowed, eyes closed, feet shoulder width apart. On his horse Martin leaned over the horn of the saddle, one hand crossed above the other, with his eyes squeezed in peculiar fervency.

Rudy's barn door was wide open in the middle of the morning. Abbie glanced at the cows dotting the nearest field and then turned toward the smaller horse pasture. The animals were all where they were supposed to be. She knocked on the house door as usual, heard no response, and went inside to leave the bread. Coming out again, it disturbed her to see the barn door open, and rather than climbing back into her cart, she strode over to the barn.

"Rudy?"

"In here." A grunt accompanied his reply.

Visions of Eber sprawled in the straw spurred Abbie into the depths of the barn. "Where are you?"

"The end stall."

Abbie kicked straw out of the walkway. When she saw him, Abbie gasped. A cow was secured in the stall, and Rudy had one arm well inside it.

"Time for the calf?" Abbie said. She had seen calves born on her own family's farm in Ohio, but the wonder of it mesmerized her every time. "Is she all right?"

Rudy nodded, his eyes closed.

He was visualizing the position of the calf, Abbie knew.

"I have one foot and the nose," he said. "Ah. There's the other foot."

Abbie moved into the stall. "How can I help?"

"Hand me the rope," Rudy said. "It's there on the wall."

Abbie handed it to him and then leaned over his shoulder to peer into the mystery of life. Rudy secured the feet and prepared to pull if necessary. The cow began to strain, and as she did, Rudy checked the position of the calf once again.

"Will it be a normal birth?" Abbie asked.

"I think so. The mother is doing well. This is her third calf."

Abbie held her breath, awaiting the cow's next round of exertion.

"Here we go," Rudy said, readjusting his position to brace for delivery.

Abbie stepped back to watch without further chatter until first the face, then one shoulder, then the other emerged. Rudy kept his hands positioned to respond to distress but otherwise let the natural process take its course. Within a few minutes, the calf lay in the straw beside its mother. Rudy examined the newborn quickly.

"Is it all right?" Abbie asked.

Rudy looked up and grinned. "A female, and she's perfect."

Abbie squatted to look more closely, taking in the angles of the legs and the curves of the head. "God is good."

Rudy calmly tended to the mother. "I'm glad you were here to see the birth."

"I am, too. I would have come ready to be more help if I had known."

"She was fast. I only started watching her closely last night, and not much happened until this morning."

"God has blessed you." Abbie stepped out of the stall. "I'll heat some water so you can clean up."

"*Danki.*"

Abbie turned for one last look at mother, calf, and Rudy, a triangle of tenderness in a bed of straw. She had not seen such contentment on Rudy's face in months—but perhaps she had not been looking.

CHAPTER 11

"Thank you for taking me to town with you." Ruthanna offered Abbie a grateful smile.

"It was no trouble. I was going anyway, and it's so much more fun to have you with me." The reins were nearly slack in Abbie's hands. Their business in Limon complete, they were in no rush to return to the chores that awaited them.

"We both did well with our eggs today," Ruthanna said. "It seems to be the only thing that gives us a bit of cash these days. Imagine what would happen if the townspeople figured out they could keep chickens in back of their houses."

"They don't like the smell and the mess. So far there are enough merchants to take eggs from both us and the *English* farmers. God provides."

"It doesn't hurt that the railroads will buy as many eggs as they can get to feed their employees."

Abbie chuckled. "Blessing comes in many forms."

Ruthanna spread her arms out in front of her. "Fresh air! I've barely been out of the house in weeks. Jake insisted it would be good for me to have an outing. He promised he would stay inside the house with Eber the whole time I was gone."

Abbie bit back the response that sprang to her mind. If Ruthanna had wanted to go somewhere, Abbie or one of her parents gladly would have stayed with Eber. Abbie visited every day, sometimes collecting eggs to sell in town, and Ruthanna never said she wished she could go, too. But she took advice from Jake

Heatwole, that Mennonite minister who obviously was looking for people to help him start a congregation of his own.

"Have you heard anything new about Noah Chupp?" Ruthanna asked. "It's already been four days since he told the committee he needed more time."

Abbie nodded. Talking about the possibility of their own minister was a far more pleasant topic. "I think he wants to be very sure, and I cannot blame him. It's an honor to be asked, and he will want to be sure of his motives before the Lord."

Ruthanna peered down the road at her approaching farm. "I do hope Eber is all right."

"I'm sure he's fine." Abbie clicked her tongue to speed the horse for Ruthanna's sake. "He seemed much better this morning when we left."

"He enjoys Jake's company, even if he has reservations about the Mennonites."

"If Eber is feeling well enough for company, I am sure our own men would be happy to see more of him."

"Willem and Rudy have been by, of course. We're out of the way for everyone else."

"Nonsense. I will mention to my *daed* that Eber might benefit from some male company." She turned into the lane that would take them to the Gingerich home. To her surprise, Eber was sitting in a chair in the yard.

When Abbie stopped the buggy, Ruthanna got down as gracefully as possible in her condition.

"Eber! You're outside!" Ruthanna closed the yards between them and put a hand on her husband's head.

"Jake carried the chair outside," Eber said, "on condition that I agree not to lift a hand with the work."

Abbie followed Ruthanna's eyes as she smiled at the Mennonite minister.

Jake picked up a rag and wiped it across his forehead. "I thought I would make some repairs to the henhouse. Hail damage, I think."

"I'm sure the hens will be grateful," Ruthanna said.

"Maybe they've gotten used to seeing the stars at night."

Ruthanna laughed. Still in the buggy, Abbie clamped her jaw

closed. This was not the time to impress on Ruthanna that Jake Heatwole's motives might include recruiting the Gingeriches.

"I should go." Abbie rearranged her grip on the reins. "As soon as I hear that Noah Chupp has officially accepted, I'll let you know."

Willem looked up when the shadow across the barn door interfered with the light he was depending on. "Noah! Good afternoon."

Noah stood in the doorway without stepping into the barn. "Do you have a few minutes, Willem?"

"Certainly." Willem laid down the short stool leg he was carving to replace one that had cracked on his milking stool. "Shall we go in the house? It's humble, but it's out of the sun."

Noah nodded, and Willem led the way. Inside, Willem turned two narrow wooden chairs toward each other. He saw the perspiration seeping through Noah's beard.

"Let me get you a glass of water."

Noah put up one hand as he sat down. "There is no need. I'm on my way into town to deliver some boots and will not take up much of your time."

Willem scratched the back of his head and occupied the other chair. The space between them would have accommodated one pair of stretched out limbs, but Willem took his cue from Noah and sat straight and upright.

Noah cleared his throat. "I told the committee I would let you know when I made a decision."

Willem held his face in solemn stillness, already suspecting that Eli Yoder was going to be unhappy with what Noah was preparing to say.

"Yes," Willem said, "we are anxious to hear what sign the Lord has given you."

"I came here because I believe you are the most sensible man on the committee who visited me four days ago."

Willem waited.

"I must decline the gracious invitation to serve as the settlement's first minister."

Willem sighed. He could not think of one settler who would

not be disappointed to hear this decision.

"People will have many questions," Noah said.

"Yes, I suppose so." Willem waited as Noah shuffled his feet and rubbed his hands down his legs.

"We each must serve out of our conscience," Noah said. "My conscience will not allow me to accept such a grave responsibility while my spirit is home to the least bit of doubt."

"Doubt?" Willem had never known Noah Chupp to be filled with anything but devout faith. "Are you doubting our Lord?"

Noah shook his head. "Our Lord is faithful, and my faith in Him is firm."

"Then what troubles your spirit, Noah?"

"Our settlement is as fragile as an old stalk of wheat."

Willem leaned forward, elbows on knees. "Yes, we are precarious. I would have to agree. But we all feel that a formal church with a minister will only be to our good. When we hear the Word preached and sing our hymns together, our bonds will surely strengthen."

Noah tilted his head. "I realize that is the prevailing sentiment."

"Is it not more than sentiment? Is it not faith?"

"Therein lies my doubt," Noah said. "We are few in number as it is. No one else is coming. We need members. We need crops to feed our families and take to market. Frankly, I believe we will lose families rather than gain them."

Willem also suspected this to be true, so he offered no dispute.

Noah licked his lips and glanced around the house before meeting Willem's eyes again. "My family will be the first to leave, Willem."

Willem sat up and scraped his chair back a few inches. "Have you already decided? I thought your livelihood was going well because you took in work from the *English*."

"It is. But I need a church as much as anyone. My seven children need a church. In a few years my eldest daughter will be looking for a husband. Am I supposed to marry her off to Widower Samuels? Or that bundle of nerves Rudy Stutzman?"

Willem had no response.

"I am on my way to Limon to mail the documents to finalize

the purchase of land in Nebraska. I am already talking to an *English* interested in my land here. He won't pay what I paid per acre, but I will go away with something to start again."

"I see. You've given this a great deal of thought."

Noah rubbed a knuckle against the side of his nose. "I may as well tell you the whole truth."

"There's more?"

"I am leaving the Amish."

"Leaving? Altogether?"

Noah nodded. "I believe the Mennonites are fine people, and not so different from us. Even the Baptists are true people of God, and many of them live as plainly as we do. I am sure we will find a spiritual home."

Willem felt his jaw drop open. He never suspected Noah Chupp would consider anyone beyond the Amish to be true people of God. He cleared his throat.

Noah stood. "I thank you for not trying to talk me out of a decision I have wrestled with in prayer for long hours."

Willem stood as well. "I know you can't have come to this easily. What would you like me to do for you, Noah?"

"Speak to Eli Yoder, please."

Willem's heart thudded. "Perhaps we can go together to speak to him."

Noah waved off the idea. "I realize he will come directly to my shop as soon as he hears, and I will have to talk to him. But I trust your sensibilities to break this news to him first."

❧

Abbie clenched her fists and glared at Willem.

"Don't look at me like that," he said. "Noah Chupp's decision is not my doing."

She kicked a rock down the rutted lane of her family's land. Willem had waited until they were beyond earshot of the rest of the Weavers to tell her the news. She huffed out the air pent up in her chest.

"I'm sorry. It just would have meant so much to the community for him to become our minister." In an established district, church members would have chosen their minister by lot from among the men. Declining would have been far more difficult. Sadness crept through Abbie that time-tested traditions of their own faith had failed to answer this need.

"I know how much you wanted Noah to accept," Willem said.

"To discern that it was not God's will is one thing. But to move away and join the Mennonites? Or the Baptists?"

"He remains a man of deep faith, Abigail." Willem reached for her hand and pulled her to his side. "*Gottes wille.* If Noah is not to be our minister, God still has a plan. We will be all right."

"Why won't any bishops come to us, Willem? That's what I want to know." She searched his face for any sign that he knew the answer to her question. "We don't live in the wilderness. Colorado Springs is not so far, or Denver. Limon has twenty-four trains a day! Traveling to us is not a great difficulty."

She could see he had no response, but the rampage in her heart was too full blown to stop. "We *need* to worship in our traditional ways. We need to go to church. We need to hear the Word preached. Our settlement could bear everything else that is happening to us if we just had our spiritual life together."

Willem nodded and lifted both her hands, turning her to face him. "Jake Heatwole is a minister. He knows all our hymns. He speaks our language. We could have church."

A *Mennonite* church service. The thought of it almost caused physical pain in Abbie's chest. She wondered if Willem knew her as well as she thought he did.

Abbie stitched feverishly that night on the tree of life quilt, full of defiance of what Willem implied. His words would not be enough to diminish her faith.

CHAPTER 12

A bbie swiped a rag cut from a flour sack across the wide-planked table one last time. Rudy Stutzman lived simply. Cleaning his house never took long. He was not particularly organized, but he was more inclined than most men to push a broom across the floor occasionally or brush bread crumbs into his hand and shake them outside for the birds. Abbie had not seen Rudy that morning. She supposed he was in the fields, though it was possible he had decided to go into Limon. His horses were not in the pasture where Rudy usually left them during the day.

She gathered her pail of cleaning supplies and stood on his narrow front step for a moment, her mind flashing to the day she had found him inquiring about train tickets. That was weeks ago. Surely he was not still thinking of leaving, not after the joy she saw on his face when the calf was born. Abbie heard chickens clacking in the yard and saw Rudy's cows nuzzling the ground for something to chew. When Rudy acquired more than one cow, many had thought it was an odd choice for a bachelor. How much milk and cheese would he need? Abbie had smiled to herself at the time. Eight cows were Rudy's investment in a future. Before long he was selling milk, butter, and cheese to *English* neighbors, claiming that the distance he had to drive to do so was well worth the income. Sometimes they paid him in meat or beans, which was almost as good as cash.

With her pail beside her on the floor of the Weaver buggy—in the heat of midsummer, she preferred the shade of the buggy to the open-air cart—Abbie picked up the reins. She was on her way next to Mary Miller's farm, having promised to sit with Little Abe for a few hours while Mary went to work on a quilt with Mrs. Nissley. Abe was past the age of sitting quietly to play on the floor while his mother concentrated on something besides him, and Abbie loved to be with him. With a glance at the sky to judge the time, Abbie opted for a detour that would take her well out of her way. Once she had made up her mind, she shut off any thoughts of reasons not to.

Forty minutes later, Abbie pulled up to the Chupp property, swinging wide away from the cobbler's workshop and instead aiming for the house. Sarah Chupp was in the yard hanging the sparse laundry she had indulged in washing. In a household with seven children, a certain amount of water had to be allotted to washing. At Sarah's feet, her youngest child pushed a fist-sized rock around in the dirt. What would Little Abe Miller do without his favorite playmate?

With a dark brown dress slung over her shoulder, Sarah turned toward Abbie. Taking in a deep breath, Abbie stepped down from the buggy's bench in no particular hurry.

"Hello, Abbie." Sarah took a clothespin from a basket and used it to hang a towel. "I suppose you've heard the news."

Abbie nodded. "I'm sorry that I didn't notice you were unhappy before it came to this."

"It hasn't come to anything. We made a decision, that's all." Sarah pinned up a tiny white shirt.

"I hate to see you go. You are a precious family. The church loves you all."

Sarah lifted her basket and moved it down the line. Abbie picked up a damp towel and two pins.

"There really isn't a church, now is there?" Sarah's tone was soft, but her words stung Abbie.

" 'Where two or three are gathered,'" Abbie said. "We could be the kind of church we all want if your husband were the minister."

Sarah sighed and scratched the top of her head just in front of her prayer *kapp*. "Noah made up his mind."

"You're his wife. He would listen to you."

"You presume I would want him to change his mind."

Abbie forced down the lump forming in her throat. "Your families have been Amish for two hundred years."

"I know."

"Then you know what it means to belong, to help each other through hard times, to care for each other."

"We have seven children to think of." Sarah bent for a moment to run a hand through her son's hair, smoothing it out away from his face.

"I am sorry we failed you," Abbie said. "I hope you will accept my apology on behalf of the whole church."

"Don't be silly, Abigail. No one failed us."

"But you want to leave us."

"It's not anybody's fault, Abbie. We made a choice to move out here three years ago, and now we have made a choice to try another place."

"But to leave the Amish church—is that not extreme?" Abbie fought the lines forming in her face.

Sarah reached out and took Abbie's hand. "You're very kind. No one is more committed to this settlement than you are, and if it succeeds I suspect it will be because of you."

Abbie's shoulders fell. "But you do not believe we can succeed."

"*Gottes wille.* But no, Noah and I both feel it is only a matter of time before the families of the settlement will face the same decision we faced. We simply have chosen to decide sooner."

Abbie failed to stifle her gasp. "Do you really think others will leave?"

"Abigail, you're an intelligent young woman." Sarah raised her palms toward the blistering sun. "You know about the drought. You know the damage the hail did. You know that everybody owes money to the bank. You know that not everyone will have any crop to sell this year."

"But your husband has a trade," Abbie protested.

"And no money to buy hides to make leather, and nine mouths to feed. Our own people cannot even ask him to make shoes because they have nothing to pay him with. We did not come all the way out here to make shoes for the *English*. Noah can do that in a place where we can join a church and teach our children the life of faith. We've made our decision, Abbie."

Sarah put her empty laundry basket on her hip, reached for her son's small hand, and began to walk toward the house.

By the time Abbie reached the Millers' house, she made sure her to banish her tears. Mary met her at the door with her quilt project bundled in her arms.

"Little Abe is down for a nap," Mary said, "but he should wake up in about half an hour. Thank you for coming!"

Mary left, and Abbie moved to the doorway of the room where Little Abe slept. She leaned against the doorframe with her hands behind her waist and watched the little boy's chest rise and fall. He was too little to know he was losing a playmate whom Abbie had hoped he would know for his entire life, too innocent to realize how precarious his own family's existence was. Abbie's mind drifted to her own quilt, the one she worked on in the evenings. Twelve trees of life were to represent the twelve founding households of the settlement. Eleven would be all wrong.

The evening cooled, though the air remained arid. Willem rode over after supper, as he often did, to see if Abbie would like a walk. One look at her face told him that Noah Chupp's decision still crushed her.

"*Gottes wille*," he said. "We will be all right."

"It's wrong, Willem." She paced so briskly that Willem expended more energy than he wished to keep up with her. "Can't you talk to Noah again? It's been a few days. Maybe he would be ready to listen to reason."

"Each man should follow his own conscience." Willem reached for her hand, trying to slow her down. "You know Noah is a man of prayer. He did not make the decision on a whim."

"But what about our community? It is the way of our people to have a commitment to one another. We all knew that a new settlement would face challenges. We must face them together, not surrender to our individual interests."

He took her by both shoulders now, stilling her and turning her to face him. "Abbie, can you honestly say that your family's life has been as you pictured it when your parents began talking about moving to Colorado?"

"That is not the point I'm trying to make." She tried to worm free, but he would not release her. He held his gaze steady until hers settled and she looked him in the eyes, unblinking.

"We all came out here not just to begin a new church," Willem said, "but because we believed we could have a more prosperous life. More land, lower prices. We have to be honest about our motives before we judge Noah Chupp."

"Of course the men must make a living and provide for their families," Abbie said. "Life here on the plains is a great deal of work for the women, too. But how can we so easily lose sight of the church? If everyone gives up and moves away, what will these years have been for?"

"God has His purposes. Even suffering forms us into His image." Willem moved one hand up to the side of Abbie's neck, and he felt the tension ease beneath his fingers as he knew it would. "Abbie, no matter what happens, we will be all right."

"You always say that." Her lips pouted, but the fight had gone out of her tone.

"Because it's true. If it is God's will for our settlement to succeed, then it will. And if everyone moves away, God will not care for us any less."

Her lips moved in and out, but Willem could see Abbie had no argument against the simple truths of his statement. He raised a thumb to her face and gently drew it across her lips before covering her mouth with his and feeling her remaining resistance dissipate.

They jumped apart at the sound of a throat clearing.

Willem peered over Abbie's shoulder. "Jake."

Abbie exhaled and took a farther step back.

"It's a lovely evening for a long walk, don't you think?" Jake smiled at both of them.

"How is Eber?" Abbie asked.

Jake tilted his head. "Today has not been as bad as many."

"Has the doctor been back out to their place?" Willem asked.

"Several times. He does not seem to have anything new to say. It may be a disorder of the stomach."

"Eber is under too much stress," Willem said.

"How much longer will you stay?" Abbie asked.

"A few days." Jake ran one finger around the rim of his hat. "I will let you know, Willem, so you and the others can sort out what to do about the chores. I don't want Ruthanna left with the heavy work."

"Of course not."

Abbie raised a hand to adjust her prayer *kapp*. "I think I'll turn in early tonight. I'll see Ruthanna in the morning." She turned to go.

"I'll walk you back," Willem said.

"That's not necessary. There's plenty of light left. You two must have things to talk about." Abbie had already recovered her brisk pace of earlier in the evening.

Willem watched her go but made no move to follow.

Jake's mouth twisted in a smile. "Where's your horse, Willem?"

Willem dipped his straw hat. "Outside Abbie's front door."

"She's a woman with a mind of her own."

"That she is. She's worried about the church more than anything."

Jake nodded. "I heard about Noah Chupp. I would offer to try to help folks, but I suspect I would only feed the discord in the council right now."

Willem swiveled his head to look at Jake. "Discord in the council?"

"My presence suggests that some believe true faith is possible outside the Amish church," Jake said. "Is that not what causes the bishops to refuse to come to your congregation?"

Willem scratched his forehead. "It would certainly be an explanation, though not one that I have heard."

"Then I hope I have not spoken out of turn." Jake lifted his own hat off his head in a farewell gesture. "Keep your distance. Don't let her catch you fetching your horse."

CHAPTER 13

Standing in the Chupps' barren yard two weeks later, Abbie refused to let tears well. Noah double-checked the harness that strapped two horses to an overloaded buggy while Sarah kept the youngest two children where she could reach them easily. Abbie stood with Rudy Stutzman apart from the mass of families who had come to bid the Chupps farewell.

"They aren't taking very much with them," she observed.

"An *English* family came in and bought it all for half what it was worth." Rudy kicked a pebble back and forth with one toe. "Noah wanted every penny he could scrape up for traveling costs."

"Will they drive the buggy all the way to Nebraska?"

"I believe that is his plan. Nine train tickets would be costly, and he wants the horses."

"What will he do for work? Do the *English* in cities even use cobblers anymore? Don't they have factories for things like that?"

Rudy shrugged. "Noah is not afraid of hard work. He will find something."

"But they cannot even go to their families if they are still intent on leaving the Amish church."

Rudy turned to look at Abbie. He gestured toward the buggy. "They are truly leaving, Abbie. You have to put them in God's hands."

"If they were in need, the rest of us would do anything we could to help, just as they would have for us. A family with seven children—they have to know what a loss this is for our community.

Why should they leave when the rest of us are here? I had hoped they cared more than that."

"Your own love for the church cannot force anyone to stay."

"You stayed," Abbie said. "That day at the depot, you were thinking of leaving, but you are still here."

Rudy said nothing.

"Rudy, you're staying, aren't you?"

"I don't want to quarrel, Abigail."

Her heart raced. "We are not quarreling. We are talking about the good of the community, about not thinking only of ourselves but how our choices will affect many other people."

Rudy gave the pebble a swift kick with the side of his shoe. "You should talk to your own Willem about that. He will do anything it takes to save his farm. Surely you know that."

"We all share that goal. If we save our farms, we save our settlement, and if we save the settlement, we save the church."

"In your mind everything is tied together like so much string in a ball. Willem doesn't see it that way."

"Who are you to say how Willem sees our life here?" Abbie ground her teeth together. Who was Rudy to think he knew Willem better than she did?

"I thought we weren't going to quarrel." Rudy spoke softly.

Abbie swallowed. "We're not."

"Ask Willem yourself, unless you are afraid to hear what he would say."

"Of course I am not afraid to ask Willem." Abbie flipped a palm up. "I'll do it tomorrow."

"Ask him what choice he would make between his farm and the church."

"Why should he have to make that choice?"

Rudy was not looking at her any longer. "The Chupps are ready. We should go wish them Godspeed."

~≈∗≈~

"Does *Mamm* know you are taking salt pork?" Levi Weaver raised his blue eyes with the question.

Abbie put the lid back on the wooden barrel outside the Weaver back door and made sure it was closed tightly. "Yes, she does."

"Is she sure we have enough food for you to take some?" Levi thumped the barrel lid himself.

Abbie carried a hunk of pork into the kitchen, where she had left a knife on the butcher block. Levi followed. "As you can see, I am only taking a little bit."

"But *Mamm* always says every bit of food counts." Levi's tone carried no accusation.

"And she is right." Abbie drew the knife through the pork and carved off five modest slices. She held one out to Levi.

The boy shook his head. "I wouldn't feel right."

"I am sure *Mamm* would want you to have it. She said only yesterday that she doesn't believe you are eating enough."

"I'm fine."

Levi was such a serious child, Abbie thought. He was not anything like the two brothers in between the family bookends that Abbie and Levi formed. Daniel and Reuben were hardworking and respectful, but they did not carry the weight of the world on their shoulders.

"Levi, we have enough food. It probably feels like we eat the same things all the time. I suppose that's true, but we have enough."

"It can't last forever."

"We have to eat, Levi. That's what food is for."

"But you're taking a picnic for Willem. Is he running out of food?"

Abbie wrapped the pork slices in a flour sack towel. "I don't think so. But he's a bachelor. We often share food with him and the others. You know that."

He shrugged one shoulder and looked at his feet.

She sat in a chair and pulled him onto her lap. "God will provide, Levi. You must believe that. God gives us food to nourish us, and when we eat it we show that we are grateful for God's gift. Do you understand?"

Levi dragged his bare toe in a circle on the floor. When had he gotten tall enough to still reach the floor when he sat in Abbie's lap? He was going to be lanky like his brothers.

"I hope Willem is grateful for the food you're taking him."

"I'm sure he will be. Now help me pack the picnic. Get me a jar of apples from the back porch, will you?"

"We didn't grow those apples," Levi said. "*Mamm* had to buy them from the *English*."

"They were too small for the *English* to sell in their market, and she got a very good price on the whole bushel. Now go get me a jar."

Abbie ran down the mental list of foods she would use to entice Willem on a midday picnic. She had fresh bread, egg salad, spiced apples, half a sponge cake, and salt pork. And she would be sure to take plenty of water. It would be an act of faith that surely God would soon send rain.

⚜

Abbie smiled down at Willem from the buggy bench, and he leaned on the fence post with both arms.

"You must have driven halfway around my farm to find me out here," he said.

"I very nearly gave up and thought perhaps you had gone into Limon and didn't mention it to me."

"Now why would I do that when you make such fine company?"

"What are you in the middle of?"

Willem liked the way her nose scrunched when she asked questions instead of coming right out with what was on her mind.

"I can't seem to grow anything," he said. "But I'm thinking of marking off a road from the back side of my property."

Abbie smiled. "We go that way all the time anyway. Might as well make it a faster way."

"I was pretty sure you would figure that out." Willem raised his hat and ran a hand through his hair. "Why have you tracked me down out here in the far corners?"

She brightened further. "I packed a picnic. Let's drive somewhere and find a nice spot."

"A picnic? For no reason?"

"Your favorite cake. Admit it. You can't resist."

Willem looked over his shoulder in the direction of his future road. He had wanted to pace off his planned route and begin calculating how many stones he would need to line the edges for the entire length. If conditions persisted, dry soil would blow off toward Kansas and leave stones uncovered. He would rather have had a good crop and have to dig rocks out. Willem looked again at Abbie's face shining under the brim of the bonnet she wore over her prayer *kapp* and admitted what he was doing did not qualify as urgent. And a man did need to eat lunch, after all.

"All right, then." He brushed his hands together to clear them of dirt. "But I want you to let me drive."

"Of course." Abbie slid over on the bench.

Willem hoisted himself into driving position and signaled the horse to make a wide turn. Abbie was a good driver but too slow. She would wander all over searching for the perfect spot—which of course did not exist. A picnic called for temperate weather, not oppressive heat. A picnic called for shade, not one exposed field after another. A picnic called for a cool breeze off a lake or river, not dust blowing in their eyes. Had Abbie even thought about these realities, or did she see in her mind's eye the river and oak trees of Ohio rather than the dried creeks and half-dead scrub oak of Colorado? Willem wondered how long it would take to grow a decent shade tree in this part of the country. Maybe their grandchildren would be able to sit under one.

Abbie spread a quilt out on the ground. The spot of shade Willem had spied was barely big enough for the two of them to sit beside a large bush, but she did not complain. They had not passed any more promising options, and at least it was a patch of green instead of unending brown dirt. Abbie still did not know the names of all the odd vegetation of the Colorado plain.

She had used an empty fruit bushel to hold the picnic food. It had seemed like plenty in the kitchen, but out here it appeared sparse. *Gratitude*, she reminded herself. At the bottom of the bushel basket were two plates, and she handed one to Willem. They paused for a silent prayer. Abbie asked for the assurance her heart craved. Of Willem's love for her. Of his faithfulness to the church. Of the only choice she could bear to hear him voice. She waited until she heard Willem moving before she opened her eyes.

"Eat!" she urged.

"This is quite a feast for a simple bachelor's lunch." Willem laid two slices of pork on his plate.

Abbie let her breath out. Willem did not require fancy food. Why had she let herself fuss? She spooned egg salad onto his plate, and he selected a thick slice of bread.

"I suppose I must eat my lunch before I can have cake," he said. Abbie chuckled. Her own plate was still empty.

"Aren't you going to eat?" Willem set his plate on the quilt and reached for the jar of apples and twisted off the cap.

"Yes, I will." She made no move to serve herself any food.

Willem set down the apples. "Abigail Weaver, something is on your mind."

She took in a deep breath and let it out slowly. "There's plenty of time to talk. I want you to enjoy your lunch."

"I thought the purpose was to enjoy lunch together."

"It is." Abbie reached for the egg salad and a slice of bread. "How long have you been thinking of making a road?"

"It has always been in the plan, when I found the time. I might get started on it this year, but soon we will all have to start laying in coal for the winter, and that's a lot of work."

"Will we have a harsh winter, do you think?" Abbie used a fork to spread egg salad around on her plate without moving any to her mouth.

"*Gottes wille.*" Willem put a piece of bread in his mouth, chewed slowly, and swallowed. "Perhaps we should talk about whatever is on your mind."

"All right." Abbie set her plate down and looked Willem in the eye. "If you had to choose between making your farm successful and staying with the church, which would you choose?"

Willem did not shift position, but Abbie could see that he was moving his tongue over his teeth, first the bottom then the top.

"Come with me," he whispered.

CHAPTER 14

"Come with you where?" Abbie felt her heart skipping beats.

"Think of the life we can have together." Willem put one elbow down on the quilt and leaned toward Abbie.

"I don't understand. Do you want to follow the Chupps to Nebraska?"

He shook his head. "I want to make my farm work. We may be peaceable people, but I am going to fight for my land. Everything I have is invested there."

Abbie moistened her lips and set her untouched plate aside. "Then what are you saying?"

Willem held her gaze with his green eyes as her breaths grew shallow. Finally he turned his head and looked to the horizon.

"Would it be so awful to be Mennonite?" he said.

"So you've made up your mind?" Abbie's heart pounded. She had waited all this time for Willem because she never doubted they would one day be together—not until now.

"I haven't decided anything," Willem said, his voice thick with earnest conviction, "except that I want this farm to work more than anything I've ever wanted."

More than you want me. The truth clanged in her mind like *English* church bells. "What has that got to do with turning Mennonite?" Abbie asked.

Willem picked up a twig, snapped it, and flicked half of it away. "Noah Chupp's decision to move away was disheartening to some of the other men."

"To the women as well."

"Noah did not think the settlement will succeed. What if he's right?"

"He will be right if we allow ourselves to think that way." Abbie stood up, unable to keep her feet still. "We'll fight this drought together. We will be all right. That's what you always say."

Willem pulled his knees up under his chin and wrapped his arms around them. "What if the threat is more than the drought? Bad weather is not the only thing that can break the back of the most determined of men."

"Willem Peters, you must not allow your mind to dwell on such things. We must encourage one another, now more than ever." Abbie paced three steps away from the blanket and pivoted sharply to return, forcing herself to sit down and discuss Willem's concern like a calm adult.

"Not everything we first heard about Colorado has proven to be wrong," Willem said. "It is a different kind of beautiful than Ohio or Pennsylvania, but it is the handiwork of God. We could have a good life here. You and me, together."

This was not the sort of proposal Abbie had always supposed she would eventually hear from Willem. His words were far too conditional. She eased pent-up breath out of her chest.

"Why should we not have a lovely life here if we choose to spend it together?" she said.

"Because the church may not be here, Abbie. You have to see how precarious the situation is."

"One family left. That changes nothing."

"It changes everything. The solidarity is broken."

"Perhaps Noah was not a true believer after all. Perhaps that is why it was so easy for him to leave."

"Easy?" Willem shook his head. "It was not easy. And I do not believe you could doubt the faith of a man like Mr. Chupp."

She flushed, knowing he was right about Noah.

"The bishop of the nearest district has not visited in over a year," he said. "We have had no visiting ministers in all that time. Noah was our best hope for a minister of our own. Adam Nissley's notion that a minister will come from Kansas denies reality. People are discouraged. Even if their farms were flourishing, they would be longing for a real church."

"As do I." Abbie laid a towel over the egg salad and started to wrap up the bread.

"As do I, as well."

Abbie stilled her hands and looked at Willem. "Then what is our point of disagreement? Why were we talking about the Mennonites?"

"Because the others may decide to sell their farms and move back to a thriving district, but I don't want to go back. I only want to go forward. I want to stay here, no matter what. If I have to go to the Mennonites to do that, I would like nothing more than to have you with me, but I will not propose marriage under false pretenses."

Abbie began to stack dishes in the empty bushel basket.

"You didn't eat anything," Willem said.

"I have no appetite. You should take the food home for your dinner."

He reached for her hand. "The last thing I want to do is upset you, but I have to be honest."

❖

Ruthanna sat on the lone chair in the yard, her hand on her abdomen. Beneath her touch the baby kicked, and her lips spread in a smile though no one was near to see it. For the third day in a row, Eber had risen at dawn. He had done the early morning chores, and when he returned, Ruthanna cracked one egg after another into the sizzling skillet and pulled fresh biscuits out of the oven. Eber guzzled coffee with a glow on his face she had not seen in many weeks.

After breakfast Eber returned to bed for a long nap, but Ruthanna had been confident he would rise again bubbling over with tasks he wanted to accomplish around the farm. A poor crop was no reason to let the fences go untended, he said, and he was going to see about getting a couple of roosters and more hens. They could do more than eat eggs the chickens produced. They could raise chickens to see them through the winter and to share with others who might have already begun to consume hens that stopped laying despite their tough meat. Eber and Jake had gone off together to cut a window in the back side of the barn. More natural light would allow Eber to create a workshop in an empty stall so he could begin building some decent furniture out of lumber he had stacked months ago, before he first fell ill.

Ruthanna hardly let herself admit that she had worried Eber would not rally. He was so weak for so long. But during these last few days he was showing signs of his old self, and Ruthanna murmured one continuous prayer of thanks all day long.

Jake approached, and she smiled.

"You have been an angel of the Lord," she said. "You brought hope when I needed it, and look at Eber now!"

Jake nodded. "He is much better, but he is not as strong as he thinks he is. You must watch him carefully and make sure he rests. I look forward to hearing good news when I return."

Ruthanna stood, one hand on her aching back. "You are leaving, then?"

"I believe it's time. Eber wants to work his own farm again."

"But you'll be back?"

"I expect I will be coming more often. I am thinking of moving to Limon soon. If I am going to open a Mennonite church, I must begin making real plans not just talking about it."

Ruthanna's throat thickened. "I am sure you will do well."

"You will always be welcome, you know."

She shook her head. "We have our people and our ways. I have faith that God will send us a minister."

Jake pointed over his shoulder toward the barn. "Eber is cleaning up. There's a place in Limon where he can get glass for that window when he's ready. I'll help him finish out the day and then be on my way in the morning."

❦

Somber muteness swathed the ride back to Willem's farm. Abbie had run out of words, and Willem seemed to know that he should hold his. When he got out and handed her the reins to the Weaver buggy, she pointed to the basket behind her.

"Please take it," she said. "We hardly touched the food. There will be plenty for your evening meal."

"I'm sure your brothers would be happy to have it."

"But I want *you* to have it." She heard an edge in her tone she had not intended and took a deep breath to restrain it. "Things are not so dismal that we cannot afford a token of generosity. Please enjoy the food. It would make me happy to know you have it, especially the cake."

He nodded and lifted the basket from the buggy. She did not look at him again as she nudged the horse forward, back toward the road that would take her to the Weaver farm.

Rudy Stutzman was right.

If Willem had to choose between his church and his farm, he would choose his farm.

Even if that meant leaving her.

Abbie felt foolish for all she had presumed in the last several years. Putting clean sheets on his bed and imagining the day it would be her bed as well. Cleaning the corners of his sitting room and seeing herself seated in a chair beside him, perhaps with a toddler at her feet. Imagining the joy of spending three days cooking when it was their turn to host their fellow Amish worshippers.

In the beginning, they were fellow settlers facing a challenge that left little respite. On neighboring farms, of course the Weavers got to know the determined bachelor. Life on the Colorado plain toughened Abbie, made her feel grown up. And of course she was grown up—old enough to have married years ago in an established Amish district. When her eyes turned to Willem in something other than a neighborly manner, he was looking back at her. Abbie knew she would marry him someday.

In all the episodes where she had let her mind drift toward a future with Willem, never had she supposed he was capable of turning his back on the center of her heart. Never.

Willem loved the Lord. Abbie was sure of that. And he loved her as much as she loved him.

But he would choose his farm. He would choose the Mennonites.

As she turned into the lane leading to her family's house, Abbie wiped the backs of her hands across her eyes and cheeks, trying to banish the heartbreak her family would see in her face.

Daed met her in front of the barn. "How was your picnic?"

"Hot. I should have known it would be difficult to find shade."

"I will cool the horse for you."

"Thank you." Abbie handed her father the reins. "*Daed,* can I ask you a question?"

"Of course."

"I know we have not been getting any new settlers because people back home have heard how difficult the drought makes everything. Is there another reason why no one wants to come?"

"What do you mean, daughter?"

"Did something happen? Something to cause division?"

"We are a people of forgiveness."

"I know. But all this time without a minister—can it not cause doubt?"

"Are *you* doubting, Abigail?"

She was quick to shake her head. "I am confused, that's all."

"Whether we have a minister, are we not still in God's hands?"

"Yes."

"And whether we have drought or rain, are we not still in God's hands?"

"Yes."

"Then, my daughter, what is there to be confused about?"

Abbie brushed dust off her skirt. This was her father's way of saying what Willem always said. We will be all right. She trusted both her father and Willem, but standing in the blazing sun at that moment, she found scarce comfort. Would her father also say, "Whether you have a husband or not, are you not still in God's hands?" She wasn't sure.

"Thank you for letting me take the buggy," she said. "I'd better go see if *Mamm* needs some help." Abbie gave her father a halfhearted smile and let him kiss her cheek.

❦

Despite all the chores awaiting her attention, and the heat that made her feel as if she were walking around in an incinerator, Abbie chose to walk through the fields to Rudy's farm the next morning. She found him in the barn with the new calf.

"How is she?" Abbie said when he looked up.

"Healthy and happy." He stroked the calf's nose.

"Good."

She watched his gentleness, never more evident than when he was caring for his animals. Abbie had thought to tell him that he had been right about Willem. Now the words caught in her throat.

"I remember the first time I helped a calf feed," he said. "I was about nine. My *mamm* thought I should stay out of the way, but my *daed* insisted I needed to learn. After that he let me help with all the new calves, helping them suckle at first and then weaning them and feeding them with a bottle."

It was a sweet picture. Abbie welcomed it into her mind. Rudy as a little boy, learning to feed a calf on a farm in Indiana, with his father watching over his shoulder and murmuring patient instructions.

"I found a scrap I thought you might use in your quilt," he said. "It's just a bit of red. I'm not even sure why I have it, but if you still want it, I'm happy to give it to you."

She smiled. "*Danki.* Yes, I would love to have it." His was the only square she had not finished cutting pieces for, waiting because she hoped he would find something to give her—and because it might mean he had surrendered his notion of leaving.

He might have been right about Willem, but the moment when she wanted to give voice to his insight eased away.

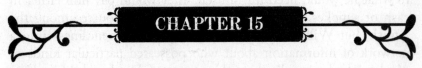

CHAPTER 15

The number of winters Willem had spent in Colorado equaled the fingers on one hand. Even in mid-August heat, his mind was on the coming cold season. The hope of a crop was gone weeks ago. He needed to keep his animals alive and healthy and try not to get frostbite himself. In many ways the Colorado climate was more temperate than eastern Ohio had been, but it seemed that seasons could shift during a casual gaze at the horizon. Winds would gust, clouds would swirl in, and a winter storm would release its fury when only hours earlier the day had promised fall pleasantries. Willem would be ready whether that day came in mid-September or late October.

The last three weeks had not been wasted. Willem had picked through his paltry wheat fields, gleaning dry wisps that might contain seed to use next spring when he would try again. And he *would* try again. His pile of stones to mark off his back road had grown considerably. Though he might not get them all laid before winter, he was now able to estimate how many more times he needed to fill his cart, and he had taken his horses back and forth over the route he planned to tramp down the straggly weeds and make the rough places plain. But soon he would interrupt this task to begin gathering coal for the minimal cooking he did, warming his cabin for the winter, and selling to the *English*.

Soft brown coal was in plentiful supply. All the Amish farmers lived within a few miles of a ravine where lignite coal was free for the digging. In places it was only a few feet below the surface, rather than thousands of feet down. Still, digging it out and transporting it to a useful location was tedious, backbreaking work, and because lignite burned quickly the homes required considerable supplies. A year ago Willem had discovered that many of the *English* around Limon were willing to pay someone else for this labor even if they had a vein on their own land. This year Willem had already made inquiries and committed to dig lignite for three families in addition to what he would need for himself. They would pay him either in cash or supplies. He preferred cash, a scarce resource among the Amish, but Willem had already parlayed his friendliness into a network of information about who possessed particular kinds of goods and who sought them. He was confident he could trade to get what he needed not only to survive the winter but also to make improvements on his farm that would last long into the future.

Willem hated to see anyone so discouraged that they would give up on their farms, but even if all the rest packed their belongings and traveled eastward, Willem would remain.

Was that not a commitment strong enough even for Abigail Weaver?

Ruthanna could hardly believe the difference the last three weeks had made in her girth. After months of feeling sick to her stomach most of the time, the sensation settled at last. She made one batch of biscuits after another and fed her ravenous appetite with them while the baby kicked to make his presence known almost incessantly. When the motions stilled, alarm flashed through her, but she reminded herself that even a babe yet in the womb would sleep at some point. Her gait reminded her of a waddling duck, but she reveled in the movement, perhaps even exaggerating it. Well past the halfway point of her pregnancy, she had begun to realize she would miss the wonder of a child growing within her. So many weeks were consumed with worry for Eber rather than rejoicing together in this mysterious fruit of their love. She wished she had savored more.

Eber was better. He was. But he was not well. He learned to pace himself so that he did not fall into exhaustion and have to return to bed for days at a time, but his energy was not what it had been. When he sat across the table from her, his shoulders stooped. His hand went to his stomach in moments of pain. In his workshop in the barn he sat on a stool rather than stand. After supper, when he read aloud from the German Bible, sometimes she could barely hear him. Then he went to bed earlier than Ruthanna had ever known him to do.

The baby would help. Ruthanna rubbed her firm, expanding middle. Eber would hold their child in his arms and dream beyond the future he could see now. This would spur him to new strength. They would warm themselves at the stove and pass the baby back and forth while one or the other of them tended to chores and they waited for the winter to pass. At Christmas they would remember the birth of God's Son by cradling their own child in love. Spring would come and they would find the money to buy new seed, even if they had to borrow it. They would plant. They would harvest. They would build. Day after day Ruthanna focused her energy on believing this.

Still, in the night as she listened to Eber's erratic breathing, Ruthanna's heart clenched. *Gottes wille.* Why would it be God's will for Eber to be ill? She knew she ought to rest in God's will, and she did not confess even to Abbie that this troubled her. A minister might be able to answer her question, but whom could she ask? Jake Heatwole was a warm, generous man, but he was a Mennonite. Ruthanna lacked confidence that she should open her soul to anyone outside the Amish church.

And who would dig their coal for them? Eber would want to do it, and Ruthanna would worry what the effort would cost them both.

※

Willem did not rush the team of horses. They would be working hard enough in a few hours when the wagon was full of coal. He calculated where along the ravine he should begin. All the men had their favorite spots. It was not a question of whether they would find coal. Geology reports assured them their farms were on the eastern edge of the great Denver Basin and lignite was abundant.

They had all found this to be true in previous years. The worst of the work was clearing away earth and rocks to expose the vein. Even though the depth to reach coal was only a few feet, the labor of making a hole large enough to work in meant that most of the men brought their sons or relatives to guard an exposed hole while they carried a load home and then returned to dig more.

Willem slowed along the side of the ravine, wondering if he should have partnered with Rudy as he did last year. They could have looked out for each other. But he was here now and might as well do what he could. He took the team down the slope of the ravine and looked for a spot to claim for his day's labor. There was nothing to tie the horses to, but unless they were frightened Willem doubted they would drift too far.

When he got out of the wagon, he took his axe with him. Spreading his feet and bracing himself, he swung the sharpened edge in rhythmic, circular strokes until he began to feel the surface give way. He pounded and loosened and shifted dirt until he spied the promise of lignite. In his mind, he pictured his wagon full and overflowing and then the pile he would have behind his house. Once he exposed the lignite it would be soft enough to break in his hands. At that point he could shovel for as long as his back would tolerate.

Willem heard the approaching horse before he saw it. Determined not to give way to distraction, he tossed another shovel of coal into his wagon without lifting his head and listened for the sound of the rider passing by.

The sound stopped. Willem shoveled.

"Willem!"

At the sound of Abbie's voice, he looked up. They had not spoken since the day of the picnic. His last view of her had been a face wrenched in disappointment, shoulders slumped in dismay. Now she sat erect and controlled on her horse.

"You look well," he said. The sun magnified the light in her wide brown eyes.

"As do you." She looked around. "Are you working alone?"

"For today." He took advantage of the interruption to wipe his dripping face.

"Reuben could help you."

"Your brother must have a list of chores taller than he is." Willem jabbed the point of his shovel, and lignite tumbled out of the wound he made in the earth.

"My father has three sons," Abbie said. "I'm sure he can spare one of them for a few hours."

"I'll keep that in mind the next time I come out to dig."

"I'm on my way home now. I'll tell Reuben you're here. I'm sure he will come."

Willem nodded. Reuben was good company, even if he was easily distracted.

CHAPTER 16

Willem waved up at Reuben. Abbie must have gone straight home and urged her brother to hurry to the ravine.

Reuben slid off his horse and peered down.

"Did you bring any tools?" Willem asked.

"A shovel. Abbie didn't say to bring anything else."

Willem tossed another shovelful of coal into the wagon. "That will be fine. I have an axe."

"Should I bring my horse down?"

"Maybe later. Right now it would make things crowded."

"Be right down."

Willem jabbed at the vein of coal with the point of his shovel, testing the resistance of the next section. Behind him he heard Reuben controlling his slide down the slope of the ravine, his shovel sometimes thudding against the wall of dirt.

"Did you help your *daed* last year?" Willem looked at the boy out of the side of his eye as he raised his shovel once again.

"Once."

"So you know what to do?"

Reuben nodded. "You already have the hole exposed. That's the hard part, right?"

"It's all hard." Willem reached for his axe. "You dig out the coal you can see. I'm going to try to widen the hole so we both have room to work."

"Your wagon is more than half full already." Reuben probed the vein with his fingers.

"I've been here quite a while." Willem paused to run the rag over his face again. He could not go more than five minutes without sweat dripping into his eyes and blurring his sight.

"Maybe you should have some water."

"Later." Willem laid his shovel down and picked up the axe, bracing again to swing it at the side of the ravine.

They fell into a pattern, swinging in opposite rhythms and keeping their hands out of the way of descending implements. Widening the hole seemed to be less intense than starting it had been, and Willem allowed himself to feel the relief that Reuben's help would bring to the task.

His axe head stuck in stubborn earth, as if it knew Willem was feeling encouraged. He yanked on it and pushed the handle back and forth trying to loosen the tool. When it did not yield, he leaned into it—and immediately regretted the movement.

Reuben froze with his full shovel in midair. "Did it crack?"

Willem sighed. "Yes." With one more twist, the split axe handle came free in two pieces.

"We can still dig what's exposed." Reuben emptied his shovel into the wagon.

"I should have brought two."

"How could you know the axe handle would break? No one expects that."

"This is going to slow us down."

"I'll come back and help you another day."

Willem shook his head and glanced up at the sun. "We still have several hours of good light before your mother will expect you home for supper. Can you stay while I ride home for another axe?"

Reuben nodded. "I'll keep digging what I can get to."

"Thank you. I don't want to leave the wagon unattended or have someone else find the hole waiting after I've done all this work."

Willem removed the harness that strapped his team to the wagon and pulled out an old saddle he stored under the bench. Unencumbered and on his stallion, he could avoid the roundabout roads and gallop across open country.

❦

Rudy knew Jake Heatwole had left the Gingerich farm. He also knew, from Abbie, that Ruthanna still was nervous about Eber's vitality. What harm could it do for a neighbor to drop by and see if he could help with something? Rudy threw down a fresh layer of straw from the barn's loft and spread it around the empty stalls his animals would occupy in a few hours. Then he went outside and whistled for his horse.

When he reached Ruthanna and Eber's place a half an hour later, he saw no sign of activity. The barn was closed up. Even the chickens were sluggish in the afternoon heat. Rudy dropped from his horse and rapped on the door, where he could hear Ruthanna's cumbersome movements within. When she opened the door, he kept his voice low.

"Have I disturbed Eber's rest?"

Ruthanna puffed out her cheeks and blew out her breath. "He's not here."

"Oh?"

"He wanted something from Limon."

"I wish I had known. I would have gone to get whatever he needs."

"That's what I said. He wouldn't wait. I didn't even want to ask what it was that could be so urgent." Ruthanna stepped outside the house to share the small space of the stoop with Rudy.

"I'm here," he said. "I may as well see if there is something I can do to help."

She shook her head. "Thank you, Rudy. That's very kind. But Eber is feeling sensitive these days. I don't want to have to explain to him how the chores got done."

"I see."

"But since you have ridden all the way over, I hope you will let me get you a cold drink." She laughed. "Or a lukewarm drink, at least. I have some tea that used to be cold."

"I would be obliged."

As Ruthanna retreated into the house, Rudy spied the chair that sat out in the yard and moved it close to the stoop where it would be in the shadow of the house. Then he sat on the step and set his feet on the ground below. Ruthanna reappeared with a glass in each hand. Rudy wondered how much time she had left before her baby would come, but it was unseemly to ask.

"Is Abbie still stopping by to check on you?" he asked.

Ruthanna sat in the chair. "Nearly every day. And we've been into town together a couple of times. She is such a sweet friend."

Rudy took a long gulp of liquid. "I am glad you think so."

"I cannot imagine how I would get by without her."

Rudy had pondered the same question lately.

Willem wasted no time at his farm, going directly to the barn to pull another axe from the rack and throwing himself astride his horse before the animal had time to even nuzzle the barren ground. As it was, more than an hour would have passed by the time Willem got back to Reuben. Even if the boy had worked steadily in Willem's absence, they could continue at least two more hours before abandoning the exposed hole. Willem was already calculating when he could dig again. If he went soon, perhaps no one else would discover that he had begun and he could exhaust that section of the vein. He dug his heels into the horse's flanks and spurred speed.

At the ravine, Willem pulled up on the reins, confused. He was sure he returned to the same place where Reuben had left the Weaver mare. His wagon should be down below.

Except Reuben's horse was missing.

"Reuben!"

Willem listened for a response that did not come.

"Reuben!"

Willem left his horse and scrambled down the side of the ravine. Reuben was nowhere in sight. And Willem's wagon was empty, with his second horse content to stand still and swish her tail. Fury rose from his gut. Everyone knew it was unsafe to leave a wagon of coal without someone to watch it. Too many came to this vein for coal who would find it much easier to take what someone else had dug out, not to mention the risk of losing his horse. Even when Amish men were the only ones digging with no *English* around them, none of them left a load of coal that represented as much as a day's labor. With two wagons backed up against each other, two men—or even one—could shovel the soft coal from one to the other in almost no time.

How could Reuben have left and allowed this to happen?

Furious, Willem stomped out of the ravine and led the stallion back down to harness with the mare and pull out the empty wagon. "Reuben!" Willem bellowed at regular intervals.

When his team had all eight feet on level ground again and the wagon was steady, Willem heard the rustle of horse feet and spun around to find Reuben approaching. He snatched the reins out of the boy's hands.

"Get in the wagon."

Reuben's eyes widened. "What happened to the coal?"

"That's what I want to know." Willem tied Reuben's horse to the back of the wagon. "I said get in. I'm taking you home myself."

Abbie handed the pail of slop for the chickens to Levi just as she saw dust swirl up in the lane.

"It's Willem," Levi announced.

"I see that." She had not expected to see him after dispatching Reuben to assist the coal-digging effort.

"Why is Reuben riding with Willem?" Levi asked. "I thought you said he rode down to help Willem."

"He did."

Reuben sat with shoulders slumped on the bench beside Willem, arms crossed in front of him. As they got closer, Abbie realized the horse Reuben had taken was trotting behind the wagon. At least it had not gone lame. She put her hand on Levi's shoulder as Willem pulled to a stop in front of them.

"Is your father here?" Willem's gruff tone overlooked any pleasantries.

"Is everything all right?" Abbie looked from Willem to Reuben.

"I need to see your father. Reuben has something to tell him."

Abbie put her hand flat on Levi's back and urged him toward the barn. "Levi, why don't you go ask *Daed* to come?"

She could tell Levi wanted to ask questions, but he left without speaking.

"Reuben?" she said.

"I thought I saw a coyote looking down into the ravine," Reuben said. "It was a chance to see where the den might be."

"I asked him to stay with the coal." Willem jumped off the bench and paced in the dirt. "I thought he was old enough to understand what that meant."

"I am." Reuben straightened his back in protest. "Not a single person came by on the road the whole time you were gone."

Willem glared. "Obviously somebody did."

Abbie stepped into the space between Willem and Reuben. "You must both be hot and thirsty. I'm sure that after some refreshment we can have a calm conversation."

"Coyotes, Willem." Reuben set his jaw. "You know what it could mean if we could figure out where they come from. How often do we get a chance to see one in the daylight?"

"Did you find it?" Abbie asked. Never had she seen Willem so angry, and it rattled her, but she wanted to hear her brother's story.

Reuben kicked the dirt. "No. By the time I got up to my horse, it was gone. I figured it wouldn't hurt to try to track it for a few minutes. I guess I didn't realize how long I was gone."

Ananias Weaver emerged from the barn with Levi at his side.

Abbie stifled a groan. "I'll get you both something to drink."

CHAPTER 17

"Did you hear?"

Ruthanna turned from the stove at the sound of her husband's voice. "Hear what?"

Eber picked up the damp rag Ruthanna had used to wipe dust from the table before setting plates out and used it to wipe his hands.

"Someone stole Willem's coal."

Ruthanna's shoulders dropped. "Surely not one of our people."

"I pray not, but we cannot be sure."

Ruthanna picked up a spoon to stir a stew of last year's paltry vegetables, which she had canned, and a rabbit Eber had trapped the day before. "I don't even want to think that one of us would do that."

"Would you rather accuse one of the fine *English* we do business with?"

"I prefer not to accuse anyone." Ruthanna tasted the stew and reached for the saltshaker.

"Of course we do not want to make false accusations."

Eber pulled a chair out from under the table, sat, and started to pull off his boots. Ruthanna wondered if he had stopped to drink anything all day. Was it her imagination that his breathing was more labored than it had been lately?

"Ruthanna, we must be very careful whom we trust."

"We trust God, do we not?"

"You know what I mean. I ran into Willem at the end of our

lane. He was on his way home from the ravine. He made the mistake of trusting Reuben Weaver to watch his load while he came home for an axe, and the boy let himself be distracted."

"He must have had a good reason. Reuben is old enough to know better."

"You would think so. But his actions illustrate that even people we trust can let us down. For right now, I think it is best if we do not trust anyone but each other."

Ruthanna laid her spoon down and took two plates from the shelf. "What are you saying, Eber? Trust no one? That's no way to live."

"I'm doing all the chores now. We don't need help anymore."

"We don't know what might happen. Caring for each other is what our people do. How can we just shut people out?"

Eber raised one foot and laid it on the opposite knee, massaging it. "I am not suggesting we be rude, only that we can be self-sufficient. We can be gracious in explaining we have no need to trouble anyone."

The baby squirmed within her, and Ruthanna rested her hand on her belly. "What about when my time comes? I will need Abbie and Esther."

He nodded. "Yes, I can see that. But we are more than two months from that day. Perhaps we will know by then who is at the root of this trouble."

⚹❖⚹

Abbie waited three days. Reuben was sincerely sorry, and she believed that once Willem cooled off he would see that he had been harsh. But he did not come.

On Saturday morning she took a horse and the buggy and rode over to Willem's. It might be unseemly for her to broach the subject with him, but she could not wait any longer. Reuben was miserable, and if she could do something to alleviate his suffering, she would. She had never been afraid to speak her mind to Willem, and if she wanted to be his wife—and she did—she saw no point in cowering now.

Willem was in the pasture brushing one of his own horses.

Abbie tied her horse to a fence post near the gate and lifted the latch.

He looked up but did not greet her with a smile the way he used to. She counted her paces in her head as a way to keep calm. *One. Two. Three.* She hoped he would speak first. *Four. Five. Six.*

She stood before him, her hands crossed behind her waist. Now she counted his strokes through the horse's mane. *Seven. Eight. Nine.*

He looked up again but still did not speak.

Ten. Eleven. Twelve.

"Willem."

"Yes."

"Reuben feels terrible about your coal."

"I know."

Thirteen. Fourteen.

Abbie took a deep breath. "Of course the coal is valuable. And you worked for hours to dig it out. It was not right that someone should come along and take it."

"No, it wasn't."

Abbie moved one hand to a hip. "Must you be so unyielding?"

Fifteen. Sixteen.

Finally he let his arm drop to his side and turned to face her. "What would you like me to say, Abbie?"

"That you know Reuben is more valuable than the coal."

Willem said nothing.

"That you know coyotes have been a bigger and bigger problem. The longer the drought goes on, the more widely they will roam."

Willem sighed.

"That whatever has gone wrong between us, you know that Reuben does not deserve this punishment."

He raised an eyebrow. "Is that how you see it? That things have gone wrong between us?"

"Haven't they?"

He raised his brush again. "I suppose so, though my feelings for you have not changed."

"Nor mine for you." If he reached out with his hand, she would lay hers in it. She would not be able to help herself. Perhaps it was just as well that he made no move toward her.

"Do you still believe the church can survive?" he said.

"Have you given up trying?"

"If you mean to ask whether I am still talking to Jake Heatwole, the answer is yes. There is a difference between giving up trying and accepting reality."

"There is no reality outside God's will. We must not give up on God's will." *Twenty. Twenty-one.* "Willem?"

"Our people live a simple life," he said. "What if God's will is not as simple as we wish to think?"

"Do you doubt the teachings of the church?" A year ago Abbie would not have imagined Willem could say such a thing, but now she could hardly keep from gasping at how far he allowed himself to stray.

"I love the church, Abbie," he said. "You know that."

"Then why do you talk to Jake Heatwole and let him fill your head?" She glared.

"Because I miss the church as well. The Mennonites live plainly and speak our language and worship our God. The longer we go without our church, the harder it is to see what is so wrong with their ways."

Abbie forced herself to exhale and inhale. *Twenty-four. Twenty-five.*

"I believe even the Mennonites would agree that we are called to forgiveness."

"So we are back to Reuben."

"Yes."

Willem nodded. "I will come over later today, and Reuben and I will speak words of peace to each other."

❧✦❧

Abbie fell into her dreams that night before the sun had been down an hour. After Willem and Reuben reconciled, her brother invited Willem to stay for supper, and after supper Levi begged their guest for a game of checkers that turned into four. Willem finally reminded the little boy that he had a cow that needed milking, and Esther affirmed Willem's departure by sending Levi to bed. Abbie cleaned up the dishes, humming to herself a favorite hymn from the *Ausbund*. By the time she finished, her mother sat at the table writing a letter and her father was nodding off in his chair with the family Bible in his lap. Drenched in gratitude for the resolution of Willem's disagreement with Reuben and the comfort of Willem's company for the evening, she went to her bed rubbery with readiness to sleep.

Shrieking hens wakened her. In the darkness, she had no idea what time it was. The thunder of footsteps in the hall told her the entire household was awake. Abbie groped for matches to light the candle at her bedside and rushed to follow her family toward the door.

"Coyotes?" Abbie's stomach hardened.

"Esther, keep Levi inside." Her father stopped for a rifle.

"I want to see." Levi pressed forward, but Esther clamped a hand on his shoulder.

Abbie trailed after her father and two brothers. Reuben held a lantern high and moved in a slow circle. Ananias put his rifle to his shoulder and fired a shot into the air. Abbie, with her candle flickering in the cooling night air, stood beside Daniel holding her breath. The torment in the henhouse had subsided.

"Abigail, did you see anything?" Ananias swept his rifle in a moonlit arc.

"No."

"Boys?"

"No, *Daed*," they answered together.

Ananias lowered the rifle. "We'd better check the hens—and figure out how a coyote got in this time."

Abbie licked her lips. A coyote needed very little room beneath a barrier to slide through. The concentration of human scent must have chased it off—that and the satisfaction of a vanquished meal. Abbie nudged Daniel forward to the henhouse and opened the door. Chickens immediately clacked and scattered. Reuben was behind her now with the lantern.

Two hens lay on the floor, lifeless. Abbie peered into every corner, counting chickens. One was missing, and she knew just which one it was.

"Three of *Mamm*'s best layers," she muttered.

Reuben grunted. "I knew there was a good reason I should track that coyote I saw from the ravine."

"You can't be sure it was the same one."

"But it could be." He knelt beside the two dead hens. "I'll take them out of here, but in the morning I am going to see if I can find any teeth marks. Then we'll know if it was a full-grown male like the one I saw."

The Sabbath passed quietly. The boys milked the cows, and Esther inspected the henhouse. Reuben studied teeth marks, though he could not be sure of a pattern. Otherwise the family ceased their labors. Levi kicked a rock around the yard. No one wanted to talk about the coyote. Abbie walked behind the barn, out of sight of the rest of her family, and permitted herself tears at another passing Sunday without a worship gathering of all the Amish families. Esther served a cold supper, and Ananias read aloud at length from an Old Testament passage about the people of Israel whining at their sufferings in the wilderness.

In the morning, as soon as breakfast was over, Abbie was surprised to see Willem's wagon approach. She met him in the yard.

"Do you feel like a trip to town? Your mother must have a good list going by now."

"Yes." She answered without hesitation. "How much do coyote traps cost?"

He stiffened. "Did you have a coyote on your land?"

She gave him the gruesome details. Some of the birds were still too frightened to lay. Even by taking what was in the pail in the kitchen, Abbie doubted she could produce enough eggs to be worth trading for traps.

"Don't worry about what they cost," Willem said. "I will figure something out that the mercantile owner will accept, and I will set those traps myself."

"We should have done it sooner."

"Don't focus on regret, Abbie. The way forward is what matters."

CHAPTER 18

"Y ou have to take me with you." As the day ended and shadows fell, Abbie put her hand through the bridle on Willem's horse to keep him from urging the horse forward away from the Weaver house.

"It's going to get dark." Willem was on the bench already, reins in hand. "I'm just going out to listen for coyotes so I can decide where to set the traps we bought."

"I know. I want to come."

"Reuben will be jealous if you are out hunting coyotes. He thinks that's his job."

Abbie rolled her eyes. "I'm coming, Willem." She lifted the hem of her skirt and raised her leg to climb into his wagon.

"And your *daed*?"

"He knows we enjoy an evening drive and has never objected." They had not taken an evening drive for several weeks, but Abbie had kept to herself the reason she and Willem saw so little of each other now. When he came to supper the previous Saturday, his family treated him as if he still belonged among them.

Willem adjusted the lantern hanging at the front of the wagon, which they would need soon enough, but did not protest further. Abbie settled in beside him, and the horse began to move.

"Where will we go?" she asked.

"To the corner where the farms meet."

Abbie knew the spot in daylight. Willem and Rudy's farms bordered on the Weaver and Gingerich farms, and while the farms were not square as quilt patches, there was a narrow point where a person could see the back fields of all four farms. Rudy was the only one who had planted his back field, and that was last year. Otherwise the land lay fallow and neglected during this impossible summer, used as nothing more than a shortcut between farms.

"I figure to get out of the wagon and sit on the ground, perfectly still."

Abbie nodded.

"The coyotes are howling every night lately. If we listen carefully, we should be able to tell which direction the sound comes from."

"Right."

"You have to promise me you won't make any sudden movements once we're on the ground."

"I am aware of the seriousness of the situation, Willem. Some of my mother's hens still have not recovered from the fright. We all know how close that coyote was to the house."

Willem was not driving fast. Stillness cloaked their path as the sun slid behind the distant mountains and gray began to blur their sight. In the fading light, Abbie raised her eyes to the ever-present Pikes Peak. It was there any time she stepped outside, unmoving and faithful. When the Weavers arrived in Colorado and she gazed on the mountain for the first time, she had tucked away the thought that it was a symbol of what their district would someday be—a church unmoved by changing times and faithful to the Word of God.

Now, though, fear welled that her mountain of hope would crumble like so much soft lignite in Willem's hands.

Willem turned the lantern to a brighter setting. The new moon was only a few nights old and cast just a sliver of light. The lantern was all they had to see by as the horse stepped forward in a slow rhythm and the wagon swayed in response.

As they rode in near silence, Abbie choked on questions. Was Willem actively helping Jake Heatwole? What prayer was in his heart these days? Did his heart clench at the thought of a future without her, the way hers did when she tried to imagine being another man's wife? Or no one's.

"Willem." She spoke softly.

"Yes?"

"Thank you for this. For getting the traps. For trying to help us."

He turned his head to look at her, but the lantern was behind his head now and she could not make out his expression in the deepening darkness.

"Of course," he said. He reached across the bench for her hand.

She knew she ought to let go. He was going to leave the church. Leave her. She closed her eyes and prayed for God to send an Amish minister to the settlement. Soon. But she did not let go of Willem's hand.

Willem took his hand back only when he required its use in bringing the wagon to a safe stop. He unhooked the lantern, offered Abbie assistance in descending from the bench, and led her a few yards away from the wagon.

"I hope you don't mind sitting on the ground." His voice was barely audible.

She lowered herself into the dirt and pulled her knees up under her chin. Willem sat beside her, the light burning between them.

"Should we turn the light off?" Abbie whispered.

He shook his head. "I am not trying to lure the coyotes. I only want to know where they are, whose farm might be next." His voice trailed into silence.

Abbie found herself holding her breath so she would not miss a valuable sound because she was listening instead to the air flowing in and out of her lungs. Willem was still as a boulder.

The howling came, distant, mournful, insistent. Following the noise, Abbie's head turned in the direction of Rudy's farm. Allowing herself a breath, she thought of his beautiful cows. Could a coyote take down a cow? Certainly the calf was vulnerable.

She tilted her head, thinking she heard something closer. A moment later, Willem leaned in the same direction.

The crack of a rifle threw them both to the ground, Willem's weight on top of Abbie.

❧◆❧

"You two all right?" Rudy lowered his rifle and moved toward Willem and Abbie.

At the sound of his voice, they sat up and then sprang to their feet.

"Rudy!" Abbie raised the lantern and turned it up to bring them all into its circle of light.

"You could have shot us." Willem took the light from Abbie's hand.

Rudy stood his rifle on the butt and held its slender nozzle in his hand. "Or that coyote could have pounced on you."

"We were only listening to them howl," Abbie said.

"This one wasn't howling." Rudy moved in the direction he had shot. "I saw his eyes. Bring that light and let's see if I got him."

Willem and Abbie followed Rudy's long stride.

"There." Rudy pointed with the end of his gun.

Rudy had caught the beast between the eyes. It lay sprawled as if its legs had gone out from under it in an instant.

"I don't understand," Abbie said. "I thought the scent of humans repelled coyotes."

"Usually," Willem said. "But Reuben did say he saw one in broad daylight at the ravine."

"And Ruthanna," Rudy said.

"What about Ruthanna?" Abbie stiffened.

"Didn't she tell you?" Rudy raised his eyebrows. "Right after it happened I was over at their place helping with chores. She was still rattled, but she didn't want to tell Eber. On the day of that meeting about whether Noah Chupp should be minister, a coyote approached her."

"She never said a word!"

"I guess she got it out of her system when she told me. Probably she wanted to make sure it wouldn't get back to Eber while he was so sick."

"Do you think it's been the same coyote every time?"

Even in the darkness with only the light of the lantern, Rudy saw the pale color of Abbie's face. "I expect so. He was probably hungry."

"But there are plenty of gophers and rabbits."

"That's what I'm planning to bait the traps with," Willem said.

Abbie raised a hand to her mouth, as if to banish the sickening image. She understood the realities of living on the Colorado plain, but Rudy knew her well enough to know she would recoil at innocent animals finding such a fate.

"We should all go home," Rudy said. "We can talk about this tomorrow."

"I am still going to set traps," Willem said.

Rudy nodded. "And I still think you should."

"I want to see where they are."

Two days later Willem looked up at the sound of Abbie's voice in his yard. "I didn't know you were coming by," he said.

"I wanted to be sure I caught you before you left and I wouldn't know where to find you."

She had no horse with her.

"You walked?"

"*Daed* wanted both the horses."

She must have set out the minute her mother finished serving breakfast. The sun already was rising hot in the sky. Light twisted in the braids coiled against her head and shimmered loveliness through her stature. If only she would listen to Jake Heatwole even one time. Could she not see Jake was their best hope of marrying at all?

"The traps are dangerous, Abbie." A dozen of them clanked against each other as Willem laid them in the wagon.

"I know that. I'm not foolish enough to set one off. I only want to know where they are. Levi sometimes wanders."

"He might have to reform that habit. I will speak to your father about having a stern conversation with your brother."

"If I know where they are, I can help Levi stay away from them."

"I saw how squeamish you were when I said I was going to use gophers for bait." Willem watched for change of color in her face, but she only straightened her shoulders.

"A human being could get hurt," Abbie said. "Sacrificing a few gophers is a small price to pay."

"The gophers are no friend to the farmers, either, you know."

"I know. *Daed* says they eat the wheat."

Willem tapped the side of the wagon. "Get in."

❧✦❧

Ruthanna met Abbie's gaze later that afternoon as they sat together in the Gingerich kitchen.

"Why didn't you tell me about the coyote?" Abbie set her jaw, and Ruthanna knew she was determined to have an answer.

"*Shh.*" Ruthanna glanced toward the bedroom.

"Is Eber sleeping?" Abbie's brow furrowed.

"Just resting. I don't want him to know."

"Is it wise to keep secrets from your husband?"

"When it is for his own good. Do you realize what he would do if he knew about it?" Ruthanna fiddled with her empty coffee cup. "It was bad enough that he insisted on going to that meeting with the other men."

"Willem set traps. Some of them are on your land. You know others will look out for you if you are in danger."

Ruthanna turned her head to look out the small window in the side of the cabin. "Eber prefers to take care of us himself."

"We take care of each other. He knows that is our way."

That would involve trusting someone, and Eber had made his feelings clear on that matter. Ruthanna got up and carried her cup to the sink.

"Ruthanna, is everything all right?" Abbie scraped her chair back.

Ruthanna turned and put a hand on her back. "Of course. I'm tired, that's all. Nothing unusual for a woman in my condition."

"You still have two months." Abbie stood up and took her own cup to the sink. "You need to save your strength. I'm going to come more often to help with washing and cleaning."

"Thank you, but that's not necessary."

"But I want to."

The bedroom door opened, and Eber stepped into the main room of the cabin.

"Eber," Abbie said, "are you unwell again?"

Ruthanna's heart sank. She had hoped it was not so obvious that her husband's health was once again declining.

CHAPTER 19

Abbie tugged her thread through the seam in Rudy's shirt one last time before tying off the knot. This was the fourth time she had repaired the same garment. Rudy needed at least two new shirts. At home in Ohio a man without a wife to sew for him could go to an Amish tailor when he needed new clothes. Abbie supposed Rudy had not had a single new item since he arrived in Colorado. She folded the shirt and set it on the shelf beside his bed, then gave the top quilt one last swipe to free it of wrinkles before calling her work inside complete.

She collected her cleaning rags and last week's empty bread bag and took them outside, putting them in the buggy before looking for Rudy. He was in the barn with the new calf. Abbie stood in the open barn door and marveled at his gentleness with an animal that had hesitated to cooperate with life on this side of the womb only two months ago. Well fed and lively, the calf now nudged Rudy's fingers to see what treat it might find there. Rudy spoke soothingly, more sounds than words.

Abbie stepped into the barn. "How are my favorite mother and daughter doing today?"

Rudy glanced over his shoulder and smiled. "They are very well, I am happy to say. This little one never wants to stop eating."

"Good." Abbie paced over to the stall. "Then her mother will be a wonderful milk cow once she's weaned."

"A dairy needs good milk cows."

Abbie relished hearing Rudy talk about the future—acquiring

more animals, expanding his milk and butter sales.

"You'll have a fine dairy one day." Abbie sat on a milking stool. "I'm so glad you didn't use that train ticket I caught you buying back in May."

Rudy scratched under the calf's neck. "I still have that ticket voucher."

"I would have thought you would have returned it for the cash long ago. You have wonderful land, and your animals are having young. Your milk business is growing even if your crops are not."

"You make a good argument for staying."

"I certainly hope so."

He looked at her now. "Twice you have persuaded me to stay, Abbie. I know how much it means to you, especially considering that the Chupps decided to leave the settlement."

The Chupps. Abbie tried not to think of them. They probably attended a Baptist church somewhere in Nebraska by now.

"I have to be honest with you," Rudy said. "I am still here because of you. I stay because I have a glimmer of hope that someday you might see something in me that would make you want me for more than the survival of the settlement."

"Rudy, I—"

He held up a hand. "Don't say anything. I only wanted to speak my mind. I know you don't feel that way right now. But things change."

He gave the calf a final pat and strode out of the barn.

Grateful that everyone else was out of the house for the afternoon, Abbie sat at the table with a blank sheet of paper in front of her and a black fountain pen in her hand. She wanted to write a report to the *Sugarcreek Budget*, the same Amish newspaper in which her family had first read about the wide open prospects of Colorado.

"Here we are located in the rain belt of Colorado," the glowing report had said. What it failed to note was that the yearly rainfall was half of what Amish farmers were used to in Midwestern states. Fifteen inches a year included snow in the winter. Moisture melting into the soil in the middle of January was helpful, but it did not make up for the lack of rain in the dry summer months when the settlers planted wheat and barley and rye. At least potatoes seemed to do well even with less water than the farmers wished for.

Abbie knew she could not write any of these thoughts. She wanted to say something enticing, something that would encourage other families to consider transplanting themselves to the Colorado plain. But Abbie wanted to be honest.

The majesty of Pikes Peak was always in view. She could say that honestly. And the winters were not as harsh as one might think, nothing like Ohio or Pennsylvania. Snowstorms were spaced widely apart, and in between, temperate days outnumbered cold days. All the farms were within a few miles of the ravine where coal was near the surface.

All these things were true. Somehow, though, they did not add up to the rosy account Abbie wished she could offer. What could she say that would interest someone in coming to a community that had not even had a church service in more than fourteen months, with none on the horizon?

Abbie lodged the tip of the pen in the corner of her mouth. Perhaps it would be more productive to write to a bishop, or two or three. She might be overstepping her role as a woman, but if a bishop visited, it would not matter who had invited him. A report from a bishop might encourage new settlers, or at least keep the existing settlers from giving up on their investments of money and spirit.

Abbie blew out her breath and put the pen down. No, she would not write to a bishop. *Gottes wille.* In God's time He would send a minister. It was better to pray fervently for this than to take matters into her own hands.

And writing to the *Budget* would have to wait until she had a clearer mind. Rudy's words were unexpected. She had only meant to befriend and encourage him, just as she sought to encourage all the settlers when she had opportunity or they had need. Rudy had been right about Willem's dalliance with the Mennonites. He had been right that if Willem had to choose, he would choose another church over Abbie's devotion to the Amish settlement. Willem wanted a thriving farm more than anything else.

But Abbie loved Willem Peters, something she could not honestly say about Rudy Stutzman.

⚡

"Are you sure you feel up to walking down the street?"

Ruthanna leaned on Abbie as she got out of the buggy. "I feel better if I move around. Eber will hardly let me leave the house for fear that something will happen while he is not with me, but he knows I am safe with you."

Abbie waited a moment for Ruthanna to get her feet solidly beneath her. "Ruthanna, is Eber working too much?"

Abbie lifted the basket of eggs from the buggy and they started down the street toward the Limon mercantile.

"He did not look well last week," Abbie said.

"He is tired. He festers over everything around the farm, even though we have no crop to speak of. Fences, mucking more than necessary, whatever comes into his mind."

"Eber should let someone help him."

"He won't."

"What about coal?"

"He will dig soon. Willem tells him that the *English* are all digging now. Sometimes there are thirty teams in the ravine. Eber prefers to avoid them."

"Does he let Willem help him?"

Ruthanna shook her head. "Willem tries, but Eber sends him away."

"But is he truly able to keep up?"

Ruthanna had said too much already. "Abbie, Eber would be troubled to think that you are worrying over him."

To Ruthanna's relief, Abbie let the subject go. Ruthanna looked down the street and brightened. "Look, there's Jake. Let's say hello."

"But Ruthanna—"

"He was so kind to us. I will never forget it." Ruthanna waddled forward before Abbie could pull her back.

Jake caught her eye and changed his trajectory to intersect with Ruthanna's path.

"Mrs. Gingerich, how good to see you." Jake offered a handshake, and Ruthanna accepted.

"Are you living in town now?" Ruthanna asked.

Jake nodded. "I was at the hotel for a few days, but I found furnished rooms for rent and picked up the key this morning."

"I hope you will enjoy your new home."

"There is some work to be done before I can call it a home, but I will have some help in accomplishing the tasks."

"I am glad to hear that." She wished Eber were in a position to repay Jake's kindness, but even if he were well in body Ruthanna knew that her husband's mind-set of distrust would not permit him to associate with the Mennonite minister's efforts to start a church that might tempt Amish households.

"Here comes my helper now." Jake gestured across the street.

Willem paced toward them.

❧❦❧

Abbie gripped the egg basket with both hands. Willem had said nothing to her about helping Jake move in. But she could hardly blame him. He would have known it would upset her.

"Hello, Willem," she said. It was not like him to come into Limon without stopping by to see if the Weavers needed anything. He used to predict with impressive accuracy which days she would want to bring eggs to town to sell while they were fresh and found reasons of his own to offer to take her.

"Hello, Abbie, Ruthanna." Willem looked from the women to the minister. "I suppose Jake has told you the good news."

"Yes, he has."

Ruthanna was overeager, Abbie thought. How was it good news that Willem was helping a Mennonite minister move into town? Until a few weeks ago Jake's decision would not have mattered to Abbie one way or another. Now it threatened everything.

"Ruthanna," Abbie said, taking her friend's elbow, "we shouldn't dally. I don't want you to get too tired."

Ruthanna laughed. "I am always tired at this point."

"Still, we don't want to stand out in the hot sun for too long."

Abbie nodded at Willem and then Jake. "I wish you success in your endeavors today."

Two black hats dipped in tandem at the women.

An hour later, with their eggs traded and a few staples in the back of the buggy, Abbie helped Ruthanna back up to the bench.

"I was glad to hear the mercantile is going to carry fruit from the Ordway Amish." Ruthanna settled herself as gracefully as she could. "God has blessed them with an irrigation system that can benefit us all."

Abbie unhitched the horse and picked up the reins. Sour jealousy brooded in her spirit. The Ordway Amish, only sixty miles away, had flourishing orchards and sugar beet fields—and two ministers and a bishop. Not only did the Limon Amish struggle to grow vegetables for their families, much less cash crops, and all without a minister, but now the Mennonites were flaunting their plans in the streets of town.

Willem was serious about the Mennonites. Of all the threats that picked at Abbie's longings, this was the most persistently painful.

If she were to marry Rudy Stutzman, a bishop would have to come. He would see how desperately the families needed their church. He would do something.

Abbie blew out her breath, chastising herself for even thinking of using Rudy that way.

Still, he did care for her.

Ruthanna turned a palm up. "I feel rain."

Abbie raised her face and scanned the sky. Clouds dense with moisture moved across the sky.

"Rain, Abbie!" Ruthanna said.

Abbie moistened her lips. She ought to feel grateful. But the rain was too late. It would not save the crop. It would not save Willem.

CHAPTER 20

A week later Ruthanna went outside to check on the laundry she left on the line an hour earlier. In the midday sun she had no doubt it would be dry already, and if she left it much longer dust would whip on the wind against it and settle into the cotton weave of sheets and shirts. Eber seemed to perspire faster than Ruthanna could launder. Bending over to transfer items from the line to the basket was a task more complex by the day.

She hummed, her way of prayer, to quell her spirit restless with impatience to hold the babe in her arms and with worry that Eber would not return to himself. With a tune stuck in her head, Ruthanna almost did not hear the approaching horseman.

"Mr. Heatwole!" Ruthanna glanced toward the barn, the last place she had seen Eber.

Jake dropped his feet to the ground. "It was delightful to see you in Limon the other day."

"Yes, a pleasant surprise." Ruthanna dropped a shirt into the basket and turned to face Jake. "I will always be grateful for what you did for Eber and me."

"I would do it again if the need arises."

"Thank you." Ruthanna watched for movement from the barn, wondering if Eber could hear the voices from his workshop.

"Now, Mrs. Gingerich, I want to choose my words carefully so as not to presume or offend, but I want to make sure you understand that you would be welcome at my new church on any Sunday you choose to attend."

"Oh. Thank you—and I wish you well—but Eber and I are quite content with our Amish beliefs."

"Of course you are. I would never try to persuade you otherwise. I only mean to make sure you know you are welcome, and I would be happy to minister to you in any way that you need."

"Thank you." Ruthanna raised one hand to point casually. "Here's my husband now."

Eber came and stood close beside her. She felt the heat rise from his skin and could hardly keep from laying a hand on his forehead.

"Isn't it nice of Jake to come by?" Ruthanna said.

Jake dipped his head in greeting. "If I can ever do anything for you, please let me know."

"You have been generous enough," Eber said. "Thanks to you, we are getting along well."

"My offer stands, should you ever need something." Jake slung himself back on his horse and waved as he left.

"What did you say to him?" Eber asked.

"Nothing." Ruthanna reached for another shirt on the line. "He's getting ready to start his church."

"He seems a sincere man, and I'm grateful for what he did for me," Eber said, "but we will not be joining the Mennonites."

"I did not suppose we would."

⋙❖⋘

Abbie threw down the damp rag, hardly able to believe her eyes. What was Jake Heatwole doing in Widower Samuels's barnyard? Mr. Samuels was away for the entire day. Abbie would not have Jake poking around looking for him. She strode across the small house and out the front door before Jake could even get off his horse.

"Why, Abbie, I did not expect to see you here."

"Mr. Samuels is not home."

"I see. Then perhaps I will come again another day." He started to turn his horse.

"I cannot imagine what business you have with Mr. Samuels."

Jake tipped his head up and looked at the sky for a moment. "No, I don't suppose you could."

"If you are making the rounds trying to convert our people, I would appreciate it if you would stop."

"It seems that you are imagining after all."

"Isn't it enough that you have Willem?"

"I don't 'have' Willem, Abbie. He is a good friend, and we find we have a great deal in common in the things of the Lord."

Abbie wiped her damp hands on her apron. "I am sorry if I sound rude, but surely you can see my point. We have no minister, and you are trying to start a new congregation."

"I do not see quite the conflict that you do," Jake said. "I only seek to offer ministry to a flock without a shepherd. I am not competing for anyone's soul."

Abbie crossed her arms across her chest.

"Willem cares for you very deeply." Jake stacked his hands on the saddle horn.

She said nothing. What would it matter how deeply he cared for her if Willem joined Jake Heatwole's new congregation?

❧

For a split second, when Rudy heard the knock on the barn's doorframe, he let himself believe it would be Abbie. She had cleaned his house the week before, but bread day had come around again. If he had not frightened her off with his doubts and declarations of the previous week, more than likely she would come to visit the animals in the barn under the guise of telling him that she had left bread on the table.

But it was not Abbie.

"Hello, Jake." Rudy would have offered a handshake if his hands had not been mired in muck at the moment.

The bundle of black and white that followed Rudy around scampered to sniff Jake's hand.

"What can I do for you?" Rudy asked.

"It is I who would like to ask that question. Can I be of any help?"

Rudy surveyed the black suit Jake wore, made of a simple cut but still more fitted than an Amish suit would be. "Thank you, but I wouldn't want to ask you to soil your clothes."

Jake laughed. "Perhaps I am overdressed for the sort of calls I am making today."

"And what sort is that?"

"We don't know each other very well," Jake said. "I just stopped by to let you know that if I can help you with any spiritual concerns, I hope you will feel free to ask me. And for the record, I am always willing to take off my jacket and do whatever needs doing."

"You proved that with Ruthanna and Eber." What did Jake mean by spiritual concerns?

"You have probably heard I hope to open a new Mennonite congregation in Limon."

"Yes. God be with you." Rudy was not aware of any Mennonite families in Limon.

"I believe He is. I am not trying to pressure anyone, but I am going around to the Amish to let them know we will have our first service soon. I know some of you have been longing for plain worship."

The Stutzman family had been among the earliest to come from Europe and settle in Lancaster County, Pennsylvania, in 1737. Amish worship was in his bones. He did not see himself joining the Mennonites, but Jake was right. Rudy did long for the deep, rich worship of his people.

Willem nailed in the last of the new baseboard Jake hoped would help to keep the mice out of his furnished rooms and pushed a sofa back against the wall. The furniture had seen better days. No wonder Jake had gotten such a good price on the rooms. Even the Amish settlers who sank all their money in their land and left little for their houses had sturdier furniture. Earlier Willem had tipped the sofa over and banged a displaced crosspiece back into position and leveled the legs of the small rustic table that would serve as Jake's writing and study desk.

The doorknob turned, and Jake entered.

"How did it go?" Willem began to pick up the tools strewn around the room.

Jake shrugged. "It is difficult to tell. I can't say that anyone was surprised."

"You've made no secret of your hope to start a church, and you've always been friendly with the Amish."

"Not everyone was home, and I called on people I was sure were not interested in the Mennonites. I did not want anyone to feel left out."

"Let me guess. The Weavers, Martin Samuels, Rudy Stutzman."

"My goodness, your Abigail was quite disturbed at my presence on Widower Samuels's farm." Jake sat on the sofa.

Willem grimaced. "Did she try to throw you off the land?"

Jake chuckled. "I have a feeling she wanted to, but Amish restraint got the best of her. She seems to think I have some sort of hold on you."

Willem dropped his hammer in his open wooden toolbox. "I try to be honest with Abbie."

"She will not come to a Mennonite church of her own free will, and we cannot force her."

"There is always the Holy Ghost," Willem said. "God's will may change Abbie's will."

"Willem," Jake said, "have you thought about what it would mean if God's will does not change Abbie's will?"

Willem straightened the black hat on his head. "Abbie loves the Amish church."

"So do you."

"I do."

"And you love her."

"Yes." Willem folded himself into a small chair upholstered in a floral print, something none of the Amish would have in their homes. "But I can also see that the will of God is bigger than the Amish church. If Abbie cannot believe that with her whole heart, then she deserves a husband who will share her conviction, and I will not stand in her way."

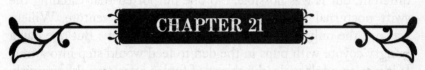

CHAPTER 21

The sky still hung in the faint ambiguous pink and gray of morning's decision to break forth again when Willem pulled on his boots and loaded his rifle. His traps were designed to kill a coyote or any other animal that found a gopher carcass attractive bait. Early every morning, before tending to farm chores or digging lignite for his *English* customers or even satisfying his own hunger with the bread that Abbie baked and brought every week, Willem made the rounds to inspect the traps. If he found an animal in one of the traps, whether predator or innocent, he would be prepared either to dispense justice or end suffering. So far, after two weeks, he had seen coyote tracks in a wide circle around a couple of traps, but none had succumbed. Today Willem took heavy gloves with him, a purchase of his last trip into Limon. If he wore them to change the bait, he hoped to minimize his own human scent on the trap.

Willem knew the coyotes were out there. He heard them every night, howling and barking whether the moon was bright or dim. Chickens were not the only targets. A coyote could kill a full-grown deer with a strategic strike to the neck. A cow would not be much different. Baby goats and calves had no defenses. The livestock of all the Amish farmers was at risk. They built their fences to keep cows and horses on their land and in pastures. Constructing a barrier that a coyote could not scale over or dig under was likely impossible, and certainly expensive beyond the means of struggling Amish settlers.

On his way out, Willem looked at his coffeepot and fleetingly longed for the sensation of thick black coffee sliding down his throat. But he did not have time for the indulgence and walked past the stove without lighting it. This might be the day that a trap held evidence of the enemy's demise.

Given the barren yield of the last two weeks in traps spread around on four farms, it was unlikely this morning would be different, but it was possible. No one purported that catching the swift nocturnal wolf-like animals was an easy venture. Willem was not the only man whose traps came up empty. But one day a hungry coyote with pups in the den to feed would step into a trap. If it was an adult male, the threat of future attack would diminish. Willem had no plans to relent on his vigilance.

Willem saddled his horse. Is that what Abbie thought—that it was possible the Amish could have a thriving congregation despite one defeat after another assaulting their efforts? Her hope kept her vigilant for the glory of God among their people. To her, it was only a matter of time and the settlement would rejoice in the triumph of worship.

He trotted the horse through his own land first, planning a wide arc.

Abbie barely slept in the two nights since Jake made his rounds welcoming any interested Amish to his Mennonite meetings. He had talked about starting a church for so long, and now he was going to do it. And he was going to take Willem away from her. The imminence of this reality dulled her appetite and robbed her sleep.

She swung her feet over the side of her bed and reached for her clothes. In a few minutes she was dressed with her hair pinned up adequately enough for the slim risk that she would see anyone on a walk at dawn. Chores during the heat of the day were inevitable, but a walk while the morning was yet cool would help her clear her mind. Abbie looked out the tiny window of her narrow bedroom and judged that the fullness of dawn was still at least thirty minutes away. But the moon had been full only a few nights before and lingered still.

As she walked, she could pray. For Willem. For Ruthanna. For Eber. For all the families. They might not be able to gather to hear sermons and take communion, but she could still pray. Even for herself, that God would quell the unrest of her spirit at the thought of losing Willem.

Abbie had traversed more than two miles on her morning quest for peace when she saw Willem on his horse silhouetted against the rising sun. Her feet stopped and she drew in a long breath. She was angry, hurt, confused, and in love. It all swirled around this man whose left shoulder sloped more severely than his right, this man who knew her heart like no other. She hated being angry with him. "Be ye angry, and sin not: let not the sun go down upon your wrath," the Bible said. And only a few verses later, "Be ye kind one to another, tenderhearted, forgiving one another, even as God for Christ's sake hath forgiven you." Ephesians 4:32 was one of the first verses Abbie's parents made her memorize before she had even learned to read it for herself. She knew it in German and in English. Sermons of her childhood had impressed on her that forgiveness was at the heart of a life obedient to Christ.

Her left foot went forward, then her right, and she counted her paces toward Willem. When she knew he had seen her, she started counting again at one.

He slid off her horse to greet her. "*Gut mariye.*"

"Good morning." Abbie hid her nervous hands in her plenteous skirt. "Are you checking traps?"

He nodded. "Are you well?"

"Very." She ran her tongue over the back side of her lips. "The Holy Ghost has convicted me that I have acted unkindly toward you and Jake. Please forgive me."

She looked into his eyes reflecting the growing light.

"Of course I forgive you, Abigail. I know that some of my choices make you unhappy. I never mean to hurt you."

"I know." She hardly heard her own voice.

"If I catch a coyote, you will be the first to know."

She smiled, wondering if he could tell how hard it was for her to do it. "Would you like to come to supper tonight? I know Levi would love to see you. We all would."

"And I would love to beat him at checkers, but I am afraid it cannot be tonight."

"Oh?"

"I have a meeting in town."

"Oh."

"It's just a meeting, Abbie."

She refused to lose her temper. "About Jake's church, I suppose." The Amish rarely held meetings in the evenings, when they preferred to be with their families. Were the Mennonites going to disparage the value of family?

"Yes."

She maintained a pleasant tone, determined not to hollow her request for forgiveness. "Another time, then."

Willem could hardly keep his eyes open when the meeting began thirteen hours after he found Abbie at the edge of the field. Other than minimal attention to farm chores that could not wait, Willem spent the day digging lignite. In mid-September residents carried out load after load of coal for cooking and heating through the winter. So far Willem's labors had yielded little coal for his own use. *English* customers with larger homes to heat were pleased with his efforts, and between cash and foodstuffs, Willem was optimistic about the coming cold season. The ravine harbored ample coal still.

The meeting was small, only Jake, Willem, and one married couple who lived in Limon. They met in Jake's sitting room.

"Thank you for coming." Jake smiled at his guests. "Tonight we remember that where two or three are, there Christ is also. Though we begin with a small group, we know the harvest is ripe. Many souls need the ministry that we begin together."

"Are you expecting many others to join the church?" James Graves put his palms on his knees as he asked the question.

"We will see how God leads," Jake answered. "At every step, we will be grateful for what God provides."

James turned to Willem. "My wife, Julia, and I have known the Mennonites before, but I am surprised to find an Amish man here for this first meeting. Are you planning to convert?"

Willem cleared his throat. "Jake and I have talked a great deal. I feel I understand the Mennonites well. We love and serve the same God."

"Do others of your people feel the same way? I've heard that you don't really have church."

"It is true that we do not have a minister," Willem said, "but we are people of deep faith."

Jake spoke. "I have been visiting Amish families. Willem is right. They have deep religious conviction, and I intend to respect them. I will not try to coerce any of the Amish to join us."

"Then why were you visiting them?" James asked.

"I want them to know they are always welcome. That's all."

Julia pressed the point. "But do you think some of them will want to join us?" She turned to Willem. "Are you going to join us, or are you merely curious?"

Willem glanced at Jake. "As Reverend Heatwole suggested, I will be waiting on God to make His will plain to me."

Jake suggested that the group take time to pray about the adventure of beginning a new church in Limon and led aloud in prayer. Then he moved the meeting on to other matters. Where would they hold services? How would they let the townspeople know of the new church? Did the Graveses have any names to suggest that Jake call on to make a personal invitation? Did any families in town have spiritual needs that a new minister might meet?

Willem said little during the course of the meeting. He had offered to make some notes of the conversation, and Jake supplied paper and a fountain pen. If James Graves tried to return to the subject of the Amish, Jake graciously redirected the conversation. Willem recorded Jake's questions and the answers that emerged from the Graveses.

By the time Jake closed the meeting in prayer, the sun was well on its way down. Willem hung two lanterns from the front of his wagon for the drive home and allowed his horse to set her own pace. He did not hear the coyotes while he was in town. Only when he was a few miles west of Limon, halfway to his own land, did he hear the mix of howling and barking.

So far Willem had not promised Jake anything, and Jake did not press for a commitment. If only Abbie would say she would come with him. But with Abbie or without her, he was not sure how much longer he could stand not to hear the Word of God preached. Even if he began with a tiny congregation, Jake planned to hold his first service within a few weeks. Willem was fairly certain he would be in the congregation that day.

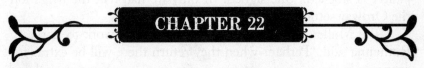

CHAPTER 22

With a basket of warm muffins, Abbie walked down the lane from her home to the main road, crossed to the other side for a fifteen-minute walk, and turned down the lane to the Miller farm. She had offered to take a buggy over to fetch Ruthanna, but her friend had assured her Eber would bring her and come back for her later. When she reached the house, she found Mary and Ruthanna sitting at the table drinking coffee. Mary gestured toward a third cup, and Abbie sat in front of it.

"I just made them." Abbie unfolded the towels wrapped around the muffins and was pleased to see that the baked goods still steamed slightly.

"They smell delicious." Mary inhaled the fragrance. "Wherever did you get blueberries?"

"*Mamm* had one last jar from last year." Abbie pulled a muffin open.

"Did either of you manage to have anything to trade for Ordway fruit this year?" Mary filled Abbie's coffee cup.

Ruthanna nodded. "I don't know how he did it, but somehow Eber convinced Mr. Gates at the mercantile to give him some on credit. I'll be canning all next week."

"I'll help you," Abbie said. "We'll just have to be sure to choose a different day than when *Mamm* wants to can. She managed to coax a few more beans and squash out of her vegetable garden, and we're hoping to trade eggs for fruit."

"The rain last week must have helped," Mary said. "It wasn't much, but it was something."

"Every drop helps." Abbie flung doubt out of her tone. "We have potatoes, too. Plenty to share, I think."

"Little Abe pulled up half of what I planted." Mary stroked the head of the little boy playing with a wooden spoon at their feet. "But Albert says we'll get some produce somehow."

"We should make a canning schedule and make sure everyone's pantry is stocked." She sighed. "If only we had half the irrigation the Ordway settlement has."

"The Mullet sons went down for a month's work to harvest," Ruthanna said. "Perhaps when they return there will be extras for everyone."

"God will provide." Mary picked up her son. "He looks like he's been eating dirt." She moved to the water barrel, where she stuck the hem of her apron in to dampen it and scrubbed at Little Abe's cheek. He protested by leaning away from her at a precarious angle. When his mother set him on the floor again, he toddled away from the table.

Ruthanna felt so enormous and full of child that she could hardly imagine her waist would ever again slim down the way Mary Miller's had after Little Abe was born. Her feet swelled more every day, and the baby kept her awake at night. Life had slowed to doing only the next thing she could see that needed doing, and she hardly thought beyond the end of the day. She cleaned the cabin, made sure Eber ate and rested, and tried to rest herself in the afternoons when it seemed that the baby was less active. The heat was becoming too much. By midday the house was stifling and did not cool again until after the sun set and the evening winds blew. At home Ruthanna kept a clean, damp rag within reach to wipe across her face as often as she felt the need.

While Mary and Abbie chatted about how the settlement families would get fruits and vegetables to can for the winter, Ruthanna put a hand across her tightening belly. Against her will her entire body contracted and she found it hard to breathe.

Pain wrapped itself around her midsection, rising in her back and making her gasp before circling around to the front again. These pains were happening every day now, one every few hours or several close together.

"Ruthanna, are you all right?" Abbie's voice cut through the pain in a distant sound.

"Breathe, Ruthanna," Mary said. "Don't close your eyes. That only makes you feel the pain."

Ruthanna had not realized her eyes were closed, but she forced them open to see her two friends leaning across the small table, inspecting her. At this unnaturally close angle, their eyes seemed awkwardly wide and the furrows in their brows alarmingly deep.

"I'm fine," she managed to say.

"False labor," Mary diagnosed. "The same thing happened to me before my time."

Ruthanna nodded. "Esther tells me it is quite common." If this was false labor, she dreaded what true labor would feel like.

"How much time do you have left?"

Mary took her hand, and Ruthanna kept herself from crushing her friend's fingers as the pain finally subsided.

"Less than two months." Esther Weaver had birthed many babies besides her own, including Little Abe. Ruthanna had no one else to trust in these matters, so she repeated the calculations Esther had made long ago.

Before Ruthanna's train trip to Ohio marked off the distinction between life there and the hardship of the Colorado plain.

Before Eber got sick and exhausted the hope she had stored up for their future.

Before Jake in his kindness nevertheless made people nervous about his intentions.

"I'm all right," she said again, and Mary released her hand.

❧❖❧

"A baby doesn't really need much." Mary took a muffin from Abbie's basket. "Whether you have a boy or a girl, the baby things don't matter. I kept Little Abe in white muslin gowns until he started to walk."

Abbie glanced at Ruthanna, hoping she was not hiding something more serious than false labor that would lead to a birth any time soon.

"The gowns are easy to make." Mary moved to the stove for the coffeepot and refilled the cups on the table. "I have a pattern. But you can use all my gowns. They are in perfect condition. Babies don't wear out their clothes."

"Thank you." Ruthanna lifted her cup and took a cautious sip of hot liquid. "Actually I've already made two from remnants of Eber's shirt fabric."

"It's generous of you to share your baby things." Abbie smiled at the toddler across the room, trying to remember how he looked when he was small enough for baby gowns. She had held him when he was new. How many months had it been now? Abbie calculated from his birthday in January and came up with twenty months.

"How is Willem?"

Abbie had been staring into her coffee and flicked her eyelids up at the sound of Mary's inquiry. "He is well."

"I know most of us don't have much crop to harvest this year," Mary said, "but that doesn't mean it cannot still be the wedding season."

Abbie felt the color drain from her cheeks. A few weeks ago she had playfully reminded Willem of the same thing. "It's hard to make plans right now."

"I suppose so. No place to read the banns. No one to perform the ceremony."

Abbie nodded politely.

"You could always go to Ordway," Mary continued. "You could get married there and stay for a few days before you came back."

Abbie put a bit of muffin in her mouth and looked around. "Where did Little Abe go?"

Mary pushed her chair back and stood up again, but she did not seem concerned. "That child. If I turn my back for half a minute, he disappears. I can hardly get anything done keeping track of him all day."

Abbie stood now. "You relax. I'll find him."

She pivoted so that most of the cabin was in sight and saw no sign of Little Abe other than a trail of small household items that served as his playthings. Abbie saw now that the Millers' front door did not catch fully when it was closed, and she pushed it open to go into the yard.

❧❀❧

Ruthanna was relieved to see Abbie lead the small boy back into the house less than a minute later. Even if Ruthanna did feel perpetually pregnant, at least she knew her child was safe in her womb.

"You little rascal." Mary picked the boy up and put him in her lap in a wooden chair with a high carved back that must have once been a fine piece of furniture. "Ruthanna, that chest right there has all the baby things. Why don't you go through them and see what you would like to use."

Ruthanna rose from the table. By the time she reached the cedar chest, Abbie had it open and lifted out a stack of neatly folded tiny clothing items.

"The gowns are in several sizes. Little Abe was growing so fast I was sewing constantly."

"They're lovely." Ruthanna found the softness of washed and worn muslin appealing as she thought of it next to her baby's skin.

"There's a quilt, too."

"I just finished making one."

"You can always use another."

Ruthanna found nothing to disagree with in that observation and took the quilt from the chest. Tiny blue and green triangles were laid on their backs against each other. Ruthanna had made her quilt with simpler squares.

"Your quilting is beautiful," Ruthanna said.

"I wish I could say I made it. My mother sent it. She was one of the best quilters in our district at home."

Mary's innocent comment sent a sharp pang through Ruthanna, who suddenly wished that her own mother were going to be present when her baby was born. Her parents had been vague about when they might visit.

"Abbie, how is your quilt coming?" Mary asked.

"I work on it nearly every night," Abbie said.

"I can't wait to see it!" Mary picked up a tiny sweater. "Don't forget this. Little Abe was born in January. If your baby comes in November, the size should be right for the winter."

Abbie handed Ruthanna a simple black knitted sweater with an open front and one tie at the neckline.

"Do you have a cradle?"

Ruthanna shook her head. "Not yet. But Eber wants to make one, something that we can use for all our children. I think he already has the wood cut out in his workshop."

"Well then, a few burp cloths and soft towels and you'll be all set."

Ruthanna rewarded Mary's generosity with a warm smile to mask her inner sense of foreboding. She wanted Eber to return and take her in his arms and to their home.

CHAPTER 23

With the smell of fresh bread rising from behind the bench and taunting her stomach, Abbie approached Rudy's farm a few days later. As she drove the buggy past the scruffy meadow and saw both his horses grazing, she smiled. He was probably home.

At first Abbie was nervous about seeing Rudy again after his confession of two weeks ago. But they were friends and fellow settlers, and she refused to think of sacrificing either dimension of their relationship to awkwardness. The Colorado plain was too desolate and lonesome to cut herself off from anyone. When the time was right they would speak again of that day, but for now she did not want him to feel spurned because she suddenly dropped away from him.

She knocked at his door and immediately opened it to let herself in, as she did every week. If he was home during the day, he did not spend his time inside the house, so she never waited for him to answer the door.

This time, though, he sat at the rugged table that he used for meals and papers. Several envelopes lay open before him. He looked up.

"Hello."

"Hello." Abbie moved to the shelf where he stored his bread and set the flour sack she carried in with her on it. She glanced around for last week's bag.

"It's there on the back of the chair." Rudy pointed.

She picked it up and folded it neatly into a small square. "What are you reading?"

"Letters from home. I had not picked up my mail in quite some time."

"Good news, I hope."

"Amusing news."

"Oh?"

"Listen to this." He read to her from the page he held in his hand. "Your little second cousin Ezra is a mischievous fellow. Though he is only nine years old, he is the master of practical jokes. Last week he hid a barn cat in a crate and put it on a shelf in his grandmother's closet. Lest you think he was being cruel, let me assure you the creature had plenty of air and was only confined for a couple of hours. Of course the thing meowed incessantly while the boy's grandmother had her quilting group over for lunch. Afterward, when she was determined to discover why there was a cat in her house and began an earnest search, he moved the crate around to another room every twenty minutes or so. She was convinced the poor thing was trapped in a wall and was about to call someone in to open the wall when the boy confessed. Fortunately she has a good sense of humor, though she threatened retaliation when he least expects it. Now the child is suspicious of everything his grandmother does. The entire family is having quite a laugh."

Rudy looked up, a grin on his face. "He was such a little boy when I left. I wish I knew him now."

"They sound like lovely people."

"They are."

A lump took instant form in Abbie's throat and made her voice thick. "What other news do you hear?"

Rudy picked up another letter.

"Amos Schrock was a good friend when we were little boys. He's getting married as soon as his family's harvest is in." Wistfulness crept out of his words.

"I'm sure he would love to hear that you are well," Abbie said.

Rudy nodded slightly and picked up a note card. "This one is from my father. He is all business. How many acres he planted, how much yield he expects, how many calves have yet to be weaned."

"He wants to know you are happy." Abbie surprised herself with the sudden insight. "He wants you to write with your own news."

"I know." Rudy's gaze drifted out the window. "They all feel so far away."

Abbie did not know what to say. They *were* far away. She had come with her parents and brothers and had not often stopped to think what it must have felt like to come alone to a new state only to discover that all was not as expected.

"Speaking of calves," she managed, "how is yours doing?"

Rudy took in a deep breath and returned his gaze to Abbie's eyes. "She is well. Do you want to see her? I let her out in the fenced part of the barnyard today. She needs to get used to being away from her mother."

"You're not going to wean her yet, are you?"

Rudy tilted his head to one side. "Soon. Two months is a long time to leave a calf with its mother. I'm raising milk cows, after all. But I don't want to separate them abruptly."

He had a soft heart, Abbie thought. Many farmers she knew thought only of what they needed from their animals. Rudy remembered that his cow and calf were also mother and child.

They walked out to the barnyard together, and the calf came easily to Abbie. She scratched under its chin and looked into its huge brown eyes. In another year, this calf would be old enough for breeding and could have her own calf and begin her work of producing daily milk.

Abbie smiled at Rudy, grateful that he was not pressing her to say how she felt toward him. She did enjoy spending time with him and keeping track of his animals.

But Rudy Stutzman did not make her heart race the way Willem Peters did.

❧

Ruthanna waddled from the house to the barn, a trek that seemed to take her longer every day. It was harder to make her legs go where she wanted them to go and keep her balance at the same time, and every day required greater effort to breathe in the thin Colorado air. She thought she had adjusted to high altitude living until she began to carry a child. Supper was ready, but Eber had not come in from the workshop all afternoon. Ruthanna was not sure how much longer she could keep the food warm without drying it out, or how much longer she could keep at bay her fear that something was wrong with Eber.

She shuffled across the dusty ground and breathed relief when she found the barn door open, uncertain that she could have managed to push it open. The heat inside the barn smacked her in the face and weakened her knees. Instant thirst made insistent demands she could not satisfy. When she did not see Eber standing in his workshop stall, Ruthanna's heart raced, and she ignored the limitations of her condition to reach as quickly as possible the place where she could look over the stall wall.

Eber lay on the stall floor.

"Eber!"

His eyes popped open.

"Are you all right?"

Sluggish, he sat up. "I'm sorry. What time is it?"

"I've had supper ready for almost half an hour."

He rubbed his eyes. "I only meant to take a quick nap."

Ruthanna hesitated to ask how long ago that had been. "It's beastly hot in here. No wonder you're sleepy."

"It's beastly hot anywhere we go, Ruthanna."

She could not argue with that.

He stood up. "Look at the cradle. I sanded everything and put it together today. I just need to put a finish on it."

Ruthanna stepped into the stall and ran her finger over the simple curved piece of each end of the cradle, then the spindles in the sides notched delicately at the centers. She pushed it gently side to side and was pleased with the way it glided.

"Thank you, Eber," she said softly. It was an exquisite gift, and Ruthanna hoped their child would one day feel as grateful as she did for the care Eber had taken.

"I told you I would have it finished before it was too late." Eber draped an arm across Ruthanna's shoulders. Though heat and dehydration would make him sleepy, she was now sure that he also had a fever.

"We still have a few weeks," she reminded him. "You don't have to make yourself ill to meet the deadline."

Abbie ignored the howling coyotes that evening. With a lantern on the table in front of her, she spread open the issue of the *Sugarcreek Budget* that she had already read three times. Beneath it were three earlier issues. As hard as she had tried to write something cheerful and encouraging to send to the *Budget*, she had instead laid her attempts in the belly of the stove and listened to them crackle into flame. If she could not be cheerful and honest at the same time, she would rather be silent. However, someone else might have written.

Most of the time the Weavers scanned the stories in the *Budget* looking for news of someone they knew. This time Abbie intended to read enough of each story to be sure she was not missing some reference to the struggling settlement, whether a comment by someone who lived within miles of the Weaver farm or someone remarking from afar on the conditions in Colorado. Two years ago a woman from Oklahoma had visited and then reported that Colorado was all right for a man who had money to spend, but a poor man had no business there. For weeks after that, a flurry of articles crisscrossed the country venturing opinions about the suitability of settlers for the demanding life on the plain.

Though she wished the woman from Oklahoma had kept her opinion to herself, Abbie understood what she meant. A settler who had sufficient money could do well carving out a life in Colorado and enjoy the beauty the state had to offer. Without money, though, the task had proven more complex than any of them expected. Most of the settlers had to just do the best they could to feed and shelter their families. Whether any of them would succeed over time remained to be seen.

Willem certainly intended to. But his terms of success would hardly attract future settlers.

Rudy aspired to a sweetness of life that was as brittle as old thread.

Abbie pored over the articles, one issue after the other. For the first time she felt the irritation of trivialities and understated criticism that wove through the articles, and the whole business struck her as an indirect way to communicate. The settlers around Limon did not have that luxury.

CHAPTER 24

A bbie did not leave the farm the next day. Tuesday was a baking day, and while the loaves rose through two yeasty cycles before going in the oven in twin sets, she cleaned the Weaver home. Her mother sat for much of the day in the shade cast by one side of the house or another, repositioning two chairs with the movement of the sun so she could listen to Levi read painstakingly from the family's German Bible and recite multiplication tables. Abbie took them plates of boiled eggs and cold ham at lunchtime and the first slices of fresh bread and milk for midafternoon refreshment. Levi had been grateful for both interruptions. He was a cooperative student even in midsummer, but Abbie knew he was not reading as well as many children his age. Esther Weaver was on her own to teach him.

Abbie had heard talk of the Amish families beginning their own school, even if it convened in someone's barn and the mothers rotated teaching duties. With the Chupps gone, though, Abbie supposed the energy for undertaking would dissipate. After all, the Chupps had five of the nine school-age children who would have attended. The remaining families, like hers, had only one child each between the ages of six and fourteen.

On the other hand, Abbie mused, an organized Amish school could be an attraction to families with young children. Occasionally she did Levi's lessons with him and surprised herself with her patience. Late in the afternoon, the baking finished, Abbie pondered this question as she swept a coating of flour blown astray from the mismatched pieces of linoleum that constituted the kitchen floor.

Soon it would be time to get supper on the stove. Abbie made sure that the doors at both the front and rear of the house were open to catch the breeze that the unobstructed plain often birthed in the late afternoons, just when the family was most weary from the heat. She stood for a moment looking toward Pikes Peak rising from the seemingly endless plain. It was miles and miles away. Still it dominated the view. Abbie hoped she would remember to come out later and watch the sun set behind the mountain. She knew better than to hope Willem would ride over to share this simple pleasure as he had so many times in the past.

But someone was riding in. Abbie squinted into the glaring late afternoon light to see Mary Miller urging her horse to pull the buggy faster. Mary was calling something, but Abbie could not hear her words over the clatter of the hurtling rig.

Finally Mary pulled on the reins, breathless.

"Little Abe is missing."

The instant pressure in Abbie's chest seized air from her lungs.

"Did you hear me?" Mary shrieked.

Abbie gulped, Little Abe's sweet face rising in her mind. "How long?"

Esther and Levi appeared from around the corner of the house.

"I don't even know!" Mary covered her eyes. Her shoulders rose and fell three times before she could continue. "He went down for a nap, and I sat outside to work on my mending. Then I went out to the garden to see if there was anything worth picking and started clearing weeds. When I realized how long I had been out there, I figured I should wake him up or he would never go to sleep tonight. But he was gone!"

"Ananias!" Esther hollered for her husband.

"Albert went into town and isn't back yet," Mary said. "I've looked and looked around the house and barn. I can't think where Little Abe could have gotten to."

Esther tapped Levi in the center of the back. "Find your *daed* and tell Reuben to bring the horses."

Levi lit off through the dust.

"Someone should be at the house to wait for Albert." Abbie started to hoist herself onto the buggy bench. "I'm going to take you home. We are going to turn over every stone and board of your place, and we are going to find Little Abe."

Esther nodded. "My husband and sons will not be far behind."

"What will I say to Albert?" Mary moaned. "How does a wife tell her husband that she has lost their child?"

"We're not going to worry about that." Abbie took the reins out of Mary's hands, which had gone limp. "When do you expect Albert home?"

"He's over working on Mr. Nissley's land. He said he would be home for supper."

"Then he'll be home soon, and you know he would move a mountain to find that boy."

Mary's tears gushed unrestrained now.

Abbie glanced over and saw her father, Reuben, and Daniel marching toward them in stride with each other. By God's grace they had all been together and not off in the far corner of the farm. She clicked her tongue and got the horse moving, leaving it to her mother to explain the urgency of her summons. Forcing herself to breathe as she drove, Abbie did a mental inventory of all the places a small boy might get lost on a three hundred-acre farm. But he was barely less than two years old, and she did not think he could have gotten far.

Unless he had never fallen asleep for his nap at all.

At the Miller farm, Abbie jumped out of the buggy and fell to her knees at the base of the house, looking for any space into which a small child might squirm.

"I already looked there." Mary hovered behind Abbie.

"He can't have gotten far."

"That's what I thought." Mary's tone rose in panic. "Don't you think I looked everywhere around the house and barn before I went for help?"

"The henhouse?"

"Nothing but hens."

Abbie sucked in her breath. "The outhouse?"

"We keep it latched way above his reach."

"But you looked?"

"Yes, I looked."

Abbie scrambled around the perimeter of the house and saw no sign of Little Abe's tiny footprints. She sat on her haunches and squeezed her head between her hands and closed her eyes, trying to picture where he would go. She did not know the Miller farm nearly as well as Mary did herself, but perhaps in her panic the child's mother had overlooked something obvious.

Esther arrived with Ananias and Reuben just as Abbie got to her feet.

"I left Levi with Daniel," Esther said. "Having him here would be a distraction we don't need. He's frightened as it is."

Abbie squeezed Mary's hand. "You stay here with my *mamm*. You won't be alone when Albert gets here."

"I want to keep looking." Mary lurched toward the Weaver buggy.

"You can hardly stand up," Abbie said. "You did the right thing to come and get us. Stay here and pray."

Esther took Mary's elbow and steered her back toward the door to the house. "Reuben," she said, "take one of the horses and ride for Willem as fast as you can. Then come right back."

Abbie marched toward Mary's buggy. "We can each take a direction. I am going north."

"Make sure there's a lantern in that buggy," Esther cautioned.

Mary gave a cry and balked in her progress toward the door. "It won't be dark for hours!"

Esther put her arm across Mary's back. "We will pray."

Abbie covered her mouth with her hand at the thought that they might not find the little boy well before dark. Surely they would find him playing in the dirt or he would look up and realize he could not see his mother and his cry would give him away. Convinced they would be passing him around a crowded room well before dark, nevertheless Abbie rummaged under the buggy bench to make sure there was a working lantern before she seated herself and picked up the reins.

❧❅❧

The longer Abbie searched, the more her chest clamped down on her breath. If anyone else had found Little Abe, someone would have ridden to the north acres to let her know. By now, well past suppertime, surely Albert had come home to find his wife a frantic puddle of anxiety and disbelief, and he would have taken his other horse out. Reuben would have returned from Willem's farm hours ago, and the two of them must be searching.

Hours.

Hours since Mary's buggy rattled onto Weaver land, and perhaps hours more since Little Abe slipped out of the Miller house undetected.

Abbie's thickened throat scarcely allowed air to pass.

Her first impulse had been to give the horse its head and hurtle toward Little Abe, scanning the countryside. But he was so small. It would be too easy to gallop past him if he had fallen asleep in a ragged field or lay frightened in the shade of a ball of thistle. Instead, Abbie mentally divided the land north of the Miller's home into calculated sections and set out to cover every square yard in a systematic manner. But when she had taken the buggy through every acre without finding him, and still no one galloped toward her with the news of a rescue, she started over, widening the perimeter of her search and slowing her pace even further.

"God," she said aloud at regular intervals, "I cannot understand Your will in this. He is an innocent child."

The horse grew sluggish, and Abbie urged it on. Periodically she slid out of the buggy and walked widening concentric circles around the horse before returning to ride to another sector. Finally she admitted she could no longer see well enough in the descending gray to trust her eyes, and she stopped long enough to fish the lantern out from under the seat and shield the wick from the rising wind long enough to light it. She heard only her own breath, a desperate, shallow, tattered effort to suppress the visions that roared through her mind.

"Little Abe!" she called out, over and over.

She listened for the slightest rustle of small feet, the faintest cry of a small boy's voice, or the gathering approach of a rider with good news. None of these sounds met her ears.

Abbie stepped farther away from the buggy in full darkness.

The only vibration to break the silence was the distant howl of a coyote.

CHAPTER 25

Standing in deepening gloom, Abbie held the lantern high, sweeping slowly from side to side in a field of dry, half-grown wheat that would probably not be worth the price of having it milled.

"Little Abe, where are you?" she said softly.

When Abbie raised her eyes to consider where she would move next, she gazed into the shadowy distance, wondering where the other searchers were. She blinked twice at a shifting shape before she realized it was Willem astride his horse.

"Willem!"

He gave no sign of having heard her shout, instead holding his pose in the pale light cast from the moon in its last quarter. Abbie could barely make him out. If it had been anyone else she might have told herself her eyes were transforming a large thistle ball into something she wished were there. But the slope of his shoulders, one raised higher than the other in his characteristic posture, made her certain.

"Willem!" Abbie swung her light from left to right hoping he would see it and be curious enough to investigate.

He shifted this time, but away from her. Willem moved slowly, no doubt for the same reasons Abbie did—to look and listen carefully for any sign of Little Abe. His horse made a full quarter turn now and began a slow pace. Abbie kicked at a small loose stone and heard it thwack a stalk of wheat six feet away. With equal desire she wanted to find Little Abe or to hear the thunder of a horse whose rider came to tell her he was found. Willem's concentration in the search told her the boy was almost certainly still missing. Willem eased out of her sight, and Abbie's heart fractured.

Keep the boy safe till we find him. She blew out her breath heavily as she pondered whether God was listening to her prayers.

The coyote's howl once again dominated the night and seemed to echo gusting in the wind. Night breezes often cooled the temperature considerably, but tonight Abbie perspired as much from anxiety as heat. Not wanting to wander too far from the buggy, she began a path that would take her in a straight line to where the horse and buggy stood at the center of her wide circles.

"Little Abe!" she called out once again, forcing conviction into her tone.

She gasped and held still. A tiny sound. Holding her breath, she listened for any swish in the wheat or footstep in the narrows rows between planting. Had it only been a noise carried on the wind?

"Little Abe!"

A cry. A child's cry, this time full and fearful and angry. Abbie turned around and hustled back through the wheat, swinging the lantern as she ran beyond the circle she had just abandoned and toward the cry.

"Little Abe! I'm coming!"

She found him face down in the ground trying to push himself up. Abbie set the lantern on the ground and knelt to fold him into her arms. Partially upright, Little Abe clung to her neck with grubby hands, his small shoulders heaving with shallow breaths and his plump cheeks smeared with dirt and tears. Abbie ran her hands over his arms and torso and legs, looking for injury. Where his right knee should have been, her hand hit earth, and she grabbed the lantern to pull it closer.

Little Abe's chubby leg was stuck in a gopher hole. Despite the warnings Abbie had heard Mary give her son time and again, the little boy remained fascinated by gophers and giggled every time he saw a round, brown face with tiny ears peek out of a hole or dash across the ground. He was too little to understand the risk of a gopher hole and just little enough for an appendage to fit into one. Abbie clasped him tight, waiting for both their hearts to calm.

Little Abe did not want to let go of her as Abbie tried to settle him in the mound of dirt that would have warned an adult that the hole was nearby.

"I'm not going to leave," she said with more calm than she felt. "We have to get your leg out, Little Abe."

He whimpered and tightened his grip on her neck.

On her knees, Abbie pried his hands off her skin and moved them to her skirt. "Here. Hold on to my dress."

She kissed his forehead, and his wide, frightened eyes stared at her, but he made no more effort to grab her neck.

The dry earth was unyielding to her fingers, and Abbie did not want to cause further injury. The boy might have hurt his ankle when he felt into the hole. Abbie banished from her mind the thought that gophers underground could have nibbled on his toes. If only she had a table knife or a spoon or anything to dig with. She felt around on the ground until she came up with a stone hardly bigger than a coin. One stroke at a time, she began chipping away at the edge of the hole to widen it just enough to pull Little Abe's leg out.

She drove with the child in her lap, his face buried against her chest and his arms wrapped around her waist. His heart beat wildly against her body, a testimony to his hours of fear, but he did not cry.

Abbie dipped her head to speak into his ear. "We'll get you home to your *mamm* and *daed*. You'll go to sleep in your own bed."

He nodded and dug his head against her as if he wanted to burrow a tunnel straight through her like a gopher. His skull against her breastbone was uncomfortable, but Abbie would tolerate whatever comforted Little Abe. When they got out of the dismal wheat field and onto the road that cut through the Miller farm, Abbie urged the horse a little faster, and faster still as the house came into view. By now Abbie drove with one hand around the reins and the other around Little Abe's tense back.

The front door stood wide open, and the light of half a dozen small oil lamps emanated out of the structure.

"We're almost there," she murmured to the boy.

"*Mamm.*"This was the first word he had spoken during the ride, though Abbie was sure he knew several dozen words.

"Yes, your *mamm* is waiting. She will be so glad to see you."

"Home." Little Abe sat up and twisted around toward the light-warmed house.

"That's right!"

A figure appeared in the doorframe, and Little Abe pointed. "*Mamm. Mamm.*"

A grin of relief split Abbie's face. She tightened her grip on Abe before he could get any ideas about getting down from the bench before the buggy stopped.

Mary rushed to the buggy and swept her child out of Abbie's lap and squeezed. Her chest heaved in sobs of relief.

"Be careful of his leg. I'm not sure if he got hurt." Abbie's own legs were melting rubber by the time her feet hit solid ground.

"Where did you find him?" Mary inspected the boy, running a hand over every inch of him.

Abbie explained the gopher hole.

Mary exhaled. "Albert has been trying to get rid of the gophers because he thinks they eat the wheat. But it is hard to find all the holes."

Abbie put an arm around Mary's shoulders, and they stepped into the house.

Esther looked up from the stove. "I'm heating water."

Mary nodded. "He needs a bath."

Abbie glanced around and settled her eyes on two tea cups. "Everyone else is still out looking?"

"The bell." Mary looked out through the open front door. "We need to ring the bell and call everyone in."

"I'll do it."

At the corner of the house, Abbie tugged on the bell and kept it clanging until she heard horse hooves beating from every direction.

❧❦❧

At dawn Rudy stood at the corner of his barn and whistled for his

168

dog, Rug. Though the small dog often wandered the acres late at night, it was unusual for him not to scratch to be let in at some point. Rudy had long ago become accustomed to opening the door at two in the morning and falling immediately back into sleep as if he had not been interrupted at all. Waking and finding the spot at the foot of his bed empty was disconcerting.

At his whistle, several cows mooed, a horse neighed, and chickens fluttered in the henhouse, but no dog appeared. Rudy paced around the outside of the barn to satisfy himself that the dog was not sleeping so comfortably under an eave that he could not bother to respond to a breakfast summons. Then he ventured to the farthest point in the barnyard and the spot in the fence where the dog was most likely to appear. Still not seeing the animal, Rudy hoisted himself over the fence and whistled again.

His whistle died half formed when he saw Rug—or the carcass that had been the dog. The teeth marks of a full-grown male coyote told the story, first clamping into the dog's neck then ripping open the abdomen.

Rudy turned around and retched. He had worked with animals long enough to see bloodier visages than this one. But the dog had been a companion in the wilderness. Rudy wiped his mouth, straightened, and went to the barn for a shovel.

⚜

Abbie's eyes widened as she forced down the knot in her throat. "I'm so sorry, Rudy. How awful for you."

"I thought you would want to know before you came over with bread and wondered where he was." Rudy sat astride his horse in the Weaver barnyard looking as dismal as Abbie had ever seen him.

Abbie nodded. She would have wondered. The dog consistently greeted her, and she reciprocated by scratching under his chin.

"Rudy," she said, "I have something to tell you as well. Little Abe Miller went missing last night."

His eyes widened.

"He's all right. He wandered off while Mary worked in the garden, but we found him after a few hours."

"God be praised."

"Yes. God is good. We all worry about our animals because we know what a coyote can do. But I can't help wondering what would have happened if that coyote had found a helpless child instead of your dog."

"The human scent would have turned the beast away."

"Would it? The coyotes seem to come closer and closer."

"Perhaps it is best if you do not mention my dog to anyone." Rudy wrapped the reins around his hand. "No point in putting a distressful notion in people's minds. But I hope Mary Miller will keep her boy close."

CHAPTER 26

A meal?"

Millie Nissley looked up from the beans in her garden. She had been more ambitious than most in what she planted, but it seemed to Abbie that her yield was as halfhearted as anyone else's vegetable patch. At mid-September, most gardens had finished for the season and Amish women were already canning.

"Nothing fancy," Abbie said. "Mary Miller and I would love to have everyone together to share our gratitude to God for Little Abe's safety." As she had already four times that morning, Abbie told an abbreviated version of the drama of Little Abe's rescue and was careful to give thanks to God for answered prayer.

"All of the families?" Millie looked dubious.

"I will invite everyone. Wouldn't it be lovely if everyone came? It would almost be like having church."

"We have no one to preach." Millie dropped a handful of beans into a basket.

"I know." Abbie was undeterred. "We can still sing and pray and be grateful."

"It's been a hard summer to think about being grateful."

Abbie nodded. "But Little Abe is safe. That matters more than anything else that has happened."

"What about food?"

"We have plenty of potatoes to roast and share. A couple of families have said they can spare a meat chicken or two. The Mullet sons have returned from Ordway with fruit. I made extra bread yesterday. Everyone will share as they are able."

"You seem to have thought of everything."

"Come at suppertime." Abbie stepped away from the garden and toward the buggy she had parked a few yards away. "We still have some light in the evenings."

Millie nodded without promising the family's attendance. As Abbie climbed into the buggy, she reviewed her mental list. She had visited five farms, and of course Mary and Esther knew the plans already. With the Chupps gone, that left Rudy, Willem, Martin Samuels, and the Troyers. She glanced at the sun approaching its zenith and judged that she still had time to talk to Mrs. Troyer, make her bread rounds, and clean Willem's house before it was time to start the potatoes roasting.

❧

Willem sank into a chair as Abbie readied her cleaning supplies. "What awful news about Rudy's dog."

"I hope I didn't sound unsympathetic when he told me." Abbie dampened a rag. "All I could think about was, what if it had been Little Abe?"

"But it wasn't."

"But it could have been."

"You must not let your mind dwell there," Willem said.

Abbie shrugged. "I'm trying not to. I'm trying to be grateful. In fact, Mary asked me to invite everyone for a meal tonight. She and Albert want to give thanks for Little Abe's safety by being with all the families."

"Everyone?"

Abbie began to wipe off the stove. "I drove around half of creation this morning making sure everyone is invited. I hope they will come." She paused to look at him. "I hope you will come."

Willem wiped crumbs from the table and into one hand but then was not sure what to do with them. "It is a good thing to be grateful."

"It will be almost like having a church service. We might have to sit on the ground, but we can be together. We can pray. We will share our food, just like we used to do after church. We can even sing our hymns. It will cheer everyone's hearts to hear the harmonies and ponder the words of God's greatness."

When she put it so simply, Willem could hardly argue. He often hummed from the *Ausbund* as he worked, and his ears ached to hear surrounding voices fill in melody and harmonies. The gathering itself was not what caused him to hesitate. Rather, it was that the common meal would feed Abbie's hope for a true Amish church when the likelihood had become all but impossible. And Willem's presence, in particular, might stir a hope that they once again were of one heart.

Abbie rinsed out the rag and started on the table, scrubbing in preparation for polishing. As rugged as his table was, she was persistent in coaxing out the best sheen it could offer. She wanted to wheedle the best of out everything. It was one of the reasons he loved her, but every day brought reasons to reconcile reality with hope. The table would never be what she wanted it to be, and neither would the church.

Willem stood up and dropped the crumbs in his hand into the slop bucket that would go to the chickens.

Abbie stopped scrubbing and turned her pleading brown eyes to him. "Please come."

Willem gave a one-sided smile, still unable to resist that expression even when he knew their future was in doubt. "A man has to eat."

With her unfolding fingers buried in the yardage of her dress, Ruthanna ticked off the weeks. She had only seen the doctor in Limon once, preferring to let Esther Weaver monitor her pregnancy. As long as there were no unusual symptoms, Esther said, Ruthanna had no reason not to expect a healthy delivery. The child turned and kicked and rested at intervals that assured Ruthanna all was well. By her best count, she had six more weeks.

At least the sun was not quite as scorching as it had been a few weeks ago. While the days still elongated in summer fashion, the height of the afternoon temperatures dropped a degree or two each day. Still, it was hot, and Ruthanna was tired of being hot, tired of lumbering around in a body that was less recognizable by the day, tired of not sleeping because she could not find a comfortable position, tired of fearing her restlessness would disturb Eber.

Abbie made sure Ruthanna had a chair and a plate of food. Two or three families had loaded benches into their buggies and arrived ready to share seating. Several of the families did not see each other often, and the shared meal on the Miller farm sparked conversation to catch up on family news while children and young people relished being with people their own age.

Not everyone came, though, and Ruthanna saw the disappointment written on Abbie's face.

"I notice that the Yutzys have not come." Millie Nissley glanced around as she settled on the bench next to Abbie. "I didn't think they would."

"Why shouldn't they?" Abbie's voice carried a note of stubbornness Ruthanna knew well. "Perhaps they are simply delayed."

"I don't think we'll see too much more of them." Mrs. Nissley pushed a fork through a potato.

"Why would you say that?" Abbie demanded.

"Amelia Yutzy never wanted to come in the first place. Her children are not much older than Little Abe. She worries about them night and day out in this wilderness."

"It's not really a wilderness," Ruthanna offered. "We're all still getting our feet under us. Even farming in Ohio is not without challenges."

Mrs. Nissley swallowed a bite and stabbed another. "She wants to go home. I think her husband is going to agree very soon."

Ruthanna flicked her eyes toward Abbie, who paled just as Ruthanna expected.

"I think perhaps I should be going." Ruthanna balanced her plate in one hand and stood up.

"But you hardly touched your food," Abbie said, "and we haven't started singing yet."

"I know. But I don't like leaving Eber."

"I'm sorry he didn't feel well enough to come. I'll fix a plate of food for you to take him and get Reuben to drive you home. I don't want Eber to feel left out."

Ruthanna nodded, grateful for the detail of Abbie's ministrations. For now it was easiest to let others think Eber was simply tired and that a woman in her condition would be more comfortable at home.

❧❧❧

Abbie waved good-bye to Ruthanna as Reuben pulled the Weaver buggy away from the other buggies and wagons lined up along the fence. She wanted to hold this vision as long as she could. They could have gathered like this long ago, buggies and horses announcing they were one body and children's voices lifting toward a future when every other Sunday morning would bring the families together. There was no reason to wait for a crisis like Monday night before being grateful and enjoying true Christian fellowship.

Esther and Mary were collecting plates to carry into the house to wash. Albert sat on a bench, leaning forward on his knees watching his son play in the dirt. Abbie spied Daniel pairing off with Lizzie Mullet to stroll outside the circle.

Abbie sat in the empty spot between Willem and Rudy on a bench. She nudged each of them with one elbow. "In church one of the men always starts the singing. It wouldn't be proper for me to do it."

Rudy gestured that Willem should begin, and Willem deferred to Rudy.

Abbie exhaled. "I know it shows humility when the men suggest another should go first, but please, you both have beautiful voices, so couldn't one of you just start singing?"

Willem cleared his throat. He had only sung a few bars when Rudy joined. The swell of eager voices rolled over the gathering in cool refreshment. Even after all this time without regular church services, the words welled with confidence. Abbie joined, though the knot of gratitude in her throat produced a scratchy sound. Around her the harmonies fell into place.

Where shall I go? I am so ignorant. Only to God can I go, because

God alone will be my helper. I trust in You, God, in all my distress.
You will not forsake me. You will stand with me, even in death. I have
committed myself to Your Word. That is why I have lost favor in all places.
By losing the world's favor, I gained Yours. Therefore I say to the world:
Away with you! I will follow Christ.

The wind flapped the hem of Abbie's skirt and caused her to
reach for her prayer *kapp* and make sure it was secure. She kept
singing, but she saw the glances around the circle. The wind
abruptly became fierce and dumped its chill over the gathering. The
temperature plummeted in an instant. Women dashed to keep food
from blowing over and reached for hands of small children. Men
hastily loaded benches.

Abbie had hoped for more than one hymn. The plain had
stolen the moment. Next time, she thought, she would arrange for
the shared meal to be held inside someone's barn. Rudy's was the
largest. There *would* be a next time.

CHAPTER 27

As soon as Rudy milked his last cow in the morning, he harnessed a horse to the buggy and trotted toward Martin Samuels's farm. Over a plate of roasted potatoes and boiled green beans with a chunk of salted pork at the Millers' gathering, Martin had asked Rudy to come look at a cow that was behaving poorly. Rudy liked to evaluate cows early in the day, after the night had dissipated body heat and before the animals had time to take on a new day's fever.

Wind had howled overnight, drowning out even the coyotes, and Rudy saw the effects. Loose thistle huddled against every fence he passed. Even weeds that withstood summer's blasts now bent in disarray. As soon as he finished with Martin's cow, Rudy planned to climb on his own roof and make sure his shingles remained secure.

Rudy turned on the road that would take him to Martin's land and began to watch for the collection of outbuildings. The house itself was small, but Martin had a good-sized barn and a shed he had built only last year out of odds and ends of lumber. Rudy slowed as he approached the compound, confused at the absence of the shed. Where it should have stood, he saw an exposed pile of lignite beside an open wagon.

Then Martin charged out of his barn with a shovel, not bothering to lift his eyes, and attacked the pile. With the shovel's point, he alternated between transferring coal to the wagon and knocking aside the splinters that had been his shed only the night before.

Rudy slowed his horse and narrowed his eyes. When he was close enough, he spoke.

"Martin."

Widower Samuels snapped his head up.

"I'm sorry about your shed." Rudy surveyed the scattered remnants. "That wind was mighty fierce."

"Yes, it was." Martin threw another shovelful of coal into the wagon.

And then the inconsistency rolling around in Rudy's mind fell into place. "Where did the coal come from, Martin?"

"The ravine, of course."

"Directly?"

"What is that supposed to mean?"

Rudy tightened the reins to keep his horse from drifting. "I thought you had not dug any coal yet."

"How else would I get it?" Martin stopped shoveling, but neither would he meet Rudy's eye.

"Thirty men a day dig in the ravine. Even the *English* remarked they have not seen you. We have been concerned you might not be prepared for the winter."

"As you can see, I have a good start on what I need." Martin adjusted the hat on his head.

Rudy moistened his lips, wishing a conclusion made sense other than the one foremost in his mind. "Martin, is that Willem Peters's missing coal?"

Martin dropped the shovel. "I appreciate that you came to see my cow. I'll show you where she is."

There were no elders to consult, no bishop to report to. Rudy had his doubts about whether Willem was doing right by Abbie, but he deserved to know what happened to a day's hard labor.

"I'd better come back another time." Rudy started to turn his rig around.

"My cow could go down if you don't help."

"I suspect I'll be back soon enough. In the meantime, make sure she's taking enough water."

Martin kicked his boot at the coal. Rudy did not look back.

Willem nodded his thanks as Abbie set a plate of hearty breakfast in front of him. Three biscuits, four scrambled eggs, and chopped fried potatoes mirrored the plate in front of Reuben. When she asked, Willem said he already had his breakfast, as Reuben did when the family had breakfast together, but neither declined her offer of another plate of food before they left the farm together to dig coal. Though she would pack food for them to take, she doubted either would stop to eat again until supper. Willem and Reuben paused for silent prayer, and Abbie held still as well. When Willem opened his eyes, he smiled at her.

"*Kaffi?*" she said.

"Please."

She had a hard time not meeting his green eyes. A few weeks ago they would have had an entire conversation in a room full of people just with chaste glances and turns of the head. Now she guarded her hope, and it was all because of Jake Heatwole. In her mind, Abbie turned the question in every direction but refused to be the one to give voice to the heaviness between them. If she asked about Jake and Willem's intention, and he said only what he had said in the past, her heart would sink yet again. And if he leaned more distinctly toward Jake, she would have to run from the room. When Willem made up his mind, he would tell her, and she would either shed her tears or let her heart burst in rejoicing.

She poured coffee for both Willem and Reuben and nudged a small pitcher of cream toward Willem, knowing he would pour generously from it.

The knock on the front door startled her. She paced through the house and returned a moment later with Rudy behind her.

"I believe I have found your coal," Rudy said.

❧❀❧

Willem took the time to unhitch his wagon only because he wanted to cut across the network of Amish farms in a direct route to Martin Samuels's house as close to a gallop as possible. The wagon would only slow him down.

"Wait." Abbie pulled at his elbow as he unfastened the hitch.

"Maybe there is an explanation. Give Martin a chance."

Willem sighed and stared into her dark eyes. At times her perpetual optimism was beyond his words. "Abigail, you heard what Rudy just said."

"Don't go in anger. Cool down first."

"And by that time will there be any evidence on the widower Samuels's farm of that coal?" He pulled out of her grasp and saddled his stallion. By now the entire Weaver family stood with Rudy in the yard. Willem did not look back at any of them as he pressed his heels into the stallion's sides.

Martin Samuels was stacking broken slats of wood along the side of the barn when Willem reined up beside him.

"I see Rudy wasted no time." Martin dropped another slat onto the pile.

"I see Rudy was right," Willem countered. A load of coal, a quantity that would have fit nicely in his wagon, was divided between a pile on the ground and the bed of Martin's wagon. "No one ever saw you digging, Martin. Not a single time."

"We still have long hours of light. No one could be at the ravine every moment of every day." Martin closed the gap between the barn and the coal.

Still on his horse, Willem followed Martin. "You have been a subject of much conversation. We were all concerned. Even Eber tried to dig before he fell ill again. But no one ever saw you."

"Perhaps I bought it from someone digging for profit. You are not the only one who does so."

Willem shook his head. "A man digging for you would have mentioned it amid our concern. And you led Rudy to believe you had been digging yourself."

"I will run my business, and you will run yours."

"Martin," Willem said, his jaw tight, "if you needed help, all you had to do was ask. You know that. You did not have to steal my coal."

"All coal looks alike." Martin turned his back to Willem. "You cannot possibly prove that this coal is yours."

"Why should I have to?" Willem's tone took on an edge. "Confession and forgiveness would be a more peaceable way to resolve matters."

"I do not owe you an explanation."

"It is no coincidence that the collapse of your shed in a windstorm is the first anyone knows of your coal supply."

❧

"Can't you go any faster?" Abbie gripped the bench of Rudy's buggy.

"This gelding is as old as the hills," Rudy said, "and I've already pushed the poor animal to race from Martin's place to yours. I thought I was just going to look at a sick cow or I would have brought a team."

Abbie exhaled and let her shoulders slump.

"Don't worry," Rudy said. "Willem is not going to hurt Martin."

Abbie remembered the look in Willem's face the day he dragged Reuben home after the coal went missing. If he had been that angry with Reuben, he would be much more angry with the culprit of the crime. *Crime.* She hated to even think of using that word in connection with any of the Amish settlers.

"Don't you know a shortcut?" Abbie kept her eyes straight ahead, watching for any turnoff that might speed their journey.

"I said I would take you." Rudy glanced at her. "But if you want to do something helpful, I suggest prayer for a demonstration of love and forgiveness."

Abbie nodded. "In my distress I cried unto the Lord, and he heard me. Deliver my soul, O Lord, from lying lips, and from a deceitful tongue." She murmured the words of Psalm 120.

When they finally pulled into the widower Samuels's yard, Abbie was relieved to see both Willem and Martin standing upright, though Martin had his feet spread and his hands on his hips as he glared at Willem. The buggy swayed to a stop beside them.

Rudy closed a hand gently around her wrist. "Stay here."

Abbie did not protest as Rudy slid his hand down and encircled her fingers, but she did not take her eyes off of Willem.

"Can you stand before God and declare that you did not take my coal?" Willem said.

Abbie sucked in her breath.

Martin crossed his wrists behind his back. "A few minutes ago you were suggesting confession and forgiveness. Now you sound like an *English* court."

Willem stepped toward Martin. "The way of confession is always open. This has been a difficult year for all of us. We must try to understand and encourage each other."

Martin picked up a piece of coal and threw it into his wagon. "I will drive the coal to your farm. You can follow me to make sure I don't take off with it."

Abbie looked from Willem to Martin, who still had not admitted wrongdoing.

"Keep the coal," Willem said, "but come with Reuben and me to the ravine today to dig. Three men will make the work go faster than two, and you will still have your coal."

"I have a sick cow to tend to." Martin's voice had dropped to a mutter.

"No one wants your cow to go down." Rudy jumped down out of the buggy. "I'll see to your cow now, Martin."

Abbie let her breath out.

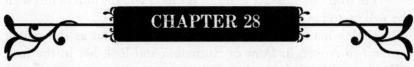

CHAPTER 28

I heard." Ruthanna gestured that Abbie should follow her away from the house and into the open yard. "News like that gets around fast."

"I didn't think you had left your farm since supper at the Millers'."

"I haven't." Ruthanna's pace felt like a sluggish elephant even to her.

"Rudy?"

Ruthanna nodded. "I don't think he meant to gossip. By the time he stopped by I don't think it was a secret anymore. He wanted to know how we are for coal."

Abbie turned the old yard chair around and indicated that Ruthanna should sit. "I know Eber hasn't been up to digging."

"I have enough to cook with, and the nights aren't cold yet." Ruthanna tried to get comfortable in the chair, a task growing in difficulty with every inch of her waistline.

Abbie stood behind Ruthanna and began to rub her shoulders. "I'll talk to *Daed* and my *bruder*. They can make sure you have what you need."

"Rudy has already offered."

Abbie pressed into her shoulder, and Ruthanna gave a sigh of bliss. "You have strong fingers. Eber cannot even rub my sore feet these days."

"He seems quite ill again, Ruthanna."

Ruthanna forced herself to breathe. "He is."

"I can take a buggy to Limon and get the doctor."

"He was here three days ago. He never has anything new to say. It might be an ulcer, and Eber needs to rest, or it might be something worse. The pain in his stomach comes and goes."

"Maybe we can get a doctor to come from Colorado Springs, or take Eber there. They will have a hospital. The trains go every day."

"He won't go. He says that if it is God's will for him to die, then he will go to his Savior gladly."

Abbie's hands ceased their comforting motion as she swung around to crouch in front of Ruthanna and look her in the face. "Did he really say such a thing?"

Ruthanna nodded.

"But our people have no objection to medical care. Where did he get such a notion?"

"*Gottes wille.*"

"Both of you should go to Colorado Springs and stay. Eber could see a specialist, and you could have the baby there."

"The child is not due for more than a month. We have no money. Where would we stay? How would we buy food? Who would look after our animals?"

"You know that the men would look after the farm. We could take up a collection for your other needs. That is our way."

Ruthanna shook her head slowly. "Abbie, no one has any cash to speak of. Everyone gets by with trading. Besides, Eber will not agree."

"This is no time for him to be proud. You should at least talk to him. We'll figure out a way."

Ruthanna changed the subject. "Rudy said the Nissleys want to have a meeting about what happened with the coal. Do you plan to go?"

Abbie lifted her shoulders and let them drop slowly as she stood up. "I suppose. It's tomorrow. Pray for us all."

❧❦❧

"If it is true, then Martin is accountable to all of us." Adam Nissley opened his blue eyes wide, creating ridges in his forehead. "Even without a minister, we all know that what he did was wrong."

Abbie stood in the back of the crowded room. Not many of the other women were present, but no one had told her she could not be present. Millie Nissley poured coffee and handed cups around the ragged circle in her sitting room. Abbie watched as Willem took his cup and characteristically blew across the surface of the hot liquid before sipping. She wished she had thought to bring a coffee cake or rolls to share, though it hardly felt like a casual social occasion. Men either sat stiffly in their chairs or leaned forward on their knees.

Other than Eber, the one man missing was Martin Samuels, and Abbie wondered whether he had declined to attend or they had intentionally left him out. It seemed to her that he ought to have the opportunity to speak to his own people in a matter that so obviously concerned him.

"It is true," Willem said softly.

"Is he willing to confess?" Adam said.

"You will have to ask him that question." Willem sipped his coffee.

Abbie crossed her arms and clasped her elbows. Despite his rush to justice on the day Rudy discovered the coal, Willem had mustered surprising calm. But Abbie saw the way his fingers wrapped around his coffee cup, indignation swelling in his clenched joints. What was happening to him? He never used to let troubles disturb him to this extent.

Albert Miller spoke up. "I would never have imagined Martin was capable of this. If we cannot trust each other, then who can we trust?"

"We will all have to look out for each other," Moses Troyer said, "to make sure this does not happen again. If any of us sees another falling into sin, let him speak up."

Abbie swallowed her thought. The point of trust was not checking up on each other. Whether or not they all trusted one another, they could trust God to care for them. Willem had been offended, but he had not truly suffered. She watched his face now, but he simply caught Millie Nissley's eye and she brought the coffeepot to refill his cup.

When the knock on the door disrupted the tone in the room and all heads turned, Abbie was closest to the door.

She pulled it open to find Jake Heatwole standing on the other side.

❧❀❧

Willem immediately stood. Color rose through Abbie's cheeks as she tensed every muscle in her face. Willem forced himself to look away from her and meet Jake's eyes.

"I don't mean to barge in," Jake said, "but I heard about the disappointment you have all endured in the last couple of days."

Willem nodded. Jake was not so distanced from the Amish that he did not understand that what wounded one of them wounded all of them.

Adam Nissley rose. "This is a private meeting, Mr. Heatwole."

Willem resisted the urge to sigh audibly. If the Amish families would listen to Jake's kindness, they would see that he meant no harm.

"I only wanted to see if there might be something I could do to help." Jake glanced around the room, unperturbed.

"I think we have the matter well in hand." Eli Yoder held his stiff-seated pose. "We will decide for ourselves what is fair."

"I did not suppose you required any assistance with that determination." Jake had not stepped any farther into the room than Abbie initially allowed. "You are all people of conscience. I suspect even Martin Samuels's transgression is a lapse due to more general difficulties."

"Are you excusing him, then?" Eli Yoder shuffled his feet slightly.

"Not at all," Jake said. "In fact, I make no judgment about the matter at all. I merely came to minister if there might be any need that I might fill."

No one spoke. Abbie still stood at the door, one hand grasping the thick panel of wood.

"Would you like some *kaffi*?" Millie asked.

Willem heard the reluctance in her voice and saw the relief in her face when Jake shook his head.

"I will not intrude further," Jake said. "But if you don't mind, Mr. Nissley, I would like to remain outside for a few minutes. Then if anyone feels the need to talk, I will not be far away."

Adam pressed his lips together, but he nodded. Jake stepped outside the door, and Abbie closed it behind him and leaned against it.

Willem swallowed his second cup of coffee in one gulp. "Thank you, Mrs. Nissley, for your kind refreshment." He nodded at the men around the room and the women on the periphery. Abbie's eyes widened, but he knew she would not speak or try to stop him in a room full of people. Willem brushed a hand against hers on his way out.

Jake stood a few yards from the house stroking the slender nose of his horse. "Hello, Willem."

Willem patted the horse's rump. "Forgiveness has a hard edge, Jake. I need prayer if I am going to face Martin Samuels with love in my heart once again."

The house quieted soon after sunset. Hours later, Abbie turned up the wick in the oil lamp that illumined her quilt square. Triangles of blue and green and purple and brown and crimson and black and white blurred together in her wearied eyes. The trunk of this family's tree—the Yutzys, in Abbie's mind—was stitched with precision, and she had started adding colors alternating with white to form the leaves of the tree. After the meeting earlier in the day, Abbie was more determined than ever to finish the quilt before further division could set in among the Amish families. Six of twelve blocks were finished, and she would not let up on the impeccable quality she chased. She had ripped out entire rows already, and she would do it again if she had to. The finished quilt must be a testament of enduring beauty, because it would represent the growth and spread of the settlement.

Abbie murmured prayers for every household in the settlement, even the long-gone Chupps, whenever she stitched. Twice she had stayed up all night, only realizing dawn would soon invade the sky when her mother shuffled into the kitchen to light the stove and start breakfast. She knew the names of every child in the settlement, though their precise ages often escaped her and she would have to calculate based on what she knew about the rest of the family. She knew whose wheat had suffered most in the June hailstorm and whose vegetables had flourished most in the July heat. She knew who might yet eke out a bit of cash from a second planting and who had given up trying. And she prayed for them all.

For Eber in his prolonged illness, that he might yet find hope.

For Willem in his temptation to leave the church.

For Rudy in his fragile dreams.

For Ruthanna and her tension-filled muscles.

For her parents and Daniel, Reuben, and Levi.

For Little Abe's safety and his parents' nerves.

For Martin Samuels and the stress that would make him do the unthinkable.

For all of them. Every leaf of every tree of life in her quilt and the prosperous future her heart ached for.

CHAPTER 29

For as far back as she could remember, humming an *Ausbund* tune had soothed Abbie's mind. She used to hum as she walked to the rural school where she studied in the early grades when she was nervous the *English* teacher might not understand her words through the thick Pennsylvania Dutch accent. She hummed when one of the farm animals was giving birth or gasping in the moments before death. She hummed as she concentrated on making bread that would meet her mother's standard.

And she hummed now as she prepared to clean Martin Samuels's house. It was his regular day. Abbie could hardly tell him that because he had stolen Willem's coal she would no longer bring him bread or sweep his floor. For nearly a week now she had hummed her way through disappointment at what he had done and the tension brooding in every conversation she overheard between men. The women were not any less suspicious. Abbie was nearly as disappointed in the shroud of distrust that fell over the families as she was in Martin. If she raised the question of forgiveness, someone was sure to point out that the widower Samuels had yet to express any convincing remorse.

Abbie had not spoken to Willem since he stepped past her with clear intent to converse with Jake Heatwole about the events rattling the Amish settlement. She should not have been surprised, but his wordless steps had settled into place the wall rising, brick by brick, between them for weeks. And that was perhaps the greatest disappointment. When she left this week's bread, she did not allow herself to look around and wonder if he might spot her and offer a greeting.

Out of courtesy, she knocked, but as usual did not wait for a response. The only time she had found Martin in his house on one of her weekly visits was when he was ill. That was more than a year and a half ago. Abbie set her bucket of brushes and sponges in the middle of his sitting room and inspected her surroundings. She could see straight through to his lean-to kitchen and the crusted dishes stacked to one side of the washtub. The disarray was notably worse than usual, which Abbie credited to the turmoil in his spirit. There was no point in taking his bread loaves into the kitchen until she had cleared a place to put them. Instead she set them on the small desk that had been in his wife's family for sixty years before her death. Abbie nudged aside a spread of paper. Once she had emptied her arms, she attempted to stack them with better order.

Abbie's eyes fell on an open letter, and the words sprang up before she could chastise herself for reading sentences not meant for her. Blinking, she picked up the two sheets of paper filled with tiny script. The more she read, the more tightly she held a hand over her mouth. She nearly tripped over her bucket in her haste to reach her buggy and turn the horse toward home.

"So it's true?" Abbie's jaw dropped as she stared at her father in the sitting room where he sat with the family Bible open in his lap. Since there was no harvest, he had taken to filling hours he used to spend on farm work by reading the German tome.

Ananias tipped his face forward so he could look at her over the tops of his round reading glasses. "Yes, what you read is true. But you should not have been reading Martin's papers."

"I told you, I didn't mean to. I was so shocked that I couldn't stop."

"That is a failure of your self-control, Abigail. What you have learned was not supposed to go beyond a private council meeting with the bishop."

Abbie flopped into a chair across from Ananias. "But that meeting was fifteen months ago. Were you really never going to tell anyone what happened there?"

Ananias nodded. "That was our intent."

"But *Daed*, don't you see? If this has been dividing us all this time, how could we ever hope for a successful settlement?" Abbie quelled the urge to stand up and stomp around the room.

"We believed it was our only hope for what we all wanted."

Abbie reached up with both hands and pulled on the strings of her prayer *kapp*. "But how could that be? If the visiting bishop would not even stay to give us communion because of your argument, how could you hope to heal such a deep spiritual divide by ignoring it?"

"*Argument* is an indelicate word, Abigail."

She put her head back on the top of the chair and stared at the ceiling. How could her *daed* remain unflustered? Abbie calmed her breath and returned her gaze to her father.

"The bishop you met with must have talked to other bishops in Kansas and Nebraska. There must be a reason they stopped visiting."

"I have no way to know what the bishops say to each other."

"Please talk to me, *Daed*. I want to understand."

"You already understand the essence. The council was not of one mind about whether there is true salvation outside the Amish church."

"That question has always been part of our history. I suspect that if you convened a meeting of all the Amish bishops and ministers, they would not all agree either."

"And you would be right." Ananias smoothed a hand across the open Bible in his lap. "But each district must decide what it will teach. Because we have families here who came from several different districts, the disparity of thought is more pronounced than it might be elsewhere."

The back door swung open and Levi charged into the house. "Aren't we going to have lunch?"

"In a little while," Abbie said.

"*Daed*, Reuben wants to know if you are going to dig coal this afternoon."

"I have not decided," Ananias said.

"If you do, can I go with you?" Levi draped himself across an end of the sofa.

"It's dangerous for a little boy," Ananias said.

"But I'm not so little anymore. I want to!"

Abbie rolled her eyes. "Levi, please, *Daed* and I are talking."

"When are you going to be finished talking?"

"Levi!" Abbie stood up, pulled the boy to his feet, and pointed him back out the door with a firm shove.

When Levi was gone, her father raised an eyebrow. "Might you have been harsh?"

"I'm sorry. I'll apologize to Levi later for my impatience." Abbie sat down again and smoothed her skirt. "I wanted to be sure we finish our conversation."

"There is not much more to say."

"Why don't the bishops visit anymore, even just a few times a year?"

"Part of the reason bishops visited was to decide whether they would want to move here. They have seen for themselves what a challenge it would be, even apart from the spiritual question."

Abbie could not dispute this observation. Even bishops had to be able to support their families. She shifted in her chair. "And what do you think on the spiritual question?"

"Abigail."

"Tell me, *Daed*."

"I am not interested in stirring up conflict."

"The conflict is already there, *Daed*. It runs under everything that happens. If we could only worship together, so many things could be better."

Ananias closed the Bible and stacked his hands on top of it.

"*Daed*, please. I am not asking out of disrespect or lack of submission, only lack of understanding."

He stood up and put the Bible on its carved stand. "My conscience tells me that I must interpret the Word of God to mean that there is no salvation outside the church."

"Outside the Amish church. Is that what you mean?"

He nodded.

Abbie sank against the back of her chair, her shoulders sagging. "So the Chupps?"

"If they have left the church, I believe they have turned their backs on the Lord's gift of salvation."

Abbie crossed her ankles and quickly uncrossed them. She could not think what to do with her feet or her hands or her face. If her father was right, Willem was in grave danger. *"Come with me,"* he had said to her on the day of their doomed picnic. She did not want him to go to the Mennonites at all, and she could not imagine going with him. As badly as he wanted his farm to succeed, even more Abbie wanted their church to succeed. But questioning Willem's salvation—or even Jake's?

"Abigail?"

She snapped her head up and found her father's gray eyes peering at her.

"Have I answered all your questions?"

"Yes, *Daed.*"

"And do you now understand why I hesitated to do so?"

She nodded.

"You must not speak of this to anyone."

"But *Daed*—"

"Not anyone."

Every sway and bump in the road seemed to punch Ruthanna in the back and steal her breath. Frightened beyond imagination, she had left Eber alone in the bed clutching his stomach. All day long she had tried to ease his pain and usher in a period of rest. It had been bad enough when he was feverish and exhausted. Watching his pain contort him sliced through her. Finally she knew she did not want to be alone when the end came, and if she did not get help, the end would come soon. It had taken her a long time to climb into the buggy unassisted. Now she was driving so fast, with both hands clenched around the reins, that she could not even raise a palm to wipe away the tears that blurred her vision. She rumbled into the Weaver yard and screamed the names of every member of the family.

Abigail rushed toward the buggy. "Are you in labor?"

"No."

"You're sure?"

"Yes."

"Eber?"

Ruthanna nodded.

Abbie spun around in a circle, her gaze sweeping the property.

"Is your *mamm* here?" Panic struck Ruthanna. Esther was Eber's best hope for relief.

"She's here somewhere."

"Please, Abbie, you have to find her."

Ananias emerged from the house with Levi on his heels.

"We need *Mamm*," Abbie said. "Right now."

"She walked over to visit with Mary Miller," Ananias said.

Ruthanna did not recognize the sound that pulled at her depths.

Abbie climbed into the wagon. "It's Eber."

"I will go for the doctor myself." Ananias slapped the haunch of Ruthanna's horse, then pivoted and started for the Weaver buggy.

Ruthanna surrendered the reins to Abbie, closed her eyes, and trusted that the Holy Ghost would translate her fear into prayer.

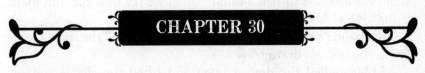

CHAPTER 30

With Ruthanna leaning against her for the short distance between where she parked the buggy and the door to the Gingerich house, Abbie focused through the quiver in her knees and her stampeding heart.

Ruthanna groaned and put her open hand against her back.

"Do you feel all right?" Abbie asked.

"Eber is what matters now." Ruthanna turned the doorknob, and they stepped inside the house before she paused to catch her breath. "He's in the bedroom."

Abbie rolled in her bottom lip and bit gently, going ahead of Ruthanna toward the bedroom. The stench made her turn her head before she got there. She indulged the rise of bile from her own stomach for only a second before swallowing it and forcing firm steps. Eber lay tangled in sweat-drenched bedding with one arm draped around a smell metal pail. Abbie did not have to look to know its contents were viscous green fluid and blood. She paced around the bed in the cramped room, picking up a towel from the dresser on her way and used it to wipe Eber's pallid face. The bed creaked as Ruthanna lowered herself onto the other side and took Eber's head in her lap.

"When did this start?" Abbie asked softly. She lifted a bowl of water and judged it had already been used several times to rinse soiled cloths.

"A few hours."

Limon was eight miles. Even if Ananias Weaver found the

doctor quickly, eight miles back would seem like a trek through the Rockies. "The doctor is coming," she said.

Ruthanna stroked Eber's matted hair and beard. "I know this is the end, Abbie."

"Reuben will find my *mamm*. She'll be here soon." Abbie turned away to cover her nose and mouth for a moment, trying to find even a minute stream of air that did not taste rancid. Taking small breaths, she turned around. "Shall we try to make him more comfortable? Clean things up?"

Ruthanna kissed Eber's sweat-caked forehead. "The spare sheets are in the bottom drawer."

Abbie pulled the drawer open and lifted the sheets and set them on the dresser. She had once seen a nurse in a hospital change the sheets under a patient who could not get out of bed. Gingerly she pulled back the sheet covering Eber. His skeletal condition, garbed only in undergarments, shocked her, but she pressed her lips together and tossed the soiled top sheet to the floor. Starting gently with one corner of the bottom sheet, she began inching it out from under Eber. Ruthanna stood to help and they managed to change the sheets and Eber's undershirt.

Abbie bundled the sheets in her arms and picked up the revolting pail. "I'll get some fresh water from the well and put these to soak."

❧❦❧

Ruthanna pushed the window open before returning to her vigil post on the bed beside Eber. She picked up another small pail and set it within reach. Not once had Eber opened his eyes while Ruthanna and Abbie cleaned up around him, and now Ruthanna wondered if she would ever see the blazing blue of his eyes again. Had she known that his last gaze would be the last, she would have fallen into the pleading pools of his eyes to soak up one final memory of his face.

She picked up a limp hand and held it between both of hers. "Does it feel better to be cleaned up? I'm sorry I couldn't manage to do that on my own."

Eber took a ragged breath, his chest barely lifting, and Ruthanna stilled her movements to see if he would exhale. Five seconds passed, then ten. She counted almost to twenty before the air moved out of him.

"I hope you know how much I love you," she whispered. "God smiled on me the day we met. I could not have hoped for God's will to be more gracious toward me."

He inhaled with a rasp, his mouth opening slightly.

Ruthanna cupped her hand around his face. "I would take away every throb of your pain if only I could."

His exhale was the faintest she had ever heard.

Ruthanna winced, moved a hand to the side of her protruding abdomen, and forced herself to exhale. The pain was longer than usual, the hardening beneath her hand more persistent. False labor pains had been striking at unpredictable intervals for weeks. Esther reminded her every time they spoke that she would know real labor when it began. That was still weeks away by Ruthanna's reckoning.

A sob clenched her chest as the vice around her middle released its grip. Her child would not know the light of its father's eyes, or the cradle of his arms, or the beat of his heart as he held the babe to his chest. Ruthanna slid down in the bed, reaching her arms around her own midsection to grasp her husband's thin form.

It seemed like Abbie had to let the bucket down a long way before she heard it splash against the surface of the well's water. It was no different on her own family's farm. Normally she was careful not to use more water than she needed, but today was no time to conserve. She dumped the water into a tub she had found outside Ruthanna's front door that now held the soiled sheets then let the bucket down again. Soaking out the stains would take plenty of cold water.

When she heard the horse's hooves she paused to look up. "Willem!"

He seemed surprised to see her. Then his eyes dropped to the tub. "The baby?"

"Eber."

When the bucket came to the top of the well again, Willem grabbed it and emptied it into the tub. "What happened?"

Abbie scratched at the back of one hand. "It's time."

Willem's eyes widened. "Time for what? I just came to see what chores needed doing."

Abbie's stomach rolled, and she wondered how many times she would have to voice these words. "I should have insisted they both go to Colorado Springs or Denver. Another doctor might have made a difference. The *English* have specialists."

Willem grasped her fidgeting wrist. "Abigail, say what you must."

"When is the last time you saw Eber?"

"A few days ago. A week."

"I would have come sooner if I had any idea." She ran her tongue over her lips and looked up at his eyes. "Eber will leave this world today."

Willem started and his eyes snapped toward the house.

"*Daed* has already gone to Limon for the doctor," Abbie said, "but it will not matter now."

"You can't be sure of that."

Abbie pushed his hand off her wrist and gestured toward the tub. "I've been in there, Willem. I've seen him. He's been a lot sicker than he let any of us believe."

Willem held a hand over both eyes.

Abbie trembled through her core. "I should go back in. Ruthanna should not be alone." She turned to go.

Willem stopped her and wrapped his arms around her. Despite her resolve, Abbie melted against him and buried her head in his chest while he stroked the back of her neck. Neither his firm hold nor solid stance quelled the dread rising from a foreign space at the pit of her stomach. She circled his waist with her arms, and still she shook.

"I have to go in," she said hoarsely.

"We'll go together." Willem unfolded the embrace and steered Abbie toward the house.

Eber's stomach had retched several times in a vain attempt to empty, but unconscious he could not lift his head to the pail. Ruthanna did her best to turn him on his side with a towel under his face so she could lie beside him and wipe the blood that dribbled between his parched lips. Relief rushed through Ruthanna when she saw Willem and Abbie come through the door together.

"Thank you," Ruthanna murmured. "Thank you both."

Abbie picked up the washbasin from the dresser and the two rags draped across its rim. "I'll get some fresh water."

"The barrel in the kitchen is almost empty."

"I can fill it," Willem said.

Ruthanna nodded, her hand once again going to the pain in her abdomen. Abbie left with the washbasin. Ruthanna listened to the familiar sounds of throwing the reddish brown water out the back door and swishing water in the basin to rinse it clean before filling it afresh. Abbie's skirts rustled with the normal movements of simple housekeeping. Ruthanna could tell Abbie had paused to pull a rag across the kitchen table and push the canisters of flour and sugar to one side.

Ruthanna groaned and tried to shift her weight.

"Are you all right?" Willem asked.

"I think I need to sit up for a while," she said. Her back ached violently as the now familiar roll of pain began a fresh circuit. She put a hand out, and Willem grasped her arm all the way to the elbow as she righted herself. Beside her, Eber's breath leaked out of him, and Ruthanna once again counted the seconds and waited for his lungs to move. The number was higher with each interval. She lost track of whether she was measuring Eber's breath or her own pain.

The front door opened, and a moment later Esther Weaver's form blocked the light coming from the main room.

"Reuben brought me," Esther said. She immediately moved to Ruthanna and laid a hand on her midsection.

"Thank you for coming."

"Are you in labor?" Esther asked quietly.

"The false pains." Ruthanna grimaced.

"They are not always false," Esther said, "not at this stage."

Ruthanna shook her head. "It's too soon." She turned her head back to Eber, trying to remember where she left off counting before Esther came in and unsure whether she had missed a breath cycle. She did not think so.

Esther rounded the bed for a closer look at Eber. Ruthanna knew better than to seek a glimmer of hope.

Eber's chest did not move. Ruthanna wiped his mouth again and laid her ear against his mouth even as her abdomen squeezed with fresh fury.

Esther lifted Ruthanna's hand, drawing Ruthanna's gaze up.

"I'm concerned, Ruthanna," Esther whispered. "This is a terrible moment for you, but we must think of the baby."

Ruthanna exhaled sharply and sucked in three quick breaths. Still she counted. Still Eber's chest did not move.

She felt the trickle of fluid between her legs.

CHAPTER 31

Eber's chest lifted. Or perhaps Ruthanna only thought it had. "Ruthanna."

She looked up at Esther's face.

Esther pointed to the puddle forming on the floor beneath Ruthanna's feet.

Ruthanna nodded in answer to Esther's unspoken question. Her waters had broken.

Esther glanced at Eber, before turning toward the door and softly calling Abbie's name.

Abbie entered the bedroom with the basin of fresh water, her eyes immediately going to Eber. Willem shuffled toward her and took the basin. Abbie sat on the edge of the bed with her arms around Ruthanna.

Ruthanna grimaced and grunted with the next pain.

"It's only been a couple of minutes since the last one," Esther observed. "Your baby is coming, Ruthanna."

"But Eber." Ruthanna huffed out her strained breath.

Abbie stood up and pulled Ruthanna to her feet as well. She held Ruthanna's face in both hands. "Eber is gone, Ruthanna. But his child will soon be in your arms."

Ruthanna wailed for the first time. Whether in pain or grief she was not sure and it did not matter. Eber had left her for the arms of the Savior.

"But what about Eber?" Ruthanna asked when the contraction subsided.

Abbie pulled the sheet up over Eber's face. "We'll take care of him, too. But we have to get you comfortable."

"Where? I can't give birth in the bed now."

Abbie looked at Willem. "Bring some hay from the barn, Willem. We'll make a pallet."

Willem nodded and left. Ruthanna gripped Abbie's hand as she led her to a chair in the main room. Eber always said that as soon as they got a bit of money they would get some decent chairs, or he would learn to make a glider for her. For now, all she had to sit on was the straight-back padless chair Eber had used when he sat outside. As she sat, she turned the chair toward the bedroom and fastened her eyes again on the shape on the bed. Esther was tucking the white sheet around Eber's form.

The next pain seized her.

Abbie was scrambling around the stove, trying to stoke the fire and looking for a pot.

"The big one is on the back porch." Ruthanna forced the words out between gritted teeth.

"You're going to be all right, Ruthanna." Abbie touched Ruthanna's shoulder before stepping out the back door.

The room suddenly went frosty. Ruthanna began to shiver. Her husband was wrapped in a sheet, and her baby was coming a month early. How could she have a baby without Eber?

She leaned forward and keened.

❧

As soon as he dragged half a bale of hay through the back door and Abbie spread the most tattered quilt she could find over it, Willem excused himself. He paused only for a scant look at Eber before dragging the now empty water barrel out of the kitchen and toward the well. The cows would need to be milked before long, and he wondered when the last time was that Ruthanna took a slop bucket out to the chickens. Eber's horse was still hitched to the buggy Ruthanna had taken to the Weavers.

Willem was glad for the chores. He could stay near without feeling in the way of the birthing work. He stood the barrel on end next to the well and began to fill it one bucket at a time.

Rudy galloped into the yard. "I ran into Ananias on his way for the doctor."

"It's too late." Willem sighed and dumped another bucket.

Rudy slung out of his saddle and folded his long form as if he had been kicked in the stomach. "God's will is surely mysterious sometimes."

Willem nodded. "There's no way to get word to the doctor that he need not come."

Rudy let out one long, slow breath. "Perhaps he will have a potion for Ruthanna. She must be frantic, but she will need to rest."

"I'm afraid it is too late for her to rest as well, although she might yet have need of the good doctor's expertise before the night is over. I assume he knows how to deliver a baby."

Rudy stopped Willem's cranking motion with one long hand. "Ruthanna is birthing her child now? With Eber just gone?"

"What we really need," Willem said, "is an undertaker. I know we usually bury our dead within a day or so, but Ruthanna will be in no condition. And she will insist on being there."

"She should be there. Eber will only have one funeral."

"Eber will have to be embalmed to give her some time to recover from the birth. A few days, at least. We could try to buy some ice to put under him, but the days are still warm. It will be difficult to cover the smell."

"You are right that he should be embalmed." Rudy released his hold, and Willem resumed cranking up the bucket. "But an *English* undertaker will want a fee."

"Yes, I suppose he will. We'll have to sort that out later."

"Maybe he would like free eggs and fresh milk for a few weeks." Rudy turned back to his horse and prepared to mount. "I will go to Limon and see what arrangement I can make."

❧❧❧

Abbie knelt at Ruthanna's head and let her friend dig her finger-nails into her arm with neither flinch nor protest. When she was not grunting against pain, Ruthanna sobbed and cried her husband's name. On the stove, the soup pot of water seemed to refuse to boil, and when Willem returned with the barrel, Abbie wanted to start another pot.

Abbie reminded herself that her mother had been an unofficial but experienced midwife at dozens of births, but still she admired the quiet calm Esther exuded as she went about getting Ruthanna comfortable on the pallet of hay with her knees up and inspecting to see how far labor had progressed.

"Try to relax between contractions," Esther said with one hand on Ruthanna's abdomen. "I do not think it will be long before it's time to push."

"It was not supposed to be like this." Ruthanna's voice was at near-shriek pitch. "Eber wanted a child even more than I did. God waited years before giving us one."

"*Shh.*" Esther patted Ruthanna's arm. "The hardest part is ahead of you. You must save your strength."

Ruthanna flopped her head back on the hay. "My strength died with my husband."

Esther positioned herself where she could look Ruthanna in the eye. "You still have a baby coming. Nothing is going to change that. You must focus on what you have to do."

Ruthanna's head swung widely from side to side. "What does it matter without Eber?"

"This child is a gift from God," Esther said softly but firmly. "When he is in your arms, you will treasure him. You will see Eber in his face every day. Right now you must birth him, nothing else."

Ruthanna's cry settled into a whimper, but when the next contraction came, she was ready.

Abbie squeezed her hand. Many Amish women her age had several children of their own, but Abbie had never before been present at a birth. It was wonderful and terrible at the same time. Her mother seemed to know just what to do. Abbie tried to imagine what it would be like when she had a child. Would her mother be able to remain calm when her own daughter travailed?

"Abbie," Esther said, "we are going to need string and a clean pair of scissors or a knife."

Abbie looked around.

"In the basket on the top shelf." Ruthanna's voice was flat but her instructions accurate.

Abbie could see the basket now, the one Ruthanna had used as she worked on her baby's quilt. When she pulled it off the shelf, Abbie could see the small quilt neatly folded in the flat woven bottom.

"The cradle," Ruthanna croaked. "It's still in the barn, but I think Eber finished it."

"There's plenty of time for that." Esther pushed Ruthanna's knees apart. "When the next contraction begins, you can bear down."

❧❧❧

The water had barely reached boiling when Eber and Ruthanna's daughter slid into the world. Esther laid the baby on a clean towel and then tied off the cord and cut it. Just as the child let out her first wail, Esther turned her toward Ruthanna and Abbie.

Abbie gasped. "She is beautiful, Ruthanna. So beautiful!"

Esther wrapped the baby in the towel and handed the bundle to Abbie. "Don't spend too much time admiring her. She'll want her mother soon enough."

Ruthanna smiled through the streaks of grimy tears on her face. "And her mother wants her."

Marveling, Abbie released the baby into Ruthanna's waiting arms and then settled in again as together they counted fingers and toes.

"She's perfect. Her father would have—" Ruthanna's voice broke.

Abbie leaned her head against Ruthanna's. She had no words for the moment.

"Poor Willem," Ruthanna said, "waiting outside all this time. You'd better go tell him."

Abbie wiped her eyes with the back of one hand and nodded.

Outside, a moment later, she stopped to gaze at Willem in the fractured instant before he sensed her presence. This was the man she had imagined having children with. The thought that they might have no future triggered tears.

Willem spotted her from where he sat on the ground with his elbows propped on his knees and his head hanging between his dangling hands. He jumped to his feet. "The baby?"

"A girl. They're both fine."

A grin cracked Willem's face. "A girl. I hope she is as lovely as her mother."

"Every bit." Abbie's throat was too thick to say more.

Willem opened his arms, and Abbie went into them for the second time that day. She breathed in the sweaty scent of a man unafraid of hard work—and a man whose salvation her own father would question if he knew what Willem contemplated. Abbie banished the thought.

"I guess my *daed* could not find the doctor," Abbie said. "He never came."

Willem kissed the top of her head. "Rudy was here. He went for an undertaker."

CHAPTER 32

The weather was not cold and dreary, as Ruthanna had supposed it would be. She had not imagined the day she buried her husband could be warm, sunny, and inviting. It was the sort of day that beckoned giggles and bare feet in a creek, picking wild sunflowers and naming clouds.

Those were the wishes of girlhood, not the order of a funeral.

Standing behind her home, Ruthanna pulled the baby's quilt away from her face and stroked a silken cheek. She had barely discovered how to feed the child comfortably, much less face the fatherless years that stretched ahead. Someday this innocent little girl would hear the story of her father's death on the day of her birth. Ruthanna would avoid the topic for as many years as she could. No child should have to learn to mingle grief with rejoicing, missing a man she never knew simply because of a coincidence of dates.

Not coincidence, Ruthanna reminded herself. *Gottes wille.* Was not everything that happened God's will and meant to teach her something? Ruthanna could not see the lesson in tragedy. She saw no hope in devastation, no justice for a little girl with no *daed.*

The back door opened. Abbie's face looked as drawn and pale as Ruthanna supposed her own was.

"Is it time?" Ruthanna asked.

"The first buggies are here."

Ruthanna adjusted her daughter's slight weight in her arms and followed Abbie into the house, where Abbie and Esther had prepared the humble home for the service. The undertaker's black wagon had come early in the morning to return Eber to his bedroom, this time embalmed and laid in an unlined coffin on a wide plank balanced over a bench. The crisp white sheet would come off soon. All other furniture in the room had been removed to the barn, save one chair for Ruthanna. Esther had insisted it was too soon to expect Ruthanna to stand to greet the Amish families who would come to see Eber. Dark cloths covered the windows, casting the room into unfamiliar midday gray shadows.

"Do you want to see him before the others come in?" Abbie asked.

Ruthanna nodded, the knot in her throat too big for speech.

Abbie stepped quietly across the room, which now felt cavernous to Ruthanna, to lift the sheet and gently fold it into a tight, small rectangle.

Ruthanna's heart pounded. Eber lay in the same unadorned white shirt and dark trousers that had been his wedding suit, with his arms folded across his chest. The undertaker had made Eber look healthier than he had been in the last few weeks, the fullness of his cheeks unlike the gaunt outline Ruthanna had become accustomed to.

Oh Eber.

❧❦❧

They all came, even Widower Samuels. Tears burned behind Abbie's eyes.

Her memory of the last time the Amish had gathered for a worship service had grown fuzzy around the edges, and she could not be sure every family had been there. As desperately as she wanted them to be a church together, she hated the occasion that summoned them on this day. A few *English* families arrived as well, tentative about the procedure but earnest in their intention. They understood few truths about the Amish, but they understood loss. Of this Abbie had no doubt.

Abbie rotated between greeting people at the door, checking to see if Ruthanna needed anything, and helping her mother organize the steadily widening array of food the visitors carried in. Her father and brothers had gathered every bench and stool from the surrounding farms, and still children would have to sit on the floor and some of the men stand. The Gingerich home simply was not spacious enough to bring comfort to a gathering fraught with distress. No one's home would have been. They had all built quickly, eager to have shelter and begin farming and expecting to expand soon.

But soon had not come for any of them. While they might have held a Sunday service in a barn, tradition demanded Eber be laid out in his home with his wife and daughter beside him. From the kitchen, where she found space on the crowded counter for yet another plate of food, Abbie could look into the bedroom and see Ruthanna cradling her four-day-old daughter. Families entered for the viewing. Some murmured to Ruthanna words that Abbie could not hear but could suppose.

"It's God's will."

"You must trust."

"We will pray for you."

Abbie believed those affirmations, yet they sounded hollow even in her own mind on this day. She picked up an empty milking stool, before someone else would discover its unoccupied state, and carried it into the bedroom to sit beside Ruthanna. In a moment, Jake Heatwole would come through the front door. Abbie had seen him trot his horse into the yard.

Jake.

When Willem suggested asking him to lead the service, even Abbie could not dispute the wisdom. The Ordway settlement was a day and a half of travel in each direction, and no one could be sure a minister would come. Even if one had, he would have been a stranger. Jake knew Eber, and Ruthanna trusted him.

If her father was right, though, and the latent fissure under the Amish settlement was a pressured crack about the salvation of a man like Jake Heatwole, Abbie could not help wondering what this moment of trying to do right by Eber would mean.

She put out her arms and offered to take the baby, but Ruthanna only ran a single finger down the tiny curve of the infant's nose.

Life unto death. This was the theme of Jake's sermon, as well it should be. Willem listened to Jake's voice rise and fall, rise and fall, in somber waves expounding the truth of John 5. The Father has given the Son authority to judge, and all people should be ready for the moment of their deaths. Jake believed that Eber had been ready. When the Book of Life was opened at the Great White Throne of Revelation 20, Eber Gingerich's name would appear on its pages.

As Willem had expected he would, Jake stood in the crowded house for nearly an hour and preached with an open Bible. He paused several times to look over the heads of the assembly and into the bedroom where Ruthanna and Abbie sat. Willem was sure they heard Jake's words, including the kind comfort he offered the grieving widow at regular intervals. With his back to the bedroom, Willem could not see Ruthanna's face. But he had seen it before the service. He had seen it many times over the last four days and could not imagine that it had gained any cheer or color.

Jake was right. Eber had been ready. Though the bishops might say that no one could be certain of another's salvation at the time of death, Willem had no doubt about Eber. He had not been a perfect man. No man was. But his heart belonged to the Lord.

Jake closed his Bible and let silence shroud the room before intoning, "Eber Gingerich was twenty-seven years old."

The *English* would have read a long eulogy, but the Amish congregation recognized this simple statement as their cue to kneel for Jake's prayer. Shuffling boots and scraping benches filled the room for a few minutes. It was not easy for Willem to unfold his lanky form and find space for his knees on the floor, but Jake waited until everyone had settled. His prayer was brief, sincere, comforting. At his "Amen" the congregation once against shifted, this time to stand for the benediction. Willem used the opportunity to look over the heads of his fellow settlers into the bedroom in time to see Ruthanna shudder.

The moment the last nail went into the coffin, obscuring Eber's face until eternity, had nearly undone Rudy. A shriek had escaped Ruthanna's control. But now Rudy gripped his corner of the coffin and nodded to Willem and the two other pallbearers that he was ready. With the ponderous dignity the task evoked, they carried the coffin to Willem's open wagon and set it in the empty bed. Reuben, Daniel, and Levi Weaver had hitched all the horses and turned the buggies around while everyone else attending the funeral shared a meal and said their final farewells to Eber. Now it was time for the entire community to process and lay him to rest. The spot Ruthanna picked out was beyond the horse pasture, closer to the bedraggled wheat field than the house, because she believed Eber would want to be there. Rudy had helped to dig the grave yesterday, mourning with each slam of the shovel into the earth. Eventually, he supposed, there would be a flat stone bearing Eber's name.

The pallbearers released their hold on the coffin almost simultaneously. Rudy could feel the tremor of regret in the movement of their hands. Regret that they had not realized sooner how serious Eber's illness was. Regret that his life had ended too soon. Regret that they did not know the words to speak to his widow.

Rudy got in his own buggy and waited for his turn to click his tongue and lift his reins to put his horse into motion. Mourners passed the field where Eber's animals grazed and the field he would never harvest and tied their horses to the fence he had built.

Abbie sat stiffly on the edge of her bed that night and watched Ruthanna sleep. She lay in the bed with her eyes closed, anyway. Abbie was not sure for a long time that Ruthanna truly was sleeping.

After Eber's death and the baby's birth, Abbie had spent two days and nights at Ruthanna's home. She cleaned up after the undertaker came for his sober task and nourished and cared for Ruthanna's physical needs. On the day before the funeral, Ruthanna moved to the Weavers' house. Abbie was more than glad to share the bed in her narrow room. Eber's cradle sat on the floor beside the bed. The baby was snuggled in a cotton sack that tied at the neck. Abbie had found it among the baby things Mary Miller had given Ruthanna.

Abbie had stroked Ruthanna's back until her friend stopped fidgeting and breathed in a deep, regular rhythm, perhaps for the first time in weeks. Now she slowly lifted her hand but was afraid that getting in the bed would wake Ruthanna, and Abbie was not willing to take that risk. If she had to, she would sit up all night.

The baby whimpered. Abbie knew she had been fed and changed only an hour ago. At the second whimper, Abbie eased off the bed, bent over, picked up the child, and slipped out of the room.

She inhaled the infant's sweetness and prayed for her mother.

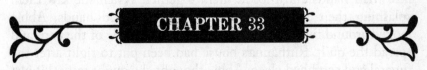

CHAPTER 33

"I could come with you," Ruthanna said a week later.

Abbie set a basket of food in the Weaver buggy. "You would get some notion in your head about helping."

"It's my farm. I should help."

"You have other things on your mind." Abbie laid a hand on the baby's head as she slept in her mother's arms.

Ruthanna blew out her breath. "Going to talk to the banker in Limon last Friday did not help matters."

"This is a new day, a new week. God will make His provision clear."

Ruthanna looked less sure than Abbie's words sounded.

"In the meantime," Abbie said, "I'm just taking lunch to Willem and Rudy. I hope to bring you word that the barn has been mucked."

Abbie kissed her friend's cheek and the baby's head before getting in the buggy. She had been going to the Gingerich farm every day since the funeral to check. Reuben's offer to bring the animals to the Weaver farm so it would be easier to care for them met with Ruthanna's resistance. It was too much trouble, she said, when she would be going home any day now.

At Ruthanna's farm, Abbie saw Willem's stallion and Rudy's gelding grazing aimlessly alongside Ruthanna's two horses. She tied her horse to the fence, leaving it hitched, and retrieved a quilt and the lunch basket of salt pork, cheese, bread, and apple cake. As she crossed the yard toward the barn, Willem emerged with a wheelbarrow. He grinned, and she could not help but smile back.

"Rudy," Willem called over his shoulder, "Abbie is here."

Rudy emerged wiping his hands on a rag.

"I hope you're both hungry," Abbie said.

Rudy's blue eyes greeted her gaze. "Just give us a moment to clean up."

Willem followed Rudy to the well, where they dumped water into their hands and rubbed them together. When she saw them splashing their faces and drinking from cupped hands, Abbie looked around for a patch of shade against the side of the barn and spread the quilt. Ruthanna's house had been put to right after the funeral and scrubbed clean. Abbie thought she ought to find it just that way when she was ready to come home. Surely Willem and Rudy would continue to help with chores until Ruthanna could pay for some help.

The men returned and dropped onto the quilt. Abbie unpacked the basket.

"We heard about what happened in Limon on Friday," Willem said.

"Something will work out," Abbie said. It seemed to her that the banker's conversation with Ruthanna should have been confidential.

"It sounds as if Ruthanna had no idea how much debt Eber took on to keep the place running." Rudy wrapped a chunk of pork in a soft slice of bread.

"They lived so frugally," Abbie said. "I can't imagine where the money went."

"Buying hay because they couldn't grow it. Lumber for fence posts. Turning the shack that was on the land into something they could live in. Building a decent barn." Willem ticked off his points on his fingers.

Abbie sighed. "I know. But so much money! No wonder Eber would never agree to a hired hand even when he was so ill."

"Ruthanna will have some decisions to make," Rudy said.

"She can sell some of the land." Abbie poured water from a jug into a tin cup and sipped it. "She does not have to farm. There are other ways to make a living."

A strange horse trotted into the yard with an *English* astride. "Ruthanna Gingerich?"

"She's not here." Abbie untucked her legs and stood up. "She's staying at my family's home right now. Can I help you?"

He pulled an envelope out of a saddlebag. "She got a telegram. Will you sign for it and take it to her?"

⋘❖⋙

Ruthanna lifted her squirming daughter from the cradle, carried her down to the Weaver kitchen, and took her place at the table. She held the baby upright over her shoulder during the silent prayer before the evening meal. Every day she learned something new about what would soothe the child or what the pitch of her cry might mean, and today's lesson in mothering had been the discovery that her baby would rather be upright and patted on the back than cradled in the arms and swayed. Ruthanna closed her eyes for a moment in a posture of gratitude she did not feel. But perhaps if she cultivated her habit of giving thanks she might one day feel grateful again.

Ananias intoned, "Amen," and the family began to pass serving dishes. Beside Levi, Esther closely supervised his portions, insisting that he should put more on his plate than the skinny boy was inclined to do. No matter how many times his family assured him they were not going to starve, Levi tried to conserve food. Abbie had expressed exasperation about this to Ruthanna more than once.

With her free hand, Ruthanna took a bowl of green beans from Daniel and set it next to her plate so she could use the spoon to serve herself. Esther had wrung the neck of a chicken a few hours ago, and Ruthanna took a thigh from the platter and put it next to the beans.

Around her the clatter of passing dishes morphed into the scrape of forks against plates, but Ruthanna did not eat. She patted her baby's back and jiggled her gently.

Esther caught her eye and said, "Abbie says you received a telegram today. Not bad news from home, I hope."

"It was from my parents," Ruthanna said. "They feel terrible that they could not get here for Eber's funeral, but my mother is coming now."

Across the table, Abbie smiled. "I'll be so glad to see her! And it will be wonderful for you to have help for a while."

"She will arrive on Thursday on a midmorning train."

"We'll be delighted to have her stay here with us at first," Esther said. "I don't want you to feel rushed to go back to your home before you are ready."

Ruthanna took a deep breath, hating that the words she prepared to speak would crush her best friend.

"I don't think I will go back to the house at all."

Forks stopped in midair. Around the table, eyes lifted toward Ruthanna.

"My mother wants me to come home with her. And I want to go."

Abbie set her fork down gently. "Of course a visit with your family would do you good. The farm will be here when you get back."

Tears burned in Ruthanna's eyes. "I hope someday I will come back to visit you and find a thriving Amish settlement. But I think it's best if I list the farm with a broker and move back to my parents' home. We'll leave on Friday."

Abbie washed the platter, the last of the supper dishes. She dried it slowly, listening to Ruthanna's murmuring to her baby in the next room. Abbie slid the platter into its place on the shelf and hung the damp towel over the back of a chair. On her way into the main room, she paused for a moment to lean against the doorframe and twiddle her prayer *kapp* strings while she watched Ruthanna. Despite her tragic start to motherhood, she was learning to know her infant well and responded to the child's fussing with calm and cooing. Finally, Abbie chose a seat where she could see her friend's face clearly.

"I know you are not happy with my decision," Ruthanna said softly. "It breaks what is left of my heart to think of leaving you, but it is right that I go."

Abbie tucked her hands under her thighs to keep from appearing as agitated as she felt. "Your whole life has changed in ten days. Maybe this is not the time to make such a major decision. You still have the farm and people who care for you."

"You didn't hear for yourself what the banker said." Ruthanna adjusted the baby on her lap so she could look into her eyes and hold both tiny hands. "After so much drought and soil erosion from the wind, the land is barely worth what we paid for it. Eber borrowed against our equity money several times. The last time he tried, the bank turned him down."

"I'm so sorry. But the rest of the settlers will not let you suffer. You can stay here all winter, if you like. Your animals can stay in our barn. In the spring, Willem and Rudy and my brothers will put your crop in. It won't always be like this."

Silence descended. Abbie held her breath.

"My husband died," Ruthanna finally said, her voice a whisper. "I have a newborn. I have overwhelming debt I knew nothing about. I cannot struggle against reality right now, Abbie. Even if I can sell the farm to get out from under the debt, I will have no money. Please try to understand. My daughter deserves a better start, and I can give her that if I go home."

"This is home."

"I certainly hoped it would be. When she is older, I will bring my daughter back and show her Eber's grave. Promise me you will make sure the marker is laid as soon as it is ready."

"Of course I will. But you could stay at least long enough to see to that."

"It would be too hard. The mound would still be fresh and would cut my heart open all over again."

Abbie's shoulders sank in defeat. "I'm sorry. I have no idea what it must be like to lose a husband."

Ruthanna gave a wan smile. "You will have a wonderful life here, Abbie. You want a church here more than anyone else. We all know that and admire it in you."

Abbie swallowed hard. "It won't be the same without you."

"Willem loves you. I hope you know that."

Abbie nodded. She did know. But did he love her enough?

❧❦❧

Ruthanna was up with the baby for a long stretch in the middle of the night. Abbie heard her get out of bed several times and saw her pacing the room with the baby on her shoulder, illumined by the moon. It was no surprise when Ruthanna did not get up for breakfast. Abbie crept out of the room as quietly as she could, pulling her dress and *kapp* off the hook on her way out. She dressed quickly in Levi's already empty room and went down the narrow stairs to the kitchen. Esther was heating the stove. A bowl of eggs shed of their shells sat on the table. Ananias's glasses were balanced at the end of his nose as he studied some papers.

Abbie took a large fork from a drawer and began to beat the eggs. "I wish Ruthanna would change her mind," she blurted.

"I know how much you will miss her," Esther said.

"She should not make a decision when she is under so much stress."

"She has to do what she believes is right. It is not for us to judge." Esther dropped a generous pat of butter into a frying pan, which sizzled immediately.

Ananias cleared his throat. "She made the right decision, Abigail."

"How can you say that, *Daed*? She hasn't given the church a chance to help her."

"We are not much of a church, Abbie. We are barely a settlement."

"But we can be if it is what we all want."

Ananias stood and tapped his fingers on the papers on the table. "I have made a decision as well. We will return to Ohio. We will go before the end of the month, before the winter turns harsh."

"*Daed!*"

Esther dumped the bowl of eggs into the sputtering pan.

CHAPTER 34

Abbie's brain tied itself in a knot, incapacitating her tongue. Her mother, silent, stirred the eggs.

"I am responsible for the family's welfare, Abigail." Ananias picked up his papers and tapped them against the table to straighten the bottom edge of the pile. "I do not come to this decision easily, but it is in the best interest of all of us if we return to Ohio."

Abbie bit her bottom lip, choosing her words carefully. "All the reasons we left Ohio are still there. Land is expensive. The county is getting crowded."

"That is true. But the reasons we came to Colorado are no longer here. The opportunities have not proven fruitful. I cannot afford to give my sons land here, either. If I cannot succeed at farming, neither will they."

"The winter could bring blizzards of snow to end the drought," Abbie said. "We could have two good harvests next year."

Esther took plates off the shelf and put them on the table.

"We also hoped more families would come," Ananias said. "Daniel is of marriageable age, but we have no young unmarried women."

"He seems partial to Lizzie Mullet."

"She is not suitable."

Ananias's clipped tone bore growing impatience, but Abbie pushed on. "Why not? She's seventeen and comports herself well."

"Her father and I are not of like mind."

The sentence punched the air out of her. "You mean about

219

whether there is true salvation outside our church?"

"Abigail!" Ananias thumped the table.

Esther stirred the eggs but turned her head over one shoulder. "What is she talking about, Ananias?"

"We will not speak further on that question."

"Daniel is still young," Abbie said quietly. She did not need Lizzie Mullet to make her point. "Many of our men wait a few more years to marry."

"They wait so they can become established financially. There is no hope for that here."

"There is always hope, surely. *Gottes wille.*" Dread gushed through Abbie's veins on the way back to her heart and lungs. "We may not get any new families now. It is too close to winter. But in the spring—"

"Abigail."

She pressed her lips together to make herself stop talking.

"Reuben is not far beyond Daniel," Ananias said. "And what about you?"

Her eyes widened.

"I mean no insult. You are my precious daughter. But I regret that I did not insist that you marry before we left Ohio. You have limited prospects here as well."

"I do not worry about my future, *Daed.*"

Esther stepped to the bottom of the stairs and called the names of her three sons to summon them to breakfast. To Abbie her voice sounded mist-like, insubstantial.

"Your Willem seems to be in no hurry," Ananias said.

"Neither am I."

Ananias cleared his throat. "I may not be able to give my blessing to your union."

"I thought you liked Willem." Abbie swallowed back her own reservations about Willem's forthcoming decisions.

"I do."

"Then?"

"I have heard that he may not be a true believer. I would want you to be wed to a man who believes in the true church. But you and I agreed we would not speak of this matter at the risk of spreading more division. Leave the family out of it, please."

The boys thundered down the stairs seeking morning nourishment.

"*Shh!*" Esther said. "Have you forgotten a baby sleeps upstairs?"

"Isn't Ruthanna getting up for breakfast?" Levi slid into his usual chair.

"She can sleep as long as the child sleeps."

Esther gestured that her daughter should sit down, and Abbie complied although the thought of eating at that moment caused her stomach to revolt. She spent the moments of silent prayer trying to quell quivering nerves. The family ate, and Ananias quoted in German from memory a passage in Deuteronomy about teaching children to follow the ways of the Lord. Abbie could barely meet his eyes when the meal was over.

As soon as her father left the table, with her brothers right behind, Abbie stood to scrape dishes. There was not much to scrape. The family had long ago learned to eat every morsel of nourishment at a meal. Even Levi had stopped claiming that he was not hungry.

Esther began to fill the sink with water.

"*Mamm?*"

"Yes."

"Did you know about this?"

"Your father is the head of the family, Abigail."

"I understand that he makes these decisions, but did you know?"

Esther dipped a plate in water and rubbed three fingers around the rim. "No."

"Do you want to go back to Ohio?"

Esther wrapped her hands in a towel and said, "Why do you ask these questions, Abbie?"

"I'm just trying to make sense of it all."

"I have always trusted your father's decisions. I will not stop now."

"But do you want to go back to Ohio?"

Esther sighed. "I have rather come to love living in Colorado. The color of the sky is like nothing I have seen anywhere. The way the mountain breaks the sunset, the peculiar vegetation, even the sound of coyotes. It all has a beauty of its own."

"I know what you mean." Abbie put her arms around her mother and whispered, "What if I don't want to go?"

"You know our way of submission. *Demut*." Esther gently released herself from Abbie's embrace and turned back to the dishes. "If you were to marry, it would be different."

Abbie moistened her lips in thought. As an unmarried woman, did she have any choice but to obey her father? On the other hand, he was right in pointing out that she was past the age when most of her friends had married. She would not be making a girlish decision. Colorado had stolen her heart, and she still believed someday there would be a flourishing church.

"What if I said I want to stay here?" Abbie finally said.

"Stay where?" Levi shuffled in from the back porch.

"I think I'll go for a walk," Abbie said.

"I thought you wanted to stay." Levi wrinkled his face.

"I was talking about something else. I do want to go for a walk—if it's all right with you, *Mamm*."

Esther nodded.

"I want to go, too." Levi widened his eyes in hope.

"I just want to do some thinking, Levi. It won't be very fun."

"Please?"

"He's been squirming the last few days," Esther said. "It would do him good for you to wear him out."

Abbie knew Levi would pepper her with a thousand questions, but she nodded.

"Where are we going to walk?" Levi followed her out the back door.

"We'll just walk and see where we end up."

"I want to walk in the fields."

"I guess we can do that." Abbie adjusted her direction to cut across the yard away from the barn and toward the path that would take them past the pasture to the forgotten wheat fields. "There won't be much to look at. You know we have no crop."

"There's still a lot to look at. I can catch some bugs for my collection."

Insects would abound, feasting unimpeded on the parched,

stunted stalks of the crop that might have persuaded her father to make a different decision.

"What did you really mean when you said you want to stay?" Levi concentrated on making his stride match hers.

Abbie put a hand on the back of his head. It would be *Daed*'s decision what to tell his sons and when. "Never mind. It's nothing you have to worry about."

"I'm not worried. I used to be worried that we would run out of food, but I'm not worried anymore."

"I'm glad to hear that. What changed your mind?"

"*Daed* takes care of the family, and God takes care of *Daed*. Right?"

"Right."

"Then God takes care of the family. That's what I decided. It's better than worrying."

"Good thinking."

"Can you give me my lessons from now on?"

"Don't you like studying with *Mamm*?"

"I like to study with you. When you give me my lessons, I always think you are a good teacher."

"Thank you." She scratched the middle of his back. "I'll think about it."

"I want to race. Do you want to race?"

She shook her head. "No. But I'd love to watch you run."

Fourteen hours later Abbie spread her tree of life quilt out on the kitchen table. She had little progress to show for the last two weeks. Eber's death had stymied her aspirations. The baby's early birth and the funeral plans had banished ordinary routines. Ruthanna's presence in the house with the baby meant there always seemed to be something Abbie felt she ought to be doing to make Ruthanna's life easier.

But nothing would bring Eber back, and now Ruthanna had decided to make her own life easier by returning to her family.

Abbie's vision glazed over as she stared at the tiny triangles that made up the finished portions of the quilt. Instead of the quilt, she saw the lush greens of the Ohio countryside, where there were lakes and dependable rainfall and proper houses and worship services every other Sunday. Her father had not yet said where in Ohio he planned to take the family. Perhaps the Weavers would end up in eastern Ohio not far from Ruthanna's family, and Abbie could see her friend across the Pennsylvania border frequently. She imagined now what Eber and Ruthanna's little girl would look like when she was two or seven or ten years old. Maybe she would have Eber's dark hair. She already had his long nose.

Abbie left the quilt on the table and stepped out the back door to listen to the rapid chatter of the magpies, the chirping crickets, the whispering sibilants of the wind. She disagreed with her mother on the beauty of the coyotes howling, still unable to banish the mental image of what might have happened to Little Abe Miller. But the rest of it buoyed her spirit regardless of the crumbling financial realities.

With a sigh she wondered if she were the only one with blinders on, or the only one still clinging to the vision that had drawn them all out here. She glanced back inside at the quilt spread in the lamp's light and pondered how many of the families she prayed for would still be here when she finished the quilt.

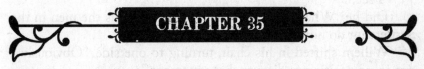

CHAPTER 35

"I suppose you heard about my *daed's* decision." Abbie laid the sack of bread on Willem's table and stood with her hands on the three mounds.

Willem nodded from his chair across the table. "He surprised us all. He went around yesterday because he wanted all the settlers to hear it from him."

Abbie absently picked up last week's bread sack and folded in half, then quarters, then eighths.

"He is doing what he thinks is best," Willem said.

"I know." Abbie did not know where to settle her blurry eyes. "He has never been one to do anything on a lark."

"Your *daed* is a good man, Abbie."

"I believe he would say the same about you." She set the flat flour sack on the corner of the table.

"We understand each other."

A gasp escaped Abbie's lips. "Not entirely."

Willem tilted his chair back and scratched under his chin. "What's on your mind?"

Abbie reached into her bucket for a clean rag and turned to Willem's water barrel to drench it. Without speaking she began to wipe off the table.

His chair hit the floor, and his hand reached across the planks to stop her motion. "You don't have to do that now."

"It is what I am here for, is it not?"

"Is it?"

She met his green eyes now. If Willem went to the Mennonites, his action would cause more division than any words her father did not want her to speak. "Before Eber. . .before the baby. . .I found out something."

"Yes?"

"My *daed* does not believe there is salvation outside the Amish church."

"I see."

Did he? What if her *daed* was right? "It seems the men in the settlement do not agree on this doctrine."

Willem shifted in his chair, turning to one side. "Obviously I am in no position to dispute that statement."

"What am I to think, Willem? If you go to the Mennonites, and if I do as you suggest and go with you—"

"Then you fear we would be condemning ourselves."

Abbie started wiping the table again. "Do you believe I should turn my back on what my father believes?"

"Whatever you believe, you father would want your faith to be based on your own conviction."

"He does not think you are serious about me."

"Ah, well. I have not confided in him as I have in you."

She said nothing.

"Come with me, Abbie. Come with me."

"So you have made up your mind?" She turned to the sink to twist the moisture out of the rag and kept her back to him.

Willem knew what she wanted to hear, but hypocrisy would be unbearable.

"Will you go with your parents?"

He saw her shoulders lift then fall, but she did not turn to face him.

"Will I have a choice?" she said at last.

"You are a grown woman."

"A grown *unmarried* woman."

"Our women sometimes find another calling."

She slapped the rag against the sink and spun around. "A

calling to keep house for a relative, for instance? I don't have any relatives around here. I have no place to go if my parents leave and you won't have me."

"I will always have you, Abbie." Willem stood now and walked around the table to stand before her and cradle both her elbows in his hands.

She wriggled against him at first, then her hands settled on his forearms. Her touch was light, hesitant, tentative. But she did not move.

After a long moment, he leaned in to kiss her. If his words failed to stir her, perhaps his lips would. The softness of her mouth welcomed him, and she made no move to break away.

When he raised his head again, he moved one hand to her cheek. "Come with me."

She stepped to the side. "You're confusing me."

"Am I?"

"Yes."

He returned to his side of the table. "At least take some time to consider your circumstances. I was in Limon the other day and saw a posting at the mercantile."

"What sort of posting?" She was listening and had not resumed scrubbing.

"A position. An *English* family I know is looking for a woman to be a companion to their young son. I believe he is recovering from some sort of respiratory illness and needs to be kept still, but they want to be sure his education continues."

"A teacher?"

He shrugged. "Of sorts. You help with Levi's lessons. This boy is about that age."

"But I have no formal qualifications."

"Perhaps that does not worry them right now. The man in the mercantile said they were more concerned to find someone temperamentally suited to being with him for a few hours a day. With the right conversation, the education would take care of itself."

"I don't know, Willem. I have never worked for an *English* family."

"They are nice people, and it's only for a few months while he recuperates."

She pressed her lips together, and he wondered if she still tasted him.

"I understand why your father wants to leave," he said, "but I also understand why you want to stay."

Rudy nodded to confirm to Abbie that he had heard the Weaver family news. They stood side by side along the fence around his pasture. He could see the sack of bread on the bench of her buggy, but she seemed in no hurry to deliver it to the house.

"The calf is doing well," she murmured as she folded her arms across the top of the wooden fence and set her chin in the crook of one elbow.

"She is fully weaned, though I find I cannot leave her in the same field with her mother or she tries to suckle still."

"She's a beautiful animal."

"You see beauty where everyone else sees potential for profit."

"Not everyone, surely."

"Just about. Even Amish cats have to earn their keep by keeping mice out of the barn."

"We used to have a dog in Ohio," Abbie said, "but he had to be able to herd. When he got too old, *Daed* shot him."

Rudy gazed at her face. Her eyes watched the calf but seemed to see right through the animal and fix on a point on the horizon. He leaned on the fence next to her. The thought that Abbie would leave the settlement sliced through him. She was the one who stopped him from selling his cows and getting on a train months ago. Without her he would have no reason to stay after all.

Wordless, he reached over and folded his fingers around her hand. The reluctance he expected did not come. Instead she turned her palm up and laced her fingers through his. In the end, he was the one to break the grasp without knowing what it meant.

Ruthanna's pulse quickened more than she had expected it would. She rode between Ananias and Abbie, who held the baby, on the way to Limon to meet her mother's train. They would be absurdly early, but Ruthanna had not wanted to risk any delay. A neighbor's wagon blocking the road, a cracked harness, a loose wheel—a dozen small incidents could cause them to be late. Even now Ruthanna prayed silently that an axle would not break or the horse would not step in a hole and go lame, as she mentally checked off the landmarks that meant they were approaching the outskirts of Limon.

When they pulled up to the depot, Ananias nodded toward the clock that hung on the outside wall.

"Thank you for indulging me," Ruthanna said. "I just couldn't bear to think of not being here the minute she gets off the train."

"Will you be all right here, then? Abbie can wait with you."

"Yes, fine."

"Do you have to rush off, *Daed*?" Abbie asked.

"We are very early for the train. I figure to see the land agent as long as I am in town," Ananias said. "I'd like to know what he thinks he can get for the property and how long he thinks it will take to find a buyer."

Ruthanna saw the droop in Abbie's face at her father's unvarnished account of his intent.

"No point in wasting time," Ananias said.

Ananias lowered himself from the bench and then offered assistance to Ruthanna. She reached for her daughter, but Abbie held the child securely with one arm and with the other braced herself to step down. Ruthanna did not object. Soon enough they would stand on this platform and bid each other farewell. She would not deny Abbie the pleasure of holding the baby now. They walked over to a vacant bench while Ananias took his seat in the buggy and urged the horse forward again.

Abbie adjusted the baby on her lap, and Ruthanna looped an arm through Abbie's elbow. "Maybe we'll see each other in Pennsylvania or Ohio someday," she said.

"Maybe." Abbie raised her eyes to Pikes Peak in the distance. "I love you, Ruthanna, but it breaks my heart to think of your leaving this place. Being here without you seems unimaginable."

"What about the job that Willem told you about?"

"Shall I consider it?"

"If it meant you could stay, wouldn't that be reason enough? No one is suggesting you become *English*." Ruthanna used the hem of her shawl to wipe her daughter's drool.

Abbie breathed in deeply and out heavily. "I am not sure how to make my *daed* understand. He would not see how working a few months for an *English* family would solve anything."

"What would he think if you said you wanted to marry?"

Abbie rolled her eyes. "I've told you about Willem. You know how he feels about Jake and the new church."

"I wasn't thinking of Willem."

"Then who?"

"Are you so blind that you do not see how Rudy feels about you? Now more than ever."

"Rudy is very sweet," Abbie said. "A tender soul."

"And he would jump at the chance to be your faithful, loving husband."

"But how could I encourage him when he knows how I feel about Willem?"

"Centuries of strong Amish marriages have been built on something other than those kinds of feelings."

Abbie twisted her neck and looked at Ruthanna with furrowed brow. "I know you married Eber because you loved him."

"He was the desire of my heart. I was blessed that God gave him to me."

"Don't I deserve that?" Abbie said hoarsely.

Ruthanna stroked her friend's arm. "I know you thought you would marry Willem, but if his choice takes him away, perhaps Rudy is God's way to give you the desire of your heart in the settlement."

A whistle blew, and a train barreled toward them.

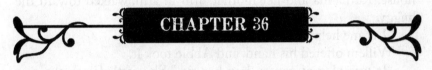

CHAPTER 36

Words formed in Abbie's mind the next morning but tangled themselves up between her tongue and her lips. She held Ruthanna's daughter and watched Willem load Ruthanna's trunk and the small bag her mother had traveled with. Ruthanna had come to Colorado with few possessions and left with fewer. She had packed only the few baby clothes she had stitched, the quilt she had made before her wedding to Eber, his Bible, and a change of clothes in case the baby spit up on her on the train. In a separate crate, packed in straw, was the cradle Eber made.

"Are they almost ready?" Willem asked as he checked the harness that strapped Ruthanna's buggy to the horse.

A nod was all Abbie could manage. She checked the knot of ribbon at the baby's neck.

"She'll write," Willem said.

Abbie nodded again and failed to resist the shiver that traveled up her spine.

"And you'll write," Willem said. "You'll still be friends."

It took three attempts before Abbie could push air through her throat. "I don't understand what the hurry is. Her mother could stay a while and see what Ruthanna's life was like out here."

"It's not that kind of a visit. Ruthanna may as well go and get settled."

"Get on with her life. That's what you mean."

"Yes. I suppose that is what I mean. Eber is gone. She can't save the farm. Raising a child alone must be frightening. Her parents want to help."

Abbie grazed one hand over the fuzz on the baby's head. It looked like it would grow in to yellow blond hair like her mother's, but it was impossible to be sure.

"I can't imagine not being able to ride over and see her. We didn't meet each other until we came here, but she is the closest thing I've known to a sister."

Willem lifted his chin toward the opening door of the Weaver house. Ruthanna and her mother, arm in arm, walked toward the buggy.

"Let me help you up with the baby."

Willem offered his hand, and Abbie took it.

"It was nice of you to buy her rig." She settled into the rear bench of Ruthanna's buggy.

"I'll send her what it's really worth when I can, but at least she has a bit of traveling money. Something to get situated with."

The buggy rocked as Ruthanna climbed in and sat next to Abbie. Her mother took the seat beside Willem.

Abbie forced a smile. Speech had evaporated once again.

❦

At the train station, Willem and Ruthanna's mother hung back. Ruthanna clung to Abbie, who clung to the baby. She pulled a slip of paper out of the sleeve of her dress and tucked it into Abbie's.

"My address," Ruthanna said. "I want you to write to me as soon as you've made up your mind what to do."

Abbie's head bobbed.

Not once had Ruthanna doubted that she was making the right decision for her child. If she had been on her own, even without Eber, she might have borrowed Abbie's persistence. She had thought she would, in those final weeks when she had to admit that life was ebbing out of her husband. But the babe in her arms, rather than her womb, changed everything.

"You are the truest friend I have ever known," Ruthanna whispered.

She felt the soundless sob in her friend's chest.

"I pray you will not feel abandoned for long," Ruthanna said.

"Don't be so stubborn that you end up alone."

Abbie dipped her head to kiss the baby one last time before transferring the tight bundle into Ruthanna's arms. "Wherever I end up, I want you to write to me about everything she does. When she smiles for the first time, when she cuts her first tooth, when she starts to crawl. Everything."

"I promise." Ruthanna put the baby upright over her shoulder and the child burped.

Abbie giggled. "I guess she wanted to say good-bye, too."

Willem and Ruthanna's mother approached.

"I suppose we should get on the train," Ruthanna said. "Thank you, Willem. For everything."

"I counted Eber a good friend," he said.

"Look after his grave for me. Don't let it grow over."

"I won't."

Ruthanna handed the baby to her mother and opened her arms once again to the friend who had never let her down, regretting that her decision could not but disappoint the settler with the greatest enthusiasm for the venture they had all undertaken. But her daughter needed to be enfolded into dozens of faithful waiting arms, not to grow up with a mother too burdened by farm chores to look after her properly.

When she kissed Abbie's cheek, she tasted the salt of tears.

Willem did not rush Abbie. They watched the train chug out of sight, and still he held his pose and awaited her readiness to turn toward the buggy. If they had been alone, rather than standing on a public railroad platform, he would have wrapped his arms around her and welcomed a release of her grief. Only when an oncoming whistle announced the next impending shuffle of passengers did she pivot and march to the buggy.

Willem helped her up to the bench, unhitched the horse, and took up the reins. She sat beside him silent and straight backed, staring straight ahead. Willem navigated away from the bustle of the train station and through the streets of Limon to the road that would gradually narrow into the route that led to the Amish farms. He drove for several miles, occasionally glancing at her unyielding posture.

"I want you to meet someone," he said at last. "It's on the way home."

"I've just said good-bye to my best friend." Abbie's tone snapped, but she did not turn her head.

"I know. But soon enough you'll have to make your own decision, and this could help."

"You mean you think I should get on with my life, too."

"I mean," he said carefully, "that you should know what choices you have."

"Is this about that *English* job?"

He nodded.

"I'm not ready."

"Your father listed his property with a land agent yesterday and has already struck a deal for his cows. If you have any hope of deciding for yourself, rather than letting circumstances dictate, you should let me introduce you to this family."

"Whatever happens will be God's will. If I wait and the job is gone, it will still be God's will." Not only did Abbie refuse to look at him, but she turned her head with deliberation in the opposite direction.

Willem slowed the horse so there would be more time to talk before the turnoff. "And if you meet the family today and you like them, that would also be God's will. Wouldn't you agree?"

He saw the twitch in her shoulders and knew she was softening.

"I'll just introduce you," he said. "If you don't want to do more than say hello, look at me and blink twice. I will politely excuse us, and we will be on our way."

She whirled on him. "You have this all figured out, don't you?"

He cranked his head away and allowed himself a quick smile. When the lane came up on the left, he made the turn.

❧⚜☙

When Abbie agreed to go inside the house with Mrs. Wood, Willem waited outside. Abbie was not sure whether to be furious or relieved. The kindness in Louise Wood's face had undone her. Willem must have known it would. Apparently the moment had passed to blink twice and be whisked out of a circumstance she felt ill equipped to meet.

The ranch house sprawled more than any of the Amish homes, but Abbie supposed the ranch itself also was better established. From the outside, even her untrained eye could discern the outline of the original house and the slight change in the width of the siding where a wing was added to one side. Inside, one foot now detected a slight ridge in the flooring under a long runner carpet as Mrs. Wood led Abbie to a comfortable sitting room. The original parlor had been converted to a music room featuring a grand piano. Otherwise, though, the house was modestly furnished, and Mrs. Wood's high-necked dress was made of a muted green calico that had seen regular washings for at least two years.

"May I make you a cup of tea?" Louise gestured for Abbie to take a seat.

"I don't want to be any bother."

"It's no bother. I was about to have some anyway. The kettle is already on."

Abbie smiled. "Then I would love some."

"I'll see if I can rustle up some cookies as well. I won't be but a minute."

When Louise left the room, Abbie leaned forward in her chair to see if she could see out the window across the room. Willem had his back to the house while he ran his hand down the horse's long nose. For better or for worse, she was inside now and he was out of blinking range. She looked around the room, and her eyes settled on a photograph of a stiff trio. Between a man and a woman sat a little boy. Abbie peered at the picture for clues as to its age. But she was unfamiliar with photographs in general. The Amish avoided them. She did not actually know anyone who had ever sat for a photograph.

Apparently now she did, because the woman in the picture clearly was Louise Wood.

"Here we are." Louise returned with a tray bearing a plate of sugar cookies and two tea cups. She set it on a table beside Abbie.

"I'm so glad Willem introduced us. We're sure to have a delightful chat."

The warmth in her tone melted Abbie.

Louise handed her a cup. "Willem tells me you have a little brother about my son's age."

"Yes. Levi is eight." Abbie did her best not to jiggle the cup.

"Now that's a nice strong biblical name. Of course, Abigail was quite a woman of courage in the Bible. I'm sure you're well named."

Abbie took a sip of tea. "What is your son's name?"

Louise laughed. "I'm afraid it's Melton Finley Wood IV. Much too much name for a little boy, but you can see the strength of the family tradition. We call him Fin."

"I like that."

"He's not a difficult child. Quite sweet in temperament, actually. But he is a bit rambunctious and used to life on the ranch. The doctor says we must keep him quiet for at least three more months."

"What does he enjoy?"

"He doesn't seem to like to read on his own, but he does like to be read to."

As Louise launched into describing her son, her eyes lit and her cheeks softened. Within a few minutes Abbie was eager to meet Fin for herself, already sure she would like him.

Keeping a recuperating *English* child entertained by feeding his mind was not so different than Noah Chupp's making shoes for *English* children. Abbie was certain she could do a good job. Still, staying behind when her family returned to Ohio for a reason other than marriage was a drastic decision.

By late morning on Monday, Abbie had scrubbed two piles of clothing against the washboard on the back porch and hung pants and shirts on the line strung between metal poles behind the house. In the middle of October, with temperatures more bearable than July, August, or even September, most days were still cloudless and the air free of any whisper of moisture. The clothes would dry and she would be back in the yard to collect them as soon as the lunch dishes were cleared.

Unless the train had run into trouble, Ruthanna was home by now.

Home.

Could Pennsylvania feel like home again after the substance of Ruthanna's married life had unfolded in Colorado? Abbie turned the question over in her mind as she carried the thickly woven basket, now empty, to the back porch. Even though she had not married, Abbie had fallen in love in this drought-ridden state. Even if she could not marry Willem, he held her heart. Would any other place ever feel like home?

She missed Ruthanna. Mary Miller was a good friend, but the bond Abbie shared with Mary was thin and crackly compared to Ruthanna's intimacy with the desires that lined the corners of Abbie's heart. Her eyes warmed with sudden tears, and Abbie wanted to be alone. Instead of pulling open the back door and going inside to help with lunch, she strode across the yard to the barn. It would have to do for now, just long enough to corral the emotions that threatened to spill through her day. Inside the barn, Abbie reached for a horse blanket on a shelf before marching to the empty stall at the back of the structure. The straw in this un-used retreat was not fresh, but it was reasonably clean. She spread the blanket, sat, pulled her knees up, wrapped her arms around them, and buried her face in the folds of her skirt. Breathing with deliberation, she tried to form her thoughts into prayer. The words wriggled away without taking shape.

Abbie lifted her head when she heard the voices approaching. One was *Daed*'s. The other she did not recognize. They spoke English, not Pennsylvania Dutch. Abbie crawled across the straw and peered around the opening of the stall.

"The barn seems solidly built." The strange man knocked on the barn wall. "That will help us set the highest price we can hope for."

"Of course I want to get a good price," Ananias said. "But I also want to sell quickly. I believe I have a realistic expectation of the market in the price I seek."

"Yes, there are several similar properties available right now—as you well know, since some of them were Amish farms. In any event, I think we can present your land in an attractive way."

"Do you have the papers you wish me to sign?"

"Right here in my satchel."

Abbie sat back on her haunches and let her shoulders sag. The land agent.

"I have spoken to a few people about equipment and animals," her father said. "I thought selling those items separately would be my best hope for cash to move my family."

"That is wise, I'm sure. I don't believe any buyers would assume the sale of anything but the land and the house and barn. But if you have difficulty, let me know. We might hasten a sale by enhancing what we include in the price."

"I am anxious to raise enough cash for train tickets. I want to be home before winter."

Home. There was that word again, coming from her own father's mouth. Even Ananias Weaver did not think of his Colorado land as home. Abbie pressed the heels of her hands against her eyes and waited for the men to withdraw through the barn door.

❦

The day was one of the longest Abbie could remember. She managed pleasantries with her family over lunch, folded the laundry, sat with Levi as he practiced his reading, cleaned the chicken coop, and mopped the kitchen floor. Supper was somber. By then the entire family, including Levi, knew that Ananias had reached an agreement with the land agent. It was hard for Abbie to know what any of her brothers thought. If Reuben or Daniel disagreed with their father, they hid it well. Neither did they avow support for the plan to return to Ohio. Levi remembered little about living anywhere but Colorado, but in time he would likely have only vague memories of his childhood here.

After supper, Abbie spread her quilt on the table. If the house were larger, she would have wished for a proper quilting frame where she could pull the project taut and be more confident in the straightness of her stitches. But with care and persistence, she had developed a system of rolling out of the way the parts of the quilt she was not working on. While she could not see the entire quilt, she focused on the square that represented each household as she crafted the angled stitching.

Twice Abbie turned up the lamp. The sounds of the family shifted from chores and conversation in the other room to bidding each other good night and shuffling steps on the stairs rising from the kitchen. Still Abbie stitched and prayed and ached to see the quilt complete.

"Abigail."

Stilling the needle between her fingers, Abbie looked up. In his nightshirt, her father stood on the bottom step. "Yes, *Daed*?"

"Are you aware of the time?"

She glanced out the window into the blackness but admitted she did not know the time.

"It is after one in the morning," Ananias said.

"I didn't realize." Abbie finished a stitch and stuck her needle through the fabric to secure it.

"I hope you will put as much determination into packing for

239

the move," Ananias said.

Abbie said nothing.

"I find the land agent a trustworthy man," her father said. "So as soon as I can raise enough cash for train tickets and shipping a few crates, we will go. It is better that none of us is caught by surprise when the time comes."

"I understand." Abbie folded her project down to its smallest size, which still covered much of the table.

"Good. I will set the boys to building some crates tomorrow. Good night."

"Good night, *Daed*."

Ananias turned and went up the stairs he had just descended. Abbie sat at the table with both hands resting on her folded quilt. Mrs. Wood had not sent word yet about the position. Her husband had not been available during Abbie's visit three days ago, but Louise felt sure he would give his approval, and as soon as he did she would send one of the ranch hands with a note.

And then Abbie would face a decision full on. Abbie put out the lamp but made no move to climb the stairs.

❧

Rudy brimmed with resolve one moment and surrendered to reticence the next. This wretched cycle had been going on for days. Weeks. Perhaps months. Tuesday afternoon was no different.

He bore no ill will toward Willem Peters, but it seemed to Rudy that Willem had set his course long ago. Not all of the settlers knew Willem as well as Rudy did. They were two unmarried men on adjoining farms who shouldered together for tasks that required the strength of more than one man, and between them they had made sure Eber Gingerich lacked for nothing either. Their conversations rarely strayed from the work before them, and they made no pretense of having similar temperament, but Rudy felt he knew Willem's drive and intentions.

It didn't seem possible that Abbie did not also know.

Rudy went to the trough his horses drank from and splashed water on his face. With his eyes closed and the chill of well water tingling in his pores, he made up his mind. He had one clean shirt. Now was the time to put it on.

❧❀❧

The back door opened and Levi stood bursting with his announcement. "Rudy is here. He says he wants to talk to you."

Abbie pulled her hands out of the dish water, where she had been wiping the last of Tuesday's supper dishes. "Then ask him to come in. Where are your manners?"

"He said would I please ask you to come outside." Levi raised both hands to scratch the back of his neck.

"Oh. All right, then. *Danki.*"

Abbie put the last plate in the rack and dried her hands. She tugged on both strings to be sure her *kapp* sat on her head evenly and went out the back door into the gray, dusky air. Sunset came so much earlier now than it did during the long, hot summer.

"Hello, Rudy. What a nice surprise to see you."

Rudy dipped his hat slightly. "I thought you might enjoy an evening stroll. We have some time before it's dark, I think."

Abbie looked to the west, where the orange fingers of the descending sun spread their grasp. "A stroll would be lovely."

They turned and fell into an unhurried pace together. Rudy had both thumbs hooked under his suspenders. Abbie twiddled one tie of her *kapp* between two fingers.

"I imagine you miss Ruthanna fiercely," Rudy said.

Tension cascaded out of Abbie's shoulders. "I hardly had a chance to get used to the idea that she would go, and then she was gone."

"I still have the urge to go by the farm and see if they need something."

Abbie smiled. "You are a good man, Rudy Stutzman." And he was.

"We were all stunned about your father's decision. It must weigh heavy on you."

Abbie's throat thickened. What a refreshing sensation it was to hear from another's mouth such truth about her own spirit.

"Will you go with them?" Rudy asked.

Abbie blew out her breath. "My *daed* certainly thinks I will."

"But you—what do you want to do?"

Abbie raised a hand toward the distant mountain. "On some days this feels like the most forlorn place on earth. But other days I can scarcely breathe for how lovely it is."

"And the church?"

Abbie stopped and turned toward Rudy. For the first time, she saw that he was perspiring, even though the evening was not overly warm. "So many questions, Rudy."

He took one of her hands, and she heard the shallowness of his breath.

"If you were to marry, your parents could not object to your remaining here."

"No, I suppose not."

"Why should you pine for Willem?" he said softly. "He will go to the Mennonites."

"I know." Her words were more a movement of her mouth than sound.

"If you were to marry me," Rudy said, "we could be the first of the settlers to marry. Surely a minister would come from Ordway for such an event. It would be a great encouragement to the others to see that we want to pledge our futures to this place."

"Is that what you want, Rudy? Truly?"

"If I can be with you, I can be happy anywhere."

Abbie's hand trembled, and she could not stop it. "I need some time, Rudy."

"I'll wait."

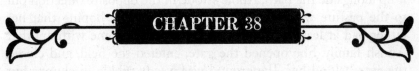

CHAPTER 38

"D *aed!*" Abbie called over her shoulder two days later and then returned her gaze to the view out the front window. "An *English* is here with a wagon."

Ananias snapped shut the accounts book in his lap. "He's here for the hay."

"You're getting rid of the hay?"

"Did you think I would crate it up to ship to Ohio?"

Abbie blinked three times at the man who patted his horse's rump on his way to the Weaver front door. "I hadn't thought about the hay."

Ananias crossed the room. "You were here the day I took delivery on hay because we had so little from our own fields. What's left is still worth something. We must use every asset."

"But the animals," Abbie said.

"The cows will be gone before the day is over. The horses can make do with grazing and straw until I sort out what to do with them."

Ananias left Abbie standing in the front room of the house and strode across the yard to greet the *English*. He gestured toward the barn and the man nodded and returned to his rig. Abbie backed away from the window as her mouth soured. Hearing her *daed* say that he wanted to leave before the end of the month was hard enough. Visible progress in his effort to raise train fare sucked breath from her chest in a way she was unprepared for. He would sell the coal, too, she realized. Though lignite was plentiful, the savings in labor would be worth something to a family who had sufficient cash. And the chickens. Either they would go to a nearby farm, or her mother would pluck and cook one every day until they were gone.

Abbie suddenly wanted to bury her face in the neck of one of the cows that had kept the Weavers in milk, cheese, and butter all this time. As the *English* man turned his wagon around and lined it up alongside the barn, Abbie strode in the opposite direction out to the pasture where the cows spent their days, hoping that her father had at least tried to find the animals a home with another Amish family. She opened the gate, entered the field, and closed the gate behind her. The ground was weedy rubble in clumps but mostly hard-packed barren earth that could not sustain the cows that swished tails against flies. Abbie tried not to look toward the barn, but when she heard the rattle of a wagon and knew it could not yet be filled with hay, she relented and turned around.

It was Willem's wagon she heard.

Willem spotted Abbie in the field with relief. He would not have to contrive some awkward reason to see her out of hearing distance of her family. He looped the reins around the top of the fence and then climbed over. The slump in her shoulders bore witness to the disappointment she carried within herself, and Willem hoped the errand that brought him to her would transform both her posture and her mood.

He strode across the grassless pasture. "I stopped by the Woods'. Mrs. Wood has sent a note."

Her spine straightened and her eyebrows rose.

Willem offered her the cream-colored envelope elegantly addressed to Miss Abigail Weaver.

"What was her decision?" Abbie tentatively fingered one edge of the envelope.

"She didn't say. You'll have to read the note."

Abbie slid one finger under the sealed flap and pulled out the note. Willem watched her eyes go back and forth as she absorbed the words.

"Well?" he said.

Abbie smiled. "The position is mine if I choose to take it."

He reached for her hand. "I knew the two of you would like each other."

"Her husband has given his approval, and she hopes it will be convenient for me to start very soon. She would like me to come for tea on Friday and meet the boy."

"And will you?"

Abbie took her hand from his and raised it to her cheek. "I was not certain until this moment what I would do, but I believe I will gladly accept her kind offer."

"So you won't leave with your family."

She turned her head toward the activity around the barn. Reuben, Daniel, her father, and the *English* man had created an efficient system for transferring the hay.

Willem followed her gaze. "I see your *daed* is following through on his decision."

She nodded.

"We all understand his choice," Willem said.

"I don't. I wish he would at least wait to see what moisture the winter brings, but he seems intent on making sure he can't change his mind."

Willem let the silence drape the space between them for a moment, knowing the comfort of his arms would only add to her confusion.

"I could carry a note back to Mrs. Wood, if you like," he finally said.

"I have nothing to write on. I'll have to go to the house and see if I can find a suitable scrap of paper." Abbie lifted a hand to control a sniffle.

"She won't expect anything fancy. She does not share our ways, but she understands them."

⋇

Thirty minutes later Abbie handed Willem the note and waved as he scrambled up to the bench of his wagon in three practiced motions.

The *English* wagon was about as full as it could be, bales carefully stacked and balanced to withstand the sway of the ride to their new home. Abbie did not know the man, nor how he had heard about the Weaver hay. Reuben and Daniel lifted the last bale into place and the *English* shook Ananias's hand. Abbie turned her head as the cash passed between them. She glanced into the field and wondered how many more hours—or perhaps only minutes—would pass before the cows would take a final nibble of Weaver land before being roped and led behind a horse or a wagon.

She resolved not to watch. There were half a dozen ways to make herself useful for the rest of the day without listening for the sound of dread to fill her spirit.

Ananias approached. "Did you see that the boys put your trunk in your room?"

"Yes." How could she miss a trunk that sat where Eber's cradle had stood only a few days ago? Abbie measured her steps toward the house so as not to seem eager to escape her father's eye.

"Let me know when you've packed it. The boys can carry it out to the barn for a few days."

"A few days?"

Ananias nodded. "Once the cows are gone I should have what I need for the train tickets."

"So soon?" Her heart pounded.

"Abigail," he said, "we've already talked about this. We may as well be expedient."

"I know." She tried to stride ahead of her father, but he kept pace.

"You can take your hope chest, too, of course. I know you've prepared those items with care for your marriage, and there is no reason they should go to waste."

Abbie struck the ground with the heel of her right foot and rolled it forward for balance, but she did not pick it up again. "*Daed.*"

"Yes?" He halted beside her.

"I have decided I want to stay." She scoured his face for a reaction and did not have to wait long.

Ananias's jaw tensed as he spread his feet under his shoulders, knees locked. "Has Willem finally chosen to take a wife?"

"Not so far as I know."

Ananias waited for more.

"I do not wish to disrespect you, *Daed*," Abbie said, "but my calling is here."

"Your calling is to your husband, though I am somewhat relieved that you and Willem realize your differences. Rudy is much more suited to you. He is less likely to wander from the true faith."

Abbie flushed. Had Rudy spoken to her father? Until now, she had not thought so.

"I have made no decision about a husband." Abbie cradled her own elbows. "I have accepted a position with an *English* family."

Ananias raised two fingers to one temple. "Perhaps I have misjudged you as well."

"No, *Daed*. My heart belongs to our people. But it also belongs here in Colorado."

"I do not hear you asking for my consent."

She paused. "May I have your blessing?"

Ananias resumed walking toward the house. Abbie trembled.

Abbie did not have one dress that was better than another. She had three, and all of them lacked in some way. One had frayed cuffs, another faded color, and the third mended seams. This had never mattered to her before, but somehow in Louise Wood's home, Abbie felt self-conscious. Perhaps it was the china arranged on the table for tea or the damask tablecloth or the wave of Louise's sweeping golden hair held in place with a pearl-ridged comb. Louise's dress was a muted solid color, but Abbie suspected it was what the *English* called Sunday best.

"Everything looks lovely," Abbie said, because it did.

"Don't mind the fuss." Louise gestured to a chair at the end of the dining room table. "Every now and again I like to give Fin a chance to practice his manners."

"I'm anxious to meet him." Abbie arranged herself in the chair.

"Excuse me while I call Fin."

Louise stepped from the room, and Abbie allowed herself to absorb the room in more detail. Yellow chintz curtains draped from three matching windows against a pale green wallpaper print. In spite of the china and tablecloth, the tea offering was fairly simple: rolls in a bread warmer, a tea pot in a cozy, a few slices of cheese, and a bowl of red grapes. When Abbie heard the shuffle of feet in the next room, she wondered if Fin was as nervous as she was. A moment later, Louise appeared in the wide doorframe that separated the dining room from the front parlor with her hand on her son's shoulder.

"Fin, this is Miss Weaver," Louise said.

Fin folded one arm across his stomach and bowed. "I am very pleased to meet you."

"And I you," Abbie said.

The boy approached her and offered a handshake, which Abbie accepted immediately.

"I hope you will feel comfortable in our home," he said.

Abbie smiled. The child was adorable in his navy blue suit and collared white shirt with his brown hair carefully parted and slicked down. She knew a boy who enjoyed being active on a ranch would not dress this way often, but he was making every effort to please his mother, just as Levi would have done.

They were going to get along just fine.

CHAPTER 39

Outside the bank on Thursday morning, Willem straightened his suit and double-checked that the seam at the top of his shirt Abbie had mended a month ago still held. An oversized envelope contained assorted papers that may or may not be relevant to the day's quest. He wanted to be prepared for any question.

Inside the bank, Willem surveyed the lobby. A half-dozen people stood in lines to see the three tellers on duty, and around the perimeter of the room were several imposing desks occupied by men with stern faces and airs of authority. Willem had an appointment with one of them, the chief loan officer. He caught the man's eye and smiled as he crossed the lobby.

"Hello, Mr. Peters. Thank you for coming in this morning. I trust things are well on your farm."

"Well enough, considering the challenges all the farms have faced this year." Willem was determined not to sound pitiful. It would only impede progress toward his goal. "I have been a conscientious steward of my resources."

The banker gestured to a chair opposite the desk. "What can I do for you today?"

Willem sat up straight with his papers in his lap. "You may be aware that several properties near mine have become available."

"I have heard this, though I am not familiar with the particulars." The banker adjusted his rimless glasses.

"Eber Gingerich passed away, and his widow decided to sell the land. And now Ananias Weaver has decided to return to Pennsylvania."

"I'm sorry to hear that." The loan officer thrummed the edge of his desk.

Willem resisted the urge to look to one side and kept his gaze fixed on the banker's face. "Both of these farms abut my property, which has caused me to wonder if this might be the time to enlarge my acreage. In the future, a larger farm would yield greater profit."

The banker leaned back in his chair. "Profitability in farming is subject to many circumstances. Number of acres is only one of them."

"I believe it to be a solid starting point. I would like to look into buying one of these farms, or at least some portion of the acres. To do so, I would need a higher line of credit."

"Mr. Peters, even the *English* farmers are having a tough go right now. The ranchers are doing a little better, but the drought has been difficult for everyone."

Willem did not move, lest any gesture suggest a crack in confidence. "Farming requires taking the long view, does it not? If we do not make plans during the difficult years, we will not be prepared for the opportunity of abundance in the future."

"Well, now, I suppose there is nothing to disagree with there, Mr. Peters. But this is a bank. I am a loan officer. Our decisions come down to taking acceptable risks."

"I don't believe I have given you any reason to regard me as an unacceptable risk."

"No, not so far. But how would you make the increased payments that would come with a new loan when your farm has yielded so little in the last two years?"

"I've brought some papers that will demonstrate my assets beyond the value of my mortgaged land." Willem slid the documents out of the envelope and laid them on the desk.

The loan officer leaned forward and began studying the papers. He flipped over several of them and looked up at Willem. "I grant you that you present a more encouraging picture than I had supposed, but it would still seem inadvisable for you to take on more debt."

"If I failed to make my payments, the land would belong to the bank."

"And it might be worth even less than it is now if drought and soil erosion continue. We would require a substantial down payment to hedge against that possibility."

"How much?"

The banker named a figure.

"If I could come up with that amount," Willem said, "would you consider my application?"

The banker cleared his throat. "I would agree to take the matter to the full loan committee, but I make no promise of the result you desire."

"Fair enough."

Willem collected his papers and returned to his wagon down the street. At the familiar lilt of a laugh, he turned his head.

"Willem!" Abbie said.

Beside her stood Rudy.

"We didn't know you were coming into town," Abbie said. "We could have all come together."

We. Willem was not sure he had ever heard Abbie use that word to describe Rudy and herself. And he was equally uncertain he could remember a time when Abbie had come to Limon with Rudy. Abbie had not laughed since before Eber died. What had Rudy said to raise her mood? Willem reminded himself he had no right to be jealous as he looked from Abbie to Rudy and observed that they stood close together.

"Have you just come from the bank?" Rudy's blue eyes met Willem's evenly.

"Yes. I had some financial business to attend to." Willem dropped his envelope of papers onto the floor of the wagon.

Rudy pushed the fingertips of both hands together. "Perhaps it is no coincidence that you see the banker just as the farms around yours become available at an attractive price."

"Rudy!" Abbie took a step away.

"Am I mistaken?" Rudy said.

Willem spread his feet in a solid stance. "Nothing in *Ordnung* prohibits a man from making a wise business transaction."

Abbie's mouth dropped open. "Would you really try to profit from Ruthanna's loss? From my father's concern for his sons?"

Her tone stabbed him, and he hoisted himself into his wagon without answering.

⫘⫘⫘

Abbie held still during the silent prayer before her family's evening meal. Behind her closed eyes, while she smelled the roasted chicken whose neck her mother had twisted a few hours ago, Abbie saw Willem driving off in his wagon. She had expected him to deny Rudy's accusation, but he had not. How was it possible that Rudy seemed to know Willem better than she did?

Her father murmured his "Amen," and the family began to pass dishes around the table. Looking at chicken for the fourth night in a row, Abbie's calculation of how many were left in the coop obstructed her gratitude. Esther could have sold her chickens, especially the ones that were laying consistently, but she seemed to have chosen to feed her family with them. Green beans from the plentitude of the Ordway Amish, potatoes Abbie had dug last week, and bread filled out the meal.

"Eat." Esther urged Levi, who had passed the potatoes to Reuben without serving himself.

"I'm only a little bit hungry."

Abbie heard the scuffling sound that meant Levi had hooked his ankles behind the front legs of his chair. He had been doing so well with eating until the last few days. She laid a piece of bread on his plate without asking if he wanted it. Levi tore off a corner and put it in his mouth.

"I have urged all of you to pack your things." Ananias sliced off a piece of chicken breast. "If you have not done so, please do so soon. We leave on Monday."

Abbie caught her fork just before it slipped from her grasp.

Ananias pulled a neat stack of small papers from his lap and spread them on the table beside his plate. Levi leaned over to examine them.

"Are those train tickets?" Levi asked.

Ananias nodded.

"But they didn't give you enough. There are only five, and there are six of us."

Abbie dropped her eyes to her plate and carefully set her fork down.

"Abigail has decided to remain here." Ananias took a bite of potato. "And I have decided not to quarrel with her about it."

Levi knocked the train tickets to the floor.

"Levi!" Esther pointed at the papers. "Pick those up right now."

Despite the reluctance in his face and shoulders, Levi complied. "Why don't you want to come with us, Abbie?"

"My heart would remain here." Abbie reached to stroke Levi's head, but he ducked away from her touch.

"Don't you love us?"

"Of course I do."

"Then why aren't you coming?"

"Love is complicated sometimes."

Levi kicked the table leg.

"Levi, behave." Ananias's words stilled Levi's agitation but not the sulk on his face.

Abbie glanced at Daniel and Reuben, neither of whom had stopped eating with their father's announcements.

"It will likely take some time for the farm to sell," Ananias said. "Abbie can remain in the house until then. She has found a job for the time being. We'll leave enough furniture for her to get by. She can keep the buggy, since no one but an Amish family would want it and none of them can afford it. Once the land sells, she will be on her own, since that is what she has chosen."

Abbie looked at her *daed*, but he did not meet her eyes.

"Who do you think will come?" Willem passed Jake a bowl of boiled eggs and then picked up a slice of Abbie's bread.

Across the table in Willem's kitchen, Jake cracked the shell and began to peel an egg for the simple breakfast they shared Friday morning.

"I don't know," Jake said. "I've spoken to a lot of families. People are polite, but that does not mean they will come. Perhaps we'll have half a dozen for our first Sunday morning worship service. Even if it is just you and me, Christ will be present and glorified."

"Are you sure you wouldn't like to wait until you're certain more people will come?" Willem slathered butter on his bread.

"It's time," Jake said. "Mennonites have been scattered in the area for five years. And all the ministers agree it is time for a mission to the Amish around Limon, since you do not have a minister of your own. In a few weeks, I will be ordained as a bishop. When people see that this is not a passing desire on my part, they will give more serious consideration."

Willem reached behind to the stove and brought the coffeepot to the table. "I'm serious, Jake. I hope you know that."

"I do. I know it may cost you dearly."

Willem filled his coffee cup. "Abbie has decided to stay when her family leaves."

Jake gave a half smile. "So there is hope for the two of you?"

Willem shrugged, thinking of the way Abbie and Rudy had stood together at the edge of the street. "I don't think that's the reason she is staying, but I hold hope in my heart. All things are possible with God."

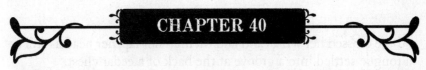

CHAPTER 40

illem lingered over his sparse Sunday breakfast. He could have managed more than coffee and a thick slice of bread, which he did not even bother to butter, but his mind was hours ahead of a dawn meal. Morning farm chores did not pause for the Sabbath. Willem had always found it humorous that while God decreed in Deuteronomy that livestock should have a Sabbath from their labors, God did not spare their owners the chores of caring for the animals. One morning a week that did not start with milking would have satisfied Willem.

He swallowed the last of his coffee, pushed his chair back from the table, and paced to the stove. If he stoked it now, when he came back from the barn it would be hot enough to boil water and he could clean up properly for church.

Church.

Willem spoke the word aloud to savor the sensation on his tongue. *Church.* Far too many months had passed since he last indulged in the anticipation of worship with others who believed. Occasionally he joined the Weavers for their somber family worship. Most Sunday mornings, after the chores, he sat alone with his Bible on his knees reading a favorite passage and trying to remember a sermon that taught him what it meant. Now he thought that if he had known he would be so long without preaching he would have listened more carefully when he had the opportunity.

But today would be different. Today he would ride in his new buggy to Limon, to Jake's humble rooms, and pray for the others whom God would send to the gathering. Together they would pray for future worshippers who had not yet heard the call but would heed it in the months ahead. Willem would feel the Spirit move in his heart telling him the hymn they should sing, and he would intone the opening notes as the words rose from his throat. When he returned to his farm and sat at the table again, it would be with the drenching satisfaction of worship washing over his soul.

Abbie crossed her wrists and laid them in her lap, her head as still as a tongue settled into a groove at the back of a cedar chest.

Reuben and Daniel betrayed no emotion about this last Sunday as a complete family. Levi had refused to meet her eye all morning, and her mother's face was drawn with unspoken resignation. When Abbie decided to stay in Colorado, she had not thought of this moment, this ache of the last.

The last full day they would have together.

The last time they would sit in the circle of their front room to hear her *daed* lead them in family worship.

She had missed the last smile on Levi's face because she had not known it would be the last. Now she doubted he would relent. The sagging disappointment in his young face told her he knew she would not relent, either.

Her father had chosen to read from the sixth chapter of Deuteronomy, where God warned the people of Israel against the sin of disobedience.

"Beware lest thou forget the Lord," he read. And a few verses later, "Ye shall not go after other gods."

And then, "Ye shall not tempt the Lord your God."

Is that what *Daed* thought she was doing? Chasing after other gods? Testing the Lord?

Perhaps he meant it as a warning against following Willem to the Mennonites.

A Mennonite church would never be the church of Abbie's heart, but surely it did not have to mean that Willem did not love the one true God.

Rudy thought Willem was trying to serve two masters. Why else would he be trying to buy the Weavers' farm, or Ruthanna's land? Willem said all the right words about loving God, Rudy had observed, but he also did not want to pass up an opportunity to increase his worldly wealth at the expense of people he was supposed to care for.

Willem was with the Mennonites that morning. He had given up trying to be discreet about his intentions. All the Amish families knew this was the day Jake Heatwole had chosen to hold his first pubic worship service. Abbie supposed next Willem would be actively recruiting Amish families to join him.

Abbie allowed herself a slight shift in position. Why should she not tell Rudy she would marry him? He was right. They were well suited to each other in ways she had not realized until a few weeks ago. Together they could coax a living from the land and with their union announce that the core of Amish families did not have to dwindle away. It *was* still possible to think of a future. If she married, her father would not object—even in the guise of a family sermon—to her choice to remain in Colorado.

Yes. Rudy was right. Willem had staked his future in his decision to worship with the Mennonites, and now it was time for her to stake hers.

Eight.

That was how many people entered Jake's sitting room for a worship service.

Jake, Willem, and James and Julia, the Limon couple who had attended an organizing meeting because they once had Mennonite neighbors they liked well.

Theresa Sutton, an unmarried middle-aged woman who took in sewing and who had mended two of Jake's shirts.

And Albert, Mary, and Little Abe Miller.

When the family of three slipped in the door just before Jake's opening prayer, Willem forgot to blink as he watched them settle. Little Abe, still several months shy of two, was born on the

Colorado plain and could not have any memory of a church service, let alone the self-discipline Amish children learned about sitting still during ponderous twelve-stanza hymns and two sermons. The seating arrangement was informal. Albert and Mary tucked their son between them on a small sofa and both kept a hand on one knee. Gratitude for their presence tingled out of the pores of Willem's skin.

He was not the only one, not the only Amish to accept Jake's invitation.

What Abbie would think when she heard what her friends had done Willem hated to consider. Abruptly aware that he was staring at the Millers, he moved his eyes to Jake. A holy hush fluttered through the room as Jake prayed.

Willem began a hymn. Within a few notes everyone but Little Abe was singing. *Where shall I go? I am so ignorant. Only to God can I go, because God alone will be my helper. I trust in You, God, in all my distress.* The small boy forgot his squirming and put one finger in his mouth while he watched the phenomenon. When Willem paused to breathe between phrases, he smiled at Abraham, who buried his face in his mother's shoulder.

Jake stood up and opened his Bible. He took his text from Colossians 3 and gently reminded the assembly that they were God's children and called to clothe themselves with compassion, kindness, humility, meekness, patience, and forgiveness.

And love. Above all love.

Jake was a gracious preacher, Willem decided. His words, his posture, his tone of voice, the way he looked each person in the eye—he showed himself to be a shepherd who would leave no sheep out of the fold.

He would be everything Abbie could hope for in a minister. So much had changed in her life in the last few weeks. She needed what Jake could give as much as he did. He could ask her one more time. The worst that could happen was she would say no.

<hr />

Abbie sat up in bed and felt around the base of the candle for the box of matches. The first match lit on one strike, and she held its flame carefully against the wick until the candle caught. She had been in bed for two hours and unable to keep her eyes closed for more than half a minute at a time. Whether wide eyed in the dark or tight eyed in bursts of determination to sleep, her mind conjured the image of her quilt, its desperate squares yearning for completion and the unity of finding their formation with each other.

Outside Abbie's curtainless window, the moon was new and dark. The candle could not find even a shadow of light to cast against and only fluttered in the breeze her own movement caused as Abbie pushed back the bed covers and felt the cool wood beneath her bare feet. If she could not sleep and could not relax and could not even pray, she may as well get up and quilt even though it was the middle of the night. She picked up her candle and crept down the stairs into the kitchen. There she lit the lamp on the table and took her quilt from the laundry basket that had becomes its home.

Abbie spread the quilt and fingered the square she had thought of as belonging to the Weaver household. She had prayed so many hours for the trees of life of the other settler families. Now she wondered if she had failed to pray enough for her own.

"I'll be sorry to miss your wedding."

Abbie gasped and turned toward her mother's face still hidden in darkness. "*Mamm!* I thought you went to bed hours ago." Abbie moved the lamp to light Esther's form sitting upright in one of the few wooden chairs left in the front room.

Esther shook her head. "I never went up. Somehow I couldn't bring myself to waste my last night here sleeping. I've been listening to the coyotes."

Abbie held still for a moment and listened as well. "Why did you say that about my wedding?"

"Maybe it won't be Willem," Esther said. "But I hope there will be someone for you. I hate to think of leaving you here all alone."

Abbie smoothed a hand across Willem's finished square. "No, I don't think it will be Willem after all."

"I've been saving some blue yardage for your wedding dress. I always hoped we would make your dress together. I'll give it to you in the morning with a prayer that you will yet use it."

"Thank you, *Mamm*." Abbie's throat swelled in an instant, and she swallowed back the knot. "Do you really think I could be happy with someone else?"

"I think we all can choose to be happy by receiving God's blessing. I hope God will bless you, and I hope you will recognize it when He does."

Abbie stood, picked up her chair, and carried it to the space beside her mother. Sitting again, she leaned her head on Esther's shoulder and said, "I have something to tell you. I've made a decision."

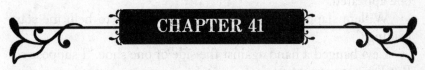

CHAPTER 41

Dawn pinked the Monday sky and slithered through the windows, but Willem was already awake, dressed, and ready to dispense with the morning chores. This was not a morning to be late. He downed the reheated coffee, collected the eggs, made the rounds in the barn, let the animals into the pasture, and hitched a team to the wagon. The weight his wagon would carry that day—in one direction—warranted the extra horse.

By the time he pulled into the Weaver farm, which had a quieted, desolate appearance, the sky was bright with October brilliance. The bottom trunk in the stack outside the front door sagged under the weight it bore, but the precision of the arrangement suggested Ananias's work. Perhaps the trunks had been outside all night awaiting conveyance to the train station in Limon. The door opened, and Levi came out and leaned against the pile to fidget with his shoes. Wearing them likely was an unaccustomed sensation for a child with toughened bare soles, but riding the train was not the same as running free on the farm. He would have to wear shoes all the way to Ohio, where it could already be cool enough that Levi would have to resign himself to shoes for the winter.

Abbie was next to emerge from the house. "*Gut mariye,* Willem. I didn't expect to see you."

"I offered to take your family to the train." Willem let himself down from the bench and approached the trunks. "Your *daed* agreed my wagon would accommodate the trunks and passengers more comfortably than your buggy."

261

"We would have managed."

She looked over his shoulder at nothing in particular, as if she did not want to meet his eyes.

"This must be a difficult day for you." Willem stepped into her line of sight. "It seemed only right for me to help."

Abbie wrapped her shawl around her shoulders more tightly and turned to look over her shoulder at the open door, though no one appeared.

Willem slapped a trunk. "Levi, do you want to help me start loading?"

Levi banged a hand against the side of one shoe. "I suppose so. But I'm not very strong."

"Even a small bit of help makes the job easier."

"You could wait for Daniel or Reuben." Abbie spoke but still looked away.

She knew he had been to the Mennonite service, Willem realized, and today she was bidding her family farewell. Still, her mood was off. There was something she did not want him to see in her face.

❧

At the train station, Abbie reached for Levi's hand, and to her relief he did not resist the gesture. He stood with her while Willem helped the rest of her family check their baggage with the porter.

"You're not going to love that *English* boy instead of me, are you?" Levi looked at his shoes as he asked the question.

"He's a sweet child," Abbie said, "but he is not my little *bruder*."

"I still wish you would come."

She stroked the back of his head now. He was getting so tall. "I know."

"You can visit. I'll ask *Daed* to send you the money for a train ticket."

Abbie doubted very much her father would consent to the request, but she held back from twisting Levi's earnest hope. "We can write letters."

"I won't know your address when you move."

"Silly. I'll send it to you."

"You don't know our address. We don't have one yet."

"*Mamm* will send it to me. And I know the addresses of our grandparents and all our aunts and uncles. They will always know where to find you."

Levi shrugged, unconvinced.

Abbie glanced at their family. Willem was shaking hands with them one at a time. *Mamm. Daed.* Daniel. Reuben. Then he hung back. Abbie realized she was holding her breath. She raised her eyes toward Pikes Peak, seeking a prayerful reminder of why she had chosen a path that would separate her from the people she could barely imagine living without.

What would happen if she watched the train pull away and changed her mind? She had a few chickens and Rudy's assurance he would keep her in milk and cheese. Louise would pay her in cash, but only twice a month.

She sniffed back the drip easing out of her nose as Esther opened her arms. When her mother's embrace closed around her, Abbie caught a sob before it left her chest. She kissed both her mother's cheeks and tasted the tears she had not seen. Daniel and Reuben nodded stiffly when she caught their eyes over Esther's shoulder.

Ananias shuffled toward her. "Abigail, I pray you find God's peace in your decision."

"*Danki, Daed.*" Thank you. She looked into his eyes and dared to hope.

Ananias put one hand to her cheek. "Good-bye, daughter."

He broke the gaze before Abbie could manage words again and pivoted toward the waiting train.

"Come, Levi. It's time to go."

Abbie constrained her emotions and watched her family file up the steps into the train. Glare on the wide windows of the passenger car sliced them from her sight as soon as the last one—her father—turned toward the bank of seats. Nevertheless, Abbie stood on the platform and waited for the whistle, followed by the roar of the engine devouring fuel and the thud of doors slamming shut as railroad employees secured one set after another. Finally the great wheels began to turn. Abbie's shoulders heaved in rhythm as the train gained steam and chugged out of the station.

She paused for a moment to compose herself before turning to face Willem. The moment would have been easier if others had come to see her family off, but she was fairly certain her father had spurned the notion of a fussy farewell. From the day he announced the family would leave, Ananias had been sparse with his social gestures and reluctant to allow distraction from his methodical march toward departure. Now she might not be able to hide the disappointment that shuddered through her from this man who knew her so well.

Abbie smelled the scent of Willem. He had left his discreet post and now stood behind her. She pivoted slowly.

"We should be on our way home." Abbie hoped Willem was not planning on errands.

"I'll take you right now."

She walked beside him to the wagon but declined his assistance getting up to the bench.

"Are you sure you want to go straight home?" Willem released the brake and raised the reins. "The house...well, it will seem empty, will it not?"

"I have to face it. There's no point putting it off."

"Abbie," he said, "if there's anything I can do to help, you know I will do it."

She craned her gaze away. "There's not much to manage. *Daed* disposed of nearly everything."

Willem nudged the team into the road.

"Are you really going to try to buy our land?" Abbie gripped the bench with both hands.

Willem waved the reins gently. "I'd like to buy some of it. The bank officers may not agree."

"*Gottes wille.*"

"Yes. God's will." He looked at her. "I don't want you to be angry with me."

"How can I be angry with God's will?"

"It will help your family if I can buy some of the acres. I would pay as fair a price as anyone."

Abbie pressed her lips together. Did he think she did not

understand that the price considered fair had dropped considerably in recent months?

"Abbie, something else is bothering you. We know each other too well for me not to notice."

She permitted herself a glance at his face but looked away quickly. Even her mother had promised not to tell her father of Abbie's decision until the train had crossed into Nebraska. Rudy deserved to hear the news that she would accept his proposal before Willem did.

"I've changed my mind," she said. "I'd like you to take me to Rudy's farm."

"Of course. We'll stop by there first. Then I'll make sure you get home all right."

"There's no need for you to wait for me."

"Abbie—"

"Please, Willem. Just take me to Rudy's."

"May I kiss you?" Rudy's face glowed in relief as he gripped both her hands.

Abbie nodded. Now that the moment had come, she wanted him to. His lips were dry, but softer than she had imagined lips so thin could be. He lingered only a few nervous seconds. Before he could pull back, Abbie leaned in with firmer pressure. Rudy's arms encircled her now. This is what the embrace of her husband would feel like, the man she would lie beside and rise beside.

"I was so sure you were going to turn me down," Rudy whispered into her ear. "I didn't even speak to your father."

"Then why did you ask me?"

"I had nothing to lose."

"Well, I didn't turn you down. So we'll have some plans to make."

He released her. "We'll do whatever you want to the house. I'll find a way. You'll see. This place can be a home."

"I know it can. It will be *our* home."

"Your family is gone. I hate to think of you alone in that house."

Abbie could not remember a time she had ever been alone in

the house for an entire night.

"When. . .how soon. . .?"

Rudy twisted his lips in calculation. "A month? We'll have to wait until the harvest is over in Ordway before we could hope a minister would come."

"Of course."

"Will you finish your quilt in time? Will it be ready to use as our wedding quilt?"

Abbie swallowed hard. When she started the quilt, she imagined it in Willem's house, not Rudy's. But she had nothing else to offer.

"It's almost finished," she said.

"Good. I don't want you to be discouraged because some families have left. I want you to look at your quilt and believe that more will come."

"You are very sweet, Rudy Stutzman."

He kissed her again.

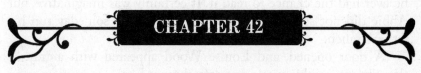

CHAPTER 42

"Can't we sit on the sun porch?" Eight-year-old Fin Wood's eyes pleaded with Abbie. "Just one more chapter?"

She nodded. "But you have to read aloud this time."

"I like listening to you read."

"I know, but we have to be sure you can read for yourself. We'll take turns with every paragraph. How would that be?"

Fin made a slow pivot and led her toward the sun porch. Once winter gusted in, the porch would be too cold. For now waning October days offered appeal. They settled in together on a brown wicker loveseat cushioned in a red-and-blue floral chintz. As she tucked her skirt, Abbie felt the smooth crispness of the fabric and noticed the bits of green and yellow at the edges of the flowers. Her fingers lingered on the curve of a broad leaf.

"Mama says this is her favorite place in the whole house," Fin said. "Mine, too."

"I can see why." The porch faced west, toward the mountains. The wide screens and the length of the porch gave a panoramic view of open ranch land.

Maybe this is what Willem wanted, Abbie thought. Acres and acres of possibility, but farm crops rather than cattle between the zigzag of fencing. She forced her mind to shift to Rudy, uncertain how she was going to break the habit of wondering about Willem.

She opened the book, *The Wonderful Wizard of Oz.* "Where did we leave off?"

"Toto!" Fin said.

"Oh yes." Abbie found the page and handed the book to Fin. He began to read, stumbling on a few words but easily gaining momentum. In her years at an *English* school, the Amish parents sought alternative assignments if they felt an *English* book was disparate from their educational goals. She read American history and biographies but never anything as fanciful as this book that enchanted Fin Wood—and would have enchanted Levi Weaver if he ever had the chance to read it. It certainly was imaginative, but Abbie did not see how it would prepare Fin to someday run his father's ranch.

A door opened, and Louise Wood appeared with a tray. "I thought you might enjoy some refreshment."

"Thank you." Abbie took the glass of lemonade that Louise offered.

"I haven't seen your friend Willem lately," Louise said. "I hope he is not unwell."

Abbie had not seen Willem in three days, not since he dropped her at Rudy's farm on Monday afternoon.

"I pray not," Abbie said. "I don't always see him often myself."

"Oh? I rather thought you two were sweet on each other." Louise handed her son a glass and set a plate of sugar cookies in front of him.

Abbie fought the blush creeping into her cheeks. "There was a time when we considered one another in that regard."

"Have you had a falling out?"

Abbie dodged the question. "I hope to always count Willem among my friends, but I have recently accepted the proposal of another man."

Louise smiled. "Of course a young woman as lovely as you would have suitors. I hope you will be very happy with your young man."

Abbie returned the smile. "We are quite compatible."

Fin pushed the book into Abbie's lap. "It's your turn to read."

Abbie waited for the stunned expression on Mary Miller's face to fade.

"I know you weren't expecting this," Abbie said. "Neither was I. But I know it's the right thing."

Mary shrugged. "It is the way of the Amish to keep courting private. Albert and I did not even drive home from singings together in Pennsylvania because we didn't want our families to speculate."

"How did you court, then?"

"We managed to find a few minutes here and there at a picnic or an auction." Mary stood on her porch and pulled her shawl snug. "In our old district the people came together all the time. I don't understand how you and Rudy courted, though. We don't even have church out here, much less singings or auctions."

Abbie tilted her head to think. She had not even thought they were courting. "It started with his calf, I suppose. We were both afraid she wouldn't make it. I fell into the habit of looking in on her when I stopped by with bread. More and more, Rudy was in the barn when I got there."

"So this is why you did not leave with your parents."

"Not really." Abbie rolled her bottom lip in but immediately pushed it out. She did not want Mary—or anyone—to think she harbored doubt. "I stayed behind because I wanted to remain with the community. I came to be a settler, and I mean to settle."

"Even if there is no community in the end?"

"The end of what, Mary? Does God's will have a timeline?" Abbie searched her friend's eyes for what she really meant.

"Come inside," Mary said. "I'll make tea."

Abbie waved off the suggestion. "Thank you, but don't go to the trouble. I've had a long day already."

"I heard about your position on the Wood ranch."

"It's just for a few weeks," Abbie said. "But I am tired, and Rudy is bringing me some milk and cheese before supper."

Mary's smile looked forced. "Another time, then. I pray you and Rudy will be as happy as Albert and I are."

Abbie shuffled to her buggy and watched as Mary called for Little Abe and herded him into the house. Too late she realized Mary had meant to tell her something over tea, and Abbie had been too distracted to listen.

❧❀❦

For three days Willem festered over Abbie's peculiar behavior on the day her parents departed. No matter how many times and how many ways he explained away her reticence toward him, he was not satisfied. At least once each day he marched to the barn resolved to saddle up his stallion and go make sure Abbie was all right. Every time, though, he put the tack back on the wall. She might not even be there because of her work schedule, and during the wagon ride home from the depot she had adamantly resisted offers of help ranging from subtle generalities to specific chores.

And going to the Mennonite church service—even though the Millers participated as well—had set his course away from her. At least that was her opinion, and it was pronounced enough that she would rather get her milk and eggs from Rudy Stutzman. She had managed to leave his bread that week without encountering Willem, even though he had not left the farm in three days. Willem had not expected she would treat him so cooly so quickly.

On Thursday afternoon, Willem decided to muck the stalls thoroughly, as if clearing soiled straw would also clear his mind. By the time he heard the sound of the approaching buggy, betrayed by snorting horses, Willem had worked up a sweat. He went outside to greet Moses Troyer.

"The news is good, *ya*?" Grinning, Moses jumped down from the bench.

"What news is that?" Willem used a sleeve to wipe the sweat from his forehead.

"The Weavers should have stayed a few weeks longer. It's a shame they will miss their daughter's wedding."

Willem cleared his throat, puzzled but determined to remain calm. "I had not heard the news."

"That sneaky Rudy Stutzman!" Moses wagged his head. "I just came from there. Who would have known he was courting Abigail Weaver?"

Yes, Willem thought. *Who would have known?*

"We all knew she was spunky," Moses said, "but I was shocked that Ananias would let her remain here once he decided to go."

"I guess they worked it out." Willem reached for the rake he had left leaning against the side of the barn.

"I suppose Ananias was determined to move before winter. Why else would they miss her wedding?"

Willem shrugged. Why indeed?

"I always thought it would be you," Moses said. His face sobered. "But considering how her father feels about the salvation of anyone outside the Amish church, I suppose I should not be surprised. She could hardly marry you and set the two of you against each other."

"I thought you had an open mind on that question, Moses." Willem twirled the rake between his hands.

"I do. It's Ananias who doesn't."

The knock, though not insistent, jolted Abbie out of a doze she had not meant to fall into. For a moment she listened for the footsteps of her mother or little brother on the way to answer the door. Standing up, she raised a hand to the back of her neck to rub the spot where it had gone stiff while she slept with her chin on her chest in an upright chair.

"Coming!" she called, unsure how long she had slept. It must be Rudy with the eggs and milk. She snatched her prayer *kapp* from the side table and put it on her head before she reached the door.

He stood there with downcast face and wounded pools of murky green where his eyes should have been.

"Willem."

"I wish you had been the one to tell me, Abbie."

Abbie stepped outside. "I'm sorry." Her murmured statement was more than words.

"I would have understood."

"Would you?" She challenged his gaze. "You wanted me to go to the Mennonites with you. You went even when you knew I couldn't. Wouldn't. Would never."

"Never is a long time, Abigail."

She straightened her shoulders. "Don't scold me. You have no right."

"I gave that up." Willem shifted his feet in the dirt. "I didn't realize your growing affection for Rudy."

"I did not realize it myself until recently. But I have found myself in the position of having to make several decisions I never expected to make, and I have no regrets."

Willem stepped away from her. "I know what it will mean to you to be married in the Amish church. I wish you every happiness."

"*Danki.*"

She covered her mouth with the back of her hand and she watched him stride away from her and mount his horse. The moment had come to truly find release from his hold on her heart.

CHAPTER 43

The sight of him made Abbie smile.

Rudy, not Willem. Rudy made her smile.

When she drove gently onto his land on Friday morning, he was on a ladder scrubbing the outside of the window at the front of the house. She had cleaned the inside of the glass more times than she could count in an effort to keep the dust blowing in from the plain from coating every inch of interior surface, but cleaning the outside was not part of her housekeeping duties, and Rudy had never raised a sponge. When she asked him about it once, he said he saw no gain from the chore. The wind would only blow dry soil against the panes before the day was over, and most of the hours he spent inside the house were after the sun was low enough in the sky that he had no reason to look out the windows. Yet here he was, scrubbing glass.

From the fourth rung, he dropped his sponge in the bucket at the foot of the ladder and grinned.

"Why, Rudy Stutzman, what has come over you?" Abbie let the reins go lax.

He climbed down and came to stand beside the buggy. "I won't be a bachelor much longer. Figured it was time I learn to behave like a man who cares what pleases a woman."

Sentiment filled her throat, making her words hoarse. "I would never ask you to change anything about yourself."

"You didn't. But a man can decide." He offered her a hand to help her out of the buggy.

She reached under the bench. "I found a jar of cherries *Mamm* left behind and made a pie. It's still warm."

When he took it from her, he cradled her hands along with the pie plate. The tingle that started in her fingers and flowed up her arms startled her.

"I don't think *Ordnung* forbids having pie in the middle of the morning."

How had she never noticed the twinkle in his blue eyes before? Or the depth of the dimple that would be covered with a red beard once they were married?

"With *kaffi*?" she asked.

"If you like." Rudy gestured toward the door. "Come and see what I've done inside. I will start the *kaffi*."

"You've done something inside?" Abbie felt like a curious schoolgirl and spurted ahead of Rudy.

Behind her, he chuckled. She turned her head and smiled at him over her shoulder. Only five days ago her mother had urged her to recognize blessing when it came. Now she did.

Mailing a single letter seemed like a feeble excuse to go into Limon. It was possible Willem would find something of interest in the mercantile, but less likely that he would decide to part with cash for the purchase. Determination to come up with a credible down payment for additional acres magnified his sense of stewardship. Every dollar mattered.

And so did the letter. It might be his best hope. When he left Ohio, Willem's father gave him the value of his share of the family farm. They both knew the money would go further in Colorado than Pennsylvania. Willem never asked for another penny—until now. He proposed a business arrangement—a loan, not a gift. He would even include his father on the title of the new land if that was what would satisfy either the senior Peters or the bank officer. And since he did not know when a specific need would draw him to Limon again, Willem chose to make the trip just to mail a letter.

Outside the post office, he tied his horse to a hitch and fingered the envelope. The laboriously crafted words ran through his mind.

It took him three drafts before he felt secure that he did not sound alarming or in need. The matter was one of timing and opportunity.

"Hello, Willem." Jake approached. "What brings you into town?"

Willem tapped the letter against an open palm. "A letter home."

"I'm sure your folks will be glad to hear from you."

Willem nodded and glanced at the post office.

"Something wrong, Willem?"

"Wrong? No. Why do you ask?"

"You seem distracted. Do you have regrets about attending the service last Sunday?"

"Of course not. I was grateful to be included."

"I heard about Abbie and Rudy," Jake said softly.

"I knew how she felt about your church."

"Still."

Willem scratched one ear. "I'd better mail my letter. Then I'm going to ask around about odd jobs. Maybe somebody needs help getting ready for the winter."

Jake brightened. "The Melton Wood ranch does. I just heard this morning that they lost one of their ranch hands."

Willem shook his head. "Abbie is working for them."

"I know. But you'd be out on the ranch, not in the house. It couldn't hurt to inquire."

"I can paint," Rudy said. "Fresh white walls. You would like that, wouldn't you?"

"You don't have to do that, Rudy." Abbie scraped up the last bit of pie from her plate.

"But you would like it, wouldn't you?" Rudy watched her face for the slightest light of pleasure.

She broke down and smiled. "Yes, I suppose I would."

"Then I'll do it. Next time I go into town I'll order the paint."

"You don't have to do all this, Rudy." Abbie reached across the table and took his hand. "We agreed we would get married without a lot of fuss. A simple start."

Rudy downed the last of the coffee in his cup. "And we will. I don't see how a clean coat of paint will complicate anything."

He did not tell her that he had started a list of what he wanted to do to make his house, which could barely be construed as a cabin, into a home. He would have to do something about the sagging, creaking bed, for instance, but it would be unseemly to speak of that. And she deserved to have matching shelves on the kitchen wall spacious enough to hold more than a dented stockpot and the one iron skillet he owned. The sale of a cow or two would provide some cash for immediate needs and perhaps allow him to hire someone to make drawings for expanding the cabin. He should have spoken up sooner. He should have risked telling her how he felt or asked her how matters stood between her and Willem. Now he would never know if she might have accepted him without first finding herself in the confusing circumstances of her parents' abandonment of the settlement.

But he had not. And it did not matter, because he would do his best to make sure that Abbie never found reason to regret her decision to marry him. She might not love him the same way she loved Willem—or at least had loved Willem—but the blessing of her affection in any form was more than he deserved.

He wondered what his own face would look like once a full grown beard covered it to indicate his married status. A year from now there could be a baby on the way. Rudy hoped all their children would have Abbie's gentle features.

The only thing missing was a church to raise their children in. The Chupps. Eber and Ruthanna. The Weavers. All gone from the community's midst. Willem was as good as gone to the Mennonites. Rudy and Abbie would have to lean on the Lord to see them through the years without church. Even as Rudy told himself that God was faithful and gracious in His will, he yearned to sit on a bench in a room full of men and women who shared his desire for worship.

❧❧❧

Willem shook Melton Wood's hand on the wide porch of the Wood house. "I appreciate your seeing me so quickly."

"No point in wasting time," Melton said. "I need a hand. If you're serious about wanting the work, I'm happy to take you on.

You did a good job digging coal for us."

"How soon would you want me to start?" Willem tilted his head and scratched behind his ear.

"Let's see." Melton looked up at the overhang shading them. "This is Thursday afternoon. I think Monday will be soon enough. How is that for you?"

Willem nodded. "That would work well. I have to confess I've never worked on a ranch before."

"But you're a farmer," Melton said. "I need somebody to help me look after the fences."

"I can fix fences," Willem said.

"I have no doubt." Melton's tanned face scrunched as he narrowed his eyes. "I meant to do a lot of repairs over the summer that I never seemed to get to. Too many sick animals to tend to. Then last week a half-dozen head wandered off of my land through a break in the barbed wire, so the matter has become more urgent. It's expensive to lose cattle just when you have them fattened up for market. I was lucky to recover them."

"I'm only too happy to help with anything that needs doing."

"You haven't even asked what the job pays." Melton's mouth turned up.

Willem scratched behind his ear. "I trust you to be fair."

"Most of the hands live on the ranch as a good part of their pay, but I'm sure we can come to an agreement that is fair to everyone. You can take your meals here if you like. My foreman will pay you in cash twice a month."

"Do you mind if I ride around this afternoon and get a better idea of the layout of the ranch?"

"Not at all. It's not a large property as ranches go, but you should still be careful not to wander so far that you can't get home to look after your own animals."

Willem extended his hand again. "I won't disappoint you."

"I wouldn't take you on if I thought you might." Melton shook Willem's hand. "I'll walk you back to your horse."

As they walked down the steps and into the open yard, Willem glanced around in involuntary speculation about where Abbie spent her time when she was here.

I'll copy the letter over so it's not so messy." Abbie smoothed the corner of the page she had crumpled while she wrote at Rudy's table on Monday morning. They had selected the minister in Ordway they thought would be most able to get away for a trip that was likely to take four days even if the minister did not stay for a visit with the Amish families. Abbie did not expect that he would, given that no one had come even to preach in such a long time.

"Why don't you read it back just to be sure we've thought of everything?" Rudy straightened his chair up against the edge of the table.

Abbie cleared her throat.

> *We greet you in the faith that binds us together.*
>
> *We are Rudy Stutzman and Abigail Weaver of the Elbert County settlement. God's will has become plain to us, and we rejoice that God leads our hearts to be wed. Our hope is to speak our vows before the end of November. We are writing to you because we could not see ourselves as truly married in the eyes of God if we could not be married in the Amish church we both love so dearly.*
>
> *Following the custom of our people, we know the harvest must be in before we turn to our celebration. As you know, the drought in our county has pressed our labors from every side. Our farms have yielded little to harvest, but we share your joy*

that Ordway's crops have been abundant. We pray God blesses your family through His gracious provision in these busy weeks.

May we ask you to pray about whether God might lead you to come to Elbert County to lead our wedding service? Being married here, among the families who share our settlement and our future congregation, is the desire of our hearts.

We implore you in the name of Christ to consider this ministry to our shared people.

Abbie looked up. "You don't think it sounds too strong?"

Rudy twisted his lips in thought. "Maybe we should offer to travel to Ordway after all."

"Are you having second thoughts?"

"Would it not be satisfying to be married in an established congregation?"

"But they would not be *our* congregation," Abbie said. "Who would want to come if they don't even know us? I don't want our families here to think we are turning our backs on them at one of the most important moments of our lives."

"Of course you are right." Rudy's volume dropped.

Abbie studied his face. "I don't want to be right, Rudy. I want us to be of one mind."

He patted her hand. "We are. We'll send the letter just as it is."

"It will only take me a few minutes to copy it fresh," she said. "We should both sign it, don't you think?"

"Yes, let's do that. I'll pour some more *kaffi*."

Abbie watched his movements as he stood, turned to the stove, and reached for the pot. They had talked about these questions several times in the week since she accepted his proposal. Why had he chosen this moment, when they were writing such an important letter, to sound uncertain?

He was in one of his funks, she decided as she copied in a firm hand the words they had chosen carefully. One of his moods. It would pass. She would have to get used to them and learn to respond with patient words—or patient silence.

When she finished writing, she handed Rudy the pen. "I think the husband's signature should come first."

He scratched his name onto the paper and returned the pen. "Do you still plan to mail the letter yourself?"

"When I go to work I'll be halfway to the post office in Limon," she said. "But if you would rather take it—"

"No. Your suggestion is sensible. You take it."

❧❧❧

Abbie gave Fin Wood a stern look. "You heard your mother. It's time for your rest."

"All I do is rest." Fin slumped in his chair and crossed his arms. "We didn't do anything."

"We played four games of checkers, cleaned the bottom of the bird cage, and read thirty-six pages in *The Wonderful Wizard of Oz*. I'd hardly say that's nothing." Abbie wondered what Levi was finding to complain about these days. "If you don't rest in the afternoons, the doctor might send you back to bed."

"I can't make myself be tired when I'm not." Fin scowled.

"You might find you are tired if you just close your eyes for a while."

"I want to feed the new calf."

She wagged a finger at him. "You know your parents don't want you to leave the house yet."

"When?"

Abbie softened. "As soon as your parents give permission, I promise our first outing will be to the barn."

"When are you coming back?"

"Tomorrow, first thing."

"Promise?"

"Promise." Abbie stood up and gathered her things. The letter to the Ordway minister lay in the folds of her shawl. She had not been willing to leave it in the buggy out of her sight. "I'll tuck you in before I go."

Despite his protests, a few minutes later Fin dropped off, and Abbie padded out of his room. She stopped in the kitchen to let Louise know she was leaving and then went out the front door.

The stallion tied up outside the barn caused her to look twice. Yes, the ears were right, and the spot on the left flank. It was

Willem's horse. Abbie did not know what his business was on the Wood ranch, but she scanned the open area around the house and hoped to get her buggy turned around before stallion and rider were paired again. She whistled for her horse in a nearby pen—and then slammed a hand over her mouth in regret.

Abbie dashed to the mare and tried to urge it through the gate. Too late.

Willem came around the corner of an outbuilding. "I thought I recognized that whistle."

"Hello, Willem." Abbie slowed her pace. It would seem rude to hurry now. "I'm surprised to see you here."

"I'm working for Mr. Wood today."

"I thought you finished digging his lignite long ago." Abbie patted her horse's neck to keep her hands busy.

"I did. I'm going to fix fences for a while, and then we'll see what else needs to be done."

"I see." He was after money, no doubt so he could buy the Weaver farm.

"I was hoping I would run into you," Willem said.

"Willem, I'm going to marry Rudy. There's nothing to talk about." She picked at the harness.

"Abbie, listen. I have something to tell you."

She said nothing and did not look at him.

"The Yutzys have decided to leave," he said.

Her eyes shot up at him. "What?"

"I only heard about it on Saturday. The bank is about to repossess their land. They have no hope of catching up on their loan."

Pain sliced through Abbie's middle like a blacksmith's fired chisel. Willem caught her elbow.

"I knew how you would feel," he said. "I wanted you to hear it from me before the rumors start flying."

"I suppose you're going to try to buy their farm, too." She shook off his touch. "Don't think I can't figure out why you want to work here."

His face fell.

"I'm sorry." Abbie composed herself. "That was an awful thing to say, especially after you found this position for me when I needed it. Please forgive me."

"Of course I forgive you. I'm sure the news about the Yutzys is upsetting."

"It's no excuse. Let me make amends. Do you need anything from Limon? Since I'm halfway there I'm going in to mail a letter." And then she would be up half the night baking the bread she would deliver to Willem, Rudy, and Martin Samuels on Wednesday as usual. She could not give a whole day to baking now. Two evenings would have to suffice.

"Thank you, no," Willem said. "If you're writing your parents, perhaps it is not too late to send my greetings along with yours."

"Rudy and I wrote to Ordway," she said, looking away again. "To the bishop."

≈≈≈

While the loaves were rising and the oven warmed, Abbie spread out the quilt on the floor of the front room. Her father had not left much furniture, so she had plenty of space. With a pair of scissors in one hand and a lamp in another, Abbie crawled around the edges of the quilt to be sure the binding was securely stitched and to trim off excess threads that caught her eye. When she had been around the entire perimeter, she sat back on her heels. Considering that she had made the entire quilt without benefit of a frame, she was pleased with the result.

Other than its physical appearance, the quilt was nothing Abbie had expected it to be. It had twelve blocks because the settlement had begun with twelve households. With the imminent departure of the Yutzys, and including Willem's departure to the Mennonites, five of the twelve would be gone. Every household had contributed at least a few patches of fabric to this quilt, and as she stitched the triangles together she prayed for God's clear blessing. She had chosen a tree of life pattern because she wanted each family to blossom and grow in faith and prosperity. Instead, one by one, the families felt the weight of discouragement that reshaped their vision. Branches bent and broke.

This quilt was supposed to cover the bed she would share with Willem. Though Abbie had been forced to abandon that expectation weeks ago, she had not reoriented to the image of this quilt covering Rudy's bed. But what else did she have?

The quilt could still carry meaning. It could still represent a fresh start, a growing faith. In addition to praying for the families that left, Abbie could pray for the unknown families who would come. She could pray for a marriage she had not expected but nevertheless welcomed. She could pray for the safety and security of God's will.

Smelling the yeasty fragrance of the burgeoning bread dough, Abbie got up to put the first batch in the oven.

CHAPTER 45

The sleepless night persuaded Rudy.

Perhaps it was the bed and knowing, when he let himself reach down inside himself, that he could not ask Abbie to sleep on it. But her father had sold the family's beds, and Abbie was sleeping on a narrow cot. Between them they did not even have a decent bed.

Or perhaps it was the news that the Yutzys were giving up. Rudy had spoken to Isaiah himself, and he had not even tried to say that since his farm had failed it must be God's will for them to move somewhere else. He just said he was giving up. Too discouraged to keep trying. Another square of Abbie's quilt would wilt before it blossomed.

Or it might have been the approaching Sunday, the second Sabbath in November, and so many weeks without a worship service that Rudy had lost count. He had been right, those months ago, when he sat in the barn with all the other men and prodded the council to speak forthrightly about why the settlement still had no minister of its own. If he had been successful, instead of letting himself be silenced or influenced by Willem's unflustered demeanor, the Amish households might have found the spiritual unity that seemed beyond their grasp. Noah Chupp might have stayed. Rudy and Abbie might have taken a buggy down the road to their own minister to speak in person, rather than labor over words that might still be misunderstood. They could have heard their banns read in their own congregation. Now even if a minister came from Ordway, would the banns would be read at all? Who was there to hear them?

He lay in bed, awake, with his eyes closed and picturing the fullness of his home congregation shoulder to shoulder on the benches, the mothers with babies on their laps and small boys beaming their delight at being old enough to sit with the men. He heard the robust harmonies of the hymns, smelled the hams baking in the kitchen, watched for a glimpse out the window of the horses gathered in their own circles in the pasture with tails swishing.

Rudy missed going to church.

He did not have to open his eyes to know that dawn was no imminent promise, but he rolled over and lit the lamp. If he did not put his thoughts on paper before the morning milking, they would torment him all day.

❧

Abbie was grateful for Saturday. Louise Wood did not expect her on Saturdays, and Abbie was certain Mary Miller would welcome a leisurely visit. While it was still warm, Abbie wrapped up a small cake she had baked as a treat for Little Abe. Louise had given her a basket of apples, and Abbie put half in a sack to take to Mary, who made the best *schnitzboi* of anyone Abbie knew. They might even work on baking together while they talked about Abbie's wedding plans. Abbie planned to cut out the pieces of her blue wedding dress that evening and begin spending her evenings stitching them together.

Abbie put the cake and apples in the buggy and slid her arms into the sleeves of a thick sweater. If it were not for the devastation the incinerating summer had wreaked on crops, the blistering days would have seemed a distant memory, a harmless turning of the seasons. She shook off the thought, determined not to let even the departure of the Yutzys dampen her wedding preparations. With her mother and Ruthanna gone, Mary was Abbie's closest friend in the settlement.

The horse established a steady trot, and Abbie's work at the reins was easy. The distance between the farms closed while she daydreamed, and Abbie nearly missed the turnoff. A last-minute tug turned the horse toward the Miller home.

Abbie tied the reins loosely over around a post and fished out the cake and apples from under the bench. She knocked on the door, listening for Mary's cheery "Come in" or Little Abe's giggle.

Instead, Mary came to the door and stood in its frame.

"Good morning." Abbie started to step up into the house, but Mary did not back away from the door in welcome.

"Hello, Abbie."

Abbie lifted the cake in one hand and the apples in the other. "A treat for Little Abe and something for your *schnitzboi.*"

"You shouldn't have bothered."

Mary's voice sounded distracted.

"It's no bother," Abbie said. "Is everything all right?"

"Abraham is not feeling well," Mary said.

"Nothing serious, I hope." Still holding her gifts, Abbie tried to look past Mary into the house.

"I'm sure it is not." Mary took the food into her own arms. "You know how little children are. He is too excitable. I think he just needs a quiet day."

Abbie nodded. "I promise not to play rough with him."

"Forgive me, Abbie, but I think it is better if we don't have company today."

Abbie blinked. She had not thought of herself as company at Mary's house, but easy friends who looked forward to breaking up their own isolation. "Can I help you with anything?"

"Thank you, but no. I'm just going to keep Little Abe in and quiet today. Thank you for the food."

"Of course."

Mary closed the door.

A moment later, Abbie was back in her buggy hating the thought that she had offended Mary and did not know what she had done. There seemed to be nothing to do but go home—or to Rudy's. Surely he would be happy to see her.

Willem walked along the tracks behind the depot in Limon, wondering why he had not seen the obvious before this. Most of the people who lived within the city limits of Limon had some connection to the Union Pacific or the Rock Island Railroad. The rail companies had tracks that crossed in Limon, and freight cars and passengers cars had to be coupled and uncoupled day and night. Baggage handlers loaded and unloaded trunks and crates. Willem was as strong as any man. If he started on the Wood ranch early in the morning, he could still offer a few hours a day to one of the railroads and get home to his animals before the milk cows got desperate. He could save enough for his down payment even more quickly. It was worth an inquiry as soon as his work at the ranch settled into a routine.

He turned up the collar of his jacket. The early November Saturday harbored a threat of winter Willem had not detected before now. A graying sky, a temperature reluctant to warm appreciably since sunrise, and a wind hopping from one ridge to another across the plain carried reminders of the change in seasons. Willem did not see how winter could be more harsh than summer had been this year.

He walked the blocks toward Main Street, where he had left his wagon to be loaded with several rolls of barbed-wire fencing. He would take advantage of the opportunity to check for mail. If he could predict his mother's rhythm accurately, he was due for a letter.

The postmaster looked at him as soon as Willem entered the building. "I've got two for you this week."

"I'll be glad to have them."

The postmaster rummaged through a cubbyhole and handed the contents to Willem. "Are you still collecting mail for the Weaver farm? I have you on file as authorized, but my understanding is they've left town."

"Their daughter stayed behind."

"Ah. Then I suppose there is no harm in giving you the mail addressed to them. It's just one letter, actually, and it's addressed to the daughter."

The return address flashed through Willem's mind before he

saw it, but it was too late to withdraw his open hand.

Ordway.

Abbie would be anxious for this letter. And he was heading back to the Wood ranch where she was working with Fin today.

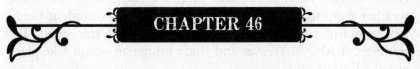

CHAPTER 46

Louise Wood glided into the sitting room, where Fin was teaching Abbie to play chess. Relieved to have a reason to interrupt the puzzle of the boy's explanations for how players were permitted to move the various pieces, Abbie looked up and smiled at Louise.

"Mr. Peters just came from town," Louise said. "He asked me to give you this letter."

Abbie's eyes widened when she saw the return address in block letters. "The bishop!"

"The bishop can only move on the diagonal," Fin said.

"I don't think that's the bishop Abbie means." Louise's eyes sparkled when she turned up the corners of her mouth.

Abbie turned the envelope at a right angle and back again. "Thank you. I'll just put it with my bag." She stood up.

"Fin," Louise said, "why don't you come in the kitchen and help me fix some tea?" She winked at Abbie as she reached to take Fin's hand.

"But it's almost lunchtime," Fin said.

"Then we'll see what we can find for lunch."

"When can I eat with the ranch hands again?"

"Not yet."

Louise and Fin turned the corner into the hall. Abbie immediately slid a fingernail under the flap to break the seal. If the news were bad, she might regret opening the letter while she was supposed to be working. But she hoped the news was good, and she did not want

291

to waste a minute wondering about it and not knowing.

Abbie unfolded the plain white paper and held it along the sides. Scanning just the first few lines allowed her to let out her breath. He was willing to marry them.

She started again and read more carefully. He was happy to consecrate their marriage, but he preferred a date in the middle of December rather than the end of November because of previous commitments. He was mindful of the added risk of inclement weather that might impede his travel, but he was confident God's will would of course be plain in the events that transpired. The wedding of Abigail Weaver and Rudy Stutzman would take place as quickly as possible.

He said yes.

The bishop was coming.

With Fin leading the way with a bowl between his hands, Louise carried in a tray of cheese, ham, and bread. As she set it down on the table beside the chess set, she raised an eyebrow.

Abbie grinned.

"Let's eat lunch, Fin," Louise said. "Then I believe Abbie has a matter she needs to take care of this afternoon."

Abbie's buggy clattered into Rudy's barnyard. She did not wait for a full stop before leaping down in two steps and leaving the reins lax. Chickens in the pen pecked at the ground outside the coop just as they always did, some of them clacking at the disturbance Abbie's arrival brought. Eight cows—no, nine, counting the calf—grazed in the pasture as they always did. The new calf, fully weaned, was with the others. The horses—all but one—meandered on the other side of the field. The trough outside the barn was full of water.

"Rudy!" Abbie clutched the bishop's letter and spun in a circle looking for some indication of Rudy's whereabouts. "Rudy!"

She looked first in the barn, where it was obvious Rudy had mucked and laid down clean straw. With no animals in the barn, he had even left the door open. Fresh air gusted in behind Abbie as she looked in every stall.

Next she let herself into the chicken pen to make sure he was not cleaning there. The day's eggs had been removed, but Rudy left no other sign of recent presence.

She ducked a head into an outbuilding where he kept a plow and a few other large farm tools, but it was dark and dusty.

"Rudy!" She called louder this time. "The letter came!"

She strode to the house, knocked sharply, and entered. Rudy had cleaned up since Saturday. Their visit had been brief. Rudy claimed a headache, making Abbie wonder if Little Abe and Rudy shared an illness and giving her hope that Mary Miller had not been avoiding her after all.

The kitchen wall had been scrubbed down since then, and the scrap bucket emptied—probably what the chickens were pecking at. The bed was tidied, and both chairs were tucked under the table at precise angles. The floor had been swept so recently that it bore not even a faint layer of dust. Abbie smiled. She appreciated the effort he was making, but she would make sure he understood that she did not mind doing the housework. After all, she had been keeping house for him for a long time already. Nevertheless, it was nice to know he would not start their marriage taking her for granted.

Abbie lit the stove and pulled the coffee canister off the shelf. She might as well have a cup while she waited for Rudy. If he was out in one of the fields, he would not be long, since he had no harvest. When the coffee was ready, she filled a mug, chose the chair facing the front door, and sipped at regular intervals.

The afternoon descended into early darkness. Every time Abbie thought she might as well go home and save the joyous news for tomorrow, she believed surely he would step through the door at any moment. The cows would need milking, for one thing. A man dedicated to building a dairy business would not put his cows at risk.

She lit a lamp and foraged in his food bins. When he came through the door, she would greet him with a meal. Before long she had a potpie of green beans and potatoes in the oven.

The darkness deepened, and the howl of a coyote pierced her solitude. Rudy would never leave the calf in the pasture exposed to the coyotes. Abbie pulled the lantern with the sturdy handle off a shelf and transferred flame. She had to get the cows in.

And milked.

She knew how to milk a cow, of course. And she was fairly certain she knew Rudy's system for caring for the milk until he could distribute it in the morning or churn it into butter or cheese. The truth was, though, that her family had never had more than two cows, and her brothers had taken on the milking as soon as they were old enough. Even Levi had milking duties. While she assumed she would learn to help Rudy with the milk after they married, she never had before this.

Where was Rudy?

For the first time in this interminable afternoon, Abbie was frightened. She tightened her sweater around her midsection and carried the lantern out to the pasture. Wherever he had gone, Rudy had taken one horse, but riding without a wagon he would have nowhere to hang a light when he came home in the dark.

By the time Abbie finished the milking—which she was sure took her far longer than it would have any of her brothers, including Levi—and got all the animals settled in safety for the night, Abbie's nascent fear had multiplied into terror for Rudy's well-being. The meal in the oven dried out beyond consumption, and Abbie made another pot of coffee to drink while she sat upright at the table the entire night. She regretted now that she had let the daylight seep away while she sat cheerfully expecting Rudy to walk through the door when she could have been out riding through his fields as the first step in making sure he had not fallen ill or into harm.

She had milked the cows later than they were used to, and now she would rush the next interval by disturbing them before dawn. As soon as daylight broke, she intended to be looking for Rudy. She tended to all the animals and left them in the coop and the barn when she struck out on her search. Before the sun had transformed from pink threads to bright orange, Abbie was certain Rudy was not on the farm.

Her heart thudded against her chest wall as Abbie admitted she would have to seek help. She rode to the Millers' and interrupted their breakfast.

"Have you seen Rudy?" she asked a surprised Albert at the door.

"Today?" he asked.

"Or yesterday." Abbie's brain muttered a scrambled prayer. *Please, God, let Rudy be all right.*

"What's wrong, Abbie?"

"I'm not certain anything is wrong." Yes, she was. "When did you see him last?"

Albert shrugged. "Last week."

The weight in Abbie's stomach threatened to explode. "If he drops by today, will you let him know I was looking for him?"

"Of course. But I don't expect him."

Abbie got back in her buggy and gauged the sky. It was still very early. She had several hours before Fin Wood would be watching out the window for her arrival. *God, show me what to do.*

She was going to have to ask Willem. It only made sense. Other than the Millers, Willem's farm was the nearest. She took a deep breath, steeled herself, and drove the buggy back out to the main road.

The fluster of activity in his coop told her he was collecting eggs. Even Levi could do a more deft job of getting the eggs without upsetting the hens. Abbie pulled up beside the coop.

❧❦❧

Willem had never seen Abbie so pale. Urgency coursed through him. "What's wrong?"

"Have you seen Rudy?"

"I'm. . .keeping my distance," Willem said. "I don't want to complicate matters."

"It's not that." Abbie twisted the reins around her hand. "I can't find him. I waited for him all day and all night at his farm, and he never came home."

"But the animals—"

"I did what I could. The animals are fine for now." Abbie's voice cracked. "I've been all over his farm, and over to the Millers'."

"What about his deliveries?"

"I can't think about that. Besides, I don't know who all his customers are."

"I meant, maybe he mentioned something to someone."

"I wouldn't know where to start, Willem. But something is very wrong."

Willem set the bowl of eggs he was holding on the ground and brushed his hands against his trousers. "What about the *English* authorities?"

Her eyes clouded. "So you agree something is wrong."

He wanted to reach up to the bench where she sat to stroke her cheek and reassure her. Instead, he slipped his fingers in the horse's bridle. "You're not a hysterical woman, Abbie. If you feel something is wrong, then something is wrong."

"What can the *English* authorities do?"

"Make inquiries. Try to determine what he has been doing the last couple of days. If you could find Rudy's account books, they could start with his dairy customers."

He saw the tremble in her nod.

"I think I know where to look," she said.

"Come inside and wash your face," he said. "Pin up your hair. We'll find it and then go into Limon together."

Abbie wanted to know the minute Rudy returned. He *would* return. She would not allow herself to consider another answer to his disappearance.

The police officer in Limon, Mr. Shelton, was too calm. He took down the information Abbie provided, including the list of Rudy's dairy customers, and promised he would let her know when he had some information.

How long would it take? she wanted to know. What did he plan to do? Who was he going to talk to? How soon would he start? She explained where she lived, where Rudy lived, where she worked. Would he promise to send a man out to find her as soon as they knew anything at all? The most the officer did was arch an eyebrow and write a few more words on his form.

Willem had to take her by the elbow and guide her out of the police station before she heard any satisfying answers. Somehow she managed her hours with Fin, though he expressed exasperation at her lack of progress in understanding the rules of chess. Because she had ridden in with Willem that morning, she had to wait for him to return from the far reaches of the ranch. She said good-bye to Fin when it was time for his afternoon rest, telling herself she would go outside and walk off her nervous energy. In the end, she stayed near the house. If she roamed the ranch, how would an *English* officer know where to find her?

Willem drove her home, though the buggy was hers.

"I want to wait at Rudy's," she said when Willem started to

turn onto the Weaver land. "If. . .*when* he comes home, that's where he will come."

Willem redirected the horse. "I'll do the milking."

"I can manage."

"But you don't have to."

While Abbie worked alongside Willem, he was three times as fast at every task.

"In the morning," he said as they finished the last cow, "we'll have to find some use for some of the excess milk or pour it out."

"Seems a shame to waste it," she said.

"We both have jobs," he reminded her. "Neither of us has time to try to find Rudy's customers or churn butter. We should focus on keeping the cows producing."

"You're right." Whatever had happened to Rudy, he deserved to come home to healthy animals.

"I'll be back in the morning."

"You don't have to do that. I'll manage." Abbie rinsed her hands in the trough outside the barn and turned to his expectant face.

He met her gaze and moistened his lips. "The turn in your relationship with Rudy surprised me. I'll admit that. But it doesn't mean I don't care about him. Or you."

She swallowed without speaking.

"I'll ride one of Rudy's horses home for the night and be back in the morning in time to milk."

⚜

"Let's play chess again." Fin made a face at Abbie the next morning. "You don't seem to be learning the rules very well."

She forced a smile. How could she explain to a housebound eight-year-old that two sleepless nights and a missing fiancé meant she had no mental energy for absorbing the rules of chess?

"We should read today," she said. "Your mother is particularly concerned that you not fall behind in school." Fin's reading had improved enough that he might not notice she was not listening carefully.

"I don't want to do math," he said.

"We won't today." The last thing Abbie's brain wanted to do

were the multiplication tables. "Your mother suggested that we read *Around the World in Eighty Days*. It might be an interesting way to learn some geography."

Fin turned around in a dramatic fashion. "I know where the book is."

They read for most of the morning in the library. When Abbie felt the boy's efforts lagging, she took the book from him and tried to inject some enthusiasm into the task. She had never read the book before, either. It was far too fanciful for an Amish education.

It was almost lunchtime when Louise interrupted them. Abbie put a finger under the line she had been reading and looked up.

"We have a visitor," Louise said. "He said he is here for you."

Rudy! Abbie snapped the book closed and stood up.

"I've put him in the sitting room so you can have some privacy." Louise gestured and Abbie paced across the hall.

"Mr. Shelton," she said when she saw the officer who had taken her report about Rudy's disappearance.

He stood in a casual stance with his hat in one hand, resting on his leg. "We have some information."

Abbie trembled. "Have you found Rudy? Is he all right?"

"As far as we know he is quite well."

She exhaled relief.

"Apparently he decided to take a trip."

"A trip?"

"It was quite a simple matter, actually," Mr. Shelton said. "This is a railroad town, after all. People come and go all the time."

"Rudy hasn't left the area since he arrived four years ago. He hasn't even been to Colorado Springs or Denver."

"The railroads keep records, you know, and the ticket masters have developed excellent memories. Since there are so few Amish men around here, it wasn't a difficult inquiry."

"What are you saying, Mr. Shelton?" Abbie crossed and uncrossed her arms.

"We traced him to a Union Pacific passenger train that left on Tuesday morning. Apparently he had a voucher from some time ago and decided to cash it in for a ticket."

"But his farm! He would never go off without making sure his animals were cared for."

"Have they been cared for?"

"Well, yes. Mr. Peters and I have been looking after them."

"Then it seems Mr. Stutzman knew what he was doing." Mr. Shelton reached for a slip of paper. "And it seems he sold the horse he rode into town to a railroad employee, tying up loose ends."

Abbie closed her eyes to calm her breath. "We are engaged to be married. Something must have precipitated his sudden departure."

"I cannot speak to that, Miss Weaver. That is between the two of you. We consider this a closed matter because there seems to be no indication of foul play."

"But where did he go? Can you at least tell me that?"

"It was an easterly train. His ticket would take him as far as western Missouri, but of course he could have gotten off anywhere."

"Can't you find out?"

"It's not a police matter, Miss Weaver."

The mare resisted Abbie's urge for speed, but she pestered the animal until it responded to commands with sufficient conviction.

Gone.

Rudy was gone. Abbie had refused to believe the officer's conclusion for two distracted hours until she could extricate herself from Fin's attention and barrel toward Rudy's farm. If he was really gone, he could have no objection to her looking through every stack of papers, every shabby drawer, every drooping shelf for the truth. She remembered now seeing the crimped corner of the voucher one day while she was cleaning. That was months ago, and in all this time Rudy had never again spoken of leaving. Now she was supposed to believe that he had after all.

Leaving the horse in the yard, Abbie stomped past the chickens and yanked open the door. With hands on her hips, she narrowed her eyes and looked around for the clue she had missed. Rudy had left the place tidy, but Abbie had been camped out there for two days and left evidence of her presence. She began by gathering the odds and ends of her belongings into a compact pile and stacking them on one chair next to the front door. A shawl, a soiled apron, the schedule she had scratched out for taking care of the farm chores. Then she moved the coffeepot from the table to the back of the stove and shifted the pots and dishes she had left drying beside the sink to the shelves above it. A tattered quilt went back to the foot of Rudy's bed.

Now the cabin was as he had left it.

And Abbie realized what was wrong. The pile of papers Rudy always left on the table, on the end that doubled as his desk, was gone. The notes about milk production, the quantity of seed he hoped to plant in the spring, the record of how he had weaned the calf. Abbie had supposed Rudy cleaned up to please her. Now she realized he cleaned up to say good-bye.

She hunted for the stack. If he truly was abandoning the farm, he would have no reason to take it, but the papers might give some clue of his intent. Abbie stood and stared at the three narrow drawers that housed Rudy's meager wardrobe. As soon as she tugged on the bottom drawer, she knew it gave easily because it was empty. The middle one was as well.

The top drawer yielded the papers, with a letter tied closed in twine laid on top of them. Shaking, she pulled the twine away and unfolded the letter.

Dearest Abbie,

First, I want you to know that my affection for you is more profound than I imagined possible. The greatest joy of my life is the moment you agreed to wed.

Second, I want you to know the depth of my admiration for your commitment to the success of the Elbert County settlement. You could have taken the easy road and gone east with your family, but your determination is relentless.

And now for two truths. I was utterly surprised when you accepted my proposal. For so long I thought it was the only thing that could tie me to this land. I have given my farm the best effort I could, and quite possibly, given time, I would have succeeded.

But I am not your Willem. Success would not be enough. I need the church as much as you do, and I am afraid I don't have your patience or optimism. So I have used my train ticket after all. I could not bear to ask you to come with me. I was too afraid you would say no and I would have to face the truth that your acceptance of my proposal was not based on mutual affection after all. I could not bear to know that for certain.

I ask you not to look for me. I am not sure where I will go, but I know there will be a robust Amish congregation wherever I end up. On a separate page, I am leaving instructions about the animals.

Fondly,

Rudy Stutzman

The knock on the door startled her, and for a flash she wanted it to be Rudy.

But of course he would not knock on his own door.

Willem stepped into the cabin. "Mrs. Wood said you didn't look well when you left today."

Abbie handed him the papers and stumbled to a chair. Willem scanned the letter before sliding it under the document below.

"He's left you the livestock," Willem said.

Abbie exhaled and spoke hoarsely. "What do I want with dairy cows when I have been abandoned by two men?"

"I'm here," he said quietly.

"I always thought you and Rudy were different as night and day." She stared out the front window. "Now I see I was wrong. Neither one of you could choose the life that included me."

CHAPTER 48

Willem twisted the barbed wire in place and snipped the excess off one end. Johnny, the ranch hand Melton Wood had sent out to help him was a young man, probably not any older than Reuben Weaver. But if he had grown up nearby, he might know the answer to Willem's question.

"If I wanted to sell a half-dozen milk cows around here, who do you suppose might be interested in them?"

Johnny straightened his thick gloves and prepared to handle the roll of wire. "Not too many folks. Milk cows are not the same as cattle raised for beef. The feed's not the same."

"Can you think of anyone?"

"Maxwells, maybe."

"Maxwells?" Willem raised his eyebrows.

"Brothers. Jason and Raymond. They'll buy most any kind of livestock and then try to turn a profit."

"So they'll take horses, too?"

"As long as they aren't ready to be horse meat."

Rudy's horses were healthy, and one was still young as far as horses went. Most of the cows had ample calving years ahead of them.

"How do I find these Maxwell brothers?"

"On a ranch a few miles northeast of here. Other side of Limon."

Northeast was the wrong direction for going home, but he would have to do it. Rudy's intentions were clear, and Abbie needed prodding to take action. She would run herself ragged trying to take care of all those animals by herself, and for no purpose. Rudy was not coming back.

Willem braced to lift the roll of wire. "Come on. We need to finish our quota early today."

The Maxwell ranch was farther out of Limon than what Willem would have called a few miles, but by the time he realized Johnny's estimate had fallen short, Willem had invested too much time to turn back. His stomach grumbled for a late supper by the time he found the ranch and sorted out which building to approach.

"I hear you might be interested in some dairy cows," he said to Jason Maxwell.

"Maybe. How many?"

"Eight. And a calf."

"The only one of your people who has that many dairy cows is Rudy Stutzman, and you're not him."

Willem resisted the urge to point out that Jason Maxwell might not know as much about the Amish as he thought he did—except he was right on this point.

"Those are the cows I'm talking about. I am inquiring on behalf of Mr. Stutzman."

"We don't pay agent fees."

"I'm not asking for anything. Mr. Stutzman is a friend."

"We looked at his cows once." Jason narrowed his gaze. "He turned us down."

"Circumstances have changed."

Jason's eyes perked up. Willem held his tongue. He would say nothing that might compromise the value of Rudy's livestock.

"I'll tell you what," Jason said. "We'll come and have a look. Tomorrow before supper."

Willem nodded. "We'll be ready."

"You'd better not be wasting our time."

❦

Abbie sighed and turned away when she saw Willem's stallion through the open barn door on Rudy's farm the next afternoon. She sat on a three-legged stool with her skirt arranged for clear access to the cow's udder and leaned her head into the animal's side. Only two minutes into the milking, and still not as fast as her brothers, she calculated she could keep her head down and her eyes averted for twenty minutes. If Willem had not left by then, she would move on to the next cow.

"Abbie," he said.

She did not answer.

"You can ignore me if you want to, but it won't change what is about to happen."

Abbie bit her lip in determination not to speak.

Willem picked up an empty bucket in one hand and a stool in the other. Abbie glanced out of the side of her eye and saw him inspecting the cows to determine which ones still needed to be milked.

"I made some inquiries." Willem situated himself beside a cow. "Jason Maxwell and his brother are coming in a few minutes to look at Rudy's livestock."

Abbie flared. "It's none of your business."

"Rudy wants you to sell. I am going to make sure you get the best value."

"I didn't ask you to find a buyer. Neither did Rudy." She listened to the rapid rhythmic squirts of Willem's efforts against the metal bucket.

Willem named a number. "If they offer you at least that much just for the cows, I think you should take it. Don't let them try to get you to throw in the horses."

"You're not listening, Willem. It's none of your business."

Squirt. Squirt. Squirt.

"When I heard you were going to marry Rudy," Willem said, "I thought I could accept that you were none of my business. But that has changed, hasn't it?"

"I'm not giving up on Rudy."

"Abigail."

Squirt. Squirt. Squirt. She was nearly keeping pace with him now.

"I just need time to find him. Eventually he'll go home to his parents. To his home district."

"He asked you not to look for him."

"I should never have let you read that letter."

"But you did. We can't undo what's done. Rudy is gone."

Abbie leaned her head harder into the cow's side, though her hands slowed. Underneath the rhythm of Willem's steady milking, she heard the hoofbeats. Two horses.

"They're here," Willem said softly. "I'll bring them in. We'll start with the cows and then see about the horses."

⌖

Willem had been surprisingly accurate in the number the Maxwell brothers would eventually offer for the cows, including the calf. Abbie met the gazes of the Maxwells with an unflinching lack of expression.

"We are mighty curious about why we are not dealing with Mr. Stutzman." Jason picked at his teeth with one finger.

"The reason does not matter," Willem said. "Miss Weaver is a legal agent for the sale."

"Maybe so," Jason said. "But if you want our full price offer, we'll need some proof of that."

Abbie looked at Willem and took a deep breath before she relented and got up to retrieve Rudy's document from the house, leaving the three men leaning over the fence watching the horses in the pasture. When she went back outside, she took a lantern with her and dutifully held it above the paper while Jason perused the details in Rudy's handwriting.

"Are you sure the livestock are not securing any debt?" Jason asked.

Abbie had no idea. She turned her face toward Willem.

"He bought them free and clear," Willem said. "One at a time when he had the cash."

"He is a good businessman." Jason handed the papers back to Abbie. "It's getting too dark to inspect the horses tonight. We'll come back tomorrow. My offer on the cows is good until then."

Abbie waited until they rode away before she spoke. "I haven't decided to sell. You can't force me."

"I'm not trying to force you." Willem took the lantern from her. "I'm trying to help you do something I know is impossibly difficult for you to do."

"I know how much a good cow is worth."

"That isn't what I mean."

Abbie turned toward the pasture gate. "I should get the horses in and finish up for the night."

"I'll take care of that." Willem reached for her arm. "What matters is you."

She was relieved it was too dark for him to see her face.

"This is hard," he said, "but you don't have to do it alone. Isn't that what a church is all about?"

Her chest heaved.

"I believe Rudy loves you," Willem said, "but he couldn't stay here. He only stayed as long as he did because of you. But I'm here."

She spun to face him. "And you're going to the Mennonites!"

"Come with me." He tilted the lantern to shine on her face. "I want you to come with me. There's a service a week from Sunday."

The light cast its circle on Willem as well, and she saw the ache in his eyes. Heat gathered in the tears she restrained in her own eyes stung. Abbie refused to blink. In a miniscule movement, Willem leaned toward her.

She stepped away. "I suppose I have no choice but to sell the livestock."

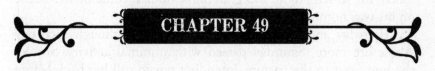

CHAPTER 49

Jason Maxwell brought three trailers and four ranch hands when he arrived on Tuesday for all the animals, including the chickens. He paid Abbie in cash, accepted the receipt she wrote out for him, shook her hand, and pulled out of Rudy's farm before supper. Abbie stood in the nearly soundless barnyard—only her own horse was there to scrape a hoof through the dirt—and turned in a slow circle before going into the house for one last desolate look around.

Rudy had not left under desperate or urgent circumstances. He easily could have taken more personal belongings or made arrangements on his own. Abbie felt the wound of his departure freshen. Rudy had left in smooth, silent stealth because of her, because she would have tried to talk him out of it. Now she held the value of his livestock in her hands, more cash than she had ever known, and she did not want it.

Someday, she resolved, she would find Rudy and send it to him. Someday she would find a way to wish him well. In the meantime, if she could not support herself in this wilderness of a settlement, she certainly was not going to live off the money of the man who had left her. She would have to write to the bishop in Ordway, but she could not do it yet.

There was no more reason to stay in Rudy's house or walk through his barn. Abbie closed the front door and drove home to the stark solitude of the Weaver farm, where she latched the door and climbed the stairs. If she paused long enough to drink a cup of coffee or scramble an egg, she would forfeit her resilience. Instead, she willed herself into an immediate deep, hard sleep of resistance.

On Wednesday morning, she rose, washed, dressed, and drove to the Woods' without breakfast. She played chess, read aloud, declined Louise's offer of tea, listened to Fin prattle about life on the ranch, and forced herself to eat enough lunch to be polite. Sufficient clues surfaced to reveal Willem was occupied in the far reaches of the ranch, for which Abbie was grateful. If he had come by her house on his way home, she would have sent him away.

Thursday and Friday repeated this pattern, though each day Abbie ate more. Saturday passed with minimal activity. She let the horse out to the pasture, intending not to call her back before dark, and collected the few eggs to be found in the coop that had once held dozens of chickens. During the day, if she felt the urge to doze, she did, fighting off the racing futile internal protest of her circumstances.

Sunday came. The Sabbath. The day of the week Abbie had always felt most keenly the lack of church services or even meal gatherings. She gathered the eggs and calculated that she had enough in the crates to be worth a trip into Limon to trade for foodstuffs that would bring variety to her diet. The flour bin was depleting, and while she could drop away from delivering bread to Willem, and he would not comment under the circumstances, the widower Samuels still relied on her. But even if she could bring herself to go to Limon on the Sabbath, Gates Mercantile would not be open.

Finished with the chickens, Abbie splashed water on her face and decided to go visit the Millers. Mary had acted so oddly the last time. If Little Abe had been ill, Abbie wanted to assure herself that he was recovered. She hitched up the buggy and drove down the road.

When she approached the turnoff, the Miller buggy threw arrows of dust from its spinning wheels as it came out of the lane that led to their house and turned in the opposite direction. Abbie pulled on the reins, put her head in one hand, and exhaled. Her only hope for friendship was swaying behind a cantering dappled horse.

Abbie sat up straight. It was unusual for Albert and Mary to leave their farm on a Sunday morning. Abbie, Ruthanna, and Mary had often found Sabbath rest and refreshment in each other's company on a day when they could release most of their obligations. She raised the reins again and followed.

As the Millers drove straight through the turns that might have taken them to the Mullets' or Troyers', Abbie's heart collected speed as well.

The Millers were going to Limon.

❧❦❧

Willem stood outside the house where Jake lived. He had arrived early because of both eagerness and anxiety. While he felt the first service a month ago had stirred his soul and made him hunger for more, he could not be sure everyone else felt the same. He was stunned to find Moses Troyer and his wife looking for the house and delighted to be able to point them to the right place. Nothing Moses had ever said to Willem suggested they would visit the Mennonite service. Willem remained outside, watching for others who might be seeking the church meeting.

When he saw the Millers' buggy ease in beside his, he allowed himself a satisfying breath. As soon as Little Abe's feet steadied on the ground, the boy pumped his legs toward Willem and wrapped his short arms around Willem's calf.

Mary hurried behind her son. "Abraham Miller, you behave yourself!" She pried him off of Willem, lifted him, and fenced the child in on one hip with both her arms.

"I'm always glad to see Little Abe," Willem said. "I'm very glad to see all the Millers today. Thank you for coming back."

"I don't know how much longer I can put Abbie off," Mary said. "I don't want to be dishonest, but it would break her heart if she knew we were here. Every time I see her, I get weaker."

"Maybe we can talk to her together," Willem said. "You and Albert and me."

"I'm sure that would be easier for me." Mary set her son on the ground again but held his hand firmly.

Albert joined her. "We didn't tell anyone we came last time," he said.

"Go on in," Willem said. "Jake is waiting for you."

Willem turned his eyes back to the street, hoping to see James and Julia Graves, who were likely to walk the few blocks from their own home, or Theresa Sutton. Instead, another Amish buggy clattered down the street, causing Willem to mentally run down the list of households who remained in the settlement and speculate who would be arriving. For a moment he was so surprised to see a fourth Amish buggy that he did not focus on the horse he knew very well.

Abbie's horse. The mare. The only one Ananias did not sell before the Weavers boarded a train. He sucked in his breath and strode toward the approaching rig.

"Good morning, Abbie."

Her narrowed eyes flashed from him to the house and then to three parked buggies. "What's going on, Willem?"

"We are having a worship service this morning. I hope you will join us."

"I followed the Millers," she said.

"Yes, the Millers are here." Willem winced. The confrontation Mary was leery of was unfolding on the side of the street.

"I see." Abbie pressed her lips together and smoothed her skirt. "Now I understand Mary's reluctance to speak to me. And of course I am not surprised to see you here. But there's another buggy."

"Come inside, Abbie. See for yourself."

Abbie had not even gotten out of the buggy. Willem expected she would click her tongue and get the mare moving again.

Instead, she met his gaze. "Where shall I park?"

With a strangling knot in her neck, Abbie followed Willem inside the house and into the room where Jake had pushed the furniture around.

Mary Miller jumped up from the sofa. "Abbie!"

Abbie gave a wan smile. "You never expected to see me here."

"I didn't know how to tell you."

The Troyers stood. "Thank you for coming," Moses said.

Abbie nodded in the smallest gesture she could manage. She had not exactly come. She had followed Mary, first out of curiosity, then confusion, then aggravation. Entering the house was simply more provocation to see for herself what the row of buggies outside meant. Her mind's eye saw two more squares in her quilt fade into frayed fragments of the beauty she intended.

The Mullets, the Yoders, Martin Samuels, the Nissleys, and Abbie. Of twelve households, only four remained. Abbie could not count herself a household. The place where she lay her head at night might belong to someone else by next week. She was in no position to bear the expense of running a farm or to manage the physical labor on her own.

Jake crossed the room. "Welcome, Abbie. Let us worship our God together."

"I'm sorry," Abbie mumbled. She bumped into Willem when she turned around and immediately pushed past him and hurtled herself toward the outside air.

She stood, planted, outside the house. Inside was an unimaginable compromise. Outside failure slapped her in the face.

"Abbie."

She should have known Willem would follow her out. "No, Willem."

"I have not asked a question," he said. "Yet."

He stood near enough that her breath drew in his comfortable, familiar scent. Every muscle in her body wanted to surrender, to drink in the assurance of this man.

"You're here," Willem said. "Your friends are here. Would it be so terrible to come inside?"

She wavered. "There's no point."

"There is every point," Willem countered. "These are people who seek God's face, and we will worship together. We will sing hymns you love and pray. Jake will teach us from God's Word. These are people who care for you and want to share their lives together. Is that not the church you seek?"

She raised her face to his, then ducked down again. "Ruthanna. My family. Rudy. You. I've lost one thing after another. Now you ask me to lose my church as well."

"You never lost me, Abigail."

"You're trying to profit from the loss of others. The man I loved would not do that." She choked on using the past tense.

Willem crossed his wrists in front of him. "Of late I have realized the ingratitude in my heart. I am choosing to receive the abundance God has already given me. I'd like your help in keeping me on my path."

"You have Mr. Heatwole." She hardened. "You chose the Mennonites."

"I chose church, Abbie. I chose worship. I chose the same thing you've been fighting for all these months."

She bit her bottom lip. "But what if my father and the others are right? What if this is not truly a church?"

"Isn't that for God to judge? What if you are starving your soul for nothing while the blessing you crave is right here?"

Abbie could not speak. Her mother's parting advice ricocheted around her mind. *I hope God will bless you, and I hope you will recognize it when He does.* She had thought the blessing was Rudy, had chosen to embrace it with all her heart. And Rudy left. Was blessing still possible after everything she had lost? Tears welled as her face scrunched and she stared into Willem's gentle, confident eyes.

"Here is the church." Willem offered an open hand to her. "Come with me."

Come with me. How many times had he said that in past weeks? The gasp pent up in her chest wriggled free like a determined goat. "I love you, Willem."

"I know. I am only waiting for you to let me love you."

Abbie drew in a deep, overdue breath. "I might not be very good at it."

"We'll learn together."

Abbie rubbed her eyes with the heels of her hands. His hand was still open, stretched toward her. As soon as she laid hers in it, and felt his fingers close around hers, the quivering ceased.

Abbie met his eyes, clear as she had ever seen them. "Let's go inside."

Author's Note

Ever since I began writing about the Amish, their history has fascinated me. Many people are intrigued by what they think is the simpler lifestyle of the Amish and their strong family values. Anyone tracking trends in church membership will find it curious that the Amish have a phenomenal rate of young people who choose to join the church—far above the larger, more well-known denominations with much less strict lifestyles.

In the early days of their history, the Amish would not have looked so different from the general population as they do today. They lived apart from people they regarded as unbelievers and practiced a form of Christianity that was not popular, but they dressed and cooked and farmed the same way everyone else did. It was the culture around them that evolved and accepted change at increasing speeds, and the Amish had the strength to ask, "Is this good for our community?"

This is the question of *Wonderful Lonesome*. And what is community? How does community intersect with faith? We each must ask and answer these questions, just as the characters in this story did.

The band of settlers in this book is based on a real settlement in eastern Colorado a hundred years ago. It failed for the myriad reasons woven into this story. I have taken some liberties with the characters, most of whom are products of my own imagination, though I've used some names from the known record of the settlement. The title comes from a note one of the settlers sent to the *Sugarcreek Budget*, the newspaper read widely among the Amish, in which she said that the lack of a church service for over a year made it "wonderful lonesome" to live on the Colorado plain. The turn of phrase caught my imagination, and the story spun out of it.

MEEK *and* MILD

PROLOGUE

Flag Run Meetinghouse
Niverton, Somerset County, Pennsylvania
1895

From the first scratch of sound to settle in her daughter's throat, Catherine Kuhn knew the coming squall would agitate a tempest in the entire row. Even as she tightened her grasp around the toddler and prepared to leave the worship service, Catherine looked across the aisle to catch her husband's eye. Hiram, the reddish hue of his beard distinguishing him in the third row of married men, kept his eyes forward. Probably he would not know she took the child out until Catherine told him later.

Clara's cry rose through her throat and burst across her lips. Catherine hastened her pace, easing herself outside the meetinghouse just before her daughter threw her head back and unfurled her distress into the unsympathetic empty air. Catherine carried the writhing girl farther from the confines of the worship service. This was no simple task. Catherine was eight months along. The energy required for moving quickly enough to contain the disturbance sapped her breath. When she reached the grass at the edge of the clearing where the meetinghouse stood, she let Clara slide down her skirt to the ground.

Clara was tired and probably hungry. When she was rested and fed, she was a delightful child full of curiosity and fluid smiles. When she was tired, though, she seemed to require a primal eruption of temper before surrendering to sleep. Catherine squelched envy of the mothers whose children slumbered during church, content in the arms of their mothers or older sisters, with their mellow baby noises exuding comfort to anyone seated close enough to hear. Catherine had expected her own baby would be like this. She took the infant to church when she was only a few weeks old, believing it was best for the child to become accustomed at the earliest possible age to the routine of three-hour services on alternate Sunday mornings. But Clara, with her feathery light brown hair in wispy curls, had not been the sort of baby to fall asleep oblivious to surroundings.

Catherine was grateful to be part of an Amish district that met in meetinghouses rather than homes, alternating between two meeting-houses, both in the southern end of Somerset County, Pennsylvania. Catherine and Hiram had married three years ago in the Flag Run Meetinghouse, Catherine's favorite. It was silly to have a favorite, since the two were identical and two more just like them existed over the border in Maryland, but Catherine enjoyed this particular clearing around the unadorned frame structure.

The year after their wedding was when the trouble started. Bishop Witmer visited to help sort it out, but the results seemed dubious.

Clara settled in the grass, rubbing her cheek in its cool texture, and Catherine saw she had thwarted the tantrum. The child already had closed her eyes and slowed her breathing. Catherine's back ached, but even if she managed to get herself down to the ground, she wasn't sure she would be able to rise when the time came. About ten feet away was a fallen log of sufficient girth to keep her off the ground and give her a fighting chance to stand up again. The log had been there for years, and Catherine suspected it was going soft at the core, but it was her best option. Still catching her breath, Catherine lumbered to the log.

She didn't mind being alone. On most days she savored a few minutes to hold herself still and notice the signs of life around her, the green of the grass, the flutter of tree leaves, the insects crawling along a wooded path, the birds inspecting the ground with their perpetual optimism of finding sustenance. On this day, though, Catherine had hoped against hope that she would be able to remain in church and hear whether the rumors were true. From this distance, she could not discern what was happening inside the meetinghouse.

Twenty minutes later, the women's door opened, and the eldest

Mrs. Stutzman emerged. She had five sons, all married with families of their own. Some of her grandsons had married as well, making "Mrs. Stutzman" an indefinite term. The youngest grandson, John, had only one year of schooling left before he would turn fourteen and join his father in the fields. Catherine had always thought he was the nicest of all the Stutzman children. Betty Stutzman now strode as purposefully as her age allowed toward the log where Catherine sat.

"Hello, Betty." Catherine reflexively laid a hand on her belly, where the baby had wakened to wriggle.

"You should go inside." Betty lowered herself beside Catherine and nudged her elbow.

A torrid burst fired up through Catherine's gut. "What's happening?" She glanced at Clara, who had thrown her arms above her head in her favorite sleeping position.

"Bishop Witmer should have stayed," Betty said. "How could he have thought this was settled?"

"Tell me what's going on." Catherine's gaze returned to the meetinghouse.

"Just go in." Betty nudged Catherine's elbow again, this time with more force.

Catherine rose. "But Clara—"

"She knows me," Betty said. "If she wakes, I'll bring her in."

Catherine was not sure Betty could lift Clara but supposed she could at least take her by the hand.

She wished her sister, Martha, were there. But Martha and Atlee were at the hub of the trouble, although they held in their characters nothing resembling maliciousness, and the decisions now stirring controversy were made nearly twenty years ago.

"What happened?" Catherine said, frustrated. "Everything's been fine for more than fifteen years. Why must we suddenly quarrel?"

Betty smoothed her skirt and interlaced her fingers in her lap. "It was peaceful at the time. When some members considered a few small changes, it was a simple thing to use the state line to indicate the preferences."

"The ministers agreed, didn't they?"

Betty nodded. "People were free to worship where they were comfortable. No one held a grudge. We were still one church, and have been all this time."

Martha and Catherine were children when it happened, too young even to have memories of the event. They had grown to womanhood understanding that congregations meeting in Somerset County, Pennsylvania, held to the old ways, while those in Garrett County, Maryland, took a wider view. Still, the differences were small. Anyone looking in from the outside would not have perceived them.

"So why now?" Catherine said. "If the ministers have held their own opinions and yet served together all this time, why now?"

Betty held Catherine's eyes. "You're worried about Martha."

Catherine forced down the bulge in her throat. "It's just a class for children and a few new hymns."

Most of the members in Pennsylvania found the notion of Sunday school hideously of the world. The Amish had lived apart for centuries, so why should they now adopt a spiritual practice that began in Protestant churches? In Maryland, where Martha and Atlee decided to live after they married, church members saw no harm, and neither did Catherine.

"Go on in," Betty said. "The outcome will not change my life. It's different for you—and your little *boppli*."

As quickly as she could, Catherine moved back toward the building and pulled the creaking door open. Inside, the congregation sat in stunned silence as Bishop Yoder spoke in the firm, full-throated manner the congregation had come to expect since he was ordained bishop earlier in the year.

"We will, of course, take a congregational vote," Bishop Yoder said. "But I will remind you that Bishop Witmer is well acquainted with the events that have occurred in our district in the last two years. Some of you met him while he visited to advise us on how we should proceed. I have presented to you the substance of his counsel to me as your bishop. Let us not respond to the division we have already suffered with more factions. I plead with you now for a unanimous vote on this matter."

What matter? Catherine wished she could pull on Hiram's arm to find out what was happening and what his thoughts were.

A man's hand went up—one of Betty Stutzman's sons—and Bishop Yoder acknowledged it.

"Are we certain this is the counsel Bishop Witmer offers? Perhaps he does not realize the extent of our family relationships with the Marylanders."

Martha. Whatever had brought the conversation to this point, it was going to involve Martha. Heartburn spread across Catherine's chest, and she did not think it was because of the baby.

Bishop Yoder straightened his shoulders. "Jesus said, 'If any man will come after me, let him deny himself, and take up his cross, and follow me.'"

Deny. Bishop Yoder was talking about shunning the Maryland families, Catherine realized. *Meidung.* He wanted her to shun her sister. To not see Martha. To not speak to Martha. For her children not to know their *aunti.* Catherine stared at the back of Hiram's head, willing him to turn around and see her, but he didn't.

"After this date," Bishop Yoder said, "any families who join the fellowship of the congregation in Maryland will no longer belong to our fellowship, and we will regard them as having abandoned the true faith."

Catherine twisted between relief that the shunning would only apply to future families who left the church and anxiety that shunning should occur at all.

Another hand went up and another man spoke. "In my conversations with Bishop Witmer, I did not find him so resolute."

Irritation flickered from Bishop Yoder's face. "I assure you that Bishop Witmer and I studied the Scriptures together. We also carefully considered the Discipline of 1837, which stresses the importance of a strict ban to maintain a vigorous church. I am sure we all want a vigorous church, do we not? When we neglect God's ordinance, the church falls away. Have we not already seen this in what happened with our former brethren in Maryland?"

Former brethren. The bishop had already cast aside Martha and Atlee Hostetler and the families who worshipped at the Maple Glen and Cherry Glade meetinghouses. How was it possible that the believers who labored side by side to build four meetinghouses should now see each other as former brethren? Catherine's body tensed. Her sister's heart had not fallen away from God. If the bishop would visit the families in Maryland, he would see this for himself.

A few heads turned now, forming pockets of whisper around the congregation. Catherine watched husbands and wives leaning forward or backward around those among whom they sat to find the eyes of their spouses across the aisle. Hiram rotated at last and caught her gaze. Catherine felt the blood siphon out of her face.

"We must vote now," Yoder said, "and I again remind you that a unanimous vote is essential to protect us from further division. You are here at Flag Run in Niverton, and not at one of the meetinghouses only a few miles away in Garrett County, because you already realize the authority of the Word of God in this matter. You understand the spiritual benefits that flow into your lives when you submit to the church and the congregation is of one mind. Consider carefully whether you want to be responsible for causing a crack in our unity with a dissenting vote."

If there had been any honest discussion of the question, Catherine had missed it. The bishop now left members of the congregation with little choice but to vote as he wished.

"All baptized members may vote," Yoder said. "I ask you to raise your hands with me if you uphold the Word of God and desire to be obedient to the teaching of the true church."

Catherine's throat thickened as she again looked at Hiram. Bishop Yoder had not asked whether people believed Sunday school violated the Word of God. He had not asked whether they agreed that the shunning was needful. He had framed his request in a way that marked anyone who disagreed with him as a heretic or an apostate.

Bishop Yoder lifted his right hand high in the air. Catherine, still standing at the back of the congregation, buried her hands in the folds of her skirt. Technically her sister had begun worshipping only on the Maryland side of the border before the ban the bishop now proposed. Catherine could still see her. Yet in her heart she was supposed to think of her as having fallen away. She could not make herself lift her hand.

Yet around the Flag Run Meetinghouse, one hand after another went up. Some lifted eagerly and some reluctantly, but the hands of baptized members present rose. Hiram's was one of the last, but he complied. Catherine knew her husband had no strong feeling on the matter of shunning those who left to join other churches—even the Lutherans—but she understood that he did not want to be the source of friction in the congregation. Who among the church would accept that role? Hiram sat in a row of men who had already raised their hands. In front of him and behind him, the men watched each other. On the other side of the aisle, the women did the same. Only because Catherine stood in the back could she withhold her vote without notice.

When the bishop asked if anyone opposed, Catherine's heart pounded. But she said nothing. Perhaps with her silence she had voted in agreement after all.

Bishop Yoder smiled in pleasure. "We have a unanimous vote. God will be pleased that we have placed ourselves in His care and have chosen His will over our own. Let us do as the disciples did and sing a hymn as we depart."

One of the bishop's sons, Noah, began the hymn, and the congregation soon joined with German words their ancestors had been singing for two hundred years.

CHAPTER 1

Somerset County, Pennsylvania
June 1916

The pan lid clattered to the kitchen floor. Clara Kuhn scrambled to contain the noise by stepping on the lid and then picking it up to press against her chest while her heart rate slowed. Three-year-old Mari had gone down for her afternoon nap not six minutes earlier. Rhoda was likely to stick her head in the kitchen and scowl at her stepdaughter within the next seventeen seconds. Expelling her breath, Clara turned around and dunked the lid back into the sink of water to scrub it again. Once she had dried it and stowed it with its matching pot on a low shelf, she ran a damp rag across the kitchen table and declared the kitchen properly tidied after the midday meal.

Rhoda had not appeared.

Rhoda's propensity to scowl at Clara was a recent development in their relationship. Clara didn't know what triggered it or what she could do to make it subside. She rinsed out the rag, hung it over the side of the sink, and drained the water. Mindful of where her skirts might catch or what her elbow might encounter, she moved out of the kitchen and into the hall leading to the front parlor. The voices were low, but with Josiah and Hannah in their last week of school and Mari napping, the house offered nothing to obscure the words. This was not a conversation Clara should walk into, accidentally or not. She halted her steps and held her breath.

"It's time Clara married," Rhoda said.

"She goes to the Singings," Hiram Kuhn said. "When she has something to tell us, she will."

"There must be any number of young men she could marry," Rhoda said. "Perhaps she's being particular."

"I was particular. After Catherine died trying to birth our child, I waited nine years to marry you even though I had a daughter who needed a *mamm*."

Rhoda's voice softened. "And I am blessed that you did. Your wait gave me time to grow up and meet you. I have done my best to love Clara as my own—I *do* love her as my own. I want what's best for her. She needs a husband and her own house to run."

"I always thought she was a help to you after the children were born."

"She was. She is. But I can manage my children without help. Clara should be looking after her own *boppli*."

Remaining still, Clara allowed herself to ease out her breath and cautiously fill her lungs again.

"Of course you can manage the children, but it's nice to have help, isn't it?"

"I won't have Clara thinking that I need her help," Rhoda said. "She must know that it's time to grow up. She's twenty-three."

"Hardly past the age of being marriageable," Hiram said.

"Very nearly. She could go to Maryland to stay with her mother's people," Rhoda said. "Perhaps she would meet someone to her liking in their church."

Clara visited her aunt Martha and her cousin Fannie often. Fannie had her own little girl now, and Clara adored Sadie. But Clara had never thought of joining their church. She certainly wouldn't look for someone to marry in the Mennonite-leaning congregation.

It was not for lack of possibilities that she had not yet married.

Andrew Raber liked going to the *English* hardware store. Whenever he had reason to do so, he allowed himself three times as long as his errand might legitimately require. If he needed a wrench he couldn't find in an Amish shop, he went to that aisle in the *English* store by way of the electric toasters. If he needed barbed-wire fence to keep horses in their pasture, he also marveled at the rolls of wire that could carry electricity. If he needed a new ax head, he first flipped through the brochures and catalogs of what could be sent for by special order. He could spend hours under the tin ceiling, walking the uneven wooden floor and investigating the overflowing shelves.

It was not that Andrew intended to purchase any of these things. It was only that he could not stifle his curiosity.

Today he was contemplating a new hoe and rake. Weeks of spring labor had made clear that handles on the cast-off overworked tools he received from his father years ago were ready for replacement. Andrew was fairly certain his grandfather had used those tools as well, and his faulty efforts to sand the long wooden handles back into service without risk of splinters in his hands had persuaded him new tools would not be an extravagance.

He would get to the tools, but right now he was looking at electric table lamps. Some were spare and efficient. Others had ornate bases and decorative glass globes. Some were sold as matched pairs and others billed as unique. Andrew had no doubt, though, that they were all wired alike. When they were plugged into a wall socket, electricity would flow through all the lamps in the same manner.

Andrew chose the lamp that appeared the least fragile and turned it upside down to see if the base might come off and give him a glimpse inside. If he had a screwdriver, he could pry it off, but the risk of damaging the lamp and then feeling obligated to purchase it was too much. He removed the shade and stared at the bare socket where a bulb would go, wishing he understood what he saw.

"Why are you looking at that?"

Andrew didn't have to look up to know whose mouth the words came from. "Hello, Yonnie."

"What are you doing?"

"I'm only looking." Andrew carefully replaced the shade and set the lamp back on the shelf. His eyes flicked to a white globe with painted flowers on it.

"We have all the light we need to read by with our oil lamps," Yonnie said.

Andrew wondered if Yonnie Yoder even heard the perpetual stern streak that ran through nearly every sentence he ever uttered. Perhaps it was just the way he spoke, his own cadence of language. They'd been boys together, and Andrew learned to disregard Yonnie's tone years ago. Lately, though, it had begun to irritate him. He had always supposed

Yonnie would grow into a more graceful way of speaking, but Andrew no longer thought he would.

"Why do you always fuss with the *English* things?" Yonnie said. "Our people do not use them."

"Maybe we will someday."

"You should not wish for something so worldly."

Andrew turned his back to the lamps. "I need a new rake."

Clara withdrew to the kitchen and then out the back door.

She was in the way. How had she not seen this years ago? It was one thing to be an eleven-year-old child whose father at last remarried and another to be twenty-three and thought to be without options.

Clara's own mother died when Clara was not yet two. Although Clara's birth was uneventful—at least that's what her father always told her—the boy her mother carried had taken too long to come. By the time he arrived—stillborn—Catherine Kuhn was exhausted. The bleeding that followed the birth quickly became uncontrollable, and within minutes Catherine was gone as well. Clara cocked her head, listening to the faraway sounds of that day. As always, she was unsure whether she remembered the screams and the rushing and the clattering of pans as she lay in her crib resisting a nap, or whether imagining the events had seared into her mind in the manner of memories.

Hiram was left with a small daughter and his grief. He was attentive and patient and sad.

When Clara was ten, Hiram met Rhoda, and the little girl saw the light in her father's eyes that she had longed for all her life.

But grief did not abandon the family with the marriage of Hiram and Rhoda. While Rhoda quickly became with child, one after another, three babies were born three and four months too early. Clara remembered the pall that fell over the house with each loss and the nervousness that shrouded each succeeding pregnancy. Though daylight streamed through the home, weighty darkness pressed on Hiram and Rhoda. After each loss, Hiram withdrew into the shadows and Rhoda instigated a frenzy of "trying again." At the time, Clara understood little of the biological process that ushered in repeated, cumulative grief, and no one thought to explain it to her, but clearly marriage brought with it great risk of sadness and disappointment.

Finally Josiah safely arrived, and then Hannah, and then Mari. Rhoda was still young enough to have several more children, if God should choose to bless her.

When Clara was a child, before Rhoda, she used to visit her aunt and uncle in Maryland and their rambunctious household. After Fannie, only a year and a half older than Clara, Martha and Atlee produced a string of boys. At twelve, the youngest was scarcely four years older than Josiah. In the summers, when she did not have school, Clara stayed for weeks at a time with the Hostetlers. Sometimes she stared at Martha when no one was watching, wondering if Martha resembled Catherine. Could she look at her aunt and see her own mother's face? Clara couldn't imagine loving Martha more if she had been her mother.

But staying in Maryland now? Away from Andrew?

Clara was not without options, as her stepmother supposed. She could have married two years ago. She could marry in the next season if she wanted to. If Clara confided in her now, Rhoda would plant extra rows of celery in preparation for a wedding as soon as Andrew had his fall harvest in.

Clara did not want to leave Andrew. She did not want to go to a strange Singing and have a strange man ask if he might take her home in his strange buggy.

But neither could she marry Andrew Raber.

Clara glanced back at the house and decided it was time to go clean the *English* household. The banker's wife maintained a busy social schedule, and three giggly daughters felt no compunction to pick up after themselves. A woman who came in to cook the family's meals was adamant she would not clean beyond the kitchen, so the family depended on Clara to come twice a week and restore order. Later in the week she would go to the Widower Hershberger's house for her regular afternoon of housekeeping.

Rhoda's words rang in Clara's ears. Maybe it was time to find more housekeeping work.

⋇

Andrew bought his rake. He had come into town in Yonnie's buggy, and now they were headed back toward their farms—Andrew to the acreage where he grew up and now lived alone and Yonnie to his parents' home, where he lived while trying to save enough money to purchase his own land.

As the buggy jostled and Andrew's eyes soaked up the scenery, he wondered how his parents could have left this place for Lancaster County. No matter what the season, beauty spilled from every vantage point. The mixed green hues of early summer or the rich rust palette of autumn, the brilliance of summer sunlight or the heavy laden clouds of winter moisture—Andrew savored it all.

A glint of dark green caught Andrew's eyes. On its own, he might have thought it a believable June hue, but it bounced the sun's light in a way that vegetation didn't, and his eye quickly followed the shape to brassy lines.

"Stop!" Andrew said.

Yonnie glanced at Andrew but did not pull on the reins or reach to set the brake.

"Stop," Andrew repeated. He positioned himself to jump down off the buggy's bench whether or not Yonnie halted the forward motion. They were not moving so fast that he would hurt himself—at least not seriously.

The horse's hooves slowed. Andrew glanced gratefully at Yonnie and saw the skeptical expression on his face. Ignoring it, he dropped down to the ground and strode toward the object that had caught his eye at the side of the road, its rear positioned under the lowest branches of a spreading red maple tree.

"Andrew, no."

Andrew ignored the warning in Yonnie's voice. The worst that could happen was Yonnie would drive off and leave Andrew here, which was a risk worth taking.

The sign painted on a large wooden square and propped against the front of the object said FREE.

"Get back in the buggy," Yonnie said. "That's for the *English*. It's not our business."

Andrew moved the sign out of the way and felt the smile well up inside him.

"Andrew!" The sharpness of Yonnie's tone escalated.

"Relax," Andrew said. "Look at this. It's beautiful." His eyes feasted. In town he always felt obliged to avert his eyes at such a sight, but out on a quiet road through an Amish district, his courage mounted.

"It's an automobile," Yonnie said.

Andrew grinned. It sure was. Shiny and clean and modern.
And free.

CHAPTER 2

A Model T.

Andrew pushed aside drooping branches and uncovered the upholstered seat with neat rows of tufted green diamonds. Hanging off the back of the seat were the neat, organized folds of the collapsed roof that left the seats open to the air. He felt the sun on his head and imagined wind in his face as the automobile rumbled at top speed. Andrew wasn't sure what the maximum speed was for a Model T, but it would be fun to discover it.

Behind him, Andrew felt Yonnie's silent judgment, but he ignored his friend's effort to bore into him with eyes of guilt. At the front of the car, brass-rimmed headlights were open eyes ready to stare fearlessly into the night. Andrew walked around the car, finding four perfectly round tires, two unbroken axles, and twin wide running boards—at least he thought that's what they were called—which would make it far easier to step into the car than it was to get into a buggy. He opened the driver's door and climbed in.

"Andrew!"

"There's a note," Andrew said, taking a card tied to the center of the steering wheel.

"It can't possibly be for you," Yonnie said. "Get out of that *English* contraption before anyone sees you."

Andrew inhaled the alien smell of the vehicle as he unfolded the card and scanned the lines.

> *Congratulations. It's yours. I've come to the end of my wits with this thing. The ownership documents are in the box under the seat. Good luck getting it running.*

Andrew allowed one side of his mouth to rise in pleasure. "Actually, it is for me. I just found a free car."

A squirrel darted across the road, and the dark gelding nickered.

"Let's go," Yonnie said. "I have chores to do and so do you."

Andrew glanced at the sky. Nothing on his farm mattered whether he did it today or tomorrow or next week. The horses had plenty of water and hay, and the two hens would lay eggs whether or not Andrew was there. He didn't keep a cow because he'd never liked milking schedules. Andrew's fingers fished for the handle again and he leaned into the weight of the door to open it, wondering how to open the cover over the engine. It could not be too complicated—a lever, a hook, a latch to displace. Andrew ran his hands lightly along the angled shape of the hood, feeling for possibilities. When he found the release latch, he paused before opening the motor's covering.

"Aren't you even curious?" Andrew gently lifted a green rectangle off one side of the motor.

"No, I am not." Yonnie's response was swift. "And you should not be, either."

"Curiosity is not a sin."

"If your curiosity takes you away from God's people, you'll have to reconsider that statement."

"Look at it, Yonnie. It's beautiful. Someone kept it in perfect condition. All I have to do is get it running."

"And what do you know about the motor of an *English* automobile?"

"Nothing. But I can learn."

Not everyone in the church spurned motor vehicles as instantly or vehemently as Yonnie did. Although Yonnie was a third cousin to Andrew—neither of them was sure of the exact connection—his family's name was Yoder, and Yonnie never loosened his grip on the responsibility he felt in also being related to Bishop Yoder.

Yonnie was still on the buggy's bench.

"Just come down and look at it." Andrew poked a finger into a greasy connection in the motor and sniffed his blackened fingertip. Oil. He understood nothing about what he was looking at, but the thirst to learn compelled him. Wires. Cylinders. Rubber hoses. Parts he had no words to describe. Somehow all of this harnessed energy that could compete with the power of galloping horses.

To Andrew's surprise, Yonnie stood beside him now with his fists balled behind him. Andrew ran one hand along the sleek, polished rod that ran from behind the lights on the front of the car to a shield of glass in front of the steering wheel.

"It's a marvel," Andrew whispered. He saw cars on the road nearly every time he ventured beyond the ring of Amish farms, but never before had he enjoyed the freedom to touch and feel and explore.

"It's for the *English*." Yonnie stepped back several feet.

"What are you afraid of, Yonnie?"

"I am not afraid." The edge in Yonnie's voice sharpened. "I take my baptismal vows seriously. I will live in submission to the church."

Andrew made up his mind. "I'm going to keep this car."

Back from the *English* house, where the electric lights and glittering trinkets held no allure for Clara, she climbed the steps to her room. Clara had slept in the same bedroom all her life. It was neither large nor especially comfortable. She supposed that if her mother had lived and her parents had more children, eventually she would have shared the room with a sister, but living alone with her father for most of her childhood allowed Clara the privilege of privacy. She was fifteen before Josiah was born and eighteen before she had a sister. By that time, no one expected her to share a room with an infant.

At twenty, Clara already had married friends with infants of their own the same ages as her little sisters Hannah and Mari. Her cousin Fannie, for instance, had a daughter barely a year younger than Hannah. Clara was certain Sadie and Hannah would like each other if they were ever allowed to meet.

A dust mop stood propped in the corner of the room, reminding Clara she had intended to clean her own room before Rhoda's words drove her from the house. She ran the mop over the bare wood floor under her bed. She did this often enough that she did not expect to encounter serious accumulation of dust, but she took satisfaction in knowing her bedroom was company clean at any moment. Her mop bumped up against the one item she routinely stored under the bed, and Clara pulled out the small leather bag that once belonged to her mother. With a rag, she cleared the hint of dust that had begun to gather around the handle.

"I wish I had a bag like that."

Clara looked up to see Hannah enter the room and throw herself across Clara's bed. She kissed her sister. "I didn't realize you were home from school."

"Only two more days."

"You'll miss seeing Priscilla every day when school lets out."

Hannah giggled. "We've promised each other we will nag our mothers all summer to let us play together."

"*Bensel.*" Silly child. Clara was certain both girls would fulfill this commitment. Whether their mothers would cooperate in their response was another question.

"Can I use your bag?" Hannah rolled over and took the bag from Clara.

"What will you use it for?"

"Maybe I can go see Aunt Martha, like you do."

Clara had used this bag for overnight visits to Maryland since she was a little girl not much older than Hannah. As soon as her sister died, Martha insisted that Hiram Kuhn allow his daughter to know her mother's family. Hiram never objected. Because Martha and Atlee had joined the Conservative Amish Mennonites before the bishop's ban when Clara was a toddler, Clara broke no rules by seeing her aunt and cousins. The shunning was not strictly enforced anyway. Most of the families in the district traced to both churches at some point in the family trees, and those who were not related by blood were connected by friendships spanning generations. Amish business serving both congregations flourished on both sides of the border. Farms on both sides of the border supplied milk to an Amish dairy in Somerset County. Dairy drivers collected the milk on daily rounds, and the dairy sold milk, cream, butter, and cheese to the *English* as well as Amish families who wanted more than their own animals produced. No one stopped to ask what date a person had joined the Marylanders.

"I could ask *Mamm*," Hannah said, "and maybe the next time you visit Aunt Martha, I can go with you. It's going to be summer. I won't miss any school. I could play with Sadie."

"We'll have to see." Clara did not want to make promises. Rhoda would be the first to point out that her children were not related to the Hostetlers in any way.

"That's what *Mamm* says when she hopes I'll forget about something." Hannah's lower lip trembled on the verge of a pout.

"She's your *mamm* and she loves you," Clara said.

"But you're my sister and you're a grown-up. You wouldn't let anything happen to me."

Footsteps sounded down the hall, and Hannah sat up in recognition of her mother's approach.

"Hannah!" Rhoda called.

"Go quickly." Clara nudged Hannah's thin form and was relieved when the child complied without arguing. The last thing Clara wanted to do right now was inflame her stepmother's mood. She would stay out of Rhoda's way, be as silently helpful as she could, and hope that the notion of sending her to live in Maryland would pass.

"Come on," Andrew said. "Help me."

"Help you do what?" Yonnie said.

"Move this car." Andrew picked up the Free sign from the ground in front of the car and carried it to Yonnie's buggy.

"You've been making me do things like this our whole lives."

Andrew winked. "We've never moved a free car before."

Yonnie turned his head to look both directions down the road. "Where exactly are you planning to move it? We're still a long way from our farms."

"So you'll do it?"

"I didn't say that. I'm just pointing out reality."

Yonnie was especially good at pointing out reality. Even as a boy, he persistently hovered over what might go wrong or which rules they might break even accidentally in the course of ordinary childhood play. Perhaps that was why Andrew had long ago developed the ability to ignore Yonnie's lack of enthusiasm. He barely heard the protests anymore.

"There's a barn," Andrew said, "just over a mile down the road. It's been empty for at least five years."

Yonnie cocked his head to think. "An *English* family named Johnson used to live there."

"That's the place. A fire took the house, and they didn't rebuild."

"If they were Amish, they would have. Everyone would have helped."

"Well, they weren't Amish and they were getting on in years. I heard they moved in with their son in Ohio."

"They must still own the land."

Andrew shrugged. "Probably. But they're not using the barn."

"It's more like a shed, as I recall," Yonnie said. "Three stalls at most. It might have served as a barn originally, before the Johnsons put up a more sufficient structure."

"Yes, I suppose so."

"But it would be a good place to hide a car."

"I'm not *hiding* it," Andrew said. "I only need a place to store it—a place big enough to work on it."

"How do you propose to get the car there?"

Andrew rolled his eyes. "You have a horse six feet away from you."

"I suppose he could pull it, but I'd have to unhitch my buggy."

Andrew waited. At this point in a conversation with Yonnie, he did not have to articulate his next argument. He only had to wait for Yonnie to catch up.

"I suppose the buggy would be safe here," Yonnie finally said. "Not many people have reason to come down this road, and no one could steal it without an extra horse and harness."

Andrew waited again.

"If we drag the buggy well off the road, it won't be in any danger. No harm has come to the car while it was parked here."

Now Andrew moved again. He had Yonnie right where he wanted him—persuaded that the job was possible and not, for the moment, entangled with his conscience.

"I'll get your rope," Andrew said, one hand already fumbling around under the buggy bench. He had no idea how to tie a rope to a car, but he supposed it could not be much different than dragging a buggy. The main thing was to not put too much stress on the axle, and he would have to figure out how to release any brake that might impede the tires' movements.

Common sense. That was the primary strategy to solving most problems. Despite Yonnie's legalistic perspective on decisions, he was loyal. Right now, Andrew counted on Yonnie's loyalty toward him to run long and deep. As long as Andrew stayed one step ahead of himself and was patient enough to learn, he would have himself a car.

CHAPTER 3

Garrett County, Maryland

The vice gripping Fannie Esh's womb, all too familiar, meant only one thing.

The womb was empty. There was no child this month. Next would come the backache, and then the flow. Heartbreak would smash through hope once again.

Once she weaned Sadie more than four years ago, Fannie assumed another child would come as easily as Sadie had, another wash of luminous wonder into the household, another joyful pitch of a baby's giggle. She and Elam had never tried to avoid a child, but now all she had to do was catch his eye over his supper plate and he would know what the expression meant. Oblivious, Sadie would chatter through the silent exchange at their small wooden kitchen table. Elam would rise early the next day and be out in the fields before Fannie could fix him a proper breakfast. He would not come in for lunch nor eat more than a few bites at supper. They would not speak of it. What more was there to say after all this time, while their siblings and neighbors and fellow church members received child after child from God's hand? Sometimes the babes were not even a year apart.

"Sadie would like a little sister, wouldn't she?" Fannie's friends used to say.

"There's nothing as sweet as the smell of a baby's head."

"Have you seen the new Stutzman baby? She's their most beautiful child yet."

Now her friends had three or four children and somberly promised to pray for God's blessing to come to Fannie as well.

Fannie yearned for another child, but she was beginning to doubt whether the arrows in the quiver, as the Bible said, were truly a measure of God's blessing. Perhaps the psalmist meant something else entirely, something that would make Fannie feel less discomforted by her inability to bear another child.

She sat at the kitchen table, where in the past she would allow herself the release of tears when this moment arrived. Fannie had abandoned tears more than a year ago. Now she simply counted off ten slow, deep breaths and composed herself.

Sadie bounded in through the back door, her cheeks scrubbed fresh by the late spring air and her eyes lit with anticipation.

"It's today, right?" Sadie said. "Today we go to for supper with *Grossmuder, ya?*"

The desire to join her boisterous family for the evening meal could not have been further from Fannie's mood, but Sadie loved to go. Especially since Fannie's brother's son began to toddle, Sadie loved to take Thomas's hand and lead him around the house or yard.

And Elam would be waiting for them there. He walked over several hours early to help Atlee Hostetler put a new door on the outside entrance to the cellar. Perhaps it was just as well. Among her extended family it would be easier to avoid Elam's eye. He could have one more day of hope even if Fannie could not.

"Shall we fix your hair before we go?" Fannie said, taking her daughter's hand. "Your braids are coming loose."

"If we must," Sadie said, "but please hurry."

Fannie took in little of what Sadie said while they repaired her hair and rode in the buggy the two miles to the Hostetler farm. Most of it seemed to be about the words Sadie wanted to teach her young cousin, though in Fannie's observation the boy showed little interest in expressing himself beyond the few simple sounds he already had mastered. There was plenty of time for that.

Fannie pulled her buggy in beside her brother's, and Sadie gripped the bench and looked at her mother for permission to get out. After Sadie once jumped out before the buggy stopped moving and nearly rolled under a wooden wheel, Fannie and Elam became stricter than their general natures about a rule that Sadie must not leave the buggy without explicit permission.

Fannie nodded. Sadie leaped down, and Fannie followed. They entered the back door together, and the little girl ran to embrace her *grossmuder*, flinging her arms around Martha's waist and laying her head against her abdomen.

"*Grossmuder*," Sadie said, "my arms don't reach around you anymore. Are you eating too much?"

"Sadie!" Fannie said sharply.

"Sorry." Sadie hung her head for a few seconds before looking up again brightly. "Where's the baby?"

Martha Hostetler laughed. "In the front room. But he's supposed to play on his blanket right now."

"I'll help him play." Sadie shot through the door.

"What can I help you with?" Fannie said.

Martha turned and removed a knife from a drawer. "I haven't done the vegetables yet."

"I'll do them." Fannie took the knife from her mother.

Amish dresses hid weight gain and shifting shapes, but in a startling moment Fannie saw what had sparked her daughter's impolite question. Her mother's bosom was heavier and her apron climbed a less defined waistline.

Martha was thickening.

❧

"Clara!"

Clara jolted at the sound of Rhoda's voice. Whatever Rhoda needed, Clara would do—dishes, dusting, sweeping.

She stepped from her room into the hall. "Yes? What can I do for you?"

"Nothing," Rhoda said. "I only wanted to say that I'm going to walk the children up to the road and see them off to school."

"I'll take them," Clara said.

"No need. I can manage."

"Then leave Mari with me." The three-year-old would only slow down the others.

"I'll take her," Rhoda said. "I simply wanted you to know I'll be out of the house for a while."

Clara glanced out the window. "It's a lovely morning to walk. Take your time. I'll start the laundry water to boil."

"I'll do that when I get back," Rhoda said. "If your father comes in, you can tell him I'll have coffee cake for him at midmorning."

"I'll mix it up," Clara said.

"I'm sure you have things to do," Rhoda said. "I know just how he likes it."

As if I don't, Clara thought as Rhoda herded her children out the front door. Clara followed them out and sat on the top step. Rhoda supported Mari on her hip with one hand while with the other she straightened the shoulders of Josiah's white shirt and smoothed his black suspenders. At the last minute, before they stepped out of the yard and onto the path to the road, Hannah turned and waved. Her expression was lost in the morning glare, but Clara was certain her mouth was a wide smile. It always was when she waved good-bye.

Clara blew out her breath and closed her eyes to focus on the sensation of the sun bleeding orange through her eyelids. The truth was, she had little to do since Rhoda had begun refusing her offers of help around the house, so she closed her eyes and raised her face to the sun. Each day was warmer than the one before, and the heat came earlier. Another week would bring unquestionable summer, vanishing the threat of retreating into the cool, damp days of spring. At least Josiah and Hannah would be out of school after tomorrow. Josiah would be eager and content to work alongside his father in the fields. Hannah would be the wriggly one. Hiram had never let Clara work in the fields, so she doubted his policy would change for Hannah. And Hannah wouldn't want to. She would prefer to flit in and out the back door doing whatever caught her fancy. Rhoda, on the other hand, would have a more structured method to keep Hannah occupied.

The approaching clatter of horses pulling a rickety wagon demanded Clara open her eyes.

Yonnie Yoder. Andrew brushed off Yonnie's mannerisms in amusement, but Clara was not so noble. Yonnie usually did the second collection route for the Amish dairy that employed him closer to midmorning, though occasionally he took a turn at the early-morning route. But what brought him to the Kuhn farm? The Kuhns did not keep extra cows. With six people in the house—and Hiram's well-known affinity for cheese—they consumed most of what their two cows produced.

Clara descended the porch steps and paced out to meet Yonnie's wagon.

"*Gut mariye,*" she said when he pulled to a stop. Who could complain about a morning greeting? For Andrew's sake, she injected an extra dose of friendliness into her words. "What brings you here this morning?"

"Your cousin was out at the road first thing this morning waving me down," Yonnie said.

"Fannie?"

"She sent a note."

"So early?" Clara took the envelope from Yonnie. "Thank you for coming out of your way to deliver it promptly."

"Are you suggesting sometimes I am not prompt?"

"No, of course not," Clara said, wondering how Andrew tolerated someone so inclined to be suspicious and snippy. She was not sure she would have the fortitude if one of her childhood friends had grown up to have Yonnie's temperament. "Thank you, Yonnie. I pray God blesses your day."

He turned the wagon in a wide circle around the yard and left. Clara tore off the end of the envelope and unfolded the single sheet inside.

Dear Clara,
    Please come as soon as you can. My heart is heavy once
again, and I have received stunning news which ought to make
my heart glad but which instead weighs on my spirit. I can tell
no one but you.
Your cousin,
Fannie

Clara read the words a second time but found no further meaning in them. An empty day stretched ahead of her. Why should she not go to Fannie now? She could walk and be there before the midday meal. Clara pivoted to scamper up the porch stairs and then to her second-story bedroom as she considered whether she ought to pack the overnight bag. When she heard movement downstairs, she expected Rhoda had returned from her errand to send the children off on their walk to school. Instead, the heavier footsteps ascending the stairs were her father's. Clara stepped into the hall.

"Hello, *Daed.* Rhoda asked me to tell you she will have a coffee cake ready by midmorning."

"I hope she does not go to a lot of trouble. I'm not feeling well."

Clara looked at him more closely. When his head drooped at the breakfast table, she had supposed he hadn't slept well. Now she could see he was pale and his breath labored.

"You should lie down," she said.

"That is my intention," Hiram said, "but I must ask a favor of you."

"Of course."

"Take the buggy and go over to John Stutzman's farm. I promised I would go to help him with roofing repairs today. He will understand that I am ill, but I don't want him to think I have forgotten him."

Clara glanced into her bedroom at the bag on the bed. "Of course."

The Stutzmans lived on one of the most outlying of the Amish farms. They were near the Maryland border, but well west of the Kuhn land. A round-trip journey, with time for polite socializing or the meal John's wife was likely to offer, would take half the day. Clara was grateful, though, that Hiram had enough sense not to go up on a roof when he felt unsteady.

Fannie would have to understand.

Fannie tucked the lightweight quilt around her daughter's shoulders and cracked the window to coax in cool air. Sadie bounced through her days with enough energy for three children. When bedtime came, she dropped into bed and often was asleep before Fannie finished murmuring soft prayers for her household. Tonight was no different.

Fannie sat on her daughter's bed and put out the lamp before listening for Sadie's even breath. She had hoped that Clara would come before the day's light petered out. Even without conversation, Clara's presence would have been a comfort.

Clara feared childbirth as deeply as Fannie longed for it. They knew each other's secrets more than anyone else. But this—who would have expected this? After five children, the youngest of them twelve years old? At Martha's age?

Elam sat in the front room studying papers about crop rotations. He knew Fannie's news now. But did he know Martha's?

CHAPTER 4

Clara lost the entire day. By the time she got home from the Stutzman farm, she'd missed the afternoon run of the milk wagon, her usual prospect for hitching a ride to a farm near Fannie's. Though she might still walk the six miles before darkness fell, she hesitated to leave without being sure her father was on the mend—or at least resting well—and Hannah was so full of after-school chatter that there was no place for Clara to break in and explain she was leaving. Clara recognized the precise moment she looked out the window and knew it was too late.

She barely slept.

On Friday morning, Clara paced before daylight the mile to the corner where she knew the milk wagon would pass. The words in Fannie's notes replayed in her mind. Though a stone dropped in her stomach when she realized the driver was Yonnie Yoder and not one of the two other—more pleasant—dairy drivers, Clara put a smile on her face and asked for a ride that went past the Maple Glen Meetinghouse the Marylanders used. At least she knew he would not require conversation beyond an initial greeting and departing pleasantries.

When he let her off, Clara ignored Yonnie's silent scowl and thanked him for obliging her with a ride. He no more approved of her visits to her Marylander relatives than he did his employer's choice to do business with the Marylanders.

None of that was Clara's concern. She only needed to see Fannie. When she knocked on the back door, Clara smelled the bacon and eggs Fannie cooked every day for Elam's breakfast. Her empty stomach gurgled in response.

Fannie fell into Clara's arms. Elam was gone to the fields or the barn, and Sadie stood on a chair with her skinny arms in the dishwater. Clara felt Fannie's tremble and squeezed her shoulders hard, while at the same time catching Sadie's grin. The girl was especially proud that she had lost three teeth and smiled wide to show her accomplishment.

Fannie composed herself and touched her daughter's shoulder. "Sadie, thank you for helping with the dishes. We're going to go see *Grossmuder*, so please tidy your bed before we go."

Sadie pulled her hands out of the water, splashing droplets on Fannie and Clara. "I'm glad you're here," she said to Clara, pulling her lips wide again.

Clara smiled at Sadie and then turned to Fannie as soon as the girl was out of sight. "We're going to see your mother? Is she all right?"

Fannie pulled the last plate from the sink and rinsed it in clear water. "Yes. As far as I know. It seems she has not been confiding in me."

"But you're very close to your mother."

"You'll see," Fannie said. "Sadie!"

Fannie would reveal little in her daughter's presence, so Clara did not press. Instead, as they walked they talked about the state of Fannie's vegetable garden and whether the hens were laying enough eggs. Sadie circled around them in her bare feet, asking the names of sprouting vegetation and pointing out the birds swooping from their nests. On an ordinary day, Clara would have enjoyed the leisurely two-mile morning stroll. Today each step twisted her anxiety tighter.

Clara heard the aching breath Fannie drew as they approached Martha kneeling between the budding rows of flowers across the front of the house. Sadie raced ahead to greet her *grossmuder*, throwing her weight against Martha's back and disturbing her balance. Martha recovered quickly, but in the effort it took to stand up, Clara saw more than the strain of age.

Martha was not an old woman. She was only forty-four and actively managed her household.

Not *only* forty-four. Clara corrected herself mentally. A woman having a child at forty-four was not the same as a woman weeding her garden at forty-four. Already Martha's balance was off. Already her back arced slightly to compensate for the rising mound in the front.

Clara swallowed hard. Worry shot through her even as she reached out to put a hand on Fannie's arm.

"But your youngest brother is twelve," Clara whispered.

Fannie's response was a choked sob.

Even as Clara kissed her aunt's cheek, she felt the color drain from her face. Once, a woman in the church was pregnant at forty-six. Even the *English* doctor said it was dangerous.

Martha patted Sadie's head. "There's strudel in the kitchen. Why don't you go get a piece?"

Sadie's penchant for strudel propelled her into the house.

"You don't have to hide what you feel," Martha said softly to the two young women before her. "Clara, you're worried something will happen to me or the baby—or both of us. Fannie, you're heartbroken even though you want to be glad."

"*Aunti* Martha," Clara said—but she did not know how to finish her sentence.

Beside Clara, Fannie pushed her breath out slowly. "You didn't tell me. You waited until I could see it."

"I didn't know what to say," Martha said. "I know how much you want another child."

Clara moistened her lips and glanced at her cousin.

"*Gottes wille,*" Martha said. God's will.

❦

They went inside for strudel and coffee. Sitting on a stool, Sadie's face was already smeared with cherry filling. When Fannie took cups down from a shelf, clinking nearly obscured the toddler's cry.

"Thomas is here?" she said.

Martha nodded. "Lizzie asked me to keep him for a few hours this morning."

Sadie wiped her mouth on her sleeve. "I'll get him."

"Be gentle," Fannie called after the girl. "Hold his hand. Don't carry him."

Thomas, her brother's son, was a year and a half old. When Fannie heard the news that he was on the way to the newlywed couple, she was genuinely glad for them. But now another two years had passed. In all that time, Fannie had not had even one delayed cycle, not one morning of conflicted signals from her body, not one morning of hope that her faithful patience was rewarded at last. Lizzie and Abe likely soon would announce that they were expecting another *boppli*, and Fannie would once again have to kiss their cheeks in congratulation.

Sadie returned to the room with a crooked grin on her face and a sleepy boy wobbling on his feet.

A boy.

A son would please Elam. A stair-step row of sons, with another daughter or two along the way, would split his face in permanent joy. Fannie wanted to give Elam that vision. She wanted to hold that vision for herself.

But after more than five years since Sadie's birth?

Fannie looked at her mother heating coffee at the stove. Perhaps if she steeled herself with enough pastry, she could say she was glad for her mother.

She wouldn't *be* glad—not yet. But she would try very hard to say that she was.

❧

Clara was grateful to be back at Fannie's house. Though the outing lasted barely three hours, it had exhausted Clara. It was not the miles they strode in lovely sunlight.

Her aunt was right. Clara was fearful, and Fannie was heartbroken.

At least in Fannie's home, neither of them had to pretend they felt differently. They only had to avoid speaking of the subject in Sadie's presence. As soon as Clara dropped into the davenport, Sadie snuggled against her and nudged her way under Clara's arm.

"Did you bring me a story?" Sadie looked up at Clara's face hopefully.

Clara stroked Sadie's hair. "No, I'm afraid I didn't think of it this time."

"Will you send me one in a letter, then?"

"I'll have to finish one," Clara said. "I'm in the middle of Joshua and the Battle of Jericho."

Sadie turned her head toward her mother across the room. "*Mamm*, do I know that story?"

"I don't know," Fannie said. "Do you?"

"You're being silly," Sadie said. "Just tell me if I know it."

Clara tickled Sadie's neck. "If you don't remember, then I guess you don't know it."

"But you do, right?"

"Yes, I do."

"Then tell me from your head." Sadie scratched one bare foot. "You can send me the paper later."

"Well, let me see. Have you ever been surprised by a very big job? Something that seemed so hard that no one could do it? Maybe it made you afraid?"

"I remember when I was afraid of feeding the chickens."

"Bigger!" Clara said.

Sadie pushed her lips out, thinking. "I used to be afraid of carrying the milk bucket from the barn when it gets too full."

"Bigger!"

"I'm not afraid to pick up Thomas." Sadie giggled. "*Mamm* is afraid I'll drop him, but I'm not. And I'm not afraid to let the horse take an apple out of my hand."

"You're a brave little girl," Clara said. "But I'm sure if you think very hard, you'll remember something that seemed like a big, huge job, and when you do, you'll know just what Joshua felt like when God told him to lead the people in a walk around the city of Jericho. Joshua had to be brave enough to lead the people, but he also had to be brave enough to believe that when he obeyed God, the very tall and very thick walls around Jericho would fall down. That's how the people would get inside the city."

Sadie's eyes were wide and bright. "Are you going to make sounds in this story? I like it when you make sounds."

"Now that you mention it," Clara said, "there are some very exciting sounds in this story. I'm going to need your help with them."

Sadie clapped.

"I'll make some lunch," Fannie said. "It should be ready by the time you get to the part about walking around the city seven times."

"We'll be hungry by then," Clara said. "Now Sadie, let's practice a trumpet sound."

Clara kept her voice cheerful for Sadie even as she watched the deepening droop in Fannie's shoulders.

After lunch, Sadie scampered outside with a promise that she would not stray far from the house. As soon as her daughter was out of earshot, Fannie turned her strained face toward her cousin. They stood at the front window watching Sadie run in circles.

"She's a gleeful child," Clara said. "I hope I didn't wind her up too much with all the marching and horn blowing."

Fannie gave a wan smile. "She'll never forget that story. She remembers all the Bible stories you tell her. And soon as she gets a letter, she makes me stop everything and read it."

"We'll have to work on teaching her to read them for herself."

"Thank you for coming." Fannie squeezed Clara's hand. "None of my friends here would understand. Everyone in the church will think it's such happy news."

It was happy news. Perhaps on another day Fannie would be able to make herself feel the gladness new life should bring.

"Have you decided whether to marry Andrew?" Fannie said.

Clara pulled her bottom lip down in a grimace. "What will I say if he asks me again?"

"Yes! You should say yes!"

"I know. I do care for him. Truly I do."

"Then don't try his patience any further. The wedding season will be here before you know it."

Fannie's mind flashed to what might happen by this time next year. Andrew and Clara could marry in the fall or early winter. By next summer, they could have a baby of their own on the way.

And it would be one more child wrenching at the grief in Fannie's heart, even though Clara would be terrified at the prospect of giving birth.

Martha's child—Fannie's own brother or sister—would be sitting up on a quilt in the sunshine, perhaps even rocking on hands and knees preparing to crawl.

Fannie swallowed the thickness of her throat. The world did not stop because God did not find her deserving of another child.

"Don't miss out on Andrew's love," Fannie said. "If there should be a child. . ."

"Let's not talk about that now," Clara murmured. "I should go."

Fannie nodded. If Clara didn't get to the Maple Glen Meetinghouse on time, she would miss the milk wagon going back across the border.

CHAPTER 5

The pressure in Clara's chest triggered tears in her eyes before she opened them the next morning. The dream had come again. Sadness trailed behind the vague shapes that never quite came into focus in those gray moments between disturbed sleep and opening day.

At least she had not wakened whimpering.

Clara hesitated to use the word *dream* for the unprovoked gloom that swam through her from time to time, as it had all her life. Nothing happened in these dreams, if that is what they were. She saw no faces, no landscape, no burning sun or swirling river water. The babies were gone before she heard their cries.

The babies. It was always the babies. Sometimes she thought she was the baby, but sometimes the baby was a boy.

Clara pushed her quilt away and swung her feet over the side of the bed. She had not woken this way for months—long enough to hope that perhaps the misery she feared had dissipated and perhaps she could marry Andrew after all. Daylight had not yet broken through the window, but Clara would not sleep again. She never did when this happened. Her fingers knew where to find the matches on the corner of her nightstand, and she lit the lamp. She might as well finish writing Joshua's story for Sadie.

She didn't want to think about anybody's baby today.

❧

This time Andrew did not linger over the electric table lamps or toasters.

On Saturday morning, he entered the hardware store with no list and no intended purchase. Instead, he sought space to wonder what he would do with the Model T. What he understood about the functioning of a motor—of any variety—was sparse enough that he could write it on the flap of an envelope. Andrew was fairly confident a hardware store was not the place to be schooled in the workings of an automobile engine. He would have to learn what the *English* meant when they said words like *piston* and *spark plugs* and *throttle*. For now he only wanted a place where he could look thoughtful and occupied while acquiring a basic knowledge of what the store might offer in terms of supplies an automobile owner might require.

Andrew stood in front of a display of motor oil. How much did an engine use? Next to the oil was a rack of gloves made especially for driving. Were they essential? What about goggles? Andrew squeezed his eyes shut and then opened them again. He wouldn't need to worry about gloves or goggles unless he got the automobile running.

And since he did not know why it wasn't running already, he faced a conundrum.

"Andrew!"

At the sound of his name, Andrew snapped his gaze up. He let out his breath. It was only John Stutzman.

"Good morning, John."

"It is a good morning, isn't it?" John nodded his head in satisfaction.

Andrew had always liked John. The nine years' difference in their ages was enough that until not so long ago Andrew had called him a respectful "Mr. Stutzman," then "Smiling John" to distinguish him from his father, and finally simply "John." A husband and father of seven children, John was in a season of life Andrew hoped would arrive for him before long. The older Andrew got, the less marked the age disparity became. They were two farmers who went to church together and shared a way of life.

John stroked his beard and glanced at the display before Andrew.

He wouldn't ask. Andrew was sure of that. John Stutzman believed that a man's conscience was his own, which was just why Andrew felt no need to hide.

"I found something the other day," Andrew said.

John's eyebrows arched. "A horse that drinks oil?"

Andrew gave a half smile. "What if I said yes?"

"Then I'd say it was a horse that didn't eat hay."

"Not so far as I can figure, no."

"Not having to muck a stall would bring certain advantages."

Andrew laughed now. "Do you want to see it?"

"Do you mean to say you've taken possession of the remarkable beast?"

The remarkable beast. The description seemed apt, both for the automobile and for Andrew's rapidly growing affinity for it.

"I have indeed," Andrew said. "Free and clear."

"I will confess that does spark a certain degree of curiosity in me."

The fine lines at the corners of John's eyes creased, offering a faint suggestion of his age. For the first time, Andrew noticed wisps of faint gray in his friend's hair curling at the back of his neck.

"Then we shall have to arrange something," Andrew said.

With their heads tilted toward each other, Andrew revealed where the Model T was and the circumstances under which he acquired it. He'd poked and tugged at every loose edge inside and outside the automobile, looking for any evidence that the note and papers giving the Model T to whoever was willing to take it off the hands of its exasperated owner were not as straightforward as they seemed. Finding nothing, he took the papers home and stored them securely where even Yonnie would not know where to find them.

John laughed at Andrew's recounting. "You're hiding an automobile and you're worried someone will find the papers?"

Andrew shook his head. "I have no regret about taking the car. The possibility of being falsely accused of how I came to possess it enters my mind."

"What about Yonnie?"

"What about him?"

"Do you trust him?"

"He's my relative and my childhood friend."

"Yes. And do you trust him?"

John looked over Andrew's shoulder, and Andrew turned to follow his gaze. Yonnie stood at the end of the aisle.

Clara sometimes wondered what it would be like to court as the *English* did—always properly chaperoned, but without secrecy. Amish pairings were not always a surprise when engagements were published in church, but until that moment, no one could be certain a young man who offered to take a young woman home from the Singing where the unmarried gathered had true affection for her or whether she returned it. If a group took a buggy and food baskets for a picnic along the Casselman River, there might be a romantically aspiring couple among them or there might not be. Three minutes of conversation beyond the ears of anyone else could be casual insignificance or stolen, treasured words. Clara had her suspicions who might be announcing engagements as the harvest season approached this year—Ruth and Peter, for instance—but she made no claim to be certain of anything.

One thing Clara did know was that if she never left the Kuhn farm, she would never run into Andrew coincidentally—or not so coincidentally. After all, was there such a thing as a coincidence? Was not all that happened God's will?

So when Rhoda casually remarked on Saturday morning that she had forgotten to purchase green thread the last time she was in town and was now disappointed that she was not equipped for the mending in her basket, Clara cheerfully offered to go to the mercantile. To her surprise, Rhoda did not refuse the help and in fact gave Clara a list of several other small but needful items that would more than justify the excursion.

Taking just one horse with a small cart, Clara kept her eyes open for any sign of Andrew, who might come from a side road because he had been visiting a neighbor or who might come from the direction she was traveling. When Clara passed the turnoff to his farm, the urge to see if he was home tempted her, but she knew a daytime meeting would be much safer out where anyone might observe it and think nothing of it.

The thought that she *might* run into him, that it *might* be God's will for them to see each other today, was enough to stretch her neck in anticipation, but she chastised her own hope with determination not to lose her grip on her errand for Rhoda. If she wanted to prove herself useful, she could not disappoint Rhoda by tumbling into distraction and failing to come home with green thread and a few practical items.

Clara got all the way to Springs, where she drove around two small squares of shops looking for a place to leave the horse and cart. The shops still had hitching posts in front of them, but every time Clara came into Springs, there seemed to be more automobiles. Irritation pulsed through her good mood. The automobiles themselves did not bother her, but why did their owners have to leave them in front of the hitching posts?

The annoyance fled when the circuit around the blocks led to a sighting of a brown stallion with a stripe of white running down his long nose.

Andrew's horse—and room to share the hitching post. Clara eased her gentle spotted gray mare into the space and knotted the reins to the post before reaching under the bench in the cart for the sack of apples her father always kept there. She offered one to the mare and one to the stallion, tempted to feed them all the apples in the bag while she loitered with the thought that Andrew would have to return to this spot eventually.

Clara wiped her hands on her apron. Rhoda would wonder whether she truly meant to bring the thread. Clara pivoted to amble down to the mercantile.

At first she passed the hardware store. Then she idly turned. The store was Andrew's favorite. She opened the door and there he was, talking with John Stutzman. Clara contained the grin welling up inside her as she shuffled down the aisle.

And then she saw Yonnie with his dour features and set jaw. He stood with Andrew and John, only coming into Clara's view when John shifted his weight to one side. If Clara wanted to see Andrew, she would have to see Yonnie as well. At least John was there with his broad smile and eyes that twinkled for no apparent reason.

Andrew lifted his head and rotated his glance toward Clara. One corner of his mouth twitched in invitation, and she moved toward them.

John dipped his head toward Clara. "*Gut mariye*, Clara. My wife will be wondering what happened to me, so please excuse my departure."

"Of course." Clara gave John a small smile. "Please greet your family for me."

Yonnie seemed to have planted his feet. Clara met his eyes with sufficient manners before fixing her gaze on Andrew's brown hair, with its ragged cut he insisted on giving himself, and the brown eyes that announced curiosity and pleasure as surely as if he spoke into a megaphone.

If only marriage did not mean bearing children.

⚜

Yonnie crossed his arms over his chest. If Andrew felt no shame for taking the abandoned car, then why should he mind if Clara Kuhn knew about it?

"Andrew was just telling John about the Model T," Yonnie said.

"The Model T?" Clara said. "It certainly has become popular among the *English*."

"At least one *English* has lost interest," Yonnie muttered.

Clara creased her brow. "I'm afraid I'm not following your point, Yonnie."

Andrew put a thumb through one suspender. "He means the one I found."

Yonnie watched Clara's eyebrows rise. It was one thing for John Stutzman to show no concern that Andrew had taken possession of a valuable *English* machine—though Yonnie thought he should have. Clara would be different. Her father was staunch in his convictions. He could have joined the Marylanders twenty years ago when the churches clustered around the border parted ways, but he chose the Old Order.

"You found a car?" Clara said to Andrew.

Andrew glanced around the store. *He says he's not ashamed*, Yonnie thought, *but he doesn't want everyone to hear*. Yonnie surveyed the store as well and saw no other Amish customers.

With soft tones, Andrew described the events of Wednesday afternoon. Yonnie was less interested in what Andrew said than in what he saw on Clara's face.

No alarm.

No shock.

Her blue eyes widened, but not in fear. It was more akin to inquisitiveness.

"Clara, what would your father think of Andrew's decision?" Yonnie asked.

She shrugged. "My father is not Andrew's conscience."

"What about you? What do you think?"

Clara smiled. "I'd like to see the automobile."

CHAPTER 6

Was it a sin to hope that Mose Beachy would be the minister selected to give the main sermon? Or to pray that this would be God's will?

Though she wouldn't speak it aloud, that was what Clara wondered during the final hymn before the sermons. In a moment, the bishop and three ministers who served the congregation would return from their private meeting and prayer, and one of them would begin to preach a short sermon. After another hymn, a second minister would bring the main sermon. Why could it not be Mose Beachy? Mose was a gentle, thoughtful man in conversation and in preaching.

But when the four men entered at the front of the meetinghouse, Clara could tell from Bishop Yoder's posture that the lot had fallen to him. Clara did not know much about lots and statistics, but it seemed to her that Bishop Yoder gave sermons more often than any of the others. She had been hearing them her entire life. He'd always been firm, but in the last couple of years, he had turned virulent. He wasn't ancient, but he was near seventy, so few men in the church exceeded his age. Lately, Clara observed, Bishop Yoder moved more slowly, as if his joints had stiffened and refused cooperation. His sons deferentially stood aside and held doors open with patience. Yet when Bishop Yoder stood to preach, his frailties seemed to leave him.

Bishop Yoder remained standing beside the preaching table, while his two sons, Joseph and Noah, took seats on either side of Mose Beachy on the ministers' bench facing the congregation. One of them would give a second sermon. Clara clung to the hope that she might yet hear Mose's words of wisdom today.

Clara settled in with her youngest sister on her lap. Mari had fallen asleep during the final hymn, and Clara doubted she would wake before the service ended. Beside them was Hannah and then Rhoda. Clara glanced across the aisle to the men's side, where Josiah recently had been permitted to sit with his father rather than among the women. He took the privilege seriously and sat somberly with his hands crossed in his lap and every muscle in his face under control. Clara nearly smiled in pride but caught herself just in time. Of all places, the worship service was the wrong place for pride.

In the row behind Hiram and Josiah, Andrew sat beside Yonnie with the unmarried men. Clara wished she could know what Andrew was thinking, but like all the worshippers, he wiped expression from his face. It pained Clara to think that even if she married Andrew, she could not sit beside him during church and feel him near.

Clara shook off all the trivial hopes and wishes that coursed through her. None of them mattered. She was here to worship and learn, though she did not have to wait for the bishop to announce his Scripture text to know what he would preach about.

Self-discipline. This seemed to be the only theme God had laid on the bishop's heart for the last two years.

Bishop Yoder began to preach.

Clara succeeded at remaining still and attentive, but under its outward form, her body ached to rise and pace across the back of the meetinghouse. Ironically, if she had a colicky baby on her hip instead of a sleeping sister in her lap, she could have done so.

She glanced at Andrew again.

At the sound of the benediction, Andrew's first thought was Clara. As she left the meetinghouse, she glanced over her shoulder at him and met his eyes. Outside, he meandered toward where she strolled without particular aim, making sure to greet several people along the way. Clara was doing the same, but Andrew knew she was waiting for their paths of greeting to cross just as he was.

"*Gut mariye*," he said when he reached her and they stood safely away from other members of the congregation—but not so far as to provoke speculation.

"*Gut mariye,*" Clara answered. "The same as always, was it not?"

They had spoken of Bishop Yoder's sermons before.

"Please don't let him upset you," Andrew said.

"He is working up to something," Clara said. "I believe he can find the theme of discipline in any part of the Bible."

"He preaches what God puts on his heart."

"Does he? Does the Holy Ghost use such judgment?"

"Will you be at the Singing tonight?" Andrew would hear Clara out later, when they were alone, and then their conversation could move on to more personal matters.

Clara nodded. "You'd better go help with the benches."

Andrew's gaze held her eyes for a few more seconds before he turned away to his duties. A few men had already begun transforming benches into tables, and Andrew grabbed the free end of a bench and entered the process.

Beside him a conversation was under way, and it had nothing to do with benches and tables.

"He's doing it again," one man said.

"He never stopped," another responded.

"Almost thirty years of this, ever since he signed that letter in 1887."

"That's history."

"Is it? Bishop Yoder has never found peace with the decision to let the Maryland churches go their own way. That's why he preaches as he does."

With the approach of footsteps, the two men cut off their conversation and carried a bench out of the way. Someone took the other end of Andrew's bench and they moved it over several yards, where it would provide seating on one side of a table. Andrew's partner dropped his end of the bench with a careless thud.

"Are you all right?" Andrew walked along the length of the bench to stand beside the man, someone about ten years older than Andrew whom he did not know well.

The man looked around. Andrew followed his gaze across the room to Noah and Joseph Yoder.

"His sons are the same way, you know," the man said. "Mose Beachy is our only hope."

"Hope for what?" Andrew probed.

They picked up another bench, but the man clamped his lips closed.

"They are all following God the best way they know how," Andrew said.

"Then why does it feel so much like they want us to follow them?" The words, hardly more than a mutter, were the man's last contribution to the conversation. He turned on one heel and found another task in another part of the room.

Andrew straightened benches under tables, seeing in his mind instead of slats of wood the sleek green metal and brass of the Model T.

"It's 1905 all over again," Barbara Stutzman said.

Bishop Yoder had eaten and said his farewells, with Joseph and Noah at his elbows. Several other families had left as well. The women were clearing away the remaining food.

Clara remembered 1905. Rhoda had lost her first baby only weeks before the truth came out at church. At home, Clara's father cared much less about controversy swirling in the congregation than the fragile state of his young wife. Clara had not understood everything that happened at church or at home, but the silence of a child was expected in both places so she dared not ask questions. She muted her curiosity and kept a respectful distance from the grieving adults in her home.

"We were duped in 1895 and again ten years later," Barbara said. "It won't turn out that way this time."

Clara liked Barbara Stutzman as much as she liked her husband, John. But never had she heard Barbara speak out with such certainty. Duped? Surely that was a strong word for the decisions the congregation made.

Rhoda appeared beside Clara. "Are you riding home with us?"

Clara glanced at the group of men sorting out the last of the benches, arranging them in neat rows in readiness for the next time the congregation would gather in the Flag Run Meetinghouse.

"It's a nice day," Clara said. "Perhaps I'll take a walk."

"That's wise." Rhoda looked from Clara to a tangle of unmarried people forming at the meetinghouse door.

Hannah tugged on her mother's sleeve. "I want to walk with Clara."

"You'll ride with us." Rhoda's tone left no room for argument. Hannah knew better than to pout.

Clara squelched the urge to say she would be glad to have Hannah with her. She and Rhoda both knew the girl would tire and begin to whine before all the miles were accomplished, but Clara also saw in Rhoda's eyes the mandate to mingle with the young people who lingered. *"Find someone to marry."* Clara heard Rhoda's voice in her mind. *"Start your own life."*

"And you'll go to the Singing tonight?" Rhoda said.

Clara nodded.

"Good. Then I'm sure you have a full Sabbath ahead of you."

Clara kissed the foreheads of both of her young half sisters and offered her stepmother a wan smile of assurance that she would not be underfoot in the Kuhn household today.

After a long service and a leisurely shared meal, the evening Singing was only a few hours away. Someone would suggest a group walk along Flag Run Creek or a sports game to pass the hours in friendship and laughter. Clara used to enjoy these afternoons more than she did now. Friends her own age had all paired off and married. She and Andrew were two of a diminishing number of people in their twenties who were not married.

And it was not Andrew who kept them in this state.

Clara reasoned that the socializing part of the day had begun and saw no reason not to join Andrew in his cluster of conversation. The circle widened slightly as Clara approached. She stood where she could see Andrew's round face. Whether to be beside him and feel him near or to be able to watch his expressions always was a choice she hated to make. But being seen beside him too often would spark speculation she was not prepared to confront. His eyes met hers but did not linger.

"Bishop Yoder has gone too far this time." John Stutzman spoke with the same conviction Clara had heard in his wife a few minutes earlier. Had they already found a private moment to discuss their feelings about the sermon? Had they decided to speak out, or was it coincidence?

There was no such thing as coincidence, Clara reminded herself. *Gottes wille.* Everything that happened was God's will.

"He said nothing he has not said before." Mose Beachy gave Clara a welcome glance. She was glad to hear his voice, calm and peaceable.

"He's been proud of his power for years," John said.

"That is a serious accusation," Mose said.

Clara shifted her eyes to Yonnie, who stood silently listening.

"Are we not to speak the truth in love?" John said.

Mose reached under his beard to scratch his chin, as he often did during fragile conversations. Clara realized she was holding her breath. Andrew tilted his head toward Mose.

"You speak well," Mose said. "The Scriptures do admonish us to speak the truth in love. We do well if we remember the fine balance of the admonition. Neither truth nor love should obscure the other."

Clara exhaled softly. This was why she liked to hear Mose Beachy preach. These few sentences were more profound—and convicting— than anything Bishop Yoder said in nearly an hour of holding his big German Bible in his hands.

"Lucy is waiting," Mose said. "The little ones will need to go home for their naps." He stepped away.

"Little ones," Yonnie said. "With fourteen children, they've had little ones longer than anyone around here."

"They have a lovely family," John said. "But Mose sets a good example. My wife will be wondering what's become of me as well."

John crossed the room to find his family. The meetinghouse was nearly empty.

Yonnie looked from Andrew to Clara. "Will you be recreating with the others today?"

Clara looked to Andrew for the answer.

"Clara and I will take a walk," Andrew said. "Perhaps we'll join the games later."

Skepticism crossed Yonnie's face, but he moved away from them.

"A walk?" Clara said.

"Do you object?" Andrew gestured toward the door.

She twisted her smile to one side. "Actually, I was hoping to see your Model T."

CHAPTER 7

Andrew turned his buggy down a dark side road. He knew, and Clara knew, that choosing this route home from the Singing would add at least thirty minutes to the ride home. Andrew intended to add much more than that. He had always enjoyed Singings, though he went less often now. Unless Andrew was certain Clara would be there, his interest in the traditional social gathering faltered.

Two lanterns hung from the front of his buggy, lighting the dim, narrow road that divided fields of adjoining farms. Even without the lights, the nearly full moon and the canopy of stars hurled across the sky would have given them safe passage. Andrew knew the road well. No holes awaited the steps of his horse.

It was the stars that brought them out here tonight. Andrew slowed the stallion. The day had been beautiful—any day spent with Clara was beautiful—and he wanted this memory in his mind when he was alone on his farm tonight. Clara beside him. The sky vast above them. The sounds of evening restful around them. The night air cool and fluttering on their faces.

"Thank you for showing me the Model T." Clara's words came on a soft ripple.

The horse clip-clopped forward.

"It means a lot to me that you wanted to see it," Andrew said.

"I love your curious mind," Clara said.

"Even if I am curious about an automobile engine?"

"Would God have made you curious if He knew it would displease Him?"

Andrew turned and smiled at her in the moonlight and slowed the horse even more.

"Have you no doubt?" he asked.

"About the gift of curiosity? No."

"And about the Model T?"

"It was you who found it," she said, "not I."

"I care what you think."

"None of the ministers have preached against the automobile," Clara said. "Not even Bishop Yoder."

Andrew slowly eased the horse to the side of the road and gave the reins a final tug. "Bishop Yoder is too busy preaching about discipline in all its forms."

"Would he not think that owning an automobile is a lack of discipline in some form? Perhaps it has not occurred to him that anyone in the church would consider owning a device the *English* have taken such a liking to."

"Until it comes to a vote in the congregation, what harm will it be for me to learn something from it?" Andrew said. "Eventually the church will have to face the issue. Mr. Ford seems determined to make car ownership affordable."

"Perhaps affordable does not also mean desirable," Clara said.

"Do you find it undesirable?"

"No. Not precisely. I am only hearing in my head the arguments others will make."

"Automobiles could benefit the congregation," Andrew said. "It would be easier for families who live on the outskirts of the district to get to church. The dairy Yonnie works for could transport milk more easily and more quickly without risking spoilage. When someone falls ill, it would be faster to summon the doctor. Those who owned cars could be generous toward others who needed to travel."

"Those are all good points," Clara said. "I spent most of a day driving across the county to tell John Stutzman my father was ill and would not be able to help him with his roof after all."

The buggy creaked and settled. The horse snorted and stilled. Around them, a chorus of insects sprang up with sounds they had not heard above horse hooves falling rhythmically and the squeaking sway of the buggy.

Andrew stared into the jeweled darkness. "'O Lord, our Lord, how excellent is thy name in all the earth! who hast set thy glory above the heavens,'" he murmured.

"'When I consider thy heavens, the work of thy fingers,'" Clara said, "'the moon and the stars, which thou hast ordained; what is man, that thou art mindful of him? and the son of man, that thou visitest him?'"

"I suppose I have told you that Psalm 8 is my favorite psalm," Andrew said.

"About as many times as there are stars in the sky." Clara's voice carried the smile Andrew could not see on her lips. "Whether in sunlight or moonlight, the sky is deep and mysterious. I can't help but think God made it that way so we would know how deep and mysterious He is."

"Do you think it grieves God when we try to make Him too simple?"

"He knows how frail we are," Clara said. "Perhaps our people should all stare at the stars together before we decide that any one of us knows better than another about the will of God."

Andrew twisted on the bench to face Clara. Moonlight threw its sheen over her blue eyes. "You are wise. I would go to your father tonight and ask his blessing on our union if only you would agree."

"I'm sure he would welcome you—though perhaps at a time when you would not be waking him."

"Ah, yes. More wisdom. I would not want to give him any reason to turn me down." He reached for her hand. "Tell me I should go to your father. Just say the word."

"Andrew." Clara withdrew her hand.

"Clara, what are we waiting for? We're ready, aren't we?"

Clara looked down at the hands in her lap. "You may think me wise, but you will not find me courageous."

"Why should it take courage to marry me?"

"No, not to marry you. It's. . .what comes next."

He was sure she was blushing. "We'll figure that out together, won't we?"

"But a child. . ."

"Don't you want to have a child—many children, if the Lord blesses?"

"Andrew, my mother died trying to birth a child. Rhoda lost three babes. Mrs. Wickey. Mrs. Eicher." She paused, and he heard her suck in breath. "The bleeding and the fever—childbirth terrifies me."

Andrew slid along the bench and put an arm around her shoulders. "I won't say it's not frightening. After all, I am not the one who would have to endure it."

She leaned her head against him. "I know. Women have babies all the time. The Beachys have fourteen children and nothing has ever gone wrong. Children *are* a blessing."

"But you're still frightened."

Andrew felt the reluctant nod of her head against his chest.

"Look up again," he said, and she did. "Can anything be more unknown than what lies beyond the planets? Yet you know God is there."

He listened to her breath, out and in, out and in.

"I promise to think more about it." Clara raised her face to him.

Andrew ducked his head down to meet her lips. She didn't pull away. He knew she wouldn't. The yielding welcome made him heady.

The clatter of a moving buggy pulled Andrew out of the kiss. With Clara still in his arms, he leaned back into the shadow of his own buggy. When the buggy passed, they let out their breath together. Clara leaned away.

Clara woke the next morning, as she always did, to the sounds of Rhoda moving through the house and into the kitchen to prepare the family's breakfast. She rose to wash and dress with the efficiency of lifelong habit and reached the kitchen in time to see Rhoda whisking eggs in a bowl. The oven was heating.

"Good morning," Clara said. "Shall I make biscuits?"

"Good morning," Rhoda said. "Thank you, but no. We have corn bread left from yesterday."

Clara looked around the kitchen for something else she could do and settled on straightening the dish towel that hung from a hook. Surely Rhoda would allow that.

"Did you have a nice time at the Singing?" Rhoda poured the eggs into an oblong earthenware baking dish layered with cheese.

"Very nice."

"Who brought you home?"

"Andrew Raber."

"Oh? He's a nice man."

"Yes, he is."

"He's brought you home before, hasn't he?"

"Several times." *Every time,* Clara thought. *For two years.*

Rhoda slid the casserole dish into the oven. "I don't hear you speak of him."

Rhoda moved swiftly from the oven to the counter where the leftover corn bread was wrapped in a worn flour sack. She unwrapped it with one hand while reaching for a knife with the other and slicing the bread into thick chunks.

"I could do that," Clara said. "Are you planning to fry the bread?"

"I can manage." Rhoda wiped the knife clean, put it away, and arranged the bread on a platter. "Andrew Raber? Are the two of you. . . ?"

When Clara was younger, the time she spent with Rhoda in the kitchen before breakfast was an opportunity to talk about whatever might pass through her mind. It was one of the reasons Clara rose in the mornings as soon as she heard her stepmother's movements. Watching Rhoda now, Clara could not be certain if Rhoda asked about Andrew as she might have in their old rhythms or because she wished for Clara to find another home.

Words about Andrew would not form. Instead, Clara said, "I'll get Mari up and dressed in time for breakfast."

"I can do that," Rhoda said. She put the egg bowl in the sink, wiped her hands on her apron, and left the room.

Clara decided she could at least set the table and took six plates from the shelf. She looked up when she heard footsteps with a distinct shuffle that identified them as belonging to Hannah.

"*Mamm* told me to set the table for breakfast," Hannah said.

"I was just about to do it."

"*Mamm* said I was to do it."

"We'll do it together, then." Clara smiled.

Insistence grew in Hannah's tone. "But *Mamm* said I must do it."

Clara released her hold on the plates. The girl was simply trying to obey her mother. Whatever changes might come in Clara's relationship with Rhoda should have nothing to do with a six-year-old child.

After kissing the top of Hannah's head, Clara wandered into the dining room. Staying out of the way for a few minutes seemed a somber way to begin the morning, yet it seemed the sensible thing.

Breakfast was warm and hearty and pinched Clara's heart. The scrubbed, earnest face of her brother, the tight, flawless braids of her sisters' hair and their bright blue eyes, the plain familiar practicality of the kitchen she had known all her life, her father's subdued, unflustered demeanor, the woman who had filled Clara's ache for a mother. Clara's appetite subsided, and for most of the meal she watched the others eat.

What had she done to make Rhoda so eager that Clara should leave?

Rhoda cleared the dishes and Hiram laid the family's thick German Bible on the table. That Bible had come from her mother's family, Clara knew. She had always supposed someday it would be hers. Now she wasn't certain. Hiram read with expression, even if he had chosen to lead the family through the book of Leviticus.

The family scattered to their chores after family devotions. Clara moved into the front room, wondering what might be a safe task to engage in. The mending basket sat at one end of the davenport. Clara remembered the green thread she brought home from the mercantile in Springs and decided to explore the basket. A dark green dress seemed to be the major item. Clara remembered that Hannah had worn it when she was smaller. Rhoda probably wanted to make it suitable for Mari. Lifting it with both hands and holding it out in front of her, Clara inspected the seams and hems and easily assessed what the garment required.

She finished restitching the main seam along one side of the dress just as Rhoda entered the room with Mari on her hip.

"I was planning to do that," Rhoda said.

"I know. I wanted to help." Clara ran the seam between her thumb and forefinger, feeling for any irregularities she had missed.

"Mari is an active child," Rhoda said. "I had in mind to double stitch."

"Certainly. I'll put in another row."

"Thank you, but I can do that later." Rhoda took the dress from Clara's lap, gave the seam a quick glance, and put the garment back in the basket.

Clara stood up, her eyes stinging. "I'm sure the henhouse could use a cleaning."

"That's Josiah's chore now," Rhoda said.

"I'm happy to help. I'll go find him."

"Your father and I are working on teaching Josiah responsibility. I would rather you didn't help him."

"Of course." Clara had always thought Josiah one of the most responsible children she had ever known. "What else can I help you with, then?"

"I can't think of a thing," Rhoda said.

"I can't think of a thing." That was ridiculous. On an Amish farm, there

were always a hundred things to do, inside and out. Clara swallowed her objection to Rhoda's logic.

"I'll watch Mari for you," Clara offered.

"She's fine with me. Why don't you go for a walk?"

Rhoda smiled and her tone was perfectly pleasant, but Clara heard meaning beyond her words.

Rhoda did not need Clara's help.

Clara was too old to need Rhoda's help.

It was time for a change.

Clara should look for another arrangement.

CHAPTER 8

Andrew stood outside the shop for thirteen minutes before he found the resolve to go in. His horse and buggy certainly looked out of place in front of this particular establishment on the road out of Springs, and Andrew himself would look equally out of place inside. This was not the same as going into an *English* hardware store or the mercantile, or even visiting the *English* blacksmith if the Amish blacksmith was too busy and the need was immediate.

The sign over the door read HANSEN'S AUTOMOTIVE REPAIR.

Inside, Andrew scanned a small, unadorned space with two chairs and a large wooden desk. Beyond that was the large work area, with four automobiles lined up. Andrew already had noted five more outside.

A man was bent over an open engine.

Andrew cleared his throat.

The man looked up. "What can I do for you?"

Andrew hesitated over the ridiculous statement he was about to make. "I want to learn to do what you do."

The man stood up straight and looked Andrew in the eye.

"Are you Mr. Hansen?" Andrew asked.

"That's right."

"I have a Model T," Andrew said, "but it doesn't run. I want to learn to fix it."

Hansen picked up a rag and rubbed grease from his hands. "I'm not in the business of teaching. People pay me to fix."

"Couldn't I watch you for a while?"

Hansen scoffed. "I can tow your car in and fix it for you."

In the far corner a young man bent over a trash can and retched. Hansen expelled breath and tossed a wrench on a shelf.

"Sorry," the young man said, wiping his mouth.

"Go home," Hansen said. "You're no help to me in this condition. But clean up after yourself first."

Even across the large garage, the smell of the man's illness wafted as he picked up the trash can and stumbled toward a rear door.

"Let me help you today." Andrew pounced on the moment. "I'll scrub down anything the boy touched and hand you any tool you need. Just let me watch as you work."

Hansen rustled through a toolbox and came up with a tool Andrew had no name for.

"One hour," Hansen said. "If by then you've proven you're not an idiot, then you can stay the day."

"Thank you!" Andrew stepped into the work area.

"Hang up your hat," Hansen said. "It will only get in the way."

Andrew put a hand to the straw brim. He was not in the habit of doing without his hat. The Amish always wore their hats when they were out of their own homes. But he took it off his head and looked for a hook.

Six hours later, Andrew squinted into the daylight again. He and Jurgen Hansen had gotten along well, and Andrew now carried a small carton with several small parts and tools, along with a general idea that the problem with his Model T was that something was obstructing the fuel going into the engine.

Yonnie drove the milk wagon to the abandoned Johnson farm the next morning and guardedly turned into the lane that would lead to the outlying shed. It was the only place he could think to look for Andrew.

Living alone, Andrew had decided it was easier to buy milk, butter, and cheese from the dairy than to keep a cow. Yonnie checked a couple of times a week on what Andrew needed. When Andrew's milk box had no empty bottles in it that Tuesday morning, Yonnie had gone inside the house. Dishes in the sink had dried egg on them at least a day old. In Andrew's bedroom, the bed looked undisturbed. It took Yonnie a few minutes to sort out what else looked wrong, but finally it dawned on him.

Approaching the old Johnson barn, Yonnie knew he was right. Andrew's horse was tethered with a long lead that allowed it to nibble the ground freely, swish its tail, and shake its mane. Yonnie left the milk wagon and pushed open the shed door.

Andrew looked up. "Yonnie! How did you know where I was?"

Yonnie stepped inside. "I stopped at your house. When I realized every lantern you own was missing, I could think of only one reason. You've been here all night fooling with that automobile."

Andrew grinned. "And I think I've figured it out."

"Are you hoping I will congratulate you?" Yonnie counted nine lanterns burning, set on shelves, barrels, the roof of the car, and flat surfaces beside the engine.

"Think what you will," Andrew said. "I'm pleased."

"If you knock over even one of these lanterns, you could burn the place down."

"I'm not going to knock anything over," Andrew said. "Besides, I'm finished."

"You don't deny that you were here all night?" Yonnie put out the lamp that made him most nervous because of its proximity to the only bale of hay left in the barn.

"Since you're here," Andrew said, "it must be morning. So yes, I was here all night."

Yonnie watched the ruddy flush of pleasure in Andrew's face. Not many things would make Andrew stay up all night. He liked his sleep. That was one reason he decided not to keep a cow, gladly reducing his early-morning responsibilities.

"When was the last time you ate?" Yonnie asked.

"Are you planning to report to my mother in Lancaster County?" Andrew used a rag to polish a small hand tool that Yonnie did not recognize.

"Where did you get that?" Yonnie said. "And what is it?"

"I could answer you," Andrew said, "but somehow I doubt the sincerity of your inquiry."

"You are getting in over your head, aren't you?"

Andrew flashed another grin. "Have you already forgotten that I said I fixed it? It was choking for fuel, and now it'll get what it needs for the engine to run."

"So now what?"

"We take it for a test ride."

"We?"

"Never mind. I know it would rattle your nerves to get in an automobile, so I won't ask it of you." Andrew bent down, found the opening, inserted the crank, and turned it. The Model T proposed no response.

Yonnie took a few steps closer, his brow furrowed. "Are you sure you know what you're doing?"

"Haven't you ever seen one of the *English* in town start a car?"

"Haven't you ever noticed how often they can't get them started?"

"Those are the older models," Andrew said. "This one is only a couple of years old." He abandoned the crank to check the levers inside the car.

"This is not wise," Yonnie said. "This automobile will consume your thoughts. You will neglect your fields at an important time in the growing season."

Andrew cocked his head. "My corn is growing just fine. All it needs right now is sun, rain, and time. I can't control any of those things."

"You're a farmer, not an automobile. . ." Yonnie was uncertain what to call a person who knew how to repair a car.

"Ah, yes," Andrew said. "I forgot this lever has to be up. Now I should feel the compression."

Andrew jumped back to the crank. He pulled up swiftly and the engine caught, its roar consuming the small barn.

"Are you sure that's how it's supposed to sound?" Yonnie shouted over the noise.

"It's running!" Andrew leaped onto the bench behind the steering wheel. "I'm going to take it out."

"Out where?"

"To the road, of course. Stand clear."

Yonnie did not move. How could Andrew not see that he would make an incriminating situation more serious if he took the car out of this barn?

"Out of the way," Andrew said. He looked down at his feet and moved the hand lever rising straight up out of the floor to the left of the steering wheel. A sound like the kick of a rifle startled them both.

Involuntarily, Yonnie jumped out of the way.

Andrew gripped the steering wheel with both hands as the Model T rolled out of the barn. He might have had a more accurate expectation of the sensation had he ever ridden in a car before. His instinct to pull on reins to control speed was no help, and instead of the brake pedal, his foot found the gear pedal and the car lurched forward.

Throttle, he reminded himself. What was it Mr. Hansen had said? Use the throttle lever to slow the engine and change gears smoothly.

The speed stabilized just as Andrew reached the farm's lane. He turned the steering wheel to the left, realized he had pulled it too far, and turned back toward the right slightly. The next turn would be better. The right front tire dipped into a rut in the road, and again Andrew tugged on the steering wheel with both fists to correct the forward motion.

"Whoa!" he said aloud, as he would to a horse. The Model T chugged forward. Andrew's eyes went from his hands to the levers as he tried to remember the notes he'd taken and what they meant. Mr. Hansen had spoken so quickly, as if Andrew understood all the terms he used. Andrew planted his feet on the floor, remembering that if he did not want to change from low gear to high or to slow the speed, his feet had nothing to do. That was not so different than driving a buggy. Looking through the glass shielding his eyes from the wind, he began to plan how to turn right onto the main road.

To his relief, no automobile, horse, or buggy was coming into his path. Without having to stop, he turned to the right, once again pulling too hard on the wheel and correcting as swiftly as he could. The Model T zigzagged across the road several times before he gained control of the trajectory.

He needed to slow down. Another driver could appear over the next rise, or a horse pulling a wagon, whether *English* or Amish.

Slow down. Find the gear pedal. Be ready with the brake pedal on the left. No, the brake is on the right. Yes, the right. Be careful not to press the reverse pedal.

While Andrew planned the series of motions, the car hit a bump. The entire automobile twitched to the left. Forgetting about the pedals, Andrew pulled the steering wheel to the right.

When he lifted his eyes again, a ditch was rapidly approaching. The front wheels dropped off the road. The car stopped abruptly, the engine died, and the right rear tire spun in the air.

Andrew let out his breath and then gulped fresh air, his heart pounding. He'd been doing so well. A horse didn't go off the road every time it hit a bump.

The soft spring earth had yielded graciously. Andrew was relieved to hear no thud or crash. He climbed out of the seat and inspected the Model T, ignoring the bump his knee had taken against the dashboard.

Yonnie slowed the milk wagon on the main road. Before his eyes lay the evidence that Andrew, in fact, did not know what he was doing. Andrew waved from beside the rear axle of the Model T, and Yonnie gave the reins a final tug.

"I'm going to need to borrow a rope again," Andrew said.

Yonnie eyed the precarious tilt of the car. "Perhaps this is the revelation of God's will for you."

"I doubt it." Andrew said. "Anyway, I can't just leave it here."

He certainly could, Yonnie believed. "I'm already late on my rounds."

"Dale won't begrudge you stopping to help someone in need."

Yonnie sucked in his lips, thinking, *Even if your own sin brought you to your need?*

Andrew approached the wagon. "This is not the time to worry about rules, Yonnie."

"If you were concerned about rules, you wouldn't have this automobile." Yonnie reluctantly got out of the wagon and lifted a coil of thick rope from where it hung on the side. "Where is your allegiance to the faith of our fathers?"

"You can preach at me later," Andrew said. "Right now we have to figure out how to get out of the ditch without breaking the axle."

Yonnie tossed the rope to Andrew, sighing in disbelief that he agreed to have anything to do with this automobile. Even the *English* owner had the good sense to abandon it.

CHAPTER 9

The walk from the Kuhn farm to Springs was six and one-quarter miles.

But Clara found no reason not to walk.

Nothing pressing took her to town, either, but she had to get off the farm. In the last day and a half, she tried to polish Rhoda's cedar chest in the front room, wipe the dust from the kitchen cupboards, and mend the tiny weak spots she noticed in the good white tablecloth. Rhoda discouraged every indoor effort, so Clara moved into the June sunshine to sweep and mop the front porch, weed the vegetable garden, and scrub out the slop bucket. Even outdoors, though, Josiah or Hannah turned up with instructions from their mother to complete whatever task Clara began. They were small children. They could help and learn—even eagerly—but on their own they could not accomplish what Clara could do.

Rhoda did not raise her voice or express impatience. She simply was firm and consistent. So Clara, who had only the cash from two housecleaning jobs to call her own and did not carry it around, walked to town and moved between the shops. Her father had accounts at a few of them. If Clara had a true need, she could make a purchase, but she knew she wouldn't. She only needed to be off the farm.

Clara stared at her reflection in the glass of the mercantile window. Down the street was an Amish furniture store, and farther down was a grocer who carried products from the Amish dairy. The bank in Springs held the mortgages on Amish farms. Clara could name many Amish families who rarely came off their farms and even more rarely transacted business with the *English*, but many others saw no harm.

The *English* and two Amish districts huddled around the border between Pennsylvania and Maryland. Most of the *English* could not tell the difference between the two types of Amish, though the Amish certainly recognized the subtle distinctions in clothing and hair coverings. Undoubtedly they knew who attended church in which meetinghouse on alternate Sundays.

When a clerk inside the mercantile looked out the window, Clara moved down the street. She had not brought even a few coins to buy a sandwich or a cup of coffee. She shuffled to the next shop window, an *English* dress shop. Realizing where she was, she didn't linger. It was better to keep moving even if all she did was walk around the block looking purposeful.

Maybe she should have walked to Niverton instead. She could at least sit on the old log outside the meetinghouse and feel less conspicuous.

Clara hadn't been to church with Fannie or any of the Hostetlers since she was a little girl, before her father married Rhoda and she used to spend long leisure weeks with her cousins. Then everything changed. Hiram became more firm that his daughter's visits over the border should conclude in time to have Clara home with her own family on Sundays when the congregation gathered at Summit Mills or Flag Run. In the last dozen years, Hiram did not explain his decision, but neither did he soften.

Would he really now allow Rhoda to dispatch Clara to Maryland to worship with her mother's family again? Or would he oppose Clara if she wanted to? Or would he insist Clara go if she did *not* want to?

Martha and Fannie and all the others would welcome Clara. They would welcome Andrew if she married him, and he would go.

And why wouldn't he go? He was no more inclined toward Bishop Yoder's sermons than Clara was. His own parents had moved to Lancaster County. His married siblings were scattered over several districts in Pennsylvania and Ohio. Nothing held him to the Old Order Amish, as they became known after the 1895 split.

Clara wished she remembered more about that year.

Perhaps it would not feel so odd to join the Conservative Amish Mennonites—or at least to visit them.

"Clara Kuhn!"

Clara turned toward the voice. Sarah Tice strode toward her with a towheaded child attached to each hand.

"It seems like we never get a chance to talk anymore," Sarah said.

It was true. Clara had gone all the way through school with Sarah. After that they often found an excuse to visit one another. The distance between their farms had not been daunting. When Sarah married Jacob Tice, though, she moved farther out. Getting to her farm north of the Summit Mills Meetinghouse required more planning. Even at church, Sarah's attention was occupied with her little ones, and it was difficult to have a satisfying conversation.

Clara realized one child was missing. "Where's your little girl?"

"I insisted Jacob keep at least one of the children with him or I'd never get my shopping done."

One of the little boys raised his arms to be lifted up.

"Will he let me hold him?" Clara asked on impulse.

Sarah nodded, and Clara bent to lift the boy. Sarah had always wanted a houseful of children. It was no surprise that she had three within five years. Clara liked children—the wonder of them, the tiny completeness of them. It was the process of carrying and birthing children that simmered reluctance. As girls, whenever Sarah gushed about children, Clara changed the subject.

"Are you still cleaning houses?" Sarah asked.

Clara nodded. "Just two right now, Widower Hershberger and an *English* family."

"You might as well enjoy a bit of pocket money while you can. I heard Widower Hershberger is getting married. He's been corresponding with his late wife's cousin in Ohio. I imagine he won't need you much longer."

Clara determined that nothing should show on her face. Mr. Hershberger had said nothing to her. It was the sort of personal information Sarah always seemed to know before anyone else.

Clara stared into the dark eyes of Sarah's little boy, waiting to ache for her own.

"We should go," Sarah said. "But let's plan a proper visit. Can you borrow a buggy from your *daed* and come to our place?"

"Maybe," Clara said. She surrendered the boy to his mother.

"Please try. The children are down for naps right after lunch."

Sarah rearranged her grip on her sons' hands and resumed walking. Clara turned back to the mercantile window, though if anyone asked her later what she had seen, her answers would be vague.

A gleeful shriek behind Clara made her spin around to see a little *English* boy, older than Sarah's littlest son but younger than Mari, galloping down the walkway. The joy on the child's face evaporated in an instant when he stumbled. Clara reached out and caught him before his tender hands and face scraped the ground. Startled, the boy looked up at Clara with a trembling lower lip. Instinctively, Clara pulled the little one into her arms and whispered reassurance in his ear.

The child's anxious mother arrived a few steps later. "Thank you! He got away from me so quickly."

"He's fine." Clara released the boy into his mother's arms and watched them continue down the street.

Was this what her future held? Handing other people's children back to them because she was frightened to have her own?

Suddenly she wanted to see Andrew.

The wrench slipped out of Andrew's grip and knocked his kneecap before falling to the barn floor. With a short yelp, he hopped on one foot. This was the third time, and he hadn't successfully adjusted his grasp.

"Are you all right?"

Andrew refrained from rubbing his knee and looked up. "Clara! What are you doing here?"

She stepped inside, put her hands behind her slender waist, and leaned against the door frame. "I was out for a walk."

"On your way somewhere?" Andrew said. Clara was a fair distance from the Kuhn farm for a walk with no purpose.

She shook her head. "Just walking."

"Is everything all right?"

Clara pushed herself away from the wall. "How's the work on the car coming?"

"I can't seem to hold on to a wrench." He bent to pick up the tool. "Are you sure you're all right?"

Clara shrugged one shoulder. "I just needed some fresh air."

"Something on your mind?"

"Nothing important." She smiled, the gesture manufactured for Andrew's benefit. "Have you figured out what you're doing?"

Andrew tilted his head to consider her face and decided not to press. They hadn't seen each other since Sunday night. Anything could have happened in two days. When she was ready, she would talk to him. He'd waited two years for her already and did not plan to give up. If they never married, it would not be his decision bringing that result.

"I had it running yesterday," Andrew said.

She moved to stand beside him, her hands still behind her waist, and leaned over to peer at the engine. With another smile—genuine, this time—she looked at him out of the side of her eyes.

"You used the past tense," she said.

"I admit to an unplanned incident. But there were no witnesses to the actual circumstances, so I won't embarrass myself by divulging the details."

Clara burst out laughing. Andrew grinned.

She stepped back and examined the car. "It doesn't *look* broken."

"It's not broken. I fixed it."

She raised one eyebrow. "So you've put the. . .er, incident. . . behind you?"

"Let me offer you an irresistible bargain." Andrew closed the cover over the engine. "Come for a ride with me."

"A ride! Now?"

He fixed on her eyes and nodded.

Clara put her hands on the car and looked inside.

"Do you even know what to do with those pedals and levers?"

"Mostly."

She laughed again.

"You're a long way from home," he said. "Wouldn't you like to get off your feet?"

She gestured toward a misshapen bale of hay in one corner. "I could sit there."

"But it wouldn't be nearly as much fun." Andrew opened the automobile's door. "Here we have a tufted seat with a full back made of the finest leather."

"Well," she said, "it's true that while I've done a great deal of thinking today, I've had very little fun."

"We'll stay on the back roads," Andrew said. After the detour into the ditch, he had found a balance between enthusiasm and caution.

Clara stepped up into the Model T. Before she had time to change her mind, Andrew reached in to set the levers, snatched the crank from under the seat, and sprinted around to the front of the automobile to insert it.

This time he got it started on the first attempt.

Clara gripped the bench with both hands, but she giggled as Andrew steered the Model T out of the barn.

"How did you learn to do this?" She raised her voice above the motor.

"After my. . .incident. . .I spent a good part of yesterday practicing." Andrew made a smooth turn onto a path barely wide enough for the Model T. After getting the Ford safely back to the barn, Yonnie had clucked his tongue in disapproval. Andrew, however, made a few adjustments that were surprisingly easy, considering his limited mechanical knowledge, and had the car running again before lunchtime. Then he gave himself some proper driving lessons around the abandoned farm.

"Today the back roads," he said to Clara. "Tomorrow, Springs."

Her eyes widened. "Would you really drive to Springs?"

"Why have an automobile if you don't plan to use it?"

"Why indeed?"

He gave her a half grin. "Well, maybe not tomorrow, but just wait. The day will come."

Gradually Clara relaxed her grip. She had imagined the sensation of riding in an automobile would feel faster, more like a constant gallop than a sedate trot. Before Sunday, when she saw the automobile for the first time, Clara had not been on the old Johnson farm. She was uncertain where the narrow road Andrew chose would take them.

"How fast can it go?" she asked.

"I'm not sure," Andrew said. "I haven't been in high gear yet."

"Are we going to try high gear?" The hopefulness in her own voice surprised Clara.

"If that's what you want."

She made no effort to contain her mischievous spirit.

"Let me find the gear pedal." Andrew let his knees fall open so he could see his feet, put his foot on a pedal, and moved the hand lever before opening the throttle. "Here we go!"

The car thrust forward. With the wind in her face, Clara noticed Andrew was not wearing his hat. She had never before seen the wave of brown hair in its entirety. Like all Amish men, Andrew was well trained to wear his hat, whether black felt in the winter or straw in the summer.

Today it would not have mattered, because a hat would not have stayed on as the car picked up speed.

A clatter crumbled Clara's thoughts.

"What's that?" she asked.

Andrew's hands were busy adjusting levers. Despite his efforts, the engine sputtered and seized, and the Model T came to an abrupt halt.

"What happened?" she said.

Bracing himself and swinging his legs over the door without pausing to open it, Andrew leaped out of the car. "I'm beginning to understand why the previous owner was so eager to be finished with this car."

"But you're not giving up, are you?"

"Of course not." He flipped open the engine cover, releasing steam. "We might have to let it cool down, but it won't take long. We haven't been driving long enough for it to be too hot."

Clara found a lever that looked like it might open the door. She got out and leaned against the car.

"That was the best four minutes I've had all day," Clara said.

Andrew joined her against the car, nudging her shoulder with his. "I had a feeling you weren't having a very good day."

The words swirling in Clara's mind were slow to find structure, but she knew Andrew would wait.

"You're a little older than I am," she said finally. "What do you remember about 1905?"

"A lot of things."

"I mean, in the church. Why would Barbara Stutzman say that last Sunday was like 1895 all over again? That the congregation had been duped then and again ten years later?"

Andrew sighed. "Bishop Yoder had just been ordained to the office in 1895. He had strong feelings about the Maryland churches separating."

"He still does. But the congregation voted, didn't they?"

"Yes. Officially. Ten years later the truth came out."

"What truth?"

"I remember eavesdropping while my parents talked," Andrew said, "although I didn't have to try very hard. They were upset. Their voices grew loud."

Clara moved away from the car to stand where she could look Andrew in the face. "What happened, Andrew?"

"When Bishop Yoder asked for the vote, he said he had consulted another bishop, Joseph Witmer. It's possible he sincerely misunderstood what Bishop Witmer meant to communicate, but my parents—and a lot of others—were convinced he knew exactly what he was doing. The congregation voted unanimously to do just the opposite of what Bishop Witmer had advised."

Andrew's soft words sank in.

"Bishop Yoder deceived the congregation?" Clara was stunned. "All these years—the sermons about shunning the Maryland believers."

"Hardly anyone really wanted to do that." Andrew picked up a pebble and tossed it into a field overgrown with weeds. "But the vote in 1895 was unanimous."

"And our people do not easily set aside such a vote." Clara pressed on her temples. "That explains why hardly anyone whose name is not Yoder obeys the ban."

"Bishop Yoder is getting old," Andrew said. "He won't be bishop forever."

"But his sons," Clara countered. "One of them could be the next bishop."

"Or it could be Mose Beachy." Andrew paced back to the engine. "Let's not borrow trouble."

CHAPTER 10

P lease!"

Hannah tugged on Clara's sleeve two days later.

Clara dropped into the grass. She had wandered away from the house with a box of letter paper intending to finish a story to send to Sadie—and not knowing that Hannah followed. Clara glanced toward the house, wondering if Rhoda knew where her daughter was.

Hannah plopped down next to Clara. "I only want you to tell me about Sadie. I already know you like to visit her and she's your cousin."

"My cousin's daughter." Clara offered the gentle correction.

"That's still a cousin." Hannah rolled onto her stomach, planted her elbows, and propped up her chin with her hands. "What is she like?"

"Lively." Clara chuckled. "She likes running and doing cartwheels, and her *mamm* has to remind her about chores."

"Just like my *mamm* has to remind me."

"She's not old enough for school yet, but I think she's going to like it when she goes."

"Just like me. I like school!"

"And she loves cherry strudel," Clara said.

Hannah sat up. "I like apple strudel, but it's still strudel."

Clara's thumbs played with the corners of the box of letter paper. Intuition told her not to mention to Hannah the Bible stories that Clara sent to Sadie.

"Do you think Sadie and I could be friends?" Hannah crossed her legs and straightened her skirt around them.

"I'm sure you would like each other," Clara said. Why shouldn't they? Hannah and Sadie were two little Amish girls going to church and learning the ways their people had followed for more than two hundred years.

"I want to visit Sadie with you," Hannah said. "I want to very, very much."

Clara reached over and squeezed the girl's hand. "I know." The farm Sadie lived on was only five miles away, but it might as well have been the desolate settlement in Colorado that Clara read about in *The Budget*.

"Ask *Mamm* if you can take me," Hannah said. "I promise to be good and clean up after myself."

"We'll see," Clara said.

"Priscilla's dog is going to have puppies."

"Oh?" Clara was relieved at the change of subject.

"In about two more weeks. I'm going to start asking *Mamm* if I can go play with Priscilla every day. I want to be there when the babies are born so I can watch."

Clara winced. Her father had delivered the young of cows and horses over the years. It happened on every farm. But Clara never wanted to watch.

Their heads turned together toward the sound of Mari's crying. Rhoda approached, one hand tight around her youngest daughter's fingers.

"Hannah, you have chores to do in the barn," Rhoda said.

"See," Hannah said. "She reminds me, just like Sadie's *mamm* reminds her."

Clara nodded but did not speak.

"Ask her now," Hannah said. She scampered toward the barn.

"Ask me what?" Rhoda said.

"It's just something Hannah wants to do," Clara said.

"Why was she talking about Sadie?"

Clara stood up. This conversation would be difficult enough without having Rhoda towering over her.

"She wants to meet Sadie," Clara said. "We could go and come back on the same day."

"Meet Sadie? What on earth for?" Rhoda released Mari's hand, and the little girl stretched out in the grass.

"She's curious. That's all. I think they would get on well together."

"Absolutely not."

Clara took in a breath. "They're just little girls. I'm Hannah's sister and related to Sadie. It's not such a stretch, is it?"

"The Hostetlers are your mother's people. I have never suggested you should not see them if you wish. But Hannah is not related to them. I see no reason to confuse her about where she belongs."

Clara looked at Mari in the cool grass, her little fingers sliding up and down a single blade. Her eyes lifted to the barn in time to see Hannah disappear inside its cavernous door. Rhoda protected where Hannah belonged but plainly would feel no loss if Clara crossed the border. Clara was twenty-three and did not understand the false line represented by the state border. How would little children understand it? Hot disappointment seared through Clara.

❦

Andrew wondered how many times he would have to bring a horse and buggy to Hansen's Automotive Repair. The Model T was safely back in the outlying barn on the Johnson land, but ever since he put it in high gear two days ago, it made a sound that unnerved Andrew.

Jurgen Hansen looked up from where he sat at a desk strewn with papers. "How's your Model T?"

"You were right about the carburetor." Andrew eyed the rack beside the door, hoping he would have another opportunity to hang his straw hat there. "The car is running now, but I don't believe it is as reliable as it ought to be."

"Automobiles are sensitive machines," Hansen said.

"I'm learning that," Andrew said. "I wonder if I might help you around the shop again today."

"I can't pay you," Hansen said.

"I would pay you if I could," Andrew said, "for teaching me."

"It's only a matter of some basic science about the combustion engine, and a little trial and error about your engine in particular."

"I suppose it's like getting to know the temperament of a horse," Andrew said.

Hansen laughed. "More like a small herd of horses."

Andrew licked his lips. "Will you help me tame my herd?"

The shop owner looked around. "If you clean up the two end bays, I'll let you watch while I work on the next two cars."

Andrew snatched his hat off his head and tossed it onto a hook.

Outside the rear door was a water spigot, and he knew where the broom and mop were. While Andrew cleaned, Jurgen Hansen rummaged through tools and assorted small parts on three shelves. Inspecting the engine and undercarriage of his own automobile meant Andrew recognized some of the shapes, even if he did not know the names or functions for everything. Andrew attacked the clutter and dirt in a manner that would have made his *mamm* proud, determined to be ready to learn by the time Jurgen Hansen was ready to work. At one point, Andrew tilted his head back and followed with his eyes the path of the electric wiring that illumined the bays.

They worked for four hours. Andrew watched Jurgen's movements closely, asking as few questions as possible so he would not provoke impatience, but enough to undergird his growing understanding of the complex challenge of keeping an automobile running. The broom and a stack of clean rags were always within reach. Andrew kept the bays clean.

The afternoon yawned ahead of them. Finally, Jurgen went outside to the water spigot to scrub his hands clean and returned to his desk, where he pulled from a desk drawer a sandwich wrapped in waxed paper.

"Let's have lunch," Jurgen said, "and then I think I'd like to see your car."

Andrew accepted the half sandwich Jurgen offered. "I don't want to take up your time."

"Nonsense. The car I drive can go forty miles an hour." Jurgen winked. "Wouldn't you like to do that?"

Andrew glanced out the door at his horse. Despite being a large stallion, the animal had never been especially fast, even at a gallop—which Andrew rarely required of him. Forty miles an hour! And in a car that was not likely to cough and seize in the performance of its duties.

They finished the sandwich, and Jurgen tossed Andrew an apple before shuffling papers around to reveal a crank on his desk.

"Don't ever leave the crank in the automobile," Jurgen said. "That's all someone would need to take the car."

Andrew was so fixed on getting the Model T running that he had not thought how easily someone else might drive off with it. *Mine* surged through his mind, the intensity of possession surprising him. He offered his half-eaten apple to his horse, made certain the lead was secured to a tree, and then climbed into Jurgen Hansen's sleek, shiny automobile. Already Andrew could tell this Model T was one of the newest versions.

"Are those headlamps electric?" Andrew said in sudden realization. He had tested the lamps on his car and discovered they required oil to produce illumination.

"Yes sir!" Jurgen said. "The horn, too."

When Jurgen cranked, the car responded with a smooth compliance rather than the clatter Andrew expected. He had further to go than he realized in achieving the best his Model T could give.

Jurgen pulled on his driving gloves, adjusted his goggles, and put the car in gear. "Which way?"

Andrew pointed, and Jurgen took the automobile out on the road. The top was down on this sunny day, and the wind against his face reminded Andrew he had left his hat behind on the hook.

"Isn't it unusual for your people to own an automobile," Jurgen said, "even one that doesn't work very well?"

"Unusual, yes."

"It's not against the rules?"

Andrew paused before answering. "The automobile raises some questions that the church will consider with great thought."

Jurgen put the car into high gear, and Andrew felt the smile pushing against the corners of his lips as he judged the speed. Trot. Canter. Gallop. More than gallop. He could not see the speedometer, but surely they had reached forty miles an hour. Andrew squinted into the wind, understanding why the hardware store sold goggles among its automotive supplies.

This was how an automobile was meant to run.

Andrew gestured a couple of turns, and they arrived at the old Johnson barn. He pushed open the rickety door and Jurgen walked in.

After only a glance at the car, Jurgen laughed in rich, deep amusement.

"What is funny?" Andrew asked.

Jurgen pulled off his gloves. "I know this car. It has been in my shop many times."

Andrew's stomach soured. "Then it will never run the way yours does."

"Of course it will." Jurgen ran a hand along a front fender. "The owner often refused my advice. He didn't give it the care it required. I suspect your attitude will be different."

"I'll take all the advice you'll offer," Andrew said. "I want to learn everything about it."

"Once you get it running smoothly, it will be worth something," Jurgen said. "Don't give up."

The milk wagon rumbled onto the dairy grounds at the end of Yonnie's afternoon rounds. Twelve tall capped metal cans rattled in the wagon bed. Every day the temperatures crept up and Yonnie perspired more with the effort of lifting the cans from the springs where they cooled on Amish farms into the wagon to haul them to the dairy. Today Yonnie had worked in the dairy early in the morning, done a large unscheduled delivery, and then went directly into the afternoon loop to farms on both sides of the border. His muscles ached, and his lunch had long ago worn off.

Dale Borntrager stomped out of the main building, where workers bottled milk and churned butter.

"Yoder, where have you been?"

Yonnie gave the reins a final tug and jumped down from the bench. "On the rounds, of course."

"You disappeared early and didn't come back."

"I made the special delivery." Yonnie's stomach tightened. "An *English* order."

"On the wrong day!" Dale said.

Yonnie slumped against the wagon. "I saw the note in the office."

"For tomorrow." Dale glared.

"Tomorrow?"

"Nobody was expecting that delivery today."

Yonnie reached into the wagon. "But I got a signature."

"From a young woman who didn't know she could do anything else. She's not even out of *English* school yet and is just helping out for the summer. She closed up right after you left, thinking her boss must have known the milk was coming and would be there soon."

Yonnie closed his eyes. "He didn't come."

"Not for hours. The milk sat outside all that time."

"So it spoiled."

"You know better, Yonnie. You rushed and misread the note, then you rushed and left the order with that young woman. Your distraction cost me good money."

"I'm sorry. Take it out of my wages."

"Of course I will. When you make a mistake, you must be prepared to face the consequences."

CHAPTER 11

Clara wasn't sleeping, or even dozing. By midmorning on Monday, she had exhausted a brief series of small chores that could just as well have gone undone—which likely was why Rhoda offered no objection to Clara's efforts—and withdrew to her room and cleaned it unnecessarily. The floor was spotless, and her dresses and *kapps* hung neatly on their hooks. On the nightstand, her small collection of books was stacked according to size. Clara saw no reason not to stretch out on the quilt of red and brown diamonds and indulge in daydreaming about the next Bible story she would write for Sadie. Jesus' parable of the servant who received mercy yet refused to offer mercy came to mind.

Rhoda's steps clipped a firm rhythm on the bare wood of the upstairs hall. Clara sat up and snatched a book from the stack to look busy. Rhoda appeared in the doorway with Mari in her arms.

"When Hannah asked if she could stay the night with the Schrocks," Rhoda said, "I promised Mrs. Schrock I would fetch her before lunch. I'm going now."

Clara scooted to the edge of her bed. "Let me go. I haven't had my walk today."

"I can see you're reading."

Clara closed the book. "Just passing the time."

"*Danki*, but I can manage."

Mari put her open palms on her mother's chest and straightened her arms, pushing back. Rhoda compensated for the disturbance in balance by adjusting her grip.

"Mari!"

395

Rhoda's tone carried a warning Clara had first recognized years ago, but Mari ignored it. Instead, the little girl shifted her hips from side to side.

"I want down!" Mari said.

Rhoda gave the child a stern look, but she set her on her feet.

"It's a long way for Mari to walk," Clara said. "I would be happy to go."

"I'm going to take the cart," Rhoda said.

"I don't like the cart." Mari threw herself to the floor.

"Marianne Kuhn, you get up this minute." Rhoda planted her hands on her hips.

Mari had been a tempestuous toddler, and even now at three years old and with a more than adequate vocabulary, she still pitched fits. Rhoda responded by striking an implacable pose. Clara was never sure who would be more stubborn, mother or child.

"Get up!" Her hands still on her hips, Rhoda now widened her stance.

"No!" Mari flung her arms over her head.

"We're going to get Hannah."

"I don't like Hannah!"

"Hannah is your sister."

"No, Clara is my sister."

Clara averted her eyes, not wanting to witness the color that would flush through Rhoda's face at her daughter's declaration.

"Please," Clara said, "let me go for Hannah."

Rhoda huffed. "Under the circumstances, all right. But take the cart. Hannah will get halfway home and start complaining about having to walk."

Clara couldn't disagree with that assessment. Hannah was likely to stop in the middle of a field and insist that she couldn't walk another step.

Clara snatched a *kapp* off a hook and set it on her head before stepping around her youngest sister's tantrum.

"I want to go with Clara." Mari sat up.

"You most certainly will not." Rhoda glared.

Mari put a finger in her mouth and glared back.

Clara took the stairs quickly, whistled for the mare in the pasture, and hitched up the cart. The horse trotted cooperatively down the lane. As Clara arrived at the Schrocks' farmhouse, the front door opened and Mattie Schrock stood on the porch.

"I'm glad you're here," Mattie said. "I was just thinking I might have to bring Hannah home myself."

Clara got out of the cart. "I hope she hasn't been any trouble. She loves to play with Priscilla."

"They played together nicely," Mattie said. "But ever since breakfast, Hannah hasn't been feeling well."

"Hannah is sick?" Clara glanced past Mattie and into the house.

"She's up in the girls' room. I made the other children leave her alone to rest."

"May I go up?"

"Of course."

Upstairs, Clara touched the sleeping girl's forehead. Heat answered her inquiry. Hannah stirred.

"I'm here to take you home," Clara said softly.

"My throat hurts." Hannah's raspy reply gave evidence of her claim.

Next to the bed, a full glass of water appeared untouched. Clara picked it up. "Will you drink some water, please?"

Hannah shook her head. "It hurts to swallow."

"Just a sip?" Clara put the glass to Hannah's lips.

Hannah took a drink, grimacing at the effort.

Clara set the glass back on the side table and slid her arms around her sister's slight form, whispering a prayer of gratefulness for the cart.

At home on the Kuhn farm, Clara carried Hannah into the house and laid her on the davenport.

"What's going on?" Rhoda came in from the kitchen, Mari trailing behind her in an improved mood.

"Hannah is sick." Clara arranged a pillow under Hannah's head.

"I'll sit with her," Rhoda said.

Clara started to move away, but Hannah grabbed her wrist.

"I want Clara," Hannah whispered.

"Clara has taken good care of you to get you home," Rhoda said, "but your *mamm* is here now."

"I want Clara," Hannah repeated, tightening her grasp on Clara's arm.

Clara winced at the effort required for her sister to speak at all. She would gladly sit all day and night with the girl, but Hannah was Rhoda's child, and Rhoda wanted to care for her. Rhoda kissed Hannah's forehead and stroked her cheek. Hannah's fingers opened and her hand slid off Clara's wrist.

"We'll make ice cream," Rhoda said. "You'll like that on your throat, won't you?"

Hannah nodded.

Clara stepped away.

"Don't go," Hannah said.

"I'm here," Rhoda said, looking at Clara more than at her daughter. "Clara can go now."

After twelve days, the Model T looked at home in the rickety Johnson outbuilding. And Andrew felt at home with it. A few days of neglect required him to tend to the chores on his own farm—Yonnie was right about that. Andrew did need to take care of his crop. But now he left most of his lamps and lanterns with the automobile so that whenever he had a few hours to work on it, he could see clearly what he was doing. At home, alone in the big house where he grew up, Andrew could move one or two lights around as he needed them, but he spent most of his evenings with the Model T. Jurgen Hansen was generous with suggestions—and even spare parts. Though he spoke English, Andrew was not a fluid reader in the language. Still, he took home the papers Jurgen gave him to study, painstakingly sounding out words his German mind did not immediately recognize.

The moon was waning now. Andrew left the Johnson land, but rather than turning toward his own farm, he let the horse amble in the other direction—toward the Kuhn farm and a path running through Hiram Kuhn's fields. Experience in the last two years reinforced this inclination often enough that Andrew waited in the dark more frequently than anyone knew—even Clara. He waited for her. She would sometimes come out for a night walk, and he would "happen" to be staring at the stars when she did.

Andrew could hardly use that excuse tonight, though. The sky had clouded over while he adjusted the carburetor on the Model T. Dense humidity clung to the air, a portent of something more than an ordinary night in the middle of June.

Leaving the buggy, Andrew began to pace. The weight of the air deterred any real speed. Already the night's clamminess stuck his shirt to his skin. He would not wander more than an eighth of a mile in either direction. It would be foolish for Clara to come out tonight into the hovering storm, but if she did, she would come to this spot.

He paced a hundred yards before pausing to consider the sky. Lightning flashed in the distance, but no thunder answered—yet. Clouds obscured any starlight. Even the moon, though visible, seemed dim.

The rain started then, at first an uncertain drizzle and then finding a rhythm. The next lightning strike seemed closer. Andrew turned back to his buggy.

If Clara would marry him, he would not have to wait for her under heavy, damp sky.

The way she giggled when they rode in the automobile, and waited patiently while he got it running again, made him more resolute than ever. Many of the church members might think Bishop Yoder was going too far in his preaching about shunning, but few would consider an automobile as easily as Clara had.

The blackness brightened again, and in that split second Clara saw the shape of Andrew's buggy. She could turn around now, and he would never know she had been there. He would never have to see the stricken lines she felt in her own face.

But why else had she come if not with the hope that Andrew would be here?

"Andrew!" she called into the dark. Clara hastened her pace in a direct path to where the lightning had revealed the buggy to be.

"Clara!"

Though she could not see his form, his voice answered with an eager ring, and Clara moved faster. The rain was steady now, a falling river that drenched and chilled.

The afternoon had stretched endlessly, with Hannah whimpering in illness from the davenport and calling intermittently for Clara's comfort. Rhoda put Mari down for a nap and fully embraced her duties to nurse Hannah's sore throat and fever. Even while Hannah slept, Rhoda did not move more than six feet away. Clara hovered in the kitchen, in the dining room, on the front porch. When Mari woke, Rhoda was firm that Mari must keep away from Hannah but remain within sight. Eventually Rhoda gave Clara instructions to put out a cold supper of items from the icebox and allowed Clara to take Mari into the kitchen to eat with Hiram and Josiah.

But she did not relent in her determination that Clara should not tend to her sickened sister.

Hiram had carried Hannah to her bed, where Rhoda intended to spend the night, arguing that if Hannah needed her, the girl would have no voice to call out. With the rest of the family bedded down, Clara had eased out the back door. Even if she'd measured the threat of rain more accurately, she would have gone.

"I'm here," Andrew called.

Clara made out his form now, returning to his buggy. They reached it together, both drenched, his hat and her *kapp* askew.

"I'm glad you came," Clara said.

"Let's get in the buggy out of the rain." Andrew offered a hand to help her climb up.

Thunder now trailed lightning by only a few seconds. Clara shivered. Though the air was still warm, the moisture was damp and chilling.

Sheltered in the buggy, they watched the rain slide out of the sky in sheets. Clara felt sorry for Andrew's exposed horse, though the animal displayed no discontent. With one fist she began to squeeze the dampness out of her dress, but it seemed a futile effort.

"The rain is a blessing," Andrew murmured. "All the farmers will be pleased in the morning. After a soaking rain like this, we'll nearly be able to watch the crops spurt up inches by the day."

Clara nodded, but words knotted in her throat.

"What's wrong, Clara?" Andrew asked softly.

Clara sighed, making no effort to hide the current of air leaving her lungs.

"Tell me," he urged.

She couldn't tell him, though. If Andrew knew Rhoda thought Clara should make her own life in her own home, he would see the obvious solution. And she could not be wed to Andrew—or anyone—as long as she feared the blessing of children.

CHAPTER 12

It was odd for Hannah to be so still, and odd for her to be sitting in her mother's lap during family devotions after breakfast on Wednesday. Rhoda had moved Hannah from the davenport in the front room to her own bed and barely allowed Clara to go near the room. For two days Rhoda pampered Hannah, who had returned to the family table for breakfast that morning. The fever had lasted only a day, and with hot tea and freshly churned ice cream the sore throat was managed through the second day.

But here Hannah was at breakfast and morning devotions. Though she was in her mother's lap, she sat up straight with bright eyes. In Clara's consideration, Hannah seemed well, though Rhoda would want to be certain three times over before releasing the girl to resume her play and chores.

Standing beside them, Mari's lower lip protruded in a jealous unacknowledged pout as she leaned against her mother's arm. She wanted to be the girl in her *mamm*'s lap. Across the table, Josiah's feet gently and intermittently thumped the legs of his chair, as if in response to a thought that flitted through his mind.

Hiram Kuhn sat reading aloud from the big German Bible as he did every morning and evening. On many days, like this one, the sound droned. The older Hiram got—almost fifty now—the more he droned. The children were well trained to sit still and appear respectful, but Clara wondered whether they heard anything more than an undulating buzz.

Rhoda's countenance was as blandly perfect as it always was. Her eyes fixed on her husband as he read, her head nodding slightly at intervals.

Outwardly, nothing about Rhoda had changed. If she suspected that Clara had overheard her say it was time for her to marry, she did not reveal it in her composure. Neither were her words unkind. An onlooker would suspect nothing.

Yet Clara twisted in confusion and frustration, her spirit wringing more tightly each day.

While her father's *Amen* still draped the room, the family scattered, Hiram and Josiah to outside chores and Rhoda and the girls to wash Hannah's hair. Clara sat alone for an instant.

Fannie. She would go see Fannie and Sadie. At least there she could do some good.

At the turn from the Kuhns' lane onto the road that led toward the border, a wagon clattered in the street. Clara stepped well to the side. The wagon slowed, and a milkman looked down from the bench.

"Looking for a ride?" he said. "I'm going over the border."

"Thanks, Reuben," Clara said, "but it's a lovely morning. I think I'll walk. Maybe on the way back this afternoon."

Reuben shook his head. "I'll be sorry to miss you. Yonnie has that run. Shall I tell him to look for you?"

Clara smiled and remained uncommitted. If she was at the Maple Glen Meetinghouse when Yonnie came by, she could face the question then whether she was in the mood to ride with him. The walk was only five miles in each direction. Clara had little else to do to pass the hours.

"I know where to catch him," she said to Reuben. "I pray God brings favor to your day."

Reuben clicked his tongue, and the horse moved ahead.

Clara doubted Rhoda would scowl even if Clara missed supper, although her siblings were sure to wonder where she was. Illness or essential overnight travel were the only reasons for missing the evening meal and devotions. In this expectation, the Kuhns were no different than any other Amish household—on either side of the border.

What did Andrew eat for supper? Clara occasionally wondered about this question. Did he cook or eat a cold plate? Did he accept invitations from families who pitied him after his parents moved to Lancaster—or who had a daughter of a marriageable age? Did the young women who eyed him at Singings turn up on his farm with casseroles or pies? Clara never asked Andrew these questions. If she would not say she would marry him, why should he not accept invitations?

Still, the thought that he might stung.

Yonnie Yoder had a younger sister who had trailed after the boys when they were children as much as she was allowed. In his telling of the stories, Andrew never seemed to mind that she was there digging worms with them or climbing the lower branches of a tree while the boys scrambled higher. She was old enough to wed now, and though Andrew's great-grandmother had been a Yoder, the relationship was distant enough to allow for a marriage.

Clara pushed the thought out of her mind. Andrew was waiting for her.

Andrew with his Model T.

Alone on the road, Clara smiled at the memory of riding in the automobile while Andrew drove. He was not afraid of the form that joy might take in his life.

Old Bishop Yoder might have other ideas.

"I can do it!" Sadie raised a shoulder to interfere with Fannie's movement. The girl knelt on a chair to stir the apples, brown sugar, and raisins for the *apfelstrudel*. Her tongue poked out one side of her mouth in concentration as her fist gripped the wooden spoon handle and she pushed through the mixture in swift, thorough circles.

Fannie returned to kneading the dough. In a few minutes Sadie would insist on helping to stretch the dough thin, and Fannie would let her. Sadie was only five, but she had a knack for baking already. She knew just what the dough should feel like as she pulled it into a rectangle to fill with the apple mixture.

As troublesome as it was to think that Sadie might be her only child, Fannie delighted in ordinary moments like this one. Sadie would forget them. She would grow up with the automatic motions of making strudel, and dozens of other dishes, flowing from her fingers. One day she would prepare food in her own kitchen, perhaps with her own little girl.

But Fannie would store up these moments in her heart, the way she was sure Mary had stored up the moments of Jesus' childhood.

"Knock, knock." The voice came from the back door, which stood open to disperse the oven's heat.

"Clara!" Sadie dropped her wooden spoon and scrambled down from the chair to throw herself at the visitor.

"I didn't know you were coming." Fannie brushed flour between her palms and wiped her hands on her apron before embracing her cousin.

"Neither did I," Clara said. "I only decided after breakfast."

"We're having strudel for lunch," Sadie declared.

"Or," Fannie said gently, "dessert after supper."

"Or both!" Sadie's eyes glistened with optimism.

They stretched the dough, filled it, rolled it, and slid it into the hot oven.

"We have something to show you," Sadie said once her hands were clean and dry. "A surprise."

"Oh?" Clara's glance moved from Sadie to Fannie.

"Can I go get it, *Mamm*?" Sadie was nearly jumping in excitement.

"Yes. Remember to take care." Fannie watched the marvel that was her daughter scamper down the hall. She gestured for Clara to move into the front room.

"Close your eyes!" Sadie called from down the hall, and Clara complied. Fannie nodded encouragement for Sadie to lay the gift in Clara's lap.

Clara's eyes popped open. "What's this?"

"It's a Bible storybook!" Sadie's enthusiasm gushed out of her. "It's all the stories you've sent me in a scrapbook, and when you write more, we'll put those in, too. Hurry up and write more!"

Clara giggled, the same girlish giggle Fannie had heard through the secret moments of their childhood. Neither of them had a sister. They were sisters to each other.

"I can't read all the words yet," Sadie said. "Actually, I can only read a few. But I know them all by heart because *Mamm* reads me your stories every night before bed."

"They're not my stories," Clara said, "they're God's stories."

"I know that, silly. *Mamm* says you're helping me hide God's Word in my heart."

Fannie sat on the arm of a stuffed chair watching the pair of blond heads meeting temple to temple as Clara and Sadie turned the pages in the scrapbook with a plain green woven cover.

"It was Sadie's idea," Fannie said. "She saw the book in the mercantile in Grantsville and told me what she wanted to do."

"It's lovely." Clara closed the book and ran two fingers across the thick weave.

"Are you going to tell me a story today?" Sadie turned her face up, her eyes wide in hope.

Clara smiled. "As a matter of fact, I was going to mail you a story, but I decided to bring it myself." She reached under the bib of her apron and pulled out two sheets of paper.

Sadie jumped up. "I'll get the paste. Let's put it in the book right now and then you can read it to me."

"Perfect," Clara said.

"You have to visit to my Sunday school class." Sadie's voice trailed out of the room.

Clara glanced at Fannie. "Why would she suddenly ask me to visit?"

"You haven't been to church with us since we were very small," Fannie said. "You really should come."

⌖

Clara watched the door slam behind Sadie as the child skipped out the kitchen door to play in the sunshine.

"You're very patient with her," Fannie said. "You didn't have to read so many stories. I'm trying to teach her to be grateful for small blessings and not demand the universe!"

Clara chuckled. "I get to go home. You're the one who will have to read more at bedtime."

Fannie cut a slice of *apfelstrudel*, still warm, and slid it onto a plate to hand to Clara. "Do you remember being five?"

"Not very well." Clara poured two cups of coffee and settled in a kitchen chair. "I remember more about visiting your family than being at home with my *daed*."

Fannie sipped coffee. "Remember when we found the litter of seven kittens in the barn and didn't tell anyone for five days?"

"I was eight. We were afraid your *daed* would drown most of them. Nobody needs that many barn cats. By the time he caught us, we'd named them all."

"As soon as they were old enough to wean, he made us drag them around in a cart until we found homes for all but two."

"I'd do it again," Clara said. "Poor kitties."

Fannie nibbled strudel.

"What about when we were older?" Clara said.

"What do you mean?"

"When we were twelve or thirteen. You must remember something."

Fannie raised an eyebrow. "About what?"

Clara chose her words carefully. "There was new information in 1905 about the vote of the Pennsylvania congregation ten years before to shun the Maryland churches. Something about a misunderstanding."

They both looked out at Sadie, who was tossing a stick for the dog Elam had brought to the Esh marriage. The dog was aged and reluctant, though.

"Obviously my parents weren't at either meeting," Fannie said. "We heard rumors. Some boys who came down to an auction were rude to my brothers."

Clara vaguely remembered. For a while Rhoda had not wanted Clara to visit the Hostetlers, at least until things settled down again.

"What did your parents do?" she said.

Fannie shrugged. "What they always did. After family devotions one night, they told us what they thought we needed to know."

"Did we ever talk about this?" Clara asked, wondering why she couldn't remember.

Fannie shook her head. "*Mamm* took me aside and said there was no need to talk about it with you. It wouldn't change anything. You were always welcome to come, and she hoped you would still want to."

"But what did they say about the vote? About the shunning?"

"People voted against their conscience to please the bishop." Fannie took an indulgent sip of coffee. "They used to talk to us often about conscience. A sense of what's right doesn't come from pleasing a man, even a bishop. They wanted us to please God."

"But the bishop must have thought he was pleasing God."

"My parents also said some things we must leave to God." Fannie brushed crumbs off the table into her hand. "So much trouble over whether or not to have Sunday school for children—it seems ridiculous after nearly forty years."

Clara lost interest in her coffee. Forty years or not, the matter was not settled. Andrew might think change was coming, but Clara dreaded the impending rancor.

CHAPTER 13

The Maple Glen Meetinghouse easily could be mistaken for the one at Flag Run or even Summit Mills. They all dated to the same effort. Yonnie's father, uncle, and grandfathers all were among the men who built four meetinghouses clustered around the border that the two groups of Amish would share. As long as they used them on alternate Sundays, no conflict rose between the two groups, despite their differences over the Protestant notion of Sunday school. Another decade passed before ministers began clearing their throats, saying what they thought, and moving to serve on the side of the border where they would be among kindred hearts. Though unchanged in outward form, the meetinghouses became symbols of opinions and convictions.

Each time Yonnie drove the milk wagon past the Maple Glen Meetinghouse—nearly every day—he felts its sting. The people who worshipped there dallied among the world. Some of the canisters of milk in his wagon came from the cows of families who thought Yonnie's family did not understand the will of God.

Yonnie emptied his lungs and pushed the dilemma out of his mind. He was past the meetinghouse now. He needed to concentrate. Once again he mentally reviewed the movements of his day—the deliveries he made in the morning, the milk canisters he lifted into the wagon in the afternoon, the routes he took, the conversations he had, the notes he made. Another mistake could be costly.

Between the rhythm of his horse dropping hooves and the patterned sound of the creaking hitch, Yonnie heard his name from behind. He glanced over his shoulder and saw Clara Kuhn running along the side of the road waving one hand widely. Yonnie pulled on the reins. Stopped, he twisted in his seat and waited for Clara.

She was out of breath when she finally reached the wagon.

"Thank you for stopping." Clara gulped air. "I didn't realize how late it was. I should have been waiting for you at the meetinghouse."

From the wagon bench, Yonnie looked down at her round face, her blond hair pulled tight away from expectant blue eyes.

"You are going back toward Niverton, aren't you?" Clara asked.

Yonnie nodded. "If you'd like a ride, get in."

Clara took the hand Yonnie offered and pulled herself up to the bench.

"Thank you," she said again.

Clara would not likely speak to him further, Yonnie knew, unless he found something to talk about. They had little in common. She was pleasantly polite, as she would be with anyone, but all she wanted from Yonnie was a ride home. For a man's companionship, she would go to Andrew.

"Have you seen the Model T?" Yonnie maintained a forward gaze.

"Andrew's?"

Did she really consider it to belong to Andrew?

"The one he found." That was how Yonnie preferred to think of the automobile.

"He has it running, you know."

"I pulled him out of a ditch."

"He told me. Thank you. But he's been practicing driving, and he's getting better."

Yonnie looked at her now. "Have you seen him driving?"

She didn't answer.

"You got in that machine with him, didn't you?"

Clara stuck her chin out. "Yes."

Yonnie drove for most of a mile without speaking. If Clara had been in the Model T, she was as reckless as Andrew.

"Do you think that's wise?" Yonnie said.

"The automobile? Is it so different from having a horse and buggy? It's a way to get from here to there."

"You know it's more than that."

"Do I?"

They returned to silence for another mile.

"Andrew has a curious mind," Clara said. "God gave him that mind."

"Andrew is a baptized member of the church," Yonnie countered.

"You don't have to preach at me."

"The Bible tells us to exhort one another," Yonnie said. "We all made the same promises to follow the teachings."

"And what does the Bible teach about automobiles?"

"We promised to follow the teachings of the church."

"Shouldn't the teachings of the church be the teachings of the Bible?"

Clara's challenge dropped an edge between them. Yonnie clicked his tongue to urge the horse faster. The sooner Clara Kuhn was out of his wagon, the better off they would both be.

Andrew saw two forms in the approaching milk wagon. Yonnie must have picked up a passenger. As the two horses drew closer, a satisfied smile shaped itself on Andrew's face.

Clara.

Andrew pulled his buggy to the side of the road and waved an arm at Yonnie. By the time the two rigs were side by side, Andrew had caught Clara's eye. He expected to see a flicker in her eye that meant she was glad to see him even if she would not appear outwardly forward in the presence of Yonnie or anyone else. Instead, the light he saw was an ember of constrained fury.

"Hello, Yonnie," Andrew said, pulling his gaze from Clara to Yonnie. He nodded toward the load in Yonnie's wagon. "It looks like you have a good haul there, along with a pleasant passenger."

Yonnie shrugged. "The usual, I suppose."

"Maybe you'd like to go straight to the dairy," Andrew said. "I can take Clara home if you like."

Clara did not wait for Yonnie's response. "Thank you, Andrew. That would be a great kindness."

"Whatever you'd like." Yonnie's belated response was moot. Clara was already out of the wagon.

Andrew jumped down from his bench to offer assistance, but Clara barely touched the hand he presented. She'd been in and out of his buggy enough times to know where to step and how to shift her weight and pivot to sit. Still, Andrew was surprised at her fleet, unassisted movements.

"I hope your evening goes well," Andrew said to Yonnie.

Yonnie had already urged his horse forward. Andrew turned to watch him go before picking up his own reins again.

"Thank you." Clara's sigh was unmistakable.

Andrew held his horse to a speed barely above grazing in a pasture.

"We're going the wrong way now," Clara said.

She was grumpy. That much was clear.

"There's a wide spot in the road just ahead," Andrew said. "We'll get turned around."

Clara nodded, expelling breath again. Andrew recognized this tactic. She was trying to regain composure after being upset.

"We'll never get there at this rate," Clara said.

"Are you in a hurry?"

"I don't want to be late for supper. Rhoda—" Clara cut herself off.

"Rhoda what?"

"Never mind." She looked off to one side, her face twisted away from Andrew.

"You know you can talk to me," Andrew said.

"I know." Her breathing slowed, but she offered no further information.

Andrew reached the wide spot in the road and slowly turned the rig to head toward the Kuhn farm. He still had a mile and a quarter before the turnoff to their lane, and he didn't think Clara was in any danger of being late for supper, so he did nothing to speed the horse.

The unhurried swaying *clip-clop* seemed to soothe Clara. In his peripheral vision, Andrew saw her shoulders relax. He waited another three minutes.

"So," he said, "what happened?"

"Yonnie," she said quickly. "Yonnie happened. I just needed a ride, and he wanted to give me a sermon."

"And what was his topic?"

"He doesn't approve of the Model T."

Andrew laughed softly. "What *does* Yonnie approve of?"

"Baptismal vows, apparently. Utter submission to church leadership."

"Ah, yes."

"How can you put up with letting him think you're not as serious about the faith as he is?"

"We did all promise to live by the teachings of the church," Andrew said.

"And the church should live by the teachings of the Bible." Her retort was swift. "Isn't that what we hold each other accountable to? When did it become impossible for us to discuss what that might mean?"

Andrew spoke with deliberate quiet. "This is about more than Yonnie and the car, isn't it?"

A sob caught in Clara's throat, but Andrew heard it.

"We're young," Andrew said. "We will see change."

"Do you keep the car because you believe that?" Clara found her voice again. "The church hasn't said much at all about automobiles, but it may be like the telephone or electric lights. If other districts vote against it, ours will, too."

"Mose Beachy has a level head," Andrew said.

"Why are you so sure he'll be the next bishop?"

"I'm not. *Gottes wille*. But he is a minister, and I am confident he speaks his mind when he meets with the others."

"But if one of Bishop Yoder's sons gets the lot, you can't be sure what will happen."

"None of us can be sure of anything except that what happens will be God's will. But God's will for the congregation may not be God's will for everyone *in* the congregation."

He met her quizzical expression without further words. They arrived at the end of her lane.

"Shall I take you up to the house?" Andrew said.

She shook her head. "I'll walk."

He squeezed her hands as he helped her out of the buggy, wishing he didn't have to let go.

Josiah was the most studious child Clara knew. Morning and evening, he leaned forward over his knees, back flat and straight, as if he feared if he sat with his shoulders against the chair he would miss the key word that unfurled the meaning of the Bible passages their father read in somber tones. Though he was a well-trained Amish child, Clara sometimes wondered if her brother—*half brother*, Rhoda would point out—couldn't wiggle at least a little and still be within the confines of worshipful manners. On more than one occasion, Josiah voiced his intention to learn to read the German Bible, and Clara had no doubt Josiah would become fluent in High German. Already he was a good reader in the

English he learned at school, and Rhoda made sure her son was also learning to read Pennsylvania Dutch.

Clara's little sisters were another matter. Mari was too young to judge yet what kind of student she would be, but Hannah's lithe form embodied enough wiggles for all of Rhoda's children. It had from the day she mastered rolling onto her back and giggling in triumph at her success. Now, at six, Hannah had mastered sitting still during family devotions, but Clara suspected the intense focus required to accomplish this feat precluded absorbing any spiritual meaning from the words Hiram read.

The Bible should be more interesting to children.

Clara realized she was not listening any more than Hannah was. Hiram had never been one to consider what his children would be interested in. Even when Clara was the only other family member to hear his twice-daily readings, Hiram chose passages of interest to his personal Bible study. Clara, and then Rhoda, and the other children, were only listening in. Generally Hiram offered little in the way of explanation, preferring instead to observe a few minutes of quiet reflection.

Clara knew what went through her mind during these silences when she was a little girl, so imagining what Hannah and Mari were thinking did not require serious effort.

Like all boys, Josiah might someday be called upon to serve as a minister, or even a bishop, in the congregation. Perhaps this motivated his serious nature. The girls, on the other hand, could be sure they would never stand before a congregation and look into expectant faces awaiting God's message to come through their words.

That shouldn't matter, Clara thought as her father closed the Bible and announced the time of reflection. Were not the girls called to a life of faithfulness just as the boys were? Was it not reasonable that they should learn to love the Bible even as little children? To look forward to its stories and themes and exhortations?

Sadie loved Bible stories. She treasured them. Resentment burned through Clara in that moment of watching her sisters labor to control their wandering eyes and maintain appropriately dour angles in their faces.

Maybe Sadie was right. Maybe Clara should visit a Sunday school class in the Maryland congregation.

CHAPTER 14

Bishop Yoder's words on Sunday stunned Clara. She moistened her lips and tucked her tongue into one corner of her mouth as she concentrated, forcing herself to listen carefully. Her mind fell back on the tricks she had employed as a schoolgirl and mentally repeated each phrase.

Streng meidung. Strong shunning.

"It is my thinking," Bishop Yoder said, "that the ban and shunning were instituted by Jesus Christ, the Son of God, and His holy apostles. I recognize them as a teaching that shall not be changed by man. Already many have done much to reduce shunning far below the status given it by Jesus and His apostles."

The bishop paused and looked intently into the congregation. Clara couldn't resist looking across the aisle to the men, wishing she could know what Andrew was thinking—or her own father.

"Jesus' teaching is more enduring than heaven and earth." Reinvigorated, Bishop Yoder resumed. "In Matthew chapter eighteen and verse seventeen, we read that Jesus said, 'Let him be unto thee as an heathen man and a publican.' How long shall the transgressor be so regarded? Till he comes to the place of which the Son of God spoke to his disciples in Matthew eighteen and three: 'Verily, I say unto you, except ye be converted, and become as little children, ye shall not enter into the kingdom of heaven.'"

Although the room was not overly warm, perspiration seeped out of the pores along Clara's hairline. Tension thickened the rows of women around her. A couple of small children whimpered, but their mothers made no move to soothe them, instead keeping their eyes fixed on the bishop. This was not a sermon the Lord had laid on the bishop's heart that morning when he was selected—again—to preach. This was a sermon he had aimed at for months—or years.

"I believe also," he said, "that those who have in regular order been placed into the ban should be shunned, even if they join another church, so that they may indeed repent, regret, and sorrow with humble hearts and become reconciled with the church from which he or she left or was separated from. Paul wrote in 2 Thessalonians in the third chapter and the sixth verse, 'Now we command you, brethren, in the name of our Lord Jesus Christ, that ye withdraw yourselves from every brother that walketh disorderly, and not after the tradition which he received of us.'"

A rustle rose from the congregation, and Clara realized her own movements contributed. Bishop Yoder spoke over the disturbance.

"If we speak loosely about the ban and shunning, as we have done, we give a testimony that our principles can be violated in this part of Paul's teaching. But when it is received in the right way before God, so that the transgressor can be brought from death to life, the one who brings the transgressor out of darkness into light is worthy of honor."

Worthy of honor? Martha and Atlee. Fannie and her brothers. Elam and Sadie. Could Bishop Yoder truly be convinced that Clara would find honor in turning her back on her family simply because they had joined another branch of the Amish almost thirty years ago? Could he be serious in his expectation that shunning in this manner would woo any of the Marylanders back to the Old Order?

Clara's spirit rebelled. Because the vote in 1895 had been unanimous, even when the truth emerged ten years later that Bishop Yoder had pressed his own feelings upon the congregation, the vote could not easily be reversed.

And if anyone was inclined to suggest a new vote, Bishop Yoder seemed intent to prevent open discussion.

Clara swallowed hard.

⚜

Andrew cringed. Bishop Yoder's sermon sucked the air out of the room. He was asking for trouble in the congregation, and Andrew suspected that this time he was going to get it.

The bishop held his heavy Bible in front of him at the plain, unvarnished preaching table made of poplar wood. "We must heed the words of Paul in Romans, chapter sixteen, verse seventeen: 'Mark them which cause divisions and offences contrary to the doctrine which ye have learned; and avoid them.' This is now our insight on how the ban and shunning should be kept by all true disciples of Christ."

The congregation was not likely to tolerate this strict stance set out in such nonnegotiable terms. *Who was causing the division now?* Andrew mused. Mose Beachy would preach a doctrine of peace. Was that not the doctrine the church had learned forty years earlier when the Maryland and Pennsylvania churches amicably chose slightly different paths to express their shared faith?

And the differences *were* slight.

In the ten years after the peaceable division, families and ministers had realigned gradually with the groups that most closely shared their convictions. Andrew had heard the stories from his own grandparents. The groups had enough in common to build meetinghouses together and continue to share them. When consciences settled, each congregation had ministers and members sufficient to flourish and live harmoniously along the roads that crisscrossed the state border.

Andrew felt his head shaking ever so slightly in dread of the dissension this sermon was sure to stir up.

Bishop Yoder ministered in the Maryland district in those days. No one thought less of him when he decided he belonged among the Old Order. He had done the right thing to follow his conscience. But for two decades, since being ordained bishop, he had preached sermons meant to convict his new congregation of their participation in the sin of their Maryland families.

He knows what he's doing, Andrew thought. *Only a fool would not see that he lacks support for this hard line.* Andrew chastised himself for characterizing his spiritual leader as a fool, though he did not temper his opinion that the congregation would resist Yoder's indictment of their own consciences on this matter.

The sermon wound down. Stern faced, Bishop Yoder nodded toward his two sons, and one of them began a final grave hymn. Andrew drew in his breath and joined the singing, though he was certain that a hymn with twelve stanzas sung at a ponderous tempo would do nothing to quell the brewing disagreement.

At the final intonation of the benediction, Andrew turned to catch

Clara's eye. Her head tilted nearly imperceptibly toward the door, and when Andrew freed himself from the entrapment he felt on the bench where he sat, he followed her outside. By the time he reached her, huddles of conversation had formed across the grass in the clearing.

"Surely he is not serious," Clara said. "Is he?"

"I'm afraid he is," Andrew said, "but he has closed his eyes to the fallout."

"But no one wants the sort of *meidung* he is preaching about."

Andrew wished he could take her hand. "Everything will sort itself out. *Gottes wille.*"

Yonnie sidled toward Clara and Andrew. Clara's face alternately paled and reddened, but her eyes never left Andrew's face, and his were fixed on her.

They were standing too close together. It was improper.

With their gazes interlocked and strained, they wouldn't notice Yonnie creeping closer one slow step at a time. He circled slightly so he would come up behind Clara. Andrew was less likely to object to Yonnie's presence. If Clara saw him, her face would tighten as she clamped her mouth closed and stepped back. Yonnie could hear them now.

"I think God must be very sad," Clara said. "The bishop's mind is hardened against anyone who does not think as he does."

"He speaks from conviction," Andrew said. "He takes seriously his role as leader in the church."

"But all the families read the Bible in their homes," Clara countered. "Any of the men could have had the lot fall to them to become a minister. Why should Bishop Yoder think that others cannot also discern God's will?"

"The lot fell to him," Andrew said, "first to be a minister and then to be bishop. Don't you believe God reveals His will in the lot?"

Yonnie turned up one corner of his mouth. Perhaps Andrew was not as rebellious in spirit as he had judged him to be.

Clara crossed her arms over her chest. "I don't know what to believe."

Yonnie stepped forward, and now Andrew lifted his eyes from Clara's face.

"If you don't know what to believe," Yonnie said, "then God has shown you that you need the bishop's wisdom."

Clara spun around. Andrew's failed attempt to catch her elbow did not escape Yonnie's observation.

"Yonnie," Andrew said quickly, "Clara and I were speaking privately."

Yonnie swept a hand around the clearing. "This is a church gathering. Anyone might hear you."

Clara blanched. "Excuse me." She turned and left them without looking back.

"Yonnie," Andrew said, "why do you treat Clara as you do?"

"I don't treat her any differently than I do anyone else."

"Yes," Andrew murmured, "sadly, I think you are right. But if you could hear our words, then you know she is upset."

"She has no reason to be upset. The bishop's authority protects all of us. He is our spiritual shepherd."

"You know Clara has close relatives in the Maryland congregation." Andrew's tone heated. "Her own mother came from one of the Maryland families. Try to look at the question from her perspective."

"And if her relatives were thieves or fornicators, would you excuse that as well?" Yonnie widened his eyes and met Andrew's locked gaze.

"How can you compare such matters to this?"

"How can you draw a line between sin that should be confessed to the church and sin that should not be?"

"Yonnie, we've been friends for a long time. I hope that means as much to you as it does to me."

Andrew stepped back, pivoted, and strode through the clearing—not back toward the meetinghouse, but along the path Clara had taken.

Fannie walked beside her husband and watched their daughter run ahead and then turn around and grin at her parents. Elam lifted a hand and waved a response to Sadie. This was not a church Sunday in the Maryland district. Instead of a shared meal at the meetinghouse, families and neighbors would form their own groups. The Eshes, as usual, would gather at the Hostetler table for the midday meal.

Fannie was not anxious to go. She suspected Elam also would have preferred to stay home. But what excuse would they give that would satisfy Sadie, and how would they send a message to Fannie's parents not to expect them? Logically, it seemed easier to go. The closer they got to the Hostetler farm, though, the slower Fannie's steps became until she finally called to Sadie not to get too far ahead.

Martha was halfway through her months of being with child. Perhaps if Fannie had learned earlier that the babe was coming, she might have accepted the news by now. But she had only learned her mother was expecting a couple of weeks ago. The wound was still fresh.

The wound.

Her mind told her no child was a wound, but her spirit sliced open afresh every time she thought of her mother receiving this blessing rather than Fannie. It was a wound that seemed to come straight from God and fester with disappointment, the puss of infected distrust multiplying every month.

Every week now. Every day.

Every day she felt the frailty of a body that could not—or would not—conceive a child because God had willed it so.

The wound oozed with the truth that Fannie did not want to see her mother right now. It was too hard. It was too hard to see Martha's thickening waistline and yet trust God that her own might also grow wider.

Sadie was becoming impatient, but Fannie would not make her feet move faster on the road toward her parents' farm. Even if she had willed it—which she did not—her feet would not have answered.

CHAPTER 15

"Did you hear?"

Fannie looked up from the mending in her lap at Elam, who poured himself a midmorning cup of coffee.

"Hear what?" she said. Who would she hear news from on a Tuesday morning when she hadn't left the farm?

"Dale Borntrager was doing his own milk run this morning. He said Bishop Yoder came down hard on Sunday about the shunning."

"He's been doing that for twenty years." Fannie moistened the frayed end of a spool of black thread and pushed it through the eye of a needle.

"He means it this time." Elam stirred sugar into his cup.

"What's different about this time?"

"Dale said it sounded like an edict. The Old Order families are supposed to shun us without exception."

Fannie dropped her needle. "But Clara—"

"I know."

Fannie pushed the mending basket out of her lap. "I must go see Clara."

"I need the horses," Elam said.

"All of them?"

"The gelding needs to be shoed, so that only leaves me two. I've decided it's not too late to plow and seed another field, but I can't waste even a day."

Fannie sucked in her lips. "All right. I'll find my own way and be home to cook your supper."

If she left now and hurried across the back field, she could still catch

Dale at the end of his route and ride to Clara's with him. Fannie bustled to the back door and called for her daughter.

"Sadie!"

A couple of chickens clucked in reply.

Fannie glanced at the clock on the kitchen wall and realized it had stopped. She didn't know how much time she had. If Dale skipped a stop or gained time, she would never catch him.

"Sadie!" Fannie began to march across the space between the house and the barn.

The girl appeared with a black streak across one cheek. Fannie grabbed her hand. She would deal with the grime later. Right now she had to persuade Sadie to move steadily across the back field.

"Are we really going to see Clara?" Sadie asked when Fannie explained the hurry.

"Yes. We must catch Mr. Borntrager or we'll have to walk the whole way."

"Have I ever been to Clara's house? I don't remember it."

Fannie startled briefly at the truth that her daughter had never seen where Clara lived. Fannie herself had met Rhoda only once at one of the *English* shops in Springs, but that was years ago. Clara was in her first summer out of the eighth grade and Fannie a year older. Rhoda was vacantly pleasant when Clara introduced Fannie to her. That was before Josiah was born, before Rhoda began drawing distinctions between Clara and the Kuhn children who followed.

"Have I, *Mamm*?" Sadie tugged her mother's sleeve. "Have I been to Clara's house?"

"No," Fannie said. It was probably unwise to take Sadie there now, but the thought of not hearing from Clara herself about the events in the Old Order church propelled Fannie past the risk that she would not be welcome on the Kuhn farm. If she had to, she would linger down the lane, hidden among early-summer leafing until she found an opportunity to see Clara alone.

"You're walking too fast," Sadie whined.

Fannie slowed long enough only to grasp her child's hand and tug her forward. They crossed the field, emerged on the road, and followed its curve toward the Maple Glen Meetinghouse. When they reached it, Fannie stood still long enough to catch her breath before spitting on a corner of her apron and scrubbing the black streak from her daughter's cheek. Sadie squirmed and scrunched her face.

Dale Borntrager rumbled toward them in the milk wagon. Fannie raised a hand to flag him.

"Your husband must have told you the news," Dale said.

Fannie nodded and lifted Sadie up to the bench before scrambling in herself.

"What news, *Mamm*?" Sadie turned her face up.

"Just something I need to talk to Clara about." Fannie smoothed her daughter's hair, glancing over Sadie's head at Dale. Her mind burst with questions Dale would have answers for. What did Bishop Yoder preach? How were people in the congregation saying? Did he think people would defy or obey the ban? But Sadie sat between them on the bench. She was a five-year-old girl who did not deserve the fear that would strike her heart if she thought Clara would never come to see her again.

Andrew cranked the engine. It caught without hesitation. He smiled.

Every time Andrew worked on the Model T, he learned something. On some days, he learned that he should not have done what he did, and he spent tedious hours backtracking and trying another improvement. On other days, he successfully thought through where the sputter or rattle might originate and made small adjustments until he achieved the desired result. In his toolbox were multiple sheets of paper with small drawings of parts he observed as he lay on his back on the barn floor studying the undercarriage of the automobile. When he found corresponding drawings in the tattered publications Jurgen Hansen loaned him, he carefully labeled what he had identified with neat notes in Dutch about what the function of the part was. Where he had a question, he made a large *X* to remind him to ask Jurgen for further explanation.

Few possessions had ever given Andrew the pleasure the Model T provided. The thrill came not only from the promise of a well-running automobile but also from the process of discovering how the complex parts worked together. Andrew had been a mediocre student in the classroom. Learning to farm from his father, he had paid closer attention. Yet nothing had made his mind feel this alive. He did not have to ask deep questions about what made the *English* invent one new machine after another. What the machine might be capable of doing was only a small part of the triumph. Andrew imagined that it was the same for the *English* inventors. Understanding how and why the machine would perform drenched him in satisfaction.

He had so much to learn.

And while Andrew worked on the car, he pushed Bishop Yoder's words out of his mind. Yesterday's sermon preoccupied enough people. Andrew would not be one of them. He had disciplined himself not to labor on the Model T on the Sabbath, but Monday morning found him on the forsaken Johnson property wearing his oldest clothes so he was not distracted by where grease might splatter.

A form blocked a stripe of sunlight coming through the open barn door. Andrew looked up.

"Hello, Mr. Hansen."

"I told you to call me Jurgen." The garage owner had both hands in deep pockets as he sauntered into the barn. "It sounds marvelous! Smooth and steady. That's what we want."

Grinning, Andrew reached inside the Model T and took the car out of gear. The engine silenced.

"I didn't know you were coming by," Andrew said.

"I can't get this car out of my mind." Jurgen walked around to the back of the car, stepped back, and examined the view. "Do you need more parts?"

They talked for a few minutes about what Andrew had done to the Model T in the days since Jurgen last saw it. Andrew had watched Jurgen work on seven vehicles. He knew that the repairs on the Model T had been minor compared to what could go wrong—and might still go wrong. If Andrew hoped to maintain the vehicle beyond the next few weeks, he would have to work alongside Jurgen for many more hours. Only because he was an unmarried man could Andrew juggle the responsibilities of his farm and the recreation of working on the Model T.

"It looks good, Andrew," Jurgen said. "You're doing very well."

"Thank you," Andrew said. "I respect your opinion. I know you're familiar with this automobile."

"A Model T can last a long time if you take care of it," Jurgen said. "Ford Motor Company may like to make new automobiles affordable for everyone, but many people will prefer to purchase a used vehicle at an even more agreeable price."

"I know your services are valuable," Andrew said. "You are generous to give me your time and advice."

Jurgen sauntered around the far side of the car now. "I have an ulterior motive."

Andrew raised his eyebrows.

"I'd like to buy this car," Jurgen said. "I've always admired it. Every time it came into my shop, I thought of how nicely it would run if the owner would let me maintain it properly."

"Why didn't he sell it to you?"

"He didn't know I wanted it. I thought if he wanted to sell it, he would come to me. The idea that he would abandon it on the side of the road never entered my mind."

Andrew's throat went dry.

"I would give you a fair price," Jurgen said. "More than fair."

"You want to buy my Model T?" Andrew was still getting used to using a possessive pronoun in the same sentence with the name of an automobile.

"I do." Jurgen looked over the hood at Andrew. He named a price.

A response stalled in Andrew's throat. Words failed to form in his mind.

"Let me sweeten the offer." Jurgen named another figure.

Andrew licked his lips. "What about the original owner?" If he received money for the vehicle—especially the sum Jurgen suggested—shouldn't the funds to go the man who left the car on the road?

Jurgen shrugged. "He signed it away. And I heard he took a new position in Indiana. Maybe it was Illinois. Or it could have been Ohio. The point is, we wouldn't know how to find him anyway."

Learning from the automobile was one matter. Profiting from it was another in Andrew's mind. Enjoying the Model T fell somewhere in between.

"Will you think about it?" Jurgen tilted his head to one side to hold Andrew's gaze. "Promise that if you decide to sell you'll come to me first."

Clara left the meetinghouse on Sunday without eating and didn't notice until Monday that the Kuhn cupboard now contained two identical pie plates. This had happened before when Mattie Schrock and Rhoda both prepared pies to serve at the congregational meal. One or the other of them ended up with both plates. On Tuesday Clara rose early, before the house heated up with late June temperatures, and baked identical pies. Now she carried a still-warm pie down the lane to the Schrock farm.

Priscilla sat in the yard with her elbows on her knees and her face drooping between her hands. She jumped up, startled, when she saw Clara.

"I'm sorry," Priscilla said.

Clara pushed her eyebrows together. "Sorry about what?"

"Never mind. I'm sorry." Priscilla dug a bare toe into the dirt, her head hanging.

Clara balanced the pie in one hand and knelt to put herself at eye level with Priscilla. "Is everything all right?"

Tears clouded the girl's clear green eyes. "I'm afraid," she whispered.

"What are you afraid of?" Clara glanced around them.

"*Daed* says I must learn to slop the pigs by myself, but I don't like pigs! They're too big!"

Clara took one of Priscilla's hands.

"The mud is slippery," Priscilla said, her voice catching, "and the noises the pigs make frighten me. And I'm afraid I'm going to drop the slop bucket, or even just spill it, and all the pigs will attack me."

The child's hand trembled in Clara's light grasp. "That reminds me of a story. Would you like to hear it?"

Priscilla nodded, her face scrunched with the effort of restraining tears.

"This is a story about Jesus," Clara said, "so you don't have to be frightened."

Priscilla looked unconvinced.

"One day, Jesus was very tired," Clara began. "He had been working very hard to tell people messages from God. When He got in a boat with His friends, He fell fast asleep."

"Did Jesus have a pillow?"

Clara pictured the words of the story in the family Bible. "Yes, He did!"

Priscilla's shoulders began to relax. Clara continued.

"A great big windstorm started blowing across the water, and the waves sloshed up over the sides of the boat. Jesus' friends started to think the boat was going to sink!"

"And did it?"

Clara smiled and shook her head. "They woke up Jesus and said,

'Don't you care what happens to us?' Jesus stood right up in the boat and He said to the wind, 'Peace, be still!' And the wind stopped. Everything was calm and peaceful again. And Jesus said to His friends, 'Why are you so afraid?'"

Priscilla looked at Clara, wide eyed. "Does it make Jesus angry if I'm afraid of the pigs?"

Clara squeezed the girl's hand. "We're all afraid of something. The story reminds us that even when we are most afraid, Jesus is right there with us."

Priscilla turned and looked toward the pigpen. "I'm still afraid."

"I know. Sometimes it feels like we're right in the middle of a terrible storm. But Jesus is there with us, and remembering that can help. Do you think you can remember that?"

Priscilla nodded.

The rattle of the approaching milk wagon pulled Clara's gaze up. She intended only to glance, but the two forms on the bench beside Dale Borntrager made her suck in her breath. Meeting Priscilla's eyes again, Clara smiled.

"Would you like to do a big job for me?" Clara said.

Priscilla nodded, and Clara held out the pie.

"Take this to your *mamm* and tell her to enjoy the pie!"

"I'm not afraid to do that." Priscilla arranged her hands around the rim of the pie plate with great deliberation.

"I know you'll do a good job." Clara watched as the child carefully measured her steps toward the house. She turned her own attention to the little girl leaning out of the clattering milk wagon and waving with vigor.

Fannie!

The wagon slowed. Fannie gripped Sadie's shoulder to keep her from leaping out of the wagon at the sight of Clara.

"Jump in, Clara," Dale said. "I'll take you all to your house."

"Yes!" Sadie clapped. "I can meet Hannah."

Clara's heart raced. How could she explain to Sadie that Rhoda's welcome would be insincere?

"Thank you, Dale, but I think we'll get out here." Fannie dropped her feet to the ground and turned to lift her daughter out of the wagon.

"But I want to see Hannah," Sadie protested.

"Not today."

Clara was grateful for the firm tone she heard in her cousin's voice. Sadie clamped her mouth closed. Dale waved and drove off.

"Do you see those rocks over there?" Fannie said. "Why don't you see what kind of bugs live under them?"

Sadie wandered away.

"I can't believe you came." Clara's embrace was tight.

"I only wish I could come to your house," Fannie said. "But we heard about your bishop's sermon. Rhoda has never invited us before. I don't imagine she'd be glad to see us now."

"No, not now," Clara said. Not with tension already scattered around the Kuhn house like hidden tree roots waiting to trip her. It was God's will for both pie plates to ride home with Rhoda and for Clara to carry a pie to the Schrocks only to discover Priscilla alone. If she had gone straight to Mattie's kitchen, she would have missed Fannie.

"Is it true?" Fannie said. "You're not supposed to see us?"

"You're still my family."

"Dale said there were no exceptions to the *meidung*."

"It won't hold," Clara said.

"But if it does?"

"It won't. You were never in our church. How can Bishop Yoder place you in a ban? That would be like saying the Baptists or the Lutherans are under a ban. He's only talking about anyone who leaves the church now." Clara took a deep breath, a whole body prayer that what she said was a right understanding. She would not accept the alternative.

"So we'll still see you?"

"Of course. But I may have to be careful for a while." Clara glanced at Sadie, refusing to imagine the absence of this wondrous child from her life.

"We should go," Fannie said.

"Find some shade and wait. I'll come back with a cart and drive you home."

Fannie shook her head. "Sadie's a good walker. You're right to be careful."

Clara kissed Fannie's cheek. "I'll see you soon."

CHAPTER 16

With her form hidden under the loose-fitting folds of her dress covered with a cape and apron, Clara doubted anyone could see that she did not fill out the dress as much as she had just a few weeks ago. She spent long hours away from the farm now, most of it walking in a manner others would perceive as recreational. Clara knew the truth. The tension at home was less severe if Clara spent most of her day away. She was present for breakfast and supper and the family devotion times that followed, but even Hannah had stopped asking why Clara often was not home for lunch anymore. Even in rising summer temperatures, Clara walked to her housekeeping jobs, to shops where she spent little money, to the homes of childhood friends too busy with their own children for a leisure conversation. Clara could hardly tell them she had too much time and too little to do.

After days of restlessness, on Saturday Clara wandered along the property line between the Kuhn farm and the adjoining Schrock farm. The crop promised an abundant yield—as long as summer rains followed the pattern all the farmers were accustomed to. Clara's bare feet sank into pliant dark earth as she ambled through rows of corn rising above her knees. With the sun full in the sky, she was hopeful Andrew was finished with morning chores and might have time to talk to her. The first stop in her inquiry would be the weather-battered Johnson outbuilding. Even if Andrew was not there, Clara could take refuge from the midday heat in its shade.

When Clara heard giggling and rustling, she paused to judge the source. Three voices still thin in timbre exuded conspiracy.

"This can be our story place."

Clara recognized that voice. It belonged to Priscilla Schrock and evidenced none of her fear of slopping the pigs. Clara crept forward with stealth until she saw three sets of little-girl bonnets nodding in a close circle.

"This story is about Jesus," Priscilla said. "Whenever you're afraid, this story will help. You might still feel afraid, but you won't feel alone."

Clara stilled her breath and gathered her skirts in both fists to keep them from brushing cornstalks. Priscilla's rendition of Jesus stilling the storm on the Sea of Galilee was earnest and factual. What she added to Clara's version were the sounds of the roaring wind. The other girls joined her in expelling loud breath and swaying precipitously as if they were in a sinking boat. Suddenly Priscilla popped up, spread her arms wide, and declared, "Peace! Be still!"

That was the moment Clara met the girl's confident, clear, green eyes.

"It's Hannah's sister!"

At Priscilla's announcement, Naomi Brennerman and Lillian Yutzy broke their concentration and jumped up as well. Clara soaked up three eager gazes.

"This is God's will!" Priscilla pushed through the stalks.

"Careful," Clara said, "don't trample the corn."

Her warning did not slow the girls.

"Did God send you to tell us another story from the Bible?" Priscilla's eyes brimmed with expectation.

Clara glanced across the field, wondering where the girls' mothers were and if they knew how far from the house their daughters had wandered.

"Please," Priscilla said. "It doesn't have to be a long one."

Naomi gently fingered a silken cornstalk. "Are there any stories in the Bible about crops?"

Clara swallowed hard, barely believing what she was about to do. "Crops and fields and soil and barns and so many things that are part of our life."

"Tell us," Priscilla said.

Clara sat on the ground and tucked her skirt around her knees. "This story is about a farmer sowing seed." Clara dug her hand into the ground and let the black soil run through her fingers. "What difference do you think the soil makes?"

The girls all lived on Amish farms. Clara described four kinds of soil and four kinds of yields, watching their heads bob in understanding.

"What kind of soil are you?" she asked. "That's the question Jesus wants us to think about."

Thoughtful silence hung for a few seconds before a mother's calling voice shattered it. The girls jumped up.

"We have to go," Priscilla said. "When can we do this again?"

Clara hesitated. She loved their attentive faces and little-girl answers to the questions she asked as she navigated through the story. But telling them they could meet like this again would be an unfair, false promise.

"You'd better go," she said. "Don't keep your mothers waiting."

The trio scampered down the row calling out to answer the summoning voice. Clara let the responses fade before she stood. It would only be a matter of time before one of the girls told an adult about the story—maybe even before suppertime that day. Most likely they would be admonished not to bother her, to tend to their chores, or to ask their questions about the Bible at home.

In this moment, though, Clara savored the flush of satisfaction.

Andrew turned a wrench and asked, "Why do you feel guilty?"

"I know it's silly," Clara said. "It's not as if I put up a sign to advertise. I found Priscilla frightened in her own yard, and I couldn't have known she would bring her friends to the field today at the same time I happened to walk through."

"*Gottes wille.*" Andrew ducked into the engine again.

"That's what Priscilla said."

"She's an Amish child," Andrew said. "She probably learned to say 'God's will' before she learned to say her own name."

Clara chuckled.

"Did you tell them anything your father would not say?"

"My father is not much given to commentary. His method is Bible reading and silent reflection."

"There's a time and a place for that," Andrew said, rubbing his hands on a rag, "but you have a gift for communicating with children that your *daed* might not share."

"All I've done is tell a couple of stories about Jesus. Why do I feel so guilty?"

"I don't know. Why do you?" Andrew caught Clara's gaze.

She picked at a fingernail. "Perhaps because their parents don't know."

"Did you make the girls promise not to tell their parents?"

"No, of course not."

Andrew turned a palm up as if his point were self-evident.

"No one but my father ever told me a Bible story, and he sticks to his favorites," Clara said. "I didn't understand most of the sermons at church. I had to learn to read High German before I could read the Bible for myself. I still have many, many questions about what everything means."

"You don't have to persuade me," Andrew said, "but you're making a pretty good argument that what you did will help those girls."

"I suppose it does not feel very much like submission." Clara studied the back of her hand. "No women in the church are teachers."

"Mothers teach their children." Andrew tossed his rag over a head-lamp and stepped closer to Clara.

"That's different. They have husbands to help guide them."

"You could have a husband," Andrew said. "And to remove all doubt, let me say that I believe you would do a wonderful job with our children and anyone else's."

She blushed. "Andrew—"

He held up a hand. "I know. You're not ready. I'm not rushing you."

Clara laid a hand on the Model T. "Do you ever feel guilty about the automobile?"

"Not especially."

"Yonnie doesn't think you are in submission, either."

"I'm not worried about Yonnie."

"He might tell the wrong person you have a car," Clara said, "just like the girls might tell the wrong person about my stories. Bishop Yoder could make us both stand up and confess before the entire congregation."

What Clara said was true—and if someone happened upon them together in this remote barn, the list of their transgressions would likely lengthen. But Andrew found fear an unlikely basis for a faithful life.

"If someone asks you not to speak to their children," he said, "I am sure you would respect their wishes. And as for Yonnie? I will not borrow tomorrow's trouble. The Bible tells us each day has enough trouble of its own, right?"

Clara nodded. She raised her eyes and looked beyond him. "You have a visitor."

Andrew pivoted and saw Jurgen Hansen striding into the barn. He'd been so intent on listening to Clara that he hadn't heard the sound of the vehicle Jurgen must have driven.

"Am I interrupting something?" Jurgen said.

"You're always welcome," Andrew said. "This is my friend Clara Kuhn. Clara, this is the garage owner I told you about."

"Are you also interested in Model Ts?" Jurgen offered a hand to Clara, who shook it awkwardly and glanced at Andrew.

"She's interested in *my* Model T," Andrew said.

"I hope she's not too attached," Jurgen said, "because I'm here to renew my offer."

"It's only been a few days," Andrew said. "I thought I had more time to consider the question."

"I realize I may be rushing you," Jurgen said. "I have a customer who wants to buy the car I drive. I'd sell it to him if I knew I could have yours."

"But your automobile runs far better than this one."

Jurgen ran a hand along a shiny polished fender. "I've been enamored of this machine since the first time it came into my shop. Have you thought about my offer at all?"

"I have," Andrew said. "How could I not after the number you named? But I'm afraid I'll have to decline. I'm quite enamored with this Model T myself."

Jurgen swung one foot and kicked up a small flurry of dust from the barn floor. "I don't blame you, but I thought it was worth asking. Consider it a standing offer."

"Thank you, Jurgen, but I don't plan to sell the automobile."

Jurgen made polite farewells. Andrew and Clara stood still as they listened to him crank the engine of his own Ford outside the barn.

"You're really going to keep the Model T," Clara said.

"I am."

"And if you're disciplined?"

"Mose Beachy will stand with me."

"And will that be enough?"

"Others will be glad to stand with Mose."

Clara's candle burned long after the rest of the Kuhn household was shrouded in rest. She resisted the urge to light an oil lamp for brighter illumination. Her father and Rhoda were just across the hall. If one of them happened to rise in the night, the yellow gleam under her door would launch a battery of questions about what would keep her up when morning was nearer than last evening's nightfall.

Andrew's modern thinking emboldened her. A box tucked deep under her bed held the scribbled first drafts of the stories she copied over and sent to Sadie. Clara had lifted the pages one by one and made a list of all the Bible stories she'd written in words Sadie would understand— or Priscilla or Naomi or Lillian. One day perhaps she could even tell them to Hannah and Mari.

Until now, Clara had written the stories stirring her own heart. Now she considered where the gaps were. Had she written enough about the history of Israel and the good kings and the bad kings? What about the prophets? Elijah's and Elisha's lives were full of miracles to encourage faith. Had she balanced the miracles and parables of Jesus? What about the book of Acts? She hadn't begun to try to put the letters of Paul into language for children.

Clara didn't know if she would see Priscilla and her friends again for a story, but if she did—*Gottes wille*—she wanted something ready in her head and heart. Sadie would always be eager for a new story. Clara resolved to copy afresh all the stories she had written up until then, and from now on to make one clean copy to send to Sadie and a second to keep for herself.

Someday she might also want these stories for her own children—if she could bring herself to marry.

She thought of the image of little Priscilla standing in the field and announcing, "Peace! Be still!"

Clara's own heart craved the assurance she had declared to Priscilla.

CHAPTER 17

For a week Dale Borntrager did both the morning and afternoon milk runs himself, leaving Yonnie with the dairy employees who bottled milk, kept the butter churns moving, checked on the process of the cheeses, and sorted orders for delivery. In the winter, everyone preferred the indoor work. At this time of year, though, Yonnie relished sitting on the uncovered wagon bench and watching summer's splendid settling in.

His exile to bottling had ended, but the route was shorter now. On Monday morning, Yonnie returned to the dairy with about two-thirds of the canisters he would have collected only nine or ten days ago. He steered the wagon tight up against the platform where he and others would unload.

Dale Borntrager scowled. "Where are the rest?"

"This is everything." Yonnie heaved a canister out of the wagon and onto the platform.

"Cows do not suddenly stop producing milk," Dale said. "This can't be right."

"There are fewer stops now." Yonnie puzzled at explaining the obvious.

Realization broke over Dale's face. "Do you mean that you didn't pick up from the Marylander farms?"

"Of course not."

Dale grabbed a canister so forcefully that milk sloshed around the edges of the closed top. "Get these unloaded. Then go back and get the rest before it's too late."

Yonnie's feet froze. "But the bishop—the ban. He was quite clear."

"The bishop has a nice, quiet farm. He's not running a business," Dale said. "The Marylander families supply thirty percent of our milk, and they buy from us as well."

"Didn't you explain to them when you made the rounds yourself?"

"I made those visits to make sure they know where I stand." Dale hefted another canister. "It seems you are the one who doesn't."

Yonnie's feet finally moved, and he gripped the handles of a milk canister. He had assumed Dale would cull his lists.

"The ministers might call on you to explain your actions." Yonnie spoke respectfully. "I did not want to put you in the position of facing discipline."

"I'll decide that," Dale said. "Your job is to do what I ask you to do."

Yonnie hesitated. He did not want to face discipline, either. Bishop Yoder's sermon last week made clear that lax shunning would no longer go unnoticed. Church members would be accountable for their interactions with the Maryland church members.

Dale straightened back, hands on his hips. "Yonnie?"

Yonnie met his employer's eye.

"You've worked for me for a long time," Dale said. "But if you're not in agreement with my business policies, I can find somebody else to drive the wagon. I'll understand if you quit, but as long as you're on the payroll, you'll pick up the Marylander milk right alongside the Old Order milk."

Yonnie needed his job. He would always be welcome in his parents' home, but he had too many brothers. The farm would not be enough when they all began to have families. His father had given Yonnie a slice of land he had never considered tillable, full of stumps and boulders. Even if Yonnie cleared it, one backbreaking step at a time, the acreage was not large enough to plant profitably. If he had any hope of his own farm someday, he needed the income that came from the dairy.

"Are we of one mind on this matter?" Dale said.

Yonnie swallowed and nodded.

❦

Clara took to morning walks that began shortly after family devotions. Each day the radius of her path widened, keeping her occupied a few minutes longer before she wondered, out of eight years of habit, what the children were doing or whether Rhoda needed help in the kitchen with the day's meals.

When Clara caught herself pacing back toward the front of the house on Monday morning, she halted. Her breath lodged in her throat, neither inhaling nor exhaling, as she wondered what might happen if she spoke her mind to Rhoda or picked up Mari and carried her out of a room over Rhoda's protests. Pressure in her chest forced a gasp, and Clara's shoulders rose and dropped three times. Stinging tears clouded her gaze, and Clara backed away, turning instead to circle around the perimeter of the yard around the house. Familiarity led her to the path to the vegetable garden. What harm could she do inspecting the burgeoning yield that would find its way to the family's table through the summer and into canning jars that would see them through the winter? She had not seen the garden closely in weeks, knowing that Rhoda kept the girls near during her daily visits for weeding and thinning.

The sight of the new section of earth her father had turned a few weeks ago buckled Clara's knees.

Celery. Rows and rows of celery.

Clara did a quick calculation and arrived at nearly four hundred plants. No one grew that much celery unless the family expected a wedding in the fall. The plants were fledgling, and not all of them would survive, but the bounty would be ample for the traditional decorations and dishes of a wedding. Any neighbor or church family who saw the rows would presume, and Clara would be the recipient of sly glances during church. Clara knelt in the dirt and raised her eyes to the clear sky, muttering halting thanks that the Kuhn garden was set back from the house, not in the front in view from the road.

Rhoda could not force Clara to marry.

Rhoda could not force her will. It was God's will Clara awaited.

Clara marched toward the house, around the barn, past the henhouse, through the back door, and straight up the back stairs to her room. She pulled out her sheaf of papers, the result of one late night after another pouring her heart out before the Lord the way she knew best.

Page after page, she had copied marked-up stories onto fresh paper in tiny script to conserve space. With her heart's ears and eyes open, she added what she saw and heard. She didn't change the stories—she would never change a jot or tittle of God's Word—but she sought what a child might see and hear in the story. Clara remembered the places where Sadie had tugged on her sleeve to pause and ask questions. She heard again Sadie's pleas to hear her favorite stories again and again.

They weren't perfect. God's Word was the only perfect book. The stories weren't even a book, just a stack of papers tied together with string to keep them from scattering in the wind as Clara walked. She doubted anyone noticed when she left the house after lunch and aimed toward the main road. A few months ago, she would have supposed Andrew was too busy on his farm to bother him—and she wouldn't have been brazen enough to seek him out there. The Model T changed Andrew's rhythms, though, and the dilapidated structure where he worked on the automobile was a more reasonable walking distance. Clara had been there several times in the last ten days, and with each visit the refuge of the old barn deepened and sharpened, whether or not Andrew was present.

Clara judged the sun carefully when she pushed open the barn door and discovered only the automobile and not its mechanic. She could wait several hours for Andrew and still be home for supper. She missed Josiah and Hannah and Mari. Hiram Kuhn discouraged chatter at the dinner table, and Rhoda hustled the children off after meals before Clara could do much more than catch their eyes and offer a smile instead of the words spoiling on her tongue. If she could not be useful with the chores or helpful with the children, what harm was there in finding refuge on the Johnson farm? Sagging and broken slats allowed nearly as much air inside the old barn as outside, and if she wanted more illumination than what filtered in jagged stripes, Clara could always light one of Andrew's lanterns. Leaning into the stubborn barn door, she closed it far enough that its disturbed state would not cause a confirming glance to anyone who passed by on the road.

She walked around the Model T twice before reaching for the latch and opening the door to climb into the comfortable upholstered seat behind the steering wheel. Clara knew how to drive a buggy or an open cart, and for the first time she wondered if she might learn to drive a car as well. Closing her eyes, she felt again the wind tickling her cheeks the day Andrew took her for a ride, leaving her rosy and glowing.

Such an unabashed sensation, one that she had never known to crave before that day.

Andrew would take her out again if she asked.

Andrew stood for a moment in the reduced opening and wondered what Clara was thinking about. He was not unhappy to see her sitting in the automobile—quite the opposite. With her hands on the wheel, she was without reticence or guile, and he was grateful to see her in such a state. Clara had made no suggestion that he should have accepted Jurgen Hansen's offer to buy the Model T. Her trust in his judgment had evoked a tenderness he had not thought possible.

He stepped into the barn. "Would you like a driving lesson?"

Her head turned with a grace that stirred him.

"I would hate to cause a breakdown," she said.

A half-dozen strides was all it took to take him to her side. She scooted over on the bench, and only then did Andrew see the papers in her lap.

"What have you brought?" He climbed in beside her.

Her nerves made her swallow with such force that Andrew heard the spongy thump.

"Stories," she said. "Bible stories. I write them for Sadie."

He raised both eyebrows. "I had no idea."

"No one in our congregation does." Clara lifted the stack of pages. "I want you to read them and tell me if they are a good that will honor God, or if they are a sinful, selfish pride that will undo me."

He took the papers but did not move his gaze from her eyes. "You know the answer to that."

She pulled a loose end of string and the knot came loose. "I know that I would be getting a man with an automobile. I want you to know what you would be getting."

Andrew gave in to a half smile. "So you're thinking about it."

Clara blushed and glanced away. "Just read some."

"Right now?"

"I'll get one of the lamps if you need it." She started to get out of the Model T, but he put a hand on her arm to stop her. He wanted her near.

Andrew dropped one shoulder to clear the shadow over the top page, adjusted his eyes to the light, and began to read silently. Beside him, Clara was unnaturally still. He hardly heard her breathe. One by one he slid the pages to the bottom of the pile.

"These are very good," he said when he was halfway through.

"Keep reading," she prodded.

Andrew smiled and chuckled and nodded and put his finger under favorite parts. When he came again to the page where he had begun, he was tempted to keep reading. Instead, he looked at her eager eyes.

"How long have you been working on these?"

"A few months. I've written a lot in the last few days."

"You have a wonderful imagination."

"Some of our people would caution me on that matter."

"Not me," Andrew said. "Never in our home."

She blushed again, but this time she did not look away.

Behind them, the door creaked open. Andrew hoped for Jurgen but saw Yonnie.

"What are you doing?" Yonnie said.

Andrew stifled a sigh and did not answer. Even he was losing patience with the tone he heard in Yonnie's voice the last few weeks, a cross between false authority and trepidation.

"I wanted to talk to you," Yonnie said, "but I see this is not a convenient time for you."

Andrew sensed Clara was going to rise and put out a hand to cover hers, away from Yonnie's view. He didn't want her to go. Clara could hear whatever was on Yonnie's mind or Yonnie could find Andrew again later.

"What can I help you with?" Andrew said.

Yonnie pressed his lips together, not in sternness but in uncertainty. When they were boys, his chin would have been drooping in a moment like this one. As an adolescent, Yonnie had learned to clamp his jaw closed when he didn't know what to say. Andrew waited.

"It's about the bishop's sermon," Yonnie said.

Andrew tightened his grip on Clara's hand. "Each man will have to seek his own conscience."

"Yes. We can talk another time." Yonnie's eyes went from Andrew's to Clara's. "I also wanted to be sure you both knew about the barn raising on Thursday."

"Mose Beachy reminded me," Andrew said.

"Then I'll see you there."

Yonnie turned to go, and Andrew released Clara's hand.

She tied the string around her pages again. "He has more on his mind than a barn raising."

❧❦❧

"You go," Fannie said to Elam.

"What will I tell your mother?" Elam poured water into his hands and splashed his face over the kitchen sink, rinsing the day's labor from his skin.

"The truth. I'm under the weather and need to rest." Fannie ached to lie down. "That's no reason for Sadie to be disappointed, and you'll get a much better meal at my mother's than I could offer you tonight."

Elam rubbed a towel over his face. "If you're sure."

"I am."

"She'll want to send some food home for you."

"I'm not hungry."

Fannie's teeth grated through the next twenty minutes of getting Sadie into a clean dress and Elam out the door with their daughter. She forced herself to stand upright long enough to return her daughter's farewell wave.

Then she went into the bedroom, climbed into the bed fully clothed, and put a pillow over her face to block the still-streaming summer sunlight.

All she wanted was to be alone in a dark, quiet space.

At church the day before, her mother's condition had become the news of the day, followed by the announcements that two other women were also expecting new *boppli*. Fannie had choked back her own grief and mustered congratulations to two women only a few years older than she was. They were still in their childbearing years. As disappointment gave way to envy in the pit of her stomach, Fannie knew she could not avoid women in their twenties or thirties having more children. It was only natural that they would.

But her own mother? At forty-four? It was too hard. Fannie craved only release from that vision. She closed her eyes and relinquished her mind to the shadows.

CHAPTER 18

Yonnie's eyes popped open and his breath caught. The room sprang into vivid focus, down to the miniscule white dust particles riding on light streaming through the shutterless window.

"Are you coming or not?" His mother's voice echoed up the stairwell. "I can't keep your breakfast hot forever."

The two beds on either side of Yonnie's were empty, though on most mornings his brothers' forms rolled and moaned at his movements no matter how quiet he tried to be. Only moments ago he was awake—at least that's what it felt like. The strength of the sunlight betrayed the true hour. Yonnie had fallen back into the deepest sleep of his night and slumbered through the morning household commotion. Even his brothers would be at their farm chores by now.

Twice during the night Yonnie got up for a drink of water, which did nothing to soothe his spirit.

By the time he finished wrestling with his thoughts, he felt like Jacob, lame from the touch of God on his hip.

When sleep surrendered its reluctance and eased its way into his body, Yonnie knew he had at best two hours before he would rise and prepare for his day's labor. It was no wonder he had examined the shadows of the room and allowed himself another ten minutes.

That was hours ago.

Yonnie's heart pounded. A milkman never had the luxury of beginning the day so long after sunrise. He did not have to consult a clock to know that by now a scowl twisted Dale Borntrager's face. On the way to the hook where his trousers hung, Yonnie paused at the water basin long enough to plunge his face into liquid that was neither hot nor cold. In one swift gesture, he snapped his suspenders into place and dropped his hands to fasten his work boots before thundering down the stairs.

His mother stood at the stove with a spatula in one hand.

"I'm sorry, *Mamm*." He whizzed past her, bending to aim a kiss at her cheek, knowing it would not land. "I don't know what happened."

Despite the allure of scrambled eggs and fried ham, Yonnie could not allow himself the indulgence of breakfast when he was so late. Maybe there would at least be coffee in the pot at the dairy.

Outside the house, Yonnie groaned in realization that his father and brothers had taken all the horses into the fields already. As late as he was, he had no alternative to racing on foot to the dairy.

His night of grappling with the bishop's message had yielded fruit in those final exhausting moments. *"Each man will have to seek his own conscience,"* Andrew had said, and he was right. Yonnie suspected Andrew meant the words as a defense of his own choice, but as they rolled through the night watches of Yonnie's mind, he heard in them the obedience of his own conscience.

The right course was to bring to Bishop Yoder's attention that one of his flock owned an automobile. The clarity that illumined Yonnie's spirit during the watches of the night now made him wonder why he had tussled so long—weeks—with the decision. In his baptism, he vowed to submit to the authority of the church. It was God's will that Yonnie had witnessed the spurious circumstances under which Andrew had allowed his commitment to falter. The strength of the church mattered more than Yonnie's personal fondness for his childhood friend.

And it mattered more than Yonnie's job. He would have to look for work that would not require him to silence his own conscience for mere financial gain. Not everyone in the congregation dismissed the bishop's leadership with the indifference of Dale or Andrew or John Stutzman. As his father liked to say, "If you are true to your faith, there are things you give up."

Yonnie barreled into the dairy without the extravagance of catching his breath. In the office, he scanned the order sheets for anything out of the ordinary. The clock confirmed the degree of his tardiness, but Yonnie pushed through the distraction and mentally calculated how he could economize his movement and trim a substantial margin off the lost time. Cheese, milk, cream, butter. He could pack three crates at a time instead of one and put more in each crate so he could make fewer trips to load the wagon. In the main room, where everything was kept cold, Yonnie moved into action.

Eventually, though, he felt Dale's glare on the back of his neck. He moistened his lips and turned to face his employer.

"I'm sorry to be so late. I overslept," Yonnie said. If Dale were in a fair frame of mind, he would acknowledge that Yonnie had never succumbed to this malady before. One incidence had no resemblance to a habit.

"And will you tell that to the customers who expected fresh cream with their morning coffee?"

"I will make every apology necessary," Yonnie said quickly. "I will ask forgiveness and make clear that the lateness of the rounds is no fault of yours."

Dale glowered. "First you spoiled an entire order of milk. Then you took the liberty to remove milk suppliers from your rounds. Now you're intolerably late."

Yonnie's gut burned. He had worked for Dale for years and knew the dairy's operation better than any of the other employees. It should not be so hard for Dale to recognize these truths.

Demut, Yonnie reminded himself. Humility.

"I will make up the time," he said. "You will find no more dissatisfaction in my work at day's end."

He would have to make inquiries soon about other work—before Dale had opportunity to spread an opinion that disparaged Yonnie. Several Amish farms were large enough that he might be able to hire himself out as a field hand. Most likely, he would not receive any salary until after the harvest and the work might be temporary, but it would be a start. Or the Amish furniture store in Springs might need help in its workshop at the edge of town. Yonnie was not much of a carpenter, but he could clean up and make deliveries.

By the time the milk wagon clattered out of the dairy, Yonnie was formulating the precise wording of his inquiries. He would have to be certain a new employer planned to properly respect Bishop Yoder's authority.

Sweat tickled Fannie's ear along a fine line from the roots of her hair down to the side of her neck, and she raised a shoulder to swipe at the irritation. Lifting a hand from her task would have been a vain effort. Tenacious humidity overpowered the air. Fannie had no thermometer, but she had lived through enough Julys not to put false hope in the notion that the weather would break into a stream of tolerable temperatures. If anything, the sweltering days would grow more intense before the turn of the earth yielded relief. Systematically, Fannie pushed a dust rag across the neglected wood surfaces of her front room. She did not much care whether the dust piled up. She only knew that keeping herself in constant motion was the most likely cure for the profound urge to go back to bed that had trailed through the hours since breakfast. Perhaps if her house was tidier, her mind would feel less cluttered as well.

At the dining room table, Sadie banged her heels against the legs of the chair and the pencil in her hand against the tabletop.

"Have you finished copying your letters?" Fannie asked, though she had only given Sadie the task to keep her from pulling items out of drawers and cupboards faster than Fannie could put them away.

"I don't want to copy letters." Sadie leaned her chin into one hand. "I'm not old enough for school yet."

"You will be soon. You can at least learn to write your name."

"I want to play. That's what I'm good at."

Fannie cocked her head and surprised herself with a smile. "Yes, playing has always been your special talent."

"Then why can't I go out and play?"

"You heard *Daed* at lunch. It's going to rain."

"But it's not raining now." Sadie's eyes rounded into solemn pleas.

Fannie tossed the dust rag on a side table. "All right. We'll both go outside." At least outdoors a breeze might flutter and divide the damp air into a small space of relief.

They went into the front yard, where Elam had dug the vegetable plot wider and longer this year. Fannie could keep her hands busy weeding and inspecting produce.

Sadie immediately threw herself into a patch of grass and rolled one direction and then the other.

"Watch me!" she called.

"I'm watching." Fannie wondered if Sadie was old enough to recognize when the expression on her mother's face was not quite sincere, though she did observe the girl's glee and remembered how cool grass close to the earth could refresh a day with little other promise. The caution that formed in Fannie's mind went unspoken. She should have reminded Sadie to take care with her dress and to roll only in the grass and not in dirt, but she lacked energy to enforce a warning so she supposed there was no point in voicing one. Needle and thread and a cool bath would remedy any damage. Fannie turned to the garden, kneeling in the loamy soil and wishing she had thought to pick up the basket on the front porch. She glanced at the sky and judged that they would not be outside for long. Elam was right. Rain seemed inevitable, and Fannie would have to persuade Sadie to go back inside.

Sadie popped up. "Look! It's *Grossmuder.*"

Stone formed in Fannie's stomach. Her mother struggled for a moment with the latch at the gate.

Pull it up, Fannie thought. Martha always seemed to try twice to open the latch by pulling it down before resorting to the opposite motion. Why didn't her mother bring a buggy? She should not have walked in this heat in her condition.

Her condition.

Martha had a definite sway now. Her waistline had seemed to explode in the last few weeks, making it impossible for Fannie to avoid thinking about the child in her womb.

Fannie might be able to hide her feelings from a five-year-old, but her mother would be a steeper challenge. She stood and smiled.

"Hello, *Mamm.*" Not since Fannie had begun going to Singings on her own had she wished this hard that her mother would go away.

"Are you feeling better?" Martha said, dabbing an apron corner at the sweat on her forehead.

Fannie had no desire to lie to her mother. Neither could she tell the truth.

Sadie tugged at Martha's hand. "Do you want strudel? We have a lot."

"Yes," Fannie said quickly, "why don't you go get *Grossmuder* a piece of strudel? Wrap it in a napkin and don't squeeze it."

Sadie skipped toward the house. Fannie felt the first widely spaced drops of rain as she turned to face her mother.

"I know why you didn't come to supper last night," Martha said softly.

Fannie said nothing.

"I prayed for years that God would give you another child," her mother said. "I still do. I never asked for this for myself. I have a house and a heart full of children, and after twelve years I was content to think that the days of new babes were over for me."

"I know." Fannie forced out the reply. She *did* know. Other than her husband, her mother was the one to soak up Fannie's heartache month after month as if it were her own.

The rain spattered with sudden force, and thunder rumbled. Sadie stood on the porch cradling a napkin, unsure what to do.

"Stay there!" Fannie called to Sadie. Raindrops splotched her apron, coming faster and harder like a certain birth.

"This child will be your brother or sister." Martha raised her pitch above the thrumming shower. "I hope you will love it as much as you do the others."

Fannie nodded, if only to bring the conversation to a close. She could not keep her mother standing out in the rain, and neither could she expect Martha to begin the walk home in a thunderstorm. She would have to invite her inside. Sadie, at least, would be delighted.

"I'll find you a cold drink to have with your strudel."

CHAPTER 19

The remains of a barn that stood for fifty years had been removed. Melvin Mast had been talking about a new barn, with more and bigger cow stalls, for close to ten years. Now, instead of a rickety weathered structure, the space beside the Mast house featured precise stacks of beams, joists, rafters, siding, and shingles. The foundation, laid last week, was already covered with floorboards. Clara could see the clear shape of the barn.

"I understand Young Dave is the boss of the raising today." Hiram Kuhn guided the family buggy to a clear spot along a pasture fence and pulled on the reins.

"His first time," Rhoda said. "I'm sure he has learned well from his father."

Clara got out and then raised her hands for little Mari. Hannah would insist she could get down on her own. Josiah was already helping Hiram unhitch the horse, and Rhoda gripped the handles of two baskets of food. Clara welcomed Mari into her arms, giving the three-year-old a quick hug and a kiss on the top of her head without looking at Rhoda.

"I want to really help this time." Josiah straightened his eight-year-old height. "I'm old enough."

"We'll see," Hiram said.

"I don't want to go with the *kinner*." Josiah's face set with his mother's determination. "I want to learn to build a barn."

Clara watched the glance that passed between Hiram and Rhoda.

"Come with me," Hiram said, "but you must obey carefully today." They walked away.

Mari tugged Clara's skirt. "Is this a frolic?"

"Yes, it is," Clara said. A hundred people or more would turn out. Glancing around, she could see most of the church families were already present.

"I like frolics, don't I?" Mari, standing beside the buggy, looked up at Clara for confirmation.

Clara smiled. "You are the best frolicker I know."

Rhoda cleared her throat. "Please don't fill her head with pride."

Clara cupped her hand around the back of Mari's head but said nothing.

"Come along, Mari," Rhoda said. "You, too, Hannah. Let's let Clara enjoy her day."

"I'll keep the girls," Clara said, gesturing at the baskets Rhoda carried. "You have other things to do."

"Thank you," Rhoda said, "but I've already spoken with Hannah. It's time she took on more responsibility. She's old enough to keep Mari occupied."

Once Rhoda turned her back, leading the girls away, Clara let out her sigh. Clara would have enjoyed her day very well with her little sisters in tow. Even when her father first married Rhoda, Clara knew she had a determined personality. Her penchant for order served the household well after Hiram's years of limited cooking skills and uncertainty about what a little girl needed. But now, the way Rhoda drew lines around her stepdaughter without ever being rude—this was something Clara would not have predicted.

Clara turned her eyes to the bustling scene. Men clustered around supplies, women unwrapped food at a series of tables, and children scooted off to find friends and have the run of the farm. Young people old enough to go to Singings would eye each other.

She would enjoy the day. As a motherless little girl, she loved any sort of frolic that brought her into the arms and attention of the church. No one today would have reason to think anything was wrong between Clara and Rhoda. She could be with people she had known all her life, doing something no one would disagree about.

Clara caught Andrew's eye across the farmyard cleared for the day of the chickens that normally occupied it. He would be working hard. She had seen Andrew's contribution to a barn raising before. He let older men lean into the poles that would raise the first bent to an upright position, while nearly two dozen others held it with ropes from falling over. As soon as the second bent was raised, Andrew would lead the scramble of agile young men up to jiggle and fit the crossbeams into place and drive in the locking pins. He had never been afraid of heights or of standing on surfaces more narrow than his boots. The men were already arranging themselves, awaiting Young Dave's call to begin raising the skeleton.

Clara decided to be useful by helping to set up a water station. It was already after eight o'clock, and in the middle of July, temperatures would soar by midmorning. A large dispenser was positioned on a table, no doubt well chilled in spring water. Clara pulled out one of several crates under the table and found glasses, which she began to set out in rows.

"Clara!"

The voice came from behind her. Clara pivoted to see Priscilla Schrock a few feet away.

"I was hoping you would be here." Priscilla bounced on her heels.

"And here I am," Clara said.

"I'm going to tell Naomi and Lillian you're here. We can have a story class."

"Priscilla, I don't think—"

The girl was already in motion, unhearing of Clara's gentle protest. As she looked round, Clara wondered if she appeared as furtive as she felt.

Young Dave strode past her, positioned himself in a central location among the supplies, and gave the first call.

Yonnie joined the crew framing doorways and windows. Uncomfortable with climbing the rising form of a barn, he was consistent in his choice of tasks that kept both feet on the ground with little risk that any sudden movement would endanger his balance. Now he wished he had paid more attention over the years to the details. If he had learned to frame a window rather than simply hand tools to the carpenter, he might have a skill to offer a new employer.

Mose Beachy turned a palm up, and Yonnie laid a tiny awl in it. At least he knew which tool was needed, even if he hadn't learned to use it himself. He watched carefully, though. The barn would have several doors and a bank of windows letting in daylight.

Bending his wide girth, Mose finished an adjustment and signaled that Yonnie should help him lift the window frame into the space left for it in the side of the barn. Outside the barn, older men marked with chalk where siding boards would cross a beam before handing the boards off to others who carried them, three at a time, and passed them to younger men stationed among the framing. The sound of swinging hammers striking nails would not abate for hours as siding boards went onto the frame in a rolling wave.

Younger boys, old enough to help but not yet trusted with tools or heights, moved around the barn and yard collecting waste wood to pile out of the way. One of them trailed Mose and Yonnie now. It was the Kuhn boy, Yonnie thought, though he never could remember the boy's name. Joshua. Jeremiah. Something like that.

Mose worked with few words. Suddenly he shouted over Yonnie's shoulder. "Watch out."

A thud launched a clatter, followed by a yelp.

"Put the window down." Mose swiftly lowered his end to the barn floor. Yonnie set his end down carefully and balanced the frame against an interior post, irritated that Mose had left him with the weight of the fragile window.

Mose knelt beside the boy, who had fallen and dropped the waste wood balanced in his arms.

"Josiah, are you all right?"

Josiah. That was the Kuhn boy's name. His eyes were closed, and he made no sound.

"Josiah?" Mose said again.

"My head hurts." Josiah raised a hand to one temple, his eyes still closed.

"It's all right. You can open your eyes." Mose pulled out a shirttail and gently wiped sawdust from the boy's face. "It's only a small cut."

"Is it bleeding?" Josiah's eyes popped wide open.

Yonnie rolled his gaze at the boy's fright. "You should have been more careful."

The boy's face crumpled.

Mose looked up through the unfinished slope of the rear portion of the barn. Yonnie followed his view and saw Andrew peering down.

"Anybody hurt?" Andrew said. "A board got away from somebody up here."

Mose looked at Josiah. The boy was startled and on the brink of tears.

"We're fine," Yonnie told Andrew.

"I think Josiah will want to go find his mother." Mose helped the boy to his feet.

"You should have been paying more attention," Yonnie said. "It's dangerous to have children in the way of the men while they're working."

"I'm helping," Josiah said.

"Look at the mess you've made." Yonnie pointed to the strewn waste wood.

"I'll pick it up again." Josiah's voice trembled.

Mose put a hand on the boy's shoulder. "The important thing is you're safe. But maybe you'd like some water or a pastry before you get back to work."

Josiah nodded.

When the boy had left the barn, Mose began picking up the spilled wood and stacking it against the wall. "You were harsh with the boy. It wasn't his fault one of the men above dropped a board."

"If fathers want to let their sons work," Yonnie said, "they should supervise more closely."

"I have fourteen children," Mose said. "Not a one of them would fail to look around and see what needs doing when the church community is together. They want to belong. Your parents taught you the same way. I can remember when you were a boy picking up waste wood."

"He has to be aware of what's happening around him." Yonnie mumbled now. "He could have been hurt."

"And if he had been, we would have taken care of him. That's what we do. Jesus teaches us to do unto others as we would have them do unto us."

The admonishment, though delivered with gentleness, stung.

Yonnie returned to the window frame. "Let's get back to work."

The men ate lunch in two shifts, selecting food from the women's offerings and findings seats at tables inside the Mast house or in the shade of trees in the yard. After the men were fed, the women and children would eat. Women shuttled around refilling water glasses and clearing plates to wash quickly for the next wave of diners. Finishing his meal with the second shift, Andrew watched Clara amble back toward the water table where she had spent most of the day so far. Stopping to greet others who spoke to him, Andrew followed Clara in a vague way. On a day like this, a working man could always use another glass of water.

On the verge of speaking, Andrew held his words when Hannah Kuhn whizzed past him and grinned at her big sister.

"I thought you were watching Mari," he heard Clara say.

"Nap time!" Hannah answered. "*Mamm* said I could go play."

"Then you should go find your friends."

"Priscilla said I should come here."

"She did?"

"Yes. She has a surprise for me!"

Priscilla, Naomi, and Lillian arrived in tangled unison.

"I told you she was here," Priscilla announced. She turned to Clara. "You don't have to stay here every minute, do you?"

Andrew's soft steps took him closer, still behind Clara. His curiosity piqued.

"No," Clara said. "I don't suppose so."

"Grown-ups can get their own water," Naomi said. "But they won't tell us a story like you will."

Andrew saw Clara's frame stiffen. Pride rose through his chest, though he did not allow it to form on his lips.

"A story?" Hannah said.

"That's the surprise," Priscilla said.

Clara's nervous glance swept the farmyard. "I'm not sure that's a good idea right now."

"It is! It is!" Lillian said. "We've been waiting all day for Mari to go to sleep so Hannah could come, too."

Andrew recognized the shift in her posture as Clara embraced the notion. His mind's eye saw again lines jumping from her sheaf of papers. He glanced at the barn, where the side boarding continued on one end and the roofing began on the other. He judged there were enough young men willing to scale the heights and do the work, and he might not have another opportunity to hear Clara tell a story.

She could not know he was there, though, or she might get shy. And he did not want his presence to inhibit the enthusiasm he witnessed in the little girls. Andrew gave Clara and the girls a head start, the girls tugging at her hands and skirts as they walked down the tree-lined lane. He could easily keep them in sight, see where they settled, and lean against a tree out of sight but within earshot.

Andrew wished he could watch her face as she arranged a circle with four little girls to tell the story of one little boy who offered his lunch—everything he had—to Jesus.

CHAPTER 20

Fannie drowsed on her bed with the door ajar. If the rhythm of Sadie's play in the other room rumbled or heightened, Fannie would hear it and judge the need for intervention. On Tuesday afternoon her efforts to stay awake and interested in her daughter's chatter had succumbed to the weight stifling her spirit as much as to the heat and humidity that tortured her relentlessly more than any summer she could remember. It was past time to start supper. Elam would come in from his work in the far field both deserving and expecting a nourishing meal, and Sadie should eat. Behind her closed eyes, Fannie thought how unfair it seemed that the person least interested in meals should be responsible for the nourishment of the small household. She mentally inventoried the cupboards and icebox, trying to come up with a meal that would not leave Elam wondering what she had done all afternoon.

"*Mamm,*" Sadie called.

Fannie meant to answer, but after a few seconds realized she lacked the energy to speak aloud.

"*Mamm!*" Sadie's tone grew insistent.

Fannie forced open her eyes to see Sadie standing in the doorway—with Clara beside her.

Clara stepped into the room. "Are you all right?"

What did *all right* mean? Fannie was not certain she would ever be all right again.

"Fannie," Clara said.

Fannie heaved herself upright. "Clara, what are you doing here?" Clara usually came in the morning. It wasn't morning, was it? Fannie

455

glanced out the window and saw that the light had shifted toward its evening arc. Panic subsided.

"Are you all right?" Clara repeated, approaching the bed.

Fannie waved her off. "I only meant to rest a few minutes. The heat." Her eyes focused on the patches of perspiration dampening Clara's clothes. Had she walked five miles while Fannie did not even sit up in bed? Fannie regretted blaming the heat.

"Sadie," Clara said, "I think your *mamm* could use a glass of cold water. Can you fetch it?"

Sadie scampered out of the room. Fannie let her bare feet touch the floor, wishing to find it cool as in winter but encountering a layer of humidity even there.

"It's not just the heat, is it?" Clara picked up a cloth from the washstand and dipped it in water to put against Fannie's face.

Fannie knew it would be tepid, not refreshing, but she let Clara wipe the cloth across her face. "No," she said. "I'm trying, but the week has been difficult. My mother is getting big so fast that you'd think she's expecting triplets."

"I felt the heaviness of your spirit all the way in Somerset County." Clara sat on the bed beside Fannie.

"Did you walk? It's so hot."

"I'm all right."

"Sadie should get you a glass of water, too."

"I'll get one in a few minutes. I'm worried about you."

Fannie plumped the pillow her head had just vacated. "I should be grateful. I have a husband, a child, a home, a farm. There is so much to do, but all I want is to lie on my bed."

Clara put an arm around Fannie's shoulder, and Fannie laid her head against her, her own chest exploding with ache.

"Let's go sit under your oak tree," Clara said. "It will have good shade at this time of day. Then I'll make supper."

"I can make supper," Fannie said.

"I know. But I'd like to."

"Doesn't Rhoda need you?" Even in Fannie's foggy state, she did not miss Clara's hesitation.

Sadie arrived with a glass brimming with water. "I didn't spill a single drop!"

Fannie smiled and sipped. "Sadie, Clara's been walking a long way."

The girl brightened. "I should get her some water, too!"

Fannie turned to Clara again. "It's not too late to catch the milk wagon back to Somerset to help Rhoda."

Clara shrugged. "There's no hurry."

Fannie fished around her mind for what Clara wasn't telling her but could not frame the thought. She tried to recall the last time Clara said anything to her about Rhoda or any of the Kuhn children. Something was wrong. Fannie ought to care, ought to probe. She took a long gulp of water, unconvinced it would help but determined to try.

The back screen door creaked open and slammed closed. Elam's heavy footsteps crossed the kitchen linoleum. He said something to Sadie that Fannie couldn't make out, and the girl's voice lilted in laughter.

"Good," Clara said. "You can sit with Elam in the shade while I prepare the meal. You'll have some extra time together with Sadie."

Time with Elam would not heal what pierced Fannie, but at least the diversion might prevent Sadie from innocently telling her father where her mother had spent the afternoon.

Dale Borntrager would never say he was punishing Yonnie with an unscheduled delivery into Garrett County to one of the Marylander households. If Yonnie had challenged him, Dale would have said it was a last-minute order and he only got the message long after the regular afternoon run was finished. Other employees at the dairy made offhand remarks that suggested this was true. Four generations of two families that had married into each other several times were gathering to celebrate the birthday of a great-grandmother and the birth of the latest great-grandson. They wanted abundant provisions for their evening festivities. Extra milk to churn into ice cream, extra butter for favorite dishes, extra cheese, extra cream. Extra everything.

So Yonnie had put the order together and turned the wagon around. Was it not enough that he swallowed his indignity in serving the Marylander families at all? No matter how many people believed that *meidung* did not apply to business dealings, Yonnie was certain the bishop intended that his congregation should have nothing to do with the Marylanders. Yet here he was, submitting to his employer rather than to his bishop.

He was in no hurry to get back to the dairy. The other employees would have gone home to their families long ago. If sending Yonnie with the extra delivery was not outright punishment for his convictions, Dale's explanation likely would have been that Yonnie had no wife and children waiting for him to come home. His parents, sister, and brothers would eat supper without him, though his parents would scowl at the notion that Dale should keep anyone from the evening meal and family devotions. And they had a point. Dale could have sent word that it was too late in the day to fill an order in Garrett County. The Marylanders would have scooped out smaller portions of ice cream and consumed their coffee black. There was no need to intrude on anyone else's family evening. But it was a large order, and Dale had made the sort of business decision an *English* would have made. The thought stirred further indignation in Yonnie.

Now the sky had grayed, descending deeper each moment toward the release of this day's troubles. Burning Amish lamps would soon be put out as families set the last of the clean supper dishes in the cupboard, closed their German Bibles, finished reading the news from *The Sugarcreek Budget*, and inspected their children's fingernails to see if the dirt had been scrubbed out. Daylight came early at this time of year; with most of their work outdoors, few Amish farmers stayed up more than an hour after darkness fell.

Yonnie let the horse set its own pace. His own gelding was grazing in Dale's pasture beside the dairy. At this hour, what did it matter if he returned Dale's horse and retrieved his own thirty minutes sooner or thirty minutes later?

In the beam of the lantern hanging from the front of the buggy, Yonnie saw a slender, dark-clad figure walking along the other side of the road. He peered more closely and saw it was an Amish woman.

What was an Amish woman doing out on this road by herself at this hour?

Clara Kuhn.

Yonnie pulled on the reins to slow the horse even further. Clara should not be out. If she had the audacity to visit her Marylander relatives in defiance of Bishop Yoder's sermons, she ought to have the good sense to get herself home for supper. If he stayed behind her for a few more minutes, she would walk past the next turnoff, and he could divert his route and leave her to the consequences of her own foolishness.

She paused then and turned around, lifting one hand to flag his attention.

❧❧❧

Clara could not have imagined she would feel such relief at the sight of Yonnie Yoder, of all people. Whatever his reason for still being out in the milk wagon did not matter. Clara was not so proud that she would fail to recognize God's provision when it trotted toward her.

She did, however, think that it could trot more briskly. Yonnie was holding the horse back on purpose. Finally he pulled alongside her.

"I thank God you're here," she said. "I need a ride. Would you be able to take me all the way home?"

A flood of questions flushed through his face. No one ever had to wonder what Yonnie was thinking. Humiliation suffused her gratitude.

"Yes, I was at my cousin's," Clara said. "I felt God leading me to visit her today."

She had said the same thing to Fannie, and it was true. Still, she hoped a spiritual response would have some influence on Yonnie's sense of compassion.

"Why didn't you ride the wagon home hours ago?" he said.

"That turned out not to be possible." Clara awaited Yonnie's permission to board the wagon.

"You do it all the time," he said, disapproval ringing in his tone.

"Today's circumstances were unusual."

"Your cousin has a husband. Why would he send you into the night alone?"

"Conditions were complicated." Clara was not going to tell Yonnie Fannie's private business. He didn't even know Fannie, other than picking up milk from the Esh farm. "My father expected me back hours ago, I'm sure."

"Then you should have gone home hours ago."

"Yonnie, please. It's dark, and it's still very warm to be walking so far."

He stared at Clara in silence, as if to say she had not begged with enough sincerity. Fury roiled, tempting her to withdraw her request and march on. When she left Elam and Fannie, she was prepared to walk the full distance, refusing Elam's offer of a ride out of conviction that Fannie should not be on her own tonight. She would have stayed the night, but she was due at the banker's home right after breakfast. Clara met Yonnie's unsympathetic expression with an unspoken threat to mention his refusal to the bishop. Yonnie would not want to risk the bishop's judgment of his lack of Christian compassion. But Clara could not count on the bishop not to defend Yonnie's choice to separate himself from church members who had been cavorting with the Marylanders.

"Yonnie, it's late," she said, trying to keep desperation out of her voice. "I ask only for a simple act of charity." *Don't make me beg.*

"I, too, am very late getting home." His response was unyielding.

"Then you understand that circumstances arise that we cannot control." If an appeal to compassion meant nothing to Yonnie, perhaps simple logic would.

Yonnie tilted his chin up and examined her beneath lowered eyelids.

Clara swept back the strand of hair that had escaped the pins in her coiled braids and adjusted her *kapp*.

"Yonnie, please," she said, humiliation burning through her.

He lifted the reins, and the horse took a few steps forward.

"Yonnie!"

He paused again before finally nodding his head toward the empty space beside him on the bench.

Anger poured another layer of perspiration through her clothing while Clara sat as far away from Yonnie as she could.

CHAPTER 21

Andrew raced his wagon to the dairy just before lunch the next day. Dale sat at a desk in the office with an account book open.

"I need to see Yonnie," Andrew said.

"He's working." Dale didn't glance up. "I'll tell him you were looking for him. He'll find you later."

"Thank you, but I'll find him now." Andrew pivoted on one heel and charged into the main bottling room. The rhythmic thud of his work boots made every head lift and turn toward the sound.

Yonnie capped off a pint of cream and stiffened.

Good, Andrew thought. *He should be nervous.*

Aloud, he said, "How dare you?"

Hands stilled around them.

Yonnie picked up an empty bottle, moved it six inches, and set it down again. "Maybe we should go outside—when I get a break."

"I can speak my mind here." Andrew planted his feet.

Behind Andrew, Dale spoke. "Your break just started, Yonnie. Whatever this is about, take it out of my dairy."

Yonnie led the way through the back door. Aggravated by Yonnie's sluggish pace, Andrew nearly stepped on his heels. They moved ten yards away from the building. Three sets of curious eyes peering out a window did not deter Andrew.

"You humiliated Clara."

"How is it she has spoken to you privately already?"

"Don't," Andrew said. "Don't think you can escape this by accusing Clara or me of wrongdoing."

Yonnie ground one boot heel into the dirt. "You said it yourself. Each of us has to follow our own conscience. My conscience says to obey the bishop."

"And leave a member of your own church stranded on the side of the road?"

"Clara was hardly stranded. She walks that road often."

"Not alone in the dark."

"She would have gotten home eventually. I was following Bishop Yoder's instructions to separate ourselves from those who have joined the Marylanders."

"Clara has not joined the Marylanders."

"But she was visiting them. She didn't deny that she had been to see her cousin."

"Did you think she would somehow contaminate you?" Andrew exhaled laden fury. "Is that what you would have said to the man on the Jericho road? You are like the religious leaders who walked past the man who had been beaten nearly to death because they didn't want to become unclean."

"It's not the same at all."

"Isn't it?" Andrew said. "Or maybe you were ready to punish Clara in your own way."

"If I can show her the way of obedience more clearly—"

Andrew cut him off. "Shall I remind you it was a Samaritan who showed compassion, not a stuffy, self-righteous man of religion?"

Yonnie stared. "You bear false testimony toward me. It is daring of you to use the words of Jesus to do so."

"I've been fond of you for more than twenty years." Andrew shook a finger. "I've defended you. I've understood you. Now you go too far."

"If Clara were your wife," Yonnie said, "I might understand this show of defense. But she is not your wife. You don't owe her this, at the peril of your own soul."

"I've heard every sermon you've ever heard," Andrew said. "Don't preach at me. And don't come around my farm."

Andrew turned and strode along the side of the dairy to find his wagon.

❧❀❦

Yonnie shifted his weight from one foot to the other and back again, hoping the movement would disguise the tremble that overtook him.

Before he slept the night before, he prayed for God's forgiveness for his weakness. Perhaps God could commend his mercy in driving Clara all the way to the Kuhn farm instead of returning directly to the dairy. Perhaps God would strengthen him to be righteous in the days ahead while church people, like Dale and Andrew and Clara, would choose their own path instead of God's.

The rear door of the dairy opened, and Dale stepped out. Yonnie moved his feet forward, determined not to falter or appear reluctant. He stopped in front of Dale.

"This isn't the place for your personal business," Dale said. "After all the mistakes you've made lately, I would have thought you would know better than to allow this to happen."

"I didn't ask Andrew to come here." Under the shame Yonnie felt at yet another scolding from Dale, defensiveness surged.

"Straighten up," Dale said. "I can't give you endless warnings if I don't see that you are at least attempting to improve your performance."

Yonnie swallowed. "I understand."

"Now get back inside. We still have dozens of bottles to fill. This display has distracted everyone."

Yonnie followed Dale back inside and returned to his tasks without meeting any gazes around him. If anyone spoke to him, he would pray for strength to resist the taunting.

When he drove the dairy wagon, he did not owe Clara or anyone else a ride. He was being paid to pick up milk and make deliveries, not to run a taxi service. Even Dale did not benefit by as much as a penny from the presumptuous way travelers on both sides of the border waited for rides. Yonnie could say no, especially if his own holiness was endangered.

He owed his allegiance to Bishop Yoder and to the decision the congregation made in 1895. Yonnie had once seen the written record of the meeting with his own eyes. The vote had been unanimous. In ignoring their own decision for the last twenty years, the congregation had only brought harm to themselves. They could have had a clean, fresh start with the *meidung*. In separation, their witness would have drawn their relatives and friends back to the true fold of God. Now twenty years of disregarding God's law, in spite of the consistent voice of Bishop Yoder and his sons, made people unwilling—or unable—to recognize their own sin.

Yonnie moved faster, knowing Dale's eyes were on him, to make up for the time he lost with Andrew's distraction. He would be a faithful worker who served God, even if his employer was spiritually lax.

❦

"Please, *Mamm*, please?" Sadie's entire body seemed to beg with expectancy. "It's a good day to go see *Grossmuder*, isn't it? We can make some pound cake and open a jar of blueberries. *Grossmuder* would like that. I know she would."

"*Grossmuder* is busy." Fannie dried the last of the lunch dishes and added it to the stack on the kitchen counter.

"She's never too busy for *me*. I'm her only granddaughter."

"You must learn not to take advantage of her." Fannie swiped a damp rag across the table, pausing at the place where Sadie usually sat to scrub at a spot of spilled milk.

"Because I'm getting big?" Sadie said. "Or because she's going to have another *boppli*?"

"Both. Besides, we have a lot to do around here."

"*Grossmuder* says the new babe will be my *aunti* or *onkel*. That doesn't make sense. How can a baby be an *aunti* or *onkel*?"

"I'll explain it when you're a little older. I want you to clean your room today, please."

"Are you going to help me?"

"You're old enough to do it yourself."

"After that can we go see *Grossmuder*?"

"By then I'll need to start supper."

Sadie's shoulders slumped. "Maybe tomorrow?"

"I have to beat the rugs tomorrow." Fannie handed Sadie a dust rag and a broom whose handle was twice as tall as the girl. "Do a good job, please."

Sadie shuffled out of the room. Fannie ached to feel the soft comfort of her bed under her weary back. Maybe she would pull a quilt over her head if she could stand the heat. She wouldn't sleep, just rest where she could easily hear Sadie.

No.

She would not go lie down. Two nights in a row Elam had asked if she felt well. There was always a chance he would come back to the house in the middle of the afternoon, and why shouldn't he? Fannie used to hope that he would.

Now, though, she did not want him to.

She did not want to speak to Elam or anyone—especially not her mother.

Resisting the urge to find her bed, Fannie instead went into the front room and sat on the davenport. She would not stretch out. She would only put her head back and pull the first quilt she ever made off the end of the davenport and into her lap.

Her guilty spirit weighed heavy. Guilt for sending her five-year-old off so she could be alone. Guilt for hoping her husband would not come in from the fields early. Guilt for not rejoicing in the new life her mother carried. Guilt for holding Sadie back from delighting her *grossmuder* with her presence. Guilt for not wanting to cook supper. Guilt for wishing she could be blessedly asleep.

At least, Fannie knew she *ought* to feel guilty about those things. The truth, though, was that she had left guilt behind days ago. Her limbs were too heavy to lift, and her lungs too weary to inflate, but no longer from guilt. Leaning back on the davenport, she closed her eyes.

Unburdening herself to Andrew on Wednesday morning had allowed Clara to breathe evenly again. For that she had no regrets. When she heard on Thursday that he had confronted Yonnie, though, doubt skulked into her peace of mind. Stirring dissension between the two of them was not her intent. By Friday, Clara wondered if the dissent had only risen to the surface as it was meant to do, as it was inevitably going to do. And by Saturday, she dreaded seeing Yonnie again at church the next day. She knew the row where he preferred to sit and could make sure to sit well behind him on the women's side of the aisle.

Clara now sat in the Schrocks' living room with a length of black fabric in her lap. She could practically make a new apron with her eyes watching evening fireflies instead of her stitches under a lamp, but cutting one out in the company of other women would pass the morning pleasantly. Their chatter would be about recipes and children and laying hens and the new threads at the mercantile. Clara would not have to think about Yonnie or the *meidung*.

Worry for Fannie scoffed her optimism, though. Never had she seen her cousin this way. The *English* would have a word for the condition, Clara supposed. Melancholy? Was that it? It was not a raging illness, but a gentle sadness that threatened to clot and scar Fannie's future.

The next time Clara visited, she would make sure to arrange with her father to take a horse and cart—or at least a horse. She could not rely on Yonnie, and perhaps not on any of the milk wagon drivers.

A small presence blew breath across Clara's cheek, and she turned slightly toward it. Priscilla Schrock leaned in and whispered in Clara's ear. "Another story, please."

The request was not unexpected, but Clara found it daring. It was one thing to wander away during a busy barn raising. It was another for the child to make this request in her own home, under her mother's watchfulness. Clara glanced down the hall and saw three more sets of eyes leaning around a corner in anticipation. Lillian's and Naomi's mothers were present, and of course Rhoda had brought Hannah to the sewing frolic.

Clara knew just the story she would tell. The wise Abigail knew how to help the great King David to control his temper and do the right thing. The girls could learn that a true friend helped others understand how to please God, even someone who was great and powerful.

It was only a matter of time, Clara realized. Four girls knew she told Bible stories, and one of them was her own sister and shared her home. One of them would innocently drop a reference to a story into conversation with a parent over farm chores or evening prayers. Clara almost wished that Hannah was not among the girls who would be tangled in confusion when the mothers began to speak to each other. But why would she hold back God's Word from her own sister?

She wouldn't.

Priscilla had scampered away after seeing Clara's slight nod. Now Clara excused herself, slipped out the back door of the Schrock house, and quickly rounded the corner of the barn.

There they were, seated in the grass and waiting.

CHAPTER 22

Clara jammed a fist against her mouth, stopping the scream rising through her sleep but helpless to thwart the wail flashing through time.

This version of the dream had faces.

Fannie's. Sadie's. Martha's. Atlee's. Hiram's.

Drawn. Pale. Stunned. Tormented. Lost.

A baby's cry faded. Martha collapsed.

Clara gasped and sat up. The morning breeze through the window, still cool in advance of the sun, blew across her suddenly sweat-drenched nightgown. Chilled, she scrambled out of bed, stepped to the washing bowl, and splashed tepid liquid on her face repeatedly until her breathing slowed.

Martha's baby. How would any of them recover if this dream proved true?

Clara sat on the bed. The vague sadness that startled her every few months now growled full terror.

From down the hall, Mari's cry sounded. Rhoda's footsteps responded.

Clara released pent-up breath. Perhaps her little sister crying in her sleep was all that triggered the dream. She should have been used to the sound. It was not unusual for Mari to cry out for her *mamm* without waking and remember nothing in the morning.

Little-girl dreams easily soothed with a mother's touch.

Clara had no *mamm* to call for when she was little. Would dreams of sadness have followed her for years if her mother had been there to stroke her forehead and hum a soothing tune? She would never know.

An early walk, before the bustle of breakfast and readying for church, would release her burning muscles and relieve her of the image of Martha's empty arms. Clara pulled on a dress and shoes. When she returned an hour later, the household had wakened. Hiram and Josiah were milking the cows, and Rhoda was braiding the girls' hair.

A normal morning. Everyone was safe.

After breakfast, Clara went to her room to freshen up. She tucked the last pin in her hair and checked her reflection in the dull glass that hung beside her bedroom door to be sure she had taken captive every rebellious strand. On this first church Sunday in August, filled with worship and socializing, she would have little opportunity for repairs.

She did not hear the footsteps coming down the hall. Bare feet in summer slapped the wooden planks more kindly than winter shoes. Instead, the swish of skirts, which the seasons did not alter, alerted Clara. It was not enough fullness of yardage to be Rhoda. She supposed Hannah, and in a moment her guess was confirmed.

"*Mamm* wants to know if you're ready," Hannah said, standing in the doorway.

"Nearly." Clara looked around for what she had done with her prayer *kapp*.

"Are you going to tell us a story today?" As it always did when she was excited, Hannah's voice rose in pitch and volume.

Clara sucked in her breath, grabbed Hannah to pull her into the room, and closed the door.

"No," Clara said softly, "we won't have a story today. It's a worship service. We'll hear sermons."

"Sermons make me sleepy," Hannah said. "I don't understand them."

"You will soon."

"We could have a story after the service."

"I don't think so."

"But it's been weeks and weeks." Hannah's pout accelerated.

"It only seems that way," Clara said. It had been just over two weeks, but to a six-year-old that must have felt like half the summer.

"But Priscilla will be there, and Lillian and Naomi. And lots of other girls."

Clara had worried the girls would speak to their parents about the Bible stories, but they had only to speak to their friends. Priscilla, after all, had initiated Lillian and Naomi by retelling a story. Another innocent child would ask her mother if she could hear the stories, too.

Before she knew it, Clara would be standing in front of Bishop Yoder with his demand that she explain herself pounding in her ears.

"We might not be able to have any more stories," she said. "At least not for a while."

"But we like them." Hannah pushed out her lower lip another half inch.

"I know." Clara straightened her sister's *kapp* and knotted the strings beneath her chin.

"I won't tell anyone if you don't want me to." Hannah's eyelashes blinked over her blue eyes in wide simplicity.

Clara ran her tongue behind her top lip. Hannah was no secret keeper. She wasn't a tattletale motivated by self-righteousness or maliciousness, but when she got excited, words gushed out when she didn't mean them to. It was a wonder Hannah hadn't already told her mother about the stories. Arranging her own *kapp*, Clara puzzled over why Hannah hadn't said anything yet. She would never tell the girls to withhold truth from their parents. A secret was too close to a lie. To a child, condoning one would be to condone the other. A six-year-old should not be responsible for discerning the difference, nor burdened with conflicting loyalties should a choice come down to the secret or a lie.

Clara blew out a soft breath. She knelt and put her hands on Hannah's elbows, trying to form a response that would neither ask the child to keep a secret nor send her running to divulge one.

The footsteps in the hall now were firm, quick, and evident of shoes.

"Where is everybody?" Rhoda's voice rang out. "It's time to go."

"Never mind," Clara said to Hannah. She pushed up out of the crouch, opened the door, and took her sister's hand to lead her down the stairs.

In the family buggy, Rhoda sat in the front bench beside her husband with Mari on her lap. In the second bench, Clara sat between Josiah and Hannah. All three of them folded their hands in their laps as they had been taught to do as a reminder to keep themselves still and not cause danger in the buggy. Clara could still remember Hiram setting her on the bench beside him and folding her little hands when it was just the two of them, with a stern warning that she must obey or she would fall out of the buggy. By the time she was old enough to be trusted not to move suddenly, the habit was long instilled.

Clara regarded the posture as fitting for preparing for worship. It quieted the body for the long service and encouraged a calming of the spirit as well. She wanted a clean heart for worship.

Her posture came from outward effort, however, while her heart rebelled against every notion she'd ever learned of being ready for church.

She did not feel guilty about telling Bible stories to little girls, but neither did she want to confuse them about right or wrong.

She did not feel guilty for knowing about Andrew's car, nor for her lack of judgment over his ownership of it.

She did not feel guilty for her intention to see her relatives in Maryland no matter what the bishop said.

No matter how tightly she wound and pinned braids against the sides of her head or how perfectly her *kapp* sat on her hair, Clara knew what was in her own heart.

At the Summit Mills Meetinghouse, Clara lingered outside while Rhoda ushered the girls inside and her father and brother took their places in the men's processional. At the last minute, before the men began to march in, she slipped into the bench at the back of the women's section where she could watch Andrew in the mass of black suits and hats. His defense of her to Yonnie had poured cleansing love over her spirit, washing away the humiliation of a dark night. But at what price? While Clara had never felt personal warmth toward Yonnie, Andrew did. Now because of her a chasm ran through their friendship—if it could still be called a friendship.

And the chasm was one more truth that did not spawn guilt.

Was it possible to feel guilty about not feeling guilty?

Andrew's urge was to cross his arms against his chest in doubt that Joseph Yoder's sermon would speak to Andrew's heart. His brother Noah certainly hadn't in the first sermon, although his point had been clear. How would the transgressors who strayed from the church turn to repentance without shunning?

Joseph now announced that his theme would look at two Josephs in the Bible. Andrew's skepticism notched up.

"Where did the brothers of Joseph need to go to become reconciled with him after they behaved so unmercifully toward him? They needed to take the distant trip to Egypt. One might say they went to Egypt only to get grain during the famine, but I believe they were sent of God, since this Joseph is an example of the heavenly Joseph, Jesus Christ. In Egypt they bowed before Joseph and acknowledged their trespasses against him. All hardened transgressors must come to Jesus in the same spirit. Joseph's brothers came in a spirit of undoneness and brokenness. So long as a transgressor has not come to that place, the status of a child of God is not applicable."

Andrew did cross his arms now.

"And let us move to the greatest Joseph of the New Testament. Mary and Joseph left the child Jesus, naturally speaking, and could not find him until they returned to where they left him," Joseph Yoder continued. "This is a lesson for us. If anyone loses a child, spiritually speaking, he should search again at the place where he lost it. Those who have been placed into the ban should be shunned, even if they join another church, so that they may indeed repent, regret, and sorrow with humble hearts and with a demonstration of a sincere lifestyle become reconciled with the church from which they left. The ban can only be lifted if the wanderer renews his commitment with God and the church on bended knees and by seeking the peace where he lost it."

Joseph Yoder's eyes panned the congregation in dramatic silence. "By holding fast to the ban, you will be an instrument of God's will, drawing the transgressor back to true peace. If we do not do so, the transgressor may draw away the entire church. Would such a disturbance of the peace please God? I do not believe so. I call upon each of you to bring to the attention of your ministers and bishop any knowledge you have of individuals who have lost their peace and threaten the peace of the church with their transgressions. Though the ban may seem difficult, we bear the cross Christ calls us to that we may pray for the transgressor's return to peace before we all share in the disturbance of our mutual peace."

Joseph paused again, letting his words sink in.

If there were a third sermon, Andrew wondered, and Mose Beachy were to stand with his Bible open, what would he say? The peace was already disturbed. Bishop Yoder disturbed it himself when he insisted on a strong *meidung* against people whose only transgression was to form a slightly different kind of Amish congregation a generation ago— two generations ago. It was sermons like these that could leave a young woman humiliated on the side of the road. Andrew saw no peace in that.

Andrew glanced at John Stutzman and then at Caleb Schrock. They held their posture better than Andrew did, but he knew their straight spines did not express their thoughts. He would seek them out even before helping to turn benches into tables for the shared meal.

Yonnie nodded his head. He was right. Dale and Clara and Andrew—and so many others—had turned their hearts from obedience to Christ. Hadn't the minister just said so?

Yonnie shifted his head slightly to glance at Dale, whose expression gave away nothing. Perhaps he had closed his heart to the truth so long ago that he would not hear the Holy Ghost knocking even through two sermons that spoke plain truth. Both sermons made clear the responsibility that had stirred Yonnie's heart for weeks, ever since the day he helped Andrew tow the Model T to the abandoned barn. He had been weak, too much under the daring influence of his childhood friend. When he later pulled the car out of the ditch, he was no better. But at last he grasped hold of the fortitude God offered when he rightly interpreted that Dale should avoid contact with the Marylander families out of loyalty to Christ. Clara was a woman. Since she had no husband, she would need the guidance of her father to find strength to shun her cousin, but Hiram Kuhn had been lax for so long that Yonnie almost counted him among those who needed to seek peace where they had lost it.

Clara was not Yonnie's responsibility, but Dale and Andrew were fellow men. Any of them could be called upon to be a minister in the future. Dale was already married, and Yonnie and Andrew would be eligible themselves once they wed. The day might come when someone would nominate one of them to be a minister and they would face the lot—a slip of paper tucked in a hymnal that would indicate God's choice.

In a flush of vindication, Yonnie resolved to seek out the bishop immediately after the close of worship to make an appointment to speak privately.

CHAPTER 23

Sarah Tice had proved right on that June day when Clara ran into her friend in Springs. The Widower Hershberger did go to Ohio to marry. A younger couple would have waited for the fall harvest season to pass, but Mr. Hershberger rode the train, married, and returned all within the space of four days. Clara's housekeeping work diminished. At least the *English* banker's family still depended on her services.

Clara spent most of her days in the far corners of the farm. Crouching among the rising corn to clear weeds always was an option, and her innate industriousness was not so far spent that she turned her nose up at the chore. At first she avoided the places where her father worked with Josiah under his wing. Gradually she began to work beside them, briefly at first, as if she had some more important responsibility at the house, and then for increasingly longer stretches. Hiram never asked why she was not occupied with more feminine labor.

Between sermons that grew more stern each time the congregation gathered and her determination not to rely on the milk wagon for transportation as long as Yonnie was driving the route, Clara hesitated to leave Kuhn property. Three days had passed since Noah and Joseph Yoder rained the latest scoldings on the congregation. She hadn't seen Fannie in three weeks—not since Yonnie would have gloated to leave her on the side of the road—and while Andrew was always glad to see her, Clara did not want to aggravate whatever trouble might be brewing for him because of the Model T. The expression on Andrew's face when he drove the automobile was adorable, and Clara loved the sensation of the car in motion, but if anyone saw her with Andrew and the car, she couldn't be sure of the consequence. Automobiles were *English* machines. Driving one had not yet faced the practical test of defiance that visiting relatives in Maryland had withstood, and certainly not a congregational vote. Clara was fairly certain who agreed or disagreed with the Yoders on the shunning. She was far less sure how members of the congregation would divide on the question of an automobile.

In the end, Andrew would be all right. It was Fannie who worried Clara with her melancholy. She had not been the same since discovering Martha was expecting a child, and Clara suspected Elam did not realize how deep his wife's emotions had plummeted.

At midafternoon on Wednesday, Clara wandered back to the house, too warm and too thirsty. She was barely in the back door when Hannah barreled at her from across the kitchen.

"You got a letter!" Hannah waved the envelope.

Rhoda rapped her knuckles on the kitchen table. "Hannah, that doesn't belong to you."

"Clara doesn't mind." Hannah looked at Clara. "Right?"

Clara glanced at Rhoda. She would not take sides between mother and daughter.

"Why don't I have a look?" Clara took the envelope from Hannah.

"It's from Sadie, isn't it?" Hannah wiggled in anticipation of the answer.

"Don't be silly." Rhoda sealed the lid on a jar of fat. "Sadie is younger than you are. She doesn't know how to write a letter."

Clara wished she could scoop Hannah into her arms the way she could have done a few months ago.

"It's from her mother," she said. "But you and Sadie will both be big enough to write letters before you know it."

"When I am, I will write to Sadie," Hannah said.

Clara resisted the urge to glance at Rhoda again. "One thing at a time."

"Hannah," Rhoda said, "let's go outside and get the laundry from the line."

Hannah constrained the pout that flashed through her lips and followed her mother. Rhoda paused at the back door, turning toward Clara.

"This is your turn to clean the Flag Run Meetinghouse, is it not?"

Clara nodded. "I'm going soon."

"You can take the cart if you like."

"Thank you."

"I want to help clean the meetinghouse," Hannah said.

"You're going to help me with the laundry." Rhoda's tone left no room for negotiation.

Clara took her letter upstairs to her room, opening it only when she was certain she wouldn't be interrupted.

Dear Clara,

Do you remember how we used to write letters over the winter when our parents did not want to take the buggies through the snow? At least I understood that excuse. The news we hear from your congregation is almost unbearable. And you do not fool me. I know you are not happy at home.

I must apologize for being such an inadequate hostess when you last visited. Whatever weighs in my heart, I should have welcomed you more ably. Sadie asks every day when you will come again, and I don't know what to tell her.

Why don't you come to stay for as long as you like? Come to the Maryland district. You would be much at home here. You can stay with Elam and me. Sadie would be thrilled—I don't have to tell you that.

I know you are fond of many people in your own congregation, but the thought that they would even consider keeping you from us casts a new light on the question of your visits.

You must come. You must.

Love,

Fannie

Clara had no doubt of Sadie's abounding glee if she were to go to sleep with Clara in the house and wake to discover she was still there. And Clara's presence might cheer Fannie—or at least keep the household running until Fannie could cheer herself. Clara prayed every night for the news that her cousin was with child.

But Sadie was Sadie. She wasn't Hannah or Mari or Josiah. Or Hiram. Or even Rhoda as she had been until recently. If Clara went to Maryland for an indefinite stay—especially if she visited the church there—her own family would be required to shun her. The silent division running through the household would widen into permanence.

Clara couldn't bear the thought.

Neither could she imagine not seeing Fannie and Sadie and Martha and all the Hostetlers.

She pushed her fingertips into her closed eyelids. How was it that the Yoders saw a clear straight line between right and wrong, and Clara saw only the wiggle of uncertainty?

Clara tucked the letter back into its envelope and slid it under the winter nightgown lying in a drawer. The meetinghouse was waiting to be tidied and swept. Bishop Yoder had already announced that the next service of the congregation would be at Flag Run. Clara loaded a bucket with rags, filled two large jugs with well water, chose a broom, and arranged everything in the small open cart before hitching a horse.

When Clara drove past the adjoining Schrock farm, she waved at Mattie Schrock, who strolled along the road with a small basket of apples braced against one hip.

Clara slowed the horse. "Good afternoon. I hope everything is well with the Schrock household."

"We are well." Hesitation wafted through Mattie's face. "May I have a word with you?"

"Of course."

"Our breakfast conversation this morning was unusual." Mattie steadied herself against the side of the cart.

"Oh?" Clara's mouth dried out in an instant.

"Priscilla asked when she was going to get to hear another Bible story from you."

Clara tightened her grip on the reins. So it had begun.

"Of course her *daed* and I did not know what she was talking about. Imagine our surprise when she explained."

Clara steeled herself to withstand Mattie's gaze. "The stories are in the Bible. I'm sure she has heard them before and will again."

"Yes, I suppose that's true. You know that we are not overly strict in our interpretation of the church's teachings about these matters."

While the words might have carried encouragement if they appeared on paper, the tone with which Mattie delivered them made Clara's breathing grow shallow.

"It is not so much that we disapprove of children hearing Bible stories," Mattie said. "Rather, it is that such instruction is the role of parents—or at least should have the approval of parents."

"I meant no disrespect. I am sure you teach your children well."

"Others might protest more than Priscilla's father and I do." Mattie shifted the fruit basket to the other hip. "I'm sure your own father would be happy to see you married and settled with children. Then you could use your gift under submission to your husband, as the Bible teaches."

Clara swallowed, coughing to cover the gag in her throat. "Thank you for telling me how you feel. You will have no reason for further concern."

"I was sure you would understand."

Clara raised the reins, and the horse trotted forward. She blinked back stinging, indignant tears for the next four miles before letting herself into the meetinghouse. With the door propped open to capture whatever breeze might stir the sweltering afternoon, Clara swept the floor before launching into a furious scrub of the windowsills and benches. The water in the bucket grayed rapidly. It was impossible to keep summer dust out of the structure. Clara hefted the bucket outside to dump it in the clearing. Above the splash of water, horse hooves clattered. She looked up to see Yonnie drive past in his own open buggy, not the milk wagon. He slowed slightly, his eyes meeting hers, before his rig disappeared behind a grove of trees. Clara rotated, expecting to see him come out the opposite edge of the cluster. When he didn't emerge, she stilled her hands and breath to listen, certain Yonnie had seen her. If he were passing on the road, he should have appeared by now. Clara glanced at the open meetinghouse door and at her own cart, pondering where her steps should take her.

The rattle in the bushes sent her scurrying toward her horse. She ran straight into the clasp of a man's hands.

"What's going on?" Andrew gripped Clara's trembling shoulders, preventing her from turning away from him.

"Nothing," she said.

Something had spooked her. "Did I frighten you?"

She turned her head and looked through the trees. "I wasn't expecting you."

"I know. But we haven't spoken in a long time. I remembered you would be cleaning today and hoped I could catch you."

She stepped away from him. "I'm glad you're here."

"What happened, Clara?" Andrew followed her line of sight to the road.

She exhaled. "Yonnie just went by. I saw him approaching, but he never came out on the other side of the trees."

Andrew paced toward the road, peering through the dense foliage. "Maybe you just couldn't see him."

"The noise stopped," Clara said. "I should have heard him coming past."

He looked at her white face. "He won't hurt you."

She said nothing, not convinced.

Realization struck. "The bishop," Andrew said.

"What about the bishop?" Clara said.

"If Yonnie turned off to go south to the bishop's house, you wouldn't have seen or heard him go past."

Clara groaned.

"I'm not worried," Andrew said.

"Maybe you should be."

"Each day has enough worries of its own," Andrew said.

"What will he say?"

Andrew shrugged. "The Model T, your visit to Fannie, my temper. Who knows?"

"He could hurt you."

Andrew shook his head. "I could tell my side of things, and Yonnie would not look innocent, either."

"No!" Clara said. "That would just stir up trouble for everyone."

"It won't matter. Despite what Yonnie thinks, Bishop Yoder is not as powerful as he once was. Someone will step forward to say the congregation must vote."

"But who? Who would stand up to the bishop?"

Andrew was unsure. "He's getting old to be an active bishop."

"Sixty-nine is not ancient."

"He's been leading a long time. We're due for a change."

"You can't know that."

Andrew looked again through the silent trees. "Mose Beachy will be our greatest hope."

❧❦❧

This was not the first time Yonnie visited the bishop's house. Even though the congregation worshipped in meetinghouses rather than homes, every household in the district found ample reason to extend hospitality to other families. And Yonnie was a Yoder, just like the bishop. Once a year, everyone descended from the Yoders who first came to Somerset County a hundred years ago gathered for an afternoon frolic. Yonnie knew the farm from a lifetime of reunions.

This was the first time Yonnie had come with a purpose as serious as the one on his mind now. Three days of patient waiting for the appointed time had not deterred him. In fact, the time had nailed in his determination. Today Bishop Yoder would know exactly what Andrew Raber was up to. And Dale. And Clara.

Maybe not Clara. And maybe not Dale, at least not until Yonnie found other work.

But nothing held him back from telling the bishop that Andrew had an automobile.

He arranged his stance on the Yoder front step and knocked firmly.

Caroline Yoder answered the door with a dish towel hanging from one shoulder. "Hello, Yonnie. What brings you out here?"

"On Sunday I made an appointment with the bishop for today," Yonnie said.

"Oh, I'm sorry you've come all this way for nothing," Caroline said. "My husband was called away a few minutes ago. He's not anywhere on the farm."

"But I made an appointment."

She shrugged. "Appointment or not, he's still gone. Emergencies happen."

"When will he return?"

"I don't have the mind of God, Yonnie."

"Perhaps I should wait."

She shook her head. "I have a feeling it would be a long wait. I'm sure you have other things to do. The bishop will be happy to speak to you. Please come by again another time."

Back in his buggy, Yonnie considered his options. He was finished for the day at the dairy. Dale had sent Reuben on the afternoon route, which happened more and more often. Dale seemed to prefer keeping Yonnie where he could see him.

Yonnie picked up the reins. Perhaps God had given him this unscheduled afternoon for a purpose. Perhaps this would be the day his inquiries about other employment would bring a favorable answer.

If they did not, Yonnie would double the time he spent praying for discernment and trust. If he gave Dale his notice, surely God would provide.

CHAPTER 24

Clara wondered if anyone would notice if she did not attend worship. It would be just once. From time to time, everyone had a reason to be absent—illness in the house, a cow birthing on a Sunday morning, a journey to visit relatives in another district. Clara had none of those reasons, though. She could hardly tell Rhoda and Hiram that she was staying home because she could not bear the thought of another sermon by the Yoder ministers.

She hadn't seen Fannie and Sadie in over a month, and she hadn't visited Martha in almost two months. By now everyone in the Maryland church must know her aunt was with child.

And Clara stayed home, on the farm, waiting for whatever was going to happen.

No more, she thought. She only needed to plan more carefully—walk the miles to Fannie's farm early in the day, before the heat bore down, or arrange with her father to have a horse and cart. He would not turn her down if she asked ahead of time.

A congregational meeting was scheduled to follow the worship service. Clara was of a mixed mind whether she wanted to be present.

But Andrew. If she excused herself from church on a pretense, she wouldn't see Andrew. Clara braced herself, already planning to mentally work on a story for Sadie during the sermons, and rode with her family to church.

Noah Yoder preached, and Clara spent the time visualizing the words on the pages of the family Bible about Jesus healing Jairus's daughter and then trying out phrases and cadence in the retelling of it.

When Mose Beachy stood to give the second sermon, though, Clara's wordplay tumbled out of her mind. For weeks she had prayed it would be God's will for Mose to preach.

The text God laid on his heart, Mose said, was Romans 12:18. "If it be possible, as much as lieth in you, live peaceably with all men."

Mose recited the verse twice, looking with deliberation around the congregation.

"This verse falls naturally into three parts, which we must fully consider with our hearts and minds," Mose said. "First, 'if it be possible.' Second, 'as much as lieth in you.' And third, 'live peaceably with all men.'"

Clara gave her rapt attention. Mose preached not only with his words, but also his demeanor. When he gazed at the congregation, he had none of the sternness of the Yoders. He did not brace his stance to exude authority but rather leaned over his Bible as if to bind his heart to those of his listeners. Clara wished she could write down everything he said.

Fifty minutes later, he concluded. "I ask you to consider three questions. If you answer them well, you will know you have this portion of God's Word in your heart. Is it possible for you to live in such a way to bring peace? In what ways does peace depend on you? And finally, who is the *all* with whom God wants you to live in peace?"

Andrew was right. If the lot to become bishop fell to Mose Beachy, things would change. Clara resolved to pray every day that this would be God's will.

Yonnie scowled, unsure what to make of Mose Beachy's sermon.

Who could disagree with a sermon about peace? But surely there was much room for misinterpretation. The bishop wanted unity of mind, and this would bring peace to the congregation. Mose spoke of a different peace. He made no mention of discipline or obedience to the church's teaching.

Yonnie stood for the brief break between the end of the worship service and the beginning of the congregational meeting. Women took children outside to let them run for a few minutes. Men clustered in conversation or rearranged furniture for the meeting. Yonnie stood still as Andrew approached, forming in his mind what he might say if

Andrew asked forgiveness for his actions on the day he came to the dairy and embarrassed Yonnie. Familiar proverbs would serve well. *Let your life story be for God's glory.* Or, *A heart at peace gives life to the body.*

But Andrew did not stop.

He did not even catch Yonnie's eye.

Instead, he walked past as if he were shunning Yonnie and joined John Stutzman and several other men only a few feet away.

A shaft of heat burned up through Yonnie's torso and lodged in his throat. Andrew's behavior only proved the necessity of the decision Yonnie had made. Regret billowed. He should never have let another ten days pass before trying again to see the bishop privately.

Mose called the congregational meeting to order. Beside him at the front of the meetinghouse sat Joseph Yoder.

"We are meeting today," Mose said, "at the request of some of our members to consider a clarified understanding of recent teaching in our church. Specifically, members have raised questions about the *meidung* that the bishop called for a few weeks ago."

Joseph Yoder cleared his throat and glanced at his father's stiff pose. "May I remind everyone that the *meidung* is not new. My father merely asks us to be obedient to the unanimous congregational vote taken many years ago."

Caleb Schrock stood up. "I believe our brother refers to the vote taken in 1895, when many of us were children or just beginning our own families. The congregation has seen many changes since then."

Does truth change? Yonnie thought. *Does the Bible's teaching change with the generation? No.*

Yonnie watched the bishop, waiting for him to speak. Slowly, Yonnie nodded in understanding. This was a time for the Yoder sons to show the strength of their own leadership. Bishop Yoder was training his sons for their calling.

Now John Stutzman stood. "Our brother Mose brought us the Word of God today. I believe God gave Mose words that we need to fully consider. What does it mean to live peaceably? Did not the church members who peacefully divided the Old Order from the Conservative Amish Mennonites live peaceably? There was no rancor in the separation of the two districts, and people were free to go where their consciences led them. The broken peace comes only with the insistence of *meidung*."

John sat down.

Noah Yoder stood. "We must not misunderstand the *meidung* as an instrument of punishment. It is an instrument of reconciliation."

That's right, Yonnie thought. He had heard this message from Bishop Yoder all his life.

The Yoders read from the Bible the command to separate from the heathen.

Mose had just finished preaching the Bible's command to live peaceably with all.

Yonnie was looking for the line that would connect these two commands. How was it possible to obey both?

As Bishop Yoder intoned a solemn closing prayer, Andrew was uncertain what the meeting had accomplished. Nothing that was said would lead anyone to a change of mind about the need for shunning friends and relatives who worshipped on the Maryland side of the border, and no one suggested a new formal congregational vote on the question. Neither those who spoke nor those who kept silent surprised Andrew.

Nothing had changed.

People milled between the benches, exchanging news and opinions. Andrew doubted anyone would forgo the shared meal. Amish farms were spread widely enough that many families did not see each other except on church Sundays or organized frolics. The fellowship was as essential as the worship or a congregational meeting.

Andrew drifted toward John Stutzman, who was restoring order to the furniture at the front of the meetinghouse.

"Thank you for speaking up," Andrew said. "Many in the congregation agree with you."

"More should speak up," John said. "The ministers should know what is on our minds."

"They know." Andrew's fingers thrummed the high back of a chair. "They've known for years." The fall communion was coming. No one would want to defy the bishop and imperil communion for everyone.

"Mose gave a good sermon."

Andrew nodded. "It's puzzling why he does not have more opportunity to preach. With four ministers, he should be preaching one sermon out of four."

"The lot only means that each Sunday Mose has a one in four chance he will be called on. What happens one week has nothing to do with the next."

It seemed to Andrew that over time the odds should even out more than they did. "Folks might find greater appreciation for the sermons if Mose preached more often."

"*Gottes wille.*" John gestured to shift Andrew's attention. "Here comes someone you might like to hear from."

"Good morning, Clara." Andrew hoped his smile was sincere without revealing too much.

"Good morning," Clara said. "I hope you are both well."

The two men nodded. Andrew considered Clara's features and coloring. The same strain that distracted her in this place the week before—when he helped clean up her bucket, rags, and broom—gripped her now. He knew her well enough to know when the smile on her face was an intentional arrangement of muscles and not a spontaneous response to what her eyes saw.

Clara glanced around. "I haven't seen any of the Brennermans today."

"I heard there was illness in the house," John said.

"Not little Naomi, I hope."

"Her mother, I believe," John said. "She's been poorly for several days."

"She must be very ill for the whole family to stay home," Clara said.

"Perhaps several of them are afflicted now," John said.

John made reasonable statements. He could not know that Clara would be particularly concerned for Naomi.

Fannie washed supper dishes while Elam sat at the kitchen table with paper and pencil in front of him. This was his Sunday evening ritual. After observing the Sabbath all day, whether or not it was a church Sunday, after the evening meal his mind invariably turned to the week ahead—what attention the crops needed, signs of ill health in the animals, the horseshoes requiring replacing, the repair of a buggy wheel.

Fannie did not mind. Elam was working hard to care for the family, as small as it was, and Fannie had her own thoughts to manage.

"I miss Clara," she murmured.

"Mmm?" Elam did not look up.

"Clara is the sister I never had," Fannie said. In the old days she would have told Elam her every thought. Lately she said little to him other than matters of the household. But Clara was important. She sat at the table across from her husband, and he finally lifted his eyes to her.

"Has she written?" Elam said.

Fannie waved a hand. "A silly letter about how the summer is passing so fast and she hopes Sadie is well."

"What is silly about that?"

"It's not the kind of letter Clara writes. Something's wrong."

"So write to her."

"I have. I invited her to come here and stay."

"You know she's always welcome."

Elam had not a bone of jealousy about his wife's affection for her cousin, something that always had endeared him to Fannie.

"We must persuade her," Fannie said. "It's not like her to be silent." She gave no voice to the abandonment she felt. Her disconnection from her own family was her doing, but she could think of nothing she had done to cut herself off from Clara.

"So write to her again." Elam shifted papers in front of him.

"She should think about joining the Marylanders. Surely Andrew would agree. His own family is in Lancaster County. He's on his own with that farm, and he's not a strict man. He would do anything to make Clara happy."

At this point, Elam put down his pencil and gave full attention to the conversation. "Just what do you know about Andrew Raber and Clara?"

"Clara speaks of him from time to time." Clara had confided Andrew's multiple proposals, but Fannie saw no reason to reveal details. She was thinking aloud when she spoke of Andrew, falling into the old habit of telling Elam everything as if they shared one mind. Fannie surprised herself. In the restraint of the last few months, the lack of a baby hung in the middle of every conversation between them, and it had become easier not to talk.

Elam raised his eyebrows.

"Never mind Andrew," Fannie said. "Clara should make her own decision about which church God wants her to be in. If she comes to visit, we will give her every reason to visit our congregation."

Elam half smiled. "Just give Sadie permission to nag."

Fannie surprised herself again and laughed softly as she returned to the dishes.

CHAPTER 25

Clara cooked on Monday—not for her family but for the Brenner-mans. When Rhoda took the children with her into Springs for some shopping, Clara took over the kitchen. By the time Rhoda returned, Clara had a pot of chicken soup, a casserole laden with garden vegetables—but no celery—and bread with sliced cheese. If one dish did not appeal, surely another would. It would all bring nourishment, even if only a bite or two at a time. Clara wrapped everything in towels to hold in the warmth and arranged the items carefully in a milk crate to put in the cart. Rhoda had her arms full of a fussy, overtired three-year-old and offered no objection to Clara's departure with the horse and cart.

Having a purpose invigorated Clara. After a summer of aimless wandering and finding her friends busy with their own young families, she relished the thought of easing Mrs. Brennerman's day. She sat up straight on the cart's bench and insisted the horse oblige with a brisk pace for the entire six miles.

The Brennerman yard was quiet, and Clara's alarm heightened. The family had seven children. Someone ought to be outside playing or weeding the vegetable garden or beating rugs. Two chickens clucked and fluttered from their positions on the front steps as Clara carried her crate to the door and knocked.

Clara hoped the only reason the windows were closed and shuttered was a defense against August heat pressing in. Finally she heard shuffling from within, and the front door opened. Mrs. Brennerman, beleaguered and pale, stood before her.

"We have sickness," Mrs. Brennerman said. "You ought not to come in."

"I only came to help." Clara gestured to the crate. "I brought some food."

"Thank you, but no."

A series of flabbergasted sounds passed Clara's throat, but none of them were words. She cocked her head.

"Naomi told me all about your stories," Mrs. Brennerman said.

"I see." The crate suddenly weighed heavy in Clara's arms. She set it on the porch. "How many of you are feeling poorly? I thought it might be helpful if you didn't have to fix food."

"Are you going to confess your sin to the congregation?"

For a woman with a houseful of illness, Mrs. Brennerman was stubborn. Clara chose her words with deliberation.

"How can stories from the Bible be sin?" she said.

"If that's how you feel, then you won't mind if the bishop knows."

Clara's spine tingled as it straightened. First Mrs. Schrock—whose rebuke at least had been gentle—and now Mrs. Brennerman. Lillian's mother would be next, and the trail from there to Rhoda would be short. Clara could not take back the stories she had told, nor did she want to. This was the moment in which the realization took full form. No, she would not mind if Bishop Yoder heard about the stories. Living in fear was no way to receive a gift from God's hand.

"Do what your conscience tells you is right," Clara said, "but my food will bring only good to your children. I hope it will offer you a moment of needed rest."

She turned and strode toward her cart without looking back.

The decision to see the bishop on Tuesday afternoon was an impulse. Andrew allowed that it might even be the prodding of the Holy Ghost. He paused only briefly at the intersection before taking the turn toward the Yoder farm. If the Bishop Yoder was not there, Andrew would only have lost an hour of his afternoon. *Gottes wille.* He murmured a prayer for a kind and merciful conversation.

The bishop opened the door himself. "Scrappy Andy."

The nickname had fallen away once Andrew's parents moved to Lancaster County and he no longer shared his father's full name in the same congregation. The bishop's use of it unsettled Andrew.

"I wonder if you have time to talk," Andrew said.

"I will heat up the *kaffi*."

"Please don't go to any trouble."

Bishop Yoder had already turned to lead the way through the house to the kitchen at the back. He lit the stove. Andrew wondered if the coffee had been in the pot since breakfast.

"What has God put on your heart to speak to me about?" Bishop Yoder pulled a chair from the table for Andrew to sit in.

He was breathing heavily, it seemed to Andrew.

"If you are unwell," he said, "I can come to talk another time."

"I'm not as young as I used to be," Bishop Yoder said, "but it's nothing a cup of *kaffi* won't help mend."

The coffee turned out to be lukewarm and bitter, which did not seem to bother the bishop. Andrew took a few polite sips before abandoning the effort.

"What brings you here?" The bishop raised an eyebrow.

"The congregational meeting has been on my mind."

"The lessons are not buried so deeply. They will find them."

"Perhaps," Andrew said, "a middle way?"

"The pages of the Bible are one."

Andrew inspected the bishop's reddening face. "Help me understand your meaning."

"We look into a glass darkly. Thus saith the Lord." Bishop Yoder stared into his cup before abruptly lifting it to swallow its contents in one gulp.

"The congregation," Andrew said.

"The ninety-nine and the one. The word of the Lord is irrefutable."

Andrew had found little to agree with in the bishop's recent sermons, but at least their meaning had been clear. These riddles befuddled Andrew—if that is what they were.

The back door opened. Mrs. Yoder entered with a basket of vegetables over her arm, black earth still clinging in clumps to blotches of green and orange.

"Am I interrupting?" she said.

"Scrappy Andy had a question, which I have just finished answering," her husband said.

Andrew stood, puzzling how he might ask Mrs. Yoder if her husband had fallen ill in the last two days. Though the bishop had been quiet during Sunday's service and the meeting that followed, no one had remarked that he seemed unwell.

"You ought to stick to your appointments." Mrs. Yoder touched her husband's shoulder before setting the basket on the counter and glancing at Andrew. "The bishop has always preferred to give careful thought to how to respond to a spiritual matter."

Illumination washed over Andrew. She was protecting her husband.

"The lessons are not buried so deeply. They will find them."

"The pages of the Bible are one."

"We look into a glass darkly. Thus saith the Lord."

"The ninety-nine and the one. The word of the Lord is irrefutable."

Caroline Yoder, Andrew realized, was not surprised that her husband might not make sense.

"Is it today?" Sadie asked.

"Is what today?" Fannie leaned forward in the glider and reached for a foot to rub. Lately her feet were not happy in shoes and not happy barefoot.

"The quilts. The ones that aren't finished yet."

"The quilting bee?"

"Yes. That's what I mean. This is Wednesday, isn't it?"

"I'm afraid we missed it," Fannie said.

"The whole thing? It's supposed to last all day, isn't it?"

Sometimes Fannie wished that Sadie did not listen quite so carefully to the adult conversations around her. She wasn't sure where Sadie gathered her information, but she'd absorbed it correctly. This was indeed Wednesday, and indeed quilting bees lasted most of the day.

"It's too late to go now," Fannie said.

"Can't we still go?"

Fannie sucked in a breath in the hope that the exhale would bring patience.

"It just didn't work out for us this time," she said. "There will be another bee."

"And we'll go?" Sadie came close and widened her eyes to stare into her mother's.

"We'll see." Fannie kissed Sadie's forehead. "Do you think you could go pick some beans for supper all by yourself?"

Sadie dashed off for a basket as Fannie knew she would. Her daughter thrived on opportunities to prove her independence.

Her mother was going to the quilting bee. Plain and simple, that was the reason Fannie could not muster enthusiasm for the event.

Fannie missed Martha—at least, the balance between them as Fannie waited for a second child. She missed confiding monthly disappointment to her mother. She missed knowing that Martha stood with her in prayer for a child. She missed being in and out of each other's homes several times each week.

Martha's pregnancy changed everything. Fannie could not look at her mother without resentment. And no matter how guilty she might feel about the attitude, she couldn't change it. Every day that passed, she cared less about it.

She cared less about everything.

Fannie leaned back in the glider and pushed it into motion. She was upright, not napping in the middle of the day. In a few minutes she would engage in a needed task. But the effort or normalcy exhausted her.

The screen door thwacked. The footsteps crossing the kitchen were Elam's. He came through to the front room.

"I'll get your lunch," Fannie said, though her muscles did not respond to the thought with movement.

"I expected I would be on my own," he said. "Isn't this the quilting bee day?"

"A bee is a long day," Fannie said. "If anyone tries to leave early, the others make a fuss. It's better to stay home if you don't feel well."

Elam did not speak. Fannie met his gaze for as long as she could bear it. Now she insisted that her feet find their place and support her weight. When she walked past him, he reached to catch her hand but she pulled it from him.

At the sound of the *English* motor roaring toward him from behind, Yonnie took his horse and open buggy as close to the edge of the road as he could without risking the ditch. Traffic on the farm roads was less threatening in the days before Henry Ford decided that every household in the country should have an automobile. Fewer and fewer of the English used horses to move around the county, and along with their former habit they had dispensed with a sense of the speed at which horse and buggies traversed safely.

Yonnie glanced over his shoulder at the approaching car, a green Model T with the roof down stirring up a cloud of dust. With an irritated groan, Yonnie pulled the horse into the middle of the road and slowed almost to a stop. If Andrew insisted on driving an *English* machine, then let him be the one to drive along the ditch.

Andrew honked his horn. Yonnie ignored it, refusing to turn his head again. The automobile crept along behind the buggy.

"Yonnie, move over!" Andrew shouted.

Yonnie hunched his shoulders but gave no command to the horse, instead maintaining his position in the center of the road at a near crawl for more than a mile. Andrew should not take lessons in impatience from the *English*.

At the widening of an intersection, Andrew accelerated past the buggy. What Yonnie had not expected was that Andrew would swing his car around to block the road, forcing Yonnie to stop. Andrew got out of the car and leaned against it.

"You can't block the road," Yonnie said.

"You did," Andrew shot back over the idling engine.

Yonnie rearranged the reins in his hands. "You could use your knowledge of machinery in other ways to serve the community. You don't have to be like the *English*."

"I have not abandoned the community," Andrew said. "It is you who presumes to know what is in my heart on the matter."

"You have no family to keep you here. What is to stop you from one day driving away from the church?"

"Do you think an automobile has more power over my actions than my own conscience?"

"You put yourself at risk."

"Do I? Or do you push me toward that edge by thinking you know what a man-made machine means to me?"

"You cannot serve both God and mammon, Andrew."

Andrew glared at Yonnie. The horse nickered. Andrew got back behind the wheel and sped off, leave Yonnie to cough in the dust.

Clara pushed the wheelbarrow through the barn, pausing at each stall to throw in a layer of fresh straw and assess how soon mucking would be required. Rhoda thought of the barn as her husband's purview and rarely entered. Helping in the barn now, with Josiah wrangling a wide broom behind her, transported Clara's mind back to the days when she was the child trailing Hiram. Those years held their grief, but the framework of life had been simple and predictable. The line between Hiram and Clara had been straight and clear.

When had life in a family become so complicated?

Clara threw her brother a smile, and his grin soothed her.

"Are you going to help me muck when it's time?" Josiah said.

"Of course." Cleaning animal stalls was Clara's least favorite chore, but if it meant she could spend time with Josiah without wondering when Rhoda would snatch him away, Clara would do it gladly.

She pushed the wheelbarrow out into the bright daylight. In a couple of weeks, summer's furnace would cease its blasts. The harvest would swallow up every free moment for farmers and their families. Hiram had already struck his deals for selling the portion of the Kuhn crop that he did not need for feeding his family and animals through the winter.

A buggy turned off the main road and progressed down the lane toward the house. Clara released the wheelbarrow handles and pulled a sleeve across her forehead before brushing off her apron.

"*Gut mariye*, Mrs. Brennerman," Clara said, surprised that the visitor who emerged was the woman who rejected her offering a week ago.

"I've brought Rhoda's pots back," Mrs. Brennerman said.

"I trust everyone is well."

"Well enough. Is Rhoda home?"

"Yes," Clara said. "Please come to the house."

Clara took the dishes from Mrs. Brennerman, hoping that that food had nourished the family after all and had not been thrown straight to the pigs. She led the way across the yard, up the front steps, and into the house.

Inside, Rhoda offered coffee to Mrs. Brennerman—not to Clara—and the two of them withdrew to the kitchen. Clara took quiet steps across the wood floor and stopped outside the kitchen, to one side of the open door. This could be the moment Rhoda learned of the stories. Clara wanted to hear Mrs. Brennerman's account for herself.

"Have you heard about the bishop?" Mrs. Brennerman said to Rhoda. "He's fallen ill—quite ill, I believe."

"We must remember to pray for him," Rhoda said.

"His wife has him in seclusion. She believes he needs complete rest. No one is to try to speak to him."

"We do have three other ministers," Rhoda said. Clara heard the cups in her hand clink.

"There are some who would take advantage of Bishop Yoder's illness."

"He will recover."

"He is quite ill," Mrs. Brennerman repeated.

Clara stepped away. Of course she would pray for the bishop's recovery to full strength.

But what if he did not recover?

Andrew had expected only to buy a box of nails while he was in town, not to hear that Bishop Yoder was too ill to see anyone. The news did not surprise him. He let pass the speculation that the illness was likely the same one that had infected other households. In a few days the bishop's appetite would return. He would be back to preaching by Sunday.

Andrew was certain that was not true.

He didn't take his buggy home to his own farm. Instead, he unhitched his horse behind the old Johnson barn with the confidence that the animal would not wander far. John Stutzman was the man Andrew wanted to talk to, and he lived on the other side of the district.

The Model T was running well these days, and Andrew had practiced enough to believe he was not a menace on the road. This would be a useful demonstration of the time the automobile would save. Andrew pushed open the barn door, cranked the engine to life, and drove onto the main road.

Andrew was relieved to find John in one of his fields with none of his sons in sight. He had been prepared to park the Model T out of sight and walk the last half mile to avoid the gawking eyes of John's family. Instead, he had only to cross the road to speak privately.

"I saw for myself," Andrew said after reporting the bishop's illness. "I was there Tuesday. He was clearly unwell. Chicken soup will not heal his ailment."

John glanced across the road at the automobile. "Thank you for coming all this way to tell me."

"Even if he recovers physical strength," Andrew said, "the question is not far off whether he is fit to continue as bishop."

They ambled up the space between rows of grain ready for harvest.

"Until he steps aside, he is the bishop," John said. "We should make sure his crop gets in."

"I'm happy to help," Andrew said. All the farmers would help each other with the harvest, moving from one farm to another during the critical weeks. "It's the church I'm worried about."

"Why should you worry?" John stopped walking and faced Andrew.

"*Worry* is the wrong word." The Bible said, "Worry not," and for the most part Andrew enjoyed the freedom that came with the command. "Surely, though, you can see there will be some commotion in the congregation if the bishop does step aside."

John shook his head. "God's will. We can do nothing to change that, nor should we try."

"But perhaps we can find a way to help each other live in peace, no matter what happens."

"Each of us must follow our own conscience."

Andrew examined his friend's face. While John did not look away, his eyes carried a cloud Andrew was unaccustomed to seeing.

John gestured to the Model T at the side of the field. "So it's running well?"

His words softly closed the door on conversation about the bishop.

✦

Hours later, Andrew stood on the side of a road admiring the sky. Whether black against starlit brilliance or incomprehensible behind hanging low clouds, Andrew loved the night sky.

So much transcendent possibility. So much wonder beyond farm fields and milking schedules. So much assurance beyond the mysterious lots of God's will.

Andrew wished he could simply knock on the Kuhn door and say he had come to call on Clara, the way the *English* courted. Instead he leaned against his buggy wondering if she would decide to take an evening stroll and come this way. If they should meet on any night, this was that night.

He stared into the deep, wondering what was beyond the beyond.

Andrew almost did not hear her arrive, turning at the crunch of a step to find her near and breathless.

"You've heard," he said.

Clara nodded. "I can't get it off my mind."

"I saw him last week," Andrew said. "He spoke gibberish as if it were chapter and verse from the Bible."

"Everyone will pray for him." Clara fiddled with the cuffs of her long sleeves.

"We should."

"I'm afraid selfishness will be like an illness in my prayers."

"Selfishness?"

She raised her eyes to his. "At least two mothers know about my Bible stories with the girls. As long as the bishop is ill, no one can tell him."

"Someone might tell one of the other ministers."

Clara shook her head. "Everyone knows Noah and Joseph Yoder don't do anything without first talking to their father."

"And they know Mose Beachy does not have much sympathy for tattletales." Andrew slipped a palm under Clara's fingers. "So you're safe."

"And safe is selfish. It's hard to pray for the bishop to get well."

"Don't be ashamed, Clara. And don't fear the gift God put in your heart."

She sighed. "What about your car? Don't you feel relief that at least for now, Yonnie can't draw attention to it?"

Andrew patted the side of the buggy. "I still use this most of the time. But I am not afraid."

"And if the ministers tell you that you must get rid of the automobile, what will you do?"

"One day at a time." Andrew grazed her face with one hand, setting his fingers under her jaw. "I do not worry what will happen to me, and if you were my wife, I would not have to worry what will happen to you, either."

She turned her head to his palm and laid her cheek in his hand. "Andrew, you know how much I care for you."

"You don't tell me what's bothering you at home," Andrew said, "but I know something is. I have a farm. We could make our own home together, and I would do my best not to fill it with anything that bothers you."

Clara laughed softly. "Even you are not that perfect."

"Tell me you're thinking about it."

"Every day."

"Whatever frightens you, we'll face it together." Andrew leaned in to kiss Clara, tasting the tart lemon pie she must have eaten after supper.

"Ruth Kaufman asked me to be an attendant at her wedding," Clara said after she broke the kiss with reluctance that pleased Andrew.

He laughed. "She is marrying Peter Troyer, *ya*?"

"*Ya.*"

"He asked me to be in the wedding party."

Clara laughed softly. "If they knew we were—"

"I know," Andrew said. "They are not supposed to ask two people who are thinking of marrying."

"Should we tell them?"

He raised an eyebrow. "Have you decided?"

She ducked her head away from his gaze.

As far as Sadie knew, they were headed to her *grossmuder*'s house. Fannie was not anxious to arrive. She had not actually agreed to a midmorning visit to her mother's, only to go for an exploring walk with her daughter. It was Sadie who assumed a destination. Fannie examined the sun's position, judging how long they had before it would rise to a height that ushered in a wilting heat. In a few more minutes, she would speak the words that would make her daughter pout and they would start the circle taking them to their own home, rather than to Martha's.

For now, Fannie inhaled deeply the fragrance of the end of summer. Late-blooming lilacs, sweet apple trees, pungent cows—the humid air swirled it all together and trailed the result in unexpected wafts. Fannie ached to savor these bits of life as she had every other summer. She yearned for them to call her back from the precarious edge of her days.

The milk wagon rattled toward them in a medley of clanging milk cans, horse hooves, and creaking wheels. Fannie reached for Sadie's hand and at the same time eyed the spot where they would turn away from her mother's house.

Sadie waved, and from the bench of his wagon Dale Borntrager returned the morning greeting and slowed the rig.

"I suppose you've heard about Bishop Yoder," Dale said.

"No," Fannie said. "What news?"

"Very ill. Some say he won't be well enough to lead again."

Fannie's pulse fluttered. "Will you have a new bishop, then?"

Dale chuckled. "We might at least have some more peaceful preaching. The lot to preach will have to fall to Mose Beachy more often."

Fannie knew she ought to say she would pray for the bishop, but she prayed little these days. Why should she pray when God was stubbornly silent?

Sadie pulled against Fannie's grip and spoke with patient politeness. "It's nice to see you, Mr. Borntrager, but my *grossmuder* is waiting."

"I'm headed there now," he said. "Why don't I give you a ride?"

"*Danki!*"

"No, thank you," Fannie tightened her hold on Sadie.

Fannie ignored Sadie's protests as the milk wagon pulled away. The bishop might get well, and everything would be as it had been for decades. Even if he stepped aside, one of his sons would likely become bishop. And if the lot fell to Mose Beachy, the Pennsylvania congregation would be unsettled. Clara had so much to gain if she simply came to the Maryland congregation, with or without Andrew. Fannie would write as many letters as it took to persuade her.

"Come on, Sadie. We have to get home."

"What about *Grossmuder*?"

"Another day."

"But I miss her!"

So do I. "We're going home, Sadie. Don't argue with me."

CHAPTER 27

Andrew followed John Stutzman, who followed Mose Beachy through Mose's field of alfalfa mown and standing in windrows.

"Two more days of drying," Mose said. "Then we'll thresh."

"With three teams, the work goes well," Andrew said. Mose tried to cut hay three times a year. Andrew, John, and Mose had developed an efficient rhythm for cutting and later threshing.

"My older boys can handle the grapple fork and getting the hay into the loft," Mose said. "One of the girls can lead the horse when it's time to pull."

They paced to the end of the field, across a path, and toward the Beachy barn.

"I need to put a new chain on the grapple fork," Mose said, "but I'll have that ready by the time you come back."

"Saturday morning, then," John said.

"*Danki.*" Mose paused in the middle of the barnyard and scratched under his beard. "I imagine you both would like to know how the bishop is."

Andrew nodded but said nothing. Three days had passed with no further news about Bishop Yoder's illness.

"Noah and Joseph were here yesterday," Mose said. "They seem to think their father needs an extended rest."

"He should take all the time he needs to heal," John said. "And if I know Caroline, she'll see to it."

"She was a bishop's daughter before she was a bishop's wife," Mose said. "She knows the demands."

"And Lucy?" Andrew said. "Would Lucy know the demands if the lot fell to you to be the next bishop?"

"It's too soon to say the lot will fall to anyone," Mose said.

"Eventually we will have a new bishop," Andrew said. "Do you not ever think about the question?"

"If I am called upon, I will serve as best as I am able, by God's grace. If God does not choose me, I will continue as a minister. In the meantime, I gain nothing from wondering what might be. God will make clear His will."

Andrew found sincere acceptance in his friend's face.

Lucy Beachy appeared on the porch and called out her husband's name.

"I must go," Mose said. "I promised to fix the stair railing today before one of the children gets hurt. Thank you again for your help with the hay."

Andrew and John watched Mose walk toward the house and then moved toward their own buggies.

"Do you think it may be God's will to disturb His people?" Andrew said.

"With the new bishop?" John swung his gaze around to Andrew.

"Of course we all pray for Bishop Yoder's recovery," Andrew said. "But many in the congregation disagree with him. I find myself wondering how the church can thrive while he leads."

"Most likely one of his sons will follow," John said.

Andrew nodded. "Wouldn't you say that many find that thought disturbing?"

"And if the lot falls to Mose Beachy? Won't others be disturbed?"

"You see my point," Andrew said, stroking his horse's long brown nose. "No matter who is bishop, the church harbors unhappiness. If this is so, should we conclude that God wills for us to be unsettled?"

"God has His purposes. His ways are not our ways."

John was giving the right answers, cautious words with which no one could find fault.

"John," Andrew said, "we are true friends, are we not?"

John nodded. "For many years."

"Then please speak freely."

John scraped a boot through the dirt. "The *meidung* will not bring unity to the church. I will not shun, no matter what the rule."

Andrew took in a long breath through his nose, waiting for the rest.

"The Yoders refuse to regard the Maryland congregations as true Amish churches," John said. "They also refuse the truth that some in our midst are prepared to join the Marylanders if they continue to push the question of shunning families and neighbors."

"I see," Andrew said. "You are considering this."

"Have you not?" John met Andrew's gaze. "You are the one with an *English* automobile."

"It is only a matter of time before the church must consider the question of automobiles," Andrew said. "I do not presume to know what the answer will be."

"And if the congregation votes that we must not follow the *English* way in the matter, will you sell your car?"

Andrew worked his lips from side to side but did not answer.

Yonnie straightened his spine against Noah Yoder's barn so tightly that he felt the seams between the slats of wood. Next to him, the window was open.

"Have you been to see *Mamm*?" Noah asked his brother. "How is *Daed* today?"

"He sleeps all day," Joseph said.

"Has the doctor been in?"

"She won't have an *English* doctor. Mrs. Weaver came by with some herbs."

A fly buzzed around Yonnie's left ear. He waved a hand. The fly circled and swooped in again, this time settling on the window ledge. Yonnie stared at it while he listened.

"I pray he recovers soon," Noah said. "I am beginning to hear talk among the church families."

"He must recover," Joseph said. "If Mose Beachy becomes bishop now, the church will lose its way."

"The lot would more likely fall to you or me. As long as we stand together, God's truth will prevail."

The fly twitched and lifted, making a straight line toward Yonnie's face. He blinked and swatted. Unthinking, he moved his left foot to rebalance.

He had not seen the slop bucket earlier. Now it clattered against the side of the barn before spilling its swill across his boot.

"Who's out there?" Joseph's voice boomed through the open window.

Yonnie held his breath, hoping blame for the disturbance would fall to an unseen stray dog or a clumsy barn cat. He dragged the side of his boot through the dirt in an attempt to dislodge food scraps. When he looked up, Noah was coming around the corner of the barn.

"What are you doing here, Yonnie?"

Now Joseph's face popped through the window. "Didn't you find our milk in the spring?"

"*Ya,*" Yonnie said. "I found it."

The brothers waited.

"I'm sorry about the bucket," Yonnie said.

"Have you come to visit, then?" Noah raised his eyebrows.

Yonnie shifted his weight. "I wonder if you might be looking for a hired hand."

"I would think you'd be plenty busy," Joseph said. "Between your job at the dairy and working on your *daed*'s farm, you must wear yourself thin."

"My brothers are a big help on the farm now," Yonnie said, "and it may be time for me to find other work. I am not proud. I would do whatever you ask of me, on either of your farms—or your father's."

"I thought you wanted your own farm." Joseph leaned both arms across the window ledge.

"I do. I'm still saving for a down payment."

"What's brought this on?" Noah asked. "You've been with Dale Borntrager for a long time."

Yonnie looked from one brother to another. "I find myself unsettled there of late."

"It's a solid business," Joseph said. "Steady employment."

"In my spirit, I discern that working for someone else would keep me obedient."

"I see," Joseph said. "So you feel it is the will of the Lord to seek other employment?"

"I do. If I were to work for the bishop's sons, both ministers of good conscience, my own position would be more clear."

"Is there something you want to tell us about Dale?" Noah said. "Perhaps the Holy Ghost has convicted you to come forward."

Yonnie swallowed. The fly buzzed at the back of his neck. "I only seek to safeguard my submission to the church."

"You have chosen wisely," Noah said. "You can be certain of our calling to protect and pass on the faith of our fathers."

"Thank you for bringing Dale Borntrager to our attention," Joseph said. "We will be sure to pay him a call."

Yonnie toyed with regret. If the Yoder brothers confronted Dale, he hoped they would not mention his name—at least not unless they offered him work. Any of Dale's employees might have gone to the ministers, he realized. They all knew Dale continued to do business with people the bishop placed under the ban. Still, Dale's suspicions would settle on Yonnie soon enough.

"Might you have work for me?" Yonnie asked again.

"We'll need to consider the question." Noah glanced at his brother. "We still have time before the harvest. Why don't we speak again in a week or two."

A scowl settled on Yonnie's face. Everything could change in a week or two. The bishop might or might not recover. The congregation might or might not have a new bishop. The Yoders might or might not confront Dale, who might or might not decide Yonnie deserved no further warnings.

"Thank you for your time," Yonnie said. He banished the word *might* from his mind. Yes, anything could happen, but God's will was certain— and how could he regret God's will?

CHAPTER 28

I don't see them." Rhoda lifted Mari from the buggy and set her on the ground outside the Flag Run Meetinghouse.

"It's still early," Hiram said.

"I don't care if he is the bishop," Rhoda said, "his wife is not going to let him come to church if he's been ill all week."

Clara was the last to exit the buggy and dallied as her family walked ahead. She spied Wanda Eicher wrestling with her toddlers. With a child on her hip and another swelling her belly, Wanda might have stood there all morning pleading for the recalcitrant boy's cooperation. Clara strode over, lifted the stunned child, and set him on his feet.

"Thank you," Wanda said. "He insists on independent thinking every moment of the day now."

"He doesn't seem the worse for wear." Clara brushed off the boy's trousers and held his hand tightly. "I'll sit in the back with you, if you like."

"Everybody wants to know about the bishop," Wanda said. They started to walk. "It's not as if he's never been ill before."

"They say it's very bad this time."

"Whoever *they* are," Wanda said. "The illness gets more severe with every telling."

Clara nodded. What Wanda said was true. In the absence of facts about the bishop's illness, rumors had crisscrossed the district all week.

They settled in the rear of the meetinghouse, each of them holding a child in her lap. The men marched in, a hymn began, and the ministers withdrew to determine who would preach. After twelve stanzas, the hymn faded and prayerful silence descended while the congregation waited for one of the men to feel moved to begin another.

When Clara heard the tenor strains, she knew the voice immediately. Andrew.

"To be like Christ we love one another, through everything, here on this earth," he sang.

Clara was one of the first to join. "We love one another, not just with words but in deeds."

The hymn mounted gently with admonition. "If we have of this world's goods (no matter how much or how little) and see that our brother has a need, but do not share with him what we have freely received? How can we say that we would be ready to give our lives for him if necessary?"

Clara watched the door through which the ministers would return. If only there were a way for Mose Beachy to preach both sermons. The rhythms of the hymn rose and fell with its centuries-old tune and High German words. Clara, who knew the words by heart, chided herself to heed their message.

"The one who is not faithful in the smallest thing, and who still seeks his own good which his heart desires, how can he be trusted with a charge over heavenly things? Let us keep our eyes on love!"

Faithful in the smallest thing.

Clara's lips stilled as she paused to absorb the challenge. All of her life felt small.

Let us keep our eyes on love!

The next worship Sunday would be the day of preparation, the final worship service before the fall communion the next time the congregation gathered. The hymn's message was a fit one for the occasion, giving everyone something to meditate on in the coming weeks. Clara stroked the drowsy head of the child in her lap while she sang and prayed that the words would sink into her own heart.

When the ministers returned, the postures of Noah and Joseph Yoder announced that the lot had fallen to both of them to preach. Clara clung to the words she had just sung as disappointment seeped through her spirit.

Lord, let me hear Your truth. Clara took the first of many deep breaths that would see her through the service. Despite the inner peace Clara cultivated for the next two hours, the end of the sermons had the effect on the congregation that became more predictable on each Sunday the church gathered.

Relief.

Clara could think of no other word to describe the aggregate sensation as she heard the rolling wave of sighs.

"Well, that's that," Wanda said after the final hymn, "at least for another two weeks."

"The singing was nice," Clara said. *Let us keep our eyes on love! Eyes and words and hearts,* Clara thought.

The boy in her arms slept soundly, a condition that overtook him at the midpoint of the first sermon. Awake, his sister squirmed in Wanda's arms.

"Let me take him," Wanda said.

Clara shook her head. She rather liked the sensation of the child limp in surrender, his mouth opening and closing in shallow breaths. "I'll just sit with him a few more minutes," she said.

Wanda winced and put a hand on her belly. Her daughter took advantage of the moment to escape Wanda's lap.

Clara's heart thudded as she caught the little girl's hand to keep her from wandering off. "Are you all right, Wanda?"

Wanda's shoulders rose and fell three times with her breath before she replied. "That was rather a sharp pain."

"How close is your time?"

"Not close enough for this." Wanda's face tightened again.

Clara looked around. "I'll find your husband."

Wanda put a hand on Clara's arm. "No. You have no idea the fuss that would stir up."

"If you are unwell, he should stir up a fuss."

"It's easing up." Wanda leaned back on the bench. "I'm all right."

The little girl tugged against Clara's grasp. "I want my *daed.*"

Clara wondered if the child was capable of finding her father and bringing him back into the meetinghouse.

"We'll go together," Wanda said. She braced herself to stand up.

"Wanda—"

"I'm all right."

"Tell somebody."

"It's nothing, Clara." Wanda steadied herself on her feet. "Odd things happen when a woman is with child. Someday you'll understand. Not every twinge means something is wrong."

That was more than a twinge, Clara thought. It *might* mean something was wrong.

Clara offered no further argument aloud, though she noticed Wanda was not walking as easily as she had a few hours ago.

The benches gradually emptied and conversations clustered and spattered the meetinghouse.

"We need another vote," a woman whispered behind Clara, who did not try to turn and see the speaker lest the boy wake. Clara had enough experience with small children to respect the final vestiges of a nap.

"If we change the vote, they will have to stop preaching these sermons."

"Undoing a unanimous vote that has stood for more than twenty years will not be easy." The second voice carried caution.

"My husband and I have given up talking about it, but I think it's time we began again. Surely some of the older men can do something."

The women drifted away with their hushed conversation. Clara caught Andrew's eye as he moved past in conversation with John Stutzman. Later, when they were alone, she would have to remember to thank him for choosing the hymn that had kept her calm.

Wanda's son lifted his head and rubbed his eyes. "Where's my *mamm*?"

Clara rearranged his shirt and straightened his suspenders, as she had done for Josiah when he was this age. With three young half siblings, she knew she could care for a child—or a half dozen. Mrs. Schrock was right. In her own home, Clara could tell as many Bible stories as she wished.

If only the thought of birthing a child did not terrify her.

The boy slid off Clara's lap, and she trailed him outside to be sure he found his mother.

During lunch, Clara moved between tables, sometimes listening to the conversation before her but just as often catching snippets of interchanges behind her or down the table.

"The bishop's sons will make sure nothing changes."

"Now is the time to ask for reasonable consideration."

"Pray for the bishop. Protect your heart from thinking ill."

"Mose Beachy should speak out more. It's his duty."

For the most part, Clara did not have to look around to know how opinions lined up. Those with a family relationship to the Yoders close enough to inspire loyalty tended more and more to band together. A few other families, headed by men who had known the bishop for decades, took their plates and sat with the Yoders and those who had married into the Yoders. The much larger group were church members with family scattered over the border between the Pennsylvania and Maryland districts.

Clara was grateful Andrew's connection to the Yoders was distant enough that he felt free to think for himself. She sponged up the last of the gravy on her plate with a final bite of biscuit and peeked at Rhoda. Mari was refusing to eat, Rhoda had barely touched her own food, and Hannah was nowhere in sight. All of this left Clara with the conclusion she had time for some fresh air before the Kuhns would be ready to depart and she would have to decide whether to go with them.

She was barely out of the clearing when two small forms popped out from behind a tree.

Clara gasped. "You startled me."

"We've been waiting and waiting," Priscilla Schrock said.

"We want a story," Lillian said.

A few yards farther away, Hannah and Naomi appeared.

"It doesn't have to be a long one like the sermons in church." Priscilla's features settled in the most earnest expression Clara had ever seen on a six-year-old. "God can speak to us in a short story."

Clara sighed. "I'm afraid we can't have a story today."

"I told you she would say that," Hannah said. "Next time you should believe me."

"Hannah's right," Clara said. "But you can have a lovely time playing together and enjoying your Sabbath."

Clara ignored the ring of dramatic scowls and hastened her stride. At the sound of steps crunching behind her, she turned to reiterate that there would be no story. But the girls were scampering in the other direction.

"Yonnie," Clara said.

"What did they mean about stories?" Yonnie's blocky form continued toward her.

"Never mind," she said. "It's nothing."

"It didn't sound like nothing."

Clara resumed walking. Yonnie kept pace. The last thing she needed was for Yonnie to get wind of the Bible stories she told the girls.

"You know the imagination children that age have." Clara rummaged around her mind for a change of subject. If she could manage something kind, perhaps the rift between Andrew and Yonnie would not seem as impassable as it had the last few weeks. "I heard talk that your father's crop is plentiful this year. I'm sure you had something to do with that. Everyone says you understand the soil."

"Our family works together," Yonnie said.

"We would all do well to follow your example."

"Better our example than others'."

Clara stifled a sigh. She pitied Yonnie Yoder. He had no notion of how smug he sounded.

"Andrew has too much joy in his automobile," Yonnie said. "It will be trouble."

"It doesn't have to be," Clara shot back, already chastising herself for being unable to sustain her good intention for more than eight seconds.

"No, it doesn't—if Andrew makes the right choice."

"What does that mean?"

"The bishop will not be in seclusion forever. If you are true to your faith, there are things you give up." Yonnie pivoted abruptly and reversed his direction.

Clara had always detested that particular Amish proverb. She balled her fists to keep herself from scooping up a handful of pebbles to throw at the back of Yonnie's head.

Her urge for a few minutes of fresh air matured into the resolution for a good long walk. If she did not turn up at the Kuhn buggy when Rhoda and Hiram were ready to leave, they would assume she had decided to go to the Singing and would find a way home later. Clara wanted to bolt for the meetinghouse, collect Andrew, and disappear with him. Instead, she bided her time by taking that long walk and ending up at the appointed barn for the Singing. Dutifully, she sat among the unmarried women and watched Andrew from across the barn. He sang with enthusiasm, his tenor piercing the gathering with its irresistible precise pitch.

The hymns passed, the evening ended, and the moment Clara awaited all day arrived. She was alone with Andrew in his buggy.

"The hymn you started this morning convicted me," she said.

Let us keep our eyes on love!

How quickly she had failed her resolve that afternoon.

"It was for my own admonition," Andrew said. "Whatever others do, I hope I will remember its message better than I have. I owe Yonnie an apology."

"I talked to him today," Clara said. "I'm not sure he's of a mind to receive an apology."

"He always was the tattletale who would go running to our mothers before anyone could be properly sorry. As the saying goes, 'Some people are like buttons, popping off at the wrong time.'"

Two proverbs in one day, Clara thought. No matter how clever, traditional proverbs would not smooth the rough edges in the congregation.

Clara said, "In this case I think he's only waiting for the bishop to recover."

For a few moments, only the sluggish drop of horse hooves punctuated the silence.

"Don't worry about what Yonnie does," Andrew said. "I don't."

"He infuriates me."

"I know."

"Where can I find love in a puddle of infuriation?"

"Love must be the pond that swallows up the puddle. I'm going to apologize to Yonnie for my anger."

"It won't change his mind."

"That is not my purpose." Andrew took Clara's hand. "Let's talk about something else. I saw you with Wanda's boy today."

"I'm worried about Wanda. She had some pains. It's too soon for that."

"She's had two children already. She'll know if something's wrong."

"What if she realizes it too late?"

"What if nothing is wrong at all?" Andrew countered.

Clara sighed. "I always think the worst, don't I?"

"Not always. Only when it comes to babies."

"The heartbreak would be too much to bear," Clara whispered.

"Joy cometh in the morning," Andrew said. "You'll be a wonderful mother."

"If I ever find the courage."

"You will. When you do, I'll be right here."

She squeezed his hand but could not form a response.

"Why don't you go stay with Fannie for a few days?" he said. "It's been weeks since you saw her, which seems ridiculous for the sake of five miles."

"I don't know," Clara said. "I don't want to stir up trouble."

"You told me Fannie was discouraged."

"She is." The words of Fannie's letters flowed through Clara's mind. She read between the lines that Fannie's doldrums were not abating.

"I'll take you, and you can send a message when you want to come back," Andrew said.

"I'll think about it."

"Why wait?"

"I don't want you to get in trouble."

"I won't."

Clara rubbed the cuff of her sleeve between thumb and forefinger. "Perhaps, but I want to be back for the day of preparation."

"Of course."

She wouldn't even write to say she was coming. A surprise visit would cheer both Fannie and Sadie. And while she was gone, tensions in her own district might settle down.

"Can you take me on Saturday?"

Andrew squeezed her hand. "Keep your eyes on love."

CHAPTER 29

"The bishop is not seeing anyone."

Caroline Yoder did not raise her voice, but Yonnie had heard this tone before. He broadened his smile.

"I come with the prayers and good wishes of my entire family," Yonnie said, sliding one foot closer to the threshold Mrs. Yoder occupied.

She did not budge.

"Surely his withdrawal from appointments does not apply to visits from extended family." Yonnie did not budge, either.

"It applies to whomever I choose."

"Should not the bishop choose?"

"The bishop requires complete rest. When he is feeling better, I'm sure word will get around the district quickly enough and he will welcome visitors."

"Might I not come in and say a prayer for him?"

"God will hear you from your buggy."

At that moment, Yonnie was grateful he was related to the bishop—even if only distantly—and not to this woman who failed to even offer him a cup of coffee. He supposed that if he traced the family lines far enough back, he would find a connection to everyone in the district, but the Yoder name is what mattered.

"Everyone missed you both in church last Sunday," Yonnie said. The service was six days old now, yet there was no word of the bishop's improvement. "You'll be glad to hear your sons preached faithfully."

"That is their way." Mrs. Yoder wiped her hands on her apron. "If you will excuse me, I have a long list of tasks to fill the day."

Although Yonnie did not step back, Caroline closed the door firmly, barely clearing the end of his nose. Yonnie stood on the porch and shook his head. He could think of no one in the district who would not at least have offered a bit of refreshment to a visitor, even while holding firm on the matter of seclusion.

After waiting this long, a few more days would not matter.

Andrew's attempt at an apology had not changed Yonnie's mind. Andrew might be sorry that he lost his temper and embarrassed Yonnie at the dairy—as well he should be—but he showed no remorse about possessing the Model T. It was only a matter of time before the bishop would call on Andrew to confess his sin.

"I'm going to take Thomas outside to play," Sadie announced.

"Sadie, I don't think—" Fannie began.

Her sister-in-law broke in. "That's a lovely idea, Sadie. He loves to roll in the grass."

"We have *lots* of grass." Sadie took the hand of her toddler cousin.

"Perfect." Lizzie smiled at Sadie and then at Fannie. "Your mother and I will be right here in the kitchen if you need us."

Against her better judgment, Fannie resigned her opposition. "I'll pour the *kaffi*."

"Thank you. The children will be fine."

"Sadie is only five." Fannie set out two cups. She glanced out into the yard, but already Sadie had taken the boy out of her line of sight.

"She has always been careful with him," Lizzie said. "It's your *mamm* I'm worried about today."

Fannie brought her gaze back indoors and fixed it on her brother's wife. "Is she unwell?"

"She'll never admit it," Lizzie said. "But I don't think she's well at all."

Fannie moved to the stove, turning her back as she gripped the coffeepot. "She's with child. It's not unusual to feel unwell. More rest would help, would it not?"

"She works too hard. There is no question of that. She claims she never let expecting a child interfere with her work before and that she's nowhere near her time."

Fannie poured the coffee, but she had already dismissed the idea of drinking any.

"She's right," Fannie said. "I never saw her slow down a day with any of the boys."

"She's not as young this time around," Lizzie said. "She won't listen to any of us. You must come and talk sense into her."

"What makes you think she would pay heed to me?" Fannie's stomach clenched.

"You're her only daughter."

"She couldn't be any more fond of you if she had birthed you. You are a true daughter." Fannie had heard Martha say this dozens of times since Abe married Lizzie.

"It's not the same." Lizzie leaned across the table and put a hand on Fannie's arm. "Outside of church, you haven't seen her for weeks. Elam comes to suppers without you. You don't bring Sadie for strudel in the mornings. Martha's heart is heavy for you."

Fannie's throat thickened.

"Why don't you come?" Lizzie said softly. "You have always been close. She's your *mamm*."

Escalating giggles outside the back door made Fannie turn her head. She was grateful for a fleeting excuse to glance away from Lizzie. Any month now Lizzie would break the news that Thomas was going to become a big brother, and Fannie wouldn't be able to look her brother's wife in the eye any more than she could look at her mother.

She moved to the sink and dumped her untouched coffee. "I'll try to go."

"Don't wait too long."

"I won't." Fannie gripped the edge of the sink in determination to believe her own words.

Lizzie stood. "I'd better get Thomas home for his nap. I could drop you off on my way."

"No," Fannie said. She gave a smile she did not mean. "There's no need to trouble yourself. I will come."

Fannie walked outside with Lizzie. Sadie protested being separated from Thomas so soon, and Fannie took her daughter's hand as a reminder of the behavior she expected. The girl's shoulders slumped but her objections ceased, and they watched Lizzie put Thomas in the buggy and signal the horse into motion.

"Can I stay outside to play?" Sadie asked.

Fannie inhaled and sighed. "Yes, I suppose so."

"Will you play with me?"

"I don't feel very playful just now."

"Then watch me play. Please?"

Fannie glanced toward an outdoor chair Elam had made for her during the summer she was expecting Sadie.

"All right," she said, "for a little while."

Sadie tumbled into the grass again. Fannie sat in the chair and lifted her face to the sun. In mid-September, the days were still full of summer but with the edge shaved off the heat.

"*Mamm*, you're not watching!"

Sadie's thin voice scolded, and Fannie opened her eyes. She would have anyway, because behind closed eyelids she saw her mother, heavy with child and refusing to slow down. Lizzie had put the image in the place where Fannie closed off her pain. If she could not retreat there, then where?

Sadie squealed and began to run along the side of the house. Fannie gasped and popped out of her chair.

Clara was walking toward them—with her small brown suitcase. Sadie took it from her, gripping the handle with both hands and leaning to one side to keep the bag from dragging in the dirt. In a moment, Clara's arms were around Fannie, and Fannie resolved that on this visit her cousin would not find her in the bed—or anywhere—unable to get up and make a meal.

Clara could not have ridden the milk wagon. The time wasn't right.

"You didn't walk, did you?" Fannie said.

Clara hesitated and then smiled. "Andrew Raber left me at the top of the lane. He'll be back Friday."

Six days together. Something soothed and brightened within Fannie. The smile creeping across her face took her by surprise.

"Andrew Raber," Fannie murmured. "He could have come down to the house for some refreshment."

Clara's face flushed.

"Sadie," Fannie said, "take Clara's bag to the spare bedroom. She's going to stay awhile."

"Good!" Sadie said. "She can visit my Sunday school class tomorrow."

Sadie lugged the suitcase into the house.

"You should visit the class," Fannie said. "Sadie loves it."

"I know it's a church Sunday for you," Clara said, "but I thought I would pass a quiet Sabbath on my own."

Fannie held the screen door open for Clara. "You haven't been to church here since we were little. You might enjoy the changes. The new hymns have lovely four-part harmonies, and the stanzas are much shorter than you're used to."

Clara did not respond as she pulled a chair away from the table to sit down.

"I have a feeling we have a great deal to catch up on," Fannie said. "Your letters have not said much."

"Let me settle in," Clara said. "And Sadie will want some attention."

"Have you brought her any new stories?" Fannie took a plate of cookies from a cupboard and set it on the table.

Clara nodded. "I can't stop myself from writing them."

"And why should you?"

Clara sucked in her breath but said nothing.

"Sadie is going to insist you visit the class," Fannie said. "She'll pester you all night."

One side of Clara's mouth turned up. "I admit I'm curious what it would be like to see what a teacher does with a class of children talking about Bible stories."

"Then come to church. The Sunday school class is right after the shared meal, before everyone goes home."

"Maybe just for the class," Clara said.

"We won't bite."

"It might. . .complicate things."

Fannie munched a cookie. The class was a start. Clara could see for herself how well she would fit in with the Maryland church. Maybe on her next visit, she would come to worship.

Clara walked to the Maple Glen Meetinghouse the next afternoon, carefully calculating her arrival to coincide with the close of the meal. As soon as the last of the food was stowed away, Fannie had explained, classes for children met around the tables on one side of the meetinghouse, while adults quietly continued their visiting on the other side. Clara stepped inside the building—identical to the meetinghouses where she was accustomed to worship—and looked around.

"There's my cousin Clara." Sadie's voice rang out, and she wiggled off the bench where she sat with a cluster of little girls. Some were even younger than Sadie, but others were older.

The teacher followed Sadie toward Clara. "I'm Ellen Benton. I'm so glad you could visit our class."

"I won't be any disturbance," Clara said. "I only wanted to see what it is like."

Ellen grinned. "You help make my job quite pleasant."

"Me?"

"Your stories, silly," Sadie said. "I showed her the scrapbook."

"Oh!"

"The girls love them," Ellen said. "They bring the Bible to life in just the right ways. And what an inspiration! I've even begun to try my hand at it, although I have not the skill you have. We teach the boys separately from the girls, of course, but even the boys' teachers enjoy your stories."

Clara did not know what to say. She knew Sadie went to Sunday school, but it never crossed her mind that Sadie—or Fannie—would share Clara's stories with anyone else. Surely the teachers had their own plans or instructions from the ministers.

"We tell the stories so the children can understand them," Ellen said. "Then we work on learning High German so they can learn to read the Bible for themselves someday. The little ones practice picking out letters."

"I'll just have a seat over here and watch," Clara said.

"Wouldn't you like to tell a story?" Ellen said. "I was planning on Daniel and the lions' den."

Clara had first told a story to Priscilla, then to two girls, then to four. Thirteen heads now bobbed around the table. Daniel and the lions' den was one of the stories in the scrapbook. Clara had written and rewritten the words a half-dozen times before she was satisfied. The taste of them saturated her tongue.

"O taste and see that the Lord is good."

"Thank you for asking," Clara said, "but I'll watch and listen and learn right along with the girls."

She sat down on a bench a few feet away, where she could hear and see clearly. A moment later Fannie slid in next to her.

"Next time visit church," Fannie said. "You'll see."

"See what?" Clara said.

"You'll see."

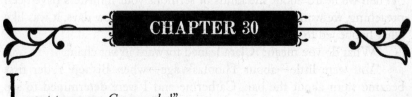

CHAPTER 30

I want to go see *Grossmuder!*"

Clara watched Sadie's bare foot lift and stomp, though her slight weight made little sound on the polished wood floor.

"We'll have to go another day," Fannie said, her eyes fixed on the mending in her lap.

"You always say that, but we never go. Isn't that a lie?"

Fannie looked up now. "Sadie Esh, you mind your tongue."

"Sorry," Sadie muttered. "But I still want to go see *Grossmuder.*"

"Let me take her," Clara said. "I've been here three days and haven't seen my favorite aunt."

Fannie poked a needle through a seam in one of Elam's shirts.

"I know it's not a good time for you to go." Clara chose her words with care. Sadie was standing right there. "But I want to see Martha anyway. Sadie may as well come with me."

Fannie didn't look up. "All right."

Sadie shot out the front door. Clara nearly had to trot to keep up with her. Martha had strudel ready, as she had for as long as Clara could remember. When she was Sadie's age, she relished a visit to Martha's kitchen as much as Sadie did now.

"Where are my uncles?" Sadie swiped crumbs off her lips with the back of one hand.

"Doing barn chores," Martha said.

"I think they want some strudel," Sadie said.

"I think you may be right." Martha laid two pieces of strudel in a dish towel cut from a flour sack. Clara remembered when her aunt had stitched the blue-and-yellow border on it.

Sadie carried her offering carefully out the back door. Clara watched Martha's movements around the kitchen as she wrapped the remaining strudel in a flour sack and tucked it away in a cupboard. Her rosy complexion was absent, and she occasionally flinched with the movement of her left leg. They moved into the front room.

"I am so glad you came." Martha finally allowed herself to sit. "When we heard about the kinds of sermons your ministers have been preaching, we wondered what would happen. For a few days, it was like what happened to your mother all over again."

"What do you mean?" Clara leaned forward in her chair.

"You were little—about Thomas's age—when Bishop Yoder first became stern about the ban. Catherine and I were determined to see each other. She didn't vote for the *meidung*, you know."

"But it was a unanimous vote."

"Not exactly." Martha put a hand on her back and winced.

"Are you all right?" Clara thought Martha looked inordinately tired even for a woman with child.

"I'll be all right." Martha blew breath slowly. "Catherine was close to her time. I was her sister. Of course she wanted me to come. As soon as the message arrived that she was laboring, I went."

Clara swallowed. She had been too little to remember the night her mother birthed a baby who never drew breath.

"She held my hand the whole time." Martha's gaze found a distant point out the window. "The baby took too long. Catherine was exhausted, but she never let go of my hand. Not until. . ."

Clara's breath stilled against her will. She knew the story. Martha had told it more than once. Catherine bled too much too fast. The baby was gone and then Catherine as well. That was the moment when her grip on Martha's hand slackened. Story and vague memories of a toddler swirled in Clara's mind, leaving her once again uncertain of the difference between what she remembered from that day and the bits of information she had acquired over the years.

Martha's breathing sounded heavy to Clara.

"Are you sure you feel all right?" she asked.

"Perfectly fit. I'm just having a baby, and I miss my sister at a time like this." Martha sighed. "And my daughter."

They dawdled through lunch, which Clara insisted on helping

to prepare. The three Hostetler sons still living on their parents' farm alternated between teasing and adoring Sadie. When the meal was over, Sadie announced she was going to help wash dishes and pushed a kitchen chair up to the sink. Clara and Martha worked on either side of the girl, both encouraging and inspecting her efforts.

"Time to go, Sadie." Clara hung the damp dish towel over the back of a chair.

"Not yet!"

"Your *grossmuder* needs to rest." Clara glanced at her aunt over Sadie's head and was relieved to see no resistance in Martha's features.

"Come give me a kiss," Martha said to Sadie.

Sadie leaned into her grandmother. "The *boppli* is getting big!"

Martha took Sadie's hand and laid it on her belly.

A few seconds later Sadie gasped. "What is that?"

"The babe is kicking."

"Is it trying to get out?"

"Not just yet."

"Wait until I tell *Mamm* the baby kicked me."

Clara pressed her lips together to keep from grimacing. Sadie chattering about the active baby would do nothing for Fannie's fallen spirits.

"Let's go, then," Clara said. She kissed Martha good-bye and promised not to wait so long before visiting again.

Sadie, who had practically run the entire distance that morning, now dragged her feet about going home. Clara kept up a brisk pace, pausing periodically for Sadie to catch up. She would see the child home, but she would not so much as drink a glass of water before setting out again.

"Aren't you coming in?" Fannie asked when Clara nudged Sadie through the front door.

"I have an errand," Clara said. "Does the midwife still live on the other side of the pond?"

"Midwife?" Fannie startled. "Surely not yet."

"How often is your mother seeing the midwife?"

"She's weeks away from her time."

"Fannie, your *mamm* is having a harder go than she admits."

"That's what Lizzie said." Fannie glanced at Sadie, who picked up her faceless rag doll from the chair she insisted was the doll's bed. "She scolded me for not visiting more."

"I can see her point."

"Not you, too, Clara!"

Clara pulled on one *kapp* string. "I know it's difficult for you."

"No one understands," Fannie said. "I don't know a single other woman who is watching her mother have the baby that should have been hers. Only me!"

They stood on either side of the threshold, matching eyes inherited from their mothers fixed on each other. Clara's heart thudded against her ribs. Only a few months ago she could not have imagined anything would separate Martha and Fannie. Their intimacy had always made her miss the mother she did not know—it still did. Clara never expected to stand between them aching for them both.

"She misses you," Clara whispered finally.

"I know." Fannie looked down at her skirt, her voice viscous and constrained. "But I can't help her right now. I just can't."

Clara nodded, a knot rising in her throat. "I'll go see the midwife."

Fannie stepped back and closed the door, pressing it softly into its frame while Clara exhaled grief.

❧❀❧

Clara visited Martha again before she went home on the following Friday and had a word with her cousins. The boys were twelve, fifteen, and seventeen—old enough not to take their mother for granted, old enough to notice how tired she was, old enough to take over some of Martha's chores without being asked.

Now more than two weeks had passed. Every day that no urgent message came from Garrett County allowed Clara to breathe another day's relief that her aunt was probably fine. She wished she could know for sure that the midwife had been to see Martha.

Sitting in the Flag Run Meetinghouse in Somerset County for the first service in October, Clara pondered the fine line between calling and regret. Her reason for not going to the worship service with Fannie's family at the Maple Glen Meetinghouse in Garrett County was that the repercussions might usher in regret. The decision was hardly an act of submission to the church. Keeping herself from a progressive church service might qualify as outward obedience—which was what people like Yonnie concerned themselves with—but it certainly was not a humble offering of her spirit to God.

The Maryland congregation would have no worship service today, but many of them would restore their souls with Sabbath visiting. Fannie *ought* to visit her mother, but *ought* and *could* were not the same thing. Clara prayed Fannie would not be mired in regret so impenetrable that turning back would be as impossible as flying to the moon.

For the first time in her life, Clara wished she could pick up an *English* telephone and tell the operator she wanted to talk to her aunt.

None of this had anything to do with the Sunday morning church service of the Pennsylvania congregation. Clara readjusted her posture, laid her clasped hands in her lap, and gave her attention to the sermon.

Clara saw no sign of Bishop or Mrs. Yoder, though one of their sons who lived in Missouri was present. She had not seen him in years. If he was home because of his father's illness, it must be serious. Joseph Yoder concluded his sermon and suggested a hymn. Noah stood for his sermon. Sometimes Clara wondered if Mose Beachy even participated in casting lots for the sermon. What else would explain why it so seldom fell to him?

After the final hymn, Noah stepped forward again.

"We have the glad news of publishing several engagements," he said.

Clara glanced at Andrew. Noah named three couples, including Ruth Kaufman and Peter Troyer. As one by one, the brides' fathers stood and issued invitations for the congregation to attend the weddings, Clara kept her eyes in her lap. She did not want to know how many eyes might be on her—including Rhoda's—wondering if yet another harvest season would pass with no wedding celebration at the Kuhn home. While she plotted how to politely slip from the meetinghouse, at least long enough for immediate stares to wear off, Joseph stood again beside the preacher's unvarnished table. At the sound of his shuffling feet, Clara tilted her head to one side, a necessity rising from her recent habit of sitting in the rear of the meetinghouse.

Joseph unfolded a sheet of paper. "I have a letter from my father to read to you."

A wave of shifting posture rolled through the meetinghouse.

" 'My beloved church,' " Joseph read. " 'As you know I have been unwell for some time. While I have faith in our Lord for my recovery, I know I am becoming older. My family encourages me to ease my load. Serving as your humble bishop all these years has brought me great joy. Now it is time that I find a new service. In obedience to God, I resign as your bishop effective October 1. May we continue together in our devotion to Jesus Christ. Humbly yours, Moses Yoder.'"

October 1. Today!

Joseph folded the paper. "The hymnals have been prepared by my father himself. Following communion this afternoon, the ministers will prayerfully choose a hymnal and discover the slip of paper that reveals the will of God."

Andrew ate little, just a slice of bread and a few beets. He watched Clara make the rounds pouring black coffee, but he did not see her sit down to eat.

Andrew's mind jumped back and forth between the careful words of the letter Joseph read and his own conversation with the bishop in the Yoder kitchen. The bishop could not have written that letter on his own. Caroline had probably insisted on the resignation.

The meal lacked the usual leisurely socializing. A baby wailed. Andrew didn't turn his head to see whose it was, instead watching the ministers. After eating together, they now stood, a signal that benches should once again be arranged for a worship service.

The fall communion service began. As the bread and wine were served, guilt pinged Andrew. This was a solemn ritual that occurred only twice a year, yet his mind was fixed on the procedure that would follow. He could read nothing on the faces of the three ministers. When his turn came, Andrew knelt to eat the bread and drink the wine and prayed that Christ's love would find a home in his heart. Though the congregation took communion seriously, it seemed to Andrew that the stillness and attentiveness around him was due to more than the somber service.

Finally the ministers returned to their bench in the front, facing the congregation. On the preacher's table were three hymnals. Each one showed the tattered wear of decades of service to the congregation. All were tied with identical string, making it impossible to discern which one held a slip of paper with a verse written on it.

Joseph Yoder was first to select a hymnal. Noah laid a hand on one of the remaining two and then changed his mind and picked up the other. Mose's task was simple. He had only to lift the last hymnal from the table.

Andrew still saw nothing in their expressions. No eagerness. No anxiety. The work of a bishop was consuming. Andrew did not envy any of them the task. *Gottes wille.* God would choose the next bishop.

One by one the ministers began untying the strings. Then together they flipped the pages of the hymnals in search of the slip of paper. Joseph reached the end of his hymnal and began shuffling pages in the other direction, consternation creeping across his face.

Andrew's heart rate kicked up, and involuntarily he peeled himself away from the back of the bench.

Noah was slower, more methodical. But he found no paper, either. The brothers maintained solemn expressions but audibly shifted their weight on the bench.

Andrew watched Mose Beachy's face and saw the instant Mose moved his eyes to the spot where his wife sat with their daughters.

A fraction of a second later, Lucy Beachy failed to contain the cry rising through her throat.

The lot had fallen to her mild-mannered, peace-loving husband. Mose laid the hymnal open across his knees and lifted the slip of paper tucked against the binding at the center of the volume.

Andrew gripped the back of the bench in front of him. Mose stood up beside the preacher's table.

"God has chosen me for your new bishop."

CHAPTER 31

Seventeen days.

For seventeen days the district buzzed with speculation. Everywhere Clara turned—in Niverton or Springs for the shops, walking through the farms as harvesting teams rolled from one to the other, visiting neighbors on the Sabbath between services or after the worship services—conversation turned to how Mose Beachy would be a different sort of bishop than Moses Yoder had been.

Reports circulated that Bishop Yoder was not as ill as he had been, but he still did not leave his farm. His sons and grandsons were bringing in his harvest. His wife, accounts said, would not allow him to return to church before he was fully recovered.

"I'm not sure he will recover," Andrew said when Clara recounted a conversation.

"Are you a doctor now?" Clara teased.

Andrew polished a headlight on the Model T. "Mrs. Yoder was right to make him step down."

"That's what you think happened?"

Andrew shrugged.

"How is it you're not working the harvest today?"

"Mose is generous with his thresher. He's loaned it out. When he gets it back, we'll help John Stutzman for the next few days, and then it's my turn."

"That's just like Mose. What would everyone do without his thresher?"

"He's skilled enough with the machinery to keep it operating."

"Like you." Clara met Andrew's eyes and smiled.

"Shall we go for a ride?" Andrew's eyes twinkled.

Clara grinned. "Are you feeling more daring now that Mose Beachy is bishop?"

He tilted his head and opened the door for her. "She's running beautifully these days."

"Is Jurgen Hansen still offering to buy?"

"Every time I see him—which is not as often now that she's fixed up."

They drove into the sunshine, still warm enough to keep the top down. Clara wondered whether being inside a car with the top up would feel much different than riding enclosed in a buggy. For now she closed her eyes and leaned her head back against the diamond tufted upholstery, relishing the breeze prickling her face as the car rumbled along a back road that had become Andrew's favorite.

She sat up abruptly. "What was that noise?"

"The knocking?" Andrew said. "She just needs a slight adjustment." He pulled over, and they stepped out into a vibrant medley of autumn hues.

"It's glorious here," Clara said, stretching out her arms and spinning in a slow circle. "They're the same trees any of the farms around here have, but somehow I never notice them at home."

"No fields to interrupt them." Andrew took a wrench out of a small toolbox he kept in the automobile now and opened the hood. "No one pays attention to this road. The Amish don't come out here."

"Do you really think Mose will change things?" Clara said.

"If he doesn't, things will change themselves." Andrew leaned over the engine and made a quick adjustment before handing the tool to Clara.

"What am I supposed to do with this?"

He grinned. "Think of me while you hold it."

Clara thought of Andrew most of the time, but she couldn't say so aloud. He would only propose again, and she had no answer for him— at least not the one he wanted. Her aunt's pale face drifted into her mind, brooding in shadow. Clara wondered again whether the midwife was watching Martha closely enough. She pushed away the thought of what might happen to Martha or the baby—or Fannie, who would never forgive herself for not reconciling with her mother if the worst came to be. Clara squeezed her eyes closed, trying to picture Martha, rosy and healthy, with a baby in her arms and swathed in lemony dawn light. But the colors collided. Rather than airy and illuminating, they were gray and dense and spinning in a certainty Clara wanted to scream against. If loss struck the Hostetler house, Clara was not certain she could ever bring herself to consider marriage again. She could never be as brave as Martha.

Clara blew out her breath.

"What's wrong?" Andrew said, taking the wrench.

"I need to visit Fannie again."

"We could take the car."

"Perhaps that is *too* daring—at least until we know what Mose would say."

"There is nothing in *Ordnung* about automobiles," he reminded her.

Whatever adjustment Andrew made cured the rattle. He needed both hands to drive, but Clara slipped a palm into the crook of his elbow.

Later, she wandered home drenched in contentment. The sight of a visiting buggy parked along the fence piqued her curiosity. Striding up the lane, she realized the horse belonged to the Schrocks. Inside the house, Clara found Rhoda setting a plate of cookies on the dining room table, where the Schrocks and her father sat. Hannah and Priscilla snatched cookies and scampered out of the room, tugging Mari by the hands.

"The Schrocks have some news," Hiram said. "Since we're their closest neighbors, they have come to us first."

Rhoda's jaw was set and her eyes more interested in the stitching of the tablecloth than her guests' faces.

"Is everything all right?" Clara said.

Caleb Schrock cleared his throat. "We've decided to join the Marylanders."

Heat raced through Clara's chest. "That *is* news."

"It seems that it is partly because of you." Rhoda's voice snapped.

"Me?" Clara fingered a *kapp* string.

"I explained how you comforted Priscilla with a Bible story," Mattie Schrock said.

Clara felt her skull squeezing. "She was frightened."

"You gave her a new attitude about her chore to feed the pigs. We can't believe the difference. I was wrong when I said you shouldn't be telling Bible stories to someone else's child."

Clara looked into her neighbor's eyes and found there assurance that she had said nothing about the other stories, or the fact that Rhoda's daughter was part of the group who heard them.

"Of course we read the Bible in our family devotions," Caleb said. "I try to explain things in a way the children can understand, but they need to hear more."

"We've talked about this a great deal," Mattie said. "This is not a hasty decision. A farm came up for sale in Maryland a few weeks ago, and recently we decided to buy it. We just signed the papers."

"But there is a Marylander church in Springs," Clara said. "Why do you not join that congregation?" Although the Pennsylvania district primarily was Old Order, there were Marylanders on this side of the border. Selling one farm and moving to another only a few miles away seemed like an extreme measure to Clara.

"We're moving for the children," Caleb said. "If we live in the Conservative Amish Mennonite district, it will be less confusing for them as they grow up."

"When?" Clara asked, a knot forming in her throat.

"Tomorrow."

"We think the Sunday school in the Amish Mennonite Church will be good for Priscilla," Mattie said. "She can go to Sunday school with your Sadie now."

Clara drew in a deep breath to offset the gasp she heard from Rhoda.

"Hannah talks about Sadie," Mattie said.

"They've never met," Rhoda said.

"Still, Priscilla is curious," Mattie said. "Whether Old Order or Amish Mennonite, we are all Amish."

"But the *meidung*," Clara said.

Mattie laced her fingers together and set her hands on the table. "We understand that some will feel they must shun us. That is another reason why it will be better for the children if we live in Maryland, among the people we will worship with."

Clara wanted to scream in objection. Instead she looked at her father and Rhoda, unsure what stance they would take. They had no family connection to the Schrocks, no intermingling business, no reason to justify continuing social contact with them.

"The new bishop will have something to say, will he not?" Clara said.

"Mose Beachy is a good man," Caleb said. "I admire him a great deal. He seeks peace, and I pray it will come. But we feel we must be true to our conscience in the way we express our faith."

Clara could hardly try to argue the Schrocks out of the decision. They had already purchased the new farm.

"Does Priscilla know?" Clara said.

"She is excited about Sunday school." Mattie's smile was tentative.

What about Hannah? Clara thought. Would Rhoda set aside the ban for the sake of her daughter's friendship?

Seventeen days since Mose became bishop. Andrew was right. No matter what Mose did or did not do, the church would change.

Relieved, Fannie let herself in the back door. The invitation for Sadie to play on the next farm over could not have been more welcome. Elam was sorting out the fields after harvesting the corn and would not be anywhere near the house for several hours. Fannie moved through the rooms shuttering the daylight out before crawling onto the davenport and cradling a throw pillow against her waist. If only a child would grow there. If only her waist would thicken with new hope.

Fannie closed her eyes. With enough practice over the last few months, she required fewer and fewer minutes to successfully retreat into sleep, her only escape.

When her eyes popped open, it was at the prodding of an insistent voice standing over her.

"You can pretend you're not here," Martha said, "but you'll also have to be like the *English* and lock your doors."

"I didn't hear you," Fannie said truthfully, pushing herself upright. "I must have dropped off."

"I stood on the porch knocking for a long time," her mother said. "I've never known you to sleep through the kind of ruckus I was making."

"I'm sorry." Fannie stared into her mother's midsection. How was it possible she was this large?

"Do you feel unwell?" One hand on her belly, Martha lowered herself beside her daughter.

Fannie scooted over a few inches, uncertain how to answer her mother's question. She had no headache, no stomachache, no dizziness, no nausea, no fever.

But no, she did not feel well.

"Do you want *kaffi*?" Fannie stood up, her eyes fixed on her mother, who seemed to have gained more weight than she had with her last three babes put together. Perhaps she had miscalculated and was closer to her time than any of them realized.

"No, thank you," Martha said.

"Something cold, then?" Fannie's brain refused to clear. She glanced at the clock. Barely thirty minutes had passed since she fell asleep, yet her body felt like a millstone dropping in a river. Even in the presence of her mother—or especially so—sleep beckoned.

"Fannie, I have not come to be entertained. I want to talk."

"I have a dozen things to do. I don't get much time without Sadie underfoot."

"You were sound asleep," Martha pointed out.

"I didn't mean to be." It was a half truth.

"It's not like you."

"Are you sure you don't want *kaffi*? I'm going to have some."

Martha grabbed Fannie's hand, pulling her back. "I had no idea things were this bad."

"What do you mean?"

"I don't see you except at church. Lizzie said you didn't look well. Then Clara came to visit without you."

"She was anxious to see how you were doing."

"And you weren't."

Fannie reclaimed her hand. "I really need some *kaffi*."

"You only drink it to be polite."

"Lately I've taken it up with more enthusiasm."

Martha braced her arms behind her and pushed herself up, abdomen first. "Then I'll come with you."

"You must have better things to do than watch me drink *kaffi*."

Martha touched her daughter's face. "I have nothing better to do than talk to you. I didn't know Sadie wouldn't be here, but perhaps it is God's will that we have this time without interruption."

Fannie took a step back.

"You're avoiding me," Martha said. "You won't come to me, so I've come to you. I want my daughter back."

Fannie said nothing.

"We've never had anything between us," Martha said. "Why must this baby separate us?"

"The baby is innocent," Fannie said.

"Then I am to blame?" Martha said. "How can you think I would want to hurt you?"

Fannie swallowed. "You wouldn't."

"Then whose fault is it that I conceived and you did not?"

If her mother said *Gottes wille*, Fannie thought she might scream. What good was prayer if God's will made no sense?

"This child deserves love," Martha said.

"Love will not be lacking," Fannie said.

"This child deserves *your* love, just as much as any of your brothers did. Sadie is excited about a baby *aunti* or *onkel*. She needs to see you excited, too."

"I'm Sadie's mother. I will decide what she needs."

Never had Fannie spoken to her mother with stinging words, but she could not stop herself.

"This is *your* baby sister or brother," Martha said. "I will decide what my child needs, and my child needs *you*."

Fannie turned away, not under the guise of making coffee but only to escape her mother's scrutiny.

Martha lumbered around Fannie and grabbed her by both shoulders, pulling her in and wrapping arms around her. "And *you* are my child. I will not watch your pain and do nothing."

Fannie tried to lean away, but Martha did not let go. Her embrace tightened the same way it used to when Fannie was young and tempestuous, annoyed by one of her little brothers or wounded by a friend's remark. Her mother would hold on indefinitely.

Fannie felt the child physically between them, her mother's womb firm and round. Martha stroked the back of Fannie's head. A sob welled up and burst out of Fannie's throat.

CHAPTER 32

Andrew walked up the path to his mailbox and extracted the stack. The latest issue of *The Sugarcreek Budget* came to him courtesy of the subscription his mother launched years ago when she lived at this address, and for which she still paid the annual fee. An advertisement for seeds and farm equipment came simply because the Rabers were farmers, not because either Andrew or his father had ever purchased from the company. Sandwiched between these two items was the envelope Andrew was genuinely interested in, a letter from his mother. Tucking the larger items under one arm, Andrew broke the seal on the flap and removed the familiar folded pages in his mother's meticulous handwriting and began to read as he walked.

Dear Andrew,

We've heard the news about your new bishop, though we are eager to hear your perspective on what this means for the church in Somerset County. Several here in Lancaster have received letters from family and friends in Somerset. I'm sure I don't need to tell you that a coin has two sides. Some write to applaud Mose Beachy because they are certain that he will at long last set aside rules that, in their opinion, have done nothing but cause unclarity and division for all the years that Bishop Yoder was in office. Others, naturally, write with downcast hearts that one of the Yoder boys was not selected. But of course who can dispute the will of God? If God selected Mose Beachy, He must have a plan for the church.

I hope that in all the fracas you will see your way clear to let your conscience guide you. In circumstances like these, your father and I have always recognized how simple it is to do what causes the least disturbance. That is, in fact, the reason we moved to Lancaster once your brothers and sisters were married and settled.

You are old enough to remember something of 1895, or at least 1905, though perhaps you did not perceive the depth of people's confusion. Whether he intended to or not, Bishop Yoder misled the congregation in the original vote about the meidung. *When the truth came out ten years later, no one was certain how to correct the matter. Someone would have had to state before a communion service that they did not agree with the teaching regarding shunning, and of course to do so would mean that communion would not occur. Who among us wants to be responsible for withholding the body and blood of Christ from the rest of the congregation?*

To this end, your father and I decided we would rather move to Lancaster. After all, we have family here. If we could not submit to the bishop, it seemed best to remove ourselves. We had no desire to be a stumbling block to anyone else. Perhaps if someone—even we—had mustered the courage to bring the issue to a new vote, the harm could have been undone long ago and Somerset would not be in crisis now. Alas, we did not. I hope we have not contributed to any discomfort you may be experiencing now.

Mose has never agreed with the shunning. Of this I am certain. But he believed that if the congregation endured all these years, then let it continue to do so. If the letters arriving in Lancaster are any indication, I doubt he can sustain this position much longer. Hearing the news across the miles, it seems to me that Somerset is going to split after all, and perhaps this would not be an entirely unwelcome event.

My prayers are with you, my son. If I had spoken plainly before moving away, I doubt it would have made a difference. You were so eager to have a go at running the farm on your own! And your father had every confidence that your temperament would both bring you success and allow you a peaceable existence in the church where you grew up.

I trust your harvest was satisfactory and will prove profitable. Do let us know the results once your crops have come in and the funds have been sorted out.

With love,
Your mamm

Andrew read the letter again once he was inside the house and in a comfortable chair. When his parents moved away and left him to run the farm, he did not ask more than a few questions.

"Are you sure?"

"Wouldn't you rather sell the farm to someone who can pay what it's worth?"

The truth was, he was eager to run the farm. Now, he realized, the advantage blinded him. And now the congregation had once again been complicit in upholding the ban. Though many disagreed, no one would speak up. No one would be the dissenting voice that deprived the congregation of communion.

Andrew moved to the desk his father had crafted twenty years ago and took a sheet of paper from the drawer.

Dear Mamm,

> *Thank you for speaking with directness about what prompted you to withdraw to Lancaster. Someday, when we have a good visit, perhaps you will tell me more.*

> *I think you are right about Mose Beachy's position. It seems to me that people have gone along with the rule for these twenty years out of respect for the office Bishop Yoder held and the conviction that God chooses the bishop. But if this is true, would it not also be so for Bishop Beachy? Perhaps God has raised our brother up for such a time as this.*

> *I do feel that since Bishop Yoder has resigned, people may feel less obligated to defer to his opinions without discussion. If the question of officially removing the ban were put to a vote, I would be surprised if it failed, though there may be some who support it because of tradition more than conviction. Of course Noah and Joseph Yoder would argue for sustaining the ban. The Yoders are nothing if not loyal.*

> *I know that Mose Beachy's father was in favor of the ban, but Mose has a mind of his own. I suppose we will see if he has the strength to express it. You may be right about a split. I pray that it would be as amicable as the decision in 1877 was meant to be when this journey began.*

> *Yours,*
> *Andrew*

❦

If Joseph or Noah had become bishop, Yonnie would have known what to do. Even if the *Ordnung* by which church members lived their daily lives did not mention automobiles, everyone knew how the Yoders felt about the *English* contraptions. If Andrew's owning the Model T was not already against the rules, the Yoders would have made an example of Andrew and the resulting rule would be clear. Joseph and Noah were still ministers. They were not without influence, and the two of them would stand together.

But Mose Beachy? Who could say how he would respond?

Yonnie chewed on this conundrum as he made his dairy rounds on Thursday.

Passing Mose's farm—not one of his stops because as a family of sixteen the Beachys consumed everything their cows produced—Yonnie recognized the distinctive white stripe in a horse's tail waving like a flag. It was Noah's horse.

If Noah was at Mose's home, Joseph likely was as well. The three of them would have many subjects to discuss. Ministers had meetings all the time.

Yonnie slowed the wagon, stopped for a moment, and then pulled to the side of the road where he could tie his own horse to a tree. He scanned the farmstead, with the house and barn dominating the assortment of outbuildings. Would the ministers meet in the new bishop's home, with his wife and children within earshot, or would they look for a more private spot? Yonnie decided to aim for Noah's rig.

As he moved alongside the house with its covered front porch, Yonnie heard voices, a blend of children too young to attend Crossroads School vying for their mother's attention. A young man, probably fourteen and in his first year out of school, intoned caution, and the rumpus subsided. Lucy Beachy's calm assurance was muffled, but the children seemed satisfied. Yonnie saw no one outside and paced toward the enormous barn.

Noah's horse turned his head and swished his flag of a tail in acknowledgment of Yonnie's presence, but he made no sound. To one side, a half-dozen hogs snorted and rummaged, oblivious to the impending fall slaughter. A hen fluttered her wings and brushed past Yonnie, whose ears focused on the drifting sound of male voices. Glancing over his shoulder again, Yonnie approached the equipment shed.

"Would you not agree," Noah Yoder said, "that it is important for all the ministers to be of one mind?"

Yonnie paused outside the open door, out of sight.

"I have been bishop less than three weeks," Mose said. "I pray each day for God's will to be clear to me."

"We cannot continue preaching our message but turning our heads from the violations we are certain of." Joseph's pitch raised in emphasis.

No one spoke for a few moments. Yonnie heard the clink of metal against metal. Mose must have been adjusting the thresher so many of the Amish farms depended on.

"Perhaps," Mose finally said, "we should agree to a period of time during which we will open our hearts to the Lord for this new season in the church."

"A church does not have a new season," Noah said. "Our responsibility is to preserve the faith as it was given to us."

Joseph spoke. "Your own father was in agreement with ours. They both signed a letter objecting to the lax enforcement of shunning."

"That was a long time ago," Mose said. "We were all boys. Now we need to examine our own consciences. The original separation of the Marylanders was peaceful. Why do we continue to fight against peace?"

"Would you have all our people join the Marylanders?"

"I would have them follow their consciences."

"They have vowed to be obedient to the church."

"And Christ is the head of the church," Mose said.

"We have *Ordnung* for our own good," Noah said. "We protect the salvation of the church members when we hold them accountable."

"Jesus said the Sabbath was made for man," Mose retorted, "and not man for the Sabbath."

"I suppose you would claim freedom to drive cars or use telephones like the *English* in the name of conscience."

Yonnie stilled his breath for the response.

"It seems to me," Mose said, "that it has always been our way for the congregation to consider such questions together. All the members may vote. Perhaps we should also vote on the *meidung* again."

Joseph's sigh could have filled a milk jug. "I see that we will need many conversations."

"That may be so. Right now, I have promised to take my thresher out to the Troyer farm so he will have it first thing in the morning."

Yonnie moved around the side of the shed and watched as the Yoders, reluctantly, climbed into Noah's buggy and turned the horse toward the road.

"Yonnie, you can come out now," Mose said.

Yonnie pressed himself against the structure.

"I know you're there. I can still see your shadow."

Yonnie exhaled and stepped into view.

"Did you get the answer you were seeking?" Mose asked.

"I don't know what you mean," Yonnie said.

"Do not cultivate dishonesty."

Yonnie licked his lips but said nothing.

"I did not ask to become bishop," Mose said. "God chose me, and I will serve faithfully as God gives me strength. I know people are watching me and wondering if there will be change. But you have come to my farm and hidden yourself for your own purposes. That is deceit, is it not?"

Embarrassment flowed in Yonnie's blood.

"Did you want to speak openly to me about a matter?" Mose said.

After what he'd overheard, Yonnie would say nothing to Mose about Andrew's car or Dale and Clara's interaction with the Marylanders.

"I must finish my rounds," Yonnie said.

Mose nodded. "That's a good idea."

CHAPTER 33

From the barn at midday on Saturday, Clara heard Rhoda instructing the girls just outside the door as they selected the chicken that would be the center of the evening meal. She unlatched the stall where one of the Kuhn milk cows stood. At the end of October, the nights were cool and the days no longer steamy and dripping with humidity, but there was no reason to keep the animals indoors. One cow was already in the pasture, and Clara slipped a rope around a second's neck and led it out into the daylight. This particular cow had never moved quickly a day in her life. Clara had long ago resigned herself to letting the animal set the pace when they went back and forth between barn and pasture.

She removed the lead, knowing the cow would immediately begin to nuzzle the ground. Clara draped the rope around a fence post and turned around to see a buggy approaching. The horse was unfamiliar, and she shaded her eyes to more clearly see who was driving.

An arm waved out one side, and a second later a face leaned out.

Andrew's face. Clara walked across the farmyard to greet the visitors. John Stutzman halted the buggy.

"Feel like an outing?" Andrew asked.

"What do you have in mind?" Clara said, though she was likely to agree to whatever Andrew suggested.

John leaned forward to look past Andrew and catch Clara's eye. "We're going to see the Schrocks' new farm. Then we could stop at your cousin's, if you like."

"I would love to," Clara said.

Andrew dropped off the bench to properly assist Clara into the buggy.

"Do you need to let someone know you're leaving?" John glanced toward the house.

"Will I be home for supper?" Clara said. Rhoda and the girls had retreated into the house with the unlucky hen.

"Long before, I would imagine."

"Then no need." Clara settled between John and Andrew.

John took the horse at an enthusiastic clip. Clara watched the landmarks of the familiar route go past—the half-painted barn, the oak tree split by lightning years ago, the trim *English* flower garden that always made her wish she could wander in and lean over to smell the fragrance of every kind of flower in sight.

Another buggy came toward them.

"That's Noah Yoder's rig," Andrew said. "The horse's tail gives him away."

"We'll wave and go on by," John said.

But Noah gradually moved his buggy toward the center of the road, making it impossible to go past unimpeded.

"Good afternoon." Joseph Yoder sat beside his brother.

"Good afternoon," John said.

"Nice day for a drive." Joseph eyed the trio.

"That it is," Andrew said.

Clara intended to say nothing.

"Heading south, I see," Noah said.

"That's right," John said.

"Be careful your horse doesn't step in the pothole about a quarter of a mile down."

"*Danki.*"

"Are you visiting one of the Old Order families in Maryland?" Joseph said.

Clara moistened her lips.

"Friends," Andrew said. There was no untruth in the response.

Joseph settled his gaze on Andrew for a long silence.

"May God bless your day," John said. "If you might take your horse to the side, we'll be on our way."

Noah made no move to signal the horse. "Perhaps we could add our greetings to the ones you carry," he said. "May I ask which friends you are visiting?"

"We will be sure to let them know you said hello." John eyed the road. Clara could see him calculating whether there was enough room to bypass the Yoder buggy after all.

Still Noah held the center of the road. Only when John's buggy came within inches of Noah's horse, causing the animal to snort and try to back up, did Noah lift the reins. John navigated past and let his mare have her head for a few yards.

Clara gripped the bench with both hands. "Surely it has not come to this."

Andrew's jaw set. "Don't let them bother you."

"It's as if they think themselves the *English* police trying to catch a criminal," Clara said. "We are not criminals. We should tell Mose."

"Tell him what?" John said. "That the Yoders greeted us in the road to remark that it was a nice day and warn us of a pothole?"

"They did more than that," Clara said.

"They said nothing objectionable."

"My objection is not to their words."

Andrew covered her hand with his. "Don't let it spoil the day."

"I hear the Schrocks have more tillable acres on their new farm," John said.

"And it's closer to the river," Andrew said.

Clara saw what they meant to do. They could make cheerful distracting comments for the next five miles and it would not change the fact that the Yoders thought themselves superior. Did they disagree with God's choice of Mose Beachy for bishop? Maybe the Schrocks were right to join the Marylanders and even to move away from their former district.

Andrew squeezed her hand, and she squeezed back.

Eventually John slowed, looking for a road. "Does this seem right?"

Andrew craned his neck from side to side. "Three oaks on the corner. That's what he said."

They took the turn and traveled another quiet mile. When the farm came into view, Clara smiled. It was a beautiful setting, the house painted white and trimmed in dark green with a bright red barn and a rolling front yard. The Schrock children chased each other through the grass, their gleeful shrieks ringing across the farm.

Priscilla stopped and watched the buggy lumber toward the house. Finally a smile of recognition cracked her face, and Clara could not help but grin back.

༺◈༻

Fannie had not withdrawn to the darkness of sleep for two days. She doubted anyone could understand the triumph, so she kept her self-congratulations silent. Melancholy was not wholly unfamiliar. Fannie had read about the subject and had known a person or two she might have described as having the melancholy, but she never expected to see its drab gray walls from the inside of her own mind or to watch the hands creep around the clock until it was legitimately time to bring the bedding up to her neck and sink into black release.

Elam was in the brightest mood Fannie had observed in months. His harvest was in. Neither insects nor weather had caused great harm this season, and the price the broker quoted would carry them nicely through the winter and into the spring planting.

Fannie, too, had reason to feel grateful. The family's vegetable garden had nurtured them well through the summer and fall, with bounty enough also for canning and stocking the cellar. Though Fannie didn't actually *feel* grateful, at least she recognized that God had provided for the household, and perhaps with enough time she would be able to express thanks.

Sitting outside in the weakened autumn sunshine, she watched Elam playing with Sadie. They balanced open cans along the top of the fence and tossed pebbles. Neither of them managed to get many into the cans, but the sound of their laughter in the effort occasionally brought a feeble smile to Fannie's lips.

When the buggy rolled onto their property, Fannie folded her arms across her abdomen. She was unprepared for her mother to return so soon. Fannie had promised to go to supper at her parents' house on the Sabbath, a visit that required Fannie to dig deep in her spirit's soil for strength. The digging was not finished.

But it was not her mother, Fannie realized. The horse was a strange one, as were the two men who emerged on either side of Clara.

Clara. They had very nearly quarreled the last time Clara was here. Fannie had been uncertain she would want to return. Six weeks had passed with only the skimpiest letters from her cousin. Tepid relief eased out on Fannie's breath. Elam paused the rock-throwing game, and Sadie hurtled herself into Clara's arms. Fannie rose and walked toward them.

"This is Andrew Raber," Clara said.

Ah. This was Andrew. On Clara's last visit he had dropped her off and picked her up out on the main road. One corner of Fannie's lips turned up. "Welcome," she said.

Andrew and Elam shook hands.

"And this is our friend John Stutzman," Clara said.

"I'm pleased to meet you," Fannie said.

"We were visiting our friends, the Schrocks," Clara said. "They recently moved to a farm a few miles south of here."

"It's lovely to have you here." Fannie very nearly believed her words. "Please come in and let me offer you some refreshment."

"Strudel?" Sadie slid out of Clara's arms.

Fannie nodded. "We have strudel, of course."

She took her daughter's hand and they led the entourage up to the house. Behind her, the three men fell easily into a conversation about crops and harvests, the topic on every farmer's mind at this time of year.

"Are you sure it's all right that you came?" Fannie said to Clara once Sadie scampered ahead of them.

"I won't ever not come," Clara answered. "I know it's been a few weeks, but I will always come."

Fannie sucked in her lips to suppress the sob that lived in her throat these days.

They gathered at the dining room table, with berry strudel, coffee, and apple slices. Sadie guzzled a glass of milk with her pastry before losing interest in the adult conversation and going to look for the dog. Fannie listened carefully to Clara's account of her former neighbors' decision to move to the Maryland side of the border.

"Have you always been Marylanders?" John asked.

Elam nodded. "Our families embraced the new music and Sunday school long ago."

John glanced around. "Your home looks no different from any in the Old Order district."

"We are Amish," Elam said simply.

"I hear some of your people own cars."

"This is true," Elam said, "though of course an automobile is expensive, and we rarely go farther than a horse can easily take us."

"I have seven children," John said. "I have a feeling they would enjoy a Sunday school class."

"You should visit sometime," Fannie said.

"My wife and I seem to discuss that idea every time we drive past the Mennonite church in Springs, where we do our shopping. We're becoming more serious about it, I think."

Fannie watched Clara, whose glance had snapped up sharply at John's admission.

"We had a good visit with the Schrocks this afternoon," John said. "I'm sure my wife will be interested to hear how they are settling in. I don't think we would sell our farm, as the Schrocks did, but what is there to keep us from visiting to see if the Marylanders might be where God leads us?"

Clara's coffee cup rattled on the way from her lips to the saucer. Andrew's arm twitched, and Fannie realized he was resisting the urge to reach out to Clara. She hoped Andrew and Clara were listening carefully to their friend. It was only a matter of time before John Stutzman would turn up in one of the Marylander meetinghouses with his wife and seven children.

First the Schrocks.

Then the Stutzmans.

What was there to hold back Andrew and Clara?

Hope flickered within Fannie.

CHAPTER 34

After church the next day, Clara pivoted at the sound of her name. Wanda paced through the narrow aisle formed by two tables. Clara could not help but notice how large Wanda was now. Each time Clara saw Wanda, relief oozed through her that her friend and her child were still well. The worry would not fully abate until news came that Wanda was safely delivered.

"I heard the bishop is looking for you," Wanda said.

"The bishop? Why would he be asking for me?" Clara set down the pitcher of water she had been pouring from.

"I think he's in the anteroom."

Clara smoothed her skirts. "Then I'll go find him."

She threaded her way between tables and benches to the front of the Flag Run Meetinghouse. Bishop Beachy had preached wonderfully that morning—finally. Whenever Clara heard one of his sermons, which she hoped would become less rare, encouragement gushed into her like refreshing spring water. So many people ignored the ban, but she hoped to see it lifted. Beyond that, it seemed to her that Mose found uplifting themes in the New Testament that made her feel that God was eager to work in her life.

Still, she had no idea why Mose Beachy would summon her on a Sunday morning. She knocked softly on the door. Someone on the other side turned the knob and opened the door.

She stared into the eyes of Noah Yoder.

"I'm sorry," she said. "I got a message that the bishop asked to see me."

"Yes, he does. Please come in." Noah stepped aside.

Clara crossed the threshold. The dim room with sparse but heavy furniture gradually came into focus. Behind a table sat Bishop Yoder. To one side of him was his son Joseph. In straight-back chairs facing the table were Andrew and John with an empty chair between them.

"Please be seated." Noah gestured to the vacant seat and then sat on the other side of his father.

"I don't understand," Clara muttered.

"Just sit down." Noah's voice was a razor.

Clara looked at Andrew, who nodded slightly, and took her place.

"Are you well, Bishop?" she said. Clara had not noticed Bishop Yoder's presence during the worship service. Perhaps her habit of sitting in the rear was catching up with her—or perhaps he had not been present. Surely she would have noticed him enter with the men, and surely conversation would have buzzed with the news of his recovery if others had seen him.

"My father is much improved," Joseph said. "Thank you for your kind inquiry."

Clara's stomach clenched, and she was glad she had not yet eaten her meal.

"Will Bishop Beachy be joining us?" she asked.

"I don't believe we need to trouble him with this," Noah said. "We can speak to you in our authority as ministers."

What was *this*? Clara could only assume the Yoders had assembled this meeting because of yesterday's encounter on the road. She wished she could reach for Andrew's hand.

❦

"I'm sure you all realize why you're here," Joseph said.

Andrew bit back his response, determined to remain nonchalant for Clara's sake if nothing else.

"Clara," Joseph said, "it is well known that you visit your mother's family even though they no longer belong to the Old Order."

"I don't deny it," Clara said. "They left the Old Order before I was born."

Bishop Yoder shuffled his feet under the table. "You must stop. They are under the ban."

Until that moment, Andrew had not been certain Bishop Yoder would speak at all, supposing his presence was merely a ruse so his sons could mislead him and the others with a message that the bishop was asking for them. But the bishop did seem much recovered. His eyes were clear and his gaze focused when he spoke. Beside Andrew, Clara crossed her ankles.

"Andrew," Joseph said, "it is my understanding that you have no family connections in the Maryland district. Is this correct?"

"Yes, it is," Andrew said.

"And you, John?" Joseph said.

"My family are all Old Order," John said.

Andrew did not have to look at John to know he was meeting Joseph's gaze.

"The lack of relatives erases any doubt about whether you can both obey the *meidung* and visit members of the Conservative Amish Mennonites. You cannot serve both God and mammon."

"You must stop," Bishop Yoder said. "They are under the ban."

"Andrew, do you deny that you visited Marylanders with whom you have no family connection?"

"No," Andrew said.

"And you, John? Do you deny this?"

"No."

"Then you are confessing your sin to us. As ministers we believe you must stand before the congregation and confess your transgression. Clara, you will confess the sin of leading your fellow church members astray."

Andrew no longer resisted the urge to turn his head toward Clara, who was pale, and John, who was red in the face.

"With all due respect," John said, "I will do no such thing. Neither will I accept your false accusations of Clara."

"The lot fell to Mose Beachy," Andrew said. "Shouldn't he be here?"

"The lot fell to him to be bishop," Noah said. "God selected us as ministers and we will serve. Sometimes our duty is unpleasant."

Andrew doubted the Yoders felt any unpleasantness in their demand.

"You must stop," Bishop Yoder said again. "The Marylanders are all under the ban."

Andrew narrowed his eyes at Joseph. "Are you sure your father has recovered?"

John stood. "You know that most of the congregation believes the ban on the Marylanders should be set aside."

"But it has not been set aside," Noah said. "Perhaps your confessions will help others to take it more seriously for the sake of the entire church."

"You cannot single us out simply because you happened to meet us on a road driving south," John said.

"If you will not submit to the discipline of the church," Joseph said, "we will have to place you under the ban as well."

"Will you place two-thirds of the congregation under *meidung*?" Andrew stood now as well, taking Clara's hand and pulling her to her feet with him.

John took a step toward the door. "The congregation will not tolerate it."

❧

Clara's eyes were wide and her lips pressed together, but she did not tremble, not with Andrew's hand wrapped around hers.

The door opened, and Mose Beachy stepped in—all three hundred pounds of him—and looked around the room.

"I was not aware there was a meeting of the ministers," he said. He closed the door behind him.

Clara breathed relief. Mose's large form shifted the balance in the room the way leaning to one side in a boat on the river threatened a capsizing.

"Our brothers propose to put us under a ban," John said.

"Only if you refuse to confess," Joseph countered. "I pray you will make the right choice."

"Threatening the ban is serious," Mose said. "Why doesn't someone tell me what happened. Andrew?"

Clara listened to Andrew relay the summons to see the bishop, only to discover Bishop Yoder in the chair behind the table. Mose paced around the room as he absorbed the details of the conversation.

"Joseph, please take your brother and your father and join your families. I'm sure they're waiting for you."

"We have not concluded our businesses," Joseph said.

"On the contrary," Mose said, "I'm quite sure you have. I did not ask to be bishop, but neither will I shirk my responsibility. You can be assured I will conclude the matter in an appropriate manner."

Noah took his father's elbow, and the Yoders shuffled out of the room.

Mose gestured to the chairs. "Please be comfortable while we talk."

They took seats.

"They should not have misled you about which bishop you would find when you came in the room," Mose said, "and they should have spoken to me about their intention."

"We were certain you would feel that way," Andrew said.

"Imagine my surprise when Wanda Eicher asked if I had finished meeting with you."

"We would have come to you," John said, "just as soon as we walked out that door."

"I have no doubt. It would have been the right thing to do."

"Thank you for understanding," Andrew said.

"Clara," Mose said, "you have done nothing wrong in visiting your relatives. I hope you enjoy many more visits with your aunt and your cousins."

"Thank you." Clara's shoulders lowered, but the hesitation she heard in Mose's voice kept her on guard.

Mose stroked his beard. "I am not going to ask you to confess to the congregation, and you will not be under a ban. But I will ask you not to see the Schrocks."

Clara gasped. "They've been my neighbors for many years."

"But they are not your family," Mose said. "And they only just left the church. It is not the same as the families who left a generation or more ago."

"They have not sinned," Andrew said. "Their only fault—and I do not believe it is a fault—is that they choose to worship somewhere else."

"It's a complicated question."

"Is it?" John said. "You're the bishop now. You can lead the church through change."

"I plan to seek counsel on that question from more experienced bishops outside our district," Mose said. "For now, I would like for the question of the Schrocks not to stir the pot."

"But we are not the only ones who will want to see them," Clara pointed out.

Mose nodded. "Surely you are correct. I will have other conversations if I need to. You are all good friends to me. For the peace of the community, I am asking for time."

Mose was the first to leave the room. Stunned, Clara trailed Andrew and John.

"We'll talk more," Andrew whispered. "We'll take the car out."

Clara nodded. Her father approached, and Andrew paced away.

"Rhoda asked me to see if you were coming home," Hiram said. He glanced at the anteroom door. "Have you been speaking to the bishop?"

The story spilled out of Clara. Hiram shook his head and sighed.

"Your mother would be horrified to see what has happened all these years later. She voted against the *meidung*."

"That's what Aunt Martha told me," Clara said. "But I thought it was a unanimous vote."

"In the way that a twisted arm is a healthy arm," Hiram said. "I was never in agreement, either, but I raised my hand. Your mother didn't. She told me later when I confessed that I was sorry I had."

"Oh *Daed*."

"I'll tell you who else did not vote—Betty Stutzman. She was outside watching you nap in the grass when the vote was taken."

"John's grandmother? With me?"

"She was quite fond of you." He chuckled. "As if she didn't have enough *kinner* in her own family. How could we know that within a few weeks, Catherine and Betty would both be gone?"

"I was hoping things would be different if Mose was bishop."

"They might yet be," Hiram said. "*Gottes wille*. We cannot expect Mose can undo all these years in one month. He'll want what's best for the church."

Clara nodded. Her father was right. Mose had been bishop for less than a month, while the vote to uphold the ban was more than twenty years old, and the division of interpretation of the Bible another twenty years older than the ban.

But time was running out. Across the meetinghouse, John Stutzman picked up his youngest child and kissed her cheek. Clara wondered how many more Sundays she would witness John's care for his family.

CHAPTER 35

Andrew left the Model T on the shoulder of the main road eight days later while he walked the final yards and stepped onto the lane leading into the Kuhn farmstead. He and John had been fortunate last week to find Clara alone and sweep her away in the buggy with minimal fuss. Andrew had no doubt that rumors already circulated about the summons to see the bishop that took John and Andrew and Clara into the anteroom with the ministers. This time Hiram or Rhoda might object to an invitation for Clara to take a ride. Certainly they would object if they saw the automobile.

Rhoda came out of the front door and snapped dirt out of a rug. Four sharp jerks loosed gray plumes, rising and then falling. Mari, too young to join her siblings at school, held on to her mother's skirt. Andrew hovered at the top of the lane as Rhoda retreated into the house. Scanning the farmyard, Andrew saw no other activity and took a few steps toward the barn. The milk cows and horses were in the adjoining pasture.

Clara could be anywhere. Hiram, full of questions, could emerge from one of the outbuildings. Rhoda could come out with another rug. But Andrew wanted to see Clara. A flash of gray fabric in the loft window of the barn drew him closer. He slipped inside.

"Clara," he whispered.

A few seconds later, her face looked down at him from the hayloft. "What are you doing here?"

"Let's go for a ride," Andrew said.

She paused. "In the Model T?"

"We'll go visit John."

She was descending the ladder now, hay caught in the folds of her dress and trapped under the edge of her *kapp*. When she reached the floor and turned to meet his eyes, Andrew wished he could capture the beauty of that simple moment, like an *English* photograph or painting. It would not be a graven image to him, but a reminder of loveliness in simple things.

"The Model T is up on the road," Andrew said, when what he really wanted to say was, *May I kiss you right here?*

Clara did not even glance back toward the house as they walked side by side up the lane. This wasn't like Clara. What was Clara doing in the hayloft in the middle of the morning? Something had been amiss in the Kuhn household for months.

But he asked none of his questions. When Clara got in the car, her blue eyes brimmed with trust. She would go with him, wherever he drove, by whatever method of transportation.

"Is John all right?" Clara asked once they were well away from Kuhn land.

Andrew shrugged one shoulder. "I feel a particular kinship with him these days. I'd just like to see him."

Clara pressed her shoulders into the upholstered bench. The top was up on the automobile now, enclosing the rectangle in which they sat. Without it, the November chill would have bitten at their faces in the wind.

They found John easily enough in one of his fields, walking with a toolbox and inspecting fence posts.

"Any more word from the bishop?" John asked as he set down his toolbox and brushed dirt off his knees.

Andrew chuckled. "Which one?"

"The only one who matters now," John said.

"No, nothing," Andrew said. "I may try to have a word with him, to hear more what is in his mind."

"Mose Beachy is a good man."

"The auction is next week," Clara said. "Will your wife be showing a quilt again?"

John cleared his throat. "Under the circumstances, we think it would be better if we did not attend this year."

"What circumstances?" Clara said.

John used a hammer to nudge a split rail into its slot more securely, testing it with one hand. His hat brim blocked any view of his face.

"John," Andrew said. "Please speak your heart with us."

John straightened and looked at their faces again. "We've decided to join the Marylanders immediately. Mose will have our letter withdrawing our Old Order membership by tomorrow."

"But John!" Clara said.

Unselfconscious in John's presence, Andrew put an arm around Clara's shoulders. "I thought you might. You asked a lot of questions when we visited Maryland last week."

"I will not shun people who have done nothing more than find another way to worship the same God," John said. "When Mose asked us not to visit the Schrocks, I knew the time had come for my family to leave as well."

"But Mose just wants time," Clara said. "In his heart he doesn't agree with the *meidung*."

"For twenty years most of the church has not agreed with the *meidung*," John said. "Yet it exists. If I cannot peacefully submit, then it is better for the congregation that I go."

Andrew tilted his head at the sentiment that echoed his own parents' choice.

"But your family is dear to all of us," Clara said.

"And you are dear to us," John said. "When Mose finally sorts things out, whether in one year or ten, we will see each other again."

"We'll still see you," Andrew said.

"No." John shook his head. "It is better if you respect Mose's wishes. We are not moving to Maryland, as the Schrocks did, but Mose will view us the same way he sees them—trouble to stir the pot."

Clara's shoulder trembled under Andrew's arm. His own tremble was inward.

They drove halfway home in silence.

"The Pennsylvania district will never change if our strongest families leave us," Clara said finally.

Andrew took a long pause. "I think that's the point. People should feel free to worship elsewhere if God leads."

"But what about the shunning? Freedom to leave is one thing, but we are pushing people we care about into a corner. They have to choose between worship or being part of the way we take care of each other."

"The Yoders, and those who agree with them, think shunning

will bring people back."

"That might work in other places where there is only one Amish church," Clara said, slapping her hands on her thighs, "but around here it's easy to go to another building on Sunday morning and find another community waiting for you."

Andrew let another long pause hang before he spoke again. "We could do that, too. Either the Schrocks or the Stutzmans would be at whichever congregation we joined."

"And how many other friends would we leave behind?" Clara's words fell in a halting cadence. "And what about my brother and sisters? My *daed*?"

Andrew drove without speaking. Leaving the Old Order district would cost Clara too much—and he would not go without her.

"The rope on the well frays more every day," Fannie told Elam.

"I know. You've told me half a dozen times."

The edge in his tone startled Fannie.

"Will you have time to replace it soon?" Fannie chose to ignore his mood and carried the last of the lunch dishes to the counter.

"I have to go to Grantsville for the rope."

"I'll go with you. Sadie would love it."

"No need."

Perhaps her own withdrawal colored her perception, but it seemed to Fannie that Elam's responses to ordinary conversation were growing terse. He remained playful with Sadie, and he'd had no trouble being hospitable and conversational when Clara and the others visited the previous weekend.

It's only me, Fannie thought.

Had he no idea of the enormous effort it took for her to remain upright? Of course he didn't. Fannie didn't tell him. She had his meals on the table at the appointed hours—for the most part—and the house remained tidy. It was the weeds in the vegetable garden that ran rampant all fall, and the mending pile that doubled every time she looked at it, and the eggs left in the henhouse until it was too late, and the fruit that went soft before canning—all details Elam would pay no attention to in the face of a triumphant harvest and caring for the animals. She would have to do better and have something to show for her efforts, something

Elam could see and appreciate.

"I know you're pleased with the harvest," she said, her spirit not nearly as bright as her voice. "Next year will be even better, I'm sure."

"I thought I would cut back next year."

"Cut back?"

Year after year Elam talked about seeding more acres even as he let some fields lie fallow. They still had at least ten tillable acres he had never touched. Cutting back made no sense.

"We can live on less."

"But I thought you wanted to expand the farm. You've always dreamed of buying more land someday."

Elam ran a finger back and forth along the edge of the kitchen table. "That was when I was planning for sons."

He might just as well have sliced through her with a harrow blade. Her throat instantly threatened to cut off her air.

"Have you given up, then?" she whispered.

"Haven't you?" He did not seek her eyes.

The answer lodged in Fannie's throat, unformed.

"Sadie will marry and move to another man's farm," Elam said. "Without sons it will be hard to work more acres than we have now."

"We could hire someone. I could help."

"There will be no need."

Sons.

Sadie burst into the room with slate and chalk. "*Daed*, will you help me with my letters?"

"Of course." Elam scooted back his chair and took Sadie into his lap. "What are we going to spell?"

"How about *boppli*?"

"What sound do you hear when you say that word?" Elam asked.

Sadie sucked in her lips and then said, "Buh."

"And what letter makes that sound?"

Sadie thought hard. "B."

Elam nodded.

Next spring, during planting season, Sadie would turn six, and next fall she would go to school. Someone else would teach her to spell and read and make sums. Fannie had always imagined that by the time Sadie's first day of school came, two more children would fill the days. Now she wondered what it would be like to be home alone, Sadie at school and Elam in the fields.

By then her mother's new babe would be pulling up on the furniture, perhaps even beginning to toddle.

Elam patiently guided his daughter's hand as she formed the letters of her selected word. He always had time for Sadie. He did not want her in the fields, where in a few seconds she might come to harm with the animals or blades while he turned his attention to some needful task, but he welcomed her in the barn and was already teaching her to milk.

They finished the word.

Elam lifted Sadie off his lap. "Your *mamm* wants me to go to town and buy rope."

The words he chose stung. *Your* mamm *wants*. The rope needed to be replaced or they would have no water in the house. It had nothing to do with what Fannie wanted.

"I want to go with you!" Sadie abandoned her slate.

"We'll have a delightful time."

"Is *Mamm* coming?" Sadie looked at her mother.

Fannie caught the flicker of Elam's eyes before he looked away.

"Your *mamm* has things to do," he said.

Fannie began scrubbing plates in the sink. Perhaps Elam observed more than she realized. Mentally she listed the tasks she could accomplish while Elam took Sadie to Grantsville. She stood on the porch and cheerfully answered Sadie's frantic good-bye waves with her own.

When the *clip-clop* of the horse's rhythm faded and the buggy was out of sight, Fannie hugged the solitude, striving to welcome it with aspirations of productivity.

Sons. Elam deserved a house full of sons to teach with patience and understanding. He had given up on sons, and with it the farm. On her.

A cow's soft *moo* alerted Fannie that Elam had fetched it from the pasture and taken it into the barn. She followed its call and scratched behind its ears to assure herself the animal was well. Elam had said nothing about why he had brought the animal in at midday. How many other decisions did he say nothing about?

Fannie could not fault Elam. She, too, felt the weight of effort to say more than was necessary.

She had come to the barn with no cloak. The brisk November day rushed through the open barn door, chilling her. Fannie reached for a horse blanket and wrapped it around her shoulders, keeping company with the cow for a few more minutes.

Then she opened the stall next to the cow, saw that Elam had freshened the straw, and sank down to her knees to pray.

She ached to pray.

She longed to pray.

But she could not pray.

She lay in the straw, wrapped in the blanket, and gave way to sleep.

CHAPTER 36

By Thursday, the news had sifted its way through the district. John Stutzman had delivered his letter to Bishop Beachy on Tuesday morning. The Yoder brothers pronounced the Stutzmans under the ban. The bishop, in office a scant five weeks, reluctantly agreed. Two churchwomen stopped by to spend a morning sewing with Rhoda on Wednesday, and every time Clara overheard a snatch of conversation, it had to do with the Schrocks and Stutzmans, who were now subjects of somber prayer for repentance.

Clara dragged through the days, finding chores to do. She cleaned the henhouse, put quilts in the buggy for the winter, and yanked overgrowth from the flower beds across the front of the house. For three days she did not leave the farm. Clara wanted to speak to no one, not even Andrew, while the Stutzman tempest brewed and settled. When she did manage to escape her grief over John's decision for a few minutes, trepidation mounted over Martha approaching labor. Incessant activity between waking and sleeping was her only path to release. On Thursday afternoon, the children arrived home from school just as Clara had readied the buggy to go to Niverton for a few items, an errand for which Rhoda gave lukewarm agreement to its merit.

Hannah's eyes lit up. "Can I come with you?"

Clara's stomach sank. Rhoda would not agree.

Rhoda stepped outside to welcome Josiah and Hannah. Josiah acknowledged her greeting before going directly inside. Hannah, though, stood beside the buggy.

"I want to go with Clara. Please, *Mamm*, may I go with Clara?"

"You've only just arrived home from school," Rhoda said, taking Hannah's lunch bucket. "You have chores to do."

"I'll do them when I get back. I promise." Hannah stroked the horse's neck.

"There's no reason for you to go."

"I just want to," the girl said. "I never get to go with Clara anymore."

"You see Clara every day." Rhoda put a hand on her daughter's back to point her toward the house, but the child did not budge.

Hannah tilted her head back, eyes pleading. "Please, *Mamm?*"

Clara squatted in front of her sister to look her in the eye. "I'm sure your *mamm* has a snack waiting for you. She always does."

"I'm not hungry," Hannah muttered.

"Still, go freshen up."

Hannah dragged her feet through the dirt, leaving a set of tracks between the barn and the house.

Clara pivoted toward Rhoda. "What have I done that makes you think I deserve your shunning?"

"I don't know what you're talking about." Rhoda hung Hannah's lunch bucket over one arm and paced toward a clothesline.

Clara strode after her, close on her heels. "It's been almost six months. You won't let me help in the house. You won't let the children spend time with me. I don't even know how Hannah feels about Priscilla moving away."

"I have told her as much as she needs to know." Rhoda swiftly removed four clothespins and draped two of her husband's shirts over one shoulder.

"And what do you tell her about me?" Clara stayed only two steps beside Rhoda, her voice rising.

"She's my daughter."

"You used to tell me I was like your own daughter."

"You are." Rhoda removed two more pins, and a pair of Josiah's trousers dropped into her arms.

"And you were the mother I didn't have when I was Hannah's age." Clara's voice cracked. "So why? I only want to know why?"

"This is for your own good. I have to do what's best for all my children."

"Hannah is my sister." Words pent up for months, a river running too high, gushed unstoppable through Clara's lips. "Will I only be allowed to see her if I marry? Do you want me out of your house so badly? Or perhaps I have to wait for Hannah to be old enough to choose for herself. Is that what you have in mind?"

Rhoda abandoned the clothesline and finally confronted Clara's insistent eyes. "This is as good a time as any to tell you that I spoke to your *English* family."

"They're not *my* family," Clara said. "I only work for them a few hours a week."

"Yesterday I let them know you're not available to come any longer."

Clara's lips twisted in fury. "I am not a child. I can decide for myself if I want to clean house for an *English* family."

"Well, it's done. He said he had in mind someone else to ask and wished you well in your marriage."

"Marriage! But I haven't said I was getting married."

"Cleaning other people's homes is as much as saying you intend *not* to marry and have your own home." Rhoda yanked two more garments off the line.

Clara swallowed hard. "When I was a little girl, you filled an empty place in me, and I will always be grateful. But this—whether I marry or where I work—is not for you to decide."

"I'm only helping you live in the way of our people." Rhoda looked around, her shoulders covered with clothing and her fists full of clothespins. "I should have brought a basket out."

"A basket! Are you more concerned with the laundry than with me?" Clara snatched one of Mari's tiny dresses from its pins and hurled it at Rhoda.

Hiram marched across the pasture and slipped through the fence into the farmyard. "Clara!"

She bit her tongue.

"You will not speak to Rhoda in this manner."

Clara forced herself to take a deep breath. "Did you know Rhoda thinks my work cleaning houses means I won't marry?"

Hiram looked from daughter to wife and back. "She has your best interest in mind."

"I'm a grown woman," Clara said.

"When you marry," Rhoda said, "you'll have a home with your husband. Until then we decide what's best."

"By shaming me? By depriving me of affection?" Clara refused to surrender to the hot tears pooling in her eyes.

"Mind your tone. Look!" Hiram gestured toward the house.

Clara saw three sets of young blue eyes looking out the front window.

"You are forgetting your place in the household," Hiram said.

"I seem to have no place in the household," Clara said, in control of her tone but still unable to filter her words.

"Think carefully about what you do and say." Hiram glared.

Clara clamped her lips closed, her face flaming. She climbed into the buggy and put the horse in motion. It was all too much. Rhoda excluding her for all these months. Fannie's melancholy. The Schrocks and the Stutzmans. The Yoders' determination to punish Andrew and her. Hannah's pleading eyes filling with disappointment over and over.

And now Clara had behaved like an impetuous ten-year-old. What example to her siblings was she now? She had just given Rhoda every reason to safeguard her impressionable children from their wild older sister's outbursts.

She could be married to Andrew within the month if she chose. He had a thriving farm and a lovely house that she could make her own. Rhoda might relax.

But Clara was uncertain she could ever forgive.

She would marry Andrew when she was ready—truly ready—and not because her stepmother held hostage three young children.

Andrew braced his feet, raised the sledgehammer, and slammed it down on a half-rotted fence post. The old wood splintered and crumbled. He stepped back, and Mose Beachy knelt in the dirt to toss aside the larger pieces and scoop rot out of the posthole. Andrew exchanged the hammer for a spade to widen the hole while Mose lifted a new post upright from the back of his wagon.

"Time matters," Andrew said.

"God's time matters," Mose countered.

"How many more families will we lose?" Andrew loaded the shovel three more times, tossing dirt and debris aside.

"As many as God chooses." Mose tipped the post into the hole and then straightened to look at Andrew.

"What if God is not choosing?" Andrew said. "What if people are simply becoming impatient?"

"Why did God make Abraham and Sarah wait so long before He fulfilled the promise?"

Andrew had often wondered. He had no answer.

"What about morale?" Andrew said. "If people realize you are going to enforce a ban that you don't believe in—"

"Who said I don't believe in it?" Mose wiggled the post snug into the bottom of the hole.

Andrew leaned on the handle of his shovel. "Do you?"

"A strong argument can be made for respecting tradition on the matter."

Andrew tilted his head as he considered Mose's response. Never before had he heard Mose take this position. "Mose, what are you saying?"

"The question is not whether to remove the *meidung* for people who go to the Marylanders," Mose said. "The question is what is best for the district. What will bring peace and unity to the church?"

"I don't understand," Andrew said. "How can it bring peace and unity to the church to watch our families leave?"

"They will not all leave."

More would. Andrew was certain of that. He had not supposed Mose Beachy to be one to lead by waiting for naysayers to leave.

"I hope that given time, we will have some productive conversations," Mose said. "In due time we might yet move ahead together on the question. Does not belonging to the community carry greater weight than being right or wrong on a single doctrine?"

Andrew pushed his black felt hat back off his forehead.

Mose chuckled. "I can see you are not persuaded."

"No," Andrew admitted. "I'm not."

"If I am to be bishop, I must care for the entire flock."

"And the sheep who wander to Maryland?"

"They will find their belonging there, I imagine. But if I lift the *meidung* with a simple announcement, then where will those who hold to it find their belonging?"

Andrew had not thought of that.

"The ninety-nine and the one lost sheep," Mose said. "Each one matters. No one is diminished."

Andrew moved dirt. "Would not those who hold to the *meidung* also submit to a new tradition?"

"Like owning automobiles?" Mose said.

Andrew's eyelids flipped up. "You know?"

"If I act too swiftly and in the extreme," Mose said, "the road to peace will become even more rocky."

Andrew lifted his hat and scratched the top of his head.

"I do not ask you to trust me," Mose said. "I ask you to trust God. All will be well in God's time. Now let's set this post before we lose the light."

Yonnie put his hands flat on the table and leaned across it, glaring into his coworker's face.

"You will see," Yonnie said. "The ban will hold."

The other young man laughed. "The ban has never held. Why should anyone take it seriously now?"

"I will pray for you," Yonnie said. "I will pray every night for the Holy Ghost to convict you."

"You seem to have taken that job on yourself."

Laughter spattered around them. Heat crawled up the back of Yonnie's neck as he set his jaw.

"What's going on in here?" Dale thundered into the workroom.

Distracted employees turned back to their tasks.

"Yonnie, please come to my office." Dale pivoted and marched out.

At a less brisk pace, Yonnie followed Dale, finding his employer behind the desk by the time he reached the office. Yonnie crossed his wrists in front of him as he spread his feet to a solid stance.

"The time has come," Dale said.

"The time?" Yonnie glanced at a clock.

Dale nodded slowly. "The time for you to find somewhere else to work."

Adrenaline broke free in Yonnie's core. His inquiries so far had led to no other employment possibilities, not even among his Yoder relatives.

"I'll count you out a month's pay to give you time to make other arrangements," Dale said.

One month. What would change in one month—during the winter when Yonnie could not even hope to find odd jobs on the farms?

"I was hoping you might settle down when Mose became bishop," Dale said.

"Settle down?"

"Become less. . .persuaded on certain matters. But since you can't set aside what you think about church doctrines or accept that others might disagree with good reason, it's time for you to go."

"They egg me on," Yonnie said. "They ask me for my thoughts and then laugh when I answer."

"I believe you," Dale said, surprising Yonnie. "But the dairy will still be more peaceful if you're not working here. I only held on this long because I heard you were asking around for work. I thought something would have turned up for you by now."

"Nothing has."

Nothing in the Amish shops. Nothing on the farms. Even at the height of the harvest, Yonnie had not found anyone who would let him run an Amish farm stand to sell to the *English*. If he had to lower himself to work for the *English*—Yonnie shook away the notion.

"Give me another chance," Yonnie said.

Dale sighed. "I don't trust you, Yonnie. Your chances are over."

Dale turned his chair and leaned down to open the small safe he kept under his desk. When he sat up he began counting bills on the desk. Yonnie was too stunned to keep track of how they totaled.

CHAPTER 37

Five days might have been five years. When her mother turned her back in the kitchen, Hannah lifted her blue eyes to Clara. When Clara opened her eyes at the close of a silent prayer before a meal with the family, she saw Hannah's wide orbs fixed on her. During family devotions, as their father read from the Bible and Hannah sat tucked in between her mother and Josiah, the sisters watched each other.

At church the past Sunday, Hannah had been the one to be brave. During the meal, she took her plate and sat down next to Clara before her mother settled at a table. Rhoda looked at the two of them, Clara avoiding her stepmother's eyes and Hannah staring into them with a dare.

I'm not moving, her posture said. *Don't try to make me.*

With Mari and Josiah, Rhoda moved to the next table, where she could watch Clara and Hannah.

It was something, Clara thought. In the safety of a hundred people having lunch together in the meetinghouse, she could at least converse with her sister.

Clara peppered Hannah with questions about school and her friends, all the while thinking how unfair it was to expect a six-year-old to understand the shift between her mother and her big sister, two people she loved and trusted. Hannah chattered, spilling overdue news of who was in her class this year and what she did when they went outside at lunchtime. Several times she said, "Priscilla used to..." or "I wish Priscilla could..." When they had finished eating, Hannah leaned against Clara, spreading an awkward embrace around her and whispering into her ear.

"I want it to be like before," Hannah said, wiggling her way into

Clara's lap even though her parents would have said she was too old for that.

Clara welcomed her, inhaling the scrubbed scent of her hair, washed just last night, and snuggling the pliant form that squirmed to fit against Clara's.

But Hannah had gone too far. Rhoda approached with firm instructions for Hannah to stack dishes. Clara nudged the girl off her lap, but not before kissing one smooth cheek.

Now, on Tuesday morning, Clara watched all three of her young siblings make their best effort to sit still and appear attentive for the morning devotions before school.

After he dismissed the family with a blessing, Hiram asked Clara to stay behind. Her mind sifted her actions in the last few days, and she gripped the edges of her apron as if to lift it and catch whatever accusation would fall out.

"I was harsh," he said. "The sermon on Sunday convicted me that I must ask your forgiveness."

This was her old *daed*, the one who was quick to admit he was wrong when she was little and he was never certain of his parenting decisions.

"Please forgive me," he said. "You have not forgotten your place. You will always have a place here."

Clara's chest tightened, and she reminded herself to breathe out.

"I loved your mother very much," Hiram said.

Though Clara had only the whisper of memories of her mother, she had always known Hiram loved Catherine. Why else would he have been huddled in grief for most of Clara's childhood?

"Martha and Catherine were closer than any other two sisters I have ever known," Hiram said. "There was nothing complicated about the decision to let you grow up knowing your mother's family. I would never have kept you from them."

"I know, *Daed*," Clara said. "I know there are some who think you should never have let me cross the border. I'm grateful you did."

He waved away the remark and stood up to put the family's Bible in its place on the shelf.

"Rhoda also has many qualities that make me cherish her," he said. "I have to think of her happiness."

"I know." Clara's gaze went to her lap.

"Your brother and sisters deserve to grow up in peace."

She felt his eyes on her and looked up into his face. "I know that, too."

Clara's heart closed around all the unanswered questions swirling in this conversation. *Do you think I am bad for the* kinner? *Don't you see Rhoda has her own form of* meidung?

"I'm going to muck stalls today." Hiram patted Clara's shoulder as he passed.

"I'll help," she said.

"There's no need for that."

"I want to."

"I can manage. You enjoy your day."

Oh Daed. Not you, too!

The sound of a racing buggy was not an easy one to ignore, even if Fannie was half asleep on the davenport on Tuesday afternoon.

"Who's coming?" Sadie popped up from the floor where she was playing with two faceless dolls and peered out the front window.

Fannie was on her feet as well. The pounding of the horse's hooves and the rattle of the hitch and buggy screamed urgency.

"It's the gray horse," Sadie announced.

Gray horse.

"*Onkel* Abe's horse?" Fannie crossed the room to open the front door.

Lizzie pulled hard on the reins and jumped out of the buggy.

"What is it?" Fannie's heart thudded.

"You'd better come," Lizzie said, breathless.

"*Mamm?*"

Lizzie nodded. "The babe is coming. It's been all day and still she labors."

"No one told me."

"She thought it would be better if we sent word after the baby arrived. That was. . .before."

"Before what?" Sadie pulled on her mother's sleeve.

"Get your shoes and your cloak," Fannie snapped.

"Are we going to see *Grossmuder?*" Excitement put a squeal in Sadie's voice and widened her eyes.

"We'll find *Daed.*" Fannie glanced at Lizzie, who nodded. "You can stay with him."

"I want to see the baby!"

Sadie was rarely petulant, but Fannie took no risk. "You will stay with *Daed* and you will not complain. Get your shoes."

Fannie fastened a cloak around her neck and snatched up her daughter, shoes still in hand, and ran toward Lizzie's buggy.

"Where is Elam?" Lizzie started the horse moving.

"I'm not sure." Fannie was at least certain Elam had not left the farm, but they said so little to each other these days. She made her best guess. "Take the wide trail that goes to the north field."

Lizzie drove while Fannie shoved Sadie's feet into her shoes and fastened them. Only then did she see that her daughter's cloak had not made it into the buggy. Mid-November was no time for a child to be out in a field without warmth. Fannie removed her own cloak and wrapped Sadie in it.

"There!" Sadie pointed. "There's *Daed*."

Fannie expelled relief and gratitude for her daughter's sharp eyesight. Lizzie raced the wagon toward Elam.

"I have to go to my *mamm*," Fannie said as she nudged Sadie out of the buggy.

"The baby's coming!" Sadie said.

Fannie fastened her eyes on Elam's. Their words may have dissipated over the weeks, but the understanding in his eyes had not. He knew she could not take a five-year-old into a difficult birth. As Lizzie started driving again, Fannie twisted in the buggy to see Elam rearrange the oversized cloak on the girl. Fannie shivered in the wintry air—and with a good dose of trepidation. The distance was only a mile and a half, but Fannie could think of a dozen things that could go wrong—a broken axle, the horse gone lame, a fallen tree blocking the road.

"How bad is it?" she asked.

Lizzie grimaced. "The midwife says the baby is not turned right. And it's taking a long time for a woman who has birthed five other children. When Martha started asking for you, the midwife said not to waste any time."

Fannie burst into the house while Lizzie tended to the buggy. Her father interrupted his pacing in the front room long enough to acknowledge her presence. Fannie touched his shoulder on her way past.

In the bedroom, on the same bed where Fannie was born nearly twenty-five years earlier, Martha writhed.

"She's so white," Fannie said to the midwife as she moved to the bed to clasp her mother's hand.

"Fannie," Martha whispered.

"I'm here."

"My precious daughter."

Fannie looked at the midwife, waiting for words of reassurance that the baby had turned or labor was progressing—something. But the midwife's face told nothing.

Fannie wanted Clara.

She went to the shelf where she knew her mother kept notepaper and pencils and scribbled a note. With a glance at her mother, Fannie strode into the front room. Two of her brothers had joined their father, and Lizzie was just coming in the front door.

"I need someone to take a message to Clara," Fannie said.

The boys looked at each other. Her father shook his head. He wouldn't leave now. None of them would.

"I'll go up to the main road," Lizzie said. "There will be somebody heading north."

"Give me the note," her father said. He turned it over and sketched a map, circling an *X* to mark the destination for its delivery.

Clara's eyes blurred as she read the note for the second time. An *English* boy brought it, shoving it awkwardly into her hand and mounting a sagging mare. Watching the animal's ponderous, slow progress back toward the road made Clara wonder just how long ago the boy took possession of Fannie's frantic scrawl on the Maryland side of the border.

Mamm in labor, it said. *Baby taking too long. Come.*

Clara put fingers to both temples. Her father had taken two horses to the blacksmith to be shoed. Rhoda had taken the buggy with a third into Springs before picking up the children from school on her way home. The fourth had a troublesome fetlock, and Hiram had told the family not to use it under any circumstance.

He could not have foreseen this circumstance, Clara thought. But she could not risk causing the horse to go permanently lame.

Please, God.

It would take at least ninety minutes to travel on foot to the Hostetler farm. If she ran most of the way, she might shave time, but running in thick shoes and long layered skirts under a woolen cloak would not make for good speed.

What choice did she have? Clara pulled the front door closed behind her, gripped her skirts to raise the hem, and established a stride at the maximum length her legs would permit. Anxiety fueled speed, and for the first mile she forced breaths.

In.

Out.

In.

Out.

Faster. Deeper.

Dread dredged her depths, burning her stomach and lungs.

Martha's last baby had been so long ago, and she had looked so unwell the last few weeks.

And the dream, with Martha grief stricken while a baby's cry faded away.

And Martha's sister had died birthing a baby at a much younger age. The absence of Clara's mother from her life stabbed her afresh. She had been too little to know what was happening to Catherine Kuhn, too little to know that the life flashed out of her mother's body, too little to know she missed her chance to say good-bye.

But Clara was not little now. She knew the danger Martha faced. Bending over and putting her hands on her knees, she paused to properly empty and refill her lungs several times.

Please, God. Please. Show me Your way in this.

Terrified that she was racing to say good-bye to her aunt, her mother's only sister, Clara resumed her trot for another half mile.

An automobile engine roared behind her, and the driver sounded the horn. Annoyed, Clara moved even farther to the side of the road. The horn sounded again.

"Clara!"

She stopped running again and spun around. "Andrew!"

He pulled up beside her, grinning. "Feel like a ride?"

"Maryland," she said, gasping. "Will you take me to my aunt's?"

His face sobered. "What's wrong?"

"I don't have time to explain. I know what Mose said, but I have to be there *now*. Will you take me?"

"Get in." Andrew leaned over to open the passenger side.

CHAPTER 38

The hours crawled into darkness.

In a narrow wooden chair with her knees pushed up against the side of the bed, Fannie held her mother's hand and folded her spine over her lap to press her forehead into the mattress. This was as close as Fannie had come to prayer in months.

"I'm so sorry, *Mamm*," Fannie murmured. "So sorry. So ashamed. Will you ever be able to forgive me?"

"Love," Martha said between labored breaths. "Love bears all things."

Martha's face transformed as another contraction sliced through her. Her grip crushed Fannie's fingers. Fannie looked up at the midwife, who spread her hands on Martha's belly and nodded.

"It's better?" Fannie asked.

"The child is in position."

Fannie let out a long, slow breath.

Atlee Hostetler came into the room, ashen. "It's never been this way before."

"Every birth is different," the midwife said.

"Why would God ask her to go through this?"

Fannie vacated her chair, making room for her father to sit beside his wife. He was never in the birthing room for the arrival of his other children. This time he shuffled in every hour or so when he seemed not to tolerate waiting in the front room, staying for a few minutes before withdrawing again. Even he felt the trepidation.

In the corner, next to the fireplace warming the room, Clara sat on a second narrow wooden chair. Fannie moved across the room and leaned against the wall beside Clara, whose face had no more color in it than Fannie's father's.

"I wasn't thinking," Fannie murmured. "I only knew I wanted you with me. I know how you feel about births. If you want to go—"

Clara shook her head. "You were right to send for me. I only wish I could do something to help. I hate how she is suffering."

"Even the midwife can think of nothing to do but wait," Fannie said.

"Then we shall wait," Clara said, "but I am praying with every breath."

They watched Atlee wipe Martha's face with a damp cloth, love still passing in their glances after more than a quarter of a century together.

"What if she doesn't survive?" Fannie's words rode a breath.

"We will pray that God brings her through her travail," Clara said.

But Clara sounded unconvinced. It was impossible that she was not thinking of her own mother's passing, Fannie realized.

"My father will not be able to manage a baby," Fannie said.

"Don't think of it!"

"I have to," Fannie whispered. "I'm her daughter. She would want me to take in the baby."

And in that moment, Fannie realized she would do so without hesitation. A helpless, motherless baby would suffer enough in the years ahead. She could give it a good start.

"At least. . .at least until he *could* manage," Fannie said. After all, the baby would not be hers. It was her sibling, not her offspring. Fannie would not try to replace the emptiness of her own womb with the fullness of her mother's. Her father would want to hold and rock his own child.

But Fannie would rouse to do whatever the child needed.

"Of course you would," Clara said. "And I would stay and do everything I could, just the way your mother did everything she could for me. But we must *pray*, Fannie. We must pray that this child will know your mother's love for many years."

Atlee kissed his wife's forehead and withdrew once again. Martha rested between contractions.

Fannie signaled the midwife, who joined the huddle in the corner.

"Tell me the truth," Fannie said.

"I don't know," the midwife said. "The labor is going into its second day, and your mother is very tired."

Fannie bore her gaze into the midwife's face. "Will she survive?"

Martha groaned.

Andrew had never met Atlee Hostetler before, but already he liked him. Nearing fifty, Atlee looked not like a sun-wrinkled, worn-out farmer, like many men Andrew knew, but like a bronzed, hard worker in robust health. The brown curls of his hair and beard showed no hint of going gray. This was Clara's *onkel*, the man who welcomed Clara into his home for weeks at a time during her childhood. Andrew studied Atlee's features, searching for some glimpse into the years before Clara Kuhn had flooded into Andrew's daily thoughts. This home, this farm, had always been a refuge for Clara. On another occasion, Atlee's eyes might have been a clearer window to Clara's history.

Atlee's face creased more deeply with each hour that Andrew observed him. Andrew had spent most of the evening on an amply stuffed davenport, while Atlee pulled a cushionless straight-back chair from the dining room—that could not have been comfortable beyond the first twenty minutes of his vigil—and positioned it in the corner of the front room nearest the bedroom. Atlee came and went from that chair, never seeking better comfort or a bit of nourishment. This was as close as Atlee could come to sharing Martha's suffering, Andrew supposed.

Atlee had sent his sons to bed hours ago. Andrew wondered whether any of them were sleeping. The oldest Hostetler son, Abe, had taken his little boy to an upstairs bedroom and stayed with him after extracting a promise from Lizzie to wake him the moment there was news. Lizzie floated between the kitchen and the front room with continuous pots of coffee and plates of food, first meats and cheese and later sweets. No one ate. Occasionally she went into the bedroom to minister to her mother-in-law in some small way.

Midnight came and went.

"Thirty-seven hours," Atlee murmured. "The others were not like this."

Andrew thought of the *meidung*. What if it were Mattie Schrock in travail and Caleb sitting stiffly in a chair? Or John Stutzman and his wife? If he was needed, Andrew would have come.

He stood up, crossed the room, picked up a dining room chair, and set it next to Atlee. He would not speak or make any pretense of understanding what Atlee felt, but he could sit beside him rather than in comfort across the room. Andrew listened to Atlee's breathing, shallow and jagged with nerves.

Lizzie came in from the kitchen with a fresh pot of coffee and filled the empty mug in Atlee's hands.

The scream that erupted from the bedroom jolted the three of them. Atlee sought a place to set down his jiggling mug, and Lizzie took it from him before he sloshed coffee all over himself.

Rapid footsteps closed the small distance between the bedroom and front room. When Clara appeared, the strain in her face lurched Andrew's heart rate up. At the same time, footsteps thudded down the stairs, and Abe appeared.

Lizzie set down the coffeepot. "I'm going back in."

Andrew stood, catching Clara's elbow. "What happened?"

"The midwife says the baby is coming soon now." Her breath came shallow and fast.

Was it still alive? Andrew left his question unspoken. He could only imagine its weight on Atlee, who stood to lose both wife and child.

Atlee rose abruptly. "I'm going to the barn. I have a cow that's been poorly."

They watched him go out the front door. Andrew looked from Clara to Abe, who seemed unperturbed at Atlee's withdrawal. Atlee had not left the house since Andrew and Clara arrived—and probably not for hours before that. A midnight visit to the barn confused Andrew.

"He's going to pray," Abe explained.

"He has claimed a sickly cow as long as I can remember," Clara said.

"Should someone be with him?" Andrew said.

Abe and Clara shook their heads.

"He is not alone. He will meet God in the barn," Abe said.

Andrew nodded. It would not be the first time God made Himself known among animals and hay.

"Am I weak for needing a break?" Clara said. "Martha has no relief."

"Lizzie went in," Abe said. "And Fannie is still there. My *mamm* will never be alone in this."

A wail came from upstairs.

"Is Thomas all right?" Clara asked.

"Probably just dreaming. I'll go back to him." Abe padded out of the room and up the stairs.

Fannie stumbled into the room, and Clara stepped over to embrace her.

"She's hardly talking." A sob disrupted Fannie's effort to speak. "She's exhausted. I don't know what to do."

The cousins clutched each other. No *meidung* could break the bond Andrew witnessed.

Fannie drew in an enormous breath. "I must go back."

"I'll be right there," Clara said. "Whatever happens, love surrounds *Aunti* Martha."

Fannie withdrew to the bedroom. Clara turned to Andrew.

"Are you all right?" he asked.

Clara blanched. "I can't help thinking about so many other births."

"They bring great joy."

"Most of the time," Clara conceded. "I was too young to come when Fannie's brothers were born, but I remember the celebrations still going on by the time I visited to see the new babies."

"Is the midwife worried?"

"She's not sure if she's hearing the baby's heart rate too slow or Martha's heart rate too fast."

Anguish passed through her face. Andrew gave no voice to the looming question. Shouldn't there be two heartbeats?

"Rhoda's first three babies came far too soon. No one would let me see them, but I know they were far enough along to look like babies."

"Don't dwell on that now," Andrew said.

"It's hard not to."

"This is not the same. This baby is ready to be born."

"When this is over," Clara said, "I have to tell you about Rhoda."

"And I'll be here to listen."

Clara could not bear the thought of watching Martha suffer. Neither could she wait outside the bedroom. A scream directed her choice. She jumped away from Andrew and pushed open the door to her aunt's anguish.

The midwife was on alert. Lizzie and Fannie were on either side of Martha, supporting her back for the final push.

"Here's the head," the midwife said. "Now the shoulders. Yes, here we go. One more big push."

Four women held a collective breath while the fifth bore down.

"A girl!" the midwife said.

Where was the cry? Clara was present when Sadie was born, and her cry filled the room immediately. Josiah, Hannah, Mari—she'd heard all their cries from down the hall. It was taking too long.

The midwife tied the cord and cut it in a well-practiced motion. "A blanket," she said.

Lizzie lurched into action, unfolding soft cotton.

"She's not breathing!" Martha reached out a hand.

The midwife turned the infant upside down. The tiny girl protested immediately. In five seconds Lizzie had her in a blanket.

"Let Clara hold her," Martha said, falling back against the pillows. "She is Catherine."

"Catherine!" Clara laid one arm across the other to cradle the child. The tiny one looked like an *English* doll, perfectly formed with long dark lashes sweeping against her cheeks. Tears filled Clara's eyes at the baby's perfection—and safe arrival. She raised a glimmering glance to her aunt. "I'm so glad you're both safe."

"After your mother died, Atlee and I always said we would name our next daughter for her." Martha laughed. "Then we produced a string of boys."

"You should hold her." Clara watched her aunt's beaming, exhausted face.

"Let me see her face," Martha said. "Then go show Atlee all is well."

Clara glanced at the midwife, who nodded as she awaited the afterbirth. All was indeed well. Seeking the fine line between holding the babe securely but gently, Clara inched up the side of the bed and turned little Catherine for her mother's inspection.

"If you ask me, she even looks like your mother." Martha cupped her new daughter's head. "That chin favors yours."

Clara smiled, uncertain that it was possible to detect a resemblance in a baby less than five minutes old. Nevertheless, it pleased her that Martha wanted this baby to look like her sister. Martha's damp hair was plastered against her skull, and perspiration stuck her nightgown to her skin. She hadn't slept in more than forty-eight hours.

And Clara had never seen her aunt look more satisfied, more grateful, more simply and radiantly lovely.

"Go," Martha said. "I want Atlee to see for himself, but I want to be cleaned up before he comes in here again."

"Should we clean up the baby first?" Clara asked.

"There's time for that later. Show Atlee."

Lizzie opened the door, and Clara walked through it with the baby.

Abe was there with Andrew, and Atlee had returned from his prayer session in the barn.

Clara choked on the effort to speak. "A girl! And Martha is fine!"

The men gathered around to admire the newest Hostetler. Atlee put a broad hand under his daughter's back, but his gaze went to the bedroom door.

"She really is fine," Clara whispered. "She'll be ready for you soon."

Release sailed out of Atlee's lungs. "So this is our Catherine, at long last." He bent and gently kissed his daughter's face.

Clara blinked against the tears as her uncle began to drift toward the bedroom, whether or not his wife was ready. Andrew put an arm around Clara's shoulder, and they leaned their heads together to marvel at the new life. Clara decided Martha was right after all. The baby's chin was like hers.

Andrew stroked Catherine's cheek. "She looks perfectly at home in your arms."

Clara was perfectly at home holding her, with Andrew's nearness stirring up a memory that was yet to be, when they would bend toward each other like this over their own child.

And they would have a child. She knew this now.

Fannie, Lizzie, and the midwife emerged from the bedroom.

"*Mamm* is already asleep," Fannie said. "*Daed* won't want to leave her now."

"We should take the baby back in," Clara said.

"There will be plenty of time for that," the midwife said. "Right now Martha needs to rest."

Lizzie moved across the room. "I'll make sure there's warm water in the kitchen to clean the new *boppli*."

The midwife trailed after Lizzie. "The room must be warm before we unwrap her."

They disappeared into the kitchen.

"Here, Fannie," Clara said. "Hold your little sister."

Fannie shook her head. "I think I'll find an empty bed and rest for a while myself so I can be some help later."

Clara watched her cousin climb the stairs. Fannie had rallied for the birth. But this babe in arms, exquisitely beautiful, was no remedy for her melancholy.

CHAPTER 39

Morning was not far off. Exhaustion settled over the house for a few hours after the midwife left, but farm rhythms did not pause for the birth of a baby.

Though Fannie had slept in the bedroom of her girlhood, when she woke a scant four hours after pulling a quilt up to her neck, she was disoriented by the silence. Elam and Sadie were the morning noisemakers at her house. Fannie threw off the quilt and went down to the kitchen. With one hand Fannie pulled her shawl more snug, and with the other she shoved wood into the belly of the stove. This was not her farm, but Fannie knew well its demands.

Her father's footsteps in the hall betrayed his effort to be quiet. Fannie raised her eyebrows and closed the stove's door.

"They're sleeping," Atlee said. "Both of them at the same time."

Fannie gave a small smile. "All's well."

"Your *mamm* thought you might come back in during the night."

Fannie fixed her gaze on the bowl of eggs on the table, four different shades of shells. "I thought I could be more useful if I rested."

The rational part of Fannie's brain justified the truth that her sister's birth had irritated a festering wound, and Fannie had run from the sight of innocent Catherine.

"The cows don't stop for a baby," Atlee said, pulling his jacket off a hook and fastening it closed.

"The boys can milk," Fannie said, glad for the change of subject. "I'll get them up."

Atlee shook his head. "I'll want to do it."

He would be praying again, Fannie knew. This time prayers of gratitude, prayers for the future. If only she could borrow his unspoken words.

Satisfied that the fire in the stove was catching and would soon both warm the room and provide heat for breakfast, Fannie padded through the house. In the front room, Clara and Andrew startled her. Fannie's own withdrawal after the birth had been so swift that she did not consider that someone should offer them beds. Even Lizzie and Abe, whose farm was nearby, had stayed through the night. Andrew and Clara would not leave before daylight. Their heads tilted toward each other, shoulders meeting, each of them asleep under a quilt from the cedar chest under the window.

Clara would have known where to find more bedding, Fannie thought. Her cousin had chosen this closeness with Andrew. Envy stirred. Everything lay ahead of them. They had not yet decided to marry, but Fannie knew Clara well enough to be sure she would not rest so easily against a man she did not love. Though Fannie and Elam had not yet observed their seventh anniversary, their unmarried optimism was a far-off land already.

Careful not to wake them, Fannie slowly opened her parents' bedroom door and slipped in.

Her father had stoked the fire before he left for the barn. It snapped and crackled behind the grate, throwing heat and orange light into the corners of the room. Her mother was in a fresh nightdress and slumbered in fresh bedding with the baby on her chest. Atlee had tucked pillows on both sides of his wife, propping up the sleeping arms holding the baby.

Just in case, he would have said. He was a cautious man. A thoughtful man. A generous man.

Fannie used to think of Elam that way.

Little Catherine's mouth started to twitch. Was she hungry? Dreaming? Stretching against the tight bundling? Tiny sounds dribbled out of her mouth, not quite cries, not quite coos. If the household had been bustling at its usual volume, Fannie would not even have heard them.

Clara had tried to hand Catherine to her a few hours ago, and Fannie could not make her arms receive the child. Now she sucked in a series of small breaths.

This was her sister.

When she thought her mother might not survive, Fannie was willing to take this child home with her. In the face of fear, her heart was wide open. Why had it closed in the face of joy? She had not even touched Catherine's tiny hand.

Fannie wondered if her father was praying for her along with his new little daughter.

Pressing her lips together, Fannie moved toward the bed and lifted the baby from Martha's chest. She stepped toward the fire and opened the quilt to see her sister. The soft white cotton dress she wore was new. Martha had long ago given away the tiny clothing her other babies wore. Unbundled, Catherine began to kick her feet and thrash her arms. Her eyes opened, and though she seemed to look at her big sister, Fannie wondered what a baby really saw.

Sadie had been like this once. New and wondrous and vulnerable and delicate and tiny. Fannie had soaked up every sensation then, and if she had known she would not have another child, she would have pondered even more deeply in her heart.

Catherine yawned, her lips hardly bigger than a doll's, making the most perfect oval Fannie had ever seen. Fannie held her diminutive hand, stilling its aimless movement through the air and kissing the row of tender fingertips. Then she tucked the quilt back around the baby.

"Thank You," she whispered. A prayer. The first in a long time.

Fannie might never have another child, and she might never know what had closed her womb after Sadie's easy arrival.

Elam might never regain his ambition for the farm in the absence of sons or a larger family to provide for.

Fannie might—*would*—have aching moments when she did not understand why Catherine had come into the world and not her own child.

But Catherine had come. She was here in Fannie's arms, two sisters a generation apart while their mother slept.

If Fannie's only prayer was *Thank You*, it would be enough.

Martha stirred, her empty arms floundering briefly before her eyes found their focus.

"My girls," she said.

As tears filled Martha's eyes, they also spilled from Fannie's.

Clara's neck was oddly stiff, and a sharp pain shot into her shoulder and made her suck in air. She had begun her sleep with her head against the back of the davenport. When she felt Andrew's shoulder under her cheek later, she was too groggy to change positions. Now her head had slipped down to his chest. The heartbeat she heard was his.

Not too fast. Not too slow. Thumping steady and strong.

This was the first time Clara had heard Andrew's heartbeat, but it would not be the last. Andrew's heartbeat on one side of her and his arm wrapped around the other was where she wanted to live.

Cautiously, she straightened her neck to relieve the pressure of the awkward position.

Andrew murmured. "Is it morning?"

Clara glanced out the window. "Almost. The sun is just coming up."

"I love morning light," he said. "His mercies are new every morning."

Clara leaned away from him and took his hand. "Let's go see it. We've never seen the sunrise together."

Above them, Clara heard her cousins beginning to move around. Abe and Lizzie and Thomas had stayed the night, but they would need to get home to their own farm and waiting cows. Her youngest cousin was in his last year of school, and in his mother's eyes even the birth of his sister would be no excuse to be late. The other two knew a full day's labor awaited them. Clara wanted this moment with Andrew, just the two of them watching the mystery of spreading orange and pink hues give way to full light.

Outside, they leaned against a post on the porch, shoulder to shoulder.

"Thank you for bringing me," Clara said, unsure whether she had expressed her gratitude for his complicity in this unscheduled trip across the border.

"It was God's will," Andrew said. "Why else would I have been on the road to your farm at just the moment you needed a ride?"

Clara smiled, suspecting that he'd had other motives than purely putting himself at the disposal of God's will. Hadn't he said something about sneaking onto the farm to take her for a ride?

"I won't ever forget this night. Martha worked so hard! Fannie thought we would lose her, and the midwife didn't offer much reassurance. But Martha held on, and Catherine is safe."

"Many prayers answered," Andrew said.

"And Martha would do it again. I could see it in her face. Whatever it took, it was worth it. I always thought of joy as something to feel. Now I know it is something to hold."

Andrew angled himself toward Clara. "Would it be worth it to you?" She met his eyes.

"I would be right there," he said. "Whatever it took, and whatever happened, we would face it together."

"I know," Clara said. "I know."

"The wedding season has only just started."

She nodded.

"We can have our banns read."

Clara nodded again, this time more dramatically. She wanted him to ask the question—again—so she could reward his patience with the answer he'd waited so long to hear.

"I can talk to Mose," he said. "Of course I should speak to your father first."

She breathed in through her nose and waited.

"Rhoda will come around, won't she?" Andrew said. "She'll help you get ready for the wedding, surely. It's what she wants, isn't it?"

Clara locked her eyes on his.

"It won't be perfect," he said. "We won't always understand God's will, especially in days of pain. But whatever it is, we will hold the joy together."

She moistened her lips and nodded.

"Clara Kuhn, are you saying that you're ready to marry me?"

"If you would ask a proper question," she said, "I would give a proper answer."

He smiled. "Clara Kuhn, will you become Clara Raber and let me love you for the rest of our lives?"

"Nothing would make me happier."

Clara leaned into his kiss, her lips tangling with his in a delicious moment that Andrew seemed keen to prolong. Clara offered no objection as she wrapped her arms around his waist and his hands took her face in his.

Atlee cleared his throat, and they jumped apart—but not very far.

"Somehow," Atlee said, "I suspect our Catherine's safe arrival will not be the only good news we celebrate today."

Clara laughed. How long had Atlee been standing there?

The sky shimmered with morning hope. Atlee went into the house, and Andrew and Clara remained on the porch to stare into future glory.

Inside a few minutes later, Clara went straight to the kitchen.

Sausage sizzled in an iron skillet, and Fannie was cracking eggs three at a time into a bowl. The smell of biscuits in the oven made Clara suddenly ravenous.

"The baby is suckling," Fannie said. "They don't all latch on so well, but Catherine seems to know just what to do."

Fannie's tone surprised Clara, along with her industrious efforts to put breakfast on the table. Clara opened a cupboard and took out plates.

"We'll need ten plates," Fannie said. "I've sent one of the boys to fetch Elam and Sadie."

The contents of three more eggshells plopped into the bowl. Fannie turned around and dropped butter into a second skillet heating on the stove, the largest one Martha had. Clara peered into the bowl and saw at least twenty yolks.

"The *kaffi* should be ready," Fannie said.

Clara's hands moved to the shelf that held coffee cups.

Fannie whisked the eggs together and glanced at the melting butter. "If you're willing to check the cellar, *Mamm* probably has some apples."

"I'll go right now," Clara said.

She stood at the back door and watched Fannie's cooking frenzy. Had hope settled on her cousin as well? Or was she merely forcing herself to do what a daughter ought to do? Clara watched Fannie's face for a few seconds. When she heard humming from Fannie's throat—a hymn of some sort but more joyous than the *Ausbund* hymns—Clara dared to believe that light had at last cleaved the darkness.

Andrew only vaguely recognized the boy who turned up at his farm the next morning. His black trousers and suspenders over a white shirt, and the child-sized black felt hat, left no doubt that he belonged to the Pennsylvania Old Order district.

A Yoder, Andrew was fairly certain, but there were so many branches of the Yoder family tree. Andrew himself hung from one of them because of his mother's maternal grandmother, but he never thought of himself as a Yoder. Whatever his last name was, this boy might not be any more closely related to Joseph and Noah Yoder than Andrew was.

He was just a boy, nine or ten years old. What were they doing sending him to summon Andrew?

"Thank you for bringing the message." Andrew took two apples from the bushel on his front porch. "Maybe your horse would like this—and one for you."

The boy hesitated but took the apples. "They said I was to make sure you come immediately."

Indignation swirled. Where did they find the gall to suggest that one boy on a sagging sorrel could demand Andrew—or anyone—comply?

"You've done a fine job delivering the message." Andrew wished he could call the boy by name. "I suppose you're already late for school."

The boy polished his apple on his shirtsleeve. "My *mamm* teaches me at home."

That narrowed the possibilities considerably, since nearly all the Amish children attended the same Crossroads School Andrew had gone to. Still, Andrew would not be hurried.

"I have some things to tend to," Andrew said, "but I'll make sure they know you faithfully carried out their instruction."

The boy looked conflicted about what he was supposed to do, but Andrew stepped back into the house and closed the door between them. When he looked out the front window a few minutes later, the boy and his horse were gone. Andrew poured himself another cup of coffee and set out the clean shirt he would don later in the day to go speak to Hiram Kuhn. Then he picked up the list, begun the day before, of all the repairs he would make around the house before bringing Clara home to live there. Out in the barn, he made sure all the stalls had fresh hay. He walked along one side of the pasture to make sure none of the fence posts jiggled.

The delays did nothing to temper his ire. He muttered prayers for self-control and resisted the urge to take the Model T for spite. Over the last few weeks he had cleared a shed of tools and equipment no one had used since Andrew was a boy. He was nearly ready to bring the automobile home to his own property.

And he would, no matter what the Yoder brothers had to say about it.

He exhaled exasperation. He had Clara to think about.

Andrew arrived at the Yoder farm at his own readiness. It should not have surprised him that this was Yonnie's doing.

"We have a witness," Joseph Yoder said, "who has taken seriously his obligation to speak to us about his brothers and sisters who choose their own convenience over the good of the congregation."

Andrew could think of no one else, other than the Yoders themselves, who fit this description. He had not noticed anyone on the road when he picked up Clara, but her distressed state had made everything fade away.

"A witness of what?" he said as he stood in Joseph's study before a thick German Bible open on the desk.

"You have made two transgressions," Joseph said. "You visited Marylanders with whom you have no family relationship, so there can be no doubt that this violates the *meidung*. Second, you drove an *English* automobile in the process."

"If you will excuse me," Andrew said, "I have a farm to run."

"I am sure you can take a few minutes from your busy day to repent," Noah said. "Our Lord is faithful and just to forgive us our sins."

"Please sit down," Joseph said. "Let us pray for you, that you might have a clean heart once again."

"I will not repent when I have not sinned."

"If we say we have no sin," Joseph said, "we deceive ourselves. We read this in 1 John."

"I didn't say I have *no* sin," Andrew said. "I only believe the actions you named are not sinful." He might have to repent if he lost his temper, but he would not repent for taking Clara to Maryland.

"Please." Noah gestured to a chair. "Come, let us reason together."

Andrew wondered if they intended to quote the entire Bible to him one verse at a time. He sat down, calculating whether they would dismiss him without a statement of repentance if in fact they could have a reasonable discussion.

"Yes," he said, "let us reason together. I will be happy to explain to you my conviction."

"You must repent," Noah said.

Andrew regretted sitting down. "And if I don't?"

"Then we will have no choice but to put you under the ban."

"The Marylanders will welcome me with open hearts."

Clara's face flashed across his mind. Would she agree to move to a new congregation and leave her family behind? And the wedding—she might not be agreeable to marrying outside their own district.

I am betrothed. Clara was aware of the silly grin on her face, but driving the Kuhn buggy alone on the road to Andrew's farm, she did not care. In a few weeks, Andrew's home would be her home. The shine of the events on the Hostetler farm had not worn off, and Clara prayed they never would. When she told Hiram the baby's name, his lips had parted and spread.

"My Catherine would have been embarrassed," he said, "but another Catherine to remind us of her. . ."

His voice trailed off, and emotion flushed through him. All these years later, with another wife and three more children, her father shared with her aunt the memory of the woman they loved.

Clara saved the news of her betrothal. Andrew had made her promise to wait until he spoke to Hiram, and Clara had made him promise not to wait very long. At home she let everyone think her light mood rose only from the baby's arrival.

Andrew was not on his farm. Thinking he might be at the Johnson place, Clara pulled the rig back out on the main road and found herself blocked by a sorrel who seemed to be resisting the reins.

"I'm sorry," the young rider said. "I only came back to make sure Mr. Raber went."

"Went where?" Clara asked, waiting for the boy to get control of the horse.

"Joseph Yoder's," he said. "They sent me this morning to find him. I don't want to be in trouble if he didn't actually go."

"I need to get by you, please," Clara said.

She zigzagged through the back roads to Mose Beachy's farm. He was a reasonable man, a kind man. And he was the bishop.

She raced onto his property. He could be anywhere on the farm, but Lucy would know where to send Clara. With the firmest knock of her life, Clara rapped on the front door.

Rather than Lucy, though, Mose answered the door.

"They have Andrew." Clara spat out the words.

The pleasant greeting in Mose's face soured. "Where?"

"At Joseph's."

Mose reached for his hat on a hook beside the door. "Lucy, I'm going out."

Clara lengthened her stride to keep up with Mose, who aimed for her buggy rather than take time to hitch up his own.

"I'll drive," he said, taking up the reins. "You tell me what this is about."

As they jostled along the road, Clara stumbled through an explanation.

The pressing message about Martha's labor.

No buggy to take from the Kuhn farm.

Andrew turning up on the road just then.

The automobile.

The urgency.

The fright.

"It's the only thing I can think of," she said, catching her breath. "It's either because he has the Model T or because he used it to drive me to Maryland."

"Andrew and I will have to talk further about the Model T," Mose said, "but I could not have made myself more clear with Joseph and

Noah about having these confrontations about the *meidung* without speaking to me first."

As they traveled, Clara wished for the speed of Andrew's automobile. They would be at the Yoders' by now if they were in the Model T.

Finally, Mose turned into the farm's lane and they scrambled toward the house, where Joseph's wife did not dare deny the bishop entrance.

Joseph's study was dark and foreboding. Clara's heart battered against her ribs.

"I speak German, Pennsylvania Dutch, and English," Mose said with impressive calm. "If you will tell me your preference, I will make sure that I am communicating clearly."

Joseph glared. "Our brother is in need of repentance, and as ministers it is our calling to guide him to it."

"He has done nothing to repent of!" Clara cried.

The Yoders remained infuriatingly calm.

"He visited a Marylander family to whom he is not related, and he drove an *English* automobile to get there," Noah said.

"I was with him," Clara said. "Were you planning to send for me next?"

"You went to see your family," Noah said. "And while you rode in the automobile, you did not drive it and neither do you own it. You have done nothing wrong."

"But we were together the whole time. What he did, I did. What I did, he did. We made the choices together. He took me because I asked him to."

"Clara," Andrew said quietly.

"You did not sin, but Andrew did," Joseph pronounced.

It made no sense to Clara. She turned to Mose.

Mose repositioned a chair and indicated that Clara should sit in it. Trembling, she obeyed. Only an hour ago she had left home with a brimming heart and the expectation of a joyous day. She wanted Andrew to kiss her while they planned for him to visit the Kuhn farm that afternoon. When they spoke to Mose—together—it would be about publishing their banns, not about whether either of them harbored sin for which they ought to repent.

"Are you prepared to dismiss Andrew from this conversation?" Mose said, still standing.

"He has not yet repented," Noah pointed out. "We would like to pray for him and await the Holy Ghost's conviction."

Clara watched Andrew's face. Though stiff, his expression told little of what might already have transpired. How long had he been there? What had they threatened him with? His eyes met hers, and he shook his head slightly.

Clara sprang to her feet. "Are you trying to chase us to the Maryland district? Is that what you want? To be rid of us?"

"Clara." Mose and Andrew spoke at the same time.

She ignored them and scowled at the brothers. "Don't tell me this is for the good of the congregation. Accusations and threats are no way to hold the church together."

Noah gave a sharp clap. "Contain your impudence!"

Mose gestured to Andrew. "Please take Clara outside and wait for me there."

"Our meeting has not concluded," Joseph said.

"Andrew, please," Mose said.

Andrew took Clara's elbow, and together they let themselves out of the Yoder home. Clara squinted into the sunlight as she pushed out a series of short breaths. Silent, they waited a few minutes beside Clara's buggy. Andrew had brought only a horse. He glanced at the house every few seconds, as if willing the door to open and Mose to emerge.

"This was Yonnie," Andrew said. "I have to talk to him."

Clara laid a hand on his arm. "Not while you're angry."

He laid one hand on her cheek. "I will not speak in anger. I will do my best to speak the truth in love."

"Mose asked us to wait for him," Clara said.

"He's taking too long," Andrew said. "I'll explain to him later. Will you be all right getting your buggy home?"

"Mose rode with me," Clara said. "I have no choice but to wait for him."

Andrew leaned in and kissed her. "Come find me later, at the Johnson place. I'll tell you everything."

He swung himself astride his horse and galloped off the farmstead.

Behind Clara, Mose's voice boomed. "Andrew!"

Andrew paused long enough to look over his shoulder. But he did not turn around.

CHAPTER 41

If there were repercussions for defying Mose's request to wait outside the Yoder home, Andrew would face them later. Clara would understand, and Mose might scowl but he would listen—which was more than Andrew could say for the Yoders. He rode straight to the dairy, confident that if Yonnie had done the morning rounds he would be back by now.

"I let him go a week ago," Dale said when Andrew politely asked for a few minutes of Yonnie's time.

"Let him go?" Andrew echoed.

"We came to a parting of ways." Dale riffled papers on his desk. "And if you know him half as well as I think you do, you know why."

"Where is he working now?"

"I haven't heard that he is." Dale stood up. "If I run into him, I'll let him know you were looking for him."

Andrew nodded at Dale's empty assurance. The dairy owner was not likely to run into his former employee.

So where was Yonnie?

Andrew mounted his horse and puffed his cheeks.

Riding out to Yonnie's family farm carried the risk that he had not told his parents or siblings of his loss of employment. Andrew knew Yonnie not half as well as Dale suspected but twice as well. And Yonnie would get up and leave the farm on his normal schedule rather than concern his parents before he was ready with an announcement that would put them at ease.

Andrew let his horse enjoy a restful pace, riding with his hands crossed over the horn of the saddle while he tried to think as Yonnie would think. Once, when they were eleven, Yonnie let himself get talked into a prank with some boys that got them all suspended from school for three days. Andrew doubted Yonnie's parents knew to this day. Yonnie left the house in the morning with his brothers and sisters and stepped out of the group just before students entered the Crossroads School. In the afternoon he caught up with his siblings along the path home. Years later Yonnie admitted to Andrew that he spent those three days hiding in an abandoned outbuilding, afraid to be seen during school hours.

An abandoned outbuilding.

At the next turn, Andrew swung the horse down a less traveled road and coaxed a canter from the animal. He approached the old Johnson place with a mixture of gratitude that he'd thought of it and trepidation for what Yonnie might be doing there.

Andrew eased off the horse and left the faithful servant tied loosely to the low branch of a tree on the outer ring of the clearing around the structure, the ground now covered with the brown, wintry decay of unmowed summer weeds that would no doubt be back with a vengeance next year. He scanned the surroundings. The decrepit barn's door was closed as snugly as it ever was—which was hardly secure—but Andrew drew no conclusions from this. He scanned the clearing systematically before staring into the surrounding woods.

Seeing nothing, he called out. "Yonnie?"

Andrew was uncertain whether the roll of shadow revealed movement within the barn or a shift in sunlight through the trees. He moved closer and pushed the door open enough to slip inside, waiting for his eyes to adjust to the dim interior.

"Yonnie?"

This time Andrew heard the shuffle and turned his head toward the sound.

In the far corner, with the Model T between them, Yonnie hunched against a wall.

Alarm shot through Andrew. Yonnie held a two-foot length of cast-off pipe.

"What are you doing here, Yonnie?" Andrew moved slowly around the automobile, hesitant to cause Yonnie to move suddenly.

"It's out of the elements, at least," Yonnie said.

"You won't make things better by smashing the car." Andrew was fairly certain now he would be able to intercept Yonnie's efforts.

Yonnie laughed. "Is that what you think I'm here for?"

Andrew said nothing as he moved closer.

Yonnie raised the pipe.

"Don't, Yonnie," Andrew said.

"I'm not going to wreck the car." Yonnie tossed the pipe to one side, where it clattered against a wall. "You can sell the car and give the money to the poor."

Making no promise, Andrew stood in front of Yonnie now, examining the circles under his eyes. He touched the torn shoulder of Yonnie's coat. "What happened here?"

"An altercation with a tree." Yonnie brushed off Andrew's touch.

"An accident?"

"Of course it was an accident. Who runs into a tree on purpose?" Yonnie met Andrew's gaze. "Have you come from Joseph and Noah?"

Andrew planted his feet, prepared to prevent Yonnie from rushing past him and out the door until they had it out.

"Yonnie, why?" Andrew said softly. All through their boyhood he had shrugged off Yonnie's quirks, rarely losing his temper and usually finding amusement. Now he had Clara to think of, and he had promised not to speak in anger.

For a long moment, Yonnie looked over Andrew's shoulder at the opposite wall. "Because it was the right thing to do."

"Was it? Where do you find such unabated certainty?"

"In the teachings of the church. In the faith of our fathers."

"What about *our* faith?" Andrew said. "What about *your* faith?"

"Don't ask ridiculous questions." Yonnie's spine slackened, and he slid down the wall of the barn.

"Yonnie." Andrew reached out to touch his shoulder.

Sitting on the ground, Yonnie pulled his knees up, rested his arms on them, and hung his head.

Andrew had not meant to hold his breath, and now his lungs ached for relief.

"Are you going to marry Clara?" Yonnie mumbled.

"Yes. She has finally agreed to have me."

"I hope you'll be very happy."

"Thank you. I think we will be." Squatting in front of Yonnie, Andrew narrowed his eyes at the odd shift in conversation.

"You're not any older than I am," Yonnie said, "and you have a farm."

"With a mortgage," Andrew reminded Yonnie. His parents had left him to take over the farm, but it was not free and clear. He had also assumed the debt.

"All the same," Yonnie said, "you have something to offer a woman. Something to make her care for you."

Andrew twisted to sit beside Yonnie, their backs against the wall. "I'd like to think I have other qualities at least equally as appealing."

"I have nothing," Yonnie said. "No farm, not enough money to persuade the bank I'm a worthy risk, no one to drive home with after the Singings. No job."

Andrew grimaced. "I stopped by the dairy."

"Then you know," Yonnie said. "The buggy I drive belongs to my father, along with everything else. I have a horse of my own that can barely keep up with a three-year-old child, and a few untillable acres on the edge of my father's farm. That's it."

Even if Andrew had not promised Clara to hold his temper with Yonnie, the urge to unleash it passed. Over the years, Andrew had seen Yonnie obstinate, gullible, fearful, and eager to please anyone he thought of as holding authority. Despondence had never colored Yonnie's features as it did now.

"It won't always be that way," Andrew said.

"What I have is the church," Yonnie said. "I have the promises that come with obedience. I can't let go of them."

"No one is asking you to," Andrew said, "only perhaps to be less. . . insistent on the forms obedience takes."

"The church must stay together." Yonnie hit the ground with the flat of his hand. "If we don't have that, we've lost everything."

Andrew ran his tongue over his teeth, resisting the urge to pursue a theological debate.

"You know," he said, "I'm alone on my farm. I could use another hand I could count on. Even over the winter there's a lot to do when it's just me."

"You've always managed."

"You should see the list of things I never get around to."

"Maybe if you spent less time with the Model T," Yonnie said.

Andrew swallowed his response. "I understand if you don't want to work for me."

"I didn't say that."

Andrew crossed his legs out in front of him. "I know you disapprove of the car, but I was putting it to good use when I took Clara to Maryland. She had a very good reason for getting there in a hurry, and I was glad to be able to help her." He still had not sorted out when Yonnie could have seen them and supposed he would never be sure.

"We have rules for a reason," Yonnie said.

Andrew counted to ten beneath his breath.

"I shouldn't have said that." Yonnie tilted his head back against the wall. "I'm envious. I'm angry. I'm lacking in love."

"Love casts out fear," Andrew said. "Love thinks the best. Love never fails."

"Let us keep our eyes on love." Yonnie sang softly from the old *Ausbund* hymn.

Andrew nodded.

The barn door opened, flooding the space with daylight. Clara stepped in.

"Oh," she said, when she spotted Yonnie. Her eyes took in the scene.

"It's all right. We're all right." Andrew stood up. "Yonnie's going to work for me for a while."

Clara's eyes widened and bulged.

"At least I hope he is." Andrew offered a hand and pulled Yonnie to his feet.

Yonnie glanced at Clara, sheepish. "I understand you've finally decided to throw your lot in with my old friend."

The sound that Clara emitted was not quite a word.

Andrew stepped toward her. "Someone had to be the first to know. Why not my boyhood friend?"

He kissed her mouth. Later she could hear the whole story.

Nine days later, Clara sat in church, still stunned that the old friendship between Andrew and Yonnie had resurfaced. They sat beside each other in the first row of single men right behind the married men.

It bothered her that Yonnie was the one who knew their secret.

The skirmish with Noah and Joseph Yoder persuaded them to wait before speaking to Clara's father or Mose. Neither of them wanted news of their engagement tangled in speculation about their future in the church. They had told each other this and agreed to wait.

Whatever Yonnie's attitude was now—and Clara was not sure she knew—the damage was done. Joseph and Noah had called Andrew to task, and with Mose's dissenting opinion, the ministers disagreed on what action the Bible required them to take. Neither Andrew nor Clara wanted their engagement lost in the swirl of the dark clouds. Andrew had waited two years for her to accept his proposal. They would wait a few more days or weeks.

Clara adjusted her shoulders, which had started to ache, and moved her eyes forward. Mose stood beside the preaching table, giving the main sermon.

"'And let the peace of God rule in your hearts,'" Mose read, "'o the which also ye are called in one body; and be ye thankful. Let the word of Christ dwell in you richly in all wisdom; teaching and admonishing one another in psalms and hymns and spiritual songs, singing with grace in your hearts to the Lord.'"

Mose looked up here, catching eyes around the room before he continued.

"'And whatsoever ye do in word or deed, do all in the name of the Lord Jesus, giving thanks to God and the Father by him.'"

Mose put one finger on the page open on the table.

"This is what the apostle Paul wrote to the believers in Colossae, and his words are of equal guidance to us." He paced a couple of steps away from the preaching table and scanned the assembly. "I do not make light of the differences of opinion among us, even as we are called to be one body. I urge peace and unity above all else, just as Paul did two thousand years ago. On the matters which confound us—and I do not believe I must list them now—I seek the wisdom of bishops in other districts. I seek the word of Christ, that I might share it with you richly. Your part is to grant me patience and continue to live in love one toward the other. Then we will know the peace of God together."

Clara hoped Mose would agree to marry her and Andrew. These were the sort of humble words she wanted to attune her heart to on the day she committed to love Andrew for the rest of their lives.

Mose did not close the door on change. Neither did he swing it wide open. He would be a wise leader. Clara would be glad to see her children grow up under his teaching.

Her children. What an odd sensation it was to permit herself to think those words without fright.

CHAPTER 42

The bride in her new blue dress paled against the charm Andrew saw in Clara's face. Clara wore the same color, starched and unsoiled, with a sparkling white apron. Andrew wondered if she would stitch another new blue dress for their wedding or choose purple or a darker blue. On the last Thursday in November, Peter Troyer and his attendants sat in three chairs facing Ruth Kaufman and her attendants at the front of the church. Directly across from Clara, Andrew watched her eyes, turning over in his mind the question of how quickly Clara would want to marry.

Soon, he hoped.

They could marry here, in the Flag Run Meetinghouse, where her parents had wed.

Andrew heard little of the sermons, but there would always be another sermon. In a white *kapp*, Clara's head tilted slightly toward Mose Beachy as he preached, but her eyes seemed to look beyond him as if boring through the meetinghouse wall. Was she also thinking about their wedding?

When the wedding party began to shift position, Andrew realized Mose had made the statement that would transition the worship service into the wedding ceremony.

"If anyone here has objection, he now has opportunity to make it manifest." Mose paused and looked at the wedding couple. "I hear no objection. If you are still minded the same, you may now come forth in the name of the Lord."

The bride and groom held hands and stood before Mose. With earnest voices, they promised love and loyalty for the rest of their lives.

Andrew's gaze moved back to Clara, who now caught his eye.

Clara's lips turned up. Anyone else would think she smiled in gladness, hearing her friend pledge her future. Andrew knew that smile was meant for him.

"I don't want to wait," she told him as soon as the wedding was over. "Talk to my father."

"Today?" Andrew said. "Now?"

"He'll give us his blessing."

"You're sure?" Andrew glanced at Hiram Kuhn.

"Aren't you?" Clara said. "What are we waiting for?"

Andrew nodded. This was their congregation. They belonged here. Speculation had nothing to do with when or where they married.

"I want the Hostetlers to come," Clara said. "I can't imagine getting married without Fannie."

"We'll ask Mose."

❧❦❧

Mose Beachy said I can have whomever I want to stand up for me.

Fannie read Clara's orderly handwriting on the crisp pale blue paper a week later.

And I want you. Please say you'll do it.

Fannie's eyes filled. Of course she would do it. After all, Clara had been her attendant when she married Elam. Fannie did not imagine an Old Order wedding was much different than a Conservative Amish Mennonite wedding.

We've decided not to wait any longer than we have to for the sake of planning and sewing the dresses. The banns will be read on Sunday, and we'll marry two days after Christmas. My daed *and Rhoda seem relieved but pleased. Daed gave his blessing almost before Andrew finished asking for it. I'm sure they will come to see how dear Andrew is. Hannah is the most excited, as I'm sure Sadie will be when you tell her.*

A tear dropped on the page just as Elam came in the back door.

He paced to the stove and peered into the coffeepot.

"The *kaffi* should still be warm." Fannie wiped her eyes with the back of one hand.

Elam gestured at the letter in her hand. "Bad news?"

Fannie shook her head and smiled. "Just the opposite. Clara and Andrew have made their plans. She wants me for an attendant."

"Then you must do it," Elam said.

Fannie felt him watching her and looked up to meet his eyes. "Do you remember, Elam?"

"Remember what?"

"When we decided to marry? When we told our families? When everything was ahead of us like a ripe, abundant harvest? When God's will was a blessing so full that we could hardly stand it?"

Elam broke the gaze and poured the last of the coffee into a cup, the slosh of the liquid the only sound in the room.

"I remember," he finally said.

"We dreamed of so much," she said.

Their arms and hearts and minds were entwined in those days. Seven years later they orbited each other on elongated paths that spun each other out for long distances before drawing near again. In those days Elam would have caught her hand in the kitchen before reaching for the coffeepot. Now, wordless, he clinked a spoon in the sugar bowl. In the void between them, Fannie heard the granules slide off the spoon and drop into the lukewarm liquid.

"Elam," she whispered.

He hesitated but met her eyes again.

"Will we always be this lost?"

He stirred his coffee.

Elam was a good man, just as good as the day Fannie married him. He might yet get past his disappointment that God's will collided with his own dreams, just as Fannie might yet find relief from the ache that plagued her.

He put his spoon in the sink. "No. God willing, no."

Hope flickered in her chest. Fannie moved toward Elam and laid a hand on his arm. He did not pull away. His hand grazed hers on the way back to his coffee cup.

Sadie was spinning slow circles as she came in from the dining room.

"Have you told her?" Elam asked Fannie.

"Told me what?" Sadie steadied herself on a chair.

Fannie could see Sadie's eyes took a few seconds to come into focus. In fine weather Fannie sent Sadie outside for her determined dance with dizziness, but in early December the weather was unpredictable.

"I got a letter from Clara," Fannie said. "She's getting married."

Sadie's eyes widened. "To that man who came when baby Catherine was born?"

"That's right. Andrew."

Sadie drew in a long, excited breath. "I liked him!"

Fannie laughed. "Clara will be glad to hear that."

"Are we going to the wedding?"

"Yes."

"All of us?"

Fannie glanced at Elam.

"Yes," he said, "all of us."

"Did Clara send me a new story?"

"Not this time," Fannie said.

"I want to write her a letter," Sadie said. "I want to tell her that I'm very happy she's going to marry Andrew, but I still want her to send me stories."

"I think it would make Andrew very happy if she did."

"Good. Are we going to go see *Grossmuder* for supper?"

"My goodness, you're full of questions today." Fannie slid Clara's letter back into its envelope.

"Well, are we?"

"We'd better," Fannie said, "because I promised to bring the biscuits and the green beans."

"I want to help make biscuits!" Sadie slid a chair across the linoleum to her favorite helping spot at the counter. "Can I give baby Catherine one of my dolls?"

"If you'd like to," Fannie said, "but she'll have to be a little older to play with it."

"I'll teach her to play."

Her daughter's wide-open heart was fresh every day. It pained Fannie to think how much of it she had missed in the months of her melancholy.

In the late afternoon they packed up the biscuits and the green beans and Sadie's favorite doll, and the three of them rode in the buggy to the Hostetler farm.

Sitting in the same rocker where she had held all her babies, Martha put a finger to her lips when they entered the house.

"Is she asleep?" Fannie whispered.

Martha nodded.

The bundle in Martha's arms seemed already to have doubled in size since the night of her frightening birth. Every time Fannie saw her tiny sister, the change in appearance astounded her. With a look warning Sadie not to wake the baby, Fannie scooped Catherine out of her mother's arms and inhaled the intoxicating new baby scent. These days Fannie's hips easily found the automatic sway that had soothed Sadie a lifetime ago. She planted a delicate kiss on Catherine's forehead.

Martha stood up and smoothed her apron. When she paused to stand beside Fannie and admire the sleeping infant, Fannie turned her head and kissed her mother's cheek as well.

How rich she was in love.

❧❦❧

"Fannie is coming?" Rhoda blinked at Clara.

"I can't imagine getting married without her." Clara stacked her plate on top of Rhoda's and took them both to the sink. Hannah and Josiah were in school, and Mari was napping. Her father was gone all day with a couple of other farmers, already beginning to plan for spring. It had been only Rhoda and Clara for a simple quiet lunch. With only a few weeks until the wedding, nearly every conversation Clara had found its way to wedding details. Without acknowledgment or explanation, Rhoda had warmed to Clara once again.

"What about Wanda," Rhoda countered, "or Sarah? You have many friends who would love to be an attendant at your wedding."

"I asked Sarah," Clara said. "But Fannie—if I had to, I would change the date in order for her to be there. Bishop Beachy has given his approval."

Rhoda looked away, picking up a napkin to fold. "I would hate for there to be any awkwardness on your wedding day."

"Why should there be?" Clara said, though she wanted to say, *How could anything be more awkward than these last few months?*

Rhoda went to a drawer and pulled out a sheet of paper. "I've got a list. Maybe it will help you."

Clara took the paper, which had two columns. On the left was a list of tasks—the *Forgeher* to usher, waiters, *roasht* cooks, potato cooks, tablecloths, *hostlers* to care for the horses. On the right, names matched up with every effort required for a traditional Amish wedding.

"Many people will want to help," Rhoda said.

"You don't think they're worn out from all the other weddings this season?"

Rhoda put a hand against Clara's cheek, a gesture reminiscent of the first time she ever touched her new stepdaughter. "This is *your* wedding. Of course people will want to give you a lovely day. *I* want to give you a lovely day."

Under Rhoda's touch, Clara twitched, stifling a tremble before it roared up and ripped her open. In Rhoda's face, Clara saw the wide-set blue eyes and high cheekbones of her little sisters.

"I've only ever wanted what is best for you," Rhoda said. "*Alli mudder muss sariye fer ihre famiyle.*"

Every mother has to take care of her family.

When Rhoda removed her touch, relief and regret warred in Clara.

"You were a good mother to me when I was young," Clara said.

"Did you think I stopped being a good mother?" Rhoda ran her hands down the front of her apron.

Clara let out her breath slowly as fragments of the last few months tumbled against each other in her mind. The times Rhoda politely said, "No thank you" or "Don't bother." The times Rhoda redirected her children away from their older sister. The rows of celery growing in the garden as if Rhoda were pushing Clara toward marriage whether or not she was ready. Weeks and weeks of feeling shunned in the home that had been hers before it was Rhoda's.

"I know you've found me hard," Rhoda said, "but it was for your own good."

These were the sort of words Yonnie would say, or the Yoder ministers. Shunning is for the person's good, to draw that person back to the church. But Clara had never left the church or her family.

Clara looked at the list in her hand. "Thank you for this. They are good suggestions."

"Your father and I are pleased with your choice of Andrew Raber."

Pleased or relieved? Clara wondered. If Rhoda thought Clara should marry and run her own household, did it matter who the groom was?

"We have much to do," Rhoda said.

Clara swallowed. Whatever Rhoda's motivations, she wanted to help and Clara needed help. Her wedding was just three weeks away.

"Hannah and Mari are very excited." Rhoda dampened a rag and wiped off the table.

"Sadie is, too." The words slipped past Clara's usual censors.

Rhoda turned to wring out the rag and hang it over the edge of the sink.

Clara pushed forward. "Hannah and Sadie have always wanted to meet each other. A day of celebration is the perfect time."

"Yes." Rhoda lifted the towel draped over a bowl of rising bread dough that had grown into a great white bubble.

"It will be all right," Clara said. "They're little girls with normal curiosity. Why should we teach them to fear or judge each other?"

"You're right," Rhoda said. "A wedding is a new beginning."

Clara's eyes sought Rhoda's, and they looked into each other. Clara saw uncertainty behind Rhoda's smile, but it was a sincere uncertainty. Rhoda's outward ways may have befuddled Clara—even wounded her—but the heart that had embraced a motherless child still lay within. Grief and gladness mingled in the smile Clara gave in return as she prayed for grace in this moment.

"I have something more than a list and celery," Rhoda said. "Come with me."

Clara followed Rhoda into her bedroom, where she opened the cedar chest at the foot of the bed and lifted a package wrapped in brown paper and tied in string.

"What is it?" Clara's curiosity was genuine. It looked like a bundle from the mercantile in Springs.

"Open it."

Clara laid the thick square package on the bed and pulled away the string. When she folded back the paper, a vibrant, piercing, rich purple burst out.

Clara gasped and plunged a hand into the folds. Smooth and soft, the fabric was perfectly dyed. The cotton may have come from the mercantile, but the color had not.

"You dyed this for me?" Clara said.

Rhoda nodded. "You always said you wanted to wear purple at your wedding."

"I still do."

"There's enough for three dresses."

"Mine and Fannie's and Sarah's."

"Actually," Rhoda said, "if we cut carefully, I think we can get two more dresses—smaller ones."

Clara looked up. "Sadie and Hannah."

"They won't be attendants, of course, but they'll think it's great fun to match your dress."

Clara drew in breath drenched in grace.

CHAPTER 43

Just because it was tradition did not mean Clara was obligated to be pleased.

She could have stayed home, in a room warmed by fire, while the rest of her family went to church. Instead she had chosen to ride with them to the Summit Mills Meetinghouse, where instead of going inside the building she transferred to Andrew's buggy—which would soon be her buggy as well—and wrapped herself in quilts to sit on the bench and stare at the meetinghouse.

From her chilly post in the line of look-alike buggies, Clara heard the hymns, slow and somber. The stolid, unchanging tempo was a reminder that although Clara felt in a hurry, no one in the meetinghouse would rush. The sermons and prayers were long stretches when no sound from the church service reached her ears. Instead, Clara listened to doves cooing and squirrels rustling through leafless trees and *English* automobile engines chugging past on the road beyond the clearing.

Clara supposed she would have to stop thinking of automobiles as belonging to the *English* if she was going to marry a man who owned one.

And that, after all, was the reason she was sitting outside rather than on the women's side of the congregation sneaking glances at Andrew across the aisle.

Today, at the end of the service, Mose would publish the news of their engagement. Tradition dictated that the bride-to-be not be present when this happened. The date would be announced for December 28, and Hiram would invite the congregation to attend the wedding.

A hymn started. *This should be the final hymn,* Clara reasoned, and then the various announcements would begin. She sat up straight and let a quilt fall away.

The door the men used to go in and out of the meetinghouse opened, and Andrew stepped out. Clara dropped out of the buggy.

"They're still singing," she said when Andrew reached her. "You'll miss the banns."

He took her hand and pulled. "You have to come inside."

"But the banns—"

"That's not the only announcement Mose is going to make. I think you'll want to hear with your own ears."

They paced back toward the meetinghouse. Clara had sat outside all this time—nearly three hours—only to be present for her own engagement announcement after all.

"What's going on?" she said.

"I wish you had heard Mose's sermon," Andrew said. "When he said he had one further announcement to make at the close of the service, I knew you would want to be inside for it."

They reached the doors. Andrew kissed her cheek and left her at the women's door. When Clara saw him slip back into the service, she did the same. She found a corner in the back, though. Behind the last row, Wanda Eicher swayed with a child on her hip. Otherwise all eyes were fixed on Mose Beachy as he stood to speak again.

"I have the pleasure," he said, "of publishing the engagement of Clara Kuhn and Andrew Raber. The couple requests that we remember them in prayer, so we will want to do so."

Mose gestured to Hiram, who stood. "Rhoda and I invite the congregation to attend our daughter's wedding on December 28 at the Flag Run Meetinghouse."

Standing in the back, Clara saw heads tilt toward nearby worshippers and heard indistinguishable whispers buzzing like gossiping bees. It happened after every engagement was published. Some claimed to have suspected, while others were surprised at the particular pairing. Smiles broke out at the happy news.

Although Clara had whispered this way many times, it was an odd sensation to watch the reaction to her own engagement. Most brides did not have this view. Wanda caught her eye and smiled. Later, Clara knew, Wanda would pry details out of Clara—when had they decided to marry; why had they waited until the end of the season; had she known she would accept Andrew's proposal? Clara had heard countless versions of these questions over the years as she watched her friends marry. Now it would be her turn to answer them.

Mose Beachy cleared his throat, and the congregation settled.

"You have heard me preach this morning that the heart of God is love," he said, one hand on the closed Bible that sat on the preaching table. "My hope is that our congregation will continue to live in the heart of God and know His love for us and in turn offer God's love to those around us.

"After searching the Scriptures for a greater understanding of certain matters, and after consulting with the wisdom of bishops who lead other congregations, my decision is that we will no longer observe *meidung* toward our brothers and sisters who leave us to worship in another church."

The congregation sucked in a collective breath.

"I have confidence that this is the will of God for us," Mose continued. "On other matters, we will continue to discern God's will. When we discuss matters of modern convenience, we will seek to understand the blessings God may have in mind for us as well as the need to protect our community from falling into idolatry. Some of you also raise the question of a Sunday school for our children. We will continue to discuss whether it is appropriate for our young ones to learn the Word of God in this way. Whether or not we choose to organize a Sunday school, we will no longer consider our Marylander brethren as having transgressed because they have chosen this path.

"I will meet with gladness the opportunity to speak to any of you privately on these matters. For now, let us share our meal and our hearts with one another in true Christian fellowship."

Clara's gaze moved to Noah and Joseph Yoder, seated in front facing the congregation and scowling. Had they known Mose intended to make this announcement? Had they tried to dissuade him?

It did not matter. Mose had spoken, and his words rolled weight off shoulders up and down the benches. If the physical reactions Clara saw were any indication, most people welcomed both his removal of the *meidung* and his invitation to conversation.

Clara wished she had heard Mose's sermon. *The heart of God is love.*

The men began to file out. Clara slipped out the women's door and stood in the clearing to wait for Andrew. His automobile, her stories—in

God's time there might yet be a place for them in their own church.

Andrew came and stood beside Clara, taking her hand in his while they received congratulations. She was glad to be marrying Andrew on the brink of a new season in the church. She was grateful to begin their life together by responding to a call to the heart of God. She squeezed Andrew's hand.

EPILOGUE

June 26, 1927

The crash that came from the upstairs bedroom made Clara blow out her breath and roll her eyes.

"Would you like me to go up?" Andrew raised both eyebrows.

"No," Clara said. "You'd better see how Little Mose is doing with the horse. I'm still not convinced he's strong enough to handle the hitch on his own."

"We have to let him try." Andrew took his black felt hat from the hook beside the back door and put it on his head. "One of these days he'll do it."

"He's only seven, Andrew. Were you hitching up the family buggy when you were seven?"

"I could let him try his hand at cranking the Model T instead." Andrew's eyes twinkled.

Clara smiled. The Model T had provided a steady flow of fond memories over the years, and Andrew had proven himself a worthy mechanic in keeping it running as it aged. He even worked a few hours each week for Jurgen Hansen, whose garage had nearly doubled in business since Andrew first approached him for help.

"I don't think he's strong enough for that, either," Clara said. "Besides, we agreed long ago not to use the automobile for driving to church."

He kissed her cheek as another crash echoed through the house. "What could those girls be doing up there?"

"Oh, let's see," Clara mused. "Katie is sprawled on the bed without having brushed her hair because she's reading one of those *English* storybooks you brought home."

"You're the one who taught her to recognize a good story by keeping a scrapbook."

Clara ignored him. "And Rachel and Rebecca are quarreling over whose turn it is to stand on the stool to clean their teeth."

"Rachel will be pointing out that she's nearly a year older and Rebecca should respect her elders."

"And Rebecca will answer that Rachel takes too long on purpose and selfishness is a sin."

"So they've knocked each other off the stool twice already."

"And Katie will claim she did nothing about it because she didn't hear anything." Andrew put a hand at the back of Clara's neck and leaned down to kiss her lips this time, letting his hat tumble to the floor.

He tasted of breakfast scrapple and blueberry jam, as he did every Sunday morning, and she welcomed the lingering kiss. Ten and a half years and four children later, she would not trade away a single day of their marriage. Now if only she could master getting four children ready for church on time.

She pulled back. "Let's not get distracted."

"It's not too late to change your mind about taking the Model T," Andrew said.

Clara slapped his shoulder. "Go make sure your only son hasn't injured himself." She had three sets of braids to tie and pin. Hopefully she would find a clean *kapp* for each of the girls. At the third crash, Clara pushed Andrew out the back door with the thought that he had the easier job. Perhaps it would be worth her while to teach him to braid. After all, her father had learned when he had no wife in the house.

Clara scurried up the back stairs of the rambling house. Despite her light step, the girls heard her coming and scrambled around to position themselves as beyond fault. Three-quarters of the way up the stairwell, Clara slowed to give her daughters time to put things right. She had no desire to catch them in the act of their transgressions. Daily life offered ample opportunity for that. Today she simply wanted to get them out the door looking suitably assembled. By the time she turned the corner into the upstairs hall, Katie was brushing her blond hair and Rachel and Rebecca were demonstrating admirable cooperation. Clara picked up a brush and began running it through the nearest head of brown hair.

With the practice of tending to the girls' hair every day, she could very nearly braid with one hand now, the fingers of the other ready with pins.

Twenty minutes later, the Raber family was in the same buggy Andrew had used to drive her home from Singings or to meet her out under the night sky at the edge of her father's farm. They were about to outgrow this buggy, though Andrew did not know that yet. Clara would tell him soon about the new babe, but not in the midst of daily chaos. She would find an evening when the children were in bed and invite Andrew to stand in the yard and admire the handiwork of God the way they used to.

They rumbled out of the farmstead and turned south toward the Flag Run Meetinghouse in Niverton, a destination that brought some relief to Clara. On the Sundays when the congregation met in Summit Mills, the Rabers were challenged to get out of the house early enough to accomplish the additional distance in a timely way. Flag Run was comfortably close. No matter which meetinghouse the congregation used, lately Little Mose had been nagging to be allowed to sit with his father on the men's side of the aisle. Soon Clara would have to let him, though it pained her to think that her little boy was old enough for this.

A buggy rattled toward them, heading north.

"Who's that?" Clara said.

Beside her, Katie leaned forward in serious examination. "Yoders," she pronounced.

"Be kind," Clara said.

"All I said was that it was Yoders," Katie said. "I recognize the horse from school."

Behind his parents, Little Mose scrambled for a look, waving his hand fiercely. The other buggy passed them without greeting.

"They didn't wave back!" Little Mose said. "That's rude, isn't it, *Mamm?*"

Clara turned her head to look down the road. It did seem inhospitable, but a larger question loomed. "Where do you think they're going?" she murmured to Andrew.

He shrugged. "Bishop Beachy's announcement two weeks ago was more than clear. He wanted to be sure we are sufficiently accommodating the families who live south of Flag Run."

"What if they weren't there?" Clara said.

"They were," Katie said. "Ezra Yoder threw a lima bean at the back of my head during lunch. I remember."

Clara glanced at her daughter, who was four months past nine. While Katie liked to hear stories and was learning to read for herself, she had never been one to make them up. If she said Ezra Yoder's family had been in church, Clara believed her.

"I'm hungry," Rebecca said.

Though the child had eaten breakfast, Clara was prepared and handed her youngest a piece of strudel. It was better to permit a snack on the way to church than endure the mood that would ensue during the three-hour service if Rebecca grew hungry before the midday meal.

"There's another wagon." Little Mose leaned over Clara's shoulder and pointed. Enthused, he began waving again.

This time Andrew lifted his hand in greeting as well and even slowed the horse. "We'll find out what's going on."

But the rhythm of the oncoming buggy did not falter.

"The Troyers," Clara murmured.

"Yoders and Troyers," Andrew said, glancing at her. "The Troyers live just on the other side of Niverton. They would have driven right past the meetinghouse."

"Why aren't they coming to church?" Katie asked.

"We don't know," Andrew said, "and we will not speculate."

"What does *speculate* mean?" Little Mose asked.

"It means guessing when we don't know the answer," Andrew said. "And we're not going to do it. That's how rumors get started."

When the Raber buggy approached the Flag Run Meetinghouse, Clara scanned the buggies and horses. Andrew parked, and they assisted the children out of the buggy.

"Those two families are not the only ones missing," Clara said softly to Andrew.

Hannah and Mari waved at Clara from across the clearing and made their way toward her. Tall and sure of herself, Hannah was past sixteen now—closer to seventeen. She had been going to Singings for a year. Josiah attended as well. If the next ten years passed as quickly as the last ten, Clara would be as reluctant to admit that her own daughter had become a young woman as she was to recognize this truth about her sister.

At thirteen, Mari's interest was simply to collect her nieces and nephew before turning back toward the meetinghouse. Hannah lingered.

"You probably heard," Hannah said.

"Heard what?" Clara reached into the buggy for the loaves of bread she had baked for the meal later.

Hannah gestured toward the diminished row of buggies. "Where everyone is."

"We heard nothing," Andrew said.

"They're at Summit Mills," Hannah said. "The Yoder ministers are meeting there."

"But Mose Beachy announced Flag Run," Clara said.

"I know. But one of the Yoders came by two days ago and told *Daed* they would be at Summit Mills and he should join them."

Clara's breath drew in quickly. "What did *Daed* say?"

"That they misread him," Hannah said. "He would having nothing to do with disrespecting Bishop Beachy."

"Of course he wouldn't," Clara said.

Andrew unhitched the horse and gave it freedom to nuzzle the ground and swish its tail for the next few hours. Clara caught his eye.

"We'll talk to him," Andrew said.

Hannah fell into step with Clara.

"Does everyone know about the other church service?" Clara said.

"They only talked to *Daed* because they thought he might come with them." Hannah tilted her head to one side. "You should have heard him telling them how the time was long overdue to make things right. I didn't understand what he meant."

"It's a long story," Clara said.

"I guess the Old Order and the Beachy Amish won't be together anymore," Hannah said.

"Beachy Amish?" Andrew cocked his head.

"We'll have to call ourselves something, won't we?"

Clara looked into her sister's face, wondering when she had grown so perceptive.

"I'd better go find my *mamm*," Hannah said. "Are you going to sit with us today?"

Clara nodded. "If you can stand to have my wiggly little ones take turns in your lap."

"I'll save you a place." Hannah slipped into the building.

Clara turned to Andrew before he would leave to take his place among the men lining up.

"This is not what you and I wanted," she said. "We hoped for change, but not this. Not two churches. Mose has always preached unity and peace. Now the Yoders are leading a split?"

Andrew breathed in long and slow through his nose. "They will say *Gottes wille*."

"Is it?" Clara challenged. "Is it God's will for the congregation to divide after so many have worked to keep it together?"

"God's ways are not our ways," Andrew said. "God is our peace. Mose will want us to affirm that above all else. It takes a century for God to make a sturdy oak."

He squeezed her hand and left her then.

Clara turned in a slow circle that allowed her to take in the entire clearing where the meetinghouse had stood for decades. The fallen log she had loved to climb on when she was as young as her children were now had long ago rotted at the center and been cleared away. Two others had been felled in its place and hosted her children's play on Sunday afternoons. Rather than going inside, Clara now paced to the log and sat.

Beachy Amish. Mose was certain to dislike the appellation, wanting neither credit nor blame for the division that seemed inevitable.

Clara placed a hand over her thickening womb.

Perhaps this child would know a church of unity.

Perhaps this child would know the church received her gifts, whatever they were.

Perhaps this child would know peace.

Clara prayed it would be so.

Author's Note

This Amish Turns of Time series brings to life turning points in Amish history. For this story, my research turned up interesting tidbits, such as writings and Bible interpretation that undergirded the position represented by the Yoder ministers, as well as information about Moses Beachy's cautious leadership toward change that seemed inevitable.

I have taken some liberties with the time frame. While the prologue, set in 1895, and the epilogue, set in 1927, rise from historical events that mark turning points in the prolonged controversy at the heart of the story, I condensed Moses Beachy's leadership. My hope was to faithfully represent his heart for peace and unity in the congregation, while showing the arc of his leadership within a few months rather than the eleven years between his becoming bishop and announcing the end of shunning those who left to join another church. I also took some license with the circumstances of age and illness that led to Bishop Yoder's resignation.

Most of my characters are fictitious, though some are based on true people. John Stutzman is based on a man named John Yoder, who in the early 1920s refused to shun. By this time, Mose Beachy was being less cautious, and his statement that he would not put John Yoder under the ban caused increased friction with his fellow ministers, Joseph and Noah Yoder. Within months, the Yoder brothers did what Beachy had resisted doing for years and led a break-off group. Since he never intended to lead a split, Beachy was not fond of having the branch bear his name. Within two years, the Beachy Amish allowed automobiles, electricity, and telephones, decisions that distinguished them from the Old Order Amish who, even nearly a century later, remain far more selective in adopting modern technology.

The Old Order and the Beachy Amish continued to share the meetinghouses in Flag Run and Summit Mills on alternate Sundays until 1953, when the Beachy Amish constructed a more modern building.

BRIGHTEST *and* BEST

CHARACTERS

Ella Hilty
Jed Hilty—Ella's father
Rachel Hilty—Jed's wife, Ella's stepmother
David Kaufman—Rachel's son from her first marriage,
    Ella's stepbrother
Seth Kaufman—Rachel's son from her first marriage,
    Ella's stepbrother

Gideon Wittmer
Betsy (Lehman) Wittmer—Gideon's wife, who died five
    years ago
Tobias Wittmer—Gideon's son
Savilla Wittmer—Gideon's daughter
Gertrude "Gertie" Wittmer—Gideon's daughter

Lindy Lehman—sister of Betsy Lehman, best friend
    of Rachel Hilty

James and Miriam Lehman—uncle and aunt of Betsy
    and Lindy

Margaret Simpson—first-grade teacher at Seabury
Consolidated Grade School
Gray Truesdale—Margaret Simpson's beau
Braden Truesdale—Gray's brother
Percival T. Eggar, Esquire, Attorney at Law
Ulysses R. Brownley—superintendent of Seabury schools
Deputy Fremont—deputy sheriff
Mr. Tarkington—principal of Seabury Consolidated
    Grade School

Amish Families:
Isaiah Borntrager Family
Cristof Byler Family
Bishop Leroy Garber Family
Joshua Glick Family
John and Joanna Hershberger Family
Aaron and Alma King Family
Chester Mast Family

CHAPTER 1

Geauga County, Ohio, 1918

Don't take another step!"

Ella froze. Her eyes flashed between the red rug on the floor in front of her and Nora Coates at the blackboard.

The schoolteacher's calico skirt swished softly as she came around the desk.

Ella relaxed her muscles but did not move her feet. "What's the matter?"

"You haven't been here in a long time, have you?" Nora stood six feet in front of Ella.

Ella Hilty was twenty-six, at least three years older than Nora. She left school after the eighth grade, half a lifetime ago, and had only occasional reason to be inside the one-room schoolhouse since then.

"The children all know how soft the floor is right there," Nora said. "The red rug reminds them, and they walk around the other way."

"Soft?" Ella echoed.

Nora grimaced. "*Rotted* is a more precise word."

Ella wasn't sure whether she felt the spongy floor yield beneath her weight or only imagined it.

"Nellie Watson put her foot through it a few months ago," Nora said. "I never heard such shrieking from a child of school age."

"I will step carefully if you would kindly advise me," Ella said.

"Take a long step to your left and you should be on solid ground again."

Ella turned her gaze to an open space under a window and

lifted her skirt just enough to accommodate the movement. Safely out of the danger zone, she squatted and lifted one corner of the red rug. Beneath it, the dank wood floor had caved in, splintered edges ringing the spot where Nellie Watson's foot must have sunk through.

"It's been wet from underneath," Ella said.

Nora nodded. "Three winters ago, during my first year teaching, Mr. King patched it, but it didn't hold."

Ella straightened the rug and stood. She understood now why Nora had asked for representatives of the parents committee to inspect the schoolhouse in the middle of July. There was time for repairs before the children returned to school in September.

"Did you attend school here?" Nora asked.

Ella nodded. She had lived in Geauga County, Ohio, all her life.

"The blackboard was new when I started," Ella said. Twenty years ago the new chalk had flashed white under the teacher's firm, quick strokes against the board. Ella had never seen anything like it. But she was six, had seen little of anything beyond the Amish farms, and only learned to speak English after she started school.

"The blackboard is still serviceable," Nora said, "but I wish one of the men would be sure it is properly secured. Sometimes the children lean on the chalk ledge when I ask them to come to the board to show their work. The creaks I hear are unnerving."

Gertie would do that. Gideon's daughter was newly six and due to begin school in a few weeks.

"I loved school." Ella moved cautiously toward the front of the room. She examined the strained wooden slats of the chalk ledge.

"Did you ever think of staying in school?" Nora's eyes brightened with curiosity.

Ella shook her head. Her parents never kept her from her books. She borrowed whatever she wanted to read from the small library in town. Besides, her eighth-grade year was also the year of her mother's death, and Ella took on housekeeping for her father. The youngest of eight children, she was the only one unmarried and living at home.

That was twelve years ago, and Ella was still the only sibling unmarried and living at home. Now, though, there was Rachel. Jed Hilty had a new wife.

Gertie Wittmer jumped unassisted out of her father's wagon. Gideon's impulse was to reach out and catch her, but she wouldn't want him to. She never did. Of his three children, the youngest was the most independent. Tobias was obedient, Savilla was sensible, and Gertie was independent. Perhaps this was because Gertie didn't remember what it was like to have a mother and the others did.

Gertie's small form hit the ground in a solid leap, and she grinned at him before running toward the schoolhouse. Perhaps he ought to warn Miss Coates to exercise extra firmness in helping Gertie adjust to the decorum of a classroom.

"Ella's here!" Gertie disappeared into the building.

His daughter's exuberance at the prospect of seeing Ella pleased Gideon. His own exceeded Gertie's, and for a moment he envied her freedom to express herself unconstrained. For obvious reasons, Ella was not part of the parents committee, which consisted of two Amish fathers and two *English* fathers. Both groups of children shared the schoolhouse, as they had for decades. Gideon had asked Ella to come, believing that a woman might see flaws in the schoolhouse that men would not.

Gideon looped the reins over a low branch of a flowering dogwood tree and followed his daughter into the school.

In the doorway, he held his pose. It was a long time after Betsy's death, when Gertie was a baby, before he saw Ella's loveliness. With an arm around his daughter, Ella raised her dark eyes toward Gideon, testing the softness at his core. Surely it was God's will that they should be together. Why else would a woman like Ella not have married years ago?

"Oh good, you're here," Miss Coates said.

Gideon's head turned toward the rattle of wagons behind him, bringing Aaron King and the two *English* fathers. They had six weeks to ready the building. Aaron's eyes would see the small flaws that could be remedied easily, but Miss Coates had already impressed on Gideon that the building needed more than fresh paint and polished desks.

The three fathers thumped in, their boots seeming heavy against the floor.

Walter Hicks rapped his knuckles against a vertical beam. "My boy warned me that things might be worse than we thought."

"Theodore is an astute young man," Miss Coates said.

Gertie ran a finger down the chalkboard and studied the resulting smudge.

Gideon glanced around. "Since we're all here, Miss Coates, perhaps you can point out to us particular matters of concern."

The teacher pointed up, above Walter's head. "I keep an extra bucket under my desk because every time it rains, that spot leaks. It got a lot worse in the spring."

"I've got a few spare shingles," Aaron King said.

Gideon watched as Gertie ducked under the teacher's desk and rattled the metal bucket.

"Gertie," he said, and the girl emerged and moved to one of the two-seater desks in ragged rows. She looked small sitting there, and the thought that his youngest child was beginning school knotted him.

Ella pointed at the red rug. "Did you know there's a gaping hole in the floor?"

Gideon was not surprised about the roof, but he had not heard about the floor.

"The windows need sealing," Miss Coates said.

Gideon crossed to a window and ran a finger along its edges. "They need a lot more than sealing." Even his slight touch broke off bits of the crumbling frame. It was likely the other five windows were just as dilapidated.

"When the wind blows in the winter, the entire building creaks," Miss Coates said.

"All buildings settle and creak," Gideon said, glancing at Gertie, who mimicked his movements on another window beside Ella.

"It's not that kind of noise," the teacher retorted. "It's the sort that makes one think the ceiling might come down. The students become quite distracted."

"How did it get to be so bad?" Walter Hicks wanted to know.

Aaron King shrugged. "One day at a time."

Robert Haney, the second *English* father, spoke for the first time. "We get busy with the summer harvest and then planting and then the fall harvest."

"And then the children are back in school," Miss Coates said. "You're all busy with your farms, but I do feel that for the safety of the children, this is the time for a concerted effort."

Gideon tilted his head back to inspect the ceiling beams. "Perhaps we should ask the school district for funds to build a new structure entirely. If we had the supplies we need, I'm sure the Amish families would be happy to build."

"One of your frolics?" Walter said.

Gideon nodded. With proper planning, the Amish erected barns in only a couple of days. A one-room school should not be difficult to organize.

"I doubt the district would underwrite the construction," Robert said. "I see in the newspaper all the time how the schools lack proper funding. And the process of requesting funds and awaiting a decision would take longer than we have before school begins again."

"Perhaps we just need to impress upon the authorities the extent of the need," Ella said.

"I've been trying and trying," Miss Coates said. "It's as if the superintendent turns and walks the other way when he sees me coming."

"Gertie," Gideon said, "come stand with your *daed*."

Walter Hicks leaned against a beam, as if to test its strength. The cracking sound pulled Gideon's heart out of his chest.

⇜❖⇝

"Watch out!" Gideon's voice boomed.

Ella lurched toward Gertie and snatched her up.

"No!" Gertie writhed in protest.

Ella held tight.

"Gertie!" The edge in Gideon's voice startled his daughter into compliance.

Ella held the girl in a viselike grip and stumbled through a maze of desks toward the back of the schoolhouse. Above her, the ceiling split open.

"I see the sky!" Gertie said.

Ella squeezed tighter, wishing she had a third hand for raising the hem of her skirt so she could see her feet and move faster.

"Ella! Gertie!"

Ella turned toward Gideon's frantic voice, a tone she had never heard from him before. She stumbled where two desks narrowed the aisle and shoved at one of them with her hip.

"I've got her," Ella shouted. "Everybody get out!"

Nora moved quickly. Mr. Hicks and Mr. Haney hesitated but headed for the door. Ella had her eye on the opening. Behind her, the front wall of the classroom groaned. In reflex, Ella turned her head toward the sound. The blackboard snapped off the wall on one end, rent down the center, and dangled.

Ella gave the obstructive furniture one last shove as the structure heaved. A fracture traveled above her head. Half the ceiling crashed down, strewing debris. Ella did not see the origin of the board that smacked the back of her head.

CHAPTER 2

Gideon shouldered past Aaron King and back into the schoolhouse.

"Ella!"

"Here!"

Her voice led Gideon to the shelter Ella had found under a
desk, her arms still clasping his daughter.

"Has it stopped?" Anxiety threaded Ella's voice.

"For now." Gideon squatted and reached to take Gertie from
Ella. "Come quickly."

With his daughter over his shoulder, Gideon reached for Ella's
hand, not caring who might see the affection between them. Only
when they were safely out in the sunlight did he realize Gertie was
limp against his neck.

"Gertie!"

The child made no sound. Gideon knelt to lay her on the
ground and rubbed a hand over her face. "Gertie!"

"She was fine when I went under the desk." Ella knelt beside
Gideon.

Gertie's intake of air came before she opened her eyes. Gideon
exhaled his own breath.

"*Daed.*"

"I'm right here."

"I don't want to go to that school."

"Does anything hurt?" Gideon put a thumb under Gertie's chin
and looked into her eyes, satisfied that all he saw was shock.

"No. Ella wouldn't let go."

"She wanted to keep you safe." Gideon turned grateful eyes to Ella. "Thank you. I would never have reached her in time."

"As far as it is within my power, I would never let anything happen to Gertie," Ella said.

Gideon looked carefully at Ella now. She was noticeably more scraped up than Gertie. Bits of wood stuck to her bonnet, and gray dust spattered her blue dress. "What about you? Are you hurt?"

She put a hand to the back of her head. "Something took a whack at me. I may have a bit of a headache tonight."

"Promise me you'll rest."

She nodded, and Gideon allowed himself to meet and hold her gaze.

"I want to go home," Gertie said. "Carry me."

"Of course," Gideon said. "First show me that you can move your arms and legs."

Gertie responded by moving all four limbs at once. "Now can we go home?"

Gideon slid his arms under Gertie's shoulders and knees and unfolded his stocky form as if she weighed nothing more than the wind.

Miss Coates stepped toward them. "I'm sorry. Even I did not realize the true condition of the schoolhouse."

"You're not to blame," Gideon said.

"If I'd had any idea, I would never have suggested that we meet inside."

"This will certainly make our case with the school district. It's time for a new building."

"It's definitely the strongest argument we could hope for," Miss Coates said.

Walter Hicks fell into step beside Gideon. "I will draft a detailed account of today's event and deliver it personally to the school superintendent first thing in the morning."

"Thank you, Walter." Gideon glanced at Ella again, looking for reassurance that she was unscathed.

Gideon carried Gertie to his wagon with everyone else following as if no one wanted to be left behind. "Can you sit up?"

Gertie nodded. "I just want to go home."

Gideon settled her on the bench of the wagon. If she got tired, she could lay her head in his lap as they drove home.

"Shall I take you home?" he said to Ella.

Miss Coates spoke. "I have my cart. I'll take Ella. You just look after Gertie."

"Yes," Ella agreed. "Take her home. Watch her closely."

"You're sure?"

"I'm fine." She brushed debris off her dress and straightened her bonnet.

Gideon noticed Ella moved more slowly than normal.

"*Daed*," Gertie said, "please, can we go?"

"Go," Ella said.

❧❦❧

The other three men left shortly after Gideon, leaving Ella and Nora Coates standing and staring at the building with its roof yawning open to the elements on one side.

"What should we do?" Ella asked. "Is there anything we should take out to keep safe?"

"I feel badly enough that you were all in the building on my account," Nora said. "I can't ask you to go back in."

"You wanted the men to see for themselves."

"I was not expecting the encounter to be quite this dramatic." Nora wrapped her arms around herself.

"I hate to think what would have happened with thirty-five children inside and you responsible for their safety," Ella said. "That would have been an unreasonable expectation—unfair to ask of you."

"Yes. From that perspective, what happened today is the lesser of two evils."

"There can be no argument now that we need a new school. Surely the superintendent will release the funds under these circumstances— and quickly."

Nora looked away. "I rather suspect he will propose another solution."

"What other solution could there be?" Ella gestured toward the building. "Even if the roof could be repaired, there are so many other things wrong."

"I don't know," Nora murmured. "I can't help but feel that there is a reason he has resisted all my requests for help before this. I wouldn't have turned to the local committee if I thought the superintendent would help."

Ella examined Nora's profile, unable to push away the sense that Nora had something else to say.

"What is it?" Ella stepped into Nora's gaze.

"I wanted to leave the school in good condition."

"Leave the school?"

"I'm not certain of anything," Nora said, "but I may not be returning to teach this fall."

Ella was certain Nora had not mentioned this possibility to the parents committee. Gideon would have told her if he'd known the school would need a new teacher. He would be responsible to help select another young *English* woman willing to appreciate the Amish ways.

"I haven't yet signed my contract for the new school year," Nora said.

"Don't you intend to?" Conflicting possible answers to the question swirled through Ella's mind.

"I must decide by the end of July," Nora said. "That would still give the committee a few weeks to hire another teacher."

"I didn't realize you were unhappy in your position."

"Oh, I'm not!" Nora was quick to respond. Then she smiled. "I'm rather hoping for a marriage proposal very soon. My beau knows that if I sign a contract we wouldn't be able to marry until next summer."

Ella fumbled for words. "That's. . .good news. I hope you'll be very happy." How difficult would it be to find a new teacher in just a few weeks—someone willing to teach in the middle of farmland and accommodate both *English* and Amish students?

"He hasn't asked me yet." Nora's laugh sounded nervous.

"But you want him to."

Nora's lips stretched into a smile. "Yes. Very much. I'm quite smitten, I'm afraid."

Ella recognized the sensation. She was quite smitten herself.

"You should teach," Nora said.

"I'm not qualified," Ella answered easily, seeing nothing to dispute. "I didn't go to high school, much less the teachers college."

"We've only met a few times," Nora said, "but I see something in you. You're qualified in other ways."

"I assure you I'm not," Ella said. She kept house for her father for eleven years before he remarried, and she gladly looked forward to running Gideon's household. She knew nothing about teaching.

"You always have a book with you."

Ella sighed. She would have to explain to Mrs. White at the library about the book she'd left in the collapsed building.

"There must be a way to demonstrate your capacity," Nora said.

Ella said nothing. She also was hoping for a marriage proposal very soon. Embarking on a teaching career was the furthest thing from her mind.

"How are you feeling?" Nora asked.

"Well enough, under the circumstances." The headache Ella anticipated had not yet materialized. She felt only a sting at the back of her head.

"Are you well enough to ride into town with me before I take you home?"

"Oh, I don't know," Ella said. "Haven't we had enough excitement for one afternoon?" Riding into town would take them miles in the wrong direction.

"I want you to meet someone." Nora raised her eyebrows with hope.

"If this is about teaching—"

"Just meet someone. A new friend."

Ella hesitated.

"We'll have a nice chat along the way. And I'll bring you home whenever you like."

"Well, all right." Ella had no need to hurry home. Rachel looked after the house now. If she wished, Ella only needed to be present for the family's evening meal.

Nora led the way to where she'd left her horse and cart. They climbed in.

"My beau has a Ford," Nora said. "As soon as he proposes, I intend to learn to drive it."

The horse began a casual trot toward Seabury.

❧❧❧

Margaret Simpson admired the three pristine erasers and set them an equal distance apart on the chalk ledge at the front of her classroom. Her list of ways she hoped to prepare for this year's class was lengthy, but she would have to accomplish many of the tasks at home. In the middle of the summer, the principal of Seabury's consolidated grade school allowed teachers limited access to the building. Margaret looked at her watch, knowing that any moment now the principal would stand in the doorway to her classroom and clear his throat. He was a stickler for rules, including the schedule on which he would open and close the building over the summer.

Few of the other teachers bothered to come into the building in the months when classes did not meet. Some had other jobs for the summer. Some helped on family farms. Some traveled. Margaret, though, seemed to have nothing more exciting to do than straighten her classroom and make lists. She decided to scoot out before Mr. Tarkington could make her feel that she somehow inconvenienced him. Pushing papers into the leather satchel she had carried since she entered teachers college eleven years earlier, Margaret readied to depart the building. She would do Mr. Tarkington the courtesy of stopping by the office to thank him for opening the building.

A few minutes later, Margaret stepped into the bright afternoon sunlight. July was not one of her favorite times of year in eastern Ohio, though January was far worse in the other extreme. At least she had mastered using fabrics and styles that allowed her clothing to breathe. She was grateful for the current fashions that did away with cumbersome underskirts and allowed shortened hems above the ankle. The new garb was far more practical than what Margaret had grown up with.

Outside the school, Margaret turned to look at it. Her first position out of teachers college had been a one-room schoolhouse in southern Ohio, but four years ago she jumped at the chance to teach in a larger—and newer—consolidated school. While she was confident she could capably teach any grade, teaching first graders was a good match for her. She shielded her eyes from the sun and looked over at the adjacent high school. From her classroom windows, when school was in session, she could see the older students coming and going from the high school. Every year they looked younger to Margaret.

Of course the students were the same age coming into high school. It was Margaret who aged. When she became a teacher, she never imagined she would still be teaching at age twenty-nine. She would meet someone, as her college classmates had. She would marry and have her own children.

It hadn't happened. And now Margaret did not know a single unwed woman her age with any serious expectation of marriage. Until a few weeks ago, Margaret would have—reluctantly—put herself in that category and focused on being grateful she had work she enjoyed. Now she was not sure.

Margaret's rented bungalow was only six blocks from the school. She owned a car because her uncle had given her one he'd tired of, but it was foolish to think an unmarried woman would own a home. The bungalow, with its low-pitched roofline and overhanging eaves, was no architectural wonder. It had come from the Sears, Roebuck catalog as a kit, arriving in a railroad boxcar. Her landlord had constructed it himself eight years ago. The home was cozy with a small second bedroom, but its best feature was the front porch shaded by an extension of the main roof. Except in the harshest winter months, Margaret enjoyed sitting on the porch with a book or her sewing.

Her shoes clicked down the narrow sidewalk in automatic movements.

When she saw him—as she hoped she would—Margaret slowed her steps to give Gray Truesdale time to catch her eye and cross the street to say hello.

Gray was the reason Margaret was not fully certain she would never marry.

She nearly melted the first time he spoke to her and was so tongue-tied that she could not imagine he would ever repeat the act of kindness. Or perhaps it had been pity for the spinster school-teacher.

But Gray Truesdale had never married, either, and he was more than mildly eligible. At thirty-five, he owned a home that had not come from a kit. One of the first men to own an automobile truck, Gray did steady business in deliveries and home repairs.

Margaret liked a man who was not afraid of hard work.

She liked Gray Truesdale. He had spoken to her again after the initial social disaster, and gradually she relaxed and enjoyed herself with him. He made her tingle up and down. It was the oddest sensation, but delicious.

Now he waved and approached. "I wondered if I might run into you."

"And you have." She smiled.

"I might be in your neighborhood later," he said.

"Oh? When might that be?" The familiar exchange had become a litany between them.

"Around suppertime, I expect," he said.

"I expect I'll be taking a roast chicken out of the oven about then."

"Is that so?"

"Yes, I do believe I will be."

"I imagine it will be a juicy roast chicken."

"That's the kind my mother taught me how to cook."

Gray nodded. "Well, then, I'll certainly be mindful."

He tipped his black hat and backed away.

Margaret tingled.

<hr />

Ella recognized the neighborhood they turned into.

"Lindy Lehman lives on this street," she said.

"That's right," Nora said. "Do you know Lindy?"

"She's my stepmother's oldest friend." Ella did not add that Lindy was the sister of Gideon's deceased wife. Most *English* had enough trouble sorting out Amish relationships. The simplest explanation was best.

Nora's brow creased. "But your stepmother is Amish, isn't she?"

"That's right."

"And Lindy. . .is not."

"No. She chose not to be baptized and join the church, but she grew up among our people. Lindy and Rachel are still close friends."

"Is that allowed?"

"No one can force another person to believe," Ella said. "Officially Lindy was never a member of the church, so she has done nothing wrong by leaving."

"She has quite a workshop behind her house."

"I've seen it," Ella said. "She's talented. Her birdhouses are popular all over Geauga County."

"It's an unusual occupation for a woman, don't you think?"

"She used to spend a lot of time watching her grandfather."

"He was Amish?"

"Yes, but he didn't see the harm in a girl learning to use a few tools."

"Perhaps I'll order one of her birdhouses," Nora said. "I wonder if she knows Margaret Simpson across the street."

"Is that who you want me to meet?"

Nora nodded. "She teaches at the consolidated grade school. If anyone could help you become a teacher, it would be Margaret."

Ella held her tongue. Nora did not understand how complicated the notion was—or that Ella and Gideon were talking of marriage.

Nora pulled her horse alongside an automobile parked in the street in front of a bungalow.

"That's Margaret's car," she said. "I confess to envy. I feel so old-fashioned to still be driving a horse and cart."

Ella gave an awkward smile.

Nora blushed. "I meant no offense. I respect the ways of your people. I know you don't use cars. But I have my eye on the future. I just don't know how Margaret affords an automobile of her own. Maybe the town teachers earn a higher salary than the rural teachers."

Envy was not entirely unfamiliar to Ella, though she had no aspirations to the *English* ways.

"There's Margaret now." Nora guided her horse to the side of the street.

Margaret stood on her front porch and waved. Nora and Ella walked up the brick path to the bungalow. Nora made introductions.

"I thought you two would enjoy meeting," Nora said. "Margaret is a wonderful teacher and a good friend."

"Do you have a child in Nora's class?" Margaret asked Ella.

"I'm not married," Ella said, "but she's been the teacher for my stepbrothers, and I have friends with children in Nora's school."

Nora sighed. "Or what's left of my school."

Margaret's eyebrows went up.

"The schoolhouse is in serious need of repair," Ella explained.

"We need funding," Nora said. "Do you have any influence with the superintendent?"

"Me?" Margaret said. "I've been in the county for four years, and Mr. Brownley barely knows my name."

"I don't want to leave the farm families in the lurch," Nora said.

"It will be hard enough to find a teacher if I don't return, but now they need a new building."

"I wish I could help," Margaret said. "I have absolutely no influence on these decisions, but I do have a fresh pitcher of cold lemonade."

Ella silently admitted her thirst. July days seemed to bring perpetual thirst. And she liked Margaret Simpson. She smiled acceptance of the hospitality.

"Gertrude, please don't play in the dirt." James Lehman's tone was kind, but he mustered a firm expression. He knew this child well. If he gave her any reason to believe his request lacked conviction, Gertie would dawdle until one of the endless tasks on the Wittmer farm distracted him.

"I'm not playing," Gertie said. "I'm experimenting."

"Then I suggest you experiment in the grass. "You know your *aunti* Miriam doesn't like you dragging dirt into the house at suppertime."

Gertie tossed her stick aside and rose from the crouch that already had left an inch-high gray ring around the hem of her dress. She moved to the grass, where she would be content to lie on her back and squint at the clouds.

Gideon came around the corner of the barn, wiping sweat on his sleeve.

"How is she?" he asked.

"She hasn't said a word all afternoon about the school falling in," James said. After six days, Gertie was beginning to believe not all schools were like the one she'd visited.

"Good. No nightmare last night either," Gideon said.

"Sit in the shade for a few minutes." James gestured to the empty outdoor chair beside him, part of a set he'd made several years earlier. "The heat will get the best of you."

Gideon dropped into the chair and glanced at Gertie sprawled on the ground. "Where are Tobias and Savilla?"

"I sent them both to the woodpile to make sure Miriam has enough for the kitchen stove for a few days."

"We could eat a cold supper more often, you know." Gideon lifted his hat and ran his fingers through limp, damp hair. "Miriam is the one who suffers most when the kitchen heats up."

"There's no talking to her when she makes up her mind to cook," James said. "Now Savilla wants to learn, which gives Miriam more reason."

Smiling, Gideon nodded. "I don't know what I would have done without you these last five years. After Betsy died. . ."

"Hush. Betsy was our niece. We loved her and we love you." James turned his gaze across the property to the *dawdihaus* Gideon had built when James and Miriam arrived to help with the house and children after Betsy's sudden death. Without children of their own, James had imagined he and Miriam would live into their old age in the farmhouse across the state that they had occupied since they were newlyweds. Miriam was the one to say they ought to move so they could care for Betsy's family.

"I'd like to have Lindy out more often," Gideon said. "My children should know their mother's sister better than they do."

"She comes if you ask."

"I know. But I also know Miriam tends to fuss even more when Lindy is around."

James laughed. "Are you suggesting I should handle my wife? What would she do with herself if she didn't have you to fuss over?"

"Put her feet up and get the rest she deserves."

James had to admit Miriam looked ragged recently.

"Still no news from the superintendent?" James asked.

Gideon pushed out a slow breath. "It's been a week since Walter Hicks took that letter into town. You'd think that this close to the beginning of school the board would act quickly."

James nodded. "They could have a special meeting or something."

"We need to make sure no one goes in the schoolhouse."

James scrunched up his face. "Who would go in there? Everybody knows half the roof fell in."

"I wish I could be sure," Gideon said. "I put up a sign and roped off the front entrance, but you never know."

"I'll go by in the morning on my way into town. I promised Lindy to help her with some deliveries."

"I've heard some call you 'Wagon James,' " Gideon said. "Do you ever say no to a delivery?"

James shook his head. "Not if I'm sure it will help folks if I deliver. A man wants to be useful."

"I should get back to the barn. One more stall to muck. Shall I take Gertie with me?"

"I've already pulled her out of the dirt over there." James gestured. "I might as well look after her until supper."

Gideon paced over to the patch of dirt. He looked up at the scene before him and back to the dirt. "It's a drawing of the horse pasture."

"How can you tell from scratches in the dirt?"

"It's not scratches. She drew what she saw. The fence is perfect."

James got up to look for himself. "Why would Gertie do such a thing?"

Gideon rubbed a boot through the dirt and scattered the stick drawing.

<hr />

Gideon could tell from the timbre of the approaching clatter that the horse pulled a cart on the brink of repairs.

"It's Miss Coates," he said.

"Maybe she has news from the superintendent."

"Maybe. She's smiling."

In the sunshine-blanketed grass a few yards away, Gertie sat up. "I said I don't want to go to that school."

"Gertie," Gideon said, "go inside and see if Miriam needs some help."

Gertie obeyed without hesitation, as if to impress on her father that she wanted nothing to do with the teacher or the school.

Miss Coates pulled her cart up alongside the barn and got out. Her face beamed. "Since you're the head of the parents committee, I wanted you to be the first to know."

"I appreciate your taking the trouble to come all the way out here," Gideon said. "Good news from the school board, I hope."

"Oh, I'm afraid I have no word on the matter of the schoolhouse. This is another matter, but not unrelated. I've accepted a proposal to be married in a few weeks. Obviously under these circumstances, I won't be continuing as teacher."

Gideon nodded. Obviously. A stone settled in his stomach.

"Congratulations," he said. "I hope your marriage brings you every happiness."

"Thank you," Miss Coates said. "I came as soon as I could. I wanted you to have every available day to begin the search for a new teacher. She'll have to be approved by the district, of course. I'm sure the superintendent will have some names for you to correspond with. I've already submitted my resignation."

"I'll contact him immediately." Perhaps this second line of inquiry would prod the superintendent to release funds for the new school.

"I hope your little girl has recovered from the events of last week," Miss Coates said.

"She's not too keen on school right now," Gideon said, "but I'm sure she'll be fine."

Miss Coates hoisted herself back into the cart. "I won't take up any more of your time. If I can help with the search in any way, please do let me know. I won't be moving away for another two weeks."

The horse trotted out of the farmyard. With a grin still on her face, Miss Coates offered a final wave.

Behind Gideon, the back door of his home opened. Miriam stepped out.

"What was that all about?" she said.

Gideon sighed. "We don't have a school building, and now we don't have a teacher, either."

"Miss Coates is getting married." James sidled over to his wife and kissed her cheek.

Miriam tilted her head and lost her gaze in James's eyes.

Pangs of loss heated Gideon's belly. He had hoped to have fifty years of Betsy looking into his eyes that way. She'd been gone five years, and now he hoped to have a long life with Ella, but still grief washed through him in odd moments.

❧

Even after being out of school for twelve years, Ella still cultivated the rhythm of opening a book every day and expecting to learn something interesting. The Seabury Public Library had a small but varied collection, and Ella sometimes checked out her favorite books every few months, either to read them again or simply because she enjoyed having them within reach on her bedside table. Since her father's marriage to Rachel, who gladly shared household chores, Ella had more time than ever to absorb what the library offered.

She was running a finger along a shelf of bird and wildlife books on a Monday morning when a pair of green eyes startled her by staring back at her over the tops of the books. She gasped.

"Hello, Ella."

The voice was familiar, but Ella could not place it immediately. Margaret Simpson came around the end of the aisle.

"Oh, it's you," Ella whispered. "I'm afraid I didn't recognize you just by your eyes!"

Margaret chortled and then shushed herself. "I was hoping they might have some new animal books I might share with my students. But first graders need illustrations, and scientists seem to prefer lots of big words."

Ella flipped through the books in her arms. "This is my favorite book on birds. There are lots of words, but the drawings are delightful."

Margaret took the book and opened it in the middle and turned a few pages. "Mmm. *Birds of Geauga County*. I see what you mean. Your favorite, you say?"

Ella twisted her lips sheepishly. "I check it out four times a year."

Margaret handed the book back to Ella. "I'll let you enjoy it again now, but I'm going to remember it when school begins. I suppose you heard about Nora Coates."

"Yes, Mr. Wittmer told me. He's on the parents committee."

"I rather think that the condition of the schoolhouse will be more formidable than finding a new teacher. Recent graduates of the teachers college will be eager to go wherever there is a position available."

"I hope so," Ella said. "We only have six weeks to sort it all out."

"What else do you like to read?" Margaret lowered her voice further, glancing toward the librarian at the desk.

"Recipe books. Agriculture. Veterinary medicine. Waterways. *The Farmer's Almanac*," Ella said. "Occasionally some American history, particularly biographies of some of the presidents."

"Goodness. I love your curious mind. I have a small library of my own at home. You're welcome to borrow anything you'd like."

"Thank you."

"I suppose you've read all the great novels. *Jane Eyre? David Copperfield?*"

"I don't generally read fiction." Ella had never read a novel.

"I'm sure we can find a story you'd like."

"I don't want to put you to any trouble." Ella did not want to imagine explaining to her father—or to Gideon—that she was idly passing the time with an *English* novel. It was one thing to read for edification or to form useful skills, but another to indulge in a story that was not true.

"The next time you're in town, feel free to knock on my door."

"You're kind." Ella clasped her stack of books against her chest. "I'd better check out and be on my way. I need to. . .well, I should. . .be going."

She stepped quickly toward the desk. Margaret Simpson was perfectly nice and seemed determined to be friends—which was what unnerved Ella. She hadn't had an *English* friend since Sally Templeton when they were fourteen years old.

⌘

"Three yards of plain white cotton fabric," Miriam said. "Watch as the clerk measures it out. Don't let him cut it short."

"I won't," James said.

"If you forget the *kaffi*, you'll have nothing to drink with your breakfast tomorrow."

"I won't forget."

"There are two baskets of eggs on the back porch for you to take in for store credit. You know what the price is on those, right?"

"I do."

"Blue thread. Two spools. The girls are outgrowing their dresses again."

"On my list."

"And don't forget to stop by Lindy's and see if she's finished painting the rack I asked her to make."

"I won't forget."

James found Miriam's fussy, bossy moods endearing. It would bother some husbands, but he appreciated her mind for details to keep both Gideon's home and their own *dawdihaus* running smoothly. He supposed that if they'd had their own children, Miriam would have focused her fussing on them. But they'd had Betsy and Lindy and their brothers and sisters to dote on, and now they had Betsy's children.

It was already hot even before midmorning. James filled a jug with water to take in the wagon.

"No rest for the weary," Miriam said.

That was what James feared. He hoped Gideon would marry Ella soon. At least when fall came, all three children would be in school for the first time and Miriam's days would ease.

CHAPTER 4

On the beige settee with green and blue tapestry pillows, Margaret sat in her front room with hands in her lap and feet flat on the floor. Almost flat. One toe wiggled in rhythm with the ticking second hand of the clock on the mantel. She refused to give in to the urge to open the oven too soon. Patience would yield impeccable golden crusts, steam rising from the precise vents she had cut in the tops before sliding two pies into the oven side by side.

Tick. Tock. Tick.

A fine red thread ran through the weave of the pillows. Margaret seldom looked at them closely enough to notice it.

Tick. Tock. Tick.

The minute hand circled the clock face seven more times before Margaret popped up and pushed through the oak door into the kitchen, where the woodstove blasted intolerable heat. Temperatures on the first of August were beastly on their own. In past summers, Margaret was content with a cold plate of cheese and fruit for her supper. Her kitchen table always had half a dozen books on it, and food she could pick up with her fingers was more convenient while she read.

That was before Gray Truesdale.

Margaret took the two blackberry pies from the oven and transferred them to the cooling rack, though she had no intention of letting them cool. She wrapped each one in a fresh white towel purchased at the mercantile only four days ago. She and Gray could cut into one tonight—still warm—and she would send the other home with him.

He stopped by two or three evenings a week now. Margaret couldn't be certain he would come tonight, but she would be prepared. It was Thursday, a day he seemed to favor. She moved the coffeepot to the heat of a front burner.

Perspiration dripped from both temples. Taking a handkerchief from her skirt pocket, Margaret dabbed at the moisture while she walked through the house. The front porch would be cooler, and if Gray didn't see her sitting in her swing on a fine evening, he might think she would not welcome a visit.

Across the street and two houses down, Lindy Lehman knelt in a flower bed. When Lindy glanced up, Margaret waved. Tomorrow evening she would wander over with a friendly offering of leftover pie.

Margaret heard the grind of Gray's truck, though it had not yet come into view. Several neighbors were outside their homes. If they were paying attention, they would soon realize that Gray's visits held a pattern. What the neighbors might think of a male visitor to a woman who lived alone was a dilemma Margaret had not faced before.

She didn't care. This might be her last chance.

Gray's truck was not loud or irregular. Margaret doubted anyone else would recognize the pitch of its engine from three blocks away, but her ears were peculiarly attuned to the sound. He eased to the side of the road down the block, exited, let the door fall closed without slamming it, and plunged his hands into this pockets for a casual stroll toward Margaret's porch.

Her chest heated up just with the thought of him, and his scent filled her mind from yards away.

"Evening," he said, turning up the brick path in front of her home.

"Evening." Margaret gave the swing a slight push, determined not to appear too eager.

"It's a fine night."

"Quite lovely."

Gray reached the bottom of three broad steps, set his foot on it, and leaned on his knee. He was a tall man, and fit. When he removed his hat, dimming rays of sunlight brightened his brown eyes.

"I was just about to have some pie," Margaret said. "I wonder if you might want to sit on the porch and have a slice."

"That's the most hospitable offer I've had all day." Gray took two slow steps up the stairs.

Margaret stood and smoothed her skirt, trying to will her heart rate to slow. "I'll only be a minute."

By the time she returned with a tray of pie and coffee to set on the low table beside the swing, he sat on what Margaret had come to think of as Gray's side. He slowed the sway to take a plate from her and wait for her to sit next to him with her own pie. Margaret played with her fork for a moment while Gray filled his mouth with steaming fruit and crust.

"Mmm. You make a fine pie, Miss Margaret Simpson."

"Why, thank you."

Gray started the swing again, a gentle, fluid wobble in rhythm with the motion of his fork rising and falling. They sat in shadows now.

"I trust you know that I come around for more than your cooking," Gray said, his eyes looking straight down the length of the porch.

"I rather hoped that was the case." Beside him, Margaret pushed a clump of blackberries first one direction and then the other. "Would you like some coffee?"

"In a minute," he said. "There's something I'd like to ask you first."

"Yes?" She felt his eyes on her and turned her head to meet his gaze.

"I wonder if I might express my growing affection for you."

Margaret's breathing stilled. *Affection.*

Gray set his pie plate on the tray and took Margaret's. Had he seen her tremble? She hoped not.

"If I have your kind permission," he said, "I would very much like to kiss you."

"You do," she whispered.

Gray laid three long fingers at the side of her chin and leaned toward her. Margaret hadn't been kissed in years, and no other beau's kiss had been as delicious as this one. Gray lingered long enough to be convincing, but not so long as to raise alarms as to his intentions.

"I'll go to bed a happy man tonight."

Whether or not Gray slept, Margaret did not know. As many times as she closed her eyes determined to sleep, each time she shut out the shadows of her bedroom, she remembered his kiss.

It was good to know she had not turned into a dried-up spinster who could not make a man feel something.

Growing affection. That was the way he put it. Not pity for her age. Not convenience because he didn't know another suitable woman. Affection.

Still glowing from her dreams, Margaret rose early on Friday morning, dressed carefully, gave thanks for her breakfast, made notes about what she must accomplish—no matter how distracted she was—and walked six blocks to Seabury Consolidated Grade School. The principal offered two hours this morning for teachers who wanted to enter the building.

Margaret carried her leather satchel, which contained the composition book she used for her lesson plans, a set of colorful alphabet cards to attach to the classroom walls, and a rag and tin of vegetable soap with which she would polish the desks in the room. Every six-year-old deserved to find school a cheery, welcoming place on the first day of a robust educational career.

She had reached the desks in the third row when footsteps sounded in the hall.

Good. It was time other teachers joined her determination to have classrooms ready when school resumed. The building's custodian had mopped and scrubbed the rooms thoroughly in June after school let out and undertaken a list of minor repairs, but it was up to the trained teaching staff to be ready at the first bell.

The footfalls ceased right outside her classroom door, and Margaret looked up from her task. Immediately, she abandoned her vegetable soap and stood erect.

"Good morning, gentlemen," she said.

Principal Tarkington stepped into the room with the school district superintendent, whom Margaret had met only once or twice in a room full of other teachers.

"Mr. Brownley asked me for a recommendation," the principal said, "and I have suggested he speak with you."

"Of course," Margaret said, though she could not imagine what the superintendent would need her help with.

"I have some telephone calls to return," Mr. Tarkington said, "so I'll leave you two to talk."

"Thank you, Mr. Tarkington." Margaret watched him pivot and leave the room.

Mr. Brownley began to pace along the wall of windows.

"I've received some correspondence," he said. "In responding, I require the assistance of a competent teacher dedicated to the principles of a sound public education, and Mr. Tarkington assures me that you meet this description."

"I've been teaching for nine years." Margaret rotated slowly to follow the path the superintendent was taking across the back of the classroom. "I believe I am accomplished in my profession."

"I'm glad to hear you sound confident. That is just the disposition I seek."

"I'm happy to help."

Brownley crossed his wrists behind him and paced along the opposite wall. "Have you much experience dealing with resistant parents?"

Why didn't the superintendent simply say what was on his mind?

"Occasionally I have met parents who do not understand the importance of regular school attendance," Margaret said.

Brownley nodded.

"And if a child presents a disciplinary challenge, I find it constructive to win over the parents to offer a united front in resolving the matter."

"Excellent." Brownley pulled papers out of his suit jacket. "I have here two items of correspondence signed by Mr. Gideon Wittmer and others."

"Mr. Wittmer?"

Brownley raised an eyebrow. "Do you know him?"

"Not exactly. I met someone who knows him."

"Then you will not be surprised that these particular parents have children in one of the outlying one-room schoolhouses."

"A school which is in need of both repairs and a teacher," Margaret said.

Brownley's face brightened. "I must say I had not expected you to be so informed on the matter."

"I'm afraid that is the extent of my knowledge."

Brownley pulled out the chair from behind Margaret's desk and sat down. "It's a delicate matter."

Margaret waited.

"This is the letter requesting funding for a new schoolhouse." He laid one sheet of paper on the desk and positioned a second beside it, precisely one inch apart. "And this is the letter asking for names of teachers the local parents committee might correspond with about the open position."

"I understand that these are considerable challenges," Margaret said, "given the limited time before school opens."

"If only it were as simple as that."

Margaret waited again.

"We will not be rebuilding the school, Miss Simpson, nor looking for a new teacher."

"Oh."

"Mr. Tarkington tells me you are one of his best teachers. Surely you can appreciate that these circumstances suggest that now is the right time to integrate these pupils into the consolidated school."

"We have a fine grade school. And the high school is excellent as well."

"I agree. And I'm confident that we can accommodate the thirty or so students being displaced by closing their school." Brownley folded the letters and returned them to his pocket.

"Of course I wish to be helpful," Margaret said, "but I feel unclear as to what you are asking of me." These were administrative matters. Shouldn't the superintendent and the principal work out the details of the transition?

"Mr. Tarkington tells me you can be quite persuasive."

Once again, not knowing how to answer, Margaret waited.

"Some parents may resist our plan," Brownley said. "I would like you to persuade them of its virtues."

"Me?"

"You did say you wanted to help. This will be a significant change for all of the families affected, but the Amish families in particular will need to understand that they must comply with this decision."

Margaret gulped.

Ella sat in a wooden yard chair she did not quite trust. It dated back to the early days of her parents' marriage, and it creaked. The sound was ordinary, especially for the age of the chair, but after the creaking and groaning of the schoolhouse ceiling before it caved in, she would have preferred a chair more respectful with its silence. She looked up from her book about the health of chickens and saw her stepbrother crossing the farmyard.

Stepbrother was not a word that settled naturally in her mind yet. She used it readily enough to describe members of other families, but attaching a first-person possessive pronoun to the word complicated its meaning. *My stepbrother.* She avoided saying the phrase, instead referring to both David and Seth by their names in conversation.

David was a nice enough boy—a young man. He was nearly fifteen, out of school, nearly ready to begin attending Singings and consider courting. If he had any objections to his mother's decision to marry Jedediah Hilty, Ella never heard him voice them. Yet he seemed to walk around wrapped in a secret Ella could not decipher. She wasn't even sure she wanted to. Her mind was full enough of her books and Gideon and Gideon's children.

Ella expected David would walk past her to the barn or into the house. He might nod or lift his hand in a brief wave. Instead, he shuffled toward her. She had already caught his eye, whether she meant to or not, so she couldn't ignore him now.

Silent, he stood beside her for a moment and stared down.

"How are you, David?" Ella said, wishing she could go back to her book.

"I'm fine."

He said nothing more. His eyes were not fixed on his feet, as Ella had supposed, but on the stack of books on the ground beside the chair.

"Do you like to read?" she asked.

He nodded. "Do you mind if I look at the books?"

"Go ahead."

He squatted and went through her pile. "You read a lot about animals."

"I like to understand how to take care of them," she said, "or just to enjoy them."

He had his hand on *The Birds of Geauga County*. "What's your favorite bird?"

Ella twisted her lips. "I love the sound of a mourning dove, but I like the name of the American coot."

He smiled. "I like the chimney swift for the same reason."

Now she smiled. "I didn't know you liked birds."

"They're interesting from a scientific perspective."

This surprised her. "You like to read about science?"

He nodded. "Sometimes. There are a lot of things I want to understand better. Not just science."

"What are some topics you're curious about?" This was by far the longest thread of conversation Ella and David had ever exchanged.

He tilted his head. "The war."

"The war in Europe?" Ella's heart spurted.

"I'm not supposed to be curious about that. But I am." He shuffled through the books again. "Do you have any novels?"

"No," she said slowly. "I don't read novels."

"Oh. Okay."

She let a beat pass before asking, "Do you read novels?"

"Only two or three. My *mamm* doesn't approve. She says only the *English* read them."

Ella closed her book around one finger.

"There's so much world out there." David stacked the books neatly. "I don't know why I'm supposed to be afraid of it."

"I don't think the point of our ways is to be afraid."

"Never mind." David stood up.

"David—"

But he was already walking away.

CHAPTER 5

Three days later, Margaret opened her composition book to a
fresh page and smoothed it down against Gideon Wittmer's simple
polished oak dining room table. Margaret could feel the solid craftsmanship of the chair she sat in and admired the smoothly sanded
end tables in the front room and the braided rug that brought
warmth to the wood floors.

Three days earlier she had never been on an Amish farm, and
now she tried not to stare at the two bearded men in plain black
suits. Though the two *English* fathers were clean shaven and dressed
in the more familiar coveralls of farm laborers, their expressions
matched the stern expectation of Gideon Wittmer and Aaron King.

"Thank you, Mr. Wittmer, for inviting us into your home," Margaret began. "Obviously we face some challenging changes."

On Friday, right after her meeting with Mr. Brownley, Margaret
had driven her Model T out to the old school and seen the shambles
for herself. She did not blame the school board for deciding against
repairing or rebuilding.

"Why didn't the superintendent come to talk to us himself?"

It was Walter Hicks who voiced the question all four men must
have been thinking. *What he really means is why did he send a woman?*
She could hardly speak aloud the responses clanging in her mind.
*Because you won't like his answers. Because he doesn't take your proposal
seriously.*

"Mr. Brownley asked for my assistance, and I am glad to give it."
Margaret spoke with more conviction than she felt.

Gideon cleared his throat. "Perhaps it would be best if you put forth Mr. Brownley's response in a clear manner."

"Yes, of course." Margaret laid a pen across the blank page in her composition book. "The board feels it will be in the best interest of the children and their families if they ride the bus and attend the well-respected consolidated schools in Seabury."

There. She'd said it. She refused to cower.

"They won't build us a school?" Robert Haney sounded stunned.

"I'm afraid not," Margaret said.

"We'll appeal the decision," Walter said. "There must be due process for an appeal."

"As a matter of procedure," Margaret said, "I'm sure there is. If you'd like, I'll find out the schedule of the school board meetings. But I must say that I believe there is little point in the effort. From an economic perspective, the decision is quite firm."

Margaret scanned the four faces, looking for glimmers of acceptance, even excitement. Surely they knew that other one-room schools around the county had been closed. The board's decision could not have come as a complete surprise.

"The schools are well run with a faculty of qualified teachers," she said. "We are broken into grades, which allow individual teachers to become specialists of sorts with particular ages. The benefits for the children will be innumerable."

Robert Haney grunted.

"The district will send a bus." Margaret forged on. "The children will have adult supervision from the moment they get on the bus in the morning until the moment they get off in the afternoon."

"It's a long day for the little ones," Walter said.

Margaret answered, "I find they adjust quite well and enjoy the additional subjects we are able to offer in the consolidated school."

Walter scratched the back of his neck. Robert twisted his lips to one side. Margaret adjusted her hips in the chair and looked at Mr. Wittmer and Mr. King.

Aaron King finally spoke. "Do you teach the basics?"

"We give students a strong foundation for learning," Margaret said.

"So the basics."

"And so much more."

Gideon's eyes widened. "We are accustomed to discussing the curriculum with the teacher. Miss Coates knew us well."

Us. The Amish. The *English* fathers would come around. The Amish parents would need more persuading.

"Why don't you come for a tour?" Margaret said brightly. "You can see for yourself the quality of education your children will receive. We can do it on Friday, if that's convenient."

⚜

"Are you sure I should be here?" Trailing behind the others four days later, Ella whispered to Gideon. "I'm not one of the parents."

Gideon could not take her hand to reassure her with the others watching, though he doubted anyone would be surprised when they announced their intention to marry. James and Miriam would be delighted that Gideon had found happiness again after Betsy. Jed Hilty would be relieved that his daughter would be taken care of. Others would find it fitting that Gideon's children would have a mother again. Aaron King's wife had come along for the tour of the school, so Ella was not the only woman.

"You'll be a parent," Gideon whispered back. Soon, he hoped. She would mother his three, and they would have more *boppli* together.

The Kings had readily agreed that Ella should join the tour, not because she was a parent, but because she read so many books. Since the Amish did not have a teacher of their own to evaluate the school, Ella was the next best thing. She could look around and know exactly what the students would be learning.

When Ella's steps slowed, so did Gideon's. They tilted their heads back to look at the three stories of sprawling brick with sober columns of white-framed windows.

"It looks so official," Ella said. "It's as big as twenty schoolhouses."

Gideon counted twelve windows across on each story, including a double-width door at the center of the ground floor, which the Kings were very near. He wished Walter or Robert had come along for the tour. They might not have any more experience than he did with large schools, but at least they were *English* and might interpret the philosophy behind the school. But Walter said he didn't need a tour to know he would do what the law said, and one of Robert's horses went lame and he didn't want to leave her.

Aaron and Alma King stopped just short of the door, both of

them turning to gauge Gideon and Ella's progress. A moment later, the visitors stood four abreast looking at the door.

"Do we ring a bell or just go in?" Alma scanned the oversized door frame.

"Why do the *English* have to build everything so big?" Aaron scuffed one shoe against the sidewalk.

Gideon stepped forward and rapped on the door.

"They'll never hear that," Aaron said.

Gideon knocked again, harder.

"Try the knob," Alma urged.

Gideon turned the brass bulb, and the door creaked inward. The click of an *English* woman's step reassured him.

Margaret Simpson's smile was unnaturally broad. "Come in!"

⚜

"We pride ourselves on our commitment to prepare students to participate fully in twentieth-century life," Margaret said as she led them down the main hall that cut through the building.

Ella caught Gideon's eye. Pride? No Amish parents would want their children learning pride, and the year printed on a calendar meant far less for a full life than friends and family. Ella held no grudge, though. The Amish had been in Geauga County a long time, but Margaret Simpson had not. She lived and worked in town and had never taught an Amish student.

"The library is right down here," Margaret said.

Ella could not help but perk up at the racks of books that greeted them a moment later.

"The children are permitted to check out three books at a time, and the teachers are free to select volumes to keep in their classrooms to supplement a unit of study."

The grid of walnut tables at the center of the library looked inviting. Ella could imagine herself finding a quiet spot and spreading out a stack of books.

"Who helps the children select appropriate reading material?" Gideon asked.

"The librarian gets to know the children, and of course the teachers will know if a book is beyond a child's ability."

Savilla would follow the rules. And Tobias was old enough to know that he ought not to pull a novel off the shelf. It was Gertie who—once she learned to read—would soak up everything in front of her. Once Ella and Gideon were married, she would have to watch carefully what came home in Gertie's book strap.

They walked farther down the hall. Margaret gestured toward two heavy cabinets.

"These are the art cupboards," she said. "We don't have an art teacher yet, but the grade-level teachers are encouraged to nurture artistic expression. I'm sure we'll be delighted to discover what artistic talent your children will bring into the school."

Ella and Gideon glanced at each other. Art certainly was beyond the Amish basics. Sketching a design for a building or a quilt top was a matter of practicality to accomplish the task, but nurturing artistic expression was another.

They continued down the endless hall.

"The music room is way at the back," Margaret said, "so as not to disturb any of the classrooms. All our students learn to read music and sing harmonies. Once they are in the sixth grade, they may take lessons on a musical instrument. We have a delightful man who comes in, and the music store on Main Street offers instruments at reasonable prices."

Margaret pointed out the paved playground behind the building. Why children would want to play on such an unforgiving surface befuddled Ella. Then she took them up a staircase to classrooms on the second floor.

Margaret was overeager, in Ella's opinion. They went into several classrooms, representing different ages, where Margaret pulled textbooks off shelves and flipped them open.

Mathematics. Literature. Science. World history. Health and hygiene. Geography. Modern inventions. Great works of art.

Ella could not help thinking of David. He was too old for grade school now, but what might he have thought if presented with these options when he was still in school?

Ella paid close attention to Margaret's explanations, moistening her lips every few minutes in concentration. Alma King bore a steady, intense scowl. Aaron looked overwhelmed. Gideon asked a few questions about some of the books. Margaret did her best to answer them, but Ella could see that her responses tightened the tension in Gideon's expression.

Margaret was friendly and talkative and enthusiastic, all qualities Ella easily admired.

But when the superintendent sent Margaret to talk to the Amish parents, he might just as well have put her on a train blindfolded.

⚜

The tour had not gone well. The expressions on the faces of her four Amish guests told Margaret that she'd said all the wrong things. For days afterward she reviewed the conversation. She was so determined to impress them, and make them *want* to send their children to the consolidated school, that she hadn't heard the true questions folded into the polite inquires.

School would begin in four weeks. And if the Amish children did not arrive on the first day, Margaret would have both Mr. Tarkington and Mr. Brownley to answer to.

Perhaps it was not too late. Perhaps she could still persuade the Amish parents that she wanted to make their children's transition as smooth as she possibly could.

For this reason, on the Monday morning after the tour, Margaret made sure she had plenty of gasoline in her Model T and headed for the Amish farmlands and the nearest *English* neighbors. She did her best to calculate the miles and judge how long the children would be on the bus. The most outlying farm could be farther than she realized. She didn't yet have a list of the students the grade school expected. For now, she made sure she knew where the hidden turnoffs were and where to look for the clusters of farm buildings that might mark the homes of students who would venture into an intimidating new school in one short month.

It was intimidating even for the Amish parents. Margaret should have seen that before now.

Her satchel on the seat beside her held the true mission of the morning.

Margaret pleased herself by finding the road to Gideon Wittmer's farm more efficiently than she had the first time she visited. A man—not Gideon—tugged a reluctant calf out of the barn and into the pasture. Perhaps she had confused herself after all.

She shut off the engine of her car. "Have I found the Wittmer farm?"

"Yes, you have." The man lifted his head and pushed his straw hat about an inch off his forehead.

"I recognize you," Margaret said. "You're the gentleman who comes to help Lindy Lehman with deliveries of the beautiful birdhouses she paints. They call you Wagon James."

"I won't deny it. Lindy is my niece—my brother's daughter. I'm James Lehman."

"I'm Lindy's neighbor, Margaret Simpson."

A screen door slammed closed, and Gideon appeared on his front porch.

"Good morning, Mr. Wittmer."

"Good morning, Miss Simpson. Thank you again for the tour of your school."

Your school. Not *the* school. Margaret resolved not to read anything into Gideon's choice of pronouns. She picked up her satchel and got out of the automobile as gracefully as she could.

"I have a bit more information from the superintendent," she said, reaching into her satchel. "This is a letter about the bus route and where the children will be picked up."

Gideon took the envelope from her but did not open it. "I appreciate the trouble you've taken to bring it all the way out here."

"No trouble at all." Margaret straightened her hat. "Mr. Brownley thought perhaps the communication should come to you first as the head of the parents committee. I imagine letters will go out to everyone very soon."

Gideon nodded but did not speak. The silence thickened, leaving Margaret feeling exposed.

"Do you have any questions?" she managed to say.

"You've been kind," Gideon said.

"I want to be helpful." She pointed at the envelope. "There's a map with the letter. Mr. Brownley asks that you verify the locations of the farms with school-age children."

"I will."

"If there's any discrepancy. . ."

"I'll make sure he knows. Thank you again for coming."

He had dismissed her. Margaret was backing up toward her car now, suddenly anxious to be on her way. The dust cloud her tires stirred up as she drove off the farm made her cough.

CHAPTER 6

Every chair in Gideon's front room was occupied. Six additional straight-backed wooden chairs from the dining room formed a back row against one wall. James Lehman was not a father, but he was interested in the education question that would affect the entire congregation. He leaned against a door frame at the rear of the assembly.

So far Chester Mast did most of the talking. Now he pounded his fist into his thigh. "How can we expect our children to grow up untainted by the world if we send them into this worldly environment?"

John Hershberger agreed. "Neither the setting nor the companions are Christian. If our children go to this school, we lose them to the world."

"The world is changing," Cristof Byler said.

"Not for the better," Chester shot back.

Gideon showed the palm of one hand to the gathering. "We must speak in an orderly manner so that all may hear." He was one father among many. If he were not on the parents committee, he gladly would have yielded leading this meeting to one of the others.

"Let every soul be subject unto the higher powers." Joshua Glick quoted Romans 13. "For there is no power but of God: the powers that be are ordained of God. Whosoever therefore resisteth the power, resisteth the ordinance of God."

"Train up a child in the way he should go: and when he is old, he will not depart from it." Jed Hilty responded to Romans with Proverbs. "It is the God-given role of parents to train up the children God gives us."

"We've been sending our children to the state's schools all along," Joshua said.

"But we knew the teachers. We oversaw the curriculum and knew what she was teaching." Cristof Byler hung his head as if in grief. "What will happen to our children if they are exposed to the world to the degree that the *English* propose?"

"Isaiah," Gideon said, "we haven't heard from you."

With twelve children, some married with little ones of their own and some still in school, Isaiah Borntrager was sure to have an opinion.

Isaiah spoke softly but with an unyielding tone. "We can teach our children everything they need to know to follow the Lord without involving the *English*."

"So you are in favor of defying the authorities?" Gideon asked.

"I am in favor of obeying God's ordinances to bring up my children in the admonition of the Lord."

"There could be trouble if we do as you suggest," Gideon said.

"It seems to me," Isaiah said, "that there will be trouble for us no matter what we do. Either we rile the authorities or we risk losing our own children to the *English* ways."

Silence.

The range of posturing and opinions collected in Gideon's home came down to Isaiah's two realities.

James pushed away from the door frame. "I am not a father," he said, "so I do not face the decision the rest of you face. I know you will also consider the good of the congregation. Several weeks remain before the start of school. Let us make it a time of prayer, beseeching the Lord for wisdom."

Men around the room nodded.

The front door opened, and six-year-old Gertie crossed through the room to find her father.

"The mailman brought a letter," Gertie whispered into his ear. "He told me it looked important and that I should give it to you immediately."

❦

The chickens raised a ruckus at the sound of an *English* automobile crunching through the gravel lane leading to the Hilty farm. Ella let a basket of wet laundry thud to the ground below the clothesline and shaded her eyes to assess the arrival. A flash of green told her the vehicle belonged to Lindy Lehman. Ella walked out to meet the visitor.

"Did Rachel know you were coming?" Ella said as Lindy closed the driver's door behind her.

"It's a surprise." Lindy walked around to the rear of the car.

"She'll be glad to see you under any circumstances."

Lindy opened the trunk, and Ella gasped at its contents. "It's beautiful!"

Lindy grinned. "David's birthday is coming up. I thought I'd bring him an early present."

Ella lifted the birdhouse reverently. She would know one of Lindy's birdhouses anywhere—the construction without nails, the precise cut of the openings, the rich hues of paint colors harkening to traditional Amish dyes.

"I only recently discovered how much David knows about birds," Ella said. Together they ambled toward the house. "I met your neighbor recently, too—Margaret Simpson."

"A friendly sort, wouldn't you say?"

"Very."

"I suspect she has a beau." Lindy chuckled. "It's sweet to watch the way he drops by casually to sit on the porch. I'm not sure what they'll do when the weather snaps."

Ella smiled. "The Amish find ways to court without much fuss. I suppose the *English* can do it as well."

Lindy turned up one corner of her mouth. "Sounds like the voice of experience."

Ella blushed.

"Gideon's been mourning my sister a long time." Lindy held Ella's gaze. "You'll make him happy. Betsy would have wanted it."

"Thank you, Lindy," Ella said. "I do love him."

Ella had never spoken to Lindy about courting. Had Gideon? Maybe it was James or Miriam.

They meandered around the side of the house.

"Will you have a booth at the auction?" Ella asked. "It's coming up soon."

"Same as last year," Lindy said. "Once I sell what I have, I'll close up and enjoy the rest of the day."

Ella pulled open the back door. "Rachel?"

Rachel appeared promptly—and dropped her jaw at the beauty of Lindy's creation.

"For David," Lindy said.

"He's out in the barn with Jed," Rachel said, "but he's going to love this."

"I heard about the school board's decision." Lindy arranged the birdhouse on the kitchen table.

Rachel sank into a chair. "I don't know what to think. At least Seth is twelve. If Jed decides he should go to school, he'll manage. I feel sorry for the parents who have little ones to put on a bus by themselves."

Like Gertie. At least she would have her sister with her, but Savilla was only nine herself.

"Consolidation might be a good thing," Lindy said.

Rachel popped out of her chair and snatched a dish towel off the pie rack. "Of course you would say that."

Ella winced.

"I'm only trying to see the positive," Lindy said. "It's going to happen, so why not find the good?"

"You chose not to join the church." Rachel's voice sharpened. "We agreed years ago you wouldn't try to turn me *English* as well."

"I'm not! Please, Rachel, let's not quarrel."

Ella decided now would be a good time to slip out and walk out to the mailbox on the road. Lindy and Rachel had been best friends all their lives. Whatever they had to work out between themselves, they would do it without an audience. Normally Ella would walk briskly out to the road. Today she took her time, and when she returned she would resume hanging the wet laundry.

The mailbox contained only one letter, addressed to Jedediah Hilty with a return address showing the school district's office on Main Street in Seabury.

❧

Gideon sent Gertie back out to play in the yard and set the envelope in his lap as he listened to the continuing discussion among the men. He had hoped that gathering the men to talk would guide them all to a decision of one mind and heart. Instead, the reasons for and against complying with the school district's ruling splintered the conversation. Gideon felt the tension hardening like bits of concrete spattered on a wall. The bumps might never be smoothed again.

Each time Gideon glanced down at his lap, the return address on the letter taunted with more insistence. As Chester Mast and Cristof Byler went back and forth, Gideon fingered the edge of the envelope. With one thumb, he tested the seal and found it loose. Raising his eyes to watch John Hershberger's face as he again lamented the undesirable influences the Amish children would face, Gideon slid a finger under the flap and slowly pulled out two sheets of paper, one a letter and one a form.

The voices faded away as he read the words on the page.

"Gideon."

He looked up to see James with eyes full of questions.

"Is this a letter that pertains to our discussion?"

Gideon gave a slow nod. "I imagine each of you will find one in your mailbox."

"Then perhaps you should read it to us now," Isaiah said.

Gideon licked his bottom lip and held the page in front of him.

"Just read it," Aaron King urged.

Gideon should have exercised the self-discipline to leave the envelope unopened until the men had left his home. He needed time to think. They had come to no helpful conclusion on what to do about the consolidated grade school. The instructions in this letter would slash all hope of reaching a peaceful agreement.

"Gideon," James urged.

Gideon cleared his voice.

"Dear Mr. Wittmer,

"This letter reminds us all of the decision of the State of Ohio to establish a compulsory age for education. State law requires students to remain in school until they have reached the age of sixteen. It is our hope that this will encourage more of our young people to complete the requirements for a high school diploma, which will in turn equip them for meaningful employment and successful lives as productive citizens.

"You are receiving this letter because our records show that you have a child or children who may meet the academic requirements of entering the ninth grade or above, or because our records regarding the ages of your children may be incomplete.

M̲argaret carried her neatly typed report along Main Street toward the superintendent's office. With Seabury Consolidated Grade School and Seabury High School on adjacent lots, Mr. Brownley might easily have his office in one of the two modern buildings rather than farther down Main Street. Without doubt, the handful of remaining one-room schools in the rural county around Seabury would soon be closed and students integrated into the schools in town, so he could administer from one of the main buildings.

She had done what she could with the Amish, answering more questions than they knew to ask, inviting them for a tour, and making sure they had the information needed for sending the children to school on the first day. She had written an account of her encounters with the Amish. Only time would tell whether she had persuasively alleviated their hesitations. The report did not contain her own hesitations or the self-chastisement over what she might have said differently.

A few minutes later, on an ordinary sunny August Wednesday morning, Margaret stood in front of the superintendent's desk as he leafed through the pages of her report.

"This is a good beginning," Mr. Brownley said. "I see several opportunities here for strengthening your alliance with the Amish as we move forward."

Alliance? Margaret would not have used that word in describing her only partially successful course of action.

"What is your next step?" Mr. Brownley removed his black-rimmed reading glasses and raised his gray eyes to Margaret.

"Is my report lacking?" Margaret said, confused.

"On the contrary."

"Sir?"

"I am not unaware of the special nature of a relationship with the Amish," Brownley said. "You've done well at communicating the stipulations of the law. Inviting their prominent parents to tour the school was a good strategy to help them prepare for the transition. But we do need to be sure they complete the transition. I suspect that even after the first day of school on September 9, we will discover we do not have uniform compliance."

"Yes," Margaret said, "I would agree that not all the parents will accept the new schools at the same rate."

"And this is why we need you to continue as an intermediary. We must have compliance. It will not be acceptable for us to turn our heads when we are aware of children who become truants."

"I hardly think it will be a case of children deciding to become truants."

Brownley waved his hand. "The end result will be the same. Whether by their choice or their parents', they'll be truant, and I will not tolerate the rate of truancy in my district that might result if the Amish children are not in their assigned classrooms."

"What about the children who are not Amish?"

"Some of their parents may resist, but they will come around. They will understand the law and adapt. The Amish may understand the law and defy."

"Is that not a harsh judgment? They have done nothing wrong so far."

"September 9, Miss Simpson. That is the day that matters. Then we will know where we stand with them. I want you to make sure we accomplish our goal."

Margaret tilted her head. "Perhaps you can be more specific in your instructions to me."

"You've shown yourself capable, Miss Simpson." Brownley rose, paced to the door, and opened it. "I look forward to your reports. Shall we say twice a week for now?"

Margaret swallowed hard. She could not force the Amish parents to send their children to school. Keeping her jaw from slackening in shock required intentional manipulation of her facial muscles as Margaret exited the building and stepped again into the sunlight. She turned vaguely in the direction of her home, walking slowly with the wide brim of her hat angled toward the sidewalk and seeing people's shoes rather than their faces.

When the sound of a pair of men's work boots fell into step with her creeping pace, she looked up.

"Gray!"

"Good morning." He smiled. "It's my good fortune to be hauling for the mercantile today, or our paths might not have crossed."

Margaret stopped walking and looked into Gray's expectant expression. Her lips opened and closed several times without producing sound.

"Margaret, are you all right?"

She gripped her satchel with both hands. Still no words came.

Gray put a hand to the side of her face, transferring his comforting warmth and sureness. Something calmed within her.

"Mr. Brownley has asked—assigned—me to continue as an intermediary with the Amish families. He has some concern they may not send their children to school. I have no idea on God's green earth what he thinks I could do about it if they don't."

Gray took her elbow and they resumed walking. "Surely he could send a man. It would be more authoritative."

Margaret bristled against the collar of her dress.

"Be firm," Gary said. "Utterly firm. It's not a personal matter. There is no question of a choice, and they must come to understand that truth. You've given them the instruction they need, and they must comply with the law."

Gray sounded as if he had been reading the same manual as Mr. Brownley. Yes, it was the law. But was there no room for humanity?

They made the turn that would take them off Main Street toward Margaret's home. Gray had pulled her hand through his elbow and covered it with his palm. The sensation stirred her.

Someone to care for her. Someone to protect her. Just when she had—nearly—talked herself out of thinking she minded missing that experience.

Margaret let out a slow breath. The Amish controversy would not always hang between them. Perhaps it did not matter if their impulses diverged on this matter. One way or another, the issue would resolve and have nothing to do with Margaret in the future. She and Gray would be all right. There was no need to openly disagree on a passing concern that would not involve them for the long run.

❧❧❧

The bishop arrived.

Although Gideon had not spoken directly with Bishop Leroy Garber since the collapse of the schoolhouse, he was not surprised that the head of the church's district would turn up on his farm while he worked with Tobias and James to make sure disease or unmanaged pestilence did not endanger the fall harvest. It was only a matter of time before the bishop, who had no school-age children, would have heard from parents who did about the impending enforcement of state law.

"*Gut mariye*." Bishop Garber dismounted his horse in the middle of a row of wheat, careful to still the animal before its hooves wandered into Gideon's crop.

Gideon brushed his hands against his trousers, loosing bits of soil in a black spray. "I'm sorry I have no refreshment to offer you out here."

"No need. I won't keep you from your work for long."

"What can I do for you?"

The bishop glanced at Tobias, whose eyes had lifted to the exchange.

"Tobias," James said, "let's check the plants in the next row."

Gideon tipped his hat forward a quarter of an inch in thanks as James led Tobias out of listening distance.

"I do not face the decision you face," the bishop said. "My children are over sixteen. But those who are married with their own children will face the dilemma soon enough."

"It's difficult to know what the right thing is," Gideon said. "I'm sure parents will seek your counsel as bishop."

"They already have. That's why I've come to you."

"I have no clear answers, Bishop."

"Perhaps not. But what is certain in my talks with other parents is that they are looking to you. Your name comes up in every conversation. They will follow your lead."

"Bishop, I don't ask for such a role. I am only a parent seeking to please God and do what is best for my children."

"That is just what any of them would say. But they seem to think you will help them find that point of intersection."

"How can I help them find what I do not see clearly for myself?" Gideon rubbed an eye with one palm.

"We see through a glass darkly," the bishop said, "but we still see."

"I will rejoice when light banishes this particular darkness," Gideon said.

"Someday you will be nominated to be a minister."

Gideon's gaze snapped into focus on the bishop's face. "We are only talking about school."

"You are a leader, Gideon. People recognize that. Your leadership on this question will be your ministry."

"I do not seek it."

"None of us ask to be ministers or bishops. God chooses us. If he chooses you now, you must serve."

～✦～

Margaret festered for two days over how to do what the superintendent asked of her. School would begin in just over three weeks, and she had looked forward to pleasantly preparing her classroom, refreshing the lesson plans she had used successfully for the last four years to teach six-year-olds to read, and closing out the summer by canning the vegetables from her garden and the bushels of fruit the mercantile sold at irresistible prices this time of year.

Making sure the Amish children turned up where the state expected them to be on September 9 was not something she knew how to do. Nor did she know what the consequences would be if she failed.

On Friday morning, she once again checked the fuel gauge in her Model T. Armed with a list from the superintendent's office of names and addresses of students they believed should enroll, she cranked the engine of her car and began to roll through the spidery miles of farms, hoping a strategy would take form in her mind as she drove.

Gideon Wittmer came to mind again and again. The only two Amish fathers Margaret had met were Gideon and Mr. King, and between the two of them, Gideon seemed the clear choice for reasonable alliance.

Not *alliance*. Margaret shivered against the word again. It sounded too much like the alliance of nations fighting the war in Europe. She did not want war, not in Europe and not in Seabury.

Conversation. That was a better word.

Margaret turned her car toward the Wittmer farm. If she was going to please Mr. Brownley, she would have to start somewhere.

"He isn't home," an elderly woman said when Margaret knocked on the Wittmer front door.

Peeking around a corner was a pair of bright green eyes in a suntanned face framed by blond hair under a gossamer headpiece, the sort all the Amish women wore. Margaret could not remember what they called them.

Margaret smiled at the little girl and said to the woman, "Do you know where I might find Mr. Wittmer?"

The woman waved a hand first one direction and then the other. "He had some errands to do, some people to see."

"Maybe I could visit another day—soon," Margaret said. "It is rather important that I speak to him."

The little girl came out from around the corner and tugged on the woman's sleeve. "*Aunti* Miriam, *Daed* told me he was going to visit Mr. King, but he would be home for lunch."

Margaret glanced at her watch. It was nearly noon now. She had the Kings' address on her list, showing several grade school children and a high school student.

"Thank you." Margaret beamed at the child. "You look like you're old enough to start school."

"First grade!"

"That's just the grade I teach. Perhaps I'll be your teacher."

The woman put a hand on the girl's shoulder. "Gertie, please go set the table."

"I'm not trying to cause trouble," Margaret said once Gertie went into the kitchen.

"I'm sure you mean no harm," the woman said. "I'm sorry I couldn't tell you where Gideon is. You know these roads. He could be anywhere."

"I understand. If you would tell him that Miss Simpson was here, I would be grateful. I'll try again another day."

Margaret drove toward the King farm, and her intuition was rewarded with an approaching Amish buggy. She pulled to the side of the road and waved. The buggy slowed, and she could see the driver was Gideon Wittmer. Margaret got out of her car and waved again.

"Miss Simpson," Gideon said from the seat at the front of the boxy buggy.

"How fortunate to run into you," she said. "I was hoping we could speak for a few minutes."

"What can I help you with?"

"I'm considering forming a Parents Committee for United Schools." The idea had sprung to her mind only moments before. "You've seen for yourself the quality of our school. Perhaps you would be so kind to serve on the committee and help other parents on the outlying farms to feel comfortable with the consolidated schools."

Gideon's fingers twisted in the reins while his horse waited patiently for instructions. "I think you'll find the *English* parents will appreciate having more information. You could organize another tour and invite anyone who is interested."

"Excellent idea! And the Amish parents?" Margaret held her breath. "As a member of the committee, you could be an invaluable partner, a bridge between the new school and the Amish parents."

He gave a guarded smile. "I'm afraid I can't help you with that."

T he late summer auction was Ella's favorite. The spring frolics, held when the ground softened into a milder season, were too
muddy for her liking. But the last week of August was perfect.
Rarely was there rain, and the edge had come off the peak of summer temperatures. The bustling Saturday brought out all the Amish
families in the district and many curious *English* looking for a bargain to showcase in their homes.

Gideon would likely spend most of the day in the auction ring,
where horses, harnesses, hitches, plows, binders, and buggies would
be sold. Gideon was looking for one new horse. He had his eye on
one from the line Aaron King bred, a two-year-old Belgian workhorse. The bidding would be competitive. Aaron's horses always
fetched a good price.

Ella preferred wandering among the large quilts, handmade
furniture, baked goods, canned foods, and crafty household items.
From year to year, she knew who would have the best home-canned
apple pie filling to save for the middle of winter or who had a
piecework quilt for sale two years in the making. The price an *English* woman would pay for an Amish quilt stunned Ella every time.
Ella walked the rows of tables and booths, looking for that irresistible item she might want to bid on. She had little money of her
own, but she wanted to contribute. The money raised today would
go into the fund that Amish families could count on in a time of
illness or financial difficulty.

A flash of familiar red-gold hair caught Ella's eye a few yards ahead.
"Lindy!"

Lindy paused, and Ella caught up with her.

"How are things at your booth?" Ella asked.

"Brisk." Lindy looked over her shoulder. "I got a spot in the main aisle this year."

"That's good! I predict that you'll sell out by lunchtime."

Lindy chuckled. "I hope so."

"Who's watching your booth now?"

"David's there. He has a good head on his shoulders. He won't let anyone talk him into a price I wouldn't take."

"I'll be happy to help if you need an extra pair of hands."

"Thanks. I'll keep that in mind." Lindy pivoted and walked backward for a few yards before turning around again. "My neighbor Margaret said she asked Gideon to be on a committee and he declined."

Ella sighed. "It's so complicated!"

"Is Gideon going to send his children to school?" Lindy glanced over her shoulder.

"I don't think he's made up his mind." Ella's gaze followed Lindy's shifting line of sight. All she saw was a buzzing crowd, a mix of Amish and *English*. She didn't recognize everyone, but who could on a day like this? A couple of tall *English* men who resembled each other carried a set of tent poles and a bundle of canvas. The auctioneer strode past with a megaphone in one hand. An Amish woman cradled a quilt as if it were her firstborn child. Everything Ella saw seemed normal for the day.

"I suppose I should get back to David," Lindy said, glancing the other direction.

"Lindy, what's wrong?" Ella asked. "What are you looking for?"

"I'm not sure," Lindy murmured. "I just get a funny feeling sometimes."

"What kind of feeling?"

"As if I'm being watched."

"There are hundreds of people here," Ella said.

"I know. It's just a feeling. Sometimes it happens in town, too." Lindy shook her head as if in a shudder. "Don't pay any attention to me. There's my booth."

Ella looked up to see David standing out in front of the booth with several other Amish boys near his age. She slowed her pace as she followed Lindy.

"My *daed* says I will go to school, but only for one year," a boy said. "He doesn't want to get involved in trouble, but I think it's silly."

"Mine will keep my brothers and me home," another boy said. "And I'm glad. I'm too old for school! My brothers know everything they need to know to help on the farm."

Ella loitered on the fringes of the booth as Lindy patted David on the shoulder in thanks and took her place among her display of colorfully painted birdhouses, children's toys, and quilt racks.

The boys were nearly unanimous in their opinion that it was ridiculous to think they needed to go to high school. One after another, they voiced the same opinion.

Everyone except David, who said nothing.

James watched his wife's face gladden at the array of goods around them. The six pies she baked for the auction sold within minutes of putting them on display. It was the same at every auction, whether spring or late summer. Everyone new Miriam Lehman's pies were the best in Geauga County.

A few moments ago, they had been arm in arm. Now Miriam had slid her arm out of his elbow to lean her head toward Mrs. King's, both of them pointing at quilts hanging from a web of lines strung between poles. James smiled, letting her go without protest. She deserved this day of pleasure and friendship, and he was glad to give it to her.

They were fourteen and finishing the eighth grade when they first began to look at each other with particular interest. They weren't even old enough to go to Singings, but they knew. James was certain first, and Miriam a few weeks later. They were young, but they would be together.

They were sixteen when they began going to Singings, and James refused to offer a ride home to any other young woman. Miriam was the one for him.

The day after her eighteenth birthday, they married. His father helped him acquire a small farm. Someday, James had thought, he would expand the acres. Someday, when he and Miriam had a houseful of children, sons and daughters, the promise of the future.

Then the children did not come.

At the beginning of December, James and Miriam would celebrate their forty-fourth anniversary and a life together that unfolded differently than either of them imagined in those early years.

They were *aunti* and *onkel* to dozens of children, the offspring of their siblings. Betsy and Lindy had always shone luminous even among their own siblings. While James still wondered what it might have been like to raise children of his own, his heart was at its most tender when he thought of the sisters.

One passed and the other chose the *English* world.

Still James loved them both.

❦

Margaret draped the quilt over the end of her bed.

She hadn't intended to purchase anything more than a few token jars of tomatoes to supplement what she had grown in her own yard, but when she saw the precise arrangement of green, blue, and purple triangles and flawless stitching, suddenly she wanted the quilt more than anything else she saw all morning.

Margaret had gone to the Amish auction accompanied by her ulterior motive—to understand more about these puzzling people who might—or might not—be the subject of considerable drama in sixteen short days. If they kept their children out of school, Margaret was sure the blame would be assigned to her failure to persuade them. If the first day of school passed peacefully, it would be no doing of Margaret's. She had no delusions of sincere victory because she had no conviction of the merits of the challenge.

The superintendent said he wanted a woman's touch in the matter. A woman's touch was personal and warm. What good could come from a heavy-handed approach? Margaret would work her way down her list of names and addresses and pay a call to each family, beginning Monday.

The quilt looked lovely in the bedroom, though Margaret would take some time deciding if it should have the place of her bedspread or instead be arranged casually on the back of the reading chair she kept beside the bed. What to do about the Amish conundrum was much more pressing.

Conundrum. Not a very friendly word.

Ice cream. Ice cream would soothe a ragged day, and making it would give her body something to do. Margaret lit the stove and pulled eggs and milk from the icebox and sugar and vanilla from the pantry. She stirred and mixed, her taste buds already anticipating a sensation still hours off.

The knock on the door, just as she took the mixture off the stove, startled her. That Margaret heard neither the approaching engine on the street nor the footsteps on her porch stairs testified to her preoccupation. At the front door, she glanced through the slender pane of glass and saw Gray Truesdale—and regretted she had not looked in the mirror before she left the bedroom and exerted herself in the kitchen. Smoothing her hair with one hand, she opened the door with the other.

Of course she was glad to see him, though befuddled how she had lost track of the likelihood that he would call tonight.

"I was in the middle of making ice cream," she said.

"I'll help," he said.

Margaret pointed to the wooden ice cream maker situated decoratively in the corner of the porch, and Gray bent to pick it up and carry it into the kitchen. He held the inner canister while she poured the mixture in and then added the dasher before securing the lid and handle.

"I hope you have plenty of ice," he said. "And salt."

"Both," Margaret said, "though I should have chipped off the ice before I began."

Gray smiled and rolled up his sleeves. "I'll do it."

She watched as he opened the bottom of the icebox and chipped enough ice to fill the wooden bucket far more efficiently than she could have. Effortlessly, he carried the assemblage out to the front porch, positioned himself on one knee, and began to crank. The muscles in his arms rippled in a captivating rhythm, and Margaret felt heat rise in the back of her neck at her inability to turn her eyes away from the movements of his lanky frame.

"I went out to the auction today." She forced herself to do something other than gawk at this man who had come into her life ten years later than she would have liked.

"I was there, too." He looked up. "Working with my brother."

"I didn't realize you had a brother."

"All my life." Gray grinned.

"Perhaps I'll meet him someday."

"I hope so." Gray's expression sobered. "He's my only family."

"Your parents?"

"Gone long ago. I'll tell you about it someday. Not tonight."

Margaret sucked in one cheek. Gray was thinking of their future.

"What kind of work were you doing today?" she asked.

"Helping to set up some tents. I left my brother on his own to get them down, but he'll be fairly paid for the extra work."

Gray cranked.

Margaret watched in admiration.

"I wanted to ask a question," he said.

"Of course."

He cranked.

She admired, hoping he did not see the unabating blush.

"Tomorrow is Sunday."

"Yes, it is."

"Church is at eleven."

"Yes, it is."

"I'd be pleased if you'd allow me to call for you at quarter till."

"I'd be pleased if you would," she said.

He cranked.

She made herself look away.

"Then I look forward to the Lord's Day all the more."

"Likewise, I'm sure."

He cranked. They made small talk—what they had seen at the auction, the fine weather, the headlines in the newspaper out of Cleveland about the war in Europe and spreading influenza. Gradually, the cranking slowed.

"It will have to sit for a while," Gray said.

Margaret crossed to the corner of the porch and unfolded a rug to lay over the ice cream maker.

"I have blackberries," she said.

"Is that so?"

"I mean, if you might like to come back after supper. We could put blackberries over the ice cream."

"Well, I believe that would be quite delicious and convenient."

She watched him saunter back out to his truck, already savoring what his kiss would taste like later that evening.

Ella stroked the nose of Gideon's new horse, hoping he had not paid too dearly for her. It was a buggy horse, though, not the workhorse she had expected him to purchase.

"I'll make sure she's well broken in before you need to use her," Gideon said.

Ella raised her face, confused.

"I have an extra cart I'll sand down," he said. "You'll always have a horse and cart available for visiting or shopping or whatever you need it for."

His eyes met hers, and she fell into them. "Gideon. . ."

"It's time, isn't it?" he said. "If you'll have me, I would like to be your loving husband."

"Of course I'll have you!" Ella's heart raced. The crowd around them lost its color, the vibrancy of the day fading in the illumined moment.

"I'll care for you, provide for you, and do my best to bring happiness into each of your days."

"Gideon. . ." She wanted him to kiss her.

He cupped her elbow and nudged her around the back side of the makeshift stable behind the auction ring, and she waited while he glanced in both directions before removing his hat and dipping his head to oblige her wish—which he evidently shared. Ella hoped Gideon's kiss would always draw her to him as it did now.

"Your father will have no objection, will he?" Gideon whispered when he broke the kiss.

"None whatsoever."

"I could speak to him today, if you like."

"As soon as possible, please."

"Wedding season is only two months off."

"We can be one of the first couples to publish our banns." What a relief it would be to talk openly about their relationship. They could speak to the bishop and set the date for the first Thursday in November, as soon as the harvest season was finished. Rachel would gladly take on the role of mother of the bride, and Ella's siblings would come from their scattered farms for a joyful day.

Gideon kissed her again, this time lingering in a delectable recognition of the decision Ella had waited so long for. He was hers.

What sort of small gift of friendship might she take to Amish families as she visited? Sampling at the auction had convinced Margaret she could not compete with their jams or jellies, and their baked goods tempted her to beg for recipes that had never been written down. She wandered through the mercantile on Monday morning considering whether packets of stationery might be appropriate for the mothers, or perhaps flower seeds to put away for next spring.

I should have asked Lindy. She used to be one of them.

Margaret picked up two packets of stationery with matching envelopes bundled together in wide ribbons. She would start with two families today. If the gift seemed to cause offense, tomorrow she would try something else.

At the counter, as she counted out the necessary coins, she was startled to see Mr. Brownley enter the store.

Their eyes met.

"Good morning," Margaret said.

"Good morning." Brownley's eyes shifted to look down the long center aisle. "Have you seen the deputy sheriff? I was told he came in here."

The clerk pushed a button and the cash register opened. "He's in the back. Saw him looking at the hammers. Said he'd be right up."

"I told him I would just be a minute and he disappeared," Brownley muttered.

"Is everything all right, Mr. Brownley?" Margaret asked.

"Everything is in hand, Miss Simpson. The sheriff and I decided to pay a few calls on the farms, that's all."

"I'm about to do the same thing," Margaret said. "I thought perhaps a gentle, personal approach—"

"School starts two weeks from today," Brownley said. "I've decided we need a firm approach, one that makes the law clear."

Margaret's jaw dropped. She clenched it closed immediately. "Did I misunderstand your instructions to me?"

"I was clear, was I not?"

"I thought so. But now you seem inclined to handle the matter yourself."

Deputy Fremont plunked money on the counter, and the two men exited the mercantile.

Margaret scrambled after them. "May I inquire about the nature of the calls you plan to pay?"

Deputy Fremont laughed. "My badge is all the explanation most folks need."

Margaret hustled to keep pace with their strides.

"I thought we'd take my automobile," the sheriff said. "It will look more official."

"Good, good. Makes a strong statement."

"Mr. Brownley," Margaret said, trailing them, "might I have a word?"

"You can come along, Miss Simpson." Brownley nodded at the deputy. "She won't be any trouble."

"Mr. Brownley, please." Margaret's pitch rose. "Ought we not act in concert on the matter? Is this really necessary?" Had he expected that in less than a week she would be able to report that the Amish families had promised compliance? Indignation rose at the insult of his assigning a task to her and nevertheless acting on the matter without so much as a consultation. He would never have treated the efforts of a man so trivially.

"As I said," Brownley replied without pausing his step, "you may come with us if you wish. But the matter is settled. Deputy Fremont suggested that a visual reminder of the strength of law might prove effective, and I think he has a point. He's certain the sheriff over in Chardon would agree. We can be done with this matter once and for all."

So this was Deputy Fremont's idea. Despite the abundant

Amish population in his district, apparently he understood their peaceable ways even less than she did. Margaret ignored the deputy's cockeyed grin.

"We can't possibly know who will turn up on the first day of school," Margaret said. "Maybe all of them will."

"Unlikely," snapped the deputy.

When they reached the deputy's vehicle, Margaret thrust herself between the officer and the superintendent. "I must forcefully remonstrate against this decision. Give me time. I will bring you a report as we agreed."

"I've changed my mind," Brownley said.

"Then the task you described is no longer incumbent upon me?"

Brownley shook his head. "I didn't say that. I'm sure the softer side of a woman will have its place, but you cannot have expected I would abdicate my responsibility and leave the matter entirely in your hands."

Fremont leaned against the hood of the car to crank the engine. Brownley nudged Margaret aside and opened the passenger door.

"What's our first stop?" Fremont asked when the engine caught.

"Now here's where you can help, Miss Simpson," Brownley said. "Who is the most influential Amish father?"

Margaret hesitated but finally said, "Gideon Wittmer." He was influential, but Margaret's brief encounters with him also led her to believe he would hold his own. The deputy's vehicle would have no bearing on his response.

"Where's his farm?"

"I'm coming with you." Margaret avoided Brownley's eyes, instead pushing past him to climb into the backseat.

❧❦❧

The boys were out back, throwing pebbles toward the side of the barn to see who could land one closest to the structure without striking it. From his kitchen window, Gideon watched Tobias competing with Jed Hilty's boys.

"We'll all be kin before too long." Jed toyed with his mug and sipped his coffee. "I couldn't be more pleased that you and Ella will wed. You'll give her a fine home. And with only sons of her own, Rachel never expected to be mother of the bride."

"Ella will appreciate her advice." Gideon returned the coffeepot to the stove. "I'm no help. When I married Betsy, her mother and sisters arranged everything, right down to how many roast chickens we needed for the meal."

Jed chuckled. "I have three other daughters. I've learned that weddings are a good time to let the womenfolk take the lead."

"The boys get along well," Gideon said, looking out the window again.

"Seth gets along with everyone," Jed said. "David is peculiar at times, but they are both good boys. Their father would have been proud."

"Will you send them to school?" Gideon had not intended to be so blunt, but with only two weeks left of the summer break, the imminent need to find his own answer to the question had begun to round the corner of polite conversation.

"Seth is only twelve," Jed said. "He just finished the sixth grade, so he should take two more years."

"But at the *English* school?" Gideon turned his gaze to the eyes of his future father-in-law. "You've decided that this is right and pleasing to God?"

"I've decided Seth will handle himself well and learn what he needs to learn. He's not a troublemaker, and he won't want to disgrace his mother."

"And David?"

Jed sighed. "Fifteen years old. I see nothing he will gain from returning to school after he's been out for a year. Rachel agrees."

"He's not even close to his sixteenth birthday."

"No, but I can't see how the *English* will find reason to bother themselves about Amish children who have already left school. It makes no sense for them to return to the rolls."

"I'm glad to hear you say that," Gideon said. "Tobias is only thirteen, but he'll soon be fourteen. I'll need him for the harvest, but then he can go to school over the winter. I'll take him out again when I need him for the early spring planting. He won't want to go back next year."

Gertie burst into the room, coming from the front of the house.

"*Daed*, two *English* men are here." Gertie's eyes widened. "Savilla said to find you right away."

Gideon swooped up Gertie and strode through the house. Jed's boots thudded right behind him.

"Savilla!" Gideon called as soon as he was on the front porch. The girl ran toward him, leaving two men standing alongside the fenced pasture.

"I heard them talking," Savilla said. "It's about school."

"And the lady who was here before came again," Gertie said.

Gideon eyed the parked car, recognizing it as a vehicle that belonged to the Geauga County sheriff's department. He set Gertie on the porch.

"Savilla, take your sister in the house," Gideon said, "or go out to the *dawdihaus* and visit Miriam."

"Is everything all right?" Savilla took Gertie's hand but looked over her shoulder at the visitors, who now fixed their stares on her father.

"I'm sure it is," Gideon said. "We'll talk about it later."

Jed kept pace with Gideon as they walked across the rolling front yard toward the fence.

"I'm Gideon Wittmer," Gideon said. He nodded at Margaret Simpson, the only one of the three visitors he recognized. "What can I do for you?"

"We just want to make sure you understand the law," said the uniformed man.

Margaret stepped forward. "This is Deputy Fremont and Superintendent Brownley. There's nothing to worry about."

"I'm not worried," Gideon said.

So this was the superintendent behind the forceful correspondence made to sound friendlier than it was.

"I'm Mr. Hilty," Jed said. "Is there something you need from us today?"

The superintendent flipped a few papers. "Jed Hilty. I don't see the Hilty name on our list of students."

"I've received your letters. I have stepsons who might be on your forms," Jed said. "Kaufman."

"So you both understand the new laws?" the deputy asked.

"We've read your letters," Gideon said.

"Do you have questions?" Margaret asked. "This would be a good opportunity to have them answered."

"No questions," Gideon said. The more he looked at Miss Simpson, the more nervous she seemed.

"Good," said Mr. Brownley. "Then can we expect your full cooperation?"

❦❧

"Rachel told me the happy news." Lindy embraced Ella in the middle of a Seabury furniture store that frequently carried Amish craftsmanship.

"*Danki!*" Ella made no effort to contain her smile.

The last two days had been a whirlwind. Though her engagement to Gideon would not be published to the church officially for weeks, already the news buzzed.

"When Betsy married Gideon," Lindy said, "he became my brother. I suppose your marriage will make you my sister."

Ella swallowed a lump that formed in an instant. "You're so gracious to me. No one can take Betsy's place, but I'm going to do my best to love her family as she would have."

"I know you will. And you can count on me for help. Just let me know what you need."

Ella glanced at a crate Lindy had set on the floor.

"Toys." Lindy leaned toward Ella and spoke behind her hand. "The owners discovered that they sell more furniture if children find a toy to play with while the parents shop. And even if they don't buy furniture, they almost always buy the toy."

Ella giggled. "I only came in to look. I'm not sure Gideon realizes how much space my books take."

"Let me make you a bookcase," Lindy said. "It will be a wedding present."

Lindy glanced over her shoulder, first in one direction and then the other.

"Are you still having that strange sensation?" Ella asked.

Lindy nodded. "I was sure someone was following me just now on the street. I was anxious to get inside. But if I don't know who is following me, how do I know the person is not in the shop now?"

Ella looked around the store. She saw an *English* couple with a small child, who likely would soon discover the treat of Lindy's well-crafted toys, and an *English* man standing in front of a dining hutch and nodding at the salesman's explanation of its features. At the back of the store, a woman wearing a light wool dress bent over an oversized ledger. They could have been in any shop in town.

"You don't see anything odd, do you?" Lindy asked.

Ella shrugged. "I guess not. Everyone looks ordinary."

"I'm probably just on edge. I get a thing in mind, and then it won't leave." Lindy waved off the thought. "I can't even describe who it is I feel watching me. Don't pay any attention to me."

Ella now turned her face toward the window that looked out on the street, where people went about their business in unremarkable ways. Some stopped for a glance in the shop's window, which featured a small table and chairs set attractively, but most walked briskly past on their way somewhere else. No one seemed to loiter.

"I'd better let the owner know the toys are here," Lindy said. "Then I'll be on my way and try to keep my spooks to myself."

CHAPTER 10

Seething irritation tarnished the shine of exuberance Margaret usually felt on the first day of a new school year. When she accompanied the deputy and superintendent to the Wittmer farm, she had nursed a frantic hope that she might buffer the encounter. Instead, Gideon's refusal to say with certainty that all three of his children would be in the consolidated school incensed both officials, sending them charging off to other farms with an even more stern approach. Margaret's efforts to coax and cajole yielded no satisfaction for anyone. When the trio returned to town, after being stonewalled at four farms, Mr. Brownley insinuated that if the Amish children did not attend school, he might have to reconsider her principal's assurance that she was a highly capable teacher.

Margaret made the rounds, introducing herself to mothers and leaving small gifts that seemed feebler with each visit, and at the end of two weeks she still had no clear inclination of what the Amish would do. In fact, she had growing doubts that even the *English* families would cooperate until after the fall harvest when they no longer needed the unpaid labor of their children.

On September 9, Margaret was outside the school even before Mr. Tarkington arrived to unlock the building. The classroom was ready. She had nothing else to do but wait for her students, but she wanted to be in an environment where she was certain she could maintain order.

Margaret straightened books. She had refrained from unburdening herself with Gray Truesdale on the Amish matter. He was a strong man. He would want a woman who could manage her own affairs.

She checked the chalk in the long tray running along the base of the blackboard, making sure a fresh piece was positioned every eighteen inches, and thought about Deputy Fremont. If ever a man knew nothing about children!

Raising the lid to every desk, Margaret ensured she had placed a sheet of art paper from the art cabinet in the downstairs corridor for each child. Her students were six-year-olds, and children who enjoyed school were more likely to learn their words and sums. Art on the first day would help set the tone.

She imagined the bus rumbling out to the farms and stopping at the designated corners to collect the children, beginning with the most outlying acres and gradually moving back toward Seabury. How many would get on?

She picked up the pages of her attendance list and seating chart and tapped them to precision at the corners.

Children are resilient, Margaret reminded herself. This would not be the first time she had students who were uncertain about entering a classroom. Very, very few failed to adjust to the classroom structure and expectations. First graders from the farms would be learning the same reading and spelling and arithmetic they would have learned had their one-room school not collapsed. There would just be a few other subjects as well.

Running a finger down the list of names, Margaret settled on the last alphabetical entry. *Wittmer, Gertrude.*

❧❀☙

"I want to go."

David's tone was respectful, controlled—and more adamant than Ella had supposed him capable of. Why had she not noticed before this how tall he was?

"Seth will go." Jed replaced the Bible he used for morning family devotions on the shelf. "You will stay here on the farm. I can't spare you."

David spread his feet, bracing his stance. "I've lived here less than a year. You always got along without my help before this."

"I've made my decision." Jed adjusted his glasses on his face.

"What about my decision?" David said. "You never even asked me what I thought was right to do."

"We'll work in the south pasture today," Jed said.

Seth stood at the door running one thumb and forefinger along his suspenders while gripping his metal lunch bucket in the other hand. Ella glanced at Rachel, who averted her eyes from the quarrel brewing between her husband and son. Ella didn't blame her. She had no wish to watch it boil over, either. Up to this point, David had not outright defied Jed. Ella sprang up from her chair, crossed the room, and put a hand on Seth's back to guide him out the door before closing it behind her.

"What is your *daed* going to do?" Seth asked.

"What he thinks is best because he cares about both of you." Ella's answer was swift and honest. "You don't mind if I walk with you to the bus, do you?"

Seth shrugged. "I know the way."

"Of course you do. But it might help your mother if she knew that the arrangements the *English* made have worked out."

Seth was a mild child, without the complexity that pulsed under David's usual outward respect of his elders. He would do whatever would be easiest for his mother.

Seth's designated bus corner—and David's, were he allowed to attend school—was three-quarters of a mile down the main road at the end of the Glicks' lane. To attend the one-room schoolhouse, Seth had walked more than twice as far last year. Still, Ella hated to think of him standing on the side of the road on a dark, frigid morning when winter came, wondering if the bus would be on time.

Mrs. Glick stood at the corner with two of her children. Ella tried to remember how old they were—was it seven and eight or eight and nine? The girls were so alike in size and coloring that Ella had trouble keeping them straight.

The Mast boys were there also, their lunch buckets already set aside to free their hands for tossing pebbles into a small creek across the road. Seth shrugged out of his jacket to join them with his superior aim. Ella contemplated their ages as well. At least one of them was older than fourteen and headed for the high school.

"David is not coming?" Mrs. Glick stood with her daughters on either side of her, arms around their shoulders protectively.

Ella shook her head.

"What a difficult day," Mrs. Glick said. "We will pray for God's care for all our hearts."

"He does not fail us," Ella said. She peered down the road in the direction Gideon would come from. His three children were also assigned to this bus stop. Ella's head pivoted between watching Seth, who showed no sign of trepidation about attending an *English* school, and watching for Gideon.

When her vigilance was rewarded and Gideon's buggy swayed into view, Ella let her breath out. She hadn't known what to think. They spoke of the question every time they saw each other, yet she hadn't been sure he would put his children on the bus. His horse clip-clopped toward Ella, and she made sure to have a smile on her face, both for Gideon and for the children.

Gertie and Savilla jumped out of the buggy in matching green dresses, black aprons, and braids securely pinned against their heads under their *kapps*. Tobias took his time. From the buggy bench, Gideon's eyes settled for a few seconds on each of the assembled children.

Ella approached the buggy.

"David didn't come," Gideon said.

"He wanted to."

"Jed has said all along that he saw no benefit in taking the boy out of the fields when he already finished his book learning."

"And you," Ella said. "You're here with all of your *kinner*."

The head of every student and adult at the corner turned toward the clattering of an unfamiliar vehicle, all of them curious about the *English* bus. The front end looked like most of the vehicles that rumbled down this road from time to time. A black hood housed the engine, with an open bench behind the steering wheel. The bus stopped in the middle of the intersection.

Mrs. Glick's girls broke away from the stance they had held so dutifully. Curiosity widened the eyes of all the children. Even the older boys abandoned their pebble tossing.

"It looks like a cage in a wagon," Gertie pronounced.

The comparison was apt. A sturdy wagon base spanned the wide rear axle, and wooden framing rose from the wagon—where she presumed there were benches—to the roof above. On a fine day like today, canvas flaps were rolled and restrained up against the roof. When winter came, they could easily be let down to offer protection from the elements. It would still be very cold.

Ella had once ridden in an automobile, but she doubted any of the children gawking at the bus had. A few hands pushed out from the interior, followed by faces looking over the horizontal timbers of the wagon's framing.

The Byler children, Ella noted, and the King children. The Henderson boy, an *English*, grinned as if he had never done anything so exciting in his entire life. Ella recognized a couple of *English* girls who rolled their eyes at the silliness around them. The bus would make one more stop, closer to town, for the last of the children assigned to this bus. At least one other bus would make a separate route picking up children who lived in the opposite direction from town.

The bus driver lumbered off his bench and down the one step to the ground. He consulted a sheet of paper. "Let's see, Glick?"

"Here," the two girls chimed.

"Climb aboard." The driver pulled a pencil from over his ear and made two check marks. "Kaufman?"

Seth raised a hand.

"Should be two," the driver muttered. "Seth and David."

"I'm Seth. My brother is not coming." Seth placed one foot on the step and hoisted himself into the bus.

Ella's stomach clenched as she watched the *English* cavern swallow the unsuspecting boy.

"The superintendent is not going to like this." The driver pursed his lips and drew a careful circle around David's name. "Mast?"

The oldest students of the corner clambered aboard.

"Let's see," the driver said. "That leaves Wittmer. Three."

Ella sucked in a breath and held it.

⚜

Gideon bent over and spoke to his young daughters. He had made his peace with this moment. Savilla was a sensible child. Gertie was simply relieved that she did not have to go to the school that had collapsed around her. She was younger and more impulsive than Savilla, and as much as it seemed impossible that his youngest was old enough for school, Gertie was ready.

"Savilla, you are the older one," he said, looking into their matching green eyes. "You must look after Gertie. Do you understand?"

"Yes, *Daed*." The girls spoke in unison.

"You do as you're told. Follow instructions. Remember your manners. Don't lose your lunch pails."

"Yes, *Daed*."

With his hands on their shoulders, Gideon turned his daughters around. They held hands as they got on the bus, Savilla patiently waiting for her small sister to manage the high step into the bus. Gertie immediately stuck her head out and waved.

The driver consulted his list again before looking at Tobias. "You the Wittmer boy?"

Tobias nodded.

"Let's go, then. We have a schedule to keep."

Tobias looked at his father.

Gideon cleared his throat. "Tobias will not be attending school. He is needed on the farm."

The driver tapped his paper. "I can't do anything about the Kaufman boy who didn't show up, but Tobias Wittmer is standing right in front of me. He needs to get on the bus."

"He's not going. I'm his father, and this is the decision I've made."

"The law says he needs to go to school."

"The law does not know my boy," Gideon said. "He was one of the brightest students in our school. Miss Coates said he was doing eighth-grade work two years ago. I need his help, and the consoli-dated school will not teach him what he needs to know to farm."

"I'm not in charge of what they teach," the driver said. "I'm just supposed to get the students to school."

Gideon looked up at the sun. "As you said, you have a schedule to keep."

The driver puffed out his cheeks and shook his head while he carefully circled Tobias's name. "You'll be hearing from the principal."

CHAPTER 11

Gideon." Ella put a hand on his arm.

"It's all right."

His eyes fixed on his little girls, Gertie hanging out of the bus to wave enthusiastically and Savilla trying to tug her sister back to safety. Ella forced herself to wiggle her fingers at the girls. Whatever she felt at their departure into the *English* world, even for a day, must be magnified in Gideon's heart.

"Not too late to change your mind," the driver said. "Be a law-abiding citizen."

Gideon shook his head.

"Are you sure?" Ella asked.

"No. Yes."

The bus's engine roared to life and the driver put it in gear. Ella's vision clouded with the dust the oversized tires thrust into the air, and she covered her mouth to cough.

"Gideon Wittmer, what have you done?"

Mrs. Glick. Ella had nearly forgotten she was there. Simultaneously, she and Gideon turned to face their neighbor's bulging eyes.

"You stood right here and watched me put my children on that bus." Mrs. Glick scraped her shoe through the dirt. "My little girls."

"My little girls are also on the bus," Gideon said.

Mrs. Glick pointed at Tobias. "The other boys got on, and some of them are older than your son."

"I cannot cross my conscience," Gideon said.

"What will the other fathers think?" Mrs. Glick jabbed a finger in Ella's direction. "And Jed Hilty! Did the two of you decide together to do this?"

"We talked about it," Gideon said, "but I don't make another man's decision."

"I know Mrs. Mast didn't want those boys to go on the bus. What are you going to say to her about keeping your boy home?"

"I do not imagine we will discuss it," Gideon said. "The matter is between Mrs. Mast and her husband."

"But the law!"

"There are new laws about education," Gideon said, "but there are also laws about religious freedom. Isn't that what brought our ancestors to America two hundred years ago?"

Mrs. Glick huffed and tied her bonnet in a firm knot before pivoting and stomping toward her home.

"Maybe she's right, *Daed*."

Tobias's voice surprised Ella, and she riffled through her memories of the last few weeks for any sentence she'd heard him speak on the subject of school or a remark Gideon might have passed on about something his son had said. She came up with nothing.

"It's all right," Gideon said.

"But *Daed*. . ."

Gideon put an arm around his son's shoulders, as Ella had seen him do countless times in the last few years.

"Are you saying you want to go to school?" Gideon asked.

Tobias hesitated. Ella could not tell whether he was considering disagreeing with his father or simply wanted Gideon to be safe.

"We'll talk more at home," Gideon said. "Why don't you drive the buggy home? I'll see you there. I feel like a walk."

Tobias looked from Gideon to Ella before shuffling toward the horse and finding the reins. Ella watched him put the buggy into motion and drive past them before reaching for Gideon's hand.

He squeezed her fingers. "It's all right."

"You keep saying that," Ella said.

"It's true."

"But it's risky." Slowly they began to walk toward the Hilty farm. "You're breaking the law."

"So is your father."

"I know." Her voice caught. "I'm worried about both of you."

"We are in God's hands."

"What if there are consequences?"

"The authorities are blustering," Gideon said.

"How can you be certain?"

He lifted one shoulder and let it drop. "Perhaps I'm not. But why will they concern themselves with Amish young people? We pay our taxes, and they leave us alone. That's the way it has always been. They are blustering for the sake of their own people, not for us."

Ella pressed her lips together. Gideon made a good point. The Amish population in Geauga County was fairly significant, but no one had ever disturbed their way of life. They lived on their own farms, took care of each other, and asked little of the *English*. Why should the *English* care now?

But the deputy had been to see Gideon with the superintendent. Official correspondence reminding everyone of the laws had arrived in the mailboxes of all the Amish families.

"What if they press the issue?" Ella said. "What if you're wrong and they do care?"

"Then I will be wrong about that," Gideon said, "but I will not be wrong about our right to express our religious beliefs. Even the *English* laws protect that."

"I'm nervous, Gideon."

"I know."

"I wish I could be as calm as you are." Ella sighed. "I should get home. Rachel and *Daed* and David—I don't know what to think."

"Seth will be all right."

"It's David I'm worried about."

At the sound of the bell, students who had attended Seabury Consolidated Grade School the previous year responded by jostling out of their social groups and into grade-level lines. Margaret's job in this annual first-day ritual was to assist and redirect any students who seemed uncertain what to do. She ambled through the recess play area while students scrambled into formation and spoke quietly to children who looked confused about the procedure, pointing toward the lines they should join. These children were in three categories: first graders starting school, older students who were new to the district, and Amish, with their expansive, startled eyes sponging up the motion around them and the details of the building before them.

"Look at them." A seventh grader jeered at two Amish boys in his line. "I'll bet they don't even know how to read."

"That's enough," Margaret snapped. "In this school, we show respect for all our students. Is that understood?"

"Yes, ma'am." The boy looked at his feet.

Margaret turned to the Amish students. "Welcome to our school. I would love to know your names."

"Seth Kaufman," one said.

"Jacob King," the other said.

"You're both in Mr. Taylor's class. You'll enjoy him and learn a great deal."

"*Danki*," Seth said.

Jacob elbowed him and whispered, "Speak English."

"Thank you," Seth said.

The last straggler found a place in the fourth-grade line, and Margaret marched alongside the first graders to greet her own students. The daily entrance into the school always began with the youngest classes. Margaret led the wobbly line of six-year-olds through the main hall on the first floor, up the stairs at the rear of the building, and into her classroom. There, she stood at the door greeting children and pointing to where they should sit. She'd already memorized the seating chart. Now she simply needed to connect faces with the names.

Richard. Franklin. Patricia. Molly. Mary. Elbert. Gertrude.

"You're the lady who was looking for my *daed*," Gertie said.

"That's right," Margaret said. "I remember you. How lucky I am to be your teacher this year."

"*Daed* says there is no such thing as luck. Only *Gottes wille*."

Beside Gertie, a thin Amish boy nodded his head, and his hat bobbed.

"Well, if it's *Gottes wille* for me to be your teacher, I am even more pleased." Margaret turned to the boy. "You must be Hans Byler."

The boy nodded again.

"I thought you two might like to sit next to each other," Margaret said, pointing. "I have two seats for you right there in the second row."

Margaret was glad Gertie and Hans had each other. Altogether six Amish students were supposed to enter the high school, and twenty-six were due to transfer to the consolidated grade school. But Margaret was certain she did not see that many outside as the lines formed. Not nearly that many. Her stomach soured at the impending conversation with Mr. Brownley about her failure in the assigned task.

Once everyone was seated, Margaret put a smile on her face and turned to welcome the first-grade class of 1918.

*M*amm, school is fine." Seth tucked the cloth napkin around the ham sandwich in his lunch pail and pressed the lid into place.

"You would tell me if something is not right," Rachel said.

"I would tell you. It's been a week, and everything is fine. I listen to the teacher, I do my work, I come home. It's not so different."

Ella tapped the loaf on the bread board. If she wrapped it now, it might still be warm when she arrived at the Hershberger farm. She had plenty of stew left from yesterday to feed the Hershberger family, which had grown last week with the birth of their newest daughter.

Seth picked up a mathematics textbook. "I have to go or I'll miss the bus."

His lips brushed his mother's cheek as he aimed for the back door. Before the screen door slammed closed, Jed came through it into the kitchen with a sigh he made no effort to disguise.

Rachel looked up. "What's wrong?"

"David has gone off already."

"The barn?" Rachel said.

Jed shook his head.

"Stables?"

"No."

"He'll be waiting for you in the field."

Ella glanced up at her father's doubtful expression and tucked a jar of strawberry jam into the food basket she was preparing.

"Every time I turn around, I've lost David," Jed said. "He doesn't come back for hours."

"He'll settle down," Rachel said. "He knows how important harvesttime is."

Ella spread a clean flour sack towel over the top of the basket. "Is it still all right if I take the buggy to the Hershbergers'?"

Jed nodded. "Please give Mrs. Hershberger our congratulations."

As Ella drove, she prayed. Thanksgiving for Seth's smooth adjustment to the new school. Mercy for David to accept Jed's decision. Grace for Rachel's palpable anxiety. Wisdom for Jed—and Gideon—if the *English* made trouble. Her prayers took her to the Hershberger farm.

As she lifted her basket from below the driving bench, the children's voices clattered through the open windows. The latest birth brought the number of children to eight. The oldest was about Seth's age. Walking toward the house, Ella cocked her head, trying to remember whether Seth had mentioned that the Hershberger boy was in his class.

She climbed the steps to the porch, listening to the cacophony of one child's wail and another's plea for maternal attention, while an older child's voice warned a sibling to get down off a stool.

Ella paused as she raised her knuckles to knock. At least four of the Hershberger children were school age, perhaps five. The bus would have come to their stop at least half an hour ago. Why were so many of them at home? She knocked, and a mumbling shuffle progressed toward the door. When it opened, Ella looked into the eyes of the eldest Hershberger daughter.

"*Gut mariye.*" Ella hid her speculations behind a smile. "Congratulations on your new baby sister."

"*Danki.* Please come in." The girl had a firm grasp on a four-year-old's shoulder. "I'll tell *Mamm* you've come."

She left Ella standing alone in the front room while she hurried down the hall toward the kitchen at the rear of the old farmhouse. A few minutes later, Joanna Hershberger appeared with an infant in her arms.

Ella smiled again. A boy and a girl, school-age, eyed her from across the room.

"I've brought some food," Ella said. "There's plenty for all of you to have a good meal. You only need to warm the stew."

Joanna tilted her head toward the oldest girl, who stepped forward to take the basket of food from Ella's arms. When she left the room, several other children trailed after her, curious about the pot's contents.

Ella turned to Joanna and put her arms out. "May I?"

"Of course." Joanna laid the sleeping infant in Ella's arms.

"Are you able to rest?"

Joanna shrugged. "Not at this age. But I will have her on a schedule soon."

Ella glanced toward the kitchen. "Your oldest daughter seems helpful."

"I don't know what I'd do without Lizzy."

"I'm sure you miss her when she's in school," Ella said. "Are they just out for a few days while you welcome your babe?"

Joanna looked away at nothing in particular. "John has decided our children will learn at home. I will teach them."

So far Ella had seen nothing to suggest organized lessons in progress—or organized anything. She returned her gaze to the baby in her arms, who yawned but did not open her eyes.

"The Borntragers also will teach their children at home," Joanna said. "We can work together on the lessons. We'll begin soon."

Ella nodded noncommittally. Her father. Gideon. John Hershberger. Isaiah Borntrager. Who else was defying the new laws?

❧✦❧

Gideon, Aaron King, and Cristof Byler huddled around the harvesting equipment in Gideon's alfalfa field. The mid-September morning brought an overcast sky. Gideon hoped it would burn off soon.

Cristof braced his foot against a stationary wagon wheel. "Don't you think it would be better if we're all of one mind?"

Gideon puffed out his cheeks in a slow exhale. "The men I've talked to seem to have made up their minds."

"What about the bishop?" Aaron said. "In all these weeks, I haven't heard him say anything."

"Why don't we meet with him?" Cristof raised his eyebrows.

"I've spoken with him," Gideon said. "He came to see me. He understands the complexity of the question."

"A church vote, then," Aaron said.

"And what would we vote on?" Gideon said. "Forbid our children to go to school in town? Let the younger ones go, but not the older ones? What about pupils who have already finished the eighth grade, and now the *English* want them to return to school? Whatever we decide, the *English* will find fault. No, I don't think a church vote is the right course."

"Then tell us what you suggest." Cristof crossed his arms over his chest.

"The apostle Paul reminds us that as far as it is up to us, we should live at peace with all men—including the *English*."

"They will only recognize peace if we do what they say we must," Cristof said.

Aaron squinted his eyes. "I think Gideon has something else in mind."

Gideon nodded. "The school board meets tomorrow. We can go to them—the entire board—and ask for an exception to their rules. We can assure them we want our children to have the education they need for the way we live—and we can provide it ourselves."

"But we don't have a teacher," Cristof said. "We don't even have a school."

"One thing at a time," Gideon said.

"It won't work." Cristof grunted and turned away.

"One thing at a time," Gideon repeated.

⊱✦⊰

"One thing have I desired of the Lord, that will I seek after; that I may dwell in the house of the Lord all the days of my life, to behold the beauty of the Lord and to enquire in his temple."

The words of Psalm 27 wafted through James's mind as his wagon reached the highest peak of the rolling hills, and he held the horses for a moment so his spirit could inhale the view. The tinge of red creeping through the leaves announced the turn of the season. The sun's glare still made him shade his eyes, but without summer's ferocity. The lake reminded him he had promised Tobias a fishing day before the weather turned too cold for an early morning outing when the fish were biting. What was missing was the white wooden tower of the old schoolhouse. Instead, James saw the hole in the roof and the slight slant of the entire building. Would the *English* have moved all the children to the schools in town if the rural structure had remained sound? Or if Miss Coates had not left to marry? The change likely was only a matter of time.

Movement caught James's eye. A figure moved to the back of the schoolhouse with a ladder. The roofline was lower in the rear. Miriam had made James stop scaling roofs a long time ago, but it was fairly simple to get on the school's roof from the back. James urged his horses forward full speed, down the sloping ground toward the schoolhouse.

"Isaiah Borntrager, what in the world are you doing?" James scrambled off his bench and stomped over to the base of the ladder. Isaiah was two-thirds of the way up.

"There's no such thing as an Amish man who doesn't know how to build," Isaiah said. "We manage to keep our homes standing. Why shouldn't we keep the school standing?"

"Half the roof fell in, Isaiah. Come down from there."

Isaiah took another step up.

"This outside wall is not trustworthy," James said. "It won't hold your ladder."

"God is trustworthy."

James sighed. He did not think this was what the scriptures meant when they spoke of trusting God.

"Isaiah," James said, "come down. Let's talk about this."

"I'll gladly accept any help you feel led to offer," Isaiah said, turning to look down at James over one shoulder, "but I'm through talking. I am a man of action."

"Does your wife know you're doing this?"

"This is not her decision."

"Just what do you plan to do when you get up there?" James gripped the rails of the ladder and braced his feet.

"Today I'm just looking around to see the true condition," Isaiah said. "Then I'll make a plan. I'm not going to sit around waiting for the state to decide what is best for *my* children. If you don't want to help, go on home."

Having seen what Isaiah was doing, James could hardly drive off now. He gripped the ladder more tightly, realizing that Isaiah's decrepit ladder was in no better condition than the school's roof. James fixed his eyes on Isaiah's left foot as it tested the next rung. James saw the step give more than it should have.

"Watch out!"

The rung cracked. Isaiah lost his balance. The ladder surrendered its purchase on the side of the building. Isaiah let go. James's sight filled with the mass of stubbornness dropping straight toward him. The last thing James saw was Isaiah's hat flying off his head.

Then James was on the ground, and Isaiah was on top of him.

❧

"What was I supposed to do?" James winced.

Miriam dipped a cotton cloth in a bowl of warm water and dabbed the scrapes on her husband's cheek again. "Isaiah could have killed himself falling off that ancient ladder—and you."

"I don't think he'll try that again."

"Unless he gets a new ladder," Miriam said. "Are you sure you don't need a doctor?"

James took the cloth from Miriam's hand and probed under his beard for a spot where he suspected the skin had split. Already his shoulders, hips, and knees ached from the sudden surprise of Isaiah's weight dropped on him. James pushed out of his mind the image of what might have happened if Isaiah had been alone when he fell.

"No doctor," he said. "I may be moving slowly for a few days, though."

"Then we'll move slowly together."

James watched Miriam as she carried the bowl of water to the sink. The spry gait she'd had since girlhood was diminished. Miriam's neck bent at a tired angle.

"Disagreeing with the *English* is no excuse for doing something foolish," Miriam said. "But we can always count on Isaiah Borntrager to be rash."

"Things were simpler when we were in school."

"That was a long time ago, old man." Miriam winked.

She started calling him *old man* on his twenty-fifth birthday, which came fifty-six days before hers. Now, James supposed, he more obviously fit the description.

The *dawdihaus* door opened, and Gertie tumbled in.

"I'm sorry, little one," Miriam said. "I didn't bake cookies today."

"That's okay. My friend Polly shared the cookie her *mamm* put in her lunch bucket."

"That was generous," James said.

Gertie climbed into James's lap, as she did every day after school. "What happened to your face?"

"God gave me this face," James said. "Maybe I got the leftovers because He was saving the best parts for you."

Gertie giggled and leaned into James's sore right shoulder.

"How was school?" James smothered his wince.

"I like school," Gertie said. "I can read twelve words now. Pretty soon I'll know enough to read a whole book to you."

"That will be great fun." James kissed the top of her head. "And the bus?"

"Polly's teaching me songs to sing on the bus."

"Oh?" Over Gertie's head, James caught Miriam's eye.

"They're not like the songs we sing in church," Gertie said. "They go fast, and they rhyme, and we do hand motions."

James changed the subject. "Did your teacher give you an assignment to do before you go back to school?"

"She said we should choose a book at home and see if we can find three words we know and read them to our families."

James tried to picture Gideon's small shelf of books. At least half of them were in German. Gertie might have to find her words in a seed catalog.

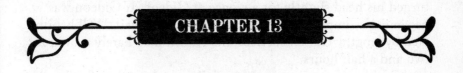

CHAPTER 13

With their black hats still on their heads, a row of Amish men sat straight-backed in the downtown Seabury building where the school board held its announced meetings. James was among them. Gideon planned to speak on behalf of the group, but he mustered the men to produce a presence that would let the board know they were earnest in their petition. He was not one man speaking on his own. Even the bishop had come in support. This was not one or two fathers disgruntled with the new regulations. It was an unsettled community that wanted to find peace again.

Gideon was warned he would have to wait until the call for new business was announced, and the board would not have a great deal of time to hear him out. James countered with advice that Gideon be prepared to hold the floor. His statement should be carefully thought through. While he might make notes, Gideon should be ready to look the board in the eye and speak convincingly.

The assembly opened with a dry reading of the minutes of the previous board meeting, followed by a motion to accept them. A spattering of *English* parents shifted in their seats, as if to get comfortable for the coming proceedings. Then the board resumed discussions of matters of old business: the budget, one unfilled teacher position, the refreshments committee for the fall harvest dance for the high school students, a new format for report cards, new tires for one of the buses, a delayed textbook order. Why the school board let the topics remain unresolved from week to week, or month to month, confounded James. The decisions did not strike him as complex—nothing approaching the significance of an unsafe rural building that technically belonged to the district or the consequences of its closure for the families it had served for more than three decades. Twice James turned his head slightly for a glance at Gideon. If Gideon was becoming as impatient as James, he did not show it. Well habituated by lengthy church services, the Amish men barely moved for two and a half hours.

"Do I hear a motion to adjourn?" the superintendent finally said.

"So moved," said one of the board members.

Instantly, Gideon was on his feet. "I believe you have overlooked new business."

Ulysses Brownley blinked at Gideon. "The hour is late. Perhaps at our next meeting."

"With all due respect," Gideon said, "we requested in advance to be heard at tonight's meeting, and we have patiently waited for you to consider your weighty matters, although all of us will have to be up before dawn to tend our animals."

Brownley cleared his throat. "Very well. We will now consider new business, but only briefly. What is the matter you wish to put before the board?"

"We wish to present our reasons for requesting an exception on religious grounds to the new educational regulations."

"We do not make the state laws, Mr. Wittmer," Brownley said. "We are only charged with enforcing them at the local level, in one small school district."

"Nevertheless, I wish to make our case," Gideon said, "in the hope that we might continue to work together for suitable education of our children as we always have."

Good for you, Gideon. James turned up one corner of his mouth.

Gideon stepped out of the row of men and centered himself before the members of the board arranged across the front of the room.

"True education," he said, "cultivates humility, simple living, and submission to the will of God. We train for life both in this world and in the next. We do not see school and life as separate spheres. The highest form of religious life is our community life, and we guard carefully against any threat to our community."

Brownley leaned back in a wide black leather chair and pulled out his pocket watch.

Gideon was undeterred.

"So long as schools were small and near our farms, we have gladly worked with teachers the district so generously provided to find a meeting of the minds. In this way, we have considered both what was needful for our children's participation in our life together and what the state offered for their good."

"Mr. Wittmer," Brownley said, "perhaps you can get to the point."

"I have four points," Gideon said, calmly ignoring the scowl on Brownley's face. "First, we believe that it is in our children's best interest to attend school close to our homes, where they can easily help with the farmwork that is foundational to our way of life.

"Second, we would like our children to receive instruction from teachers committed to and respectful of our values. This will require special qualifications that may not coincide with those the state would measure.

"Third, our children need only basic skills in reading, writing, and arithmetic. All other training should be conducive to our religious life. These goals do not require that our children remain in school after the eighth grade.

"And last, our children need to be trained for our way of life, not the *English* way of life. Our hope is not that they achieve earthly success, but that they are prepared for eternity."

James wanted to stand up and clap. Gideon's late nights formulating his thoughts had yielded a polished presentation in which he did not look down at his notes even once.

"Since the form of education is an expression of our religious life," Gideon continued, "we respectfully request that the board relent and allow our children to attend school close to home and in a manner that allows for parents to consult freely with the teacher for pupils up through eighth grade. After that, our children will withdraw from school."

James watched the superintendent's face as he made a show of consulting his pocket watch once again.

"We will take it under advisement," Brownley said, "with the reminder once again that our duty is to execute state law, not formulate it. Now, I will once again entertain a motion to adjourn."

Gideon allowed himself a sigh of relief.

He could have said far more, but Ulysses Brownley had heard enough for one evening. The seed was planted. By God's grace, it would grow.

Aaron King clapped him on the back. Joshua Glick shook his hand. Grinning, John Hershberger dipped his head toward Gideon. Jed Hilty gave a satisfied nod. Cristof Byler looked red in the face from holding himself back, but he had held to the agreement that only Gideon would speak for the group. Even Isaiah Borntrager was pleasantly composed. Amid the unspoken congratulations, it was James's eyes Gideon sought, and his reward was a smile that said James could not be more pleased.

At the front of the room, board members whispered in huddles before dispersing. Spectators trickled out of the meeting room.

"I'll get the buggy," James said.

"I'll be out in a few minutes," Gideon said. His mind needed two minutes of quiet before the spirited ride home. The men would return together to Gideon's home, where they had left their rigs. No doubt the conversation would be animated. Isaiah and Cristof and John would unfurl all the words they guarded during the school board meeting.

Gideon slipped down the corridor and turned into a side hall where he hoped to lean against the cool brick wall and catch his breath.

His refuge dissipated before he could close his eyes and utter a prayer of thanks. Heavy footfalls made him stand up straight.

"Mr. Wittmer." It was Brownley.

"Yes?" Gideon moistened his lips.

"The laws exist for a reason," Brownley said, his words a snarl.

"We are peaceful, law-abiding people," Gideon said. "But we take our faith seriously."

"Education and religion do not mix."

"I beg to differ."

"I'm warning you," Brownley said. "If you and your ragamuffin friends persist in this dissent, you must do things properly. Go through channels."

"I believe that is what we were doing tonight," Gideon said. His neck suddenly ached. "Is not the school board the right authority to meet with on the question of education? If we should go elsewhere with our concerns, we welcome your counsel."

"Don't placate me," Brownley said. "I can manage my own school district. You'd be wasting your time pressing the question. The law is clear. I will provide you a printed copy in its entirety upon request."

"That won't be necessary," Gideon said.

"I notice that your son is on our truancy list." Brownley shook a finger. "Send that boy to school starting tomorrow and I will instruct the teachers to go the extra mile to help him catch up. The same offer stands for your friends who are breaking the law."

Gideon pressed his lips together and said nothing.

"I will be monitoring the attendance reports personally. If these children do not turn up in school soon, you will face the full consequences under the law."

Gideon exhaled softly. "Perhaps we should arrange a meeting to discuss our concerns when the hour is not so late."

"Discussions will not change the law, Mr. Wittmer. Put your children in school."

⤙⥼⤚

"He's gone again," Jed muttered as he walked past Rachel, who rummaged through the vegetable garden looking for autumn squashes. Pulling overgrown bean plants from the fence two rows down, Ella stiffened at the irritation in his voice.

"Where?" Rachel said.

"He doesn't leave me notes," Jed snapped. "I asked him to throw down some hay in the barn, and he left the job half done. I haven't seen him in hours."

"It's never been like David to act like this," Rachel said. "I don't know where he could be going."

Ellie busied her eyes searching for dry beanstalks to pull, but she could do little to divert her ears.

"I can't watch him every minute of the day," Jed said. "Nor should I have to. He's fifteen and capable of doing a man's work."

"Perhaps you should talk to him again."

"And say what? I've said it all before. Would he have defied his father this way?"

Ella held her breath. Rachel gave no answer.

"I have to see to the hay myself. The animals shouldn't suffer because of David's willfullness." Jed grunted and tramped out of the garden.

Ella yanked another bare stalk and tossed it in the pile. Either Rachel refused to see the obvious or she was more naive than Ella thought. It could not be coincidence that David's odd behavior began the same week school resumed session. He was not gone every day, nor all day, but his absences roughly coincided with the same hours Seth was legitimately off the farm to attend school. How David was getting to Seabury and back, Ella didn't know. But she did not have be an *English* professor to know where he was spending his lapsed hours.

Looking over the waning vegetation, Ella gave her stepmother a flimsy smile, grateful in the moment that it was not her place to advise what Rachel should do with her recalcitrant son.

"I told Joanna Hershberger I'd bring some cotton cloth she could use for the baby," Rachel said. "I don't think I'm up to taking it. Will you go?"

"Of course. I'm almost finished here."

Ella waited for Rachel, sniffling, to finish collecting squash and haul the basket toward the house before raking through the soil at the base of the spent bean plants and returning the rake to the tool shed. She went to the well to pump water over her hands, her mind muddled over whether the Hershbergers had made the right choice to keep their children home.

News of Isaiah Borntrager's impulsiveness had spread through the farms in the last ten days. Jed had driven over to the abandoned school to see for himself the further damage Isaiah's shenanigans had caused. On James's behalf, Gideon had taken a horse and ridden out to speak privately with Isaiah before mounting freshly painted signs on the old school warning off additional disturbance. If the school district did not do something soon, Gideon told Ella, he would gather a crew to safely dismantle the structure before anyone else got hurt. Gideon's report of the school board meeting two days ago—and Mr. Brownley's hostility afterward—did not suggest the board members were concerned with the decrepit building.

Ella fetched the cotton from the house and hitched up the open buggy. She would use it for as many days as the weather remained fine. Winter would come soon enough and necessitate enclosed transportation.

The Hershberger infant seemed no closer to a routine than the last time Ella visited, and Ella saw no books or papers to indicate schooling was under way for the older children. In fact, the baby screamed over much of the brief conversation Ella had with the tiny girl's exhausted mother, who gave one distracted instruction after another to her eldest daughter about the care of the younger ones. Ella's presence only added to the chaos, and she did not stay long.

When Ella went past the school on her way home, she paused to gaze on the broken shell, still stunned to see what had become of the school she had loved. Most of the teachers came straight from the teachers college and only stayed two or three years before marrying or moving to a more progressive school. As a pupil, Ella was always curious about each new teacher who arrived with untarnished energy and dedication. Only one of them ever expressed exasperation with Ella's barrage of questions about what they read or her perseverance to complete the work of a higher grade level.

Tobias and Savilla had experienced this school, where teachers found ways to feed the minds of the Amish pupils without crossing their parents. Gertie's impressions of school were in the hands of Margaret Simpson, who was a kind individual but who believed in progressive education. The old school stirred warm memories. The new school reminded Ella more of a sleeping, unpredictable monster.

A black-capped chickadee settled on a haphazard pile of crumbling roofing, its orange-hued sides shimmering in the September sun as it dipped its head and pecked, searching for edible tidbits. Ella wondered if David had seen this bird.

Ella sighed. *David. This is not the way.*

The wagon coming toward Ella could only be Aaron King's. His hitch had been unbalanced for years, causing the team to pull slightly to the right. Aaron insisted it was hardly any trouble to compensate with the reins and saw no reason to repair or replace the hitch. Trying not to laugh at the spectacle, Ella gave him wide berth in the road and returned his wave.

Aaron carried a full load of lumber, some of it hanging precariously off the open back end of his wagon. Ella scrunched her face.

Aaron's barn was fairly new, raised at a frolic only three years ago. The last time the church met at his home, Ella hadn't noticed it was in need of repairs—certainly not enough to explain the size of the load in his wagon. Besides, he was headed east, not south toward his farm. Curious, Ella turned her cart around in the road and urged her single horse into a canter to keep Aaron in view. With each turn he took, Ella became more persuaded of his destination.

The Mast farm.

Ella followed Aaron to the west end of the Mast farm, to a pasture Chester had left fallow the last two years. Her eyes widened at the view.

Two buggies, three wagons, and a total of nine men and older boys. They descended on Aaron's wagon to unload. Chester had been the boss at the last two barn raisings. Now he glanced at each piece of lumber and pointed to where it should be laid.

Ella glanced across the Mast acres. The crew was a long way from the house or barn, and the shape taking place before her eyes was too large for an ordinary outbuilding.

A gasp caught her by surprise. Chester strode toward her.

"Keep your eyes in your head," he said.

Slowly, she rotated her head to look him in the eye. "You're putting up a school." The layout was identical to the collapsed building.

"We won't get it up today," Chester said. "We need a lot more lumber, and some glass for the windows, and a woodstove. But yes, a school."

"But. . ." Ella did not know how to finish her sentence. She swallowed. Did Gideon know about this?

"Gideon did a fine job speaking to the school board," Chester said, as if reading her thoughts, "but I know a stubborn face when I see one. That Mr. Brownley has no intention of altering an iota of his plan."

"Surely he will not sit idle and let you build a school."

"I don't require his permission. It's my land. I'll build whatever I want on it. The building won't belong to the *English*. It will belong to us, and we'll use it as we see fit."

Ella's heart boomed. "You're very bold."

Chester swung his arm wide at the other fathers and sons. "We are bold together—bold in obedience."

The men's movements were fluid, cooperative, effective. Aaron's load had not been the first to arrive. Already four trestles were laid out, ready to answer the call to hold up a roof.

"It's a fine place for a school, wouldn't you say?" Chester beamed. "A quiet corner with a view of God's goodness, but close enough to the road that it will not be difficult for our families to reach."

Ella nodded. Chester had chosen well. Pupils could come out of school and look toward an expansive sky with a band of deciduous trees fluttering against the horizon. Mast wheat would rise in golden rolls before their eyes to the east, and Borntrager cattle would dot the verdant pasture to the west. Amish children would know that the land was God's generous gift and learn their role in caring for it.

"It will be lovely," she said. "Truly. But Mr. Brownley will still consider our children truants. We won't be authorized to hold classes."

"We do not need the state's approval to educate our children. We are perfectly capable."

"But we don't even have a qualified teacher."

"We'll find one. And when we do, we'll be ready."

James Lehman entered the Seabury Consolidated Grade School without fanfare. No bell. No knocker. He pushed open the oversized door and went in. The interior of the school resembled many *English* buildings constructed in the last decade or so and matched what James expected.

Standing in the main corridor, he sought his bearings. Tasteful signs in modern script announced the purposes of the rooms or gave cryptic instructions. ART. MUSIC. LADIES. GENTLEMEN. PRINCIPAL'S OFFICE THIS WAY. CLASSROOMS ABOVE. PLEASE USE STAIRS AT REAR.

James was not there to speak to the principal, and he was not curious about *English* art or music lessons, which would have no relevance for the Amish children. He wanted to see Gertie in the setting that seemed to make her happy, look in on Savilla because she seemed less happy, and take Gideon a report.

He passed the office—where he saw no one in attendance anyway—and followed instructions to use the broad rear stairs. On the second floor, another set of scripted signs gave pertinent information. It was not hard to find the one that said, GRADE 1, MISS SIMPSON. James turned the knob, and the door opened easily.

Chalkboards, desks, books, a globe, cheery letters and pictures of animals attached to the walls. It looked like any classroom ought to, but was brightened by a bank of electric lights.

The woman at the front of the room paused with her chalk in midair. "Can I help you?"

"Miss Simpson?" James said.

"That's right."

"Then I'm in the right place." He stepped into the room.

"Sir—"

Gertie squealed, slid out of her seat, and hurtled toward him. "This is my *onkel* James."

James warmed with the enthusiasm of the introduction and received Gertie's hug, lifting her the way he would have after school in the *dawdihaus*.

"Is Gertie needed at home?" Miss Simpson set down her chalk.

"All is well at home," James said. "I only wanted to see for myself."

"Class is in session," Miss Simpson said. "If you'd like to come back after school, I will be happy to answer any questions you have."

James surveyed the rows of desks and the pairs of eyes of their occupants. On one side of the room, a little boy squirmed. At the back, two little girls leaned their heads together and snickered.

Did they snicker at Gertie that way? Which one was Polly?

He set Gertie down and turned back to Miss Simpson. "I won't disturb you. I'll stand in the back."

The teacher's jawline tightened, but her voice retained its cordiality. "The principal did not mention to me that I should expect a classroom visit. I might have been better prepared."

"I haven't spoken to the principal," James said. "I only wanted to observe the class." The request seemed unremarkable to James. At the old school, he stopped in three or four times each year. Others did the same. The children were part of the church community. Why should adults not be interested in their surroundings?

"Gertie," Miss Simpson said, "would you mind taking your seat, please?"

Gertie tilted her head back to look at James, who nodded. Smiling and waving over her shoulder, she returned to her seat next to Hans Byler.

Miss Simpson took several steps closer to James. "I'm afraid that without Mr. Tarkington's knowledge—and approval—I cannot invite you to stay."

Why did he need an invitation? He was already there.

"You see," she said, "our policy is that visitors should make arrangements through the office."

"I was in town on other matters," James said. "It's on my way home."

"I understand, but I must ask you to leave. Make the proper arrangements, and you will be welcome to visit another time. It's in the best interest of the children."

"I don't require any special attention," James said. If she had simply let him go to the back of the room when he came in, the children would have forgotten he was there and her penmanship lesson would be well on its way to completion.

"I'm afraid I must ask you to leave," she said. "I have the principal to answer to on the matter."

It was the most ridiculous thing James had heard in a long time. Why would the school discourage families from knowing what happened in the classroom? But Miss Simpson seemed like an earnest young woman trying to do the right thing, so he nodded in reluctance.

⊱✦⊰

Margaret drew lunchtime recess duty. She welcomed the brisk breeze on her face, though she could not help raising her hands to be sure her hair remained tucked into its bun. The rumble of Gray's truck bounced around her ears, and for a moment she thought she had let her imagination go too far. Then a truck pulled up to one of the wide doors at the rear of the building, and Gray emerged from the cab. He looked up, caught her eye, and smiled. Margaret wanted to wave, but she could not bring herself to do it in front of a playground full of children and teachers. Gray opened the back of his truck and began lifting out desks. She'd heard one of the upper grades needed additional seating. Even from this distance, Margaret saw the muscles in Gray's forearm ripple and had to avert her eyes.

Miss Hunter, from the third grade, sidled up to Margaret. "Did you hear what those people are doing?"

"What people?" Margaret pointed at a boy. "Elliott Lewis, you keep your hands to yourself."

"Your friends the Amish," Miss Hunter said. "They're in the office now."

Margaret's brow furrowed, and her heart sped up. "Who?"

"I don't know their names. You might, since you visited them."

Margaret returned her gaze to Gray, who now pushed a cart stacked with four desks toward the entrance.

"Go see," Miss Hunter said. "I'll watch things out here."

"I'd better get the door for that delivery," Margaret said, already stepping away from the playground.

She reached the door just in time to hold it open for Gray. Circumspect, he nodded his head in appreciation and pushed the cart through.

"Where do you suppose these go?" he said.

"Someone in the office will want to deal with them," Margaret said. "This way."

Until now, Gray's courtship and Margaret's work were separate spheres orbiting her life but not crossing paths. It was oddly delicious to see him in the middle of the day, his nearness fluttering her heart as usual. Walking beside him down the wide corridor, she forced herself not to hope he would kiss her, as she would have at home. That was simply out of the question here. She took a deep breath and clicked her heels along the tile a little more energetically.

The door to the school office was propped open. Simply walking down the hall with Gray had been enough to make Margaret forget Miss Hunter's remark that there were Amish in the office. Now she tried to absorb the scene. Mr. Tarkington stood with hands in his suit coat pockets, scowling at two sets of Amish parents. Margaret fished around in her brain for their names. The Masts and the Borntragers.

"I'm afraid that is not how things are done," Mr. Tarkington said.

"Is it against the law?" Chester Mast asked, holding his gaze on the principal.

The principal opened his mouth, closed it, and finally formed a sentence. "I'll have to check the regulations and consult with the superintendent. This is highly unorthodox."

"You've been telling us to put our children in school, so we are here to do that," Isaiah said. "In the eighth grade."

"But these pupils have already completed the eighth grade. They belong in the high school next door." Mr. Tarkington turned to Chester Mast. "I was under the impression that your son was already studying in the ninth grade."

"And now he's going to study in the eighth grade," Chester insisted, "along with the Borntrager boy. They'll soon catch up on the lessons."

"I imagine so," the principal said, "since they completed the eighth grade two years ago."

"The law says they have to go to school," Chester said, "but I don't believe it says what grade they have to be in. These children will go to the eighth grade."

Tarkington scoffed. "Do you intend to retain them in the eighth grade until they reach sixteen years of age?"

This possibility had never occurred to Margaret.

"I'm going to need a signature for my records," Gray said. "I can't just leave the desks in the hall."

Margaret turned to him, one ear still cocked toward the commotion in the office. "Will it suffice if I sign? Mr. Tarkington has his hands full."

"I suppose." Gray handed her a sheet of paper and a pen. "I'm glad not to be in his shoes. They seem like stubborn people who are not about to do what he wants."

Margaret scribbled a signature. Superintendent Brownley was not going to like this any more than the principal did.

"They're not stubborn," she said. "They want what is best for the children."

Unconvinced, Gray exhaled through his nose as he lifted one of the desks off the cart and lined it up against the wall. "It would be a lot easier for everyone if they just did what they're supposed to do."

Margaret already anticipated a summons to the superintendent's office and a mandate to talk some sense into the Amish.

CHAPTER 15

In the eleven months since Rachel and her boys entered the Hilty household, Ella had become accustomed to the sound of an automobile rattling down their lane. Lindy Lehman turned up at unpredictable intervals and was always welcome. This time, though, instead of the engine's revolutions slowing and its intrusive tumult tapering as it approached the house, the car roared at high speed.

Ella stood in the yard on Monday with a large basket of straw, getting ready to freshen the henhouse. She started to wave but opted to step out of the way as the car veered toward the spot she occupied.

Lindy braked hard and the car lurched to a halt.

And Ella saw David hanging his head on the passenger side of the bench.

Lindy got out. "I hope Rachel is here."

Ella nodded. "What's wrong? Is David all right?"

"It's best if I talk to Rachel."

"Go on in."

Lindy glanced at David. "I'd better stay here. Would you ask Rachel to come out, please?"

"Of course." Ella brushed straw off her hands.

David had begun to squirm and his fingers gripped the door handle.

"Stay right there, David." Lindy's tone made no allowance for discussion.

Ella found Rachel in the boys' bedroom upstairs, changing the linens on their beds. Rachel dropped the pillowcases and raced

731

down the stairs. Ella followed, determined to keep silent but unable to turn away from the commotion. Obviously David had left the farm again early Monday morning. Where Lindy found him was the curious question.

"David!" Rachel said, startled.

"You can get out now," Lindy said.

"You're supposed to be in the field with Jed." Dread seeped through Rachel's voice.

"He was a long way from the field," Lindy said. "David has something to tell you."

David opened the door now and got out of the car. "I'll go to the field now."

"David," Lindy said. "You know what you need to do."

"Can't you just let me go find Jed? Isn't that what you all want?" Ella's gaze snapped up. David's complexion flushed.

"Sneaking around is not the way," Lindy said. "You have to talk to your mother."

David exhaled heavily. "There's an assignment due in my literature class. If I don't turn it in today, I'll get a zero."

School. Just as Ella thought.

"Literature class?" Rachel echoed. "You've been leaving Jed with all the work so you could go to that *English* school?"

"I *like* school, *Mamm*," David said. "What is so wrong with wanting to learn?"

Rachel calmly pivoted to face Ella. "Would you please take the cart, find your father, and tell him it's urgent that he come to the house?"

Twenty minutes later, Jed had little to say as Ella drove the cart back from the field where he had abandoned his tools and tasks to answer his wife's summons. When they reached the house, Lindy's car was still there. Ella stopped the horse long enough to let her father out of the cart before pulling alongside the stable to unhitch the buggy and send the horse into the pasture.

She grimaced slightly as she opened the back screen door, which tended to both creak and slam. The kitchen was empty. Voices wafted from the front room. The worn state of her shoes made little sound as she crossed the kitchen linoleum and leaned against a wall to listen.

"How many days have you been to school?" Jed demanded.

"I don't know," David mumbled. "I haven't been counting."

School started only two weeks ago. Based on his absences from the farm, Ella reasoned David had been to school at least half the time.

"Why would you contradict my express wishes?" Jed said.

"What about *my* wishes?" David said.

"David!" Rachel's tone was sharp with warning. "Don't speak to Jed that way."

Ella peeked into the front room. David slumped deep into the davenport.

"Where did Lindy find you this morning?" Jed leaned forward, hands on knees.

"Does it matter?" David said.

"I want to know."

"I hitched a ride into Seabury."

"I saw him getting out of a car," Lindy supplied. "He should talk to you. A calm conversation would be better than sneaking around."

David huffed and turned his face to Lindy. "Can't you see where this is getting me?"

"I hope it will keep your relationship with your mother honest," Lindy said.

"So you're on her side."

"I'm not on anybody's *side*—"

"You could have fooled me."

Rachel choked back a sob. "David, please."

"I'll fix some *kaffi*." Lindy stood. "Perhaps we all need a moment to calm down."

"Yes," Rachel said, "and I have coffee cake."

Ella looked from the coffeepot on the stove to the cake on the counter.

"I don't need cake and *kaffi*," David said. "I want to go to school and turn in my literature paper. It's the first real grade of the year."

The pleading in his voice pierced Ella. How much had David been holding inside all these months?

"David's right," Jed said. "We don't need cake and *kaffi*. We have work to do."

"Jed, please," Lindy said. "Let's figure this out."

"Your friendship means a great deal to Rachel," Jed said. "But I am her husband. We have already talked about this and made our decision."

"But David—"

"David will not go to school."

Ella grimaced. Her father was not an unreasonable man, but once he made up his mind, he rarely saw the purpose in revisiting the same question.

"He's fifteen," Jed said. "He's capable in the fields, and I need him. If he wants to read in his spare time, he is free to do so. I've never kept my own daughter from her books as long as the work was finished."

David rolled his head against the back of the davenport.

Jed stood. "Come on, David. We've lost enough of the morning already."

Ella ran her hand across her face. *David, David, David.* The boy did not know what he was up against.

Jed strode across the room, opened the front door, and waited. David unfolded his reluctance into a shuffle and followed Jed out. Lindy turned to embrace Rachel.

Ella lit a burner on the stove and filled the coffeepot with water. Lindy entered the kitchen alone.

"Where's Rachel?" Ella had supposed they would both come.

"I told her I would bring *kaffi*."

Ella scooped ground coffee into the percolator receptacle. "You did the right thing by bringing David home."

Lindy shrugged one shoulder. "It doesn't seem to have done any good."

"He shouldn't be sneaking around." Ella set two slices of coffee cake on a plate and nudged it down the counter toward Lindy.

"I agree. But he'll do it again."

"Maybe not," Ella said, though she thought Lindy was right.

"Jed should let David go to school. He'll be sixteen in a year anyway."

"What if he wants to stay in school long enough to graduate high school?" The coffee started to bubble.

"He'll be old enough to decide," Lindy said. "I wasn't in school, but I was sixteen when I knew I wouldn't stay with the Amish."

A fork shook in Ella's hand. "Is that what you think David wants? To leave the church?"

"I haven't asked him," Lindy said, "and I won't. But I've known him all his life, and I've never seen him behave this way. Rachel and Jed have to listen to him and find out what's in his heart."

Ella removed a tray from a cupboard and arranged the cake plate and two coffee cups on it.

"Are you going to say that to Rachel?" Ella said, tucking two napkins under the edge of the plate.

Lindy paused before saying, "Rachel means a lot to me. I want her to be happy."

CHAPTER 16

A glance at the sun told James he was running later than he planned, but he wouldn't leave the farm on Wednesday morning without kissing his wife. He stroked the horse's nose, with an unnecessary warning not to gallop off with the loaded wagon, and started toward the house.

As he rounded the corner of the barn, a fleeting sound—a faint footfall—made him pause and look over his left shoulder. But he saw nothing unexpected. His biggest canvas tarp secured the lumpy load he was taking into town. He was transporting two end tables, the usual assortment of eggs in a range of colors, and a carefully packed quilted wall hanging Miriam had just finished. The mercantile owner now kept a list of customers who were interested in Amish handiwork. Most likely he wouldn't even put Miriam's latest creation on display, because it would sell before his best customers could answer their phones to learn it was there.

James turned back toward the *dawdihaus*, where he hoped to find Miriam with her feet propped up after the morning skirmish of getting the girls readied and to the bus stop on time.

Miriam looked up as James entered. "Will you be long today?" she said.

"I don't expect to be. I'm just stopping at the mercantile and then on to Lindy's." He could have sanded down and refinished the end tables himself, but Miriam had insisted they ask Lindy to do it and pay her a fair price.

"Good." Miriam nodded.

He kissed her and ambled back out to the wagon to take up the reins. At least the bus had come and gone. If the road was clear, he might make up for lost time and still be at the mercantile when the owner opened the doors.

When James took the wide turn onto the main road, something in the load softly slid and came to a stop against the side of the wagon. He scowled, trying to think what he had forgotten to tie down. He hoped it was not the crate of eggs. Few things were more aggravating to clean up than broken eggs. And if the eggs soiled the wall hanging—James refused to dwell on that possibility.

The mercantile came into view. Two women and a man stood on the sidewalk awaiting its opening. James pulled up as close as he could and tied the horse to the hitching post. Pacing along the side of the wagon, for the third time that morning he heard a sound he couldn't place. The bottom of a brown work boot now protruded from under the tarp.

James swiftly untied the corner of the canvas and flipped it back. "David, what in the world are you doing here?"

"I needed a ride," David said. He retrieved a book that had escaped his grasp and scooted out of the wagon.

"Does Jed know where you are?"

David avoided James's eyes.

James exhaled. "This is about school, isn't it?"

David's gaze went down the street in the direction of the schools.

"Answer my questions, please," James said.

"Yes, I'm going to school," David said. He looked James in the eye.

"Have you snuck into my wagon before?"

David twisted his mouth and nodded. "You usually go into town on Wednesdays."

The boy was right. James nearly always went on Wednesdays, with other days determined by needs of the household or neighbors.

"I can't imagine you only sneak off to school on Wednesdays," James said.

"I'm also getting very fast at running," David said. "And the *English* are curious enough that they'll almost always stop to pick me up if I put my hand out."

"I see," James said. "You are defying your father."

"He's not my father!"

"He's your mother's husband, and you live in his house."

"I'm not seven years old."

"This is not our way, David."

"I'm late." David pivoted and sprinted down the sidewalk.

⚜

Margaret led her ragtag line of first graders down the rear stairs of the grade school with firm instructions that they hold the railing and watch the feet of the pupil ahead in the line. At the base of the stairs, she directed them to line up quietly outside the music room. As soon as the older students came out, the little ones would go in. And then she would have forty minutes to catch her breath while the music teacher had charge of her class.

When the last of the first graders straggled into the music room and the teacher clapped her hands for the students' attention, Margaret raised the hem of her skirt to take the stairs more swiftly. Before the time came to fetch her class again, she wanted the arithmetic lesson to follow to be fully organized, including a set of problems on the board.

Voices in the upstairs hall startled her.

"So it turned out high school was too hard for you." A boy's voice cracked mid-taunt. "Maybe if you took your hat off, you'd be able to think better."

Two other voices laughed. Margaret hustled her upward steps.

"Look at the big lug," the first boy said. "He can't even think what to say."

More laughter.

Margaret entered the upstairs corridor. Why these eighth graders were out of the classroom was unclear, though one of two Amish boys had his hands on a rolling wooden cart stacked with books.

"I hear they don't fight," an *English* boy said.

"Let's find out." A second boy pulled back his fist and swung at Elijah Mast, hitting him squarely on the jaw. Thrown off balance, Elijah stepped back but made no move to retaliate. Only a few months short of sixteen, he was taller and broader than any of the *English* boys. Margaret had no doubt he could have put them on their rumps with one swift movement.

A boot slammed into Elijah's shin, causing another step back.

"Stop!" Margaret shouted. She closed the yards between herself and the boys. "This will stop immediately."

The *English* boys cowered at having been caught. Margaret turned to the only one she had not witnessed actively bullying.

"You go get Mr. Tarkington immediately," she said. "And be sure you come back with him."

Relief and shame mingling in his face, the boy darted down the hall toward the stairs.

"Are you all right?" Margaret said to Elijah, who had his hand on his jaw now.

He nodded. The boy with the cart, Luke Borntrager, shuffled his feet.

"I'm sure Mr. Tarkington will want to speak with both of you," Margaret said, "but for now why don't you go back to your class?"

The cart was in motion within seconds. Margaret was certain Elijah and Luke could ably defend themselves if they had chosen to. She glared at the bullies.

"Let's see, you're taller than your friend. Does that make you better?"

"No, ma'am," they mumbled, eyes on their feet.

"Or does your black hair make you better than his blond hair?"

"No, ma'am."

Margaret glared at the boys. "Different is just different. It's not better or worse. The two of you are old enough to understand that."

Mr. Tarkington's feet thundered up the stairs, followed by the more reluctant steps of the third boy.

"Down to my office, all three of you," the principal said. "This is inexcusable."

Margaret exhaled relief for the moment.

"Miss Simpson," the principal said, "I'll speak to you later for a full accounting of the facts."

He left with the boys. Margaret leaned against the wall. How could the Amish children learn anything if they felt a constant dread of mistreatment? Perhaps their parents were right. Perhaps it would be better for everyone if they had their own school where they could practice their peaceful ways without threat. On the other hand, why should they be removed from sight in order to be safe?

Margaret would tell Mr. Tarkington what she had seen, but she doubted the boys would face serious consequences. More likely, blame would be laid at the feet of the Amish parents who put their older children back in the eighth grade.

None of this was fair.

⚜

James took his rig down Lindy's quiet street and drove to the back of her lot, where her workshop sat behind the small house. With another needless playful warning to the horse, he strode to the workshop door and knocked.

No answer came. She might be in the house or on an errand of her own, or she simply might not have heard him. James turned the knob. The wide door opened.

James stifled the impulse to call Lindy's name. Something was off. Taking care where he stepped, he entered the workshop and softly closed the door behind him. Two drawers from a half-stained dresser lay splintered on the workshop floor. The contents of a tool shelf were clustered on one end. A bucket of blue paint lay on its side, the dense liquid settling into its own irregular shape on the sloping floor.

James stood still, his ears attuned to a slight noise across the workshop. He saw no one and crept toward it.

At the last minute his eyes flicked up to the board swinging down toward his head, and he raised an arm to block the stinging blow.

Someone gasped.

James turned toward his attacker.

"*Onkel* James!"

James grimaced. First Isaiah Borntrager fell off a ladder and landed on top of James. Now his own niece took a swing at him with a two-by-four. How would he ever explain to Miriam the bruise certain to form on his arm?

Lindy let the board clatter to the floor.

"What happened?" James asked.

Lindy blinked several times. "I went out for a few minutes. When I came back, the door was ajar. I'm sure I closed it when I left."

"Did you lock it?"

She shook her head. "I have too much Amish in me to lock a door, I guess. When I heard someone outside again, I got scared."

"Well, it's just me. I didn't see anyone else outside." James picked up the pieces of one of the dresser drawers.

Lindy groaned. "I'll have to make all new drawers."

"I can help you with that." James looked around. "Other than the obvious damage, is anything missing?"

Lindy's eyes took slow inventory of her workshop, and she let out a cry. "My best carving tools were on that shelf."

James put an arm around her shoulder.

"I had three carved birds ready to sell in the Amish crafts store." She broke away from him and went to her workbench. "My birdhouse templates! They're gone!"

"All of them?"

"Every single one. I had them out because I was going to cut some pieces today."

James righted the paint bucket. "I'm sorry this happened to you."

"The quilt rack!" Lindy said. "I was painting birds on the side pieces for Mrs. Tarkington."

"She'll just have to understand," James said.

"I don't even understand," Lindy said. "I do just enough work to support myself. My prices are fair. I mind my own business. I'm a quiet neighbor. Why would anybody do this to me?"

"We should get Deputy Fremont over here," James said.

"I have never liked him," Lindy said.

James understood. He did not much like Fremont, either, especially after his strong-handed approach to the Amish in recent weeks.

"I know," he said, "but he is the law."

CHAPTER 17

Gideon's here," Rachel said the next day, her gaze out the front window.

Ella sprang to her feet. Gideon's buggy swayed down the lane toward the house.

"Tell him the celery is coming along nicely," Rachel said. "We should have plenty for the wedding."

Ella smiled and picked up her shawl. She doubted Gideon cared about the details of the traditional wedding celery, but it was sweet that Rachel was monitoring its progress. Ella stepped out onto the front porch in time to watch Gideon wrap the reins around a fence post and amble in her direction. She would spend her life with this man, loving him, loving his children, loving the *boppli* they would have together. If God ever smiled, surely He smiled now. The day was golden.

"Do you have time for a walk?" Gideon asked.

"Of course." Ella descended the steps. "Let's go out to *Daed's* fallow field."

Once they were away from the house, Gideon took Ella's hand.

"I want to ask you about an idea," he said.

Gideon might not care about celery, but they had other wedding details to work out. They still had to choose their attendants and finalize the date.

"Shall we try to see the bishop?" Ella said.

"I know you want to marry soon," Gideon said.

The pressure in Ella's chest was immediate. "Don't you?"

"Maybe we should let others go first. After all, we'll have our whole lives."

743

Ella said nothing but kept walking. Obviously she did not know Gideon's mind as well as she thought.

He squeezed her fingers. "We will find the right date. I am not having doubts."

"Then what?"

"I would like to see the school question settled first—or at least take myself out of the crux of it."

"How will you do that?"

"First I have to do what I think is best for my own children. I want you to teach my daughters at home."

"I heard about what happened to Elijah Mast," Ella said. "But nothing like that is going to happen to Gertie and Savilla."

"I pray not," Gideon said.

"They like school and have made friends."

He nodded. "I am not going to give up with the school board. If other children hear their parents talking at home about the Amish 'problem,' as they like to call us, how can we know what might happen? It's my duty as their father to keep them safe."

"I understand." Questions flooded Ella's mind. Would Gideon keep the girls home temporarily? Would he get their lessons from the teachers at the school? Did the girls want to study at home? Why did he think she knew the first thing about making lesson plans or what a first grader and a fourth grader ought to be learning?

"Besides," Gideon said, "I am not comfortable having them in the *English* school. They will be attracted to *English* ways."

"But you teach them our ways at home," Ella said. "They will always know truth." She banished the image of David's rebellion rising in her mind.

They walked a few yards in silence.

"Do you have hesitations about teaching them?" Gideon asked.

"I don't know very much about teaching." The intrigue of teaching collided with the reasons Gideon asked it of her.

"But you understand a great deal about learning," he countered. "You are more than capable of teaching them to read and do basic math and enough history to know where they come from."

"I suppose so."

"If you are going to be their mother—and I hope they will see you that way—then it is fitting that they learn from you."

"But what about the laws?" Ella said. "You've already been warned to put Tobias in school."

Gideon shrugged. "I didn't do it, and nothing happened."

"You may be asking for trouble by taking the girls out."

"I made our case with the school board that the Amish can teach our own children. We need to show this is true. If they are watching me, that's all the more reason I need your help."

Ella moistened her lips. "Can I think about it?"

As much as she loved learning, Ella had never seriously considered teaching. Why should she? The one-room school always had an *English* teacher—and not one who had been out of school for twelve years.

"Prayerfully consider it," Gideon said. "I won't say anything to the girls until we're sure."

❦

"Did you hear what I said?"

"Mmm?" Margaret lifted her eyes to Gray's face across the table at the modest restaurant on Main Street.

"I was saying what a fine September we've had," Gray said. "I suppose October will bring a change in the weather."

"Yes." Margaret turned up the corners of her mouth. "I believe October is my favorite month of the year."

"I'll take note."

They were seated at a table near the window for an early supper, before darkness fell. Margaret could not quite see well enough from this distance to discern the two figures across the street.

"Margaret."

Gray's voice recaptured her gaze.

"I'm sorry," she said. "What did you say?"

"You've barely looked at the menu. Shall I order for you?"

Margaret dropped her eyes to the printed sheet in front of her. "Yes, please. I'm sure it's all delicious."

"You seem quite distracted," Gray said. "If you're not feeling well, I'll take you home."

"I feel fine," she said, resolving to pay better attention. "Quite hungry, actually."

"Would you like to tell me what's on your mind? It might help to talk about it."

She looked out the window again. "One of the pupils in Miss Hunter's class has missed more than a week of school due to illness. In fact, she's missed more school than she's attended this year so far. We're all starting to be concerned."

"I would think so. That's a long time for a child to be ill."

"The odd thing is, I'm fairly certain that's her across the street with her father."

Gray turned his head. "Where? I don't see anybody but that Amish man and his buggy."

"Yes, that's him."

"How can you be sure? They all look alike."

Objection rang in Margaret's ears, but she said nothing. A girl in a dark gray dress began to skip, only to be reprimanded with one gesture from her father.

"She doesn't look sick to me," Gray said.

Nor to me.

Gray laughed with abandon.

"What's so funny?" Margaret said.

"That Amish man is *lying* to the school authorities."

"Let's not jump to judgments," Margaret said. Perhaps the girl had been sick and was now recovering. Her parents might be keeping her home as a precautionary measure. Across the street, the girl climbed into the buggy—without assistance—and disappeared into its dark interior.

"You can see with your own eyes," Gray said. "That child is fine. There's no reason she shouldn't be in school tomorrow."

"Tomorrow's Friday. They may decide to let her finish out the week resting at home and start fresh on Monday."

"Or it may be a ruse."

The horse began to pull the buggy away from the curb.

"Let's not let the Amish problem come between us," Gray said. "Let's enjoy our baked fish and roasted red potatoes."

Amish problem. Margaret bristled at the phrase, although Gray was not the first person in town to use it. Still, it soured her stomach to think that he would adopt it. These were children. They were not a problem.

"Of course," she said. "That sounds delicious."

His features crinkled with his smile, his eyes dancing as he looked at her. Margaret wasn't sure any man's gaze had ever warmed her at the core the way Gray Truesdale's did. The disadvantage of not asking him to take her home right then was the interminable wait for his lips to find hers before the night was over.

⌘

Monday was art day. As the fourth week of school opened, Margaret selected art supplies from the cupboard in the downstairs corridor, arranged them in a basket, and carried them up to her classroom. This would be the first real art project of the year, other than some simple coloring with Crayolas. Up until now, Margaret focused on introducing a solid curriculum of reading and arithmetic as she assessed each pupil's ability. The children had been working hard for three weeks. They deserved to spend the last hour of the day exploring what they could do with charcoal pencils on thick paper. Art was required in the consolidated curriculum, and Margaret was determined to demonstrate its value to dubious parents.

When the primers were stowed and the oil cloths draped over desktops, Margaret held up one of the hand mirrors she had brought from home.

"Take turns with the mirrors," she said. "You can hold them for one another. Draw what you see in the mirror. It's called a 'self-portrait of the artist.' "

Margaret's expectations were appropriately low for what the completed projects would look like. She was more interested in observing the process of the children's efforts. They were only first graders, after all, and it was only the beginning of the school year. Most of them still struggled to control their thick pencils even to form the letters of their names.

Around the classroom, giggles and groans, jubilation and frustration greeted Margaret. She walked up and down the aisles, complimenting the effort her pupils made and touching their shoulders in encouragement. Lopsided eyes, uneven ears, disproportionate noses, oddly shaped faces—whatever the result, Margaret buoyed her students in the process of looking carefully and moving the charcoal with control.

She reached Gertie Wittmer's desk beside Hans Byler. Hans's project looked like most of the others around the room.

"I can't do this," he said.

"All I ask is that you try," Margaret said.

"But mine doesn't look like Gertie's."

"Why should it? *You* don't look like Gertie."

Hans laid the charcoal down. "Gertie, show Miss Simpson your picture."

Gertie had turned her drawing upside down. "I'd like to see it," Margaret said.

Slowly, Gertie flipped the paper.

Margaret's eyes widened. Gertie's features stared up from the desk. Margaret lifted the paper at the edges.

"Gertie, this is wonderful!" Margaret had never seen a six-year-old produce such a recognizable self-portrait, even the reflection of light in her eyes as it bounced off the mirror. "I can't wait for your father to see this."

Gertie reached up and tugged on a corner of the drawing. Margaret released it, lest the paper tear.

"Don't you want your father to see this?" Margaret asked.

Gertie shook her head.

"Why not?"

Gertie shoved the paper into her desk but did not answer Margaret's question.

"All right," Margaret said. "But please be careful with it. I'll collect them when everyone has finished."

❦

Jed's voice carried up the stairwell.

"It gets dark earlier every day," he said. "David is not carrying his load. Before school started, he never once complained about working alongside me."

"He still doesn't," Rachel said. "I haven't heard him say one word of criticism or complaint about helping you."

"Then why is he never around to do it?"

Upstairs, Ella tucked folded towels into a narrow cupboard. The conversation was becoming tiresome. Her father had always been one to mutter. It was his way of getting something off his chest. In the old days, though, Ella never would have discerned his downstairs grumblings if she were on the second floor of the Hilty home. Lately Jed's voice rose. It was hard not to hear Jed and Rachel having a slightly different version of the same conversation every few days.

Ella padded to her room and softly closed the door to block the voices. In a moment, Rachel's would break in disappointment, and Jed would either promise to be more patient with David or pull the front door closed behind him with more force than necessary.

David got up early and stayed up late to keep up with barn chores. He never missed a family meal. Some days he turned up on the farm shortly after lunch. What could her father do? Tether David to a post to physically prevent him from leaving? Ella supposed his comings and goings depended on what was happening at school—when he had an exam or an assignment due. Vaguely she wondered what high school must be like. Perhaps if she had attended high school, she would feel more prepared for what Gideon asked of her now.

She shook off the thought. Savilla and Gertie were nine and six. How difficult could it be? The half-collapsed schoolhouse still contained shelves of textbooks. Gideon would find a way to get what she needed—if she agreed to his request.

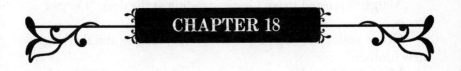

The children concentrated on copying short sentences Margaret had written on the chalkboard. On the desk in front of her lay her attendance book, her grade book, and a stack of lesson plans. Soon she would divide the first graders into two groups, a smaller group who seemed on the path to independent reading and might even be ready for second-grade primers by February, and a larger group who were mastering reading at a more predictable rate for six-year-olds. Margaret made notes on a pad as she considered each child's progress, gazing out the windows along one side of her classroom from time to time. Outside, russet and bronze had displaced variegated green on most of the trees, and the sky, while still dazzling, was less glistening than in the summer months. October had arrived, and seemed to rush into full flame by its second day. Margaret had not been making conversation when she told Gray it was her favorite month. She looked forward to the season's change every year.

She scanned the classroom to make sure no child faltered in the task, knowing that some would produce more legible papers than others. Little tongues stuck out the corners of several mouths, and other children scrunched their faces in concentration, but everyone's pencils were making regular contact with paper. Her eyes turned to the view outside, soaking in the autumn colors that framed the high school next door. A flash of black caught her eye and she looked more closely, finding a dark-clad Amish boy hustling up the sidewalk, approaching the front door of the school. Out of reflex, Margaret looked at the clock in her own classroom. The boy was considerably late for the start of the school day. He seemed in a hurry, though. Perhaps he had a good reason for his tardiness. He slipped through the door.

"That was David."

Margaret startled to see Gertie standing at the desk. "Do you know him?"

Gertie nodded. "I'm going to have a new *mamm*, and that's her new brother."

Margaret blinked, waiting for the puzzle pieces to fall into place. "Who is going to be your new mother?"

"Ella Hilty. I can't wait."

Hilty. Margaret visualized the list of Amish students she had studied several times. Jed Hilty was listed as stepfather to David and Seth Kaufman.

"David is not supposed to go to school," Gertie said. "I heard my *daed* talking to my *onkel* James."

From Margaret's brief glimpse of David, he certainly appeared young enough that he belonged in school, and he carried a bundle of books. She pulled her eyes from the window and focused on Gertie.

"Do you have a question?" Margaret said.

"I'm finished." Gertie produced a neatly scripted page of sentences. "Do you have something else I can copy?"

"Of course." Margaret rummaged beneath the papers on her desk and produced a reading primer the class had not yet begun. "Try this."

Gertie took the book. "It looks easy."

The girl sauntered back to her desk. Margaret had not noticed any of the children watching where she gazed, but if any of them would, Gertie would. She was bright, observant, talented, hardworking, and eager to please. Margaret made a mental note to speak with Gideon Wittmer about his remarkable child.

❧❀❦

The next afternoon, Ella pushed open the library's heavy door, her arms overflowing with this week's curiosity. Tucked in between her usual topics were two frayed textbooks bearing stamps inside the front covers as evidence they had once belonged to the same college that had supplied teachers to the one-room school for the last three decades. Both addressed the topic of preparing to instruct young children. When she discovered them, Ella felt as if she had made the winning bid on an auction for one of Miriam Lehman's full-size quilts. She signed them out and stacked them between her other selections, hoping she would be able to get them up to her room before anyone wondered what they were. Ella had kept Gideon waiting for nearly a week. Soon he would ask her for an answer. Perhaps these books would help her know if she was making the right choice.

Outside, Ella held the books against her chest while she traipsed to the end of the block and around the corner to where she left her horse and cart thirty minutes earlier. Stops at the mercantile and the post office had justified the excursion into town. The number of children on the sidewalk told Ella the schools had just let out. Soon it would be time to begin preparing the evening meal, a task she and Rachel shared amiably. She secured her books under the cart's bench, beside the mercantile bundle wrapped in brown paper, and gave the mare a friendly greeting. The horse nickered, and Ella smiled. She would miss this horse once she moved to Gideon's home, but his new animal awaited her there.

If only they could settle on their wedding date.

Ella climbed up to the bench, raised the reins, and took the cart into the slight traffic of Seabury. Down the street, the adjoining schools loomed as a reminder of the decision she had yet to make about the future education of Gideon's daughters. For the most part, the premises showed signs of the end of the day—few vehicles or horses nearby, a forgotten lunch pail, papers tumbling in the breeze when they were supposed to have boarded the bus with their owners.

In a small lot added last year to accommodate the increasing number of automobiles that teachers acquired, an engine cranked to life. The sound demanded Ella's attention. She recognized the car as Lindy's and started to lift her hand in a wave. When she saw a passenger leap over the side door and into the seat, though, Ella stilled her hand.

David.

At lunchtime, her father came in for the meal but said David preferred to stay in the field. He had claimed he wasn't hungry and didn't mind the extra work, telling Jed he would finish the task and there was no need for him to hurry back.

Ella couldn't hear what David now said, but Lindy's laugh in response floated on the breeze and made Ella's stomach clench. A minute later, the car rumbled past Ella. If either Lindy or David noticed her, they gave no indication. Lindy accelerated in the direction of the Amish farms.

"Let's go, girl," Ella said to her horse before clicking her tongue and raising the reins. Quickly, she urged the mare to a trot and then to a canter. A full gallop seemed inadvisable with the rickety cart in tow without risking the collapse of an axle or a wheel spinning off.

Apparently Lindy enjoyed fast driving. Ella couldn't keep up. With a sigh, she slowed the rig.

Lindy had done the right thing the day she brought David home when she found him in town. Was she now abetting his deceit?

James held a folded list in his hands. The girls were already home from school, and he had accomplished few of his intentions for the day.

Inspecting the fences, examining the shoes on all the animals, going into town to check on Lindy, and a half dozen other tasks remained unattended. The list was too long to accomplish in one day, but he had expected better progress.

But Miriam was slow and pale, and James had insisted after breakfast that she take it easy. All day long she fussed around the *dawdihaus* despite his repeated encouragement that the items on her own day's list could wait.

"Please lie down," he said now.

"I should see about the girls." Miriam started to push herself out of her chair.

"Tobias is looking after them."

"I haven't even started supper."

"We'll find something." James put a hand on Miriam's shoulder with gentle pressure. "The bedroom is right over there. If you get out of the chair, the bed is the only place I will allow you to go."

"You're getting bossy, old man." Her words protested, but her eyes moved to the bedroom.

"I'll sit with you," James said.

Miriam nodded. James held out a hand to help her up and walked with her to the bedroom, where she sat on the bed and removed her shoes. James pulled a chair to the side of the bed and held her hand as she stretched out. Within three minutes her breathing deepened and evened.

James released her hand but made no move to leave the room. He did not want her to wake and find him gone from the *dawdihaus*, or to wake and become too ambitious about the evening meal.

Besides, he welcomed time to sit still before the Lord and clear his heart and mind.

Even after all these weeks, parents remained in disbelief that the old school was gone. Building a new one seemed a risky venture without official approval to hold classes. The school board was no friendlier toward the wishes of the Amish than it had been two months ago. Discovering David in his wagon and the vandalism and theft in Lindy's workshop rattled James. Even Gideon, with his propensity for sensible decisions, was conflicted.

The quiet life James and Miriam had enjoyed together for nearly forty-four years seemed elusive now.

The bedroom window allowed just enough outside light to read for a few minutes. James reached to the nightstand for his Bible and turned to Proverbs.

"The name of the Lord is a strong tower: the righteous runneth into it, and is safe."

James murmured prayers that he would see the strong tower.

<hr />

Gertie's self-portrait lay protected by a large envelope on Margaret's automobile seat. For three days she had stared at it multiple times each day, and every time she was equally astounded that a child Gertie's age could produce something so remarkable. Margaret was tempted to go to the library and see if she could turn up information on the childhood works of some of the world's great artists. If the request was too specific, Mrs. White, the librarian, might know of a volume she could request on loan from a Cleveland library.

She could not believe that any parent would not want to know about such an exceptional ability. Gideon was entitled to see for himself what his offspring could do. Imagine what Gertie might accomplish with proper training, perhaps even private lessons.

Margaret certainly did not have the ability to teach Gertie what she deserved to learn.

If he had a telephone, Margaret could have called and arranged a proper meeting. Instead, she hoped she would at least find him home.

She stopped her car at what seemed like a respectful distance from the house and barn and crunched along the gravel for the remainder of the distance on foot. Just as she reached the front porch, someone called her name. Margaret turned to see Gideon beside a well pump at the side of the house, wiping his hands on a towel.

"Mr. Wittmer," she said. "I hope you are well."

"Very well, thank you," he said. "And you?"

"Very well also. I was hoping I might have a few minutes of your time."

"Is Gertie giving you trouble?"

"Oh, goodness, no. She's a delightful child—probably my best student, though I'll have to ask you not to repeat that to any of the other parents." Her laughter sounded more nervous than she meant it to.

"I'm glad to hear that." Gideon gestured toward two chairs on the porch, and they sat. "Are you here on behalf of the school district?"

Margaret took a seat and arranged her skirt. "I wanted to show you a piece of your daughter's classroom work."

Gideon took the envelope Margaret offered and unwound the string that held the clasp closed. The art paper slid out into his lap.

"Miss Simpson," he said, "who drew this?"

"Why, Gertie did! That's what's so remarkable. I've never seen such talent in a child of her age."

"I see." Gideon stared at his daughter's face but did not pick up the paper.

"Mr. Wittmer," Margaret said, "I daresay I was expecting a good deal more enthusiasm for Gertie's effort. She's seemed averse to presenting it to you, but the more I looked at it, the more I thought you should see it."

"Miss Simpson," Gideon said, "this is an example of why the Amish need our own schools."

"I beg your pardon?"

"A six-year-old should not be asked to choose between pleasing her father and pleasing her teacher."

"I assure you, I had no intention of putting Gertie in such a position." Margaret's heart pounded. What was he accusing her of?

"Gertie made the picture because you asked her to, but she knows that our people do not use graven images."

"And I assure you I do not teach my pupils to worship idols." Margaret's back straightened. "A charcoal drawing is hardly a golden calf, Mr. Wittmer."

"Gertie's dolls do not even have faces, Miss Simpson. Images may create pride or attachment to something other than God. In the future, I would appreciate it if you would find other work for Gertie to complete while the *English* students study art."

"Surely not!"

"Please understand, Miss Simpson. We both want what is best for Gertie."

"Yes, we do," Margaret said as she stood up. But how could anyone think it was best for a little girl to deny a talent that could have come only from God?

Friday morning breakfast and family devotions proceeded just as they did any other day of the week. Antsy, and with one eye on the clock, Seth jiggled his knee while Jed read from his German Bible. David sat still, but with an expression that suggested to Ella he wasn't hearing much of what came out of Jed's mouth. Rachel watched her sons more than she did her husband. Jed calmly refused to rush. This had been the pattern for weeks, ever since the start of the school year.

At the "Amen," Seth popped out of his seat, kissed his mother's cheek, grabbed the books bundled by a strap of leather, picked up his lunch bucket, and dashed out the door to catch the bus.

"We'll do as we did yesterday," Jed said to David, "but to the east in the field."

David nodded. "There's no need for both of us. I'll go."

"Thank you," Jed said.

Ella took control of her jaw to keep it from going slack. Did her father really think David intended to go out to the field?

She watched David slip his arms into a lightweight jacket and arrange his hat on his head before going out the back door and disappearing behind the barn.

Ella took her shawl off its hook and straightened her prayer *kapp*. She would leave the cart behind this morning. The route was uncertain, but Ella was determined to follow David's movements. As quietly as possible, she saddled a horse and led it out, going behind the stable. David was gone, as she expected he would be, but the grassless ground around the barn bore no evidence that David's footsteps had turned toward the fields of crops. Rather, he had rounded the barn and angled off toward the main road. From the house, his movements would be unseen.

On her horse, and from a distance, Ella followed. Once David entered a plot of vegetation, footprints were harder to find, but Ella was certain David would emerge on the road. She could take her own path and find him. This time, since he was on foot and she was on horseback, she would have the advantage of speed.

Ella reached the road and stilled the horse, waiting and scanning in both directions.

One minute passed, and then two. Perhaps David had found the road ahead of her after all and was already out of sight.

Three minutes, then four and five. Ella nudged the horse forward slowly. Movement in the bushes drew her attention to one side.

At last.

David broke through and, startled, halted.

"What are you doing here?" he said, shifting his books to the other arm.

"I wondered the same thing about you," Ella said. "I saw you get in Lindy's car after school the other day."

He said nothing, instead starting to walk and peering down the road in hopes of an automobile's arrival.

"Are you waiting for Lindy now?"

"No."

"Is she helping you?"

He pressed his lips closed.

"David, this is not right."

He raised his eyes to meet hers now. "I'm not giving up school."

"But sneaking around—it's defiance. It comes from pride."

David shrugged. "I'm hardly sneaking anymore, am I? Everyone knows. My *mamm* pretends she doesn't, but that's only to make herself feel better."

Ella blew out her breath.

"Besides," David said, "as long as I show up at school, I keep Jed out of trouble. They won't come after him for not enrolling me. I'm doing a good thing."

"Disobeying his wishes is *helping* him?" In all the discussions about the new school laws, this was the most convoluted logic Ella had heard. "You can take my horse and go home before anyone realizes you're gone."

"I have a math test this morning. I can't afford another zero in that class because of an absence."

David waved his hand at an approaching automobile, which slowed. Ella didn't recognize the driver. Of course, she knew only a few people in Seabury. David showed no hesitation about the process of finding a ride. He leaned in the open car window, exchanged a few sentences with the driver, and got in.

❧

Gideon decided to see for himself. Ella had been the first to tell him about the school Chester Mast was intent on building, but it hadn't been long before other parents wondered what he thought. At the last church gathering—in the spacious Byler home—Gideon could hardly eat his midday meal without an interruption every two bites from someone seeking his opinion. It was time to ride out and see what Chester was up to. If the construction seemed unrealistic, Gideon would escape forming any opinion at all. On the other hand, if it was progressing in a convincing manner, the existence of a new school building might signal to the school board that Amish families meant business about their children's education.

Hammers clattered in ragged rhythm, ringing across open land and becoming louder as Gideon approached. He recognized the wagons and teams. Cristof. Isaiah. John. Chester Mast was guiding a boy a year or two older than Tobias to find the right angle before he hammered. Gideon remembered the boy had begun the school year riding the bus with his girls. Gideon would try to remember to ask Savilla later if he still attended school. Isaiah Borntrager was up on a ladder—a more secure one than he had dragged to the shambles of the old school, Gideon was relieved to see. John Hershberger was perched on a high beam making sure a joint aligned perfectly.

"You here to help?" Chester approached Gideon.

Was he? Gideon scanned the scene again and slid off his horse.

"Where do you need help?" Gideon said.

Chester's curly brown beard shifted as his mouth shaped a grin. "Somebody has to make sure Isaiah doesn't kill himself up there."

Gideon nodded. Heights had never bothered him. He rolled up

both sleeves as he strode toward the ladder. As he walked, he spied one more wagon he recognized, and its owner was unloading two buckets of nails from the back.

"James," Gideon said.

James looked up. "You found us." He set the buckets at his feet.

"I didn't know you would be here," Gideon said.

"Just trying to do my part," James said.

"But building a school?"

"There's no law says Chester can't build on his own property," James said. "We can be ready when the time comes."

Gideon worked his lips out and in. The only reason his girls were still in the *English* school was that Ella had not yet decided to take on the challenge of teaching them. He could hardly blame the other fathers for making their own preparations.

"I thought you were going into town with some of those tables Joshua Glick builds," Gideon said.

"They're popular at the furniture store." James nodded toward the load in his wagon. "I'll be on my way soon."

"I don't see Joshua here."

"Nope. He's still quoting Romans. Says what we're doing is rebelling against a God-ordained government."

Gideon certainly did not feel rebellious. Why would God ask him to hand his innocent little girls over to the *English* world, where they learned to make graven images and sing frivolous songs? If the school would stick to a simple education, perhaps the brewing conflict could have lost its heat before now. Instead, Gideon saw no way to avoid contentiousness. Perhaps he was a rebel after all.

"Will you check on Lindy while you're in town?" Gideon asked.

"I may stop in to see the deputy, too," James said, nodding. "I'm not persuaded he's even trying to find out what happened at her workshop."

"Tell Lindy to come for supper one night," Gideon said. "The children would love to see her."

"I will."

James reached into his wagon and extracted a hammer. "If you're with us, you're going to need this."

Gideon grasped the sanded wooden handle. His goal had been to persuade the school district the Amish needed their own school with a teacher who understood their ways. Chester was right to forge ahead. It was an act of faith that God would bless their obedience.

❧

"I've spoken with Mr. Brownley."

Margaret stiffened against her will and met Mr. Tarkington's eyes. He had come to her classroom door in the middle of the day and asked her to step into the corridor.

"I'm sure you are aware that the Amish problem has not resolved."

Why did everyone insist on labeling the situation the *Amish* problem? The Amish were not the ones who changed the unspoken agreement by which everyone had lived side by side for decades.

"First they refused to enroll some of their children," Mr. Tarkington said. "Then they put some of them back in grade school when they clearly belong in the high school. Now too many of them are absent too often, claiming they are ill."

"I read in the newspaper that influenza is spreading," Margaret said. "The soldiers are bringing it home from Europe."

"Now, Miss Simpson, your tendency to give people the benefit of the doubt is a charming trait," Mr. Tarkington said, "but we both know that influenza is not ravaging the Amish farms."

"It might be."

"We've only had three cases in all of Seabury," he said, "and those were in households where family members had visited Cleveland."

"The paper says they may close the schools in Cleveland. We should not take it lightly."

Mr. Tarkington cleared his throat. "Let's not be distracted from our own matters. Mr. Brownley would appreciate it if you would once again do what you can to gather reliable information."

"I rather thought I disappointed Mr. Brownley with my previous efforts."

"Then you shall have a chance to redeem yourself," the principal said.

"These things take time to sort out," Margaret said. "We need to find common ground through understanding each other."

"The sheriff's office is losing patience."

"I will see what I can do," Margaret said, though she had little idea of what that might be. Her meeting with Gideon Wittmer over his daughter's artwork made plain that the Amish notions about education were more entrenched than she had judged.

Margaret stepped back into her own classroom, where she had left the children reading silently. Her eyes went to Gertie Wittmer and the empty seat next to her. After perfect attendance since the beginning of the year, Hans Byler now had missed two days.

Gertie turned a page. If the girl knew anything about Hans, or about other students whose attendance was becoming erratic, she showed no sign. The other teachers would allow Margaret to look at their attendance records, which might tell her whether the principal and superintendent were reacting in a more extreme manner than the evidence suggested.

At the end of the school day, Margaret lined up her class and led them out the front door, where some met their parents, others scattered on the street to walk home, and others found their buses. Margaret scanned the flow of students out of the school, looking for patches of black and the rich hues of Amish dyes, and counted. It did seem as if there ought to be more Amish students.

Margaret crossed the pavement to the line of buses and caught the elbow of the oldest Amish student in the school.

"Yes, Miss Simpson?" he said.

"I hope things are well with your family," she said.

"Yes, ma'am."

"And. . .your neighbors? Is there any sign of influenza?"

"None that I've heard of," the boy said.

"Good." Margaret glanced around. "I notice some of the children have not been in school. Perhaps some other illness?"

The student shrugged.

"And you?" she said. "Should we discuss with your father returning to the high school?"

"My *daed* has made his decision. It is not my place to challenge it."

"I see. So the children who are missing school are simply doing what their fathers have decided?"

The bus engine howled. The boy looked over his shoulder at the idling vehicle.

"Go on," Margaret said. "Don't miss your bus on my account."

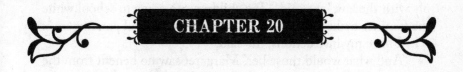

Margaret festered all weekend. Even Gray Truesdale's invitation for a Saturday afternoon stroll did not banish from her mind the Amish *dilemma*, as she preferred to call it. Even that seemed a harsh word. *Conundrum? Mystery?*

By Monday, Margaret had resolved to do whatever was within her power.

On Tuesday, she decided to start with the deputy sheriff. If the county sheriff was as impatient as Mr. Tarkington led her to believe, then perhaps reasoning with Deputy Fremont would buy her more time. She gave her pupils one assignment after another to work independently while she scratched arguments and wording onto sheets of paper, crossed out, revised, and finally memorized. As soon as the children were safely dismissed after school, Margaret braced her shoulders, lifted her chin, and walked to the local sheriff's station. If Deputy Fremont would not listen, she would take her car to Chardon the next afternoon and deal with the county sheriff himself.

Deputy Fremont kept Margaret waiting so long she was ready to pound on his desk. By the time she had his attention, she remembered almost nothing of the reasoned arguments she had spent the day preparing and instead blurted out her frustration.

"I will deal with this matter," she said. "I am here only to ask you to communicate to the sheriff in Chardon that he need only wait with more patience for a favorable outcome."

Deputy Fremont chuckled as he stood and picked up his jacket from the back of his chair.

"You can't seriously think we are going to overlook the exceptional level of truancy among the Amish children."

"I will speak to the fathers and make clear that they must comply with the law," she said. "The children can come to school while the families make their case within appropriate legal parameters."

"I have my instructions," he said.

"And what would those be?" Margaret saw no benefit from the deputy screeching his tires onto Amish farms again with blustering threats.

Deputy Fremont picked up a stack of papers from the corner of his desk. "These are official notices of fines that are the consequences of Amish flagrancy."

"Amish flagrancy! Can you not see the hyperbole in such a term?"

"I suppose you are entitled to your opinion." The deputy picked up the crank that would start his automobile. "But frankly, it has no bearing."

Margaret stood and leaned over the desk. "Are you truly going to inflict fines over a matter that might yet be solved by conversation?"

"The time for conversation is past."

"The time for conversation is never past."

He laughed again. "Miss Simpson, you were supposed to help the Amish consolidate. You failed. Now it's time for me to do my job. I represent the sheriff's office. My duty is to enforce the law, not to turn my head the other way."

"I must protest!"

"If you like." He gripped the papers in one hand. "I have work to do, starting with Mr. Wittmer. I think you were right when you pointed us to him as the most influential of the fathers. If we set an example with him, the others will come in line soon enough."

Margaret swallowed and composed herself. "Deputy Fremont, perhaps if you and I work together, we could be more effective."

He shook his head. "I have my orders from the sheriff."

Deputy Fremont strode past Margaret and into the street, his papers in one hand and his crank in the other.

Margaret trailed after him, but once outside, she turned sharply toward home. She would take her own automobile out to the Amish farms.

She had not counted on finding Gray Truesdale standing on the corner where she needed to turn toward her bungalow. His back was to Margaret, and she halted her steps before he twisted around. If only she could ask for his help. If only she could ask anyone's help. But right now Margaret could not afford further delay. This was no time for flirting or explanations or wondering if he was going to kiss her.

Gray's head began to rotate, and then one shoulder dropped.

Margaret pivoted, retraced her steps for half a block, turned down the wrong street, and muttered sincere prayers that Gray would not decide to go to her house—at least not before she could arrive, get her own crank to start her car, and pull away in a direction that would allow her to avoid eye contact. It wasn't that she meant to deceive him, but only that she had no time to be polite.

Moments later she cranked the engine and put the full weight of her foot on the pedal. There was a reason her uncle had given her this old car, though. It wasn't fast enough for him, and at the moment, neither was it fast enough for Margaret.

By the time she arrived at the Wittmer farm, Deputy Fremont and Gideon were squared off in front of the barn. Margaret braked with a lurch and leaned against the door, willing it to open smoothly. She groaned when she saw the official yellow form already in Gideon's hand.

"Deputy, please," Margaret said, approaching the men.

"I've done my duty here," Fremont said. "I have several other stops to make, and my wife would like to have me home for supper."

"I refuse to believe we cannot have a reasonable conversation about this matter," Margaret said.

"Miss Simpson," Gideon said, creasing the paper, "your assistance is not necessary."

Heat flushed through her face. "I represent the school in this matter."

"It's a matter for the law now," Fremont said. He shuffled through the remaining papers. "I will move on. Mr. Hershberger's children haven't been to school at all. Mr. Borntrager, Mr. Mast, Mr. Byler. Yes, I think I've got everyone sorted out."

Gideon seemed far calmer than Margaret felt.

"I think you'll find the fine modest," Fremont said. "I would hate for matters to escalate, so I'll remind you to take note of the date specified on the form. We'll need to see all the children properly enrolled and attending regularly by that date. And I stress *regularly*."

The deputy marched to his car. Margaret fixed her eyes on Gideon, who disappeared into his barn.

⋘ ❧ ⋙

Gideon murmured the "Amen" and closed the Bible. He had chosen to read, "Children, obey your parents" from Ephesians the next morning not to assume a disciplinary posture but as a gentle reminder to his three children that he had their best interests in mind.

"Gertie," Gideon said, "please go check and see if we missed any eggs last night."

"But I do that after school," Gertie said, fumbling to tie her *kapp* under her chin.

"Today I want you to do it this morning." Gideon looked into Gertie's eyes, her mother's eyes, and waited for the protest to pass through the muscles of her face.

Savilla slid off the davenport, her eyes focused on the clock on the mantel. "I'll get the lunch buckets. Hurry up, Gertie."

Gideon put the German Bible on the shelf. On most school days, the girls would be six minutes away from leaving for the bus stop. Savilla hated to be late for anything and knew well the consequence for missing the bus.

Tobias stood up. "I noticed the stalls need mucking. Shall I do that today?"

Gideon nodded. "This morning, please. After midday, Aaron King will come to help us get the last of the hay into the loft."

Tobias nodded and left.

Savilla returned with two lunch buckets. "I forgot where I left my shawl."

"What do I always tell you about that?" Gideon said.

"Hang it on the hook." She set the lunch buckets on the floor next to the front door. "I think I left it on my bed."

Four minutes.

Savilla's steps on the stairs were light, rushing, scampering. She returned with the shawl over her shoulders and took custody once again of the lunch buckets.

Three minutes.

"Gertie's taking too long," Savilla said.

"We're all right," Gideon said.

"No, we're not. We'll be late."

"It's all right, Savilla."

"If we miss the bus, you'll have to take us to school, and I know you're busy." Savilla stuck her head out the door. "Gertie!"

"Savilla, please sit down."

"I can't, *Daed*. It's time to go."

"I asked you to sit down."

She plopped into a chair, her eyes shifting between the waiting lunch buckets and the ticking clock.

Two minutes.

"We're going to have to run," Savilla said. "Gertie doesn't like it when I tell her to run for the bus."

"You won't have to run," Gideon said.

"I don't understand why you asked Gertie to get eggs in the morning. She dawdles."

"We'll just wait for her."

One minute.

Gertie burst in, breathless. "I looked in all the nests and there's not a single egg."

Savilla popped up, and Gideon motioned she should sit again.

"I need to talk to both of you," he said.

"Your eyes are not smiling, *Daed*," Gertie said.

"I've made a decision," Gideon said. "I've decided that the two of you will learn at home from now on."

Savilla's eyes widened. "We're not going to school?"

Gideon shook his head. "I think it's best for you to stay on the farm and study here."

"But who will teach us?"

Gideon brightened his tone. "Today you will have a school holiday! Play outside. Get some fresh air."

Gertie squealed her delight.

Savilla scowled her doubt.

When Gideon's buggy approached, Ella set aside the bird manual and leaned on the fence to wait for him.

"I took the girls out of school," he said.

"I thought you might," Ella said. "I was at the Hershbergers' when the deputy arrived with the papers yesterday. He said he had already been to your farm."

"I will pay the fine, but I will not be bullied into sending my children to a school that thinks so little of them that they would make no effort to understand their home."

"Miss Simpson seems very nice." Ella's heart pelted her chest. This conversation could have only one end.

"She's quite pleasant." Gideon nodded. "But she is one teacher, and despite her intentions, she seems to have no voice in the decisions."

Ella swallowed. Living alone or having a job or even owning an automobile did not mean *English* women were equal to their men. Lindy had said as much many times. But once she decided she didn't want to marry, Lindy chose to live among the *English*. Better to be an *English* old maid than an Amish one, she reasoned. Ella wasn't so sure. Margaret Simpson did not seem to be any better off for her *English* upbringing and independence.

"I'll do it," Ella whispered.

Gideon raised his eyebrows.

"I'll teach the girls," Ella said. "I won't have any idea what I'm doing, but I'm willing to muddle through if you are."

Gideon's brow wrinkled. "I want you to be certain."

"I am." And she was.

I'm old enough to decide." David spoke with surety two days later. "If I'm old enough to do a man's work on the farm, I'm old enough to decide I want to stay in school."

"But if you go to school, you won't be here to do a man's work," Jed said.

"David, no," Rachel said.

"I'm going to live with Lindy. She's like an *aunti* to me. You always tell me that."

Ella held her breath. The breakfast she'd swallowed a few minutes ago threatened to work its way up. When she saw Lindy pick David up after school, she never imagined it would come to this. At least David waited until after morning devotions and Seth's departure, sparing his brother this scene.

"I already packed," David said. "I don't mean to hurt anybody. If you want me to, I'll come home on Saturdays and work from dawn to dusk."

"That won't be necessary," Jed said.

Rachel blanched. Ella's stomach sank.

"Lindy has been my friend since we were small girls," Rachel said. "I can't believe she would do this to me."

"I haven't talked to her about it yet," David said. "But she'll say yes."

Ella's eyes flicked up. With his bag packed, David seemed certain.

"I'll ask her not to," Rachel said. "She'll know I don't approve."

"Then I'll go somewhere else," David said softly. "I'll find a place to camp, or get a job after school and rent a room."

"You would really do that?"

David met his mother's eyes. "Wouldn't you rather I be with Lindy? I know Lindy would rather know I'm safe."

Ella forced some air out of her lungs, wishing David had waited two more minutes until she'd at least left the room, if not the house. She could have been cleaning the henhouse or sweeping the porch or mixing bread dough or on her way to Gideon's. Anything but listening to this. Slowly she stood up from the end of the davenport.

David stood as well, and without speaking he climbed the stairs. Ella crept out of the room and hovered at the doorway to the kitchen.

"Are you going to just let him go?" Rachel said to Jed. "You didn't even try to stop him."

"He has made up his mind," Jed said.

"Don't you think of him as your own son?" Rachel said, her pitch rising. "Would you let your own fifteen-year-old son do this?"

"When we married, I took responsibility for the boys," Jed said. "But he already runs off half the time even though he knows our decision. How do you propose that I make him stay?"

"Forbid him to go."

"And if he goes anyway?"

"He's my son, Jed. He's going to the *English*."

"Lindy went."

"But my son! It's different."

David's footsteps returned, heavier. Above his mother's eyes, he caught Ella's gaze.

She shook her head. David bent to kiss Rachel's cheek and went out the front door with a duffel.

⌘

Younger men arrived to scramble up the ladders, hoisting shingles over their shoulders in a way that made James's shoulders ache just watching them. Chester Mast had driven all the way to Chardon to order lumber and supplies. The school would be finished soon. Already, while the roof crew enclosed the top of the building, others sealed windows in their frames, whitewashed the walls and floor, hammered in shelves, and sanded the wall where the chalkboards would hang.

Today's effort had been a sort of frolic among the men and any boys not in the *English* schools. Earlier progress came from a few men at a time turning up to do what they could between the long hours of their harvests, but all agreed that a frolic that brought nearly twenty men together would speed them to the finish line. The chalkboards would be the last large pieces to transport, once they arrived.

The women were at the Glicks' with a promise to arrive with lunch for everyone when the hour came. James had dropped Miriam off with a crate full of ingredients.

With his hands crossed behind his back, James stood at the rear of the school and imagined the room alive with children. Gertie and Savilla. Hans and the other Byler children. All those Hershberger girls whom James couldn't quite tell apart. The Glicks. The Borntragers. The Kings. Jed Hilty's stepson. The names of others in the church district drifted through James's mind.

Cristof Byler sidled up. "It will be a fine school."

James nodded. "What do the *English* think?"

Cristof laughed. "Not too many *English* school authorities come out this way. Chester's boys are in school—for now—so they have no reason to visit his farm."

"Will you take your children out?"

"Just as soon as we have a teacher. I'm already keeping Hans home some of the time. Gideon says he's working on finding a teacher."

A new voice spoke. "James."

He turned toward Isaiah Borntrager.

"The women sent a message," Isaiah said. "Miriam collapsed."

The pressure in his chest stopped James's breath.

"They said you should come," Isaiah said.

James gulped air. "Of course."

He strode to his buggy, checked the hitch and reins, climbed to the bench, and put the rig in motion.

At the Glick farm, three women hovered over Miriam on the front porch, one fanning her, another urging her to sip water, another arranging a pillow behind her head in the deep Adirondack chair. James nudged his way past them and knelt in front of his wife.

"What are you doing here, old man?" Miriam said.

She grasped a glass of water, and James was relieved to see it did not wobble in her grip.

"What happened?"

"I felt a little tired, that's all."

"She nearly passed out," Mrs. Borntrager said.

"I'll take you home." James put one hand behind Miriam's back to help her up.

"I promised you lunch," she said.

"I'm not hungry."

"I'll find something at home."

"You're going straight to bed." He took the water glass out of her hand and handed it to Mrs. Borntrager.

As soon as they arrived home, James once again pulled a chair up to the side of the bed to insist that Miriam rest. He would have to talk to Gideon about expecting less from Miriam with the main house and children. Surely Gideon would marry Ella in a few weeks, and the pressure would ease on Miriam. And he would have to be more direct with Miriam. It was no sin to admit she was tired.

Forty-four years. James wanted forty-four more with his bride.

❦

Saturday brought the men together again for a morning of finishing work. Gideon tied his horse to a tree and hefted his toolbox out of his buggy.

"Where's James?" Cristof wanted to know. "I was hoping he would help us sort out what we need to build the desks."

"He can't leave Miriam," Gideon said. "She'll refuse to rest if he's not there to make sure she does."

"Then he is where he should be," Cristof said.

"We should talk to Lindy Lehman about the desks," Gideon said. "She's a better carpenter than most people realize, and she'll appreciate the need for simplicity."

"I can't get used to the idea of a woman carpenter. It's not fitting."

"You have one of her birdhouses in your yard."

"That's different."

"Only in size."

Joshua Glick broke into their conversation. "Gideon, I just heard that you took your children out of school."

"That's right." Gideon gripped his toolbox with both hands and looked Joshua in the eyes.

Joshua gestured to the nearly finished school. "Someday we'll have a school. In the meantime, though, we should obey the law."

"In my mind," Gideon said, "the question has become more complex."

"Perhaps we should all pull the children out of the *English* schools," Cristof said. "If we were united, it might send a strong message."

"It would get more of us in trouble," Joshua insisted. "Several men have already been fined."

"It's a small amount," Gideon said. "The deputy is blustering more than anything."

"The Bible tells us to live in submission to the government," Joshua said. "Are the apostle's words not clear?"

"They are," Gideon said.

Cristof spoke. "Maybe the time has come for a church vote."

"No." Alarm spurted through Gideon's gut. "Asking for a vote would only inflame matters further."

Joshua kicked at the dirt. "People look up to you, Gideon. You should set an example."

"Perhaps I am," Gideon said.

"I mean an example of doing the right thing," Joshua said.

"Perhaps I am," Gideon repeated.

"That's right," Cristof said.

Gideon began to wish Cristof would go find something else to do.

"Joshua," Gideon said, "you are in favor of running our own school, aren't you?"

"I am—when it's legal."

"That may take some time." So far Gideon had not been able to persuade the superintendent to grant him an appointment to discuss the matter calmly. He was quite sure cooperating to make an Amish school part of the district had not entered Mr. Brownley's mind.

"We have to go through the proper procedures," Joshua said. "While we wait, the children should be in school."

"And what becomes of our children in the meantime?" Gideon said. Gertie's self-portrait took form in his mind, along with the frivolous novel Savilla had been assigned to read. How would a book called *The Secret Garden* prepare Savilla for a quiet life on an Amish farm?

Ella happened to glance out the window of her second-story bedroom and saw the automobile before she heard it. She dropped her dust rag on the small desk and leaned toward the windowpane. Three seconds later, she pivoted and flew down the stairs.

"Rachel! Rachel!"

"In the kitchen," came the answer.

"Where's my *daed*?" Ella burst into the kitchen, where Rachel held a long wooden spoon and stirred coffee cake batter.

"I'm not sure. He left right after breakfast." Rachel tilted her head in question. "What's so urgent?"

"The deputy's car is coming down the lane."

Rachel dropped her spoon, spattering batter on table and floor, and raced out the back door calling her husband's name.

The knock came on the front door. Ella smoothed her apron and focused on not hunching over as she answered it.

"Hello," she said, stepping out onto the porch.

"It's a fine Monday morning," Deputy Fremont said.

Superintendent Brownley was with him this time. His gloomy scowl was the only expression Ella had ever seen on his face.

"We are thankful for each day God gives," Ella said.

"Is your pa here?" Deputy Fremont asked.

"My pa?"

"Or whatever you people call your father. Jed Hilty. I need to speak to Jed Hilty."

"It's a large farm and it's harvesttime," Ella said. "I'm not sure I can say where he is just now."

Rachel came around the corner of the house, her faced blanched but her spine extended, her shoulders back.

Good for you. Ella liked seeing determination in Rachel.

"Are you Mrs. Hilty?" Fremont asked.

"I am. May I be of assistance?"

"Can you tell us where your husband is?"

"No, I can't."

"Can't or won't?" Mr. Brownley muttered.

Rachel returned his stare but said nothing.

Brownley cleared his throat. "Would you give your husband a message?"

"Of course."

"We're pleased he has cooperated and we see David Kaufman in school, but his attendance has been erratic."

"I'm certain it will improve," Rachel said.

"I understand you are the boy's mother."

"Yes, I am."

"Then you can appreciate the gravity of the situation."

Gravity? Ella thought. That seemed a severe word.

"Your son's attendance borders on truancy. He's often late or leaves the building early without authorization."

"As I said, I believe you will see improvement," Rachel said.

"Your husband has the opportunity to be an example of cooperation that other parents can emulate."

"I'll tell him you said so."

"Thank you."

Ella stood on the porch and watched the two men retrace their steps to the deputy's automobile, crank the engine, and roar off the farm.

Only then did Jed appear.

"*Daed*!" Ella met her father's eyes. Had he been there all along?

"I couldn't find you anywhere," Rachel said. "The horses were all here. I thought you must have walked out to one of the fields."

Ella believed Rachel had looked diligently for her husband. Surprise burned its way through Ella's chest. Jed had not wanted to be found. Had he seen the car coming even before she did?

Rachel gave a rapid account of the conversation.

"I have half a mind to take Seth out of school," Jed said.

"But he's only twelve," Ella said. "Seventh grade."

"They wanted David and now they have him," Jed said. "Are we also going to give them Seth?"

Why should Seth be a pawn to trade with the school district, one boy for the other? Ella's father had backed down so easily at the moment of David's ultimate defiance, but now he would take a sweet, earnest, contented boy in exchange? Ella pressed her lips together to keep disrespect out of her words.

"Other families are teaching their children at home. Your Gideon, for instance."

Ella swallowed.

"If you can teach Gideon's girls, you can teach Seth."

Ella found her voice. "I'm not even sure I can do a good job with the girls. Seth's lessons would be more advanced. It might be too much."

Jed looked again at the empty lane where the car had been before pacing across the yard to the barn.

CHAPTER 22

In church the following Sunday, Gideon mulled over the reality that so far the bishop had not publicly addressed the education of Amish children. He supposed the *English* would call it the "elephant in the room." By now any member in church could look around the congregation and know which decision each family had made, including his.

Joshua Glick had been right. As soon as word got out that Gideon was keeping his girls home from school, other households did the same. No matter how many times Gideon said that he did not judge another man's conscience on the matter, other fathers seemed to look to his example.

Yet the closest any of the ministers had come to preaching on the subject was to choose a Bible passage exhorting kindness to neighbors, as they might have done at any Sunday worship service of the year.

Gideon bowed his head, making a prayer of the final hymn.

Where shall I go? I am so ignorant. Only to God can I go, because God alone will be my helper. I trust in You, God, in all my distress. You will not forsake me. You will stand with me, even in death. I have committed myself to Your Word. That is why I have lost favor in all places. But by losing the world's favor, I gained Yours. Therefore I say to the world: Away with you! I will follow Christ.

Gideon made sure Tobias remained with the men to transform the benches of worship into tables for a meal in the King barn. He was glad for his coat this morning, and grateful that the next Sunday service was scheduled in a heated home large enough to accommodate the congregation. A juicy, steaming morsel of pork dangled from his fork on its way to his open mouth when Gideon felt a little hand thudding against his back. He turned to see Gertie. The girls were supposed to be eating with the women, under Ella's supervision. Miriam was home ill.

"*Daed*," Gertie said, "Katie Glick said that you're going to jail because I'm not in school. I don't want you to go to jail."

Gideon swung his legs over the bench so he could take her in his lap. "I am not going to jail."

"Promise?"

"Only God can promise. You know that."

"I'll go to school, and I won't draw any pictures or sing any songs. I'll only read the alphabet and do my sums."

"Don't you like learning at home with Ella?" Gideon said.

"Yes, I do. She makes everything interesting."

Gideon nodded. "Then let's keep doing that."

"But you'll go to jail, *Daed*!"

"I'm not going to jail." He kissed the top of her head. "Now go find Ella and finish your lunch."

The men around the table chewed silently, some of them staring at Gideon as he picked up his fork.

"She might be right," Aaron King said. "We could all go to jail."

"The fine was barely more than the cost of cotton for a child's dress," Gideon said. "It's hardly a foreshadowing of jail."

"I've been thinking," Chester Mast said. "Perhaps our children should all be in school for now."

"Chester!" Gideon's jaw dropped. "You're the one building a school on your own land."

"And I intend to see it used someday—sooner rather than later. My boys have been out of school the last few days, but I'm going to send them back tomorrow with a proviso."

Gideon lifted both eyebrows. The clinking of forks ceased.

"Some of the subjects the older children study are beyond what any of us regard as necessary, so in those subjects I will instruct my sons not to complete the assigned work."

Isaiah Borntrager laughed. "Chester Mast, you have spoken the word of the Lord."

Hardly. Gideon ran his tongue across his bottom lip while he thought.

"Health, world governments, art, other frivolous classes—my boys will be present in class, and I cannot control what falls on their ears," Chester said. "But I do have a say in what they focus their minds on, and it will not be these subjects."

"Gideon, what about you?" Aaron said. "Will you send your children back to school with these instructions?"

Gideon pictured Savilla's copy of *The Secret Garden*. Gertie's graven image was hidden in his dresser. He might need to present it to the school board as an example of unacceptable instruction.

"No, I don't think so," he said.

⚜

Gideon opened the accounts ledger lying at the center of the desk in the small alcove where he kept his papers. A shadow fell over the paper, and he looked up.

"May I interrupt you?" James said.

"Of course. How is Miriam today?"

"That's what I want to discuss," James said. "It broke her heart not to be well enough for church yesterday."

"Everyone asked after her."

"I will stay home and make sure she rests," James said. "But she will not want to stay down long."

Miriam was like her niece in that way. Right up until the week that Betsy died, Gideon had urged her to stop trying to do everything on her own.

"I want to help," Gideon said. "What can we do for Miriam?"

"A few changes will make things easier for her," James said. "Small things that she won't argue against."

"Whatever you have in mind."

"First," James said, "I want to put up a railing. We have only two steps up into the *dawdihaus*, but I would feel better if she had a railing."

"That's a simple thing," Gideon said.

"And I want to bring a comfortable chair into your kitchen," James said. "She needs to be able to get off her feet but still keep an eye on the stove."

"There's plenty of room under the corner window," Gideon said.

They should have done it years ago.

James scratched his head. "I'm concerned about the stairs up to the bedrooms, but I can't think of a way to keep her from going up and down."

"I'll talk to her," Gideon said. "I'll say the children are old enough now that there's no reason to coddle them. They can carry up their own laundry, and I'll put a broom and a dust rag in the hall closet. Miriam won't have to go upstairs."

"She'll be suspicious," James said. "She won't like the idea of the children doing her work."

"It won't be her work. It will be their work from now on." Gideon paused. "Do you really think she'll be all right, James?"

James looked out the window. The delay in his response caused an extra heartbeat in Gideon's chest.

"James?"

"I'm sure it's temporary," James said. "She needs more rest. But she will always think taking care of somebody else is more important than taking care of herself."

"I can ask Ella to stay around more," Gideon said. "She doesn't have to run off the moment the day's lessons are finished."

James nodded. "Miriam enjoys Ella."

"And Ella enjoys Miriam."

When Gideon and Ella married, Miriam could really let go of daily responsibilities. Miriam would respect Ella's new role to manage the house and children. Ella had ably managed her father's home for eleven years. She had learned well from her own mother and older sisters the skills she needed for cooking and gardening and canning and milking. At the same time, Gideon had no doubt that Ella would enjoy having Miriam nearby for advice or companionship, someone to sit with on the front porch and snap peas or husk corn, without letting Miriam exhaust herself.

Perhaps James was counting on this scenario, and counting the weeks until the date Gideon and Ella would arrange with the bishop.

Looking back, Gideon could not imagine how he would have managed during the last five years without James and Miriam, and he hoped they would feel no compunction to leave when he married again. Their departure would leave a gaping hole in his children's hearts. But they had taken on the care of three young children at an age when most people were enjoying grandchildren, not running after toddlers.

Miriam deserved the rest that the union between Gideon and Ella would bring her.

The plan suffered from one consequential complication.

How long would Gideon's kitchen table serve as adequate space for daily lessons with two girls?

"Where's Miriam?" Gertie asked.

"She's resting." Ella tapped the primer page. "Can you sound out the next sentence?"

"She's been resting since Saturday," Gertie said. "That's three days. When is she going to be finished resting?"

Savilla sighed. "When she's feeling better, silly."

"Don't call me names."

Ella gave Savilla a warning eye.

"Sorry," Savilla muttered, lowering her gaze back to her own book about the nocturnal habits of small animals.

"Are you going to make us lunch?" Gertie asked.

"I suppose so," Ella said. Lunch was several hours away.

Gertie swung her feet under the table. One shoe came into contact with Savilla's shin.

"Ow!" Savilla glared at Gertie.

Ella wasn't sure she had ever seen that expression on Savilla's face before. Perhaps both girls were always on their best behavior around her, cautioned by their father to mind their manners. Now that she was teaching them and would soon be living with and caring for them, she was bound to see another side to their relationship.

"Keep your feet to yourself, please," Ella said.

"That's not what Miss Simpson says." Gertie folded her hands and placed them in her lap. "She says, 'Hands and feet, nice and neat.'"

After nearly ten years of teaching, Margaret Simpson would have a long list of pithy reminders for classroom behavior.

"Miss Simpson always asks how the bus ride was," Gertie said.

"That's thoughtful of her," Ella said, tapping the page again.

"Then she makes sure everyone has a lunch bucket. She doesn't want anyone to be hungry at school."

"She's very kind."

"Can we pack lunch buckets?" Gertie looked up, hopeful.

"We don't need buckets, sil—" Savilla cut herself off. "We're sitting right in the kitchen. We can have lunch with *Daed* and Ella and James and Miriam."

"Let's concentrate," Ella said. "Then you can surprise everyone with the new words you learned."

Gertie put a finger under the first of three simple sentences on the page. Ella watched the girl's delicate lips go through the motions of finding the right formation for a *p* sound and silently add the other letters before pronouncing *put*.

Gertie looked up. "Are we going to have a chalkboard? At school we had a chalkboard."

"We could ask your *daed*," Ella said, "but since it's just us, we can use paper."

Savilla closed her book around a finger. "May I go in the other room to read, please?"

Ella nodded. "You can tell me later about any parts you didn't understand."

It would be impossible for anyone to concentrate through Gertie's chatter. Savilla tucked in her chair, as she always did, before leaving the room with relief.

"Miss Simpson gave us silent reading time," Gertie said. "We were supposed to use it to try to sound out new words."

"Would you like to have silent reading time, Gertie?" Against the left side of Gertie's head, her coiled braid sagged, and Ella reached over to adjust a pin.

The child shook her head. "I didn't like that part. It was more fun when we got to talk."

Gertie missed the other children, a factor Gideon may not have taken into consideration in his decision to keep her home. Margaret Simpson's classroom was in an *English* school, but she was an experienced, qualified teacher. Margaret would know what to say right now to encourage Gertie to focus on the task before her. While Gertie had been in school for just a few weeks, Margaret's class was her only experience of formal instruction. No wonder she measured the experience of sitting at the kitchen table with Ella against being in the classroom of a trained teacher.

"Let's read for fifteen more minutes," Ella said. "Then you can decide whether you would rather work on sums or handwriting while I see how Savilla is doing."

They were just two sisters in two grades, and already Ella wondered how the teachers in the old one-room schoolhouse had managed with thirty or forty students spanning eight grades.

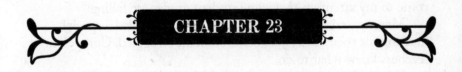

Margaret packed the leather satchel she carried between home and school. Today's teachers meeting had not been on the Thursday afternoon schedule. Mr. Tarkington came around to the classrooms only an hour ago requesting that teachers remain after school. Margaret had escorted her pupils to their waiting buses and returned to her classroom to pick up her things, planning to leave as soon as the meeting concluded. Gray would be waiting for her at the diner for lemon cake and coffee.

The music room was the only space in the school that would accommodate the assembled staff—other than the gymnasium, which would swallow speech in its cavernous hollow and throw back the echo of children playing. Margaret walked through the abandoned upstairs corridor, still chasing from her mind the voices of her own students. She'd had near perfect attendance that day. Only Gertie Wittmer was missing. Her desk still held her books and pencils and the oilcloth she used during art projects, but Margaret suspected Gertie would not be back. Hans Byler still attended— usually—but he looked lonely now when he turned his eyes to the empty desk beside his. Gideon had not formally withdrawn his daughters, but both girls were gone. That was no coincidence.

She should have done something. But what?

Allowing herself an indelicate audible sigh, Margaret shook off the thought. After Deputy Fremont slapped fines and hissed threats at the Amish fathers, Margaret considered herself relieved of responsibility to coax cooperation from them. She had never been one to play the fool, and if she had the opportunity, she would tell the school superintendent exactly what she thought of his tactics.

Mr. Tarkington cleared his throat to open the meeting. "It has come to my attention that some student grades are falling."

Margaret raised one eyebrow. The principal called a special meeting for this? Every year some students struggled. Competent teachers knew what to do.

"I have four of them in my class." Mr. Snyder taught the seventh grade. "I've spoken to Mr. Vaughn at the high school. The same thing is happening there."

Miss Hunter gave voice to Margaret's question. "What exactly is happening?"

Mr. Tarkington pushed his lips out. "Those of you teaching the younger grades may not have observed what is happening in the older grades."

"If they would simply turn in their work," Mr. Snyder said, "the grades would correct. As it is, I will have to give failing grades for the first quarter."

"I understand," Mr. Tarkington said, "that these students refuse to complete work, but only in certain subjects."

"Let me guess," Margaret said. "Assignments are missing in health and hygiene, literature, and world geography. At the high school, we might add higher mathematics, world history, art, and music."

Mr. Tarkington checked notes jotted on a sheet of paper. "That is correct."

"And the pupils you're referencing are Amish students," Margaret said.

"That is also correct."

"The Amish are not accustomed to those subjects," Margaret said. "I would go so far as to guess that the parents of these students would say that the subjects are not relevant to salvation or the practice of their religion."

Mr. Tarkington shifted his weight. "I'm a churchgoing person. I would venture to say that every person in this room is. But we offer an education that prepares students for the modern century. While we certainly hope to impart proper moral values to our students, our direct aim is not the furtherance of religion."

"I think you'll find the Amish don't make that distinction," Margaret said.

"Nevertheless," the principal said, "our task is to ensure the pupils conform to the standards we have established."

Margaret's mind withdrew from the discussion that ensued. The law said the children had to be in school, and many families complied. But just as the law did not say which grade they must enroll their children in, neither did it specify that the children must earn passing marks. Failing marks would ensure both that the students would not learn the objectionable material and also that they would not advance to higher grade levels. Margaret's lips curved in slight admiration at the ingenuity of the Amish strategies.

❧

"I'll feel better if I see for myself that David is all right."

Rachel's determination greeted Ella as she pulled the buggy onto the Hilty farm after spending most of the day on lessons with Gertie and Savilla. Ella relaxed the reins in her hands but did not get out.

"Right now?" Ella asked. There was barely time to go into town and back before supper.

"The meal is in the oven," Rachel said, "with enough wood for a slow heat. I don't want to wait another day. I hope you'll come with me."

Ella offered a smile and a nod. Rachel climbed into the buggy, and Ella signaled the horse again. Tomorrow would make two weeks since David's departure. Perhaps it would help Rachel's recent temperament if she saw for herself that David was safe and cared for.

Rachel fidgeted all the way into town, and although Ella infused her words with optimism and cheerfulness, Rachel did not settle. Any mother would want to know her child was looked after, but at least half of Rachel's nervousness might be in anticipation of what she would say to her old friend under circumstances neither of them would have imagined when they were girls—or even a few weeks ago.

After a while, Ella abandoned attempts at easy conversation and concentrated on coaxing better speed from the horse. Finally they turned onto Lindy's street. Ella let her eyes linger for a moment on Margaret Simpson's bungalow, wondering if Margaret missed Gertie as much as the little girl seemed to miss her. Ella tied the horse up in front of Lindy's house, and she and Rachel paced to the back of the lot where Lindy's workshop sat.

"What was that?" Rachel hurried her steps.

"I didn't hear anything," Ella said, trying to keep pace.

"There it is again," Rachel said.

Scraping and scuffling. It could just be Lindy pushing a piece of furniture across the room.

Thud.

A splintering sound.

A yelp.

The door of the workshop opened, and a man darted out and across a patch of grass before disappearing behind the neighbor's thick hedge. Ella caught a glimpse only of a blue shirt. She didn't recognize the man.

Rachel and Ella burst into the workshop. Splintered against the far wall were the remains of several birdhouses. A bookcase lay on its back, the bottom shelf kicked out of place.

"Lindy?" Rachel called.

A moan. A foot.

Rachel cleared the debris and found her friend, taking Lindy's face in her hands. "Open your eyes! Talk to me!"

With a sigh, Lindy complied. "Did you see him?"

"Who was that?" Rachel asked.

"I don't know." Lindy raised a hand to her head. "I've already got an egg on my scalp."

"Who would want to do this?" Ella scanned the shambles.

Lindy pushed herself upright, leaning on one arm and delicately exploring her ankle with the other. "He came in and went crazy before I could ask what I could do for him. I tried to stop him, but he pushed me, and I tripped."

Ella righted the bookcase. Rachel knelt beside Lindy and pushed up the woolen trousers to examine the injured ankle.

"I'll never get used to seeing you in men's trousers," Rachel said.

"I only wear them when I work." Lindy winced under Rachel's touch.

"It's already swelling," Rachel said. "Do you have ice in that *English* kitchen of yours?"

"The ice man was here just yesterday." Lindy exhaled.

Ella stepped around Rachel to the other side of Lindy. "We'll help you up and into the house."

Gingerly, they got Lindy to her feet. Immediately it was clear she guarded the ankle against her own slight weight as she leaned on Rachel and Ella.

"We'll go slowly." Ella glanced toward the open workshop door. A flash of blue, on the sidewalk in front of the house, made her blink twice. The man moved out of view.

Why would he come back?

"What is it?" Rachel said, following Ella's gaze.

"Nothing," Ella said. Lindy was hopping at a painstaking but tenacious pace, and Ella would not suggest they should now follow a distraction from her care.

Ella was sure it was the same man. She didn't recognize him, but she would know him if she saw him again.

❦

Gideon regretted the action as soon as he put it in motion, but it was too late to stop the hay from tipping off the end of his pitchfork in the loft onto the man standing below him in the barn the following day.

Deputy Fremont sputtered. "Are you looking to give me a reason to issue an additional violation? I will write up as many fines as you'd like to pay."

"I doubt it's a crime against the state for a man to move alfalfa hay into his own stalls," Gideon said. He may have regretted the action, but he had not yet repented of the sentiment.

"I'll ask you again to come down," Deputy Fremont said.

"As you can see, I'm busy." Gideon stuck the pitchfork into a broken bale but restrained himself this time.

"You're going to want to look at this closely." Fremont picked hay out of his uniform.

Gideon doubted that.

Fremont waved a paper. "Apparently our last communication two weeks ago was not sufficiently clear. Rather than put your boy in school, you took your girls out."

Gideon wiped perspiration from his forehead with one sleeve. "It was clear enough."

"Then it was not sufficiently persuasive."

"There's a bench along the tack wall," Gideon said. "You can leave it there."

"Whether you look at it now or later, it's not going to change."

"I didn't expect it would."

The deputy stomped across the barn, found the bench, laid the paper down, and dropped a worn rein on top of it. Gideon threw down a generous shower of hay.

Fremont left the barn door wide open. Gideon waited for the sounds of the automobile engine coming to life and tires spitting gravel before he climbed down the ladder.

The fine was much stiffer this time—no slap on the hands. He was penalized for each child separately, and now he had three truant children rather than one. He scratched the top of his head while making mental calculations. He did not yet know the market price he would receive for the portion of his harvest that he did not need to keep for his own family and animals. Some of the repairs he planned to make over the winter might have to wait. His children were worth the price.

For others, though, the choice might be more difficult. The Hershbergers already were heavily mortgaged. Fines for four children would be beyond John's means. And Isaiah? Chester? Gideon was not sure.

⋘⋙

The lessons were finished for the day, and the girls had gone to the *dawdihaus* to cheer up Miriam, promising to heed Ella's warning not to be rambunctious. They could offer to read to Miriam, Ella had suggested, or ask her to tell a story about when she was their age, but they were not to ask for cookies or a game. Stew was on the stove, and corn bread cooled on the counter.

Ella debated looking in on Miriam. She seemed more rested than she was a week ago and unlikely to accept coddling for much longer.

The back door opened, and Gideon came in.

He glanced around. "Where is everybody?"

"Tobias is in the barn with James, and the girls are with Miriam," Ella said.

A silly grin crossed Gideon's face. "Good." He leaned in to kiss her on the mouth, something he never did when the children were within sight.

She would never tire of the taste of him.

"Let's go for a ride," he said.

Ella tossed the dish towel in her hands onto the table and reached for her shawl.

"What will you do about the fines?" she asked as the buggy rumbled onto the main road.

"Pay them," he said.

"You can't just keep paying fines," Ella said. "They're sure to get steeper."

"I have a plan." Gideon clicked his tongue to speed the horse. "Did James get into town to check on Lindy today?"

Ella nodded. "The doctor says it's only a bad sprain. Lindy needs to stay off her feet for a few days."

"Then it will be handy to have David around," Gideon said. "I hope he's helping with the chores around the house."

"Rachel wishes he would come home, and I don't blame her. Someone has broken into Lindy's shop twice. How is Rachel supposed to know David is safe? Lindy could come, too. I'd be happy to help look after her."

"But David won't come home, will he? Not unless Jed agrees to let him go to school."

"No."

"Then it's better that he is with Lindy for now."

"I don't understand why anyone would want to hurt Lindy—twice." Ella exhaled. "Rachel is organizing meals. James will make deliveries."

"Good."

She leaned forward, realizing Gideon's route. "Are we going to the new school?"

Ella hadn't seen the construction since it was hardly more than framing. The Mast farm was far enough off her usual routines that she did not cross their fields often.

A few minutes later, Gideon eased the rig to a stop in front of the one-room school and helped Ella out of the buggy. He held open the door to the building. Even in the waning afternoon, windows channeled light inside.

"The blackboard is up!" Ella said.

It was pristine, still rich in its slate hues, unclouded by layers of chalk smeared across the surface. Desks were lined up in precise rows, not yet subject to the jostling of squirming children. Three different sizes bore witness to the mixed ages the room was meant to serve. The simplicity and efficiency of the space beckoned beauty.

"All we need is an Amish teacher," Gideon said, "and I think I know someone who would do a wonderful job."

Ella's eyes widened. "You can't mean me."

"Of course I can."

"I haven't even got my legs under me with the girls. I wouldn't know what to do with an entire school."

"Of course you would. You'd figure it out, just the way you figure everything out."

"It wouldn't be legal," Ella said. "I'm not qualified."

"Let me figure out that part." Gideon took both her hands. "Just tell me you'll think about it. And it would only be temporary. I'll correspond with the teachers college and impress upon them the urgency of finding a suitable candidate as soon as possible."

CHAPTER 24

N

o, you are not going to work today." James could be adamant when he chose to be. "I brought strudel, with biscuits and pot roast for later."

"*Aunti* Miriam's pot roast?" Lindy's face brightened. "With mashed potatoes, peas, and gravy?"

"That's right. Enough for you and David to eat two or three times."

"Just like she used to make on Sundays, but it's only Saturday."

James had tried to persuade Miriam to prepare something simpler, but she brushed him off and began peeling a mound of potatoes. James adjusted the pillow under Lindy's swollen ankle.

"Tomorrow Mrs. Borntrager will bring a roast chicken," he said, "and the day after that Mrs. Mast has in mind a casserole."

"Did you arrange all this?"

"Rachel did," James said.

"I suppose everybody knows David is staying with me."

"You know how it is." James handed Lindy a mug of steaming coffee. "Word gets around on the Amish farms."

Lindy looked down into the dark liquid. "I suppose she came on Thursday to make sure David is all right. Now she'll think I can't take proper care of him."

"A better question is whether he's taking proper care of you." James moved Lindy's crutches within reach of her chair.

"David's already cleaned up most of the mess in the workshop," Lindy said. "He's out there now, trying to cut pieces for birdhouses. I had customers waiting for the ones that. . ."

"Your customers will understand," James said. "You need rest. No work."

After extracting a promise that Lindy would remain in the house and not try to hobble out to the workshop, James returned to his wagon. He let the horse clip-clop slowly while he worked his jaw from side to side, thinking. Rachel and Ella had insisted Lindy telephone the sheriff's deputy to see the wreckage in the shop for himself, but his examination had not gone beyond a cursory inspection. So far Deputy Fremont had not seemed compelled to investigate.

James took firmer control of the reins and steered the rig toward Main Street, where he parked in front of the local sheriff's office and went in.

Deputy Fremont looked up. "Mr. Lehman, isn't it?"

"That's right," James said. "I'm here to make an inquiry on behalf of my niece, Lindy Lehman."

Fremont reached for a folder at one end of his desk. "Simple breaking and entering."

"Don't forget that Lindy was physically harmed," James said. No doubt the *English* had a word for a crime in which someone was injured. "Do you have any suspects?"

Fremont shrugged one shoulder. "Not much to go on."

"Ella Hilty saw a tall man wearing a blue shirt and dark trousers," James said.

"That describes half the men in Seabury." Fremont scanned James from head to toe. "Probably *all* of the Amish farmers as well."

"Why would an Amish man break into Lindy's shop?"

"Why indeed?"

Heat flashed through James's neck. "You are going to look for this man, aren't you?"

"As I said, there's not much to go on. Perhaps if there's another crime that fits the same pattern, we'll have more information to work with."

The same pattern? Lindy's shop had twice suffered wreckage. Another episode in the same pattern would put her at risk a third time.

"I have other pressing matters," Fremont said. "Perhaps if your people would abide by the law and send their children to school, Seabury would return to being a peaceful town."

James swallowed his response. The smirk on the deputy's face made James wish he had a bale of hay to pitch down on his head.

~·❦·~

Ella spotted David approaching from the corner on Monday after school and slowed her movements so she would be pulling the stew of chicken and potatoes out from under the buggy bench just as he reached Lindy's property line. She made sure to catch his eye.

"Hello, Ella." David shifted his books, hanging by their leather strap, to the other shoulder.

"You look well." Ella focused on the details Rachel would want to know. His face retained its round shape with color perched high on his cheekbones. In fact, David looked better than Ella had seen him since he first moved to the Hilty farm a year ago.

"Everything is fine," David said. "That's what you can tell *Mamm*."

"Why don't you tell her yourself? Better yet, come by and show her."

David's head turned toward the clatter in the tree in Lindy's front yard. "Barn swallows," he said.

"They won't be around much longer," Ella said, eyeing David. "I'll miss them."

"The school library has a book about winter birds. I might check it out."

"I'd like to see it," Ella said. "Bring it when you come by."

David's gaze rotated back toward Ella. "You know I can't do that."

"Of course you can. We all want you to. . .visit."

"I offered to help on Saturdays. Your *daed* made it clear I needn't come."

Ella exhaled softly. "Your *mamm* wanted to see you the day Lindy got hurt. That's why we came."

"It's good you were here. *Gottes wille*."

"Yes." She paused. "Rachel seemed unsure where you were, though."

They had called the doctor and waited with Lindy until he came. Then the sheriff's deputy came for a disinterested look around. And all the while, Rachel festered over why David had not come straight home from school that day.

"I was bird-watching," David said. "I told Lindy. She probably forgot because of everything that was going on." He let his bundle drop off his shoulder, unstrapped it, and pulled a sheet of paper from between the pages of a book.

Ella admired the sheet. "It's a brown thrasher. Did you do this drawing?"

The muscles around David's mouth twitched in a suppressed grin. "Does it really look like a brown thrasher?"

"I recognized it, didn't I?" The head was slightly elongated and the angle of the wings not quite right, but David had captured perfectly the downward angle of the beak and placement of the yellow eyes, along with dark spots on the white breast.

"It's the first time I tried sketching one. That's why I remember it was that day. When I got home, Miss Simpson from across the street was sitting with Lindy."

"Miss Simpson was kind enough to look after Lindy when Rachel and I needed to go home."

"I've already been over to thank her."

The stew pot grew cumbersome in Ella's hands under a wave of guilt. She knew the church's position on high school as well as David did, but somehow she could not bring herself to wish he would give it up.

"Come and see your mother," she said quietly.

"That would only cause her distress when it was time for me to leave." David buckled his books together again.

"What about church? We'll be at the Garbers' next time."

He met her gaze. "You know what that would be like."

Stares and whispers. Side glances. Heads shaking in sympathy and then bowed in fervent prayer for Rachel and her rebellious son.

"There's Lindy now," David said.

Ella looked up. Lindy stood framed in the front door, light from within outlining her form bent over two crutches. Ella followed David to the door.

❧❀❦

Margaret sat on the front porch with an untouched slice of cherry pie in her lap and her fork slack in her fingers. She looked in both directions down the quiet street. A week after coming home and finding a sheriff's car parked in front of Lindy's house, Margaret remained unsettled. Locking her doors at night and when she was away from the house, which she had never done since arriving in Seabury, was insufficient assurance that the vandal would not return to the vulnerable block. Every evening, as she checked on Lindy and scanned the neighborhood, she saw nothing to alarm her, but she could not shake off images of Lindy's white face that night.

"Penny for your thoughts," Gray said, his plate already cleared of all but the slightest indication of what it had held.

Margaret scraped her fork along an edge of pie crust. "I'm still thinking about Lindy. Deputy Fremont doesn't seem to have done anything to make sure it won't happen again to someone else."

"You're safe," Gray said.

"I'm sure Lindy thought she was safe."

"But she took in that boy."

Margaret raised her eyes from her pie plate to Gray's face, shadowed just outside the feeble beam of the porch light. "What do you mean?"

"She took in that Amish boy."

"He's her best friend's son, and he wanted to go to school."

Gray shrugged. "It's a warning."

"A warning! That's ridiculous." Heat fired up the sides of Margaret's neck.

"It's best if folks stay out of the Amish problem."

"I wish people would stop calling it that!" Margaret set her plate on the side table with too much force, and the fork clattered to the porch floor.

"Whoever broke into Lindy's shop wants her to stay out of the business of what happens with the Amish." Gray gently lifted Margaret's hand and wrapped his long fingers around it.

No matter what Margaret's mood, when he did that, yearning shivered through her. A man's touch. A husband. A family. A future.

"It's a matter for the sheriff," Gray said. "It's better if everyone leaves it be. Then there won't be any trouble."

"David Kaufman is a perfectly nice young man," Margaret said. "Why should anyone think he would be trouble?"

"He belongs at home with his parents," Gray said, as if it were obvious.

Margaret flushed, uncertain whether the sensation rose from fury at Gray's words or the touch that made her tingle.

"I'm glad," Gray said, "that you're not in the middle of that business anymore. I can rest more easily knowing there is no reason anyone should target you."

"They're children," Margaret said. "I still have Hans Byler in my class."

"Do your job," Gray said, "but there's no reason to be personally involved."

"It's my job to care about the welfare of my pupils."

"You wouldn't be the excellent teacher you are if you didn't care," Gray said. "But sometimes you have to draw a line. Let the authorities handle this. The fines should bring all the families in line."

Margaret's heart sank a fraction of an inch. How could a man whose hands and lips made her go soft at the center also spike distaste at the back of her throat?

"I'd like to escort you to church on Sunday," Gray said. "May I?"

In the evening's obscurity, she could not see his eyes, but she smelled the cherry pie on his breath and felt the stroke of his fingers on the back of her hand.

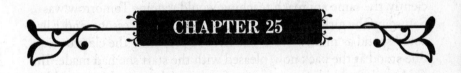

The answer came to Ella during the family's Friday morning devotions after her father's brief meditation on Isaiah 26:3: "Thou wilt keep him in perfect peace, whose mind is stayed on thee: because he trusteth in thee."

In the last week, since Gideon asked her to take on teaching the Amish students temporarily, Ella had gone out of her way three times to pass by the new school building on the Mast farm. Each time she paused to pray, wanting only *Gottes wille*. If she took on this challenge, God's will must be certain in her heart. On the Wittmer farm, gradually, Gertie had settled into the new routine, and Savilla remained as steadfast in her work as she was in most things. The time they spent on lessons seemed more efficient each day, and Ella began to see how it would be possible for her to rotate between groups of children learning at different levels.

When she opened her eyes on Friday morning, Ella felt the peaceful certainty she had sought all week. Seth was soon out the door to catch the bus—perhaps for the last time—and Ella was soon on her way with the family's buggy.

This time she entered the one-room school with her mind buzzing with plans. She started at the back of the classroom, pulling the larger desks slightly farther apart. Memories of being in the seventh and eighth grades with inadequate space for lengthening legs had come to her in the middle of the night. Then she re-spaced the front desks, resolute in tolerating the jagged aisles in exchange for the certainty that no child would have to wrestle with whether to admit she couldn't see the board. On the teacher's desk—her desk—at the front of the room sat a tin of new chalk. Ella took out a piece, reached high, and began printing letters, capital and small in pairs, across the top of the chalkboard. She worked carefully but efficiently, the same approach teaching would require. Tomorrow was Saturday. The girls would not be expecting her for lessons, and Ella could spend as much time as she needed preparing the classroom. She stood at the back now, pleased with the start she had made. The mercantile would have packages of paper, and the students would know to bring pencils. A bookcase at the front of the room awaited textbooks, which Gideon had promised to retrieve from the old school after he shored up a beam for safety.

Ella had not said anything to her father yet. She supposed she ought to ask his permission; she was not a married woman yet. But Jed would support an Amish school. He would see all the reading Ella had done in all the years since she left school herself as divine preparation for this moment. Like Esther in the Bible, she was called "for such a time as this."

Her wedding day was less than two months off. Gideon believed God would provide a teacher who could begin right after Christmas. Ella would burn the candle at both ends helping Rachel scrub down the house in preparation for the wedding while also planning lessons, but Rachel would be grateful to have Seth out of the *English* school. *All things work together for good to them that love God and are called according to His purpose*, Ella reminded herself.

If she wanted to catch Gideon before he left the house for his own work, Ella couldn't dawdle all morning in the schoolhouse. She gave the door a satisfied tug behind her and put the horse into a canter.

Miriam was standing on Gideon's porch shaking out a rug when Ella arrived.

"The girls are ready for you," Miriam said. "I told them to wait in the kitchen and not to make you spend half the morning looking for them."

Ella smiled. Savilla would be doing exactly as she was supposed to be doing. It was Gertie who might wander off distracted by any one of a hundred things.

"I'd like to see Gideon first," Ella said.

"I think he's working on his papers."

Ella stood behind Gideon's desk in the alcove for nearly a full minute before her presence disturbed his concentration. He met her gaze, and his eyes crinkled.

"You're going to do it, aren't you?"

"It makes my heart pound in terror to think of it, but yes, I want to try." She would be married in a few weeks. If she did not try now, she would never have another chance to find out if she could manage a classroom.

Gideon stood, and Ella was certain he wanted to be alone as much as she did. But neither of them would risk one of the children—or Miriam or James—finding them in an embrace.

"I'm nervous," she said. "Civil disobedience has never been my strength."

"But obeying God has always been your strength," Gideon said. "Can you start on Monday?"

Three days—only two if she did not count the Sabbath.

Ella nodded. "Eight o'clock." She would be ready, even if Savilla and Gertie were still her only students.

❧

The dispassionate warning in Gray's tone the evening before lingered in Margaret's mind for most of the night. She doubted he wished harm to anyone and believed he wanted her to be safe. He simply saw no reason for the sheriff or the school officials to concern themselves with what became of the Amish.

Gray had never mentioned conversing with any of the Amish men. He had helped them set up for their auction, and most likely that had not been the first time. Certainly he would have no occasion to speak to an Amish woman, but if he ran into one of the men in the hardware store or the mercantile, would he greet him? Could he truly hold himself so separate from the Amish that he could not at least nod his head and say good morning?

It wasn't so easy for Margaret. She had been to the farms. She had shared small gifts with the mothers, met with the fathers, and kept a protective eye on the children while they were in school. Margaret had tried telling herself they weren't her responsibility—just what Gray was saying. All her efforts to befriend the Amish and understand their ways were undercut by Superintendent Brownley's impatience and Deputy Fremont's utter lack of humility.

Mr. Brownley had asked her to take on a task and then ensured she would fail.

Yet when Margaret stood in her classroom every day and looked at Hans Byler, she thought he was the bravest little boy she had ever known. He was the youngest and smallest of all the Amish children in the school, and since Gertie Wittmer had stopped attending, he was alone in the classroom with his black suspenders and bowl-cut hair under straw hat. Nearly every day, as Margaret took attendance and checked off twenty-four names of children who resembled each other and one who did not, she thought of Jesus' parable of the shepherd who left ninety-nine sheep to find the one lost lamb and carry it home on his shoulder.

On Friday after school, Margaret walked home, changed into more comfortable shoes, and took her car out. In her own mind, she could not think what to do for the Amish children. Never one to consider prayer confined to church walls—or any walls—Margaret wondered if God might yet show her what to do and give the courage to do it. No matter what Gray Truesdale thought.

A sign, she murmured. *A sign.*

She drove out toward the Amish farms, trying to remember details of the turns she had taken when the summer sun was still high in the sky, even at this hour of the day, and optimism propelled her awkward attempts at befriending families she understood almost nothing about. The superintendent might just as well have assigned her to make sure the Creoles of Baton Rouge, Louisiana, reported to school in Seabury, Ohio. She'd fumbled the job. They all had. The only difference was that Margaret would take another approach if she had a fresh opportunity.

The automobile whizzed through an intersection. Margaret was a hundred yards down the road before recognition niggled at her. *Intersection* was an overstatement. It was only a narrow lane that came up on one side from a farm.

An Amish farm. She couldn't remember the family's name. The faces of two older boys floated through her mind. Mace? Macky? Mast? Elijah Mast had been the boy attacked in the upstairs hall at school.

That was it. But something looked altered.

She told herself it was only the bare branches, whose leaves in full summer bloom would have hidden untold details. But it was more than that. A flash of shiny whitewash had caught her eye, and she distinctly remembered the Mast house as being a nondescript gray.

Margaret braked, turned the car around, approached the lane, and navigated into it.

And there it was, in the corner of a fallow field. A one-room school that looked like so many dotting the Ohio countryside, except this one was brand new.

Outside, an Amish horse, still hitched to a buggy, nuzzled the ground in the shade. Realization dawned. Margaret shut off her engine, stunned. At least four minutes passed before she felt her breathing was under control and her heart would not explode through her sternum. Fumbling for the handle on the driver door, Margaret slid out of the automobile.

At the school's door, with her fingers on the knob, Margaret filled her lungs. She had dared to ask God for a sign. Was this it?

"Hello?" she called before the door was fully open.

"In here," came the response.

Margaret stepped into the immaculate room and stared into the face of Ella Hilty.

"Your people have built a school!" Margaret said.

"I won't try to deny it." Ella spread her arms wide.

Margaret envied the excitement in Ella's voice.

"On the day I first met you, Nora Coates was trying to persuade you to be a teacher," Margaret said. "But. . .I'm confused."

"But I'm not qualified," Ella said. "It's all right to say it. I know that truth better than anyone."

"So you've found another teacher?"

"Not yet," Ella said. "Gideon is making inquiries. I'm only going to fill in for a few weeks so the students don't lose ground."

"I want to help." The words tumbled past Margaret's lips before her mind caught up with their meaning.

Ella's eyes widened.

❧❦❧

The benches were loaded in the wagon to be taken to the next home that would host worship in two weeks. The young people were organizing a walk along the river and probably would not be back until it was time for the evening's Singing. With a basket of empty dishes hanging from one arm, Miriam was herding Gideon's daughters toward the buggy, while Tobias and James hitched it to the team of driving horses.

Standing beside his buggy and clutching her shawl around her shoulders, Ella offered Gideon a smile across the yard. It was time.

Gideon touched the elbows of Isaiah Borntrager and John Hershberger.

"Ready?" Isaiah said.

Gideon nodded. He had waited until the last minute intentionally, preferring to avoid a lengthy discussion. Persuading other fathers what they must do was not on his mind. He only wanted to be sure they all received the same information upon which to base their decisions. They would meet in the barn, but they would not be there long enough to need seats.

"The school is ready," he said a few minutes later. "Classes will begin tomorrow. For now Ella Hilty will teach, until I hear from the teachers college about someone who might come in the middle of the school year."

Gideon glanced up and saw Bishop Garber enter the barn.

"I cannot afford any more fines," Aaron King said. "I'll have to leave my children in school in town until we're sure everything is in accordance with the law."

"I understand," Gideon said. "I respect the decision of your conscience."

"I don't see how the *English* are suddenly going to leave us be," Joshua Glick said. "They'll only see this as more reason to object to our ways."

"Maybe so," Gideon said. "But we have to prove we can manage a school on our own."

"My *kinner* will be there," John Hershberger said.

Gideon nodded. Mrs. Hershberger was sure to be relieved of the expectation that she should manage lessons along with eight children, including a colicky baby. His eyes went from one man to the next, and he was fairly sure what each one would say. Opinions had not changed much over the last two months.

"We're not here to argue today." Gideon said. "Every man has to decide for himself, though I'm sure if any of you wants to talk, the bishop would be happy to help."

The bishop nodded.

"And of course you can talk to me privately," Gideon continued. "Today I only want some idea of how many children Ella should expect tomorrow. It's only fair that she know. Now raise your hand if you intend to send your children to an Amish-run school beginning tomorrow."

John Hershberger's hand shot up. Gideon smothered his chuckle and waited for others, mentally tallying the number of school-age children each man had.

CHAPTER 26

T he morning, the first Monday in November, still carried the overnight chill, and Ella poked at the wood in the potbelly stove once again to coax new flames to cast their heat into the schoolhouse. She smoothed her apron and adjusted her *kapp*, but she wasn't ready to throw off her shawl. As long as she was cold, she presumed the children would be cold, so the fire was warranted.

Unless it was her nerves that drained the heat from her body.

Ella had wound the clock on her desk as soon as she arrived, but she checked it again now. At the center of the desk, where only she would see it, was the day's schedule—or at least Ella's best guess about how the day might go. The wide, high windows welcomed abundant morning light, but lamps stationed around the room were at the ready, their bases filled with oil.

Moistening her lips for the umpteenth time that morning, Ella paced down the center aisle to look out the window on the front of the building. She was determined to welcome her pupils individually as they arrived. Gideon estimated she might have sixteen or seventeen, but it was hard to be certain. Fathers might change their minds in either direction—put their children on the buses as usual, or send them to Ella even though they had not raised their hands when Gideon asked. Sixteen students would not include everyone up through eighth grade, but it was a solid beginning.

John Hershberger was first. Four children scrambled out of his buggy. Ella mentally rehearsed the girls' names: Lizzy, Katya, and Esther. Or was Katya the youngest one? Panic surged up her throat, and Ella took a deep breath. Miriam had told her three times that

Esther was the youngest of the four school-age Hershbergers. Ella didn't know why she had such trouble remembering. The lone Hershberger boy was simple, named for his father but called Johnny.

James arrived with Gertie and Savilla, and Ella was grateful for the familiar faces. Isaiah Borntrager came, and then the Bylers. Seth loped over the hill, and the two Mast boys were the last to appear, though their house was within view.

They all looked startled to Ella, and with good reason. At best, some of them learned the previous afternoon that the school would open, but others learned only that morning at the breakfast table or intercepted on their way out the door to meet the bus. Several arrived with books in their arms—books someone would have to return to the school in Seabury.

The older ones knew what to do in the one-room school. The Mast boy walked straight to the stove and satisfied himself it was performing, and Ella supposed this had been his task in the old building. Lizzy Hershberger settled her stair-step siblings according to where children of the same ages would likely sit.

By three minutes after eight, Ella stood behind her desk, returning the stares of fifteen pairs of eyes.

"*Gut mariye,*" she said.

"*Gut mariye,*" came the unison response.

"This is an important day for all of us," Ella said, "and you might have been expecting a very different day when you woke up this morning. I want each one of you to know how glad I am to see you here, where we can help each other learn. I hope you'll be patient with me, and I promise to do my best to be patient with you. If we're kind and respectful, we can enjoy a wonderful school together."

Ella had meant to reassure the children, but as she listened to the words she had rehearsed a dozen times, her own pulse slowed. She believed what she said.

"I need time to get to know you," she said. "If you are fourth grade or older, please take out two sheets of paper and a pencil. While I listen to the younger ones read, you may work on an essay that will help me discover your abilities. On the board, you'll see three questions. You may choose the one that interests you the most and construct an essay with at least three supporting points. If you are in grades one, two, or three, please gather around my desk, and we'll take turns with the primer. Are there any questions?"

No hands went up. Instead, older students shuffled papers as they began their work, and younger ones shuffled their feet as they took places around her desk. Today would be language skills. Tomorrow she would find out what arithmetic skills the pupils had mastered.

A little hand tapped Ella's shoulder, and she smiled at an earnest face. "Yes, Gertie?"

"May I read first?"

"Thank you for volunteering," Ella said, pressing open a primer along the binding.

"And then Hans," Gertie said.

Ella's two youngest students seemed equally satisfied to be together once again.

❧❦❧

After dropping the girls off at school, James took a team of two horses and his wagon into Seabury. Rather than the mercantile or Lindy's workshop, though, his first destination was the Seabury branch of the county sheriff's office.

"I wondered what news you had about the man who attacked Lindy Lehman." James looked Deputy Fremont in the eye and braced his feet shoulder-width apart. "It's been ten days."

Fremont poised a fountain pen over an official-looking sheet of paper. "Unfortunately, ten days is plenty of time for the trail to go cold."

"May I ask whom you have interviewed?" James asked. It seemed to him Deputy Fremont had done nothing but throw ice on the trail to ensure it went cold.

"Your niece and a couple of neighbors. No one saw anything helpful."

"What about Ella and Rachel Hilty?"

"The Amish women?" Fremont used his pen to sign his name on a form.

"The witnesses," James said.

"I beg to differ," Fremont said. "On the afternoon of the incident, they both confirmed that they did not see the attack as it happened."

James set his jaw. "They might have seen something they did not realize was significant."

Fremont looked up again. "Shall we make an agreement? You do your job, and I'll do mine."

If James felt even minimal assurance that Deputy Fremont would in fact perform his duties, this conversation would be unnecessary.

"The matter has nothing to do with you," Fremont said.

"Lindy Lehman is a family member."

"You're not her husband or her father," Fremont said. "Neither are you a witness to the events in question. I'm afraid if you want information, you'll have to read it in the newspaper like everyone else."

Or I can uncover the information myself. Never in his life had he read an *English* newspaper, nor was he in the habit of gambling his money on long odds.

James left the sheriff's office determined not to return but equally determined to discover who would hold a grudge against someone as mild-mannered as Lindy.

He pulled up to her workshop a few minutes later, prepared to load and deliver items she had ready. Seeing her through the glass of the locked door, he knocked. Lindy hobbled on one crutch to let him in.

"David made me promise to lock myself in," Lindy said. "And my neighbor Margaret was on his side. I couldn't defy them both at one time."

"Don't apologize," James said. "Under the circumstances, he's right."

"What circumstances?" Lindy said. "We don't know what happened or why."

"Your shop was vandalized twice. You were attacked."

"I choose to think it was a vagrant who won't be back." Lindy settled herself on a stool and picked up a paintbrush. "Not when he knows somebody other than me might have gotten a look at him."

"Just how good a look did you get?" James asked.

"I didn't see his face, *Onkel* James. I told you that already."

"But you might have had a sense of how tall he was. Maybe you saw his boots, or noticed a limp."

"I wish I could tell you any of that," Lindy said, dipping her brush in blue paint and touching a birdhouse with the delicate point. "I guess I'd say he was taller than average. But I didn't notice his hat or his boots or anything else. I'll take Ella's word for it that he was wearing a blue shirt."

"Think carefully, Lindy," James said. "Any detail could be important. Maybe he was left-handed. Maybe his knee creaked."

Lindy laughed. "You sound like an *English* police officer—and a better one than Deputy Fremont."

Gertie would ask more questions than Deputy Fremont. James kept this thought to himself.

"Feel free to look around," Lindy said, "but I just want to get back to normal, and I'm not going to live in fear. That's not the way of our people, is it?"

"No, it's not." Her use of "our people" softened him.

"Are you still going to make my deliveries today?"

"Of course."

"I left my list in the kitchen." Lindy set down her paintbrush and reached for her crutch.

"I can get it," James said.

Lindy shook her head. "I can do it. While I'm gone, you can start with the two quilt racks for the furniture store."

James clasped his hands behind his back to squelch the impulse to offer support to Lindy's elbow—she would only swat him away—but he watched to be sure she safely crossed the patch of grass between the workshop and the house. Then he turned to her workbench before pacing to the wall used to shatter birdhouses ten days ago. James had seen the damage for himself. Now he wished David had not followed instructions to clean up the mess. Almost certainly Deputy Fremont would have overlooked a meaningful remnant, if there was one.

James carried a quilt rack out to the wagon and secured it. Before returning to the second one, he glanced across the street, unsure which house belonged to Margaret Simpson.

❧

Ella had not known exhaustion and exhilaration to be twins before, birthed from the same labor.

At two thirty in the afternoon she stood at the school door saying good-bye to her students, making sure they had collected shawls and lunch buckets and primers. Lizzy corralled her sisters and brother for a long walk home, the Mast boys shot off toward their house, and the Byler children's mother showed up with a buggy to collect them. Ella admitted relief to herself when she saw Gideon's buggy clattering down the lane.

Ella bent over and tied the strings to Gertie's prayer *kapp*. It was a preventive action. Gertie had a tendency to run out from under an untied *kapp* when she was set free outdoors. Savilla chased her sister, and both girls were in their father's arms a minute later. Gideon looked over their heads, his face a question. Ella watched as he helped his daughters into the buggy and then ambled toward the school. Ella slipped back inside the building.

"I'm sure you had an extraordinary first day." Gideon caught her hand and closed the door behind him.

Ella blew out her breath. "I think it went well, but I'm sure the girls will give you their opinions."

Gideon put his hand against her cheek. "You are so brave. I could not admire you more."

She breathed in his scent, holding it until her lungs begged for a fresh exchange of air.

Gideon glanced out the window. Ella followed his gaze. Two faces leaned out of the buggy and fixed on the schoolhouse.

Gideon laughed. "If we take two steps to the left, we'll have time for one short kiss before they burst out of the buggy to see what is taking so long."

Ella tugged his hand and took two steps.

CHAPTER 27

James had not meant to spend so much of the day in Seabury, but Miriam was the last person he wanted to disappoint, so he stood in the line at the mercantile waiting to pay for three spools of black thread. A markdown on canned beans caused an unusual midafternoon glut at the counter.

Four people ahead of him in line at the counter inched forward. Then three. Then two. Then one. With each ding of the cash register, James slid forward a couple of feet. Then a tall man stepped in from the side, nearly putting his boot down on James's toe.

"I ordered those long screws three weeks ago," the man said to the clerk.

"I'm sorry, Mr. Truesdale," the clerk said. "They haven't come yet, but they should be here any day."

"I'd better not find out that you didn't put the order in immediately."

"The order went in. It just takes time to get the length you asked for. They probably have to come from Chicago."

The man thumped the counter with both palms. "I'd think you would have figured out how to use the telephone by now. You're not the Amish, after all."

Truesdale looked down his long nose at James and brushed past him.

"I apologize," the clerk said to James. "That's Braden. His brother, Gray, is a much more pleasant person."

James set the thread on the counter and watched the man exit the store before handing the clerk his coins. By the time James reached the sidewalk a couple of minutes later, he saw no evidence of Braden Truesdale's presence.

Across the street, in front of a narrow house painted brown with yellow trim, a sign announced the business within: PERCIVAL T. EGGAR, ESQUIRE, ATTORNEY AT LAW. James worked his lips in and out a few times before tucking the thread under his wagon bench and crossing the street. As far as James knew, no member of the Geauga County Amish had ever engaged the services of an attorney. The Bible clearly said that true believers ought not sue each other in the courts of unbelievers, and right living kept them on the right side of the law.

Until now.

James came into Seabury more than most of the church members. Until a few weeks ago, he never paid much attention to the yellow and brown house. Lately, after two rounds of fines and the audacity to open their own school, James wondered how much trouble the Amish fathers might be in.

In the front room of the brown house, a young man at a typewriter looked up at James.

"I'd like to see Mr. Eggar," James said.

"Is he expecting you?"

"No, sir."

The secretary raised an eyebrow at the hat still on James's head and his simple black wool suit coat with no lapels or pockets.

"I'll see if he has time to meet you now." The young man straightened his rimless glasses as he stood.

James suspected this would be the attorney's first meeting with an Amish man. If nothing else, curiosity might secure the meeting.

James watched the gray suit disappear through an inner door, speculating that the attorney's private office had once been the dining room of the house. Perhaps the upstairs was still in use as a residence. Electric lamps testified that the structure had been modernized. James eyed a chair, unsure whether to take the liberty of sitting down.

The inner door opened. The young man returned.

"Mr. Eggar will see you," he said, gesturing that James should go in. As soon as James crossed the threshold, the secretary quietly closed the door behind him.

James was relieved to see a man of more maturity rising from a large desk and coming around it to shake his hand. Immediately he liked the friendly light he saw in Mr. Eggar's eyes and the firmness of his grip as he guided James to a high-backed chair upholstered in reddish-brown leather.

"Now, this is unusual," Mr. Eggar said, taking his seat behind his desk. "But if a man like you has need of my services, I give you my word that I will listen carefully."

The grace of God appears in needful moments.

The buses arrived and departed barely half full, making Margaret think that school administrators had underestimated from the start both the number of rural Amish students attending the one-room school in the past and the tenacity of Amish parents to influence the education of their children. The buses still carried students who were not Amish, but it seemed that each week fewer straw hats and prayer *kapps* dotted the view of children lining up at the buses. Margaret stood on Monday afternoon with other teachers making sure the bus pupils were accounted for before the engines roared. The afternoons were cooler now, and the drivers had lowered canvas siding on the wood frames of their buses to cut the wind.

"Have you none of them left in your class?" Miss Hunter, the third-grade teacher, said.

"None of whom?" Margaret said. She refused to cater to the tendency to speak of the Amish students as *them.*

Miss Hunter rolled her eyes. "You know what I'm talking about. You still have an Amish boy in your class, don't you?"

"Hans," Margaret said. "He was not in attendance today." She pictured him in Ella's classroom and hoped he got to sit next to Gertie.

The last of the buses pulled away from the school, and the teachers drifted into a huddle where they could brace the afternoon's brisk breeze together.

"The school district ought to give them what they want," Mr. Snyder from the seventh grade said. "Give them their own school. Things could go back to normal around here."

Margaret pressed her lips closed. If the other teachers did not yet know that the Amish had built themselves a school, she would not be the one to tell them. She only found out three days ago herself.

"I had not noticed the Amish children were particular trouble,"

Margaret said. Gertie and Hans were quite sweet.

"That's because you teach first grade," Mr. Snyder said. "You don't have to contend with older students not doing their work, or pupils who are obviously too old for the classes they are in. They're bored, and it's not my job to entertain them when they belong in the high school."

"Still, they deserve an education," Margaret said. "We have to admit that some of our students have been distinctly unwelcoming."

She stopped short of expressing her opinion about the general insufficiency of Mr. Tarkington's response to pupils who taunted the Amish children. He hauled offenders to his office, but Margaret suspected nothing of consequence transpired once they got there. She'd seen the smirks on the faces of students as they emerged from the principal's office.

"It's all an unnecessary distraction," Mr. Snyder said.

"The teachers in the one-room schools had no trouble accommodating a variety of students." Margaret thought of Nora Coates.

"That's hardly the same as teaching in a town school," Miss Hunter said.

Margaret's spine straightened, but she pushed down the retort forming on her tongue. "It's getting chilly out here," she said, turning toward the building.

Mr. Snyder might well be right that the Amish students would be better off in their own school. On that conclusion he would find common ground with Amish parents regardless of the position the superintendent and principals took. It was Mr. Snyder's reasons that were convoluted. Margaret could find no agreement there. Viewing the Amish students as an inconvenience to established comfort infuriated Margaret.

Margaret's offer to help Ella Hilty was sincere. For the sake of the children, she had to figure out how to carry out her word.

❧

Gray grinned at Margaret across the bench of his truck three days later.

"At this time of year," he said, "you never know how many pretty days we'll have left."

"Thank you for inviting me for a drive." Margaret dipped her head in a manner she hoped was coy, though she wasn't sure. "The fall colors are spectacular."

"We could drive all the way to Cleveland if you like." Gray's eyebrows raised in question.

Of all his endearing expressions, Margaret liked this one best. "What would we do in Cleveland?"

"Have supper," he said. "Then we'll see."

It was tempting. Ride all the way to Cleveland with the smell of him swirling into her every breath. Walk down the street holding hands. Stare into his brown eyes over the flame of a candle and not care who might think she was behaving in an unseemly manner. Feed him pie off the end of her own fork.

But the papers were full of news of influenza. They might not even find a restaurant open to serve them.

"It'll be dark soon," Margaret said. "Maybe we could just find a spot with a nice view and watch the sun go down."

He stopped at a corner and looked to the west. "I know a spot, if you don't mind driving past the Amish farms."

Her stomach soured. "Why would I mind? It's beautiful countryside."

"I would think you'd get enough of them at work."

"Get enough of them?"

Gray accelerated the truck into motion again. "Don't get testy. I was only thinking of you."

"I'm sorry if I sounded testy." Margaret stared straight ahead.

"I understand if it's a sensitive subject for you."

His tone was tender. She wanted to believe him.

"The sooner Brownley and Fremont knock some sense into them," Gray said, "the sooner things will be easier for you."

"Things are not difficult for me. Every school year has its challenges, but I'm grateful for any experience that makes me a better teacher."

"Did you know they built their own school?"

Against her will, Margaret's gaze snapped in Gray's direction. He met her eyes for a moment before turning back to the road.

"You did know, didn't you?" he said.

She wouldn't straight-out lie to him. "Yes, I did. I didn't realize it was common knowledge yet."

"I don't know that it is," Gray said, "but it will be soon enough.

Fremont got wind of it today. He went livid as an angry bee."

Margaret stifled a groan.

"They're causing a lot of trouble, Margaret. A lot of people are spending time and attention they ought to be using on other things."

She said nothing. She could see Gideon Wittmer's farm in the distance.

"They have to consolidate," Gray said. "It's the only way to let everyone move on. It will be better for everybody."

"The Amish don't seem to think so."

"They'll be made to see."

Gray Truesdale was a gorgeous man in any woman's eyes. Margaret was sure of that. That he would court her all these weeks was a phenomenon beyond her ability to explain. When his eyes latched onto hers, a loveliness surged through her that she had not known was within her. If they could just ride out this storm, perhaps the stone forming in her gut at this moment could soften again.

Or perhaps that was something she told herself when she ached for one more delicious moment, one more tantalizing kiss, before hope turned to vapor.

"Would it distress you if I changed my mind about taking a drive?" she said. "I think perhaps I should spend the evening in after all."

"I've upset you," he said, contrite.

"I wouldn't be very good company tonight," she said. "As you can imagine, I have a lot on my mind."

Gray pulled to the side of the road and turned the truck around. They rode in silence back toward town, but when he reached across the bench for Margaret's hand, she gave it to him.

In front of her house, he parked and walked around the truck to help her out.

"I'd like to escort you to church on Sunday," he said, "and then we can have dinner with my brother. It would please me if the two of you met."

Margaret hesitated.

"We can set all this aside for a day, can't we?" Gray said, putting a finger to her chin to turn her face up. "A Sabbath?"

Margaret swallowed hard. "I would be delighted to meet your brother."

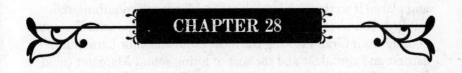

M argaret disliked the stares. This was not the first time she had arrived at church with Gray. Two hundred people turned up at this church every Sunday morning. Why should it raise eyebrows when two of them chose to sit together?

"Good morning, Margaret."

The cheery voice belonged to Mrs. Baker, who had been the first person to speak to Margaret on her first Sunday in town, four and a half years ago. At the time, Margaret thought her friendly and welcoming. Over the years she had realized Mrs. Baker simply liked to know everything that went on.

"Good morning, Mrs. Baker," Margaret said. Gray's light touch on her elbow steered her away from the encounter.

"People are starting to whisper about us," Gray said into Margaret's ear.

Margaret was well aware. People whispered if she and Gray sat together in church, and they whispered if they did not. She had not meant for her relationship with Gray, as ill defined as it was, to come under speculation. Rumors would fly if she broke it off with him—or if she didn't.

They sat in Gray's regular pew. When she came on her own, Margaret sat on the other side of the sanctuary and farther back. Everything felt odd from this perspective. The minister's voice intoned more deeply. The organ swells sounded reedy. The angle of the light coming through the front windows washed out the faces of the choir. The scent of flowers on the altar tickled Margaret's nose. More than once, as the choir sang an invocation and the minister announced the opening hymn, the urge to flee to the comforts of her own habits circulated through Margaret's veins.

And then the congregation stood, and Gray opened a hymnal and placed it so they could both see it. Margaret's mouth moved, but little sound came out. Instead, she was enthralled with the notes coming from Gray. He sang the most exquisite tenor harmonies, earnest and confident and the sort of lilting sound Margaret could listen to for her whole life and never tire. Margaret had not heard Gray sing outside of church. What else did Gray sing other than church hymns? Folk songs? Love songs? Ballads? Opera? Perhaps nothing.

As the third stanza began, Margaret tried to sing more robustly. Her voice was no match for Gray's.

Perhaps she was no match for Gray at all. Her stomach solidified every time they talked about the Amish. They never disagreed about anything else that Margaret could remember. It wasn't that she thought husband and wife must agree on every point. But if Gray could think as little of the Amish as he seemed to, who else would he be willing to dismiss for his own convenience?

Once Gray knew that Margaret intended to help Ella Hilty get the Amish school running smoothly, that could be the end of them.

And perhaps it should be.

If they stopped now, they might maintain a sincere friendship without expecting more from each other. Margaret would find a way to gradually see less of Gray. She would get used to being on her own again, as she had so long expected to be, and his attentions could turn elsewhere.

If only she didn't love having him near.

After church, Margaret took the arm Gray offered for the stroll to his brother's house. During the weeks of their casual courtship, the only time Gray had spoken of his brother was the day of the auction.

"What does your brother do?" Margaret asked. "When he's not setting up tents."

"Whatever he likes," Gray said.

"Is that a way of saying his employment is. . .unstable?"

"You might say that. He used to run the old farm after our parents. . .but he ran it into the ground. I had to insist he sell and move into town. Sometimes I hire him to help me, but he's picky about what he's willing to do."

Under her fingers, Margaret felt the muscle of Gray's arm stiffen.

"I'll warn you. Braden is Braden," Gray said. "A little rough around the edges. Don't take him too seriously."

"It's kind of him to have us for Sunday dinner."

"He knows I've been courting someone. I wanted to wait until you and I knew each other better before introducing Braden."

Margaret fought the grimace her face seemed determined to form. She never should have agreed to meet Gray's brother, not under the weight of doubt that they were meant for each other.

They ambled toward a gray-shingled house on a corner.

"Here it is."

Gray knocked on the door and then patted Margaret's hand while they listened to the shifting footsteps inside. When the door opened, Margaret stared into the familiar features of Gray's face. The eyes were a lighter brown, but they were set at the exact distance from the nose as Gray's—the same slender nose with its gentle slope. The black curly hair was cut slightly longer than Gray's with more flecks of gray, but the widow's peak notched the forehead in the same spot.

Margaret's breath caught and she glanced at Gray.

"Are we twins?" Gray said. "No. Just one stubborn combination of genes."

Margaret smiled through the doorway at the man who had not yet spoken.

"Braden," Gray said, "I would like you to meet Miss Margaret Simpson. Margaret, this is my older brother."

"Please come in," Braden said. "It may take me a few minutes to get everything on the table."

"I would be happy to help," Margaret said, stepping into a hall that ran through the lower story of the house, with a parlor and dining room on one side and—she supposed—the kitchen on the other side at the back, behind a room with a closed door.

"Not necessary," Braden said, turning to walk to the back of the house.

Gray nudged Margaret's elbow. They stepped into the parlor, and he leaned in to whisper, "I warned you he's rough around the edges."

Margaret looked at the adjoining room, where a table had been laid with a level of care that suggested a woman's touch.

"Is Braden married?" she whispered.

Gray rolled his eyes. "Goodness, no."

Braden emerged from the kitchen with a platter of sliced ham in one hand and a bowl heaped with mashed potatoes in the other.

"I told her there were only three of us," Braden muttered, setting the dishes on the table.

"Her?" Margaret said

"The housekeeper," Braden said. "She never listens. She made two vegetables. Who needs two vegetables?"

Braden disappeared into the kitchen again.

"Let's sit down," Gray said, gesturing to the table. He pulled a chair out for Margaret, and she arranged herself in it.

Braden returned with two hot vegetable dishes. "If things are overcooked, it's her fault. I only followed the instructions she left to put everything in the oven."

"It all looks lovely," Margaret said.

Braden grunted and sat down.

"I agree," Gray said. "You should try to hang on to this one, instead of chasing her off like all the others."

Braden glared at Gray. The fire in his eyes startled Margaret.

"I could say the same to you," Braden said, glancing at Margaret. "Are you going to hang on to this one?"

"If meeting you doesn't frighten her off," Gray said, "I just might."

Margaret's legs were ready to bolt, but her mother had been a stickler for manners, so she concentrated on keeping her feet flat on the floor under the table.

"Let's eat," Braden said.

"Margaret likes to return thanks before a meal," Gray said, bowing his head.

Margaret bowed also, listening to the simple prayer of blessing for the meal that Gray spoke. When he finished, Braden picked up the platter of meat and offered it to Margaret.

"I heard about the trouble on your street," Braden said. "Twice now, isn't it?"

"Yes." Margaret guarded her response as she laid a slice of ham on her plate.

"You should be careful," Braden said. "I would hate for any harm to come to my brother's friend."

⚜

Gertie and Savilla gripped the sides of Ella's cart while she rumbled to Gideon's farm after school on Monday. Each day, it felt more and more natural to spend her afternoon hours with Gideon's family, and the children had gotten used to having her there, even Tobias. The wedding was less than six weeks away. Ella found comfort in establishing some routines now, before she married Gideon. The adjustment in December would be easier for everyone, including Miriam. Ella pulled around to the side of the barn and unhitched the cart to let the horse graze in the pasture. The girls ran ahead into the house. By the time Ella got there, Savilla stood in the kitchen with her face scrunched up.

"What's the matter, Savilla?" Ella said.

"It's almost three thirty," Savilla said.

"Yes, that's right." Ella set a stack of books on the counter.

"Look at the food."

Ella glanced around the kitchen. Two winter squash from the garden. Eight potatoes, three of them cut in half. A plate with half a beef roast.

"It looks like Miriam is getting a head start on supper," Ella said.

Savilla shook her head and picked up a cut potato. "This is turning brown. She wouldn't leave food around to turn brown." Savilla touched the roast. "And this isn't cold. If she had just taken it from the icebox, it would still be cold. She hasn't been here in a long time."

Apprehension shivered through Ella.

"*Aunti* Miriam always has a snack out for us," Savilla said. "Milk and cookies or some strudel."

Savilla was right.

"Go see if she's upstairs."

"*Daed* told her the upstairs was our responsibility now," Savilla said.

"Let's just make sure," Ella said. Miriam could be stubborn.

While Savilla scampered up the stairs, Ella stepped out on the back stoop to scan the yard. Miriam could have decided to hang sheets to dry, pull overgrowth from the depleted vegetable garden, or

825

do something else equally innocuous.

Savilla thundered down the stairs. "She's not anywhere in the house."

Gertie's shout came from the *dawdihaus*. Ella and Savilla raced across the yard and burst into the small home where James and Miriam lived and ran through to the bedroom.

"She won't wake up," Gertie said.

Ella gulped air. "Has she said anything?"

"I can't understand what she's saying," Gertie said. She thumped Miriam's shoulder.

Miriam lay on the bed, pale, but beginning to thrash against the quilt.

"Napping," Miriam said. "Just. . .a few minutes."

Ella touched Gertie's shoulder to nudge her out of the way. "Miriam," she said, "are you feeling unwell?"

"No," Miriam said, trying to push herself up on one elbow.

Ella looked into Miriam's unfocused eyes. "Perhaps you should rest a little longer."

"I'll make supper," Miriam said. "It will just have to be simpler than I planned."

"I'll look after supper," Ella said. "The girls and I will start by making you some soup."

"Soup is for sick people," Miriam said. "I may be a tired old woman, but I'm not sick."

"We'll find something else, then. But you don't have to worry about it." Ella turned to Savilla. "Can you finish chopping the potatoes?"

Savilla nodded.

"And Gertie," Ella said, "you can set the table for supper. I'll be there in a few minutes."

"Is *Aunti* Miriam coming?" Gertie asked.

"Shh," Savilla said, grabbing Gertie's hand. "Come on."

Miriam was sitting up now. Ella debated between encouraging Miriam to lie down again and taking her to the main house where Ella could keep an eye on Miriam and the girls at the same time.

"How about some tea?" Ella said.

"James will want *kaffi*," Miriam said, rubbing an eye with one hand.

"*Kaffi*, then," Ella said. "I'll make a pot here and you can take a cup over to the main house."

The door opened, and a man's footfalls approached.

"James?" Miriam said.

He appeared in the doorway. "What's going on in here?"

"I took a nap," Miriam said. "Ella and the girls are determined to make a fuss."

Ella exchanged a glance with James.

"Well, if you're tired," James said, "you should have a nap. You know I'm always telling you that."

"It's nothing." Miriam leaned on James's arm and stood up. "How were things in Seabury today?"

"Our prayers for peace have been answered at last," James said. "The war in Europe is over. The armistice was signed this morning in Paris. It's all the *English* are talking about in town."

Miriam put her hand over her heart. "Many mothers and fathers will be glad to have their sons home again in one piece."

"I was just going to make *kaffi*," Ella said.

James smiled. "*Kaffi* is always a good decision."

Miriam threw off James's supporting arm. "I'll make the *kaffi*."

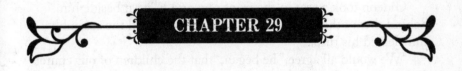

Are you sure you'll be all right on your own?" James evaluated the features of his wife's face. Extra lines fanned out from the corners of her eyes, and the color of her cheeks lacked its usual height.

"Old man, just go," Miriam said. "Did you think I wouldn't notice that you've neatly arranged the day so I won't be alone for more than thirty minutes?"

That much was true. James had invited the group of Amish parents, both fathers and mothers, to meet at the new schoolhouse after the students left on Tuesday afternoon. Ella would stay for the meeting, but the children would go home from school and Tobias would stay within shouting distance while he did the barn chores. If something happened, Tobias could take a horse and gallop for help.

"Well, if you're sure." James kissed Miriam's cheek.

"I was tired yesterday," Miriam said. "Can't a person take a nap without everyone declaring it a medical emergency?"

It was not just one nap. It was more and more naps. It was lost color in the face. It was a slower walk than James had ever seen in his spunky wife. But he knew when to keep his thoughts sealed.

"I'll try to make the meeting short and to the point," he said before leaving.

His extra moments with Miriam meant that when James arrived at the schoolhouse, parents already milled, awaiting someone who would take charge. Ella was dragging the smallest desks out of the way and encouraging parents to take seats in the desks large enough to accommodate them. Aaron King had thought to bring three of the church benches and was setting them up around the perimeter of the room.

"Shall we start as soon as everyone has a seat?" Ella asked.

The one person James most needed was nowhere in sight. James would have to do his best and hope the guest would still turn up.

Gideon took a seat in the front row, and Ella sat beside him. Behind them others quieted. James stood and faced the assembly and cleared his throat.

"We would all agree," he began, "that the children of our church district are the future of our congregation. As a church, our obligation to them is to prepare them for eternal life in the kingdom of God. For this reason, the nature of their education is important to all of us."

James paused and glanced out the windows behind the rows of parents. He assumed his guest would arrive in an automobile. The row of horses and buggies would assure him he had found the right location. James wasn't sure how much further into the meeting he could go on his own.

"Although I am neither a father nor a minister," James continued, "I want the best for our congregation. I want to know our children are on the path to salvation and not ensnared by worldly ways. For this reason, when Chester Mast began building this school that shelters us now, I was happy to help. Some of you have chosen to send your *kinner* here for Ella Hilty to be their teacher. Others are concerned about *English* retribution if your children do not attend their schools."

The sound of an automobile caused a few heads to turn. James breathed relief.

"I have taken the liberty of speaking to an *English* attorney," James said, "and I'm happy to see that he has just arrived. My hope is that he will help us understand the *English* system more fully."

A car door slammed. Restless parents squirmed to see who would enter the building. James paced to the back of the room and opened the door.

"Thank you for coming," James said softly.

"I'm sorry I'm late," Percival Eggar said. "These farm roads and oak trees all look very much alike. You really do 'live apart.' "

James led the way to the front of the room. "This is Mr. Percival Eggar," he said. "I met with him last week in his office, and I am confident that he can help us understand the risks and consequences of the choices fathers face as individuals, as well as our congregation, as we look for a way to stand together."

Percival set a briefcase on Ella's desk. "In my office, Mr. Lehman laid out for me the events to this point—the notices from the school district, the pressure to enroll your children in the consolidated schools in Seabury, the fines as a consequence of noncompliance, and the decision to open and operate this school as a private institution not subject to the regulations of the school district."

Isaiah Borntrager raised a hand. James acknowledged it.

"Why do we need an attorney?" Isaiah said. "They're our children, and we'll do what we think is best for them."

"I'm only here," Percival said, "to help you understand your legal standing. I'm afraid the fines you've paid are only the beginning of your exposure."

"The United States is a place of religious freedom," Chester Mast said. "That's all we're doing with opening this school."

Percival pointed at Chester. "That is exactly right. But the right to practice religion in a manner that conflicts with established law is bound to cause complications of interpretation."

"Don't we have a right to believe what the Bible says?" John Hershberger said.

"Of course you do," Percival said. "The question is whether we can establish that your actions with regard to the education of your children fall into the category of religious belief. Some would argue that you are free to believe as you choose, but you still must obey the law."

"If we hand our children over to the *English* school," Chester Mast said, "we will lose the next generation of our church. We can't separate how we interpret the Bible from how we educate our children."

"James," Aaron King said, "did you invite this gentleman because you believe we should take formal legal action? You know the way of our people is to stay out of the *English* courts."

James nodded. "I do know. I hope and pray for a peaceful solution without compromising the Word of God."

"They may not do anything more than occasional fines," Cristof Byler said. "As long as we pay them, they'll have no reason to bother us."

"What about those of us who cannot afford the fines?" Aaron King said. "Don't you think we'd like to have our children in our own school as well?"

Percival took a step forward. "I believe you should have that right, and I'm willing to help you fight for it."

A lull descended as the hope offered by Percival's pledge trickled through the assembly.

"If there can be peace in Europe," James said, "surely there can be peace in Seabury."

Isaiah grunted. "But at what cost did the peace in Europe come?"

⚜

Gideon twisted in his seat. He wanted to see the faces of the other parents. Before today there had been no discussion of involving an *English* lawyer. James had made these arrangements on his own, but when Gideon discovered what James had done, he did nothing to discourage assembling parents. This moment would be one they all remembered—the moment they did or did not engage the services of someone outside their own community.

Another *English* automobile announced its presence. While Gideon admired—from afar—the usefulness of a gasoline engine, it seemed to him that the *English* with all their education ought to find a way to make it less noisy. The sound was unnatural.

When Gideon saw who it was, he jumped up. A moment later, Superintendent Brownley shoved open the door.

"What in tarnation is going on here?" Brownley demanded.

"May we help you, Mr. Brownley?" Gideon said, calm and smooth.

"We'll shut down this school," Brownley said. "You've wasted your time and materials in building it."

"If that's what you've come to say," Gideon said, "you can be assured we have heard you."

Brownley strode along the side of the room. "What is this meeting about?"

"It's a private meeting," Gideon said, "on private property."

Brownley's eyes scanned the group. "It may not be illegal to build a structure on private property or to use it for private purposes, but you can be certain that using this building to keep pupils out of school will have repercussions."

"Duly noted," Gideon said.

"Furthermore," Brownley said, "whoever is posing as a teacher is in a precarious position."

Involuntarily, Gideon glanced at Ella, whose face paled.

"This so-called teacher will find herself in the middle of legal action if she continues without credentials," the superintendent said. His eyes settled on Ella. "The state establishes certain minimal standards for all teachers."

"Mr. Brownley," Gideon said. "If you would be so kind as to make time at the next meeting of the school board, I'm sure we would be happy to continue this discussion in an appropriate setting."

"Don't threaten me!" Brownley said. "Remember that I have the law on my side."

Percival Eggar stepped between Gideon and Brownley.

"What are you doing here?" Brownley asked.

"I will be representing the parties present. In the future you may address your concerns to my office."

"You?" Brownley scoffed. "Are you telling me that the Amish are engaging legal representation?"

"We had not quite worked out the details of our arrangement before your unseemly interruption," Percival said, "but now is as good a time as any."

Brownley glared.

Percival turned to the assembly. "I would be honored to represent anyone present in this room on the questions of compliance with recent changes in education regulations as they pertain to the free expression of religious conviction. I'm sorry that I was not able to meet each of you individually before our conversation was disrupted, but if you would like to accept my representation, I ask you to signal your intention by standing."

Gideon, already standing, stepped forward.

"This is absurd," Brownley said.

Chester Mast stood, followed by Cristof Byler. Jed Hilty. Isaiah Borntrager. John Hershberger. Joshua Glick. Aaron King. One by one, every man in the room rose. Gideon worked hard at smothering a grin. The wives joined, standing with their husbands. Whether parents were sending their children to the schools in Seabury, keeping them home, or taking advantage of Ella's tutelage, they were united on this question. They welcomed an *English* of Percival Eggar's education and standing in the community to their side.

Brownley glowered, first at Percival, and then at the fathers on their feet as most of the wives present also stood.

Was this what it was like to feel proud? Gideon had of course been pleased with the accomplishments of his children from time to time. When Tobias helped to deliver a new calf. When Savilla baked bread for the first time without consulting a recipe. When Gertie, only a few weeks ago, sounded out an entire verse from the morning Bible reading in German, even though at school she was learning to read English. But in those instances, and many others, he reminded himself of the border between *pleased* and *proud*. If he was proud, even of his children, he might begin to think himself better than others. But at this moment, seeing the parents of his congregation voting bodily, Gideon crossed the border. He was proud of their courage, proud of their resolve, proud of their resistance against their own inner fears.

Ella stood with the parents. This gave Gideon pure pleasure.

Percival gripped Brownley's elbow and turned him toward the door. "I'm sure you understand the need for confidential conversation with my clients," he said, walking Brownley out. "You and I will have ample opportunity to speak reasonably and honorably about the matter."

Gideon caught James's eye. If James had asked him in advance, Gideon might have cautioned against involving an *English* man of the law. But the trust Percival Eggar had engendered in a room full of Amish strangers was testimony that James had done well.

Percival closed the door behind Brownley and paced back to the front of the room.

"You all have work to do and families to care for," he said, "so I want to make efficient use of our time. Mr. Lehman has given me a basic understanding of the dilemma you face and the range of responses represented in this room. I am happy to meet with any of you individually if you seek counsel about your particular circumstances. For now, I invite questions that may be of interest to the group as a whole."

If Gideon were not sitting in the front of the room, he could have seen which hands were going up.

Percival pointed at a hand. "Yes?"

"What if we can't find a teacher the state will accept?" Joshua Glick asked. "I want my children to go to an Amish school, but I also want it to be according to the law."

So far, the Glick children had remained in the Seabury school. Joshua was one of the more cautious Amish fathers.

"I understand Mr. Wittmer has already begun making inquiries on that matter," Percival said, "and on your instructions I will prepare additional documents and send them with a courier to the teachers college."

Murmurs of approval circled the room.

"May I also suggest," Percival continued, "that we explore alternative methods for how Miss Hilty may be properly credentialed for the position."

Ella sucked in her breath beside Gideon. He slid his hand off his lap and let it rest on the edge of the chair until his little finger touched hers. Their wedding was only weeks away.

❧❀❧

The fury on Mr. Brownley's face had punched the breath out of Ella, and now Mr. Eggar was suggesting she formalize her role as a teacher. She had only promised Gideon a few weeks. Her permanent promise to him was to be his wife.

Less than an inch of Gideon's hand touched Ella's, and for only a few seconds, yet she took comfort. He was near. He understood. Perhaps James had neglected to mention her betrothed state to Mr. Eggar. Even an *English* attorney would know that a woman would not continue to teach after her marriage.

"Miss Hilty has only begun teaching. Do I understand correctly?" Percival said, glancing at Ella.

Ella nodded.

"Other than formal education," Gideon said, "she is well suited to the task. Before beginning to teach here, she taught my daughters at my home for several weeks, and I saw daily the leaps in their learning."

Percival nodded. "We may need you to testify to that effect."

Testify? Ella's brows furrowed against her will.

"My girls love her," John Hershberger said. "Lizzy and Katya said Miss Hilty is every bit as good as Miss Coates was."

"Miss Coates?" Percival said.

"The *English* teacher we had until a few months ago," Gideon explained. "John is right. Ella has a curious mind and understands the needs of our children."

"Ella has done nothing wrong," Isaiah Borntrager said. "She hasn't lied about credentials she does not hold. All she has done is choose what is best for our community, something the state has no interest in."

"The state would argue they have the best interest of your children in mind," Percival reminded the group.

"Has the state met our children?" Isaiah countered. "Has the state worshipped in our services? How can the state have the best interest of our children in mind?"

"All good points." Percival nodded. "And we may be able to raise them in an argument about the exercise of religious liberty. At the moment, though, the superintendent would argue that as an untrained teacher, Ella is in over her head."

Ella's breath came in gasps at irregular intervals when she could no longer hold it in. She *was* in over her head, with only her instincts and love of learning to rely on. The day would come when a bright student would ask a question to which she did not know the answer, or a second grader would be unable to grasp the basics of borrowing to subtract and Ella would have no new strategies to help him master the concept. She supposed that teachers who attended the teachers college learned how to handle these challenges. They learned methods of instruction and ways of making proper lesson plans that kept them ahead of the questions their students would ask.

In truth, Ella was not sure she had made the situation better by agreeing to teach temporarily. In the eyes of the law, the Amish families had dubious standing as it was. If Chester Mast had not begun building the schoolhouse in which they all now sat, perhaps this moment would not have come.

"But if we focus on finding a state-qualified teacher willing to teach Amish children according to our values," James said, "Ella will not have to face these hurdles at all."

Thank you, James. Ella relaxed her spine. *Let's stay focused.*

Gideon shifted his weight in his chair and lifted his hand, ready to ask the looming question. "What can the state really do if we do not send our children to the schools in town—especially the older ones who already completed the eighth grade?"

"I pledged to Mr. Lehman that I would be candid and honest with all of you," Percival said. "It's almost certain that the fines will grow increasingly burdensome. I know that some of you already choose to keep your children in the town schools for that reason, so I will look for grounds to challenge the legality of the fines."

"And beyond the fines?" Gideon asked.

Percival gave a slight shrug. "The laws are new. This kind of case is untested. I can only tell you what is possible within the current language of the law, not what is likely in the eyes of a judge or jury."

By the time the meeting ended, Gideon felt as if he had harvested an entire field of alfalfa hay without even the help of his team of workhorses.

Percival Eggar lingered to answer individual questions and collect a few coins from each man who wished to avail himself of the offer of legal representation. James would have explained to Mr. Eggar that farmers struggling to pay the fines imposed on them by the state would not have unlimited funds for an *English* lawyer's fees, but Gideon trusted that James had come to a manageable agreement or he would not have invited Percival to meet with the parents in the first place. The few dollars Percival collected that day only ensured each family would benefit equally from the outcome of the legal case.

The legal case. The phrase springing up in Gideon's mind astonished him. Along with Cristof and Chester, John and Aaron, Joshua, Jed, Isaiah, and the others, Gideon was party to a legal case with the potential to wend its way through *English* courts.

After asking their questions and establishing themselves as clients of Percival T. Eggar, Esquire, Attorney at Law, the parents drifted out of the schoolhouse. James walked Percival to his waiting automobile.

Alone in the building, Gideon blew out his breath and offered Ella full-faced encouragement.

"It will all work out." Gideon met Ella's uncertain gaze.

"Maybe the children should have stayed in the town schools for now," Ella said. "There would not be so much at risk."

"There might be less legal risk," Gideon said, "but what of the risk to our children if they spend their days in the *English* world?"

Ella shuffled to a row of desks and began to straighten them. "We don't know what the authorities might do to the children."

Gideon joined her in straightening the room. "Why should they do anything to innocent children? Their argument is with the parents. They understand that minor children do not make these decisions for themselves. The fathers are all doing what they think best. The children are safe."

"And me?"

Gideon almost did not hear Ella. When her whispered words sank in, he abandoned the task of cleaning up and lifted her hands from the bench she pushed against a wall.

"You are not alone," he said.

Ella let out her breath. "But I am unqualified. Am I breaking the law by doing the work of a teacher?"

"You *are* a teacher," Gideon said. "You may not have a piece of paper sealed by the State of Ohio, but you have courage and faith and natural gifts. You have the support of your community. Even Miss Simpson has offered to help you."

Ella shook her head. "I don't want to get her in trouble."

"Miss Simpson strikes me as a person who makes her own decisions," Gideon said.

Ella met his eyes. "If we are to marry on December 19, our banns should be published in a few weeks. Rachel has pages and pages of lists to be sure the house is ready."

Gideon nodded. "We have all the way to January to find a teacher, and now we have Mr. Eggar to help."

Ella dropped her eyes again, but Gideon tipped her face up to kiss her. She was not the only one eager to marry on December 19. He wanted her in his arms and in his home, her face the first he would see in the morning and her lips the ones he would kiss each night.

❧❀❧

Margaret was late getting home from school that afternoon. The Amish *quandary*—the word she was trying out this week to describe the conundrum of Amish and townspeople trying to understand each other—weighed down her shoulders like a row of cement bricks. This was enough of a distraction to put her behind in planning her lessons and correcting the papers of her pupils. Gray's entrenched attitude that the Amish *problem* was not her concern magnified the distraction, and his brother's veiled warning unnerved her. As a consequence, while her pupils did quiet independent work, Margaret was spending too much time mentally muddling her way out of the cage she found herself in.

A blur in her peripheral vision made Margaret turn her head just as she reached the walk leading to her home, and she paused to turn her head and fully discern the sight.

Braden Truesdale skulked across her side yard, cutting through the garden that had yielded the last of its autumn bounty and heading toward the front of her lot.

"Braden!" she called as he came to the edge of the house.

His head jerked up, startle flickering through his eyes. The flour sack over his shoulder bulged in peculiar angular points.

"I didn't know you came through my neighborhood," she said, approaching him. Gray had never given a clear answer about Braden's employment, so Margaret could think of no good reason for him to be in her yard.

"Never know where I'm going to be," he said, tightening his grip to seal the sack.

Were his words a simple statement or another veiled warning? And what in the world was in that flour sack?

"I'll walk with you," Margaret said with false brightness. "I'm on my way to pay a call on a neighbor."

Braden pressed his lips into a tight, straight smile and nodded. Margaret watched his glance and followed his cue, turning back in the direction from which she had come.

"Is your workday nearly finished?" Margaret asked.

"Just about."

Margaret let herself fall back a half step and eyed the bag. The bulge in Braden's muscle, even under his shirtsleeve, suggested the bag carried items of weight. Books? Candlesticks? Jugs? The sour sensation in Margaret's stomach bubbled up through her throat.

"Here's my stop," Margaret said, across the street from Lindy Lehman's house. "Now that we're acquainted, I'll see you another time, I suppose."

"S'pose."

Margaret stepped into the street to cross to Lindy's. Braden marched toward Main Street. Margaret walked slowly, perusing his progress, before approaching Lindy's workshop. She could not always keep her neighbor's property safe, but on this one day, she could make sure Braden Truesdale did not stop there. Unless he had already been there and she'd caught him in a circuitous departure.

Gray would never believe her if Margaret told him she suspected Braden was responsible for the burglary and vandalism of Lindy's shop. But in that moment, Margaret was as certain as if she had witnessed the acts herself.

CHAPTER 31

J ames wandered down Main Street on Wednesday afternoon in no particular hurry. With Gideon's assurance that he intended to stay close to the house and barn today, James had taken his wagon into town with items from several Amish farms to trade for credit at the mercantile, and then picked up birdhouses, quilt racks, and toys from Lindy to deliver to the furniture store that kept her items on hand to attract customers who appreciated Amish craftsmanship. He caught her just before she left for a shopping trip in Chardon. With his tasks complete, James left his horse and wagon with the blacksmith at the edge of Seabury to reshoe the mare and relished the idea of an unhurried walk in the brisk fall air.

When James had enough of studying the *English* display windows and trying to fathom what the women found so compelling about the rising hemlines and the attraction of homburg hats and striped waistcoats for men, he moseyed toward the hardware store. Browsing there was never without benefit. James bypassed the aisles of electrical gadgets, which seemed to take up more space every year, and instead inspected the latest unadorned tools and work gloves that would serve a practical purpose. He had a hammer in his hand, testing its weight, when the voices from the next aisle wafted over the bins of nails and screws.

"Deputy Fremont is on his way now," one man said.

"What for this time?" his companion responded.

"Don't know for sure. My wife just talked to his housekeeper. He was in such a hurry that he left half his lunch uneaten."

"The Amish farms, you say?"

James's breath stilled.

"The paperwork came through, I guess."

"Paperwork?"

"The housekeeper didn't see all the details. Just saw a few names. "Hilty. Hershberger. Wittmer. Several others, I think."

"More fines, I suppose."

"I think the law has something more in mind this time. He just needs a judge's signature. If those families can't take proper care of their children, then the state will."

The hammer clattered out of James's hand and he bolted up the aisle, past the counter, and out the door.

At Percival Eggar's office, James burst through the door. The bespectacled secretary looked up, startled.

"I need Mr. Eggar," James said. "It's an emergency."

"I'm afraid he isn't here," the young man said. "He went to Cleveland today."

Cleveland!

"When is he due back?"

"I'm afraid I couldn't say. His instructions were that I should close the office at six o'clock because he did not expect to return before then."

James wheeled back out to Main Street. The blacksmith was a good mile and a half away, a distance not in the least daunting under leisure circumstances, even for a man James's age, but more fearsome when every moment was of the essence. James set off with a brisk pace and soon forced himself to trot. If he could get back to the farms soon enough, he could warn the others. There were dozens of places to hide on the farms where Deputy Fremont would never think to look. James covered the distance in eighteen minutes.

"I need my rig," James told the blacksmith. "I'll have to bring it back another day."

"I just got all the shoes off the mare."

"I'll have to take her anyway."

The blacksmith shook his head. "You know better, James. You can't take a horse used to being shod out barefoot and expect her to handle the roads between here and your farm. She'll be far too tender."

James sighed. The man was right.

"How long will it take?"

"Now, James, you know the answer to that. I haven't begun to clean the hoofs yet, and I'm not going to rush and risk an ill-fitting shoe. It's not fair to the horse and won't do you any good in the end, either."

Right again. "Then I need to borrow a horse. I don't even need a saddle." He could leave the wagon and ride bareback.

"Look around," the blacksmith said. "I don't have any to spare. I'm not running a livery."

James rubbed his temples. Lindy was gone in her car to Chardon, where she sometimes took orders and collected supplies. "I need a ride in your automobile. It's an emergency."

"The wife took the car to go visit her mother. I thought it would make things easier if I taught her to drive, and now she gallivants all over the place."

James blew out his breath. "Can you keep the mare overnight, then?"

"What's going on, James?"

"I'm not sure," James said. "I just know I have to get home."

When he was a young man, James had been a strong runner. He used to win all the races at the frolics by several strides. He prayed that his muscles would still know what to do all these years later.

⁂

Maybe James was right. Maybe Miriam was just feeling her age and refusing to accept the limitations it brought. Miriam was in the kitchen when Ella walked home with Gertie and Savilla. Still-warm cookies adorned the table beside a jug of milk from that morning, and Miriam was in the midst of slicing onions, celery, and squash on a cutting board at the counter. A chicken in a roasting pan was ready for the oven. Still, it seemed to Ella that Miriam was moving slowly, with slumped shoulders in need of rest. Ella would feel better if she could talk to James. She left the girls to enjoy their snack and chatter with Miriam and went in search of James.

"He's not here," Gideon said when Ella found him in the barn. "He went into town for the day. I imagine by now the blacksmith has finished with the mare and James is on his way home."

"Miriam needs to slow down," Ella said.

"I know. James knows. Even Miriam knows," Gideon said. "I had to stop her churning butter this morning. If she would take it easy for a few weeks, she could get properly rested."

"And I'll be here in a few weeks," Ella said. "She won't have to feel like she's responsible for everything around the house."

Ella expected immediate agreement. Instead, Gideon's gaze shifted.

"Gideon?"

"You're right," Gideon said, meeting her eyes again. "Another woman on the farm would take the load off of Miriam."

Another woman. Ella hated the distance in Gideon's choice of words. His face gave nothing more away. Ella pulled her thoughts back to James.

"Would you mind if I took your small buggy and went to look for James?" she asked.

"You know you're always welcome to the buggy," Gideon said, "but James will be home well before supper."

"I have an odd feeling about all this."

"I'm sure everything's fine. I knew it would be a long day away for James. That's why I promised to stay close to the house."

"I can't explain it, Gideon. I just want to go see if I can meet him on the road. Besides, I'd like to talk to him about Miriam without worrying that she's going to come into the room."

"She does have an uncanny way of appearing when we're whispering behind her back," Gideon said. "I'll hitch up the buggy for you."

With the reins in her hands a few minutes later, Ella took the team out to the main road and turned toward town. She did not push the horse for speed. Rather, her impulse was for care in what she noticed. James might have turned off somewhere with a delivery Gideon was unaware he planned to make, or perhaps he had detoured to give someone a ride home from Seabury. As she drifted along the side of the road, leaving ample room for passing automobiles whose drivers would be frustrated by her strolling pace, Ella leaned forward to look down the lanes for any sign of James's rig.

An approaching driver leaned on a horn—unnecessarily, since Ella was not impeding his path. The vehicle's high speed, churning up dust and gravel, alarmed Ella. When she saw it was one of the sheriff's cars, her heart lurched. Close behind was a bus similar to the ones the children rode to school in town. But the canvas sides of the bus were rolled up, and Ella could see that it was empty. The two vehicles seemed to be keeping pace with each other. Ella stopped her buggy as she watched them pass in the other direction.

"Why should they do anything to innocent children?" Gideon had said barely twenty-four hours ago. *"The children are safe."*

Ella was not so sure.

She scanned for a spot in the road wide enough to turn the buggy around. The horse's ears lay back as it pulled toward the edge of the road.

"Whoa!" Ella tugged on the reins, wary of going into the shallow ditch.

To Ella's relief, the horse stopped. Only then did she hear the moan. She jumped out of the buggy.

James lay in the ditch with a lump the size of a chicken egg swelling out of his forehead.

"James!" Ella knelt beside him.

He moaned again. Ella looked around. Where was his wagon? Had the mare spooked at the speeding sheriff's car and bus?

"Too fast," James said. "I went too fast but not fast enough."

"You're not talking sense." Gently, Ella touched the lump on his head.

"I got dizzy," James said. "I was running too fast."

"What happened to your horse?"

"At the blacksmith's." James labored to catch his breath. "She had no shoes. I wanted to warn everyone."

Ella's gut plummeted. "Is this about Deputy Fremont?"

James sat up slowly. "Good. You have a buggy. We can still let them know. Gideon's on the list."

Ella peered down the road. The sheriff's car was long out of view. Even the dust it had displaced in its path had settled again.

It was too late.

❦

Margaret rapped on the workshop door before shading her eyes to look in a window and determine that Lindy was not inside. She paced to the back door of the house and knocked again.

When the door opened, it was David Kaufman's eyes looking back at Margaret.

"Is Lindy here?" Margaret asked.

David shook his head. "She went to Chardon. She called a

little while ago and said she decided to stay and have supper with a friend."

"So she's safe."

David's eyes flashed from side to side. "Did you see something?"

"How long have you been here?"

"Ever since school let out. I came straight home."

"Good. Just let Lindy know I was checking on her. You know where to find me if you need something."

David nodded. "Thank you."

"And David, look around. Make sure you don't notice anything missing from the house."

Exhaling, Margaret turned to cross the street. She had no appetite for supper. She only wanted to think.

And pray.

There had to be an answer to all this perplexity.

And there he was, Braden Truesdale still standing on the street a block and a half down. If he had good reason to be in the neighborhood in the first place, certainly he'd had plenty of time to finish his business and be on his way.

And what was in that ridiculous bag?

Margaret marched down the street. He saw her coming and made no effort to move.

"I feel compelled," Margaret said, meeting his eyes, "to ask you once again what your business is on this street."

"Does Gray know you're so nosy?" Braden said.

"We are not discussing Gray." Margaret gripped the handle of her satchel, prepared to swing it if necessary. "What's in that flour sack?"

"Not your business."

"I'll have a word with Deputy Fremont," Margaret said. "He may find it interesting that you were on this street on this day with that bag in your possession."

"Deputy Fremont is otherwise occupied," Braden said. "And if I were you, I'd stay out of the Amish problem, because it will soon be messier than you ever imagined."

"I demand that you explain yourself."

Braden laughed and sauntered up the sidewalk.

CHAPTER 32

Gideon put both hands on the back of Miriam's shoulders as she stood in the kitchen and leaned forward to speak softly into her left ear.

"Take a rest," he said. "I've given the girls chores to do upstairs. They won't bother you."

"Your *kinner* are never a bother to me." Miriam continued to layer cut vegetables around the chicken in the roasting pan.

"I know my children," Gideon said. "Savilla is settling down as she gets older, but Gertie can still be a handful. Go put your feet up for a few minutes while they're occupied."

Miriam laid her wooden spoon on the counter and rotated to face him. "I could do with a cup of *kaffi*."

"I'll make it." Gideon reached for the coffeepot on the stove before Miriam could get to it.

"It just needs warming," Miriam said.

"Then I'll warm it." Gideon pointed to the comfortable chair he and James had positioned in the kitchen weeks ago. "Go. Sit."

Miriam settled in with a sigh while Gideon added wood to the stove. "Don't get the stove too hot," she said, "or it will be too much to roast the chicken."

"Just enough to get the *kaffi* hot quickly," Gideon said. He set out two mugs. If he drank coffee with Miriam, she would rest a few minutes. If he left the room, she would set her mug aside after the second sip and discover a task that had transformed from unseen to urgent.

Gideon was pouring the coffee when a solid knock sounded at the front door.

"What in the world?" he said, standing.

849

Miriam tilted out of her chair. "I'll get it."

When the door did not open immediately, the knock became a pounding. Gideon followed Miriam through the dining room and across the front room.

Miriam opened the door, and Gideon stared into the eyes of Deputy Fremont.

"I paid the fine promptly," Gideon said.

"We're beyond fines." Deputy Fremont pushed Miriam aside and entered the house, leaving another uniformed man on the porch.

Indignation burned through Gideon. "You will treat Mrs. Lehman with respect." Behind him two sets of young feet clattered down the stairs.

"Gideon Wittmer," the deputy said, "you are under arrest for contributing to the delinquency of three minors, Tobias Wittmer, Savilla Wittmer, and Gertrude Wittmer."

"I know my children's names," Gideon said.

"Apparently the fines did not make you see the error of your ways," the deputy said. "Perhaps jail will make a stronger impression."

"*Daed!*"

Gideon looked over his shoulder at his daughters. "You listen to *Aunti* Miriam and do what she tells you to do."

"Don't worry about the children," Fremont said. "We have a plan for them as well."

"Miriam," Gideon said, "send Tobias to town to find Mr. Eggar."

"I'm afraid Tobias is not going into town," Fremont said. He cocked his head toward the bus parked in front of the house.

The back door creaked open, steps crossed the kitchen, and Tobias appeared. Confusion clouded his eyes.

"Take care of the girls," Gideon said. "Miriam, remember, Mr. Percival Eggar. He will know what to do."

⚓

Ella helped James into the buggy and urged the horse to maximum speed. By the time they arrived at the Wittmer farm, only Miriam remained, tearful, leaning against a post on the front porch. She straightened when she saw James emerge from the buggy.

Ella took his elbow. "Are you sure you're steady enough to walk?"

"What in the world happened to you?" Miriam came down the steps of the porch.

"I have to admit I've never had such a headache in all my life." James divided his weight between Miriam and Ella until they got him settled in a chair on the porch. Miriam chipped ice off the block in the bottom of the icebox and wrapped it in a towel to press against her husband's head.

"We're too late, aren't we?" James said.

"The sheriff's officers took Gideon," Miriam said, "and they took the children in a bus—all three of them."

Ella's heart thudded. In one afternoon, intuition had grown into fear, and fear into reality.

"Your father is on the list," Miriam said.

"But the boys both have been going to school," Ella said. "Seth has only been in my class since last week."

"Before that, he wasn't doing his homework. That's negligence and delinquency according to the papers."

"Show me," James said.

Miriam produced the papers Gideon had left with her.

"Ella, you need to go," James said.

"But you're hurt," Ella said, trying to look over James's shoulder and scan the legal papers for herself.

"Take the buggy and go. Now."

His tone mobilized Ella. She raced back out to Gideon's buggy, picked up the reins, and clicked her tongue. The horse circled the yard to get turned before falling into a familiar trot up the lane.

Faster. We have to go faster.

The more she urged the horse, the more the buggy swayed. Finally she was at the final intersection, and she tugged the reins to make the turn.

Her father stood in the yard, twenty feet from the deputy's automobile. Ella urged the horse to pull the buggy parallel to the vehicle.

"Gideon!"

Smudged glass separated them, but at the sound of Ella's voice, Gideon turned toward her. Ella leaped out of the buggy.

"Step back." The voice was male, deep, unyielding.

Ella looked up now and saw Seth being loaded into the bus she had seen on the main road. Gideon's three children leaned out of the bus. Tobias had one arm around each sister. Ella ran to them, squeezing the girls' outstretched hands.

"God is with you!" she said. "God will not leave you!"

"They're taking your *daed*," Seth shouted.

Ella spun around in time to see her father pushed into the waiting vehicle. At least neither Gideon nor Jed was alone.

The engines of both vehicles sparked and caught, and Ella was left with her father's stunned wife trembling and falling back into her crumbling flower bed.

⋘⋙

"It's Ella," Miriam said.

James took the bundle of melting ice off his forehead and followed his wife's gaze out the wide front window.

"She brought Rachel with her," Miriam said.

"She wouldn't want to leave Rachel on her own," James said.

Miriam opened the front door before Ella could knock and admitted the two guests.

"I was too late—again," Ella said. "Deputy Fremont was already there."

"So they've taken Jed?" Miriam said, gesturing that Ella and Rachel should sit.

"And Seth," Rachel said. "I promised to put him back in their school if they would just leave him alone, but their minds were made up."

"James, how is your head?" Ella peered at the bruising lump.

"Never mind my head," James said. "I'm just sorry I couldn't warn anyone. They could have hidden. If I'd just had a horse."

"It wouldn't have made a difference," Ella said. "Even a horse could not have raced against an *English* automobile to get to all the farms."

"But some of them might have hidden their children. I can think of a dozen places Tobias and the girls would have been safe."

"Where have they taken them?" Rachel asked. "The men will go to jail. I understand that. But where will they take the children?"

James reached for the papers Gideon had left behind, shaking his head. "State custody. That's all it says. I suppose they will go wherever neglected children go."

"My son is not neglected!" Rachel moved to the edge of her seat.

"Neither are Gideon's children," Miriam said.

"We have to find out where they are," Ella said.

"'Mr. Eggar,'" Miriam said. "That's the last thing Gideon said.

Mr. Eggar will know what to do."

"Ella, go find this Mr. Eggar," Rachel urged. "Do you know where his office is?"

"Yes," Ella said, "right on Main Street."

James painfully shook his head. "He's not there. I tried. The young man in his office did not expect him back before he closed the office at six."

Ella studied the clock on the mantel. Chasing around half the county all afternoon had consumed more time than she anticipated. Dusk enveloped the house. "It's past six now," she said.

"Someone in town will know which house is his," Rachel said. "You'll just have to keep asking until you find someone who does. Start with Lindy, or that *English* teacher who lives on her street."

Ella's gaze went to James and Miriam. James was once again pressing ice to his forehead, and Miriam was ghastly pale.

"I will look after James and Miriam," Rachel said.

"I don't need looking after," James protested.

"Neither do I," Miriam said.

Ella met Rachel's glance.

"I don't want to wait alone," Rachel said. "We'll all want to know what Ella finds out."

"I should be the one to go," James muttered.

"Old man," Miriam said, "you're going nowhere."

Ella drew a deep breath. "I'll make sure the lanterns on the buggy have plenty of oil."

✦

"You knew this was going to happen?" Margaret could hardly believe her ears. It was all she could do to remain seated on the davenport in her parlor.

Across the room, Gray Truesdale's lanky form overpowered the chair he had chosen.

"It should come as no surprise," Gray said.

"It most certainly does come as a surprise," Margaret said, her pitch rising against her will. Fury roiled through her midsection. "The fines were ridiculous in the first place. But arresting the fathers? Taking well-loved children into state custody as if they were abandoned orphans?"

"The lawmen are only doing their jobs," Gray said mildly. "It has nothing to do with you. Don't let it get you into a bothered state."

"A bothered state?"

"Your tea is getting cold," Gray said.

Margaret was tempted to toss her cold tea in Gray's lap. How was it possible that he could maintain this dispassionate demeanor when children were being stolen from their homes under the guise of the law?

"The men will take care of it." Gray lifted his teacup. "Will you freshen this for me?"

Margaret glared but picked up the teapot and refilled his cup.

"You're overreacting," Gray said between sips. "You have to let things take their natural course."

And just what was the "natural course" of a situation as complex as legislators and sheriffs and school boards refusing to view the circumstances through a lens other than their own? Margaret did not waste her breath posing the question to Gray.

"I saw your brother earlier," she said instead. "He was acting quite odd."

Gray shrugged. "You met him at Sunday dinner. You know he's odd."

"He was right here on my street, carrying a flour sack I'm certain did not contain flour."

"People use old flour sacks for all sorts of things," Gray said, forking into a sliver of pie. "Potato sacks, too. When we were young, the Amish around here were always glad to have sacks my mother didn't want to use."

"He made me nervous," Margaret said. "I think I will have a word with Deputy Fremont about it. Perhaps there have been some thefts in the neighborhood."

Gray put down his fork. "You think my brother is a thief?"

"I'm saying he was acting in an eccentric manner. If you want me to put such confidence in the sheriff's department, wouldn't it seem prudent to mention my observations?"

Gray took a bite of pie and chewed slowly. "You have misunderstood me."

"Have I?"

"Margaret, we were having a pleasant evening before I mentioned the Amish problem. I'm sorry I brought it up. Let's forget about it."

"Those children must be frightened half out of their minds."

Gertie's face loomed in Margaret's thoughts. Then one by one the other Amish children who had stopped attending school marched through her vision like a moving picture.

"They'll be well looked after," Gray said.

"You can't know that. I have to do something."

"I must insist that you stay out of this."

Margaret raised her eyebrows.

"I know you are a woman of strong cause," Gray said, "and on the whole I find it an admirable quality. But when we are married, I hope you know it will not be your place to involve yourself in matters I do not approve of."

Margaret stood up now. "We have spoken around the matter of marriage," she said, "and I confess I had hoped we would find a common mind. But I think we both know now that we are not as well matched as we had supposed."

Speaking the words aloud jolted electricity through Margaret's body.

Gray stood. "I can give you a comfortable life. You won't get a better offer."

"No," she said softly, "I don't suppose I will."

A knock on the door startled them both. Margaret moistened her lips and answered the door. Ella Hilty stood under the porch light.

"I'm sorry to disturb you," Ella said. "I need to find Mr. Percival Eggar. I wonder if you know where he lives?"

"Come in," Margaret said.

Ella glanced at Gray. "I'm intruding."

"This is Mr. Truesdale," Margaret said. "He's finished his pie, and I'm certain he will understand your need for assistance."

"I'm grateful for any help you can give me." Ella's words lost their fluidity. "My father. . .Gideon. . .the children. . .I don't know where to begin."

"I think I know the basics," Margaret said. "I'm sorry I don't know where Mr. Eggar lives, but we can get the telephone operator on the line. She will know how to reach him."

Margaret picked up the telephone on the table at the bottom of the stairs. With heavy, deliberate steps, Gray Truesdale left the house and closed the door behind him.

CHAPTER 33

It's late. You must stay the night," Margaret said after Mr. Eggar left her bungalow with two sheets of notes recording Ella's account.

Ella shook her head. "Miriam and James and Rachel—they'll all worry that something happened to me as well."

"I'll drive you, then," Margaret said.

Again Ella shook her head. "James's wagon is already stranded in town. I can't leave Gideon's buggy here all night. We'll need it in the morning—and what would we do with the horse?"

Ella was just being practical. She wrapped her shawl around her shoulders and thanked Margaret again before stepping out into the darkness. On most evenings, Amish farms would have quieted by now, lanterns turned low for one last look at sleeping children before parents retired themselves. Morning light would soon enough usher in the labor of another day of farm chores.

On this night, though, the lanterns would burn deep into the darkness, beacons of hope for what the new day might bring.

James, Miriam, and Rachel had hardly moved from where Ella left them hours earlier, though Rachel said she had been out to milk the cows for the night. The Hilty cows were long past their evening milking, so Ella spoke rapidly. There had been little Percival Eggar could do with state and legal offices closed for the evening. He promised to give his full attention when the business day began and to find out where the children had been taken. It was sure to be one of the state orphanages, he said. The men would be in the county courthouse in Chardon, and he would bargain for their release. In the meantime, Mr. Eggar suggested, they should all hope and pray for a firm legal outcome in their favor.

Hope and pray. After milking the Hiltys' cows—a task Seth normally assumed—Ella dragged herself back into the house, where she sat on her bed to sort out which came first—hope or prayer. Did she pray because she had hope for the answer she sought, or did she hope because of the comfort of prayer?

In the morning, the women descended on the Hilty farm before Ella cleared away the dishes of Rachel's uneaten breakfast. At last Ella had her answer about how many fathers had been arrested and how many children were deemed neglected.

Gideon Wittmer; two girls, one boy.

Jed Hilty; one boy.

Cristof Byler; one girl, three boys.

John Hershberger; three girls, one boy.

Isaiah Borntrager; two girls, three boys.

Chester Mast; two boys.

Six men and nineteen children. How the women had known to come to Ella, she did not know. Perhaps they had found each other one by one because they knew the men who chose to send their children to Ella to teach.

"Mr. Eggar is working hard for us," Ella assured the circle of anxious mothers.

"When will we know where our children are?" Mrs. Hershberger jiggled her restless infant on one knee.

Ella swallowed a lump of impossible words. "Most likely, they are at an orphanage."

"But they are not orphans!" came the nearly unanimous response.

"My Ezra was not at home when they came," Mrs. Borntrager said. "Will they come back for him?"

"They'll be back," Mrs. Byler said. "They'll accuse us of neglecting the little ones as well."

"They'll take my baby." Mrs. Hershberger held the child tightly to her chest.

"They could come for David," Mrs. Byler said, looking at Rachel.

"David goes to school," Rachel said.

"But they'll wonder what neglect caused him to run away from home."

"We'll have to hide the *kinner* still with us," Mrs. Hershberger said. "The *English* cannot steal children they cannot find."

Ella put up her hands, palms out. "Let's not jump ahead of ourselves. We have God on our side, and we have Mr. Eggar. He will come to the schoolhouse at three this afternoon to tell us what he knows."

Everyone's eyes moved to the clock on the mantel, ready to count down seven and a half excruciating hours.

"I have to take James into Seabury to fetch his horse and wagon," Ella said. "And we must care for the animals. Let us not be afraid to ask for help when we need it."

She wanted to add, *I'm sure they'll all be home soon.* This was the prayer of her heart. But could she sustain hope if the prayer went unanswered?

❧

The Wayfarers Home for Children. That was the name Percival Eggar uncovered in the legal documents he had demanded. At least—as far as they could tell—all of the children had been taken to the same location. They might have been scattered around eastern Ohio. For now they were together.

It was Saturday. Margaret owed no time to the Seabury Consolidated School District.

Three days after their arrests, the Amish fathers were still in jail in Chardon, and their children were still temporary wards of the state.

It was unconscionable.

Margaret had heard nothing from Gray since Wednesday evening, nor did she expect to. He had wanted her for his wife. Margaret had no doubt of this. He was courting in polite stages, and Margaret had given him every encouragement.

Until this. Until the Amish mystification.

The pressure in her chest waxed and waned through the days and nights. Seeing Gray around town would stir up visions of what might have been.

It was better to find out now, she told herself.

The children were what mattered. The Wayfarers Home for Children was thirty miles from Seabury. Margaret supposed few of the Amish families ever had reason to be thirty miles from their own farms. Had the sheriff's department done this on purpose— taken the children beyond reasonable reach of their mothers?

Margaret owned a car and could afford the gasoline. The least she could do was drive thirty miles and ascertain the welfare of the children.

She found the building without trouble. A blockish brick structure, it was set back from an entrance arched in wrought iron. Despite the expansive lawns calling for tumbles and giggles, Margaret saw no sign of children. She scowled at the thought that residents of the Wayfarers Home for Children attended classrooms even on Saturday. The driveway wound toward the building, and Margaret saw no reason not to park as close to the front door as possible.

At a reception desk a few minutes later, Margaret politely explained the nature of her visit. She wanted only to take assurance to the mothers of the Amish children of their well-being.

"The children are being suitably looked after," said the graying woman behind a narrow desk, "which is a great advancement beyond the actions of their parents, as I understand it."

Margaret bit her tongue. "I would like to see them. Many of them will recognize me from their days at the Seabury school where I teach."

"This is an unorthodox request. I would have to consult the director."

"Please do." Margaret seated herself on the edge of a wooden chair that rocked on one uneven leg. "I will wait."

"He may be engaged." The woman pushed spectacles up her nose.

Margaret smiled. "I teach six-year-olds, so I am well acquainted with patience."

The woman's chair scraped the tile floor, and her buttoned shoes dragged down the hall. Margaret's investment paid its return in the arrival of a man who was perhaps forty years old.

"I understand you want to see the Amish children," he said.

Margaret stood. "That's correct."

"I'm afraid children are not allowed visitors so soon after their arrival," he said. "We find it only distresses their adjustment."

"Surely they won't be here long enough to have to adjust," Margaret said.

"We have our policies." He gave a tight smile.

Margaret's blood raced. "You don't mean to tell me you would withhold them from their own mothers."

"The policies are quite clear on this matter. The children are here because they were neglected. Any visit would have to be closely supervised."

A supervised visit would be better than no visit.

"So if I return with the mothers on another day," Margaret said, "have I your word that they would be permitted to see their children?"

"Briefly," he said, reluctant. "No more than one hour, and only if I have adequate staff available to meet the supervision standards."

Margaret met his eyes and held them hard. "I will be back."

❧❦❧

Getting there had been easier than James imagined it would be. The first glimmer of opportunity came when Miriam insisted on going with Ella to a meeting with the women, leaving James alone in the *dawdihaus* with his bruised forehead. Regardless of what he might look like, he was not seriously hurt. Without Tobias and Gideon, the farm chores had fallen to him. If he could handle that work, he was fit enough for what he had in mind.

In the unexpected solitude, James scribbled a note and left it in the middle of the table, where Miriam would find it easily. He would not be home for supper. Only the fingers of one hand would be required to count the number of times he was not home for supper with his wife in the last forty-four years.

Once he heard Margaret's news, James wanted to see for himself. But thirty miles was a long way to take a horse and buggy. James might find a train for part of the way, but he would be tied to schedules he did not know. David's method seemed more direct and efficient. If *English* drivers would stop for David when he sought a ride into Seabury, why would they not stop for James as well?

He had changed automobiles twice, but here he stood in a gently descending expanse of shadows behind the Wayfarers Home for Children. One by one, lights flickered on inside the building as late afternoon slid into evening. James suspected an approach to the rear of the building held more potential for his goal.

James waited under the spreading barren branches of an elm tree, breathing in and out with care and surveying the ground-floor exits.

A door opened. A woman came out, her arms filled with a basket of undetermined contents, and followed a path toward the corner of the building. It mattered not what she carried, only that she had left the door ajar. In a stealth moment, James found himself in a small pantry.

He stood still and listened for movement in the adjoining room, which he reasoned must be a kitchen, large enough to prepare food for hundreds of children and staff. Hearing nothing, he padded out of the pantry and across the kitchen. Voices came to him now. Children's voices. One lilted above the others.

James had known that voice when it was nothing but the babble of a *boppli*. A half inch at a time, he pushed open the door that separated him from Gideon's children—at least Gertie.

He almost did not recognize her. Gone was her prayer *kapp*. Rather than braids coiled against her head, her blond hair hung loose around her shoulders. A pink ribbon at the top of her head matched the pink dress she wore with a splash of lace down the front.

The children's voices settled as a woman at the front of the room clapped for their attention. Rows and rows of children. As his eyes adjusted to the reality of looking for Amish faces above *English* clothing, James spotted them one by one. Savilla and Tobias—with his hair trimmed in *English* fashion—and Seth Kaufman beside him. The Hershberger girls and their brother, Isaiah Borntrager's children, the Bylers, the Masts. They were all there, but separated, each of them seated with other children their own age rather than with their siblings.

The woman explained the next day's schedule. A Presbyterian minister would come in to hold a morning church service. Children assigned to set up and clear after meals should be prompt. In the afternoon, if the weather was fine, there might be organized outdoor games before the evening prayer meeting.

James settled his gaze again on Gertie, who sat at the end of a row. Her eyes began to wander, and she turned her head toward him. When her blue orbs widened, her lips also parted and she drew in breath as if to speak.

James put a finger to his lips. Gertie clamped her mouth closed. He stepped back into the kitchen, determined to find a way to get the children back. For now it was enough to see that they were unharmed—except for the silly clothes and hair arrangements.

"Who's there?" a voice called. The weight of a box thumped against a butcher block table.

"It's dark in here," another voice said. "Turn on the light."

"I can't find the string to pull."

James slithered back through the pantry.

Hustling out the rear door, still ajar from his entrance, James plunged into the surrounding darkness. Most of his white shirt was covered by his black wool coat, one that Miriam had made for him only last year. For a few minutes he pressed himself up against the same tree that had sheltered him on arrival, waiting for his breathing to compose its rhythm enough that he would be able to find his way around the building without fearing collapse.

James could hear the words Miriam would speak to him if she were there. *"Old man, what have you done now?"*

By now he had missed his supper, but food was far from his mind. The pleading expression on Gertie's face lingered in his mind. Would she have a chance to tell Savilla or Tobias she had seen James? He hoped so. He wanted Gideon's children to know they were not abandoned.

"Gottes wille," he muttered. "Lord, keep them safe."

As soon as he got home, James would sketch what he had seen—the corners of the mammoth building, the doors opening in the back, the path to the large room where the children gathered. As soon as tomorrow's Sabbath was over, James would find a way to get to Chardon to visit Gideon and the other men. And he would visit Percival Eggar in Seabury every day if he had to.

James prayed it would be God's will for an obliging driver to happen by just as he arrived at the road. An even more gracious answer to his prayer would be a driver whose destination was Seabury and who could carry an unexpected passenger safely to his home. He took off his black jacket now, exposing his white shirt and hoping it made him more visible in the headlights of passing automobiles. Miriam would disapprove of his shivering in the night wind, but Miriam would disapprove of most of what James had done today.

Two cars passed without stopping. James began to walk in the general direction of home. If God did not send a ride, it would take him all night to get to the farm.

The lights of another automobile swung around a curve, accompanied by a particularly noisy engine. James waved one arm in a wide swath, expelling his breath again only once it was clear the driver was slowing. James paid no attention to the variations in *English* automobiles. He supposed this one was one of Mr. Ford's inventions. A young man with a broad smile and wavy hair leaned across the seat to look out the window at James.

"Are you stranded?" the man asked.

"You might say," James said. "Are you by any chance headed to Seabury?"

"I could be. Is that where you're headed?"

"A farm near there."

"Get in," the man said, pushing the handle so the passenger door would open. "I'm Edwin."

"James Lehman." Grateful, James settled into his seat. He had been in Lindy's car a time or two, but it still seemed an adventure to ride through the night behind a motor.

Edwin cocked his head as he put the car back into gear. "You're one of those Amish."

James slipped his arms back into his jacket and nodded. "How long do you guess it will take to get to Seabury?"

"Less than an hour," Edwin said. "Do you mind if I ask a question?"

"Of course not." James could hardly deny conversation to God's answer to his prayer.

Edwin accelerated. "What brings you so far from home at this hour?"

⁂

Ella had no students. She had returned to the schoolhouse on Monday long enough to put away what little there was of value and to make sure the windows and doors were closed securely. Each day winter howled a few degrees colder.

Monday. The children and the fathers had been gone five days. Households with older sons sent them around to be sure women with younger families had enough help with the animals, and each day the women seemed to find each other and congregate in another home.

Percival Eggar filed documents with Latin names at the courthouse in Chardon and assured the families that he had seen their men and they were fine. But the judicial process seemed to be in no hurry to come to the aid of a handful of rural farm families, and Mr. Eggar offered no estimation of when the case might come before a judge.

Leaving Rachel in the gentle care of Mrs. Glick, Ella took the buggy into Seabury to turn in her pile of library books, and because the slow ride to town would give her time to think about all that had transpired in the last few days.

Mrs. White, the cheery librarian, checked in Ella's books. "Your bird book is back on the shelf, in case you're looking for it again."

"Thank you." Ella was not much in the mood to contemplate what to read in her shrinking leisure hours. She was tempted to ask Mrs. White if the library had any books about the legal system.

"I have to say," Mrs. White said, "I was surprised by that article in the newspaper, weren't you?"

"Our people don't read the newspaper," Ella reminded the librarian.

"That's what I thought," Mrs. White said. "I was doubly surprised to find that one of you had given an interview to a reporter."

Ella rubbed one tired eye. "I'm sorry. What did you say?"

"There's a long article in the paper out of Cleveland." Mrs. White pushed a neat stack of books to one side of the desk. "You should read it."

"No, I couldn't." An interview? A Cleveland newspaper? Ella could not make sense of Mrs. White's words.

"Follow me." Mrs. White came out from behind the desk and with short, clipped steps led the way to a section of the library Ella had never before explored. Two rows of racks had newspapers hanging over them. Mrs. White plucked up the one she wanted and swiftly opened to the page of interest.

AMISH CHILDREN VICTIMS OF NEGLECT, the headline said.

Ella gasped and took the newspaper into her own hands. "I don't understand."

Mrs. White pointed to a phrase in the first paragraph. "An exclusive interview with a Geauga County Amish man."

"No," Ella said. "We wouldn't do that!" She scanned the article. *Children kept out of school. Fathers stubbornly defy state laws. Illegal private school.*

"Well, someone did." Mrs. White flipped the paper to show Ella what lay below the fold.

Ella stared into the faces of her father and her fiancé, bearded and behind bars.

"I don't know how a reporter got that picture on a Sunday," Mrs. White said. "I guess he was determined to get the scoop for the Monday morning edition. Some people have no respect for the Sabbath."

***

"Perhaps we need to pay Mr. Eggar a larger fee," Isaiah Borntrager said.

"He's doing all he can," Gideon said. "He's been to see us every day. We can't blame him for how slowly the court system works."

The six Amish men occupied two jail cells side by side. Gideon and Jed tended to pace the limited square footage, while Isaiah sprawled on a lower bunk in a prolonged sulk. On the other side of the wall, the restless shiftings and murmurs of John, Cristof, and Chester told a similar story from the other cell. A guard walked past them every hour or so, but in between they were free to lean against the bars of the jail cells and speak so all could hear.

"Five days," Isaiah muttered.

"And we still don't know what happens next," Jed said. "Whatever happens to me, I want Rachel to have her son home."

Percival Eggar had brought enough news for the men to know that no further harm had come to their families—no more children taken, no threats against wives left behind. But what of the children already removed from their homes? No matter what flowery language Mr. Eggar constructed about the safety of the Wayfarers Home for Children and the competency of the staff who served there, every father in the jail cells thought constantly of their children foundering in a sea of *English* expectations without even the comfort of coming home to their own farms and families at the end of the day.

"We should pray," Gideon said.

"All I do is pray," John Hershberger said from the other cell. "My every thought is prayer."

"Together," Gideon said. "We have already seen how prayer together, aloud, brings us encouragement. Let us not fall away now. Remember the faithfulness of the martyrs in our hymns and learn from their steadfastness in times of trial."

Isaiah swung his feet off the bunk. "We've cowered long enough, depending on the *English* lawyer to free us. Only God can free us."

The six men lined themselves up along the iron bars, hands hanging through the openings as if grasping for the freedom on the other side.

Gideon spoke aloud. "Lord God, You ordain our lives. You ordain our moments. We cleave to You in this our time of trial. Keep us free from the night of darkness of temptation and sin. Instead, lead us in the light of Your divine mercy. The psalmist tells us, 'The Lord God is a sun and shield: the Lord will give grace and glory: no good thing will he withhold from them that walk uprightly.' We depend on You to keep our steps upright and lead us into Your goodness and glory."

John cleared his throat. "May Your merciful eyes be upon us even in this place where we cannot look on Your beauty in the land. Forgive us our weaknesses for the sake of Your dear Son. Turn darkness to light before our very eyes."

Booted footfalls thudding against the hall floor pried Gideon's eyes open and he put a hand on Isaiah's arm.

"Praying again," the guard said. "Doesn't it occur to you that it might be God's will for you simply to obey the law?"

Gideon said nothing, instead moving his eyes to Percival Eggar standing beside the deputy.

"If you would please," Percival said.

The guard rattled a ring of keys. "I know. You want a confidential conversation with all of your clients in one room." He unlocked both cells and herded the prisoners together in one cell. Once the attorney stepped in as well, the guard locked the cell and retreated from sight.

"I had hoped," Percival said, "that the authorities simply wanted to make a point by detaining you through the weekend when the courts would be closed. I'm afraid the news I have today is not encouraging. They are prepared to jail you indefinitely, right up until trial."

"When will that be?" Gideon asked.

"The dockets are full." Percival shook his head. "Weeks. Months, perhaps. We'll use the time to prepare our case."

Jed separated from the group. "And if we lose the trial?"

"Let's not jump to that," Percival said. "We can make a strong case on the grounds of the free exercise of religion."

"What are our wives supposed to do in the meantime?" Chester asked.

"I'll try to arrange a visit," Percival said. "And there are rules that will allow them to see the children."

"What will it take to end all this?" Gideon slowly paced toward the rear wall of the cell.

Percival shrugged one shoulder. "Agree to put your children in the consolidated schools until the age of sixteen. And I'm sure there will be another fine."

"No compromise?" Chester said. "No reasoning together?"

"I'm not giving up," Percival said. "The question is how long you want to persist on the path to lasting justice for your people."

⊱⊱⊰⊰

Gray startled Margaret. She had stayed late in the school building on Monday, hearing other teachers close their classroom doors and fall into step with one another down the back stairs more than an hour ago. It was essential that lesson plans were clear and specific for the following day and all supplies arranged in an orderly fashion. When Margaret finally left the building, exiting through the front door so the woman who worked in the office would know the last teacher was gone, she did not expect to find Gray Truesdale waiting for her.

He leaned one shoulder against the brick of the building, straightening when he saw her come through the door.

"Mr. Truesdale," Margaret said, reverting to the neutral cordiality of the early days of their acquaintance.

"May I speak to you?" Gray said.

"Of course." Instantly, a lump formed in Margaret's throat.

"I may have spoken harshly the last time we met," he said. "And I missed sitting with you in church yesterday. I looked for you after the service."

"I didn't feel up to attending," Margaret said.

"It's your church, too," Gray said. "I would never want you to stay away because you are angry with me."

"I'm not angry," Margaret said. She ached with disappointment over his views, with grief for what might have been.

Gray ran his thumb and forefinger over the brim of the hat in his hand. "The preacher spoke about humility. Maybe I need to learn some."

Optimism flickered, struggling against the harsh wind of the words they had spoken to each other.

"I'd like to come for pie on Thursday," Gray said.

Margaret shifted her satchel to the other hand. "I have preserves made from the blackberries you brought me. It seems only right that you should help eat them."

He offered that crooked smile Margaret found so difficult to resist.

The lump in her throat softened. She would make pie. It was a small town and they attended the same church. One last evening of pie might make it easier to find the necessary geniality for an amicable break.

If Margaret had told Gray what she intended to do the following day, she was certain he would have changed his mind about the pie.

$\mathbf{M}$argaret pulled the car up close to the Hilty farmhouse and checked once again to be sure she had not left clutter on the seats. Living alone and driving alone most of the time cultivated a habit of leaving books and papers on the backseat as if it were an ordinary storage shelf in her bungalow. But today the seats had to be cleared. Today she needed space for six passengers. It would be tight, but Margaret was certain the Amish mothers would do whatever it took to see their children.

Rachel and Ella were waiting on the porch and descended the steps. Margaret scurried around the car to hold a door open for them.

"What about your class?" Ella asked once they were on their way.

"I arranged for a substitute teacher," Margaret said. "It's allowed under extenuating circumstances."

"I'm surprised your principal would consider this extenuating circumstances," Ella said.

"I said I had a personal matter that required immediate attention." It was none of Mr. Tarkington's business what Margaret did with her day. In four years of teaching at the Seabury school, Margaret had only availed herself of the services of a substitute on two other occasions, both involving abrupt illness. By now the substitute would be reviewing the clear and specific lesson plans Margaret had left. Her pupils would notice no difference in classroom routine.

"I don't have the words to thank you for taking us." Rachel was squeezed in between Ella and Margaret, leaving the backseat available for four more mothers.

"It's the right thing to do," Margaret said. "Where do we go next?"

"To the Glicks'," Ella said. "Mrs. Hershberger is leaving her *boppli* there. The littlest Borntrager boy will stay with Mrs. King."

Margaret nodded in satisfaction with the plan. Margaret had warned the mothers there would not be room in the car for their small children still at home and that she was uncertain whether young ones would be admitted at the Wayfarers Home. The Masts and Bylers did not have any children younger than those who had been removed.

"I'm so worried about Seth," Rachel said, rubbing a hand over her eyes.

"He and Tobias are close in age," Ella said. "They're probably together. And the Mast brothers. They'll all help each other."

Just like their parents. Some of the boys were old enough to be in high school. They would be fine. The girls were younger, though. Margaret couldn't think of any Amish girl at the Wayfarers Home older than eleven or twelve. Who was looking after them?

After several more stops, four mothers crammed into the backseat and settled care packages on their laps. Margaret did not have the heart to tell them they might not be allowed to leave gifts.

This time she knew just where she was going and drove confidently up the long driveway before parking outside the front doors and turning off the engine.

Rachel's eyes widened at the enormity of the brick building. "It would take three or four of our church districts to fill this place."

"This is no place for children," Mrs. Hershberger muttered from the backseat. "Couldn't an *aunti* or a *grossmudder* take in a child who is truly orphaned? Have they no families at all?"

"I don't know," Margaret said. "Let's focus on the nineteen children whose mothers are right here in this car."

"Do they know we're coming?" Ella asked.

"I phoned ahead." Margaret opened her car door and stepped out. "Let me speak on your behalf while you pray to see God's mercy in the faces of your children."

❧❦❧

Margaret led the way. Ella intentionally fell to the back of the line, watching to be sure the other mothers were holding themselves together as they approached a structure that could have contained all their homes and still had room for chickens and cows.

Other mothers. Ella loved Tobias, Savilla, and Gertie. Together with Gideon, they were going to become a family in a few weeks. She would throw herself in the path of danger for any one of them. If Ella's maternal instincts surged as hard as this, she could only imagine what this day was like for the women whose wombs and arms had carried their children since the first spark of life.

Margaret held open the front door, and the Amish mothers shuffled inside, uncertain.

Margaret pointed. "We'll go to that desk. They are expecting you."

A man met them in the hallway. While the gray-haired woman Margaret had met on her first visit stared at the huddle of rich-hued dresses and black aprons, Margaret introduced him as the director of the children's home. One by one the mothers gave their names and the names of the children.

"I'll Ella Hilty," Ella said. "I'm here to see Tobias, Savilla, and Gertrude Wittmer."

The director arranged his glasses on his nose and consulted his list. "My information indicates that the Wittmer children have no mother."

"I'm engaged to their father," Ella said quickly. "Our wedding is only a month away."

A wave of sympathy flushed through the man's face, but his words were firm. "I'm afraid we have no provision for such a circumstance. Anyone might come in and make such a claim. It's for the safety of the children. You understand."

Ella's mouth fell open, her heart beating its way up her throat.

"We most certainly do not understand," Margaret said calmly. "The children know Miss Hilty well. They understand that their father will marry her soon. I have observed no discord between them on this matter."

Ella forced herself to breathe, and the air flowing out of her lungs cradled a prayer of gratitude for Margaret's presence.

"Think of how the Wittmer children will feel," Margaret said. "The other Amish children will see their mothers, and the Wittmers will know someone came for them as well and you prohibited the visit."

The director cleared his throat. "I will have to consult the state guidelines, but I make no guarantee."

"What about our children?" Mrs. Hershberger wanted to know. "Where are they?"

"They'll be brought to you," the director said. "They are in classes throughout the building, so it will take some time to gather them."

"We had an appointment," Margaret said. "Why are the children not ready?"

Ella put a hand on Margaret's arm and said to the director, "Just tell us where you'd like us to wait."

He turned to the woman at the desk. "Will you please take the mothers to the visiting room where they may wait more comfortably?"

"And the others—Miss Simpson and Miss Hilty?" the woman asked.

The director sucked in his lips slightly and turned to Ella and Margaret. "I'll have to ask you to wait out here until I have ascertained your status."

"I will gladly wait out here," Margaret said, "but I will insist that Miss Hilty see her children. Otherwise you will hear from Mr. Eggar, the attorney representing the children's fathers."

"Mr. Eggar has already been in touch," the director said. "We are both responsible to the court for our actions. I intend to be above reproach."

"I hope that does not also require you to be above compassion," Margaret said.

Again, Ella touched Margaret's arm. One might think the director held hostage Margaret's own offspring.

"I'll wait out here," Ella said. "Is that bench acceptable?"

The director gestured toward the bench directly across from the reception desk. "Please make yourselves comfortable. The rest of you may follow the receptionist, but let me remind you that this visit will be closely supervised."

The director withdrew to his office.

Ella and Margaret sat on the backless bench. Ella did not even wish for a chair with a back or any other comfort that might compromise her vigilance. She watched the five mothers trail after the woman to a door, which she held open for them. Ella leaned forward for a glimpse of the space where mothers and *kinner* would be reunited.

"This is not right," Margaret muttered.

Though her heart begged for release from captivity within her rib cage, Ella sat with her hands calmly crossed in her lap. A moment later, three young women left the director's office, dispatched—Ella hoped—to bring the children from their classrooms.

"If the director does not return promptly, I will advocate once again for you to see your children."

Ella's shoulders softened and gratitude again overflowed for the *English* who understood her heart. Perhaps Margaret's own experience as a teacher helped her know how quickly and firmly affection might grow with a child.

One by one, the young women returned, shepherding children into the visitation room. Most of them moved quietly through the halls.

The first time the door opened, Mrs. Mast shrieked at the sight of her boys.

The second time, it was Seth who came down the hall and Rachel's sobs that escaped the visiting room.

Then Mrs. Borntrager.

The young women returned to the classrooms, returning each time with one or two children. It seemed to Ella that they had begun with the older grades and were working their way down to the younger classes.

"They didn't bring Tobias," Ella said.

Margaret took her hand. "You *will* see your children."

The students grew younger with each escort. Mrs. Hershberger's voice went shrill at the sight of her children.

"They skipped Savilla, too," Ella said.

"Has the man no heart?" Margaret said. "Gideon's children are bright. They will see that the others are going and know that someone has come for them."

The Byler children came at last, Hans trailing after his older siblings. Ella swallowed hard.

The sound she heard next was the most beautiful cacophony ever to reach her ears. Down the hall, a child's demands grew more insistent with each clattering step.

"If Hans gets to go, why can't I?"

Margaret and Ella grinned at each other and stood up.

"Gertrude!" The young escort spun on one heel, holding tight to Hans Byler's hand. "Go back to class immediately.

"Is Hans in trouble?" Gertie asked.

"No. Go back to class."

Ella's eyes widened. Gertie's yellow hair fell around her shoulders above a blue plaid jumper and white blouse intended for a girl at least two years older.

"What have they done to our children?" Ella whispered.

"I won't go back without Hans." Gertie stomped a foot, something she never would have done at home.

The young woman escorting Hans opened the door to the visiting room and gave him a gentle push between the shoulder blades through the door frame before sealing the room again.

"What's in there?" Gertie wanted to know.

Then, in a moment that Ella wished she could ponder in her heart for the rest of her life, Gertie's curls bounced with the rotation of her head and her gaze found Ella.

Ella started toward Gertie. The receptionist was on her feet. Gertie was already hurtling toward Ella, out of reach of the young escort's efforts to contain her.

"Go," the receptionist whispered. "Hurry."

Ella raced down the hall and scooped up Gertie in her arms.

The director appeared from his office. "What's going on?"

Ella ignored him. It was quite obvious what was going on. Gertie buried her face in Ella's shoulder.

The clipped steps behind Ella belonged to Margaret.

"Now if you would please send someone for Miss Hilty's other children," Margaret said.

"This is thoroughly unorthodox," the director said.

Ella took Gertie's face between her hands to examine every inch of it. "Are you all right?"

"I don't like it here," Gertie said loudly. "They never let me talk to Tobias and Savilla. I only get to see Hans when it's time for our reading lessons. And they won't tell me why Hans went in that room."

Tears blurred Ella's eyes. "Hans went in there to see his *mamm*."

Gertie kept her hands clasped behind Ella's neck.

"You can see their affection is genuine," Margaret said to the director. "If you care for these children at all—"

The director tilted his head, and the young woman awaiting his bidding started down the hall. She opened the door to the visiting room.

"You won't have long," he said.

Inside the room, tears and laughter intermingled. The children hated the clothes they were forced to wear, and no two of them had been assigned to the same dormitory room. They sometimes saw each other across a classroom or the assembly room, but rarely were they allowed to speak freely with each other and it must always be in English, not Pennsylvania Dutch. Ella's chest felt as though it might cave in with the isolation they described. Sitting in opposite corners, two women in navy blue wool dresses watched the movements in the room. Every few seconds, Ella's eyes went to the door, looking for Savilla and Tobias.

When the door opened, it was Gertie who saw them first and shot off to greet her siblings. Whatever manner in which they might have irritated each other at home dissolved in the embrace. Ella waited for their eyes to lift and opened her arms to Tobias and Savilla.

Questions spewed from all three of them, and Ella had few answers. She could only tell them that Gideon was with the other fathers. She hadn't been to see them—none of the women had managed a visit to Chardon—but Mr. Eggar brought news that they were well. Tobias promised to pray for his father.

The large round clock opposite the door seemed designed to greet everyone who entered the visitation room and remind them that their minutes were few. As if on cue, exactly one hour after the mothers had entered the room, the two women in blue stood up and announced it was time for the children to return to their classrooms. One of them opened the door to reveal the three younger women who would escort their charges on their return.

Ella held on to Gertie as long as she dared. In the end, it was sensible Savilla who wordlessly pried Gertie's grip off of Ella's neck while a visible lump formed in Tobias's throat.

And then they were gone. The room fell into a choked hush.

❦

Margaret drove most of the way home hearing only the machinations of her automobile, the shifting gears, the rhythmic thump of tires, the engine threatening to sputter for more fuel.

"I want my children back," Mrs. Hershberger finally said.

"And my husband," Rachel said.

"I never thought I would say this," Mrs. Borntrager said, "but it's time for them to do whatever is necessary."

"Whatever is necessary for what?" Mrs. Mast challenged. "To bring our families home, or to do what is best for them in the long run?"

Margaret kept her eyes on the road. Beside her, Ella took in a long, slow breath.

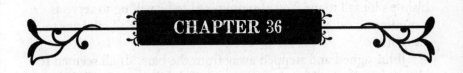

I t's the bishop!" Isaiah lurched toward the bars of the jail cell.

Gideon, who had been praying silently at one end of the bottom bunk, opened his eyes immediately and pushed himself off the bunk. Men in both cells lined up along the cell doors and watched a uniformed guard escort their spiritual leader into this forgotten corner of the *English* justice system.

"This is our pastor," Gideon said. "Please admit him."

The guard shrugged. "He's not on the list."

"What list?"

"I have a list of approved visitors on my desk," the guard said. "He's not on it. He stays on this side until your attorney comes."

Bishop Garber nodded. "It's all right. Mr. Eggar brought me in his automobile. He will park and then come in."

The guard withdrew to the end of the hall, and through the bars the bishop shook each father's hand with a prolonged grip.

"Bishop," Isaiah said, "have you come to tell us what we must do?"

"I have come to pray with you and for you," the bishop said. "You are caught between obeying God's command to submit to the government He has ordained and obeying God's command to train up your children in the way they should go. I don't make light of the decision you face."

The decision had become considerably more complex after six nights in jail. The men's resolve to act as one faltered more with each day away from their wives and children.

"When we were baptized," John Hershberger said, "we all promised to submit to the church. Bishop, if you tell us what to do, whatever it is, none of us would find shame in submitting to you."

The bishop shook his head. "I've never been that kind of bishop, and you know it. I didn't ask to be a minister, much less to have the bishop's lot fall to me. You also promised to be willing to serve as a minister, if called upon. In this situation, we must all minister to each other."

John sighed and stepped away from the bars. "It all seemed so clear in the beginning—at least to me. I didn't want my children in that town school. Now they will go to an *English* school whether or not I like it, so I might as well have them at home with me at night."

Chester Mast shuffled his feet.

"Chester?" the bishop said. "Would you like to speak?"

"We've come this far," Chester said. "We'll never know what might come of it in the end if we don't see it through."

Determined footfalls approached.

"Here's your Mr. Eggar," the bishop said.

Two guards accompanied the attorney and allowed all the men to file into one cell before withdrawing down the hall to monitor from a distance. The fathers leaned against the walls, eager for Mr. Eggar's report.

"I continue to work toward your release," Mr. Eggar said. "We have an arraignment hearing on Thursday morning. I've confirmed with the judge's clerk that we are on the docket and stressed that the delay is approaching the outside limits of 'unnecessary delay.' "

Gideon worked his lips in and out as he listened. The sheriff's department seemed to rely on the general ignorance of the Amish about specific rights within the legal system.

"What does that mean?" Jed asked.

"They'll formally read the charges, and we'll enter a plea of not guilty," Percival said.

"But we are guilty, aren't we?" John asked.

"We're not giving up," Percival said. "We want this to go to trial. That's where we get to make our case."

"What if we lose at trial?" Jed asked.

Silence fell.

"What if I said I would pay the fine and send my children to school?" John asked finally.

"Then you would plead guilty," Percival said. "Is that what you wish to do?"

"I know I want to go home to my family," John said. "What if the long way around is a lot longer than any of us imagined?"

Gideon stepped away from the wall, paced the center of the small cell, and turned in a complete circle.

"If Mr. Eggar determines that it is an option to pay the fine and obey the school laws," Gideon said, "then each man must decide whether this choice is in the best interest of his family."

"I want to go home," John said.

"I want to see it through," Chester countered.

The others stared at one another, silent.

❦

Margaret slept more deeply on Tuesday night than she had in weeks. It might have been simply because the day's emotions had exhausted her, along with the Amish mothers, but she preferred to believe she slept the sleep of the righteous. She had done the right thing. She had acted on behalf of the defenseless. She had cared for the—temporary—orphans and widows, just as the Bible told her to do.

The morning sky was still gray when Margaret left her home on Wednesday morning ready to resume her normal responsibilities at the school. If the substitute had encountered any difficulties or been unable to get through all the lesson plans, she would have left notes. Margaret wanted to review the situation long before her pupils arrived. The woman who worked in the school's office was always first to the building, making her rounds with the keys, and Margaret intended to be the second arrival.

In her classroom, she reached for the switch that would rouse the electric lights to overcome the dim gloom of early morning. Margaret had taught long enough in a one-room schoolhouse that was never electrified to be grateful for the transformation that came with the simple touch of her fingers. She scanned the room. The rows of desks were in satisfactory alignment, and on the center of her own desk was one white sheet of paper with neat script. Margaret pulled out the chair and sat down to read the substitute's report.

Four students absent on Tuesday, it said. One more than on Monday, and all with influenza. At least that was the substitute's opinion.

Steps in the hall so early—well before she expected any of the other teachers—startled Margaret, and her spine straightened as she cocked her head toward the open classroom door. A moment later, a man's form filled the space. Margaret rose to her feet.

"Mr. Brownley," she said. "Good morning."

"Good morning." Brownley stepped into the room. "I understand you were not present here yesterday."

"That's correct." Margaret's throat went dry.

"Now, Miss Simpson, you and I have known each other for some time now."

Brownley began to pace the perimeter of the room, a habit that irritated Margaret more each time she witnessed it.

"Four years," she said, though only in the last few months would the superintendent have recognized her as one of his teachers in any circumstances outside her classroom.

"And you are happy working for our school district?"

Margaret stretched her lips into a wan smile. "Quite."

"Then I must admit I find it confounding why you would put your position at risk as you have." Pace. Pace.

"I'm afraid I don't understand."

"Ah, but I believe you do." Brownley stopped moving at last and turned to face her, hands behind his broad back. "I have it on good report that you were seen yesterday driving off one of the Amish farms with a number of Amish passengers. This happened at a time of day you should have been here discharging your duties."

"I followed protocol in requesting the time away," Margaret said, "and made suitable arrangements for my classroom."

"I originally engaged your help to be sure the Amish students consolidated with minimal disturbance," he said. "I'm sorry to say your efforts disappointed me."

"Perhaps," she said, "if you had not taken matters back into your own hands without waiting for the benefits of the woman's touch you espoused to desire, I would have succeeded."

There. She'd said it. She might as well continue.

"You asked for my help, and I gladly rose to the challenge," Margaret said. "With a bit more time, I might have been able to assure the Amish families that our school administrators were capable of listening to their very reasonable concerns. Instead, you ensured that they would see me as no more than a puppet without even the strength of strings to do as it was told."

"Your job was to serve the interests of the committee." Brownley glared.

"I am a teacher, Mr. Brownley. My job is always to serve the interests of the children." Margaret returned the glare.

Brownley resumed pacing. When he reached the door, he turned once again face her. "Miss Simpson, when is your contract due to expire?"

"Not until June 30."

"Ah." He put one hand on the door. "You do understand that there are always extenuating circumstances that may void a contract."

The door closed behind him. Margaret dropped into her chair, trembling but without regret.

CHAPTER 37

M y advice is to accept the offer." Percival Eggar looked at each man's face on Wednesday afternoon. His eyes settled finally on Gideon.

"It's what they always wanted," Chester Mast mumbled. "We've sat in jail for a week for nothing."

"I've spoken with your wives again as well," Percival said. "They are most anxious to have the children home."

"And the only way the children can go home is if we give in and put them in the town school," Gideon said.

"This is not the end," Percival said. "Everything that happened during the last week can work in our favor when we take the case to court."

"Court. I don't know." With seven people in the cell, there was no room to pace. Instead, Gideon lifted himself up on his toes and then lowered his heels.

"It's the next step," Percival said, his eyes insistent through his spectacles. "You file your own suit to establish infringement of your religious liberty and free speech rights. Sending the children to school will take the focus off the truancy question and allow us to explore the issues that can settle this question once and for all."

"Can we make an offer of our own?" Gideon asked, pushing up on his toes again.

"I'm not sure we're in a position to counter," Percival said. "We want to get you out of here."

"I want their promise that if we do this, our children will also be returned to our homes—today."

Percival nodded. "More than reasonable."

"Do they know you are thinking of a court suit?"

"I have not said so overtly," Percival answered.

"Then we do have something to bargain with. Tell them we will pay the fines and send the children to their schools. Then tell them you will delay the suit if they agree to sit down with our bishop and a few of our men to listen to our viewpoint. Perhaps we can still avoid starting our own legal action."

"Don't you want to settle this permanently?" Percival said. "This could be a landmark case."

"I do not wish to be a landmark," Gideon said. "I wish to be a father whose children are brought up in the nurture and admonition of the Lord."

"And if the authorities do not agree to such a meeting?" Percival said.

Gideon shrugged and looked around the cramped cell. "Then we speak of the court question again."

Murmurs circled the room.

"You all agree?" Percival asked.

The men nodded, and Percival called for the guard to let him out of the cell.

"I'll have to speak to the sheriff," he said, "and then see the judge. I don't know how long it will take."

"We'll wait."

A minute later, Gideon watched Percival disappear through a door.

The six fathers remained in one cell, some sprawling on bunks, some leaning against walls, some shifting their weight from one foot to the other and back again in a slow, swaying rhythm.

"Will we really go to court?" John Hershberger asked. "Will the bishop allow that?"

Gideon took in a slow, deep breath, praying it would not be necessary to answer John's question.

They waited.

Lunch arrived, and they picked at the trays.

They waited.

Someone came for the abandoned trays.

They waited.

Finally Percival's solid footsteps approached. All six men crowded against the bars.

"Get out of the way," the sheriff said, turning a key in the lock. He swung the door open. "Your attorney has taken care of the fines. You're free to go."

"And our children?" Gideon said.

"The paperwork is already in progress," the sheriff said. "We'll take you all home in a bus and send another for them."

"Thank you." Gideon was the first of the men to step out of the cell.

The sheriff pointed a warning finger. "Those children had better be in school tomorrow. I've already notified Superintendent Brownley. The principals will know to expect the return of their wayward students."

⁂

"How long?" Ella asked David. She laid a hand against Lindy's hot cheek.

"She felt fine yesterday," David said. "Then this morning, she didn't get up. I couldn't go to school and leave her like this."

"Of course not."

"I'm fine," Lindy muttered. "Just a little under the weather."

"A lot of students have been absent with influenza," David said.

Ella moistened her lips. She did not have to read *English* newspapers to know that influenza had decimated Cleveland, thirty miles away. Authorities had closed schools, theaters, and even churches in an effort to contain the disease. She looked again at Lindy. Perhaps it was not influenza.

"We should call the doctor." Ella glanced toward the telephone in the front room.

"No doctor," Lindy said. "I'll be right as rain tomorrow."

Ella doubted this. And if David stayed out of school, the authorities might take him to the Wayfarers Home for Children along with the others.

"David," Lindy said, gasping for sufficient breath. "I want the new birdhouse. I'll feel better later, and I can paint it in the kitchen."

"I'll get it when you're ready," David said.

"Get it now, please."

Ella nodded at David, certain it would do Lindy no good to get worked up in a minor argument.

"I'll get another cool cloth," Ella said. She went into the kitchen, found a drawer of small towels, and tentatively turned the knob next to the faucet. Water coming straight into the house certainly would have advantages. Cold water drenched the towel, and Ella wrung out the excess. As she filled a glass with water as well, she wondered how quickly influenza might infect the Amish. Had she already invited germs into her own body by touching Lindy? What about the men in jail? The children at Wayfarers? The students in the consolidated schools already experiencing absences? When Cleveland closed its schools, towns like Seabury ought to have done the same.

Ella was not going to leave Lindy suffering because of her own fear that she might catch the disease—if it even was influenza. Without hesitation, she carried the damp cloth and the glass of water to Lindy's bedroom.

David returned just as Ella coaxed Lindy to sip the water.

"It's not there," he said.

"My birdhouse is gone?" Lindy pushed away the glass. "Has someone smashed in *again*?"

"No," David said. "There's no sign of vandalism this time. But there are a few things missing. And I found this on the workbench."

He handed a note to Ella.

You're getting what you deserve. Stop helping those people.

"That's it," Ella said. "I'm going to see Deputy Fremont."

"What does it say?" Lindy asked.

Ella ignored the question and turned to David. "You're staying here, right?"

He nodded.

"Fluids," Ella said. "Whether or not it's flu, she needs fluids. I'll be back."

Ella marched through the Seabury blocks until she reached the sheriff's outpost. Deputy Fremont looked up and raised an eyebrow. Ella pressed the note flat on the desk in front of him.

"Someone left this for Lindy Lehman," Ella said. "Is this not grounds for further investigation?"

Fremont glanced at the note. "How do I know where the note came from?"

"I just told you. Someone left it for Lindy. David Kaufman just found it on her workbench—and more items are missing from her workshop."

"Why isn't Lindy here on her own behalf?" Fremont asked.

"She's ill."

"Not the influenza, I hope."

"'I suppose that would be for a doctor to say."

"Is the boy ill?"

"No," Ella said. "Not so far."

"I can't go where there's flu," Fremont said. "That will only spread the sickness."

"But someone is threatening Lindy," Ella said, "and it's because of her kindness to the Amish in the school question."

"That's a moot point now." Fremont nudged the note to one side of his desk. "I just had a phone call from Chardon. The men have agreed to send their children to school."

❧

Finally Gideon's farm was in sight, the familiar roll of ground under barren trees wrapped in a warning of the winter to come. Had it snowed while he was in that windowless cell picturing his children crying themselves to sleep or his betrothed hustling between Rachel's bereft spirit and Miriam's frail health?

The truck did not make the turn down his lane. Instead, the driver, wordless, stopped where the paved road gave way to gravel in one direction and simply waited for Gideon to disembark. Gideon shook the hands of the two remaining passengers, supposing their throats to be as thick with anticipation as his own. He had taken nothing with him when the sheriff came last week, and he carried nothing with him now. One of three horses in his pasture noticed him and trotted to the fence, where Gideon scratched its neck. Then he turned his head toward the house. With each step, he hoped for an outburst of some sort. Savilla impatient with Gertie. Pans clattering from the kitchen. Miriam chastising chickens who had dared too close to the front porch.

But he heard nothing, which only made his chest clench more deeply.

Without going in, Gideon rounded one side of his home and followed the path to the *dawdihaus*. He knocked softly. The door swung wide, and Miriam tumbled into his embrace. When she pulled her neck from the curve of Gideon's neck, she shouted for James, who emerged from the bedroom and strode across the sitting room.

"A cake!" Miriam pronounced. "We need a cake. I'll put jelly between the layers."

Gideon laughed and tried to pull her back, but Miriam was already headed out the door to the main house where she kept her best baking dishes.

"There's no stopping her now," James said.

"I was afraid she might be unwell," Gideon said.

"She is," James said quietly. "In an hour, she will refuse to admit how tired she is."

"Then we should stop her," Gideon said. "I don't need a cake."

"No, but she needs to make you one."

They had ambled outside as they spoke, and now Gideon raised his head to the welcome sight of the Hilty buggy traversing the hardened cold ground. He ran to greet Ella, and she leaped off the bench into his arms and leaned fully against him. Her winter bonnet slid off her head, and even through her prayer *kapp* Gideon could smell the invigorating scent of her hair. He inhaled and wrapped his arms around her, resolving not to be the first to disturb the embrace.

Finally, without letting go of him, Ella turned her face up. Gideon kissed her mouth before she could release the torrent of questions rising through her throat. She tasted of the brisk air she must have been gulping all the way to his farm.

"The children?" she finally said.

"Not yet," Gideon said. "But they promised today."

Arm in arm, they went inside the house, where Ella deftly took over the responsibilities of stirring cake batter, arranging wood to produce the proper temperature, and setting the pans in the heat.

When the pans came out of the oven and the children were not home, the mood sobered.

When the cake was cool enough to frost and still the children were not there, silence shrouded the darkening kitchen.

Gideon watched the sky grow gray. James coaxed Miriam into the front room where she could rest more comfortably. Ella frosted the cake and sat down at the kitchen table beside Gideon.

"I want to be here," she said, leaning against his shoulder, "but. . ."

"But Rachel is waiting alone," Gideon said. He kissed the top of her head. "Go. If Seth comes home, you will know my children are also home."

"I'll come first thing in the morning," Ella said. "I know they have to go to school, but I can't wait all day to see them."

Gideon walked Ella to her buggy for a reluctant good-bye. Then he followed the buggy up the lane and watched her disappear around the curve in the road. He stood for ten silent gloomy minutes, praying that it would be God's will for the sheriff to keep his word, before he saw the flicker of an automobile headlight.

Then came the sound of the motor.

Then came the shadowed shape of a bus.

Then came the cries of his children's voices.

Then came the tumble of arms and legs of his offspring safe in his embrace.

＊＊＊

Margaret never liked to admit to favorites among her pupils, but the sight of Gertie Wittmer back in her seat, swinging her feet, warmed Margaret with satisfaction. Beside Gertie, Hans Byler sat straight and attentive. Even with his hat on his head, Margaret could tell it would be weeks before his hair would grow back out to a proper Amish boy's haircut. At least they had not cut Gertie's hair. Her braids still wound neatly against the sides of her head.

But even with Gertie and Hans back, the number of students absent from Margaret's classroom had risen to five. In a sober impromptu meeting with all the teachers after the final bell, Principal Tarkington relayed the somber news that Geauga County officials were dispatching nurses to make the rounds and determine the severity of the influenza outbreak that had reached even Seabury.

Margaret gathered her things and walked the six blocks to her house, which had grown cold in her absence. She turned the knob on the radiator in the front room and heated the oven in the kitchen.

She had promised Gray a pie. Probably the last one. Perhaps

they would not even get so far into the evening as to eat it. His last visit to her home had ended in an argument. What might he be expecting tonight?

When she had the pie in the oven, Margaret found she could not bring herself to sit quietly and wait for Gray. The sun was long set, but Margaret did not care. She donned a coat, took a bushel basket from the back porch, lit a lantern, and pulled dead growth from the spent flower bed along the side of the house.

She had expected to have time to straighten herself up before Gray's arrival, but he startled her with an early appearance. Surely it was not seven thirty yet. She pulled her gardening gloves from her hands and raised her fingers to her cold cheeks. In the darkness, he drew near.

Margaret wanted him to kiss her. This might be the last kiss in her entire life, and in this moment, she wanted it very much. His warm breath settled on her face as he leaned in, and she willingly raised her lips to meet his. His kiss deepened, more than ever before, and she allowed it. Once they began to speak, the exquisite moment would be gone, and she might never know another like it.

Finally, dizzy with the truth she must speak, Margaret pulled away.

"I have to tell you something," she said.

His hand on her waist, he sought her mouth again, but she stepped back, her knees weak.

"It's important," she said. Her words raced. "I took the Amish mothers to the Wayfarers Home for Children. I didn't think it was right to keep them apart, and I went to their farms to pick them up and drive them over there."

He put a finger on her lips. "I can forgive that."

Margaret took another step back. She had not asked for his forgiveness. In fact, she felt no need for repentance. Her lips parted in preparation of saying so when the thrash in the bushes made them both turn their heads.

Margaret bent to lift the lantern on the ground beside them. Gray lunged toward the noise. Someone had stumbled and fallen into the overgrown hydrangea bush and was now flailing in a foiled attempt to find the way out. Gray reached into the shadowed mass with one long arm.

"Braden!" Gray said as he pulled the intruder into the light of Margaret's lantern.

Margaret's eyes rolled to the flour sack Braden gripped in one fist. This time she did not hesitate to snatch it away from him and pull it open.

"These things belong to Lindy," she said. She tipped the open end toward Gray.

Gray pulled the lapels of his brother's jacket. "What are you doing with someone else's property?"

"What is it to you?" Braden's eyes flashed. "The Amish are no friends of yours, either."

"Whatever happened in the past," Gray said, his jaw barely moving, "there is no call for this."

"If Lindy Lehman had married our farmhand, he never would have run out on me."

"That's water under the bridge," Gray said.

"I'm just paying her back for ruining my life. I could still be on the farm instead of selling for half what it was worth."

"You could have hired another hand, but you're so mean no one wanted to work for you."

"Do you mean to tell me this is all over some old grudge?" Margaret twisted the top of the flour sack closed. "I'm going in to telephone the sheriff's department."

Saturday's quilting bee had even more children underfoot than usual. None of the mothers whose children had been away wanted them farther than the women could call. Even Seth, Tobias, and the Mast boys were there on the Glick farm with instructions not to wander off. Fortunately for the older boys, a creek ran through the Glick property, and as long as they could stand the brisk temperatures, Ella was certain they would occupy themselves. If they got cold, they could retreat to the barn and find something to do there. Hans Byler, though, was required to remain at his mother's side in her place around the quilting frame that filled most of the room. He leaned against his mother with one hand on her back. Under ordinary circumstances, he might have been whispering in her ear that he wanted to go play with the bigger boys, but Ella was fairly certain that the six-year-old was right where he wanted to be.

"They're not required to ride the bus," Mrs. Mast said. "They're only required to be in school."

"It's a long way to walk." Mrs. Hershberger held up a needle to the light to find its eye with her strand of white thread.

"My boys are old enough to take a buggy on their own," Mrs. Mast said. "They would have room for others."

Gertie sat on a chair between Ella and Miriam with a square of fabric on which to practice her stitching. Hans was nearby. The stair-step Hershberger children dotted the room. Perhaps the *kinner* ought not hear this discussion.

"Isaiah said he is going to take ours himself," Mrs. Borntrager said.

Gideon had said the same thing—either he or James would transport the three Wittmer children. Tobias had handled his first two days in the consolidated school well. The teachers had given him a long list of assignments to get him caught up to the other pupils. Gideon still hoped it would only be a matter of a few weeks before the Amish would be in their own school.

"Let's talk about something else," Miriam said, for which Ella was grateful.

"We have a wedding coming up." Mrs. King's eyes twinkled. "Less than a month to go."

Mrs. Hershberger smiled behind one hand. "Shh. We aren't supposed to know until the banns are published in church."

Ella carefully poked her needle through the block she was quilting. Mrs. Hershberger was right, according to tradition, and Ella usually shied away from being the center of attention. Maybe her wedding memories would always include the shadow cast over her engagement by the new education laws, but she hoped not.

Rachel laughed heartily aloud, a sound Ella had not heard for weeks. "Of course the banns will be published," she said, "but it's time to buckle down and get the house ready, so it will hardly be a secret what's going on."

From there the conversation turned to the usual tasks of preparing a home for a wedding—moving the furniture, scrubbing down the floors, arranging the food. Ella listened but said little. Everyone seemed relieved to be talking about something normal.

Ella pulled her needle up through the layers of backing, batting, and quilt top and turned to glance at Gertie.

The girl's chair was empty.

"Miriam," Ella said, "where did Gertie go?"

They both looked around.

"I'm surprised she sat still as long as she did," Miriam said.

Ella pushed the end of her needle into the quilt to mark her spot. "I'm going to find her."

Gertie might have gone outside, and she didn't want the child playing alone along the frigid creek. Instead, she found Gertie swinging her feet below the kitchen table while the tip of her tongue poked through one corner of her mouth. Gertie was bent over a sheet of paper, pushing a thick pencil.

"Gertie, did you get into Mrs. Glick's things?" Ella sat down across from Gertie.

"It was on the table," Gertie said. She stilled her hands in her lap.

Gently, Ella slid the paper away from Gertie. "You should have asked if you needed something."

"It's just a list for the mercantile," Gertie said, "and everything was crossed off."

Ella didn't see the mercantile list on the back side of the sheet. She saw only a meticulous rendering of the quilt pattern the women were working on in the other room. Ella knew little about art, but she had studied enough drawings of birds to recognize a close likeness when she saw one. The detail. The shading. The proportions.

It seemed to Ella to be as close to the real thing as one might hope for, apart from a photograph that an *English* might take.

"Are you going to show it to *Daed*?" Anxiety crossed Gertie's face.

Ella licked her lips. She wasn't sure. Gideon would not be pleased, but she was on the brink of marrying him. Keeping secrets about his children hardly seemed the right thing to do.

The kitchen door opened, and Rachel bustled in. "I've got to go. Mrs. Byler is not at all well. I'm going to take her home."

Ella stood up. "I'll go with you."

"No need," Rachel said. "I'll just make sure she gets home and come back. There's plenty of quilting yet to do."

Rachel left, and Ella turned to Gertie. "Let's go back and help with the quilt." She folded the drawing in half and tucked it under the bib of her apron.

"It's the flu the soldiers have been bringing home from Europe, now that the war has finished," Mrs. Mast said as Ella took her place around the quilt frame.

Ella thought of finding Lindy hot and clammy a few days earlier. James had been to see Lindy and assured Ella she was mending. If Mrs. Byler had the flu, how many others would fall to it? A quilting bee had seemed like an innocent return to Amish friendship after the tension of the last few weeks. Now Ella was not so sure.

Gideon hardly knew what to think. His six-year-old daughter had created a stunning drawing of a traditional Amish quilt pattern. As a boy, he had slept under one very similar that his own mother had stitched.

"It's like a picture in a library book," Ella said.

The children were upstairs. The girls were supposed to be sleeping, and Tobias working on school assignments. James and Miriam had just withdrawn to the *dawdihaus*. Soon Gideon would tell Tobias that he was taking Ella home.

Only a few more weeks, she told herself, and no one would have to fret about how she would get home on a night heavy with winter air. She would already be home. Right here in this kitchen, with her husband beside her. Then they could talk all night if they wanted to.

"She has a gift, Gideon," Ella said.

"It's not the kind of gift our people are used to," he said. "It's the kind of gift that may lead to pride in what she has done—something that others cannot do."

"But it's beautiful, just as the quilt itself is beautiful," Ella said. "How is it so different?"

"The women quilt for practicality," Gideon said. "We need warmth."

"Then why don't we just sew together squares of burlap?" Ella countered. "Couldn't we stuff them with old copies of *The Budget* and be just as warm?"

"The beauty in a quilt is a thanksgiving for God's provision of our need," Gideon said. He put a finger on the drawing. "This is a vain display."

"We hang quilts over racks," Ella said, "or on walls. Even spreading a quilt on top of a bed is a way of displaying it. It's all beauty that comes from God's hand. Is it so wrong for Gertie to learn her own way of this same beauty?"

Gideon scratched under his beard. "Last summer she was drawing in the dirt with a stick. Even then I could tell she saw more than other children. And then there was the picture from school."

"What picture?"

Gideon left the room and returned a moment later with Gertie's self-portrait. He laid it on the table beside the quilt drawing.

"We must help her know what this means," Ella said, looking from one drawing to the other. "If she grows up afraid of it, we may lose her."

Gideon took the hand Ella laid open on the table. "You are the mother's heart my children need."

She smiled, and he leaned across the table to kiss her.

"Now I must go check on Miriam," Gideon said. "Then I'd better get you home."

With their coats buttoned up against the dropping temperatures, they walked together to the *dawdihaus*, where lamps still glowed within.

James and Miriam were sipping tea in the sitting room. Miriam was sitting up, and her bright eyes greeted them. Ella exhaled relief. She had been afraid that the long day of quilting, which Miriam had refused to curtail, would have worn her out.

"I trust Mrs. Byler will recover quickly," Ella said.

"I hope it's not the influenza," Miriam said. "It would be so much nicer if she is unwell because she is with child."

"Time will tell," Ella said.

"Speaking of influenza," James said, "I wish we had word about Lindy. I'm going to town first thing Monday, as soon as the Sabbath is over."

"David would let us know if she took a turn for the worse," Gideon said. Even without using a telephone number to call, a boy savvy enough to find a way to school in town right under his parents' noses would find a way to send a message to Lindy's family.

⚜

James scrutinized Lindy's movements on Monday. She hardly limped at all. The forced bed rest necessitated by the flu had probably been good for her injured ankle. And five days after Ella found her stricken with sudden illness, Lindy seemed determined—and able—to return to her routine. She poured coffee for both of them while she told the story of Margaret Simpson catching Braden Truesdale red-handed with a bag of wooden toys from Lindy's workshop.

"It's as if he thought he was invincible," Lindy said, "parading around the neighborhood like that a whole day after we discovered the items were missing."

"And the note?" James said.

"It was handwritten," Lindy said, "so it was easy enough to match up to Braden's handwriting. Even Deputy Fremont managed to get a confession."

"But why?" James wanted to know.

"Braden doesn't like the Amish, and I'm the closest person he knows to the Amish." Lindy added milk to her coffee.

"Lindy," James said. "I'm you're *onkel*. I know when you're not telling me everything."

Lindy stirred white milk into black coffee, her eyes set on the resulting caramel color.

James waited.

"I could have married, you know."

James would wait, no matter how slowly Lindy wanted to unfold the truth.

"When Peter Kaufman was courting Rachel, I used to go riding with a young man named Ezekiel. His father had all sons and Ezekiel was the youngest. He had no land left to give Ezekiel, so Ezekiel looked for other work so he could save up a down payment on his own. He hired himself out to the Truesdale farm."

"Truesdale? A farm?"

Lindy nodded. "Ezekiel worked there for years. Gray moved into town, and his parents died within months of each other. The truth is, Braden wasn't much of a farmer. He just liked living out in the middle of nowhere all by himself. It was Ezekiel who kept the farm running."

"So what happened?"

Lindy looked down into her coffee. "He wanted to marry me. I said no. He moved to Kansas. I moved into town."

"And the farm?"

Lindy shrugged. "Braden lived out there on his own, I guess. But he never found another man who would put up with his eccentric ways. Last year I heard that the farm sold to a young Amish couple from Illinois."

James folded his arms across his chest. "Braden must have known who you were."

"I don't know why he would."

"I'm sure Ezekiel talked about you," James theorized. "Braden knew your name. He blames you for losing his farm."

"That's ridiculous."

"Of course it is. That doesn't mean it's not true."

"But *Onkel* James, I never even met Braden Truesdale. I would not have known him if I met him on the street."

"That's what he was counting on. When he moved into town, he discovered you were here. Everyone in town knows you and your crafts. It can't have been hard to find out where you live, especially after David moved in. He still dresses Amish. Anyone could have followed him."

"I would never do anything to endanger David." Lindy's voice cracked. "He's the closest thing I'll ever have to a son of my own."

"I know."

"Even if you're right, it's over." Lindy pushed her coffee away, untouched. "He's not out there skulking anymore. I won't need to look over my shoulder every time I leave the house."

"Where is Braden now?"

"He spent a night in the jail in Seabury before being transferred to Chardon to see a judge. I suppose that will happen today or tomorrow. He already confessed, so it's only a matter of what his sentence will be."

Braden deserved to be in jail for a long time. "Perhaps he will leave town when he gets out," James said.

"Margaret will certainly be watching out for him."

"She's done so much for us," James said.

"It has cost her dearly. I don't expect to see Gray around the neighborhood anymore. He may not be the unstable brother, but he's no friend of the Amish, either."

James sipped coffee and then set the cup down carefully. "What have we done to offend them so?"

Lindy shrugged. "Sometimes all it takes is being different."

James sat silently, looking over Lindy's shoulder to the view outside her window.

"One day we will forgive them for all they have done," Lindy said softly. "Braden, Brownley, Fremont—all of them."

"You have a big heart," James said.

"I'm not so un-Amish that I don't understand the power of forgiveness."

James pushed his cup away. "The important thing is that you are on your feet again. I promised to make deliveries."

"I have a few things that Braden didn't find," Lindy said. "But before you go, tell me how *Aunti* Miriam is."

"Good days and bad." James stood and adjusted his hat. "I don't like to leave her for too long. I'll make the deliveries and then head back to the farm."

"There's a meeting with the school board this afternoon." Lindy set her coffee cup in the sink. "Will you be there?"

"I'll have to see." James doubted he would leave Miriam on her own again that day.

Margaret had not been invited to the late-afternoon meeting of the school board and representatives of the Amish families, but that was the least of her concerns. She closed up her classroom—still five pupils absent—and marched down to Main Street to the building where Mr. Brownley conducted such meetings. In the hall, she paused to compose herself before slipping into the room where the meeting was already in session.

"This is a closed meeting," a young man said.

Margaret recognized him. He worked in Mr. Brownley's office. He had popped up from a seat in the rear of the room where he had been taking notes on a yellow pad.

She smiled pleasantly and said, "I believe I'll stay."

"The men in this room are quite capable of conducting themselves without your assistance," he said.

Annoyance welled, but Margaret contained it.

"I am an appointed member of the consolidation committee," she said. Her official resignation letter was folded in an envelope in her satchel, but she had never submitted it. "I'm quite sure you know who I am, and I assure you I will not bite if you simply permit me to sit beside you."

Margaret lowered herself into a stiff-backed chair against the back wall. With a huff, the young man picked up his pad and began scribbling, no doubt documenting her unwelcome intrusion.

She was relieved to see that Percival Eggar had insisted on meeting around a table, rather than the usual arrangement for school board meetings, where the board members sat in elevated chairs behind a long wooden desk and townspeople were left to present their positions from behind a railing, as if in a courtroom.

Mr. Brownley spoke from the front of the room. Naturally he had taken the seat at the head of the table.

"We agreed to this meeting," he said, "and we will keep our word. But I must warn you that I see few grounds—if any—for altering the arrangement the law demands."

Margaret ground her teeth. He had gotten what he wanted. The Amish children were in school. Now he had the gall to persist in his unflinching position even after he agreed to hear out the Amish fathers.

Percival Eggar spoke from the other side of the table. Margaret was glad to see he had chosen his seat in a manner that balanced Brownley's position.

"We will now begin presenting our case," Percival said. "We understand this is not a courtroom, and we trust that you will honor your word to hear us out."

"I don't have all day," Brownley muttered.

Percival was unperturbed. "We have a number of people who wish to speak, beginning with Bishop Leroy Garber."

The bishop rose and stood behind his chair. "Thank you for agreeing to meet with us. We are peaceful people and have no wish to antagonize anyone. You have acted in what you believe to be the best interests of children for whom you are responsible—on one level. This motivation is one we can admire. However, we respectfully disagree with the belief that what is best for your children is also best for ours. We ask that you hear not only our words, but also our hearts. I have asked Gideon Wittmer, one of the fathers whose children are affected by this crucial decision, to present the substance of our religious views and how they bear on our views of public education."

Margaret wanted to applaud. She had never met the Amish bishop before, and no doubt Percival Eggar had coached him carefully, but she found his speech stirring even if it was merely a preamble to what Gideon had to say.

The bishop seated himself, and Gideon stood. Margaret laid her satchel flat in her lap and settled her hands against the leather.

"We find joy in work," Gideon said simply. "We find joy in

working with our hands, in laboring along with animals created by God, in tilling the soil, in cultivating our gardens. And we find joy in caring for one another, worshipping together in our church district, building together, harvesting together. We find joy in living apart from the ways which seem more 'normal' to you so that we may seek with all our hearts to be closer to God."

Margaret leaned forward, watching Gideon closely as his feet began to wander away from the table.

"Nature is a garden," Gideon continued. "Man is caretaker. God is pleased when man works in harmony with nature, the soil, weather, cares for plants and animals. Christian life is best maintained away from cities.

"We are preparing our children for eternity. Your concern is to educate them for life in the twentieth century, but our concern is that they be prepared to serve God both in this world and the next. The education you propose to offer them—to demand for them—will teach our children to despise the work which we have thrived on for hundreds of years. Colossians 2:8 warns us, 'Beware lest any man spoil you through philosophy and vain deceit, after the tradition of men, after the rudiments of the world, and not after Christ.'

"It is our firm conviction that education beyond the eighth grade, which will lead our children into philosophies of this world, will not prepare them for eternity. Instead, it will lead them away from the ways of the people who know them best and love them most. How will advancing in the ways of this world be in their best interests if it takes them away from their own people?

"Because of these convictions, we cannot separate what we wish our children to learn in school from what we also teach at home. We do not put our religion in one stall of the barn and our learning in another with a wall in between. All of life is in God's hands, and it is there we wish for our children to abide."

Gideon found his chair again. Margaret let out the breath she had been holding, lest even this slight sound distract from Gideon's message. It was Percival Eggar's turn to stand.

"Gentlemen, as you can see, the Amish religion is not about believing something on Sunday and setting it aside for the rest of the week. The Amish truly *believe*. The course that Mr. Wittmer has so ably described is their way of following God. It is their deeply felt faith. I ask you, how can the freedom to demonstrate their beliefs in their actions be denied them in a place like America, which was founded on such liberties?"

✌✦✦

"You should have gone," Miriam said to James. "It would have made the most sense for you to stay in town all day."

James shook his head. "What would I have done all day?"

"You could have stayed at Lindy's and you know it," Miriam said. "You should be at that meeting. You only came home because you think you have to look after me."

James lifted the lid on the soup pot, trying not to think about how much of the afternoon Miriam had spent chopping the vegetables and browning the meat. At least she had done most of the work in the small *dawdihaus* kitchen. If she needed to, she could go lie on the bed for a few minutes. But moments ago the bus had dropped the children off at the top of the lane, and now Gertie pressed up against him.

"Are we going to make biscuits to go with the soup?" Gertie asked.

"Maybe there's some bread in the bread box," James said.

"But I like biscuits," Gertie said. "I like when they are fresh from the oven."

"We can make biscuits," Miriam said. "But let's do it in the big house. Then we can put them in the oven the minute your *daed* and *Onkel* James come home from the meeting. By the time they get washed up, it will be time to eat."

Over Gertie's head, James narrowed his eyes at his wife. He had planned to be at the meeting alongside Gideon, but he had already seen Miriam pausing to catch her breath three times that afternoon.

Gertie tugged on Miriam's hand. "Let's go now."

Miriam stumbled slightly, catching herself against the sink.

"Gertrude," James said softly. Instantly, she dropped Miriam's hand and crossed her wrists behind her waist.

"I didn't mean it," Gertie said.

"I know." James reached for the girl's hand. "Let's go see what your brother is up to."

"Lessons and lessons and more lessons," Gertie said.

This was true. Gideon had spoken somberly with Tobias about

908

his responsibility to represent the Amish well by working hard to catch up with the weeks of school he'd missed, even though they all hoped he could leave school soon. But between Tobias and Savilla, surely they could manage Gertie for a while.

"I'm fine," Miriam said. "Leave her be."

But James led Gertie back to the main house. He would get her settled within eyesight of Tobias and then he would make sure Miriam rested for a few minutes.

"I'm sorry, but Rachel isn't home," Ella said when Lindy turned up at the Hilty farm. "I know she'd be so glad to see you well enough to make a visit. Can you wait for her?"

"When do you expect her back?"

As she always did when she visited Rachel, Lindy had exchanged her *English* men's trousers for a modest skirt and blouse. It seemed to Ella that despite living in town among the *English* and taking up a livelihood usually left for the men, Lindy never strayed too far from the rich hues of Amish dyes in her clothing.

"She took a meal out to the Bylers," Ella said. "Mrs. Byler was feeling poorly on Saturday, and none of their children is old enough to cook properly."

"I pray she is better soon," Lindy said. "I admit I'd like to rest a bit myself. I feel so much better than I did that day you found me, but between you and me, I'm not quite myself yet."

"Please sit down," Ella said, gesturing toward the davenport.

Lindy sank into the cushions. "I wanted to tell Rachel in person how well David cared for me. I had to insist that he go back to school this morning. He's such a tender boy."

"Let me get you a glass of water," Ella said. It couldn't have been wise of Lindy to drive all the way out here on her own.

"Actually," Lindy said, waving off the offer of refreshment, "I'm glad I caught you. James came to check on me this morning and make a few deliveries. I got the idea that Miriam is not as well as she might be."

Ella sighed. "I'm not sure what to make of her. James says she has good days and bad days, but I think more likely she manages to push through better on some days than others. I do as much as I can. It will be easier after the wedding."

"Let's go see her," Lindy said. "I have my car. It won't take us ten minutes to drive over there."

"Are you sure you're up to it?"

"It's only a few miles. I'll rest better myself if I know Miriam is all right."

Ella nodded. "Let's go."

Ella felt as if she had barely settled herself into the automobile seat before Lindy pulled onto Gideon's farm.

"Let's try the *dawdihaus* first," she suggested.

James answered the door, but Miriam was right behind him.

"Well, now, there's a sensible solution," Miriam said.

Ella and Lindy looked at each other and then at Miriam.

"This old fool ought to be at that meeting in town," Miriam said, "but he refuses to leave me. He thinks I'm going to fall into the soup pot or something."

"It's too late now," James said. "By the time I get there, the meeting will be over."

Miriam rolled her eyes. Ella laughed nervously.

"Ella can stand guard," Miriam said. "You'll have no excuse to stay. We'll go over to the big house and make sure Gertie minds herself."

"I'd be happy to," Ella said.

Miriam pointed at Lindy. "And you, my dear niece, can drive your stubborn *onkel* into town in your motorcar while there's still a chance for him to hear what is happening at that meeting."

Lindy grinned. "I'll crank it up."

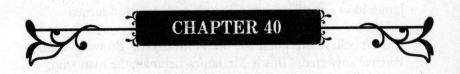

CHAPTER 40

Had the young man always been so arrogant?

At the whispered pronouncement that the meeting was nearly completed and spectators were not being admitted, James merely stared at the young man. No one could mistake James for anything but an Amish man, and denying admittance to the Amish would defeat the point of the meeting. James nodded slightly at Margaret Simpson and stepped past the young man.

As he approached the table, his eye on an empty chair, Superintendent Brownley scowled.

"You have presented some interesting ideas," Brownley said, "but I am afraid I've heard nothing that allows me to interpret the law in a way that excuses your children from regular school attendance at least until the age of sixteen."

James watched the faces of the other members of the school board. At least one of them appeared sympathetic, though James could not be certain what was going through the man's mind.

Percival Eggar cleared his throat. "You may be right, Mr. Brownley."

Amish brows furrowed around the table.

"You may be correct that this question is beyond the scope of your authority to decide."

"I have wide authority," Brownley said. "I assure you I don't take my responsibilities lightly."

"I would never accuse you of such a thing," Percival said. "But it seems clear after today that the question is one for the courts."

"That's an extreme measure." Brownley shifted in his chair.

"I am prepared to represent my clients right through to the Supreme Court of the United States, if that is how they will find justice and the freedom to exercise the religion of their choice."

James blew out a loud, heavy breath, and attention turned toward him.

"I don't believe this guest has been introduced," Brownley said.

Percival answered, "This is Mr. James Lehman, the man who first engaged my services on behalf of the Amish. I would be quite interested in what he has to say at this juncture."

Brownley leaned back in his chair. "Very well."

Percival nodded at James, who looked from Percival to Gideon. What had the others already said?

"I'm at a disadvantage," James said. "I was not able to be present for the earlier portion of the conversation."

"That's no problem," Percival said quickly. "We will all benefit from your individual expression of your views."

"All right, then." James adjusted his hat. Miriam hated that nervous habit. "We accept that others do not believe as we do. We do not judge or try to convert anyone who does not come to us sincerely seeking to follow God and with a willingness to make whatever sacrifice that requires.

"Our work, whatever it may be, is for the welfare of the community we share. We do not seek individual prestige. Jesus said, 'My kingdom is not of this world.' The apostle Paul said, 'Be not conformed to this world.' Our people seek to believe these statements wholeheartedly, as the true word of God."

James glanced at Percival, uncertain whether to continue. He had not intended to speak at all. Surely Gideon and the bishop had explained these matters.

"Please go on, Mr. Lehman," Percival said.

"As I'm sure you have already heard," James said, "we do not separate school from life. But how can our children know this connection if we send them from our world into a world far from our homes to learn from teachers who know nothing of our ways? And if they are trained for a way of life that is at odds with our community, then how are they to know where they belong? Have any of us served the best interests of the children if we create this confusion for them?

"It is our firm belief that eight years of schooling, close to home and focused on the basics of reading, writing, and mathematics, suffice for preparing our children to contribute to the community to which they belong. Beyond this, public schools impart worldly knowledge that is not useful for living spiritually in this life and for all eternity."

James swiftly pulled out the empty chair and occupied it. From the back of the room came the sound of two hands patting each other with enthusiasm.

❧❧❧

Margaret rose to her feet, letting her satchel slide to the floor, and applauded with as much gusto as she could muster. Around the table from which she had been excluded, every head turned in her direction. One pair of startled eyes after another fixed on her.

"Bravo, Mr. Lehman," she said. "Bravo."

Mr. Brownley let one hand fall heavily against the table. "Miss Simpson, please contain yourself."

At first, Margaret pressed her lips together, but before a single second passed, she began to march to the front of the room.

"I cannot hold my tongue any longer," she said. "Have you not heard the fine rhetoric of Bishop Garber, Mr. Wittmer, and now Mr. Lehman? Does it not strike you that each of these men has achieved an impressive level of articulate expression without the benefit of education in a consolidated school? I cannot think of a more remarkable illustration of the power of values that come from the heart, rather than a textbook."

"Thank you, Miss Simpson." Mr. Brownley glared, as he always did. Scowl and glare, scowl and glare.

Margaret ignored him. "Mr. Brownley originally asked me to serve on the consolidation committee. My approach was very different than his, however. While at first I was eager to present the virtues of our town schools and the many benefits the rural students would enjoy, gradually I realized the error of my way. If the Amish children are to have any benefit from attending our schools, it can only come if we make an effort to understand them.

"I am a classroom teacher, and I have spoken with teachers of other grades. It has been clear to all of us that the Amish children are more than capable of completing the work we assign, which is a credit to the Amish families and a testament to the schooling they received in the smaller settings that we have arrogantly come to regard as insufficient. I have not heard one account of an Amish child instigating a disturbance among the students. In contrast, I am ashamed of some of the town children, who have been rude bullies intent on ridiculing people they don't know just because they are different. And where, I ask you, did they learn such behavior?"

Margaret stared hard at Mr. Brownley, then moved her eyes with deliberation to the other members of the board.

Mr. Brownley pushed back from the table and stood up. "Miss Simpson, I must ask you once again to contain yourself. This is not a matter for you to decide."

"Isn't it?" Margaret retorted. "Would you rather it go to the Supreme Court, as Mr. Eggar suggests, than we learn from our Amish friends and find a way to care for our own? If the state truly wants what is best for the Amish children, we will listen to what the parents have to say. We will find a way to work together, rather than at odds."

"Please take your seat." Brownley nearly growled.

Margaret glanced at the chair she had abandoned against the back wall. Then she walked to an empty chair between two board members and sat down.

Gideon could hardly believe that Miss Simpson was capable of such oratory, and in the presence of men. He watched Brownley carefully.

"I must insist that we return to some semblance of order." In his chair again, Mr. Brownley shuffled papers in front of him. "I fail to see how threatening to take a local matter to the Supreme Court of the United States accomplishes anything. We all know that such a process takes years."

"I have all the patience in the world," Percival Eggar said. "I will ensure that my clients receive due consideration."

"My hands are tied, Mr. Eggar," Brownley said.

"We would be glad to help you untie them, Mr. Brownley."

Gideon moistened his lips. "May I suggest what I consider to be an ideal solution?"

"Please do, Mr. Wittmer," Brownley said. The words were correct and polite, but Gideon had no confidence the superintendent would see the virtue in his proposal.

"As you know, we already have a school building that was constructed at no cost to the public school district, the town of Seabury, or the county of Geauga."

Brownley's eyes narrowed, but he was listening.

"All we ask now," Gideon said, "is permission to operate a private school to serve Amish students."

"It seems to me that is what you already attempted," Brownley said.

Gideon nodded.

"But your teacher was not qualified."

Actually, Ella was well qualified. Gideon said, "It has been our intention all along to attract a teacher whose credentials the state would recognize. I regret that this process has taken longer than I had hoped, but it is still the course of action we intend to pursue."

"Surely," Margaret said, "this is a reasonable compromise at least for the younger children."

"But this teacher would not be Amish," Brownley said.

Gideon kept silent. This gathering was not the place to reveal the fullness of his middle-of-the-night wrestlings with almighty God.

"Perhaps," Percival said, "all we need at this point is your agreement that the Amish families will be unhindered in their pursuit of establishing a private school. I will work closely with them on the necessary legal details."

"Suppose we were to agree to this proposal," Brownley said. "Am I correct in assuming that such a school would only go through the eighth grade?"

All the Amish fathers at the table were quick to nod.

"Then we will have solved only half of the problem," Brownley said. "I cannot recommend to the state authorities a solution that does not guarantee that the older children will also receive an appropriate education."

Gideon was well aware of this dilemma. Next year Tobias would be old enough for high school. Even if the girls were safely in the care of a teacher who understood the Amish ways, Tobias would be expected to enroll at the high school—unless Gideon insisted that his son remain in the eighth grade for three years.

"With all due respect," Percival said, "the point my clients—and Miss Simpson—have argued today is that for Amish children, completing the eighth grade *is* an appropriate education."

Brownley shook his head. "But the law is specific. Students must attend school until the age of sixteen."

"Unless they have work permits," Percival said.

Gideon's shoulders straightened.

"We are not talking about children who will be idle or unsupervised," Percival said. "They will not be lurking around the streets stirring up trouble or burdening society. When the Amish students leave school, they take up their share of work on the farm or in the family business. In fact, it is my understanding that the labor they provide is essential to the financial success of Amish enterprises."

Percival glanced at Gideon and the bishop, who both nodded.

"If they have work permits and demonstrate that they are in fact working, students between ages fourteen and sixteen may be excused from school."

Gideon marveled that Percival had not mentioned this to him before.

"That seems a stretch," Brownley said, predictably.

"Not to me." For the first time, a new voice spoke.

Gideon looked across the table at a member of the school board who had remained in Brownley's shadow for the duration of the meeting—and for all the weeks preceding.

"I think we should consider that possibility," the board member said.

Gideon looked around the table. Chester Mast and Isaiah Borntrager had allowed smiles to form behind their beards. Miss Simpson was grinning.

"I will prepare a full presentation," Percival said. "My assistant will contact you to establish a date to meet and ensure that every point of law has been adequately covered in our agreement."

❧❦❧

"I heard what you did."

Gray's words did not surprise Margaret. That he would speak them at all had been uncertain in her mind for all of the preceding twenty-four hours, but she had known he would hear of her bold actions on Monday afternoon. All of Seabury must have heard by the time they finished dessert on Monday evening. Margaret would not have been startled to discover her presence at the school board's meeting had made the headline of the Seabury newspaper.

And now here was Gray, leaning casually against the brick wall of the school as he often did, as if he just happened to be there when she exited the building.

Few occasions in her life had stolen her words, but this was one of them. She stepped an extra foot away from him, out of the circle of his scent. She would need her wits about her.

"I had hoped you'd gotten it out of your system when you took those mothers out to the home," he said.

Margaret's throat went dry. "I've only done what I truly thought was the right thing to do."

"Speaking at that meeting, Margaret? What were you thinking?"

In their last conversation, he had said he could forgive her for getting involved with the mothers. They had not gotten so far as establishing that she was not sorry. She wasn't sorry then, and she wasn't sorry now.

"If I. . .caused you any. . .embarrassment," she said, "please know that was never my intention."

He turned his head to one side and chuckled. "And we thought the ladies at church were gossiping about us just for sitting together in worship."

"Yes. I suppose they've moved on to more consuming matters now."

"Why is it so important to you that you would. . ."

"You can say it, Gray. Why is it so important that I would risk the fondness that has taken such gentle root between us?"

"You have a prettier way with words than I ever will," he said, "but that's the gist."

Margaret gripped her satchel handle with both hands, bracing herself to look Gray in the face without wishing he would take her face in his hands and kiss her persuasively.

"Who else was standing up for them?" she said.

"Maybe they didn't need anyone to stand up for them." Gray shuffled his feet. "I thought they liked to mind their own business."

"I wish you could have heard them speak yesterday," Margaret said. "They want nothing more than to care for themselves and do what is best for their families and their church. *We* are the ones who wouldn't let them."

"Things change, Margaret. This is not the sixteenth century anymore—or even the nineteenth."

"I know. But their *children*, Gray. The sheriff's department took their *children* just to send a message about who was in control. I suppose that was the last straw for me."

"It's over now, isn't it?"

"I hope so. We'll see if Mr. Brownley will keep his word."

Gray shrugged. "They have Percival Eggar now. They won't need you."

Margaret reached into her satchel and pulled out an envelope. "I'm going to drop this off with Mr. Brownley now. It's my official letter of resignation from the consolidation committee."

"Does it even matter now?"

"Maybe not to the superintendent. It matters to me. I don't want anyone thinking for even one more day that I in any way approved of the tactics used against the Amish."

"Then that's that," Gray said. He inched closer. "We won't ever have to talk about this again. We'll look back on it as a disturbance and nothing more."

"We'll look back on it." He still offered hope. He would still have her.

But the strings already constricted her heart. He would have her because he believed nothing would ever prompt such behavior from her again, or because he believed that once they married she would better adapt to the decisions he would make for the both of them. That he would indulge in this wishful thinking revealed how firmly he had begun to regard their futures as intertwined, and this thought softened her posture.

"I'm sorry, Gray." As soon as Margaret spoke the words, she recognized the space they left for misinterpretation, so she continued quickly. "I'm sorry to disappoint you. I'm sorry I hurt you. I'm sorry that I won't get to bake pies and wait for you on Thursday evenings or sit beside you in church."

I'm sorry I won't be your wife.

I'm sorry we won't grow old together.

I'm sorry I let you hope for this long.

The Amish children would never be behind them, but between them.

Ella stood for a moment on Wednesday outside the schoolhouse before going in, savoring her mind's image of children carrying their lunch buckets and books, arriving to greet the teacher and begin the day.

She turned toward the touch on the back of her shoulder. Gideon's approach had escaped her perception, but the sight of him warmed her.

"What are you thinking?" Gideon asked.

"I was imagining the school open and thriving," Ella said, looking at the man who would soon be her husband. How good God was to turn Gideon's heart toward Ella.

"We *will* thrive," he said.

"We just need a teacher."

His answer came a few seconds later than Ella expected. "God will provide."

She allowed silence to linger as they gazed at the schoolhouse and Gideon's fingers grazed hers. Only three more weeks and she could be in his arms every day. Every night.

"It will be odd not to have *English* students like the ones we knew when we were children," Ella said. "Sally Templeton and I sat side by side for four years. I sometimes wonder whatever happened to her."

"High school, I suppose," Gideon said.

"Yes, no doubt." Sally would have gone to high school in town about the time Ella's mother passed away. Ella had always expected to take her share of the farm chores after she finished school, but having to keep house for her father on her own was a startling surprise. Not a day had passed in the last twelve years that Ella did not think of her mother and how her own life might have been different if her mother was still the woman keeping house and tending children on the Hilty farm.

Ella looked around. "Where are the *kinner*? I thought they had the afternoon off of school for the Thanksgiving holiday tomorrow."

"Miriam insisted Gertie would be underfoot here," Gideon said. "The sensible thing was to keep them all home. James is coming later."

"In time for the meeting?"

Gideon nodded. "We should go in."

They walked together down the gentle slope. Chester Mast had propped open the door, and his sons were carrying in a set of shelves.

"A place to put the lunch buckets and coats," Gideon said. "This time when we open, we'll be more than ready. Percival says we must not give Mr. Brownley any reason to suggest that we are falling short even in a small way."

Inside, while the Masts debated the most useful position for the heavy shelving, Ella and Gideon exchanged one last smile before parting. Gideon crossed the room to join the men stacking wood for the stove in one corner, and Ella joined the women organizing supplies.

"Here's Ella now," Rachel said.

Lindy stood beside her friend, looking more stable on her feet than Ella had judged her to be two days ago.

"Ella," Lindy said, "did you find it more useful to keep extra paper for the pupils in the teacher's desk or in a separate cupboard?"

Lindy gestured, and Ella's eyes widened at the wide cupboard on the side wall.

"It's lovely!" Ella said. The young woman who accepted a position teaching here would have every reason to be pleased with the schoolhouse and its furnishings.

"It's probably a good thing we had nothing like this when we were girls," Rachel said. "I would have hidden in the cupboard to avoid spelling tests."

Lindy laughed. "And I never would have told the teacher you were there."

"What about when you were a teacher?" Rachel asked. "Did you have students like that?"

Ella drew a startled breath. How had she forgotten Lindy's years in the classroom? Ella had been ten or eleven, old enough to remember her teachers. What else had she blotted out in the years after her mother's death?

"I was never a teacher." Lindy waved a hand. "It was all my parents' idea. The *English* teacher needed an extra pair of hands with the little ones, so I came in to help. I was sixteen, and my parents didn't know what to do with me after. . ."

Ella knew the unspoken end of Lindy's sentence. After she decided that she did not want to be baptized and join the Amish congregation as an adult member.

"Did you think about becoming a teacher?" Ella asked.

Lindy shook her head. "Rachel married Peter Kaufman when we were nineteen, and it was time for me to make my own way. Marriage was not for me. I moved to town and started selling small crafts."

"You've done well," Ella murmured. She stepped toward the cupboard and ran her fingers over the smooth pine finish. Surely Gideon knew Lindy had once assisted a teacher. He must. Lindy was his sister-in-law. Betsy would have told him. Ella glanced across the room at Gideon, who was stoking the woodstove. The room was chilly, and he would want it warm enough for the meeting that everyone would be attentive.

Someone opened the front door again, and cold air whooshed into the schoolhouse. Ella shuddered against the sudden sensation and, like everyone else, looked to see who had arrived.

"It's Miss Simpson," she said, surprised.

Margaret's arms overflowed with books and binders, and Ella rushed to catch the items threatening to topple off the precarious stack.

"I've brought things a teacher might like to have," Margaret explained as she divested her load on the nearest desk. "This will be such a nice place to teach. So cozy!"

The room was warming nicely, and Margaret shed her coat.

"I have some old textbooks for the younger children that have plenty of wear left in them. After all, learning to read doesn't change much, does it?"

Ella picked up a thick gray binder. "Neither does making sums, I guess."

"Those are old lesson plans," Margaret said. "They worked well for me when I taught in a one-room schoolhouse. Maybe another teacher would find them of help in getting started."

"I'm sure any teacher would be grateful to have all this," Ella said.

"Any progress on the search?"

Ella shook her head. "The teachers college has no candidates to recommend at this point in time. Apparently Gideon was about to respond to an inquiry when Deputy Fremont arrested him. When she didn't hear back from him, the candidate took another position."

"That is unfortunate," Margaret said.

Margaret flipped open a binder and began explaining its contents. Ella listened politely but not attentively. All of this would make sense to a trained teacher, so Ella did not need to absorb the information. Instead, she wondered whether Margaret had burned her bridges with the school district. Would she be seeking a new position? After all Margaret had done for the Amish families, Ella could think of no solution more perfect.

"Margaret," she said.

"I know what you're thinking," Margaret said without looking up from the binder. "But I don't expect Mr. Brownley will be eager to continue our association, and if this school is going to succeed, the last thing you need is a teacher he regards as an adversary."

Ella swallowed back her hope. Margaret was right.

"What will you do?" Ella asked.

"My sister writes me letter upon letter about how much she misses me," Margaret said. "I'm thinking of returning to Columbus next summer."

A stone of disappointment sank down into Ella's abdomen. She raised her gaze at the somber sound of Gideon's voice.

"Let's gather," he said.

❧❧❧

"As you know," Gideon began, "we are here today because all of us would like to see our own school open as soon as possible."

The nods Gideon expected greeted him.

"An Amish teacher would be best," he said, "and I'm sure you would agree that we are opening a school in the first place because we want the best for our children."

He dared not meet Ella's eyes. Not in this moment. Not when his resolve must not fail.

"That's a cockamamy idea," Aaron King said. "We tried that. It got us arrested."

"A *qualified* Amish teacher," Gideon said. "Even Mr. Brownley would not object to this teacher, because she would demonstrate beyond question that she is more than capable for the job."

Lindy stood up. "I would like to volunteer to teach."

Chester Mast shuffled his feet. "I don't understand," he said. "What qualifications do you have?"

Gideon hoped that having the school on Chester's land would not make him feel he had a particular role above the other parents in the decisions they faced. They would need to form a proper school committee made up of several fathers.

"It's true I haven't been to teachers college," Lindy said. "But for two years I did assist an *English* teacher. I went to a one-room school myself. I understand the environment. I am willing to become qualified if Mr. Eggar can determine a route to qualification other than the teachers college. I might be a bridge between the school board and the church."

"But how long would that take?" Joshua Glick asked.

"Perhaps there is some sort of probationary status," Lindy said, "some way they could let me teach while I prove myself."

Gideon had not expected Lindy's offer. He let his eyes drift to Ella now. Even when she began teaching his daughters and a few others, the plan had always been to find a permanent teacher. The stack of correspondence with the teachers college, on his desk at home, proved this intention. Only the last letter mattered now.

We are unable to assist you further at this time, it said. *We will of course retain your inquiries, and perhaps next summer we will have a recommendation for you when we have new graduates.*

When Gideon began writing to the college, he had hoped for any teacher who might come to a classroom where all of the students were Amish. Only later, within the confines of the small cell he shared with the other men, had his thoughts turned in another direction.

When the church gathered next and the worship service ended, Jed Hilty would rise and invite the entire congregation to his youngest daughter's wedding. How could Gideon speak aloud the thought that pressed more firmly into his mind each day?

He did not want to break Ella's heart.

❧❦❧

Leaning against the wall, James watched heads angling toward each other and listened to the buzz that rose.

It was an enthusiastic buzz, the sort of sound that filled a space with hope. And after the last few weeks, the people in this room deserved hope.

"I know some of you are uncomfortable with me," Lindy said. "You may even wonder why I am here. I chose not to be baptized into the Amish church. I moved to town. I drive an automobile. I have a telephone. But a teacher from the teachers college would do all those things as well. The difference is that I understand you. I *know* you. I *know* what is in your hearts for your children. You may see the differences between us, but I see the ways our hearts are still one."

It was a speech that made James's chest swell. This was his niece generously offering to set aside the quiet, orderly life she had made for herself to serve the community that had raised her.

But it would not do.

"Well," Isaiah Borntrager said, "we ought to carefully consider this matter. Mr. Eggar has assured us that he will help us see this through. Surely he will uncover some provision in the law that would work in our favor."

Mrs. Hershberger spoke up. "It does seem the next best thing to having one of our own members teach."

"And it might go well for her because she is not Amish," Aaron King said. "Mr. Brownley might be more willing to come to an agreement with a teacher who is not Amish, but Lindy would not teach what we do not wish our children to learn."

"I promise to work closely with the parents," Lindy said.

James caught Gideon's eye. Gideon's nod was so slight that no one else would have discerned it, but James did.

"Might I speak?" James pushed his weight off the wall and

turned his face toward his niece. "Lindy, you are offering a sacrifice that tells me once again what I have always known. Your spirit is right with God, and you love His people."

"*Onkel* James," Lindy said. "I want to do this."

"I believe your heart. But in my judgment, if we are going to demonstrate that we are capable of educating the children of our own community, we must have an Amish teacher from the start."

"I am Amish," Lindy said, "in language and culture and history—all the ways that will matter in the classroom."

James said nothing. Telling his niece that she lacked one qualification, the most essential one in his mind, did not come easily.

"A member of the church," Isaiah said. "That's what you mean."

James met Lindy's eye and nodded.

"I don't see a problem," Isaiah said. "Lindy did not break her baptismal vows. She never made them. She can still be baptized and join the church."

Still James said nothing.

"I have a strong faith," Lindy said quietly.

"Then you will have no trouble with the baptismal vows," Isaiah said.

"If Lindy wants to join the church," James said, "of course we will welcome her. But it's a serious decision. We cannot ask her to stand among us now and make such a promise."

Lindy sat down.

"I'm tired of fighting," John Hershberger said. "If we can have our own school and an understanding teacher, that's enough for me. In my mind, she doesn't have to be a church member."

"We cannot keep having the same discussion—dispute—with Mr. Brownley on this matter," James said. "It is imperative that we prove once and for all that we can teach our own children. Then let him test them and see how well they have done. We must be above reproach. If we have an Amish teacher and the children do well, the matter will be settled."

"Teachers get married," Cristof Byler said. "That's what started us down this road in the first place. We'll just end up back here."

"Right now all we need is the first Amish teacher," James said. "That will give us time to prepare other young women who might feel the call to serve God and the church this way."

The heads turning toward Ella did not escape James's notice.

The door opened and cold air gusted the length of the structure.

"Tobias," Gideon said.

James lurched two steps away from the wall.

"You said to come if *Aunti* Miriam. . ."

CHAPTER 43

They kept vigil. James and Gideon and Ella.

Miriam had appeared well enough on Wednesday morning, other than the fatigue that had been growing for months, but was stricken suddenly in the afternoon, moments before Tobias turned up at the schoolhouse. The ache in her legs had made her surrender to the comfortable chair in the corner of Gideon's kitchen. James had found her there when he rushed home from the schoolhouse meeting. She made a pretense of irritation that Tobias had raced off needlessly, but her protest was insincere when James half carried her to her own bed in the *dawdihaus*. Still, if Miriam had a choice in the matter, she would not have sent for the *English* doctor. But James insisted, and Gideon rode into town and the doctor arrived.

Unquestionably, it was influenza.

Even robust young men were felled within hours by the virulent strain that had circled the globe in the waning months of the world war. In fact, the doctor reported, the young experienced more severe symptoms than the elderly. The important point to remember, the doctor emphasized, was that most people made a full recovery.

Lindy had recovered.

A week after her illness, Mrs. Byler was still weak but recovering.

In the throes of watching his wife's suffering, James prayed for God's mercy. *Most people* did not give him the reassurance he sought. The medicines the doctor left seemed to bring no benefit.

No Thanksgiving turkey baked in the oven on Thursday. Miriam's fever raged. Her arms ached, she said. Her head ached. Her legs ached. No, she did not want to eat. She wanted another quilt. She wanted no quilt at all.

On Friday, Gideon encouraged the children to eat the food Rachel carried over, but the adults had no appetite. Miriam coughed most of the day. When she spoke, raspy, it was to complain how sore her throat was.

James left Miriam's bedside only when he had to and only for a few minutes at a time. Gideon tended to the animals. Ella kept Gertie occupied and periodically set out cold food for the children. James, Gideon, and Ella rotated through the bedroom of the *dawdihaus* determined that Miriam would not spend a moment alone, even when she slept. When she woke, and was not thrashing against the pain of her ailment, they coaxed water, tea, or a bit of bread into her.

James sat alone with Miriam in the abating shadows of Saturday morning, his elbows propped on his knees and his head hanging between his hands.

Had he brought this home after visiting Lindy in town or going to the meeting with the school board? Had someone coughed on him in the mercantile, and he carried the disease home to Miriam while his own body fought it off? Had Miriam been too close to Mrs. Byler, who had succumbed last weekend but was improving?

Gottes wille.

He prayed to accept God's will. But he prayed for God's will to deliver his beloved.

Gertie whined about not being allowed to see Miriam, but somber Savilla understood the gravity. If Gertie turned up at the *dawdihaus* door, Savilla would be right behind her to tug her back to the main house. Ella scrubbed everything she could think to clean in both structures.

James had always worried what would happen to Miriam if God should call him home. Somehow he had never imagined that Miriam would be the first to see the Savior's face.

Gideon slipped into the room. James looked up.

"She seems to be resting better," Gideon whispered.

"In and out," James said. "I persuaded her to sip some tea before she fell asleep again."

Her breathing was too shallow. James's hand on her cheek told him her temperature was climbing again.

"Maybe you should have something as well," Gideon said. "Mrs. Borntrager brought food."

James shook his head. He would not leave. Not now.

A gasp from the bed startled them both. Almost immediately, Miriam exhaled heavily. James knocked over the chair in his rush to get three inches closer to Miriam. Her eyes fluttered but did not open. James waited for her to take another breath.

"Miriam," he said, jiggling her arm.

She moaned, but she opened her mouth and inhaled.

The door opened. James did not take his eyes off Miriam. In his peripheral vision he saw Gideon reach for Ella's hand.

Miriam's chest fell slowly. James inhaled in harmony and held his breath, waiting for Miriam to release hers.

No rush of air came, no leaking breath, no rise of the rib cage. Finally James could hold his breath no longer and emptied his lungs against his will.

This time when he jiggled Miriam's arm, she did not moan.

Outside, the sun broke the horizon.

＊＊＊

Gideon's tears burned the backs of his eyes. They had burned this way five years ago, when it was Betsy's eyes that fluttered but did not open, Betsy's chest that fell but did not rise.

Grief blurred memory then as it did now.

Had it been fair to send a boy not quite fourteen years old to tell the nearest neighbor? Ella had offered to go, but Gideon wanted her near. Tobias had done the job well, and the news spread across the Amish farms rapidly enough that church members streamed to the Wittmer farm in a steady flow throughout the day. They came first to the main house. Ella somehow enticed them to remain there, with only a few at a time walking to the *dawdihaus* to see James.

Some were relieved by the separation, lest they unwittingly take the influenza home from the *dawdihaus* to their own households. They preferred instead to express their condolences to Gideon. James made brief polite appearances at the main house between his long stretches of vigil beside Miriam. Ella and Rachel had bathed and dressed Miriam in her blue wedding dress and prepared her for the viewing. Gideon had seen for himself how most of the people who ventured to the *dawdihaus* to pay their respects chose to do so from a distance.

How many tens of millions had the influenza taken as it circled the globe? Why, in God's will, should Miriam, on a remote farm near a small town in eastern Ohio, be one of them?

Four men organized a crew to dig Miriam's grave not too far from where Betsy was laid to her final rest, and Chester Mast and his sons were building the pine casket.

The details had to be looked after. Later, James would be grateful that church members executed the traditions swiftly and capably, just as Gideon had been five years ago.

Unabashedly, after Ella pulled the sheet over Miriam's face, the two men embraced. Grief had brought them together when Betsy died and Miriam insisted she and James must help Gideon with his young family. Now grief bound them once again in the vacuum where Miriam's voice belonged.

The touch at Gideon's elbow made him jump, but it was Ella. Was it only eight hours ago that they had together witnessed a soul leave this world while they gripped the flesh-and-blood future they dreamed of together? Ella's face was drawn with exhaustion, emotion, efficiency. Gideon conjured a wan smile.

"Look." Ella tilted her head across the room.

Rachel, Lindy, and David were huddled in a triune embrace.

"Have they. . . ?" Gideon asked.

"Life is precious," Ella said. "Why should we waste any of it separated from people we love?"

"I'm happy for them," Gideon said. Even James would give thanks if reconciliation came out of this day that had wrenched his life inside out. Gideon had a vague awareness that he had not seen any of his own children in some time. He said, "Where are my girls?"

"Savilla has the Hershberger girls upstairs," Ella said. "I'll look for Gertie."

She started to move away but paused as the front door opened for the umpteenth time that day. Margaret Simpson stepped tentatively into the front room.

❧

Margaret felt out of her element. She knew nothing about Amish traditions upon the death of a loved one, and the extent of her relationship with Miriam Lehman was the conversation they had at the

Wittmer door last summer when Margaret had called and Gideon was not home. But in recent weeks Lindy had progressed from being a neighbor Margaret waved at to a friend she cared for, and Miriam was Lindy's aunt and Gertie's great-aunt. And Margaret felt some affinity for Gideon and the battle he led for the education of the Amish children.

Lindy crossed the room toward her and said, "I didn't know you'd come."

"It seemed only right," Margaret said.

After Lindy stopped long enough that morning to give Margaret the news before heading out to the Wittmer farm, Margaret reasoned that grief was grief. She did not have to be closely connected to Miriam to know that many others would feel the weight of a boulder on their chests today—and probably for weeks or months to come. In a black skirt and shirtwaist, at least Margaret did not introduce thoughtless color into a somber occasion. The men were in black suits and white shirts, and the women in black dresses and black aprons.

"You know a few people," Lindy said. "The mothers you drove out to the children's home will never forget your generosity."

Margaret spied Mrs. Borntrager standing next to the fireplace and Mrs. Byler firmly holding the hand of her young son. Hans shyly waved at Margaret, and she gave him a smile.

"I'll bring you something to eat," Lindy said.

"I don't need anything," Margaret said.

"There's plenty. Everybody shows up with food. In this way the *English* and the Amish are not so different."

And in which category did Lindy put herself? Her faith had been formed in the Amish church, yet she had not joined. And would not. If Lindy had decided that her offer to teach was a good enough reason to join the church after all these years, Margaret would have heard by now.

Margaret didn't see James, but Gideon appeared purely stricken. Perhaps by the time she reached him, the words she ought to speak would come to her.

"Margaret," Lindy said, her eyes filling, "it really was kind of you to come."

Margaret ran her tongue across her teeth behind her lips. "Is there something special I should say?"

"Speak your heart," Lindy said. "I'll be back with something to refresh you."

Margaret reminded herself that she was the same woman who stood up to Superintendent Brownley, the same woman who drove mothers desperate to see their children across the county, the same woman who said good-bye to a man she might have loved for a long time to come—because she had done what she thought was right for the people in this room.

Gideon never seemed to be left alone for more than a moment at a time. Margaret made her way through the crowd in his front room, listening to snippets of conversation. Most of it was in Pennsylvania Dutch. Occasionally an English phrase fell on her ears as someone slipped back and forth between the two languages. But Margaret did not need to understand the language the mourners spoke to understand the language of their hearts.

Words of hope.

Words of love.

Words of loss.

Words of tenderness and compassion and care and encouragement.

Why would anyone want to interfere with creating this sense of belonging for another generation? If she never did any other good thing with her life, if she never found another teaching position, if she never loved another man, Margaret would always know she had done the right thing for the families in this room.

❧❧❧

Ella first looked upstairs, supposing Gertie would want to be with Savilla and the other girls. But Gertie was not among the growing assembly in the girls' bedroom. Savilla's eyes bore a stunned stare. Ella had seen Savilla go upstairs with two Hershberger sisters, but now there were eight girls. Several of them, too young to discern what Savilla might be feeling on this day, giggled about something or other.

Rescue me, Savilla's eyes pleaded from the center of her bed.

Ella stepped into the room. "Savilla, would you help me find your sister?"

The nine-year-old swiftly unfolded her feet and took Ella's hand.

"It's a hard day," Ella whispered in the hall. "They don't know."

Savilla nodded, sedate. "I didn't get to say good-bye."

"I know. It was too dangerous."

"I don't care if I might get influenza," Savilla said. "You and *Daed* might get sick, and you were there."

Ella squeezed Savilla's hand. How could she explain that parents sometimes took risks themselves that they would not allow for their children? How could she explain that she and Gideon couldn't leave James alone? How could she explain that it might have frightened Savilla if she had seen Miriam at the height of her illness?

They started down the back stairs.

"I think I know where Gertie is," Savilla said.

"Let's go there together, then."

Savilla led the way through the kitchen and out the back door. On the final day of November, as the sun arranged its setting glory, the air was cold. As they passed the hooks on the back porch, Ella snatched a couple of shawls.

"She goes to the loft," Savilla said. "*Aunti* Miriam always told her not to go up there by herself."

Ella swallowed. Gideon would not approve of his rambunctious six-year-old climbing the ladder on her own. Even Ella didn't like to make the ascent.

Savilla was right, though. As soon as they entered the barn, Ella caught sight of Gertie's prayer *kapp*, a bright spot against the yellow and brown hues of the hay loft.

"I don't want to go up," Savilla said.

"You don't have to."

"Do I have to go back in the house?"

Ella shook her head. "Not if you don't want to."

"Can I go in the *dawdihaus*?"

Ella glanced out the open barn door. "Maybe we should talk to your *daed* about that first."

"I'll wait here, then." Savilla sat on the bench under the tack rack at the entrance to the barn. Ella wrapped a shawl around Savilla before taking in a slow breath, slinging the second shawl over one shoulder, and gripping both rails on the ladder. One step at a time she proceeded upward, resisting the temptation to look down.

Gertie sat up straight, surprised to see Ella come over the top of the ladder. Damp streaks striped her cheeks. Ella crawled around a bale and opened her arms. Gertie trembled in them as Ella wrapped her in the shawl. Ella pulled off the girl's loose *kapp* and stroked her head. They sat silently. Ella would wait as long as it took for Gertie to stop sniffling.

"Is it my fault?" Gertie finally said.

"No, sweet girl. It's not your fault."

"Maybe it happened because I didn't obey. That's what made *Aunti* Miriam so tired."

"No, Gertie, no. That's not why people get sick."

Gertie leaned into her, silent again.

"Why do people die?"

Ella knew she should say that everything that happened was God's will, but she could not make herself speak the words to a grieving child.

"I know my *mamm* died," Gertie said, "but I don't remember her."

The truth of the statement stabbed Ella.

"I don't remember her, so I don't feel sad. Sometimes that makes me feel naughty."

Ella kissed the top of Gertie's head. "That's because Miriam came and took such good care of you."

"Am I going to forget *Aunti* Miriam, too?"

"You're much older now," Ella said. "You'll remember more. And your *daed* and I will help you remember—and Savilla and Tobias and *Onkel* James."

Ella had feared she would not know what to say when she found Gertie, that it should be Gideon's role to comfort his child.

"Is your *mamm* dead?" Gertie asked.

"Yes, she is."

"Do you remember her?"

"Yes, I do. But I was a big girl when it happened—older even than Tobias."

"Do you miss her?"

"Every day," Ella said, her throat swelling. "I miss her because she doesn't know how much your *daed* loves me. I miss her because she doesn't know how much I love you."

Gertie snuggled in. "I'll help you remember your *mamm* if you help me remember *Aunti* Miriam."

"We'll take care of each other."

"You'll be my *mamm* now, and I'll be old enough to remember you."

"That's right. We'll be together a long time."

"Twenty days?"

"Much longer than that."

"No, silly," Gertie said. "*Aunti* Miriam told me you and *Daed* would get married on December 19. I've been counting, and it's twenty days."

"That's right," Ella said. "December 19."

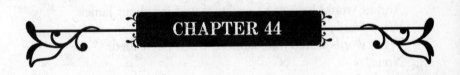

CHAPTER 44

*D*aed!" Savilla jumped up from the table. "The eggs are burning."

Gideon dropped the fork he was using to so patiently toast a piece of bread over the front burner. The implement bounced once and skittered across the kitchen floor while Gideon reached for a towel to wrap around the handle of the iron skillet where the eggs had quickly become inedible.

Before today, he had never felt unable to feed his own children. Fried eggs and toast hardly constituted a challenging menu.

His mind had been on James and whether, once the children were on the bus to school, he would be able to coax their great-uncle to eat something. The counters and icebox were still mounded with food left from the visitation on Saturday and the funeral on Monday. He should have let the children have whatever they felt like for breakfast rather than feeling obliged to prepare the breakfast Miriam would have given them.

It was bad enough that he was sending them to school today—and on the bus. Now their bellies might be empty as well.

Gideon set the skillet in the sink, where it sizzled in the half inch of water he'd forgotten to drain last night.

"How would you like ham sandwiches for breakfast?" he asked, tossing a loaf of Mrs. Glick's bread to the table and spinning around to get Mrs. King's ham from the icebox. He had already packed Mrs. Glick's roast beef in the lunch buckets.

Tobias picked up a knife and began slicing ham.

"Will Ella be here when we get home from school?" Gertie asked.

"I think so," Gideon said. After yesterday's service, she said she would be back to restore order to the kitchen, but Gideon maintained that there was no need for her to come as early as breakfast. He could manage.

And he would have, if he were not worried about James.

What words would suffice?

What words would have sufficed when Betsy died?

None.

But James must eat before he endangered his own health.

"Is it sixteen?" Gertie asked.

"Sixteen what?" Gideon muttered.

"*Daed*!" Savilla said for the second time in as many minutes. Gideon looked from one daughter to the other.

Tobias plopped a slice of ham on a plate and slid it toward Savilla, who cut a clumsy chunk of bread from the end of the loaf before passing both items to Gertie.

"She means the wedding," Tobias said. "Sixteen days until the wedding."

"Am I subtracting right?" Gertie asked. "December 19 minus December 3 equals sixteen days.

Gideon opened the icebox again, looking for nothing in particular but hiding his face from his offspring.

"Yes, you're subtracting correctly," he said.

"And then Ella will cook our eggs?" Gertie said.

Gideon dodged her question. "I promise not to burn them tomorrow."

"Maybe we should just have leftover apple strudel tomorrow," Gertie said, unconvinced.

"Finish your breakfast," Gideon said. "I'll drive you to the bus stop today."

When they climbed out of the buggy at the bus stop twenty minutes later, the bus already rumbling toward them, Gideon scrutinized his children once again and hoped he was not forgetting something that might embarrass them later. They had their lunches. The girls' hair was not as tidy as Miriam would have managed, but neither was it as disastrous as it might have been. Their *kapps* covered most of the mess anyway.

"We'll be all right, *Daed*," Tobias said. "I'll make sure they're all right."

"We'll get better at this," Gideon said.

"Sixteen days!" Gertie said.

Gideon pulled over to the side of the road and waited for his three to board the bus with the other children. Watching the bus grow smaller as the distance increased hardened his stomach, and he puffed his cheeks and exhaled slowly at what he was about to do.

"Gideon."

Ella's voice startled him as she stepped out from behind a tree on the side of the road. He had planned to go home first, to check on James.

And to muster his resolve.

But here she was. He saw now that her horse and cart were nearby.

"I told you to rest this morning," he said, "and not to come for breakfast."

"I didn't come for breakfast," she said. "I just wanted to make sure. . ."

"I know. Thank you." He got down from his buggy bench. "I want to talk to you."

She glanced around before turning her face up for a kiss. Gideon obliged, hoping Ella would not sense the regret in his lips.

"What's wrong?" She stepped back.

He held her hand, studying the spread of her fingers in his palm. "Ella, I think you should be the person who becomes qualified to teach at our school."

She pulled her hand out of his grasp and stepped back farther. "But Gideon—"

"I know. Sixteen days. Gertie is counting."

"Don't you want—"

He reached for her hand again and pulled her toward him. "Of course I do." With his hand cupping her chin, he held her face and her gaze.

"I don't understand. We can't. . .not if. . .especially now. . .after Miriam. . ."

"I know it's not what we planned," Gideon said quickly. If she came to his house today, she would see for herself the mess he had made of things, and it was only the first morning on his own. What would it be in a month or a year? "I wanted to talk to you last week, on the day of the meeting, and then Miriam got sick."

"We've hardly had a moment alone," she said.

"James is right. We need an Amish teacher, and it would be wrong to ask of Lindy what Isaiah suggests."

Fright passed through Ella's eyes.

Gideon inhaled and exhaled with deliberation. "I love you, Ella Hilty. And you will be my wife. We have our whole lives ahead of us. We must think about the community right now. Can we live with ourselves if we do what we choose only for ourselves at the cost to so many others?"

"But I've never heard of a woman who continued to teach in a one-room schoolhouse after she married. Even the *English* would not do that."

"I know," he said softly.

"But the children," she whispered.

"We'll talk to them together. Gertie will see you every day. You'll be her teacher!"

"Oh, Gideon."

Disappointment racked her features. What had he done?

"I'm not qualified," Ella said. "They'll never approve me."

"Mr. Eggar tells me there is a test you can take. Mr. Brownley has agreed to administer it next week."

"Next week!"

"If you pass it, you will receive provisional qualifications. They will test the children in June to determine their progress. I *know* you can teach the children what they need for their test."

"Next week, Gideon?"

He kissed her. "This changes nothing between us except the date that will appear on our marriage license."

⸎

"I have to think. To pray."

Even in the morning chill, heat flooded Ella, and she let her shawl drop from her shoulders. Gertie was not the only one counting down the days until the wedding. Her trunk was half packed to move to Gideon's. They had waited for Jed and Rachel to marry and settle in. They had watched other couples marry as soon as the harvest ended. It was their turn. Ella was ready to marry. Her siblings, scattered in other districts, had made arrangements to travel. Rachel, even amid the distractions and travails of the last few weeks, was slowly scouring and rearranging the house for a winter wedding.

This winter.

Now Gideon wanted to wait—how long?

"Of course you should have time to think," Gideon said. "I'm sorry that circumstances mean I had to blurt out my thoughts so clumsily. But Mr. Brownley will want a prompt answer, or he may put off the test date for weeks, even months."

"I don't even know what I need to study to be ready for a test next week," Ella said. Panic welled. "Even if I did agree to finish out this school year, what about next year?"

If Gideon and James were set on an Amish teacher, would they not merely postpone the question? How long did Gideon expect Ella to wait? Who else was willing to take the test next?

"You ask wise questions. I wish I had all the answers," Gideon said. "But sometimes we must walk along the path looking only at the light on each step."

Ella's chest heaved, and her narrowing throat held captive the words spinning in her mind.

"No Amish teacher will have the formal training the state looks for," Gideon said. "The point is to demonstrate a teacher doesn't need it—that she can teach what the children need in her own way. Perhaps all your years of reading library books, and all the times your father allowed it when others might have disapproved, have brought us all to this moment."

Ella's lungs burned.

"I'll go," Gideon said. "You asked for time."

She nodded.

"Will you come to the house later—whatever your answer?"

Another nod. Sentences collided in Ella's mind, their phrases tangling up in each other. Gideon turned to his buggy, hoisted himself in, and picked up the reins. As his horse began the habitual responses to Gideon's signals, Ella slowly walked back to her own horse and cart.

The horse neighed and she scratched its ear before arranging herself on the bench. Gideon had turned the corner and was out of her range of vision.

Ella squeezed her eyes shut, flushes and chills taking her by turn.

Gottes wille. How could she know God's will? Was it even possible?

Was it God's will for Nora Coates to marry and stop teaching, or her own desire?

Was it God's will for the roof of the old school to fall in? Would it have been God's will if Gertie had been hurt that day?

Had it been God's will for Chester Mast to build a school on his land, or stubbornness to have his own way?

David's rebellion. The vandalism in Lindy's shop. The arrests. The children taken to the home. Influenza. Miriam.

Was it all God's will? Would this precise moment have come if any of these things had not happened?

The horse began to move, tugging the cart to the left. Ella opened her eyes.

"Whoa," she said, fumbling for the slack reins.

But the horse continued, and by the time Ella had a firm enough grip on the reins to pull the horse where she wanted it to go, she laughed aloud.

The horse knew the way to Gideon's farm, a route Ella had taken countless times, especially in the last few months. Perhaps even this moment, when a restless horse presumed to know the human mind, was part of God's plan.

Ella had never known such a prompt answer to prayer.

She and Gideon could have forty years together, a dozen children, dozens of grandchildren.

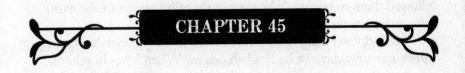

CHAPTER 45

You can do this." Margaret shifted a pile of books to the right.

Ella had moved into Margaret's house three days ago when she agreed to take the examination. Every morning, before Margaret left the house to teach her own class, she assigned Ella new topics to study and arranged the relevant books on the dining room table.

"My mind is overflowing," Ella said. "I can hardly tell the difference between the seventeenth century and the eighteenth."

"You're doing very well," Margaret said.

"I have to sleep sometime." Ella squeezed her head between her hands. She had expected this week to be busy and next week to be worse—with wedding plans. Instead, she spent three solid days reading and making notes. In the evenings, under electric lights, Margaret quizzed her.

"We'll rest on the Sabbath," Margaret said. "Or at least we'll limit ourselves to conversing on these matters without resorting to opening the books. But it's only Friday evening. We have all day tomorrow, and then Monday and Tuesday before the exam on Wednesday."

"I can't learn all of this," Ella protested. "You went to high school and then the teachers college. You had years to absorb all of this."

"And you check out more books from the library than anyone in Seabury," Margaret responded. "It's only a matter of organizing what you already know."

Ella had always thought of herself as one of the most organized people she knew. Looking around at the piles of paper on the dining room table, she concluded she had misjudged the last twenty-six years.

"We have the questions that have been published in the newspaper for the last five years in three different counties of Ohio." Margaret thumped the stack of old newspapers that the library had allowed them to borrow. "We are not shooting arrows in the dark. The questions on your test will be very similar."

"That doesn't help!" Ella said. " 'Trace in early American literature some influences of its English origin.' When I was in school, our parents approved everything the teachers assigned. I didn't learn how to answer a question like that."

Margaret slid three sheets of paper out of an American history textbook. "You've already studied my college notes and outlined a fully suitable answer."

"But I haven't actually read any early American literature." Ella picked up a newspaper and said, "And how about this one? 'How does the knowledge of a scratch on the hand reach the brain? Would knowledge of an injury to an internal organ locate so accurately the place and nature of the hurt? Does the brain control the processes of the internal organs?' "

"Basic science," Margaret said. "You read veterinary books all the time because you find them relevant to caring for farm animals. Think about how you would care for an animal showing signs of sickness."

"At least I know this one," Ella said. " 'Name three kinds of corn and discuss each in such a way that they may be recognized by the description.' Now that's something every Amish pupil needs to know."

"You'd be surprised how many teachers would have to study for that one, yet you know the answer. You can do this."

Ella blew out her breath and set a fresh sheet of paper in front of her. "Let's keep going."

"That's the spirit."

They pored over the questions listed in the newspapers, reviewed basic mathematical formulas and their applications, and studied standard vocabulary lists. Ella filled one page after another with notes.

Mark diacritically: cafe, sacrifice, Panama, Sahara, Colorado, psychology, perfected.

A piece of work costs for labor $233.75, the workmen receiving wages *at the rate of $1.50 for a day of 9 hours. What would the same work cost if wages were $1.40 a day of 8 hours?*

Show how the environments of the American colonies were conducive to union.

Mention three principal mineral products of (a) England and (b) the Rocky Mountain region of the United States.

Discuss distillation and fermentation.

A man bought 50 cords of wood for $225 and sold 15 percent of it for $45. What percent was gained on the part sold?

Why was the destruction of the public buildings of Washington in 1814 by the British condemned?

What cargo would a ship be likely to carry from Odessa to London?

A and B engage to do work for $170. A worked 3 days more than ⅝ as long as B, and received $70. How many days did each work?

Show accent and sound of vowels of the following adjectives: reputable, estimable, Philippine, recreant, imitative. Use correctly in sentences the five words.

Give a model for parsing a noun, an adjective, and a verb.

Explain Standard Time.

Describe muscles as to uses, kinds, forms, structure, and motions produced.

For every question that gave Ella confidence, another drained hope. Science, mathematics, history, language. The arithmetic question bouncing constantly to the front of her mind was how many hours remained until the time of testing.

⚜

On Saturday, Margaret cooked a hearty, filling breakfast. Lindy joined them for constant quizzing and looking up answers. They drank one pot of coffee after another.

Ella wondered what Gideon was doing that morning. What Gertie really thought about the idea that if Ella passed this test, she would be Gertie's teacher rather than her *mamm*. Whether Percival Eggar had another legal strategy up his sleeve if Ella failed. How dreadful it would be to learn that she failed only by a point or two.

On Sunday, Ella stayed home while Margaret went to church. Then they bundled up against the brisk wintry air, donned sturdy shoes, and went for a long constitutional, which Margaret claimed was refreshment for the mind as well as the body and during which she worked a range of academic topics into conversation.

On Monday, Margaret returned to her own school, leaving Ella once again to study amid the stacks of textbooks and notes written in Margaret's neat script from her college years.

By Tuesday morning, Ella could not absorb one more new sentence. She stacked the books tidily at one end of Margaret's dining room table, sorted her pages of notes according to topic, and began reading through them line by line.

Margaret topped off Tuesday's supper with a pie as delicious as any baked by an Amish woman and sent Ella to an early bedtime in the spare room.

On Wednesday, Margaret walked with Ella to the superintendent's office before proceeding to school.

"Don't let Mr. Brownley intimidate you," Margaret said.

"I'm sure he would like nothing more than for me to fail," Ella said.

"Don't give him any reason to think you might. And remember, he is only proctoring the exam. He didn't write the test, and he won't be grading your answers."

Ella nodded. Her heart pounded, pushing adrenaline through the physiology system she had learned so much about in the last few days.

"I'll come back as soon as school is out for the day," Margaret said. "I'll be here waiting when you finish."

Ella moistened her lips and pushed open the heavy door.

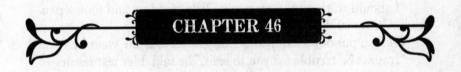

CHAPTER 46

I'll go to the bus stop," James said.

"I can do it," Gideon said.

"Or I will," Ella added.

James took his coat off the hook in the kitchen. "I want to be useful."

James's shoulders slumped more than they did two weeks ago. Over the last few days, Gideon had made several attempts to talk himself out of this observation, but each time he came to the same conclusion: James had aged five years in the two weeks since he buried his wife.

Gideon and Ella watched James go out the back door and head toward the buggy. Tobias would say it wasn't too far to walk from the bus stop to the farm, but each day seemed colder than the one before, and Gideon didn't want his children to suffer one moment more than necessary. They had suffered enough already in the bumpy fall months.

"I hope James believes me," Gideon said, "when I say he'll always have a home here."

"The girls would be heartbroken if he left," Ella said.

"Tobias, too."

"Besides, where would he go?"

"He still has a brother in Lancaster," Gideon said.

"We could invite him to visit," Ella suggested.

Gideon nodded. "In time, perhaps." He remembered those early days of being stunned that in a matter of hours the land under his life had rolled and reformed. Even after more than forty years together, James had been as unprepared to lose Miriam as Gideon had been to lose Betsy after eight. Gideon jerked his thoughts back from what it would be like to lose Ella, even after forty years.

"I should work on the casserole." Ella stood up and took a pan from a lower cupboard.

Gideon put out a hand, and Ella grazed it as she went by.

"It must be terrible for you to wait," he said. Her test results were due today—at least Mr. Brownley expected to have them today. How quickly he would pass them on to Ella was uncertain.

"It will be what it will be." Ella selected five large potatoes from a half bushel in the corner where Miriam's chair used to be.

The children had just spilled into the house and released their book straps and lunch buckets onto the kitchen counter when the sound of an automobile penetrated Gideon's consciousness and he got up to look out the front window.

"It's Lindy," he said.

Ella followed him, wiping her hands on a dish towel. "Were you expecting her?"

"No. She probably wants to see how James is."

"Or all of you," Ella said softly. She opened the front door to invite Lindy in.

"Come on," Lindy said. "Get in the car. Let's go."

"Where?" Gideon asked.

"Town. There's no reason Ella should wait another hour for the results. We all know Brownley probably got them first thing this morning."

Gideon and Ella locked eyes.

"I would like to know," Ella confessed.

"Then you should go," Gideon said.

"Come with me," Ella said. "James is here for the children. You heard him say he wants to be useful."

Gideon nodded. "I'll tell him we're going."

In the car, Gideon's hand kept wanting to reach for a brake lever to pull. Betsy always said that even when she was driving a buggy, Lindy liked speed, and this was Gideon's consistent experience with her. Ella showed no reaction. Perhaps she was grateful for the motor that would carry her to her test results and home again while there was still time to make supper.

Mr. Brownley kept them waiting. They arrived without an appointment, so Gideon had some sympathy for the time it would take for Mr. Brownley to rearrange his afternoon. The longer they sat in the reception area, though, the more Gideon resented the wait. How long would it take to say yes or no to the question of whether Ella had performed acceptably on the examination?

Finally Brownley opened the door to his inner office and gestured that they should enter and be seated.

"I understand you were to be married," Brownley said.

"We still are," Gideon said.

"Oh? I was given to understand that you realized that young women who marry cannot be teachers. It's not done."

"I do understand," Ella said evenly. "I am prepared to accept the responsibilities that come with a teaching position."

"Even at personal sacrifice?" Brownley said, one eyebrow raised.

"Yes."

Gideon's foot began to thump slowly.

"Miss Hilty, how did you feel about the exam?" Brownley asked.

"It was a privilege to be allowed to take it," she answered.

Gideon's foot thumped faster and more audibly.

"You didn't find it overly difficult, considering your own limited educational opportunities?"

"A person who loves learning will always find a way," Ella said.

"That is an admirable perspective," Brownley said. He settled back in his chair. "Was there a particular portion of the test that you found more difficult than another?"

Gideon interrupted the exchange before his foot would begin to stomp. "Mr. Brownley, it is our understanding that you have the results of Ella's test."

"Yes, I do. They arrived this morning. Of course, if you had a telephone, I might have saved you a lengthy buggy ride into town."

"Lindy Lehman was kind enough to bring us by automobile," Gideon said. "So if you also would be so kind?"

Brownley sighed. "Yes. Miss Hilty, your test score ensures that you will be duly credentialed as a teacher in Geauga County."

❧❦❧

Margaret answered the knock at her door.

"Ella!"

Margaret looked past Ella's grinning face to where Lindy and Gideon leaned against Lindy's car across the street. Her eyes came back to Ella's.

"You passed!" she said, stepping back to open the door wider. "You should all come in."

"I can't," Ella said. "James is at home with the children, and I've hardly seen them at all today, and I promised them supper, and Gideon will need to do the milking, and I—"

"Okay, okay," Margaret said, laughing.

"I just wanted you to know," Ella said. "I could not have done it without you."

"You earned this. You worked hard. You deserve the recognition."

"It is only for God's glory," Ella said.

"Then may His glory shine through the gifts He has given you," Margaret said. "I'll help you in any way I can. We can work on lesson plans and grading together, and I can give you a list of the books about teaching that I've found most helpful."

"Thank you. All of that would be wonderful," Ella said, "but I hate to impose. You've done so much for us already."

Margaret glanced at Gideon again.

"You gave up your wedding for this," Margaret said quietly. "At least you have a good man waiting for you once everything is resolved. He believes in you."

This was more than Margaret could say for herself.

"Yes, he does," Ella said, "sometimes more than I believe in myself."

"God has blessed you." Margaret squeezed Ella's hand. "When will you open the school?"

"In three days!" Ella put a hand to a cheek. "Three days! How can I ever be ready?"

"Why not wait until January—a fresh start in a fresh year?"

"Mr. Brownley will test my students in June," Ella said. "We have to be ready. Every day matters."

"Nora Coates would be so proud of you," Margaret said.

"No. No pride," Ella said. "Only obedience. A calling."

Margaret nodded. "I'll be praying for you."

"And I for you."

Margaret watched Ella scamper back to Lindy's car. She closed the front door and leaned against it.

"No pride. Only obedience. A calling."

Gray was gone. But like Ella, Margaret had obedience. Like Ella, she had a calling.

And she could ask God for no greater gift.

⊱⊰

Ella would be the first to admit she was nervous. This time when the students arrived, there would be more of them. None of the families left their children in the town consolidated grade school because they feared retribution if they did not.

The schoolhouse was warm. The books were out, the chalkboard filled with assignments and instructions. Despite the outside temperature, Ella stood outdoors and welcomed her pupils.

The King children.

The Mast children.

The Glicks.

The Hershbergers.

The Borntragers.

The Bylers.

Her stepbrother, Seth.

Gideon's children.

Every family with school-age children was represented.

Ella welcomed each child by name.

Gideon sent his children inside. "Maybe we should make sure the window on the side of the building seals properly," he said to Ella.

"I've noticed no problem," she said.

His lips turned up on one side. "Let's be sure, shall we?"

Ella looked toward the door. "My pupils—"

"We wouldn't want one of the little ones to sit in a draft."

"No," she agreed. "We wouldn't."

She followed Gideon around the side of the building that faced away from the road. There, he took both her hands.

"This was to be our day," he said.

A lump stole her throat. "Yes."

"I promise you I will always remember this day."

"As will I."

"I don't want you to be disappointed."

"I'm not. I promise. I'm not."

"December 19, 1918."

Ella smiled. "The day I became a teacher."

"No," Gideon said, "the day you believed in yourself."

He leaned in to kiss her. The words tumbling around in Ella's mind told her, *Not here. Not now.* But her lips returned Gideon's soft pressure, and her fingers returned his grip on hers. The moment lingered, and Ella savored the sensation.

It was the giggling that made them step apart.

Gertie covered her mouth with a hand. "*Daed* is kissing the teacher!"

Author's Note

I chose to set this story in Geauga County, Ohio, because this was the place of the earliest recorded conflict between Amish parents and state officials over the schooling of their children. Three Amish fathers were fined because they would not send their children to high school. My story is not a retelling of that incident, of which little is known. In fact, it is not a retelling of any one specific conflict over this issue but a fusion of principles and posturing that began in Geauga County in 1914 and continued until the Supreme Court of the United States ruled in 1972. Interestingly, in more recent decades Geauga County was again the site of discontent when a school superintendent attempted to eliminate the tradition of providing used textbooks and furniture to Amish schools. This was in hope of stirring up Amish parents to vote in favor of a levy rather than remain neutral and apart on the issue.

Because my story is a conflation, I have not strictly followed the chronology history gives us but have compressed events that happened over years or decades, and over several states, into a few months in one fictional town. Historically the Amish sent their children to school to study alongside non-Amish children through the eighth grade. Rural schools, often with mixed grades in one room, allowed Amish parents close involvement in what their children were learning. A movement that began in the 1910s to "consolidate" small rural schools into larger town schools, along with new compulsory attendance laws that took children past the eighth grade, gave rise to a sort of resistance movement among Amish parents. On January 12, 1922, eight children from Holmes County, Ohio, were taken to the Painter Children's Home and their parents charged with neglect because of their position on education.

Over the next few decades, Amish parents stood up against law enforcement because of the strength of their conviction. They paid fines, they spent time in jail, they kept their teenage children home to work on the farm, they established their own schools in defiance of standards of state law, they were charged with child neglect and contributing to the delinquency of minors. Fathers who were convicted used the court system to appeal. School districts that lost also appealed. Multiple issues emerged: Was the instruction untrained Amish teachers offered equivalent to the instruction given in public schools? Which was paramount—the state's interest in educated citizens or parents' religious convictions? Did the state have the power to close private schools?

In 1972 the determination of the Amish to educate their own children—and only through the eighth grade—reached the Supreme Court in *Wisconsin v. Yoder*. Chief Justice Warren Burger wrote: "A State's interest in universal education. . .is not totally free from a balancing process when it impinges on other fundamental rights and interests, such as those specifically protected by the Free Exercise Clause of the First Amendment."The Amish had successfully argued that enforcing the state's compulsory education laws would gravely endanger the free exercise of Amish religious beliefs.

I find an issue like this one interesting to write about because similar questions linger a century after Ella and Gideon and their real-life counterparts. We continue to need to understand each other better and learn to see the world through someone else's lens. (And for a little fun, I borrowed names from a variety of legal cases on record to populate the Amish farms around the fictional town of Seabury.)

I am particularly indebted to *Compulsory Education and the Amish: The Right Not to Be Modern*, edited by Albert N. Keim (Boston: Beacon Press, 1975), especially the chapters, "Who Shall Educate Our Children?" by Joseph Stoll and "The Cultural Context of the Wisconsin Case" by John A. Hostetler, and *The Riddle of Amish Culture* by Donald A. Kraybill (Baltimore: Johns Hopkins University Press, 1989) for an understanding of the religious and legal issues at play.

Thank you to Barbour Publishing for allowing me to explore these historical questions and ponder intersections with modern public discussion. Their team of editors, designers, and marketers turn a manuscript into a book. And as always, thanks to my agent, Rachelle Gardner, for walking this publishing journey with me with the grace and encouragement of the good friend she is.

ACKNOWLEDGMENTS

I am grateful for Annie Tipton at the Shiloh Run imprint of Barbour Publishing for receiving my original proposal for this series positively and shepherding it through to publication. JoAnne Simmons, coming alongside me in the details of the manuscript, is incredibly smooth to work with. My agent, Rachelle Gardner, rallies to the sometimes obscure things I like to write about. I was especially enthused about writing Amish stories firmly rooted in historical events, and having companions on the journey made it that much easier.

In the writing of this book, I was especially grateful for people I've never met but who have taken great care to preserve pieces of Amish history and make them available for me to find easily in the age of the Internet.

The Historian, a publication of the Casselman River Area Amish and Mennonite Historians out of Grantsville, Maryland, yielded several rich, specific articles: "History of the Amish Mennonites in the Forks of Garrett County, Maryland" (October 2001) and "Church History in the Summit Mills Area" (January 1998), both by David I. Miller, and "The Preachers' Tables" by Joanna Miller (January 2004). The September 1986 issue of *Mennonite Life* gave me "Memories of an Amish Childhood—Interviews with Alvin J. Beachy" by Robert S. Kreider. Alvin was the son of Bishop Moses Beachy and his wife, Lucy.

The Small Archives Collections of the Mennonite Church in Goshen, Indiana, turned up an interview with Henry Yoder from June 2000 (transcribed by Dennis Stoesz) recounting his understanding of the events that led to the split between the Old Order and Beachy Amish. Henry was the grandson of Moses and Caroline Yoder.

Olivia Newport's novels twist through time to find where faith and passions meet. Her husband and two twentysomething children provide welcome distraction from the people stomping through her head on their way into her books. She chases joy in stunning Colorado at the foot of the Rockies, where daylilies grow as tall as she is.

The Amish Turns of Time Continues with. . .

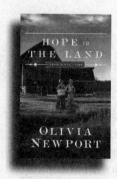

Hope in the Land by Olivia Newport

When Henry Edison turns up in Lancaster County to survey farm women about their domestic contributions during the 1930s, the last thing Amish housewife Gloria Grabill has time for is the government agent's unending questions. Gloria's hands are already full with a farm to run alongside her husband, a houseful of children and extended family, and an *English* neighbor, Minerva Swain, who has been trying Gloria's patience for forty years. Gloria's oldest daughter, Polly, wants nothing more than the traditional path of an Amish farmer's wife, but everything she does seems to push Thomas Coblentz further away. As their lives entangle, Gloria digs deep to find the grace to see past Minerva's irritating habits to her unspoken fears, while Polly and Henry brave unforeseen shifts in their dreams.

While the Great Depression shadows the country in gloom, can Amish and *English* neighbors in Lancaster County grasp the goodness that will sustain hope?

Paperback / 978-1-63409-655-3 / $14.99